Glyn Hughes has published five other novels, as well as poetry and autobiography. His first novel, *Where I Used To Play On The Green*, was about Patrick Brontë's predecessor as incumbent of Haworth. It won the Guardian Fiction Prize and the David Higham First Novel Award. It was followed by *The Hawthorn Goddess*, *The Rape Of The Rose*, *The Antique Collector*, which was shortlisted for the Whitbread Novel of the Year and the James Tait Black Prize, and *Roth*. Glyn Hughes lives in West Yorkshire.

Praise for *BRONTË:*

'Major Brontë biographies abound . . . What is left for a novel about novelists to add? Against all odds, the answer in Glyn Hughes's case is a great deal . . . Oddly, by fictionalising the Brontës, Glyn Hughes has succeeded in bringing them out of the realms of fiction and back to the true astonishment of their lives and achievements'
Washington Post

'A synthesis of scholarship and imagination even the Brontës surely would not scorn'
The Buzz

BRONTË

Glyn Hughes

BLACK SWAN

BRONTË
A BLACK SWAN BOOK : 0 552 99583 5

Originally published in Great Britain by Bantam Press,
a division of Transworld Publishers Ltd

PRINTING HISTORY
Bantam Press edition published 1996
Black Swan edition published 1997

Set in 11/12 pt Melior by
Hewer Text Composition Services, Edinburgh

Black Swan Books are published by Transworld Publishers Ltd,
61–63 Uxbridge Road, London W5 5SA
in Australia by Transworld Publishers (Australia) Pty Ltd,
15–25 Helles Avenue, Moorebank, NSW 2170
and in New Zealand by Transworld Publishers (NZ) Ltd,
3 William Pickering Drive, Albany, Auckland

Reproduced, printed and bound in Great Britain by
Cox & Wyman Ltd, Reading, Berks.

ACKNOWLEDGEMENTS

I have been at pains to be accurate in the details of this novel – something that needs to be said when much of the writing about the Brontës consists of fantasy. My novel can therefore be read as what I believe to be an accurate, though interpreted, account of their lives and circumstances. This also needs to be said because in some details I depart from some widely accepted views, for example, in the sources of inspiration for *Wuthering Heights*; also I have taken some trouble to make a different sense than the usually accepted one of what must have been the often-changing sleeping arrangements in Haworth parsonage.

A book about the Brontës could not be written without debt to a canon of biography and scholarship. This has meant some happy days at the Brontë parsonage in Haworth and with the Brontë collection in Keighley Public Library. The librarians of both institutions have never failed in their helpfulness, but the major part of my time was spent at Haworth, where all were as welcoming as they could be, and I must especially thank the librarians, Kathryn White and Anne Dinsdale, for whom nothing was too much trouble. I owe special thanks to my editor, Jim Cochrane. Also to Jane Mackay, who commented upon my novel in the construction stage. Juliet Barker gave me a print-off of her biography, *The Brontës*, to plunder before her publication date (a most unusually unselfish act, in my limited experience of the groves of academe) and has always made herself available at the end of a telephone line to talk about the Brontës. There are many others deserving thanks: Ruth Silman of the Royal Eye Hospital in Manchester who sent me information about Mr Wilson who performed Patrick Brontë's eye operation, and the staff of the Huddersfield Infirmary library who found accounts of how cataract operations were performed; Nigel Herring and John Spencer of the Bankfield Museum in Halifax who helped me with J. B. Leyland and who put flintlock guns in my hands, showing me how to load and fire them; Mr and Mrs Crowther of Clough House in Hartshead, who let me wander through it from cellar to attic; the friends who supported me through this obsession, and finally, Yorkshire itself, which has been so kind and inspiring to me. When, exhausted by writing, I have walked out among the stone walls and stone slates and moorland rises, under sun, rain, or starlight, of my own village twenty miles from Haworth, I have felt a kinship, been grateful, and known that after their work, their fantasies, the excitement and the loneliness, the Brontës walked through a similar place.

CONTENTS

IN MEMORIAM

Patrick Brontë, born 17 March 1777, County Down, Ireland. Married Maria Branwell, 29 December 1812. Died 7 June 1861 of bronchitis, aged 84, Haworth, Yorkshire.

Maria Branwell, born 15 April 1783, Penzance, Cornwall. Died 15 September 1821 of cancer, aged 38, Haworth.

THEIR CHILDREN

Maria Brontë, born January 1814, Hartshead, Yorkshire. Died 6 May 1825 of consumption, aged 11, Haworth.

Elizabeth Brontë, born 8 February 1815, Hartshead, Yorkshire. Died 15 June 1825 of typhoid and consumption, aged 10, Haworth.

Charlotte Brontë, born 21 April 1816, Thornton, Yorkshire. Author: *Jane Eyre*, 1847: *Shirley*, 1849; *Villette*, 1853; *The Professor* (pub. posthumously) 1857. With her sisters: *Poems*, 1846. With Branwell Brontë: *Angria*. Died in pregnancy, 31 March 1855, aged 38, Haworth.

Patrick Branwell Brontë, born 26 June 1817, Thornton, Yorkshire. Author (unpublished). Painter. Died 24 September 1848 of consumption, aged 31, Haworth.

Emily Jane Brontë, born 30 July 1818, Thornton, Yorkshire. Author. *Wuthering Heights*, 1847. With her sisters: *Poems*, 1846. With Anne Brontë: *Gondal*. Died 19 December 1848 of consumption, aged 30, Haworth.

Anne Brontë, born 17 January 1820, Thornton, Yorkshire. Author: *Agnes Grey*, 1847; *The Tenant of Wildfell Hall*, 1848. With her sisters: *Poems*, 1846. With Emily Jane Brontë: *Gondal*. Died 28 May 1849 of consumption, aged 29, Scarborough, Yorkshire.

ALSO

Arthur Bell Nicholls, husband of Charlotte Brontë, born 6 January 1818, Co. Antrim, Ireland. Died 2 December 1906, aged 88, Banagher, Ireland.

Elizabeth Branwell, sister of Maria Branwell, born 2 December 1776, Penzance, Cornwall. Died 29 October 1842, aged 65, Haworth.

PROLOGUE

ARTHUR BELL NICHOLLS

Except when we had visitors, Patrick Brontë and I, his daughter's widower, did not eat in the front 'dining-room parlour' of the Haworth parsonage where his famous children had written their novels and poems. If we ate together, it was in the kitchen, hardly speaking. We were reconciled now, Patrick was old, and everything had been said. When he stirred his porridge, just so, ever so slowly, with his wooden spoon, as he had done since he was a boy in Ireland, hesitating even over food as mild as porridge for he had become such a hypochondriac, and when the slowness irritated me as I anticipated the scratch and pause of the spoon around the bowl, I could put up with the agony because of what we shared: the knowledge of his daughters, and of his son, all dead.

He outlasted them to become a tall old stick of eighty-four. Even indoors he wore a quaint, white silk cravat pulled up to the edge of his lips. Draughts. And fear of damp. His face, fringed with white hair, was gaunt, sharp, peering. His tiny spectacles did him little good. He saw almost nothing of the outside world, though he spent much time in staring at the walls or ceiling. Visitors thought he looked venerable, but odd; he had grown to appear peculiar because he had little idea of what he looked like, being hardly able to see even into a mirror.

I was forty-three by then. His daughter, my dear wife, Charlotte, had been dead for six years. Following her Indian summer of health after our wedding, sickness had made one

11

of its regular winter returns to Haworth and she, too, had begun to sweat, vomit and grow delirious, at around the time she had been declared pregnant; we had been married seven months. How could that little thing bear a child at thirty-eight years of age? What I had so much feared had come to pass. She weakened over the winter and never recovered.

She died in March, nine months into our marriage, and the church was packed for her funeral. The great and the humble came. My beloved was remembered for acts both great and small. There was a blind girl who insisted on being led four miles over the hills to attend, because Charlotte had been kind to her in her poverty. The Mechanics Institute remembered her for making the tea at their meetings. She enjoyed being a curate's wife. Perhaps more than being a novelist.

I loved her so . . . I fondle and sniff her clothes. The dress and mantle that she wore for our honeymoon. I like to rustle them, in the cupboard. Should a clergyman admit to such things? When the scent of her died in them, it was then that I could have left Haworth.

Instead, I spent six years with only her father's company in the moorland parsonage, caring for him. Visitors for us grew fewer and fewer. The reason that the old man was a popular parson in Haworth in later years was because he 'meddled wi' nob'dy' (as someone told me once, approvingly – I think I was being advised on how to behave as his curate) and in return they 'didn'a meddle wi' 'im'.

The clock on the stone stairs ticked and chimed, a pan was dropped by a servant, or there was a burial in the churchyard, and that was nearly all the sound there was except when it was windy and rainy at the top end of the town. The parsonage had once been so busy, such a hive. Now it held only our memories. You could almost touch our silent thoughts.

I departed Yorkshire, on an October day in 1861, because Patrick had died, of the bronchitis which he'd always feared. He had finally let go of a life that everyone else could see was not worth living any more. Pity him, wherever he has gone to. (I'm not sure that I am a believer any more). His was a soul on fire. The 'soul on fire' is commonplace rhetoric, but I have actually felt my soul burning, like coals or paper in the grate. Though it was nothing like the experiences of poor old Patrick Brontë.

When I went from Haworth I felt as old as him with whom I had spent so many days in moody silences. Yet we had comforted one another. His was the greater sorrow because he had lost a wife and all his family of six children, whereas I had lost merely – merely! – a wife and one unborn child. There was nothing very unusual about that in a Yorkshire village where, for all the rain and water everywhere, the springs were fouled, habitations were crowded, and work, whether in new factory or old workshop, was _unhealthy,_ starting too soon in life and ending too soon also, often without the joy of retirement. Still Patrick Brontë, clenched upon an awesome sorrow, had lasted way beyond the Biblical span. Eighty-four! He had been a survivor.

I was torn apart by those last six years, like a finch in the talons of a hawk. Or maybe of an owl, for ours was a twilit existence. It was said loudly – and they did speak loudly in Haworth – that I had stayed in expectation of being given the living as Patrick's heir, and now that the trustees of Haworth Church (that hard-to-please brood!) had not granted it, I was leaving. But that was not it. If it had been that, I would have flattered them. I stayed with the old owl who had once hated me for wooing his daughter because, nevertheless, we two were the only ones who understood one another – loved one another. And I was awed by his religious certainty and power.

It was not that we did not want to talk to the strangers brought to our door by the fame of his daughters. I don't know what Patrick's thoughts were, for who did? But with what diabolical confusions I watched the arrivals! Looking down from the window of the old man's study where we waited, yet again hopefully, yet again hopelessly, we saw them, among the black stones, under the flutter of jackdaws in their mourning feathers as they were driven out of the tower. The visitors rarely saw us two old clerics peeping. Generally they were looking at their feet, worrying about breaking their ankles or their delicate shoes on the cobbles, or on the edges of graves if they came via the churchyard instead of turning off into the front garden from Parsonage

Lane. We both needed someone else to talk to. Would it be him? Her? No, it never was. They gushed with consolations – for the inconsolable. But it was not Charlotte Nicholls they asked about, it was Charlotte Brontë. They wanted anecdotes that they could put into books. When I told them . . . when I told them . . .

Oh, never mind. The point is that they did not wish to reach, well, the grief; the unspeakable: that it was a sort of murder that had taken place here. Not intentional, of course, but murder by circumstance. Patrick, a truly kind man, had inadvertently killed off his children by staying here.

Though it was I who had killed Charlotte. I am a big man, and she was so very tiny. He hadn't wanted me to marry her because of what he believed marriage would do to her.

He should know.

We had no need to talk to one another. We could do without that.

CHAPTER ONE

PATRICK AND MARIA

I

It had been in 1811 that Patrick Brontë had taken his first Yorkshire living, at Hartshead, following a short curacy in Dewsbury, five miles away. 'Mester Bron-*teh*!' his parishioners called him. They shouted, rather; harshly, with metallic emphasis on the final syllable. They opened their mouths wide and shockingly – unlike Lord Palmerston and the Sixth Duke of Devonshire, fellow students when he had been a poor sizar at Cambridge, who had kept their lips pressed together, seemingly unwilling to let their valuable words escape. 'Yorkshire folk' were not meaning to be harsh. They were merely pretending command of an unfamiliar name. Trying to get to know him – an Irishman who had crossed the social barrier. It was never easy.

He was an ambitious clergyman, Evangelical, and Yorkshire was a frontier of Evangelicism. John Wesley had said about this, his favourite county: 'that place suits me best where so many are groaning for redemption,' and Patrick agreed. Yet he hadn't intended to stay in the north of England. If he could rid himself of his Irish accent, he'd probably move on to a bishopric.

For the time being, the mysterious minglings of land, light and water of the moorland at Hartshead suited him. Wet underfoot and most often wet and windy in the sky, his parish was on a plateau above Huddersfield. Hand-loom weavers dwelled in scattered cottages and farms, which knotted into bleak hamlets without the shelter of healthy trees. In his first weeks, he had learnt that even the renowned 'muscular parsons' of neighbouring parishes could not cure the hand-loom weavers and woolcombers from going on night raids to smash machinery in the new factories. They were 'Luddites', and if they could read, they read Tom Paine. They had suffered a dreadful winter; the war against Napoleon disrupted trade, and new machinery further reduced their livelihoods. Patrick went into Dewsbury, purchased a brace of flintlock pistols, and practised by firing at walls and trees – as he had at Cambridge when preparing under the young Palmerston for an invasion by Napoleon. Patrick did not see his parishioners as some others saw them, as 'wild beasts', but certainly they were dangerous to authority, and authority was represented by clergymen.

Patrick's dilapidated church stood a mile from the village. It was unsheltered and brazen, like the Yorkshire people, and had merely a group of cottages and a farm nearby. It was Norman: a barbaric style by the taste of the day. It had a thick, stone roof that swept almost to the ground, to stop the wind from getting under and prising it off. Inside it had a gallery for musicians and grim, high, carved box pews that swallowed his congregation from sight of one another, though not from himself, whose eye was upon them from the pulpit. Catching their expressions, sometimes he was glad that they had seen him practising with his pistols.

At a quarter of a mile's distance, across fields, were his lodgings with the Bedford family at Thorn Bush Farm. Stiles were built and, across newly enclosed moorland, a footpath was beaten to the church for his use. Everyone called the farm 'Lousy Thorn', and with good reason, but why pick on this place? Every other thorn and tree was twisted; which was a metaphor for a sermon that Patrick remained too kind to preach, his character being kind, soft, bending and hopeful in those days.

Lousy Thorn reminded him of his Irish home. He had to stoop in the low buildings, where man and beast mingled intimately, as if he was bowing to his own origins – a surviving Celt, repeating the ceremony of stooping beneath a Roman *furca*, back into his traditional slavery. He knew what it meant: the tremble at the fear of a bad harvest, or of a cow falling sick. He himself had laboured in cornfields and ditches, and in a blacksmith's shop. The Bedfords thought their life was hard but Patrick, sprung from 'the most notoriously benighted peasantry in Europe', had known worse. He had the authority to tell them, and all the rebellious weavers, cloth-dressers and farmers, what he truly, shiningly believed: that it was only God's promise of an eternal purpose that justified life.

But at the moment he also had earthly love on his mind. Mary Burder had at last ceased to haunt him from five years ago, for he had met Maria Branwell.

Patrick was a heartthrob. He was an Irish laughing-boy, with his bold expression, and mop of dark, auburn hair. He could get away with murder because of his tall, slender form and romantic air. He looked distinctly Celtic and different from the usual run of clergymen, did Mester Bron-*teh*. His eyes, though weak from a youth spent poring over books, were of a pale blue colour and were piercing as he looked down, sheltering his eyes from the light. The ladies, looking up into them, saw the kindness, also the spirituality, and were lost. With his passionate, earnest wooing, with his poems, with his scholarly mind and fine appearance, he had a knack of creating mayhem: it was a common enough dilemma for handsome clergymen.

Now he often left Hartshead to walk twenty-four miles there and back to Woodhouse Grove School, a Wesleyan boys' academy at Apperley Bridge. Maria was staying there.

It would be dawn when he set out, the farms twinkling into life, the lamps hopping between kitchens and barns. As well as his loaded pistols, he handled a thick stick. A small silk cravat was wound about his neck, for after delivering the last rites to those who had died coughing in hovels, Patrick had seen that his greatest enemy in damp Yorkshire might be a chill settling on his chest. The white cravat sat on his black form as jauntily as froth on a jug of Irish stout. As he crossed the bogs he could view, across valleys sunk from sight, the Pennine peaks, rising like silver islands — usually rain-blown. He dropped into a valley scattered with factories. He climbed and descended

17

again, where more new factories were spreading dirt from their tall chimneys. He strode northwards, over the hills and through the villages lying between Bradford to the west and Leeds to the east. Excitedly, he descended into the Aire Valley, where Woodhouse Grove lay.

Everyone guessed what took him off. A woman feeding her hens pretended not to be nosy. A carter's lad grinned. They could see that Patrick's step was a lover's. Such palpitations in the heart of a man of thirty-five! But the fact was that he was still virgin, for his affair with Mary Burder had not flourished.

His failures had not been caused by timidity, and desire gave him joy in a place which was beautiful as well as dramatic. In 1811, the light was purer, the flowers were only lightly tainted with smoke, and even the lark's song seemed sweeter – either because of his later imagination, or because he had a new love on his mind.

Maria Branwell was at Woodhouse Grove because an 'accommodating' woman was needed for the sewing that kept seventy boys in trim. Her Cornish family had been decimated and, following the deaths of her father and mother, then that of an uncle and a cousin, Maria, in mourning, had come north to live as matron in the school where her other uncle, John Fennell, was headmaster. A long journey by sea and coach, but it was somewhere to go, something to do.

She was as tiny as Patrick was tall, and was twenty-nine years of age. In contrast to his ruddy, out-of-doors appearance, her complexion was pale. She had brown eyes and light brown, thin hair, a long and not elegant nose and a small, pert mouth. Despite not being graced with remarkable beauty or strong constitution, her features were transformed by her spirit. She was a light shining through parchment, in defiance of her mourning. There was an aura around her frail body.

Also her delicacy had struck Patrick, in the headmaster's drawing-room where he had first met her. John Fennell and his daughter, Jane, had been sitting with Patrick's old friend, the Reverend William Morgan – who had introduced him to Woodhouse Grove, and who was courting Jane. Maria, this bird-like creature settled in a litter of spools and schoolboys' caps which she was mending as she talked, on a June day hugged the fire. Patrick's first sight of her had roused his tenderness. Although overwarm from walking, he had considerately closed the door behind him, so that she lifted her eyes and flashed him a look of gratitude. Of instant communication.

Her inner strength, he soon found, sprang from a source he admired: from her religious conviction. Maria Branwell's father had been a pious tea-merchant and grocer in Penzance; a town councillor, who had owned property – a brewery, a public house, and a warehouse on the quay. Her brother had recently been the mayor. Patrick, after his turmoil upon finding that Mary Burder was a Dissenter when he was looking for a career in the Established Church, was relieved that Maria was Anglican; though she belonged to the Society of Methodists within the Anglicans, that merely meant that her faith was as earnest as Patrick's own.

Her religion had been imposed on Maria since her birth. But while her firmness of mind belonged to Methodism, and her confidence came from the worldly substance of her family, yet her gaiety and teasing sprang from within; a kind of secret of hers, but confided deliciously to himself, he had decided in the first weeks after he had met her. It was a native Cornish, Celtic spirit, with which he, being Irish, was in harmony. He was sure she would be 'good' for him. She made him, an over-serious man, feel happy.

Patrick was appointed examiner in classics at Woodhouse Grove. Following his report, the classics teacher was sacked. Maria Branwell was impressed by his strength of mind throughout.

They would sit talking in Mr Fennell's drawing-room, or in her sewing-room, and once he said something extraordinary. 'I believe that boys and girls should be educated equally,' he said. 'Talent should be fostered wherever it is found, amongst rich or poor, boys or girls.' To her, he sounded more radical than a Luddite.

They began to take strolls through the gardens, across the lawns to the river bank. Timidly they ventured into the woodlands; a little further on each of his visits. 'Oh, look, Patrick – look!' Their noticing together a trout leaping in the river, or a marigold in a meadow, seemed to set fire to these

19

things, make of them lights that would burn for ever in their imaginations.

But Maria was soon out of breath, so they would sit on the grass. He spoke of Wordsworth and Rousseau. They discussed their shared reading – Milton's *Paradise Lost* and Bunyan's *Pilgrim's Progress*. Maria saw life as a pilgrimage. He noted with pleasure that it was one of her favourite words.

One spring day she asked him, in her soft, Cornish accent, what it was like in Ireland. With a glazed stare into the distance, 'There's nothing there,' he answered. 'It is a place *in vacuo*.' By contrast, she told him about her life in Penzance. Patrick learned that the far western port was cosmopolitan as nowhere was in Yorkshire, west of York, (which was fifty miles away), and very unlike his Ireland. It was prosperous and gay, it had concert and assembly rooms.

Tragedy had struck, though. Beside her parents, out of nine brothers and sisters Maria had lost four, and she had spent recent years immured in mourning with two sisters, Elizabeth and Charlotte, reading novels from the Ladies' Book Club, or sewing.

'I hope you will stay here,' he said, though he could not see why she should. When she jumped, he added – with a flash of impatience, even of temper at perhaps being misunderstood – 'A little longer. Maybe you will soon find it more cheering here.'

They returned across the playing field, towards a little iron gate in the fence that kept the boys out of the rose garden. The pupils formed an ill-fed, over-confined, callow swarm, dressed in their wasp-like uniforms of dark-blue jackets, corduroy trousers and caps striped red and yellow. Maria observed his bearing among them.

'You carry yourself like a soldier,' she remarked.

'I once considered a military career. I drilled under Lord Palmerston at St John's.' He thought about whether to confess more, so early on, before adding, 'I changed my name from Padraigh O'Prontaigh to "Brontë" after Lord Nelson, who was created the "Duke of Bronte" in Italy. When I went to Cambridge I could not bear to be looked down upon as Irish.' He did not speak bitterly. He was quiet but positive, leaving it to her to feel what an unearned indignity had meant. 'When I registered, the clerk wrote my name as "Pranty". I returned the next day and gave as mine the most glorious name I could think of. "Brontë, sir?" he said. He was a little fellow. It was the first time he had shown me respect. "Yes," I said. *"Brontë!"'*

Maria laughed. Pleased. All the Evangelical clergymen whom she knew said that 'unrest' called for the clergy to show soldierly virtues.

Yet revolution by weavers and factory workers seemed remote to her. Much of the local countryside was parkland, for Woodhouse Grove had been a gentleman's country seat until, in the previous January, it had been sold to the Methodists. There was just one small factory, up-river. This was no more forbidding than a large workshop, where women went in the early mornings, and where child apprentices from distant workhouses were housed in dormitories (admittedly with the windows barred). There was little machine-breaking in the neighbourhood, and his accounts of murderous factory-hands and weavers in Hartshead seemed to belong to a foreign country, as far away as Wellington's Spain.

Most women of Maria's age had become sensible matrons rearing a family, or they were reconciled to being spinsters, but Maria was in a youthful tizzy over love. Her handsome man combined earthly and spiritual beauty, yet showed enough weakness to make him still human. How could she resist? Patrick's first kiss, lightly on the top of her head, electrified her. Through the hours that they were together, at the back of her mind she waited for the ecstasy to be repeated. She was saving a great deal up, for someone: she would give her all.

She abandoned mourning dress shockingly early and, to please Patrick, went to Leeds and spent a large part of her annuity on a dress of dove-grey silk – so deeply in love she was. She thought of Tristan and Iseult. Tristan, also, was Irish, and Iseult was Cornish. Was this strong man her rescuer, come in the nick of time?

She quivered like a girl whenever she was about to commence a letter to him. 'My Dear Friend . . . I do indeed consider you as my friend. Yet, when I consider how short a time I have had the pleasure of knowing you, I start at my own rashness, my heart fails . . .' she confessed. Hearing Jane's footsteps, she picked up her sewing, dreading to be considered 'idle'. She wondered what on earth practical Jane would think of her. Some weeks later, madly overstepping the bounds of propriety, quite mad with love: '. . . neither can I walk our accustomed rounds without thinking on you, and, why should I be ashamed to add, wishing for your presence,' she wrote.

The fact was that Maria had grown dependent on their 'accustomed rounds'. She was haunted by the scent of his maleness, and by the appearance of the back of his hand, large, freckled and strong from labouring in his youth.

Next, she was frightened that love might take her away from God. Maria Branwell had something of the bride-of-Christ's spirit. When her letters spilled over into raw emotions she sealed them quickly, lest she think twice about them.

There were times when, in panic, she accused him of loving her less than she loved him. She confessed that there had been a *Sunday morning*, of all times, when she had found her heart 'more ready to attach itself to earth than to heaven'. She had panicked and been distraught. She did not admit that by Monday she had longed the more for him.

She began to tease him as 'My Dear Saucy Pat'.

Just as she had sewed for the schoolboys, so now she occupied herself for Patrick. She worried about the dyspepsia that she learned had troubled him since his disgusting diet of oatmeal bread and buttermilk in childhood. She wanted to know whether her lover had caught a cold, and had he slept well, and how was his eyesight?

Such care – he found – also gave her the right to reprimand him. She told him off for not writing when she was aching for a letter. Once, she accused him of forgetting to forewarn them at Woodhouse Grove of a visit by his landlord, Mr Bedford, and his wife, so that there had been no-one to greet them.

'Mr Fennell said you were certainly *mazed*, and talked of sending you to York asylum . . . and even I began to think that *this* bears some marks of *insanity*!' she wrote to him, tartly.

The Bedfords' visit had been a business one, to do with supplying blankets, woven in the Hartshead district, to

Woodhouse Grove. How could he have forgotten? He did not know himself. To the Bedfords he gave the same excuse that he made to Maria. His mind had been too much upon God's business, which he hoped would be a pardonable fault.

Patrick found Maria's quick-grown, ferocious love so overwhelming that her letters put him in a dither over whether to open them at once, or save their passions, and their equally passionate scoldings, for quiet moments away from his parishioners. He would take the farm dog for long walks, and read them.

One day, looking at a flower in the sheep-cropped turf of his churchyard – the bogs and hills shining around him – because he was in love, he felt a sense of all eternity contained in the moment. Through a yellow cinquefoil, he felt a bliss that was at once calming and exciting. The boundaries of his flesh seemed to dissolve.

He compared his feelings for Maria with his ones for Mary Burder when he had been in Essex. He had been sure that had been love, too, and it surprised him how completely Mary had now been consigned to the past.

His occasional forgetfulness did not prove that his feeling for Maria was slight, as she 'hysterically' feared in her letters. On the contrary, love consumed him, also. But he saw this early stage of their love (he trusted that it would blossom) as one of those gentle spring mists which farmers like so much, cocooning the meadows and hills, hiding detail and definition, yet encouraging nature to flourish, grass and flowers to grow.

The couples, Patrick and Maria, William Morgan and Jane, chaperoned one another on picnics. Maria would arrange for a servant to be sent ahead in a trap to meet them with a hamper, while they walked, probably, along the river bank. A favourite excursion was downstream to the ruins of Kirkstall Abbey.

Their Welsh friend, Morgan, was full of heartiness on these trips. He was red-faced and stout, had a rounded forehead, close-cropped hair, a beak-like mouth, and from his manner of thrusting forward while he told jokes, he reminded Maria of a bespectacled turkey cock.

There came a day in September when the heather was in bloom, the colour of the trees was riotous, while in magical contrast – it seemed to Patrick – Maria, in her soft, dove-grey silk purchased for his benefit, appeared moth-like, delicate.

Patrick had thought about proposing for some time and had discussed it with Morgan. Perhaps it was because of her dress that Patrick did the deed then. Morgan, sensing something in the wind, had sauntered off with his Jane. Their picnic of roast beef, a roast fowl, stewed fruit, cheesecakes, and bottles of claret, had put everyone in a good mood, and the servant was happy sitting on the other side of the ruins with two bottles of ale and the leg of a roast duck. When the field was clear: 'My health is quite good, I think,' Patrick said, tapping his chest. 'Although, as you know, I am a little absent-minded.' He smiled. 'You know my habits to be studious,' he added.

'But you are always out of doors!' she mocked; for it seemed so, to her.

'That is because of my work.' He hesitated. 'Although my stipend is only sixty-two pounds per annum, doubtless it will improve, with preferment. Maria, will you marry me?'

Having seen where this speech was leading, she teased him by smiling for a couple of minutes, then clasped his hands and answered: 'Yes, Patrick Brontë, or Padraigh O'Prontaigh, or whoever you are or may prove to be, my heart is yours, to honour you and obey, and may we enjoy, what I have always desired above all else, both a spiritual and an earthly love – And children,' she added, blushing. 'Many children, if we are so blessed?'

'Many children! Boys!'

They remained holding hands, even after the return of William and Jane, hardly aware of them, so silly they were.

A week after being accepted, Patrick wrote a poem about Kirkstall – quietly, in his cell-like bedroom at Lousy Thorn. Not great verses, but expressing what was strongest of all between them: their shared faith.

> Here, faith may stretch her wings and fly,
> To regions far beyond the sky,
>   And dwell with God above;
> Whilst each celestial flame will play

> Around the heart, with melting sway,
>   And all the soul, be love.

'Patrick, don't you feel so changed that you expect the whole world to be different?'

'I do, I do.'

It was a surprise to see it going on just the same, with the seasons drifting on in their familiar way. But indeed the early, northern autumn gave place to fogs and chills. She felt them; she clutched nervously at her throat.

Patrick still took her for walks by the river. Often he strode ahead, until he paused, in a poetic trance. 'Yonderly,' they called him – fond of staring into yonder, into the distance. She would stare after him. Generally full of admiration, yet more than once she was stabbed with horror at spending her life here because of his work, enduring its early winters and late springs.

'For years I have been my own mistress, yet I do not fear to trust myself to your protection! But do you think it is really wise for us to stay in a living here? Do you think it is a good place in which to rear children?' She blushed. 'It may not be healthy, Patrick. With public unrest, it may be dangerous.'

He thought of woman's weakness, which he *must* not give in to. St Paul had commanded it. To a woman, he could not put it into so many words, of course.

'You should wear something around the throat, then it would be all right, you would be protected from the chills,' he answered, firmly.

'That is not what I meant. I meant that I do not always find it "cheering" – as you once put it, when we first met. Remember?'

He did not seem to remember.

At Wethersfield in Essex, when compelled to sacrifice Mary Burder because she was a Dissenter, the Gospel's warning against counselling by women had composed the greater part of his battle with inner demons. He must protect and guide Maria, but not give in.

'Wearing cotton and linen is dangerous because of the risk of fire,' he said. 'My father always told me that. But if you wore a silk or a wool scarf, it would protect you. I must buy you a present, Maria.'

'*I do not know if this is a good place in which to live*,' she repeated, as emphatically as she dared.

He stiffened and frowned.

'But it is my intention to be a dutiful wife,' she added, and smiled.

Having won his own way, he shone again, and she, gratified that she could transform him with love, could look up to him once more as her God. A few days later he gave her a silk scarf, and she wore it, largely from fear of him. He was so manly and powerful, and did not realize it. The question hanging over a future in Yorkshire was not raised again.

Maria couldn't bear to visit Cornwall, in case it broke her heart. Saying it was to avoid an expensive journey, she wrote to her relatives telling them how happy she was in her sweetheart, and asking them to send on her personal possessions. Soon there was another matter of which she made light, although it felt like swallowing broken glass. Nearly all her books, clothes, jewellery, portraits and other memorials of her parents, had been in a vessel wrecked on the Devonshire coast.

'If this should not prove the prelude to something worse *I* shall think little of it, as it is the first disastrous circumstance which has occurred since I left my home,' she told him, soothingly. 'I have been so highly favoured, it would be ungrateful in me were I to suffer this to dwell much on my mind.'

The couple were married in December 1812 in a joint wedding with Jane and the Reverend William Morgan. The two clergymen officiated at each other's weddings. Maria moved to Hartshead. After she had visited Lousy Thorn, '*Do* let us live somewhere light and airy!' she begged, 'a *family* home,' and Patrick leased Clough House.

The ground floor held two high-ceilinged living rooms and a kitchen. Above were five bedrooms and two attics. It stood on the junction at the top of the hill, looking down Clough Lane. Lousy Thorn had been sunk in a plateau without a view, while Clough House surveyed his domain. From his study at the front, he could see his visitors from far off. There was only a narrow strip of garden, so the house encouraged the casual knock on the door. Patrick thought that a good preacher should encourage casual callers, particularly in these times which were so troublesome for the poor.

At the foot of the hill was a stream by a small factory, from which a path led to his church a mile away, its tower visible from his window. At the rear, the house opened onto the fields. Over a rise, it fell away to the stream on the banks of which stood Rawfolds Mill.

It was following an attack on Rawfolds Mill that the Luddite movement was crushed by the hanging of thirteen men in York.

It was thus in a new atmosphere, one in which gentry and tradesmen felt able to sleep safely in their beds again, that Maria conceived her first child, a girl born in January 1814, and christened Maria.

By the time that Maria had grown to 'look like an angel' – as everyone said – with a down of fair hair of such softness that Patrick could hardly keep from stroking it, the second child was born. It was almost exactly one year later, in February of 1815, and again it turned out to be a girl, christened Elizabeth.

Refusing to be disappointed at not having a boy – everything must be welcomed as God's will – Patrick, with his small family and their servant, celebrated each morning and ended each day with a thanksgiving prayer. Why, the very light coming through door and window seemed a blessing; seemed Grace itself, seemed Grace abounding.

II

Patrick had once seen a farm cart bringing orphans from the workhouse of a southern town to be enslaved as 'apprentices' at a factory in the Spen Valley. He had seen a starving old woman burdened like a donkey to carry warps for a weaver over hill and dale in order to earn a few pence. In the last winter he had been brought out to a dead beggar frozen to a wall.

The level of pity shown by some of his fellow clergy felt as uncomfortable to his soul as their cutlery and their cut-glass goblets felt in his hands. Such a one was the Reverend Thomas Atkinson of Thornton, who occasionally came to preach at Hartshead. He turned his nose up at the Sunday board at Clough House, which was surely not unbearable. He preferred to dine with the Walkers at nearby Lascelles Hall.

One day he pressed Patrick and Maria to attend midday dinner there. As the company ate their way through game soup, fried perch in 'Dutch Sauce', and *tendrons de veau à la jardinière*, Patrick toyed with his cutlery and refused much of this feast. It only provoked him to wish he could do more for the poor. He would be capable of more if he was offered preferment. It was then that Atkinson, seeing Mr Brontë's discomfort, and, as if he could read his mind, said: 'You and I should exchange livings.

'You look stunned,' Atkinson added. 'Can't you understand your good fortune?'

Atkinson's Thornton incumbency was worth twice as much as Patrick's Hartshead one, and Thornton was a *town*, on the outskirts of the large, rich and growing town of Bradford.

'No, I can't,' Patrick Brontë admitted.

'As you may have noticed, I have a bird to catch here, and I've had enough of travelling. As a man of experience, Mr Brontë, don't you think Miss Walker is worth the trouble of snaring?'

Patrick agreed to the exchange. Atkinson was rich enough not to be in need of the money from a living. His choice of parish, being dictated by love for a woman, was not something of which St Paul would approve, yet did not God's will work through mysterious ways? After having spent two years in Clough House, and following a short delay so as not to disturb Maria's lying-in following the birth of Elizabeth, the family with two babies moved.

Never in his lifetime did Patrick Brontë feel that he could afford a horse, not even a rough cob as used by many a country parson. There was the stabling, the grazing, the cost of a boy to take care of it, and the occasional vet. They travelled in a gig, hired from the local 'job master' and driven by his apprentice. Followed by carts loaded with furniture, and conspicuously a poor parson and his family on the move, they followed almost the same route that Patrick had walked northwards so many times to Apperley Bridge. Maria nursed Elizabeth, Patrick sat with the dog on his lap or at his feet, except when it ran alongside the gig, while baby Maria was seated between her parents.

Although Thornton had shops, tradesmen, a doctor, a lawyer, and gentry, otherwise it turned out to be still not much of a town. Such weaving communities were already grim, before the smoke really poured from factory chimneys. Maria's heart sank and she now saw another reason why Atkinson had flown up to a moorland living.

Thornton straddled the road from Bradford, halfway to Halifax, Haworth and Keighley. It clung to the side of a hill, near to the top, overlooking the Pinchbeck Valley. There was one main street. After climbing from Bradford it descended gently again from a point close to the parsonage. Dividing a tangle of 'snickets', as narrow passageways were called, shops, public houses and unbroken terraces of grey dwellings, it became Lower Kipping Lane as it sank into the Pinchbeck Valley.

A clog-maker's family lived in two rooms of a cellar half below street level. Children in overcrowded houses slept in the dust around the looms in the upper storeys and attics. Babies were regularly born in sheds. It was not long before Maria was arranging for orphans to be placed in orphanages, girls to be accommodated 'in service', and paupers to be decently buried. She went around with a basket of loaves, or fruit purloined from the glut at the local mansion, Kipping House.

From the state of most of his parishioners, Patrick saw that he had no reason to complain about his parsonage, although it was an unattractive building, and not so large as Clough House, being one storey lower. There was a small garden at the front – another token strip. Their new home was crammed in by its neighbours and the Brontës were overlooked from across the street. The carts passed by the door, as at Hartshead. Horses, dogs, herds of cattle and pigs left their droppings. Beyond the houses opposite was a mill, so that if the wind was blowing up from the valley, the smoke came straight over the rooftops to them. Chest and throat complaints, bronchitis and consumption, were common. In the Bradford Subscription Library, which he often visited, Patrick looked up books on medicine and sanitation. He conjured plans for a drainage system and for clearing choked springs.

Before long, Patrick's wife was confined once more, in the downstairs room chosen for her. She could not bear, yet again, to feel perfectly well except that she was bored and frightened, so before labour pains were upon her she scared the midwife and half of Thornton by insisting that the curtains be pulled back while, in immaculate longhand, without spilling a drop of ink as she drew her pale little hand across a portable writing-desk set upon her coverlet, she composed a tract. It was called, *The Advantages of Poverty in Religious Concerns*. 'Free from the pride and prejudice of learning and philosophy, the poor man's mind is prepared to receive the truths that the Bible inculcates,' she wrote. And so forth.

Though Maria was never poor, as she witnessed poverty around her, yet she was impoverished, despite the move. So much of the spiritual aspect of her marriage 'pilgrimage' was going into coping with life on one hundred and twenty pounds a year plus her own legacy of fifty pounds, and in tholing the strains of child-bearing. In six years, she produced six children. Starting at her late age of thirty-one, she completed her cycle by the age of thirty-seven. The birth of the last, Anne, on 17 January 1820, was on the anniversary of the first child, almost to a day. She surely had to be the last. From the beginning, Anne could not breathe easily: it was as if she was lucky to be born at all, and had a mere toe-hold on life.

It seemed as though Maria's producing life was a vain attempt to fight off the sulphurous sterility of her surroundings, more and more polluted by factories. Each conception exhausted her more, and seemed more pitiless than the one before. Their most important visitor became not the verger, nor neighbouring parsons, nor local society, but the midwife, attending Maria in her confinements and fussing over her afterwards, and various other busybodying females officiating on behalf of the mysteries of women.

Patrick's first, powerful experience of fatherhood was to feel left out.

Maria's elder sister, Elizabeth Branwell, fussed up from Penzance. It was in June 1815, a week before Waterloo, so the eventual bells, parties, flags, parades, cannonades and the erection of monuments seemed to be for her benefit.

She was of the same short stature as Maria, but plumper. She was not at all as humorous and biddable as Maria. Though proud of her brother-in-law – a parson esteemed by his peers – yet she was not intimidated by him.

'Too much child-bearing will kill your wife,' she warned him. She had that defensive look of those who feel they know more than their betters.

Patrick, in his turn, found *her* quite a trial. 'Why does Elizabeth still wear mourning?' he asked Maria. 'It is six and seven years since your parents died. Three years since your uncle's and your cousin's deaths. *You* don't wear black. I am sure she puts off any suitors.'

Elizabeth wore a voluminous black silk dress, over it a silk 'spencer' – a decorative jacket – and, out of doors, a black silk cloak and large black 'coal-scuttle' bonnet. On a tall, aristocratic woman it would have looked grand. On the dumpy daughter of a tradesman, it was ridiculous.

'My sister is thirty-eight,' Maria answered. 'She thinks no-one will want to marry her now, so she is making a virtue of necessity, pretending that she does not wish to marry and claiming the virtuousness of eternal remembrance.'

Elizabeth set the whole of Thornton at a distance, especially by wearing silk. She was being 'superior'. The town was not to know that the dress was in the fashion of fifteen years earlier, when Elizabeth with her parents alive had been well enough off to posture around elegant Penzance. In the north, while silk was beyond the purses of the poor, many of the trading rich, who made their money out of wool, thought of her dress as treachery. Elizabeth Branwell did not appreciate this nicety. 'You canna tell that Miss Branwell much,' as people were soon saying.

Also, Thornton took her wearing of a spencer, a cloak and a bonnet in June to be her way of rubbing it in that theirs was an inhospitable climate. She said so, often enough, in her queer accent – which, while acceptable from gentle Maria, seemed another insult when coming from brusque Elizabeth.

She thought that the Brontës neither dressed nor entertained as they should. She did not like Patrick's dog, nor any other animals such as the cats being in the house. She thought they should live and breed in the unused stable at the back.

While Maria talked of her 'pilgrimage', her sister's favourite words were 'shouldn't', 'can't', 'wrong', and 'punishment', especially the eternal sort. Her Methodism, presumably, made her try to impose irritating timetables. When out of breath from fussing, and from complaining about her afflictions, the damp, the cold, and the draughts, she would sit in the 'parlour', spread her dress, take snuff, and denounce Yorkshire and its folk. Methodist or not, she would boast about the fashionableness of Penzance, and of her *beaux* there. There seemed no doubt that it was out of envy for her younger sister who possessed not a mere beau, but a husband, plus a fine house and children to boot.

Elizabeth Branwell went back to Cornwall. After her, the other important figures in the household included Nancy Garrs, the servant girl taken on to replace Elizabeth Branwell, and Sarah Garrs, Nancy's sister, who soon joined the ménage. They were daughters of a French refugee shoemaker originally named de Garrs, who were recruited from the School of Industry in Bradford, and even these twelve- and thirteen-year-old children, merely because they were female, seemed more important than any man, though he be the Vicar of Thornton himself.

The third daughter, Charlotte, was conceived during the celebrations for Waterloo.

The year after her birth, there at last emerged a boy, named Patrick Branwell; the only one of the six children to be proudly given names from both the mother's and the father's side, in the Irish way. Then followed Emily Jane and Anne; all of them christened in the Thornton Chapel where Patrick preached.

So much work and busyness! Each new baby was sewn into

layers of clothing which had to be unpicked and re-stitched several times per day. Patrick's province became his study, plus an upstairs bedroom. The remainder of the house was commandeered by women, girl infants and babies; over it always hanging a smell of milk. Distantly, Patrick watched this baffling, screaming, uncontrollable community, saw Maria's weakness, and feared his joy in sex.

He felt guilty. He had consoled so many weeping widowers, surrounded by too many children, who confessed their sorrow at what they had demanded of their wives. 'Better marry than burn,' St Paul had said. But Patrick thought he could restrain both what might murder Maria and what might consign him to Hell.

'Am I not heartless and selfish in my demands?' But he soon found that he could not restrain himself, and so he renewed his conflict of joy and guilt.

Maria, clearly 'sickening for something', was often ill, with fevers, colds, and obscure pains. She had grown unable to feed her babies satisfactorily. Often the important issue in the house was not the urgent need to repair the church, or the aftermath of the victory of Waterloo, but the obtaining of a wet nurse, or of herbs and medications. Maria often seemed defeated, and began to withdraw from her family. Patrick could do little except depend upon God's wisdom, go for walks with the dog or plunge into his studies.

Women! Everywhere, they left him out, over matters of house, hearth, food, as well as birth. He met them in the street and their enquiries were about his wife. At home, they seemed to crowd the rooms and he feared that they might set the place on fire, brushing their clothes against lamps, or standing too close to the grates. Back in Ireland, he had heard it said that there were three things that a man should fear: sea, fire, and women. He did indeed fear them, and answered by avoiding all three.

Until at last, unable to bear the strain, he would emerge from his study, rub his weak eyes and blink as he tried to see more than he was able, before he went to practise with his pistols against the barn wall. It was an odd and dangerous exercise for one with poor eyesight.

If he could not get free of his parsonage because of the

weather, he would sometimes burst into rages that hushed the women and set them a-tremble.

The ladies, when not busy with confinements and sickness, had a fondness for 'getting with' Miss Firth who lived at Kipping House.

When they were not there, Patrick, too, would stride down Lower Kipping Lane, ostensibly on parochial duties, really for his own share of tea and sympathy. He would enter from the lane, through the back door which was generally left open. 'Coo—ee!' he would call, until a cook put her head out of the kitchen, smiled, greeted him and withdrew. To be taken for granted was the warmest, surest welcome of all. Then down a passage that ran the width of the house, with glimpses of the gardens beyond. A more formal maidservant would usher him into the big drawing-room, with its view down the gentle valley.

The mixture of tenderness and piety in his relationship with Miss Firth reminded him, faintly, of his courtship of Maria and also of Mary Burder. Miss Firth, too, came from a family of Dissenters although in time the Firths had moved towards the Established Church.

From her religious concerns one might assume that Miss Firth was elderly, but she was eighteen, a frilly little thing with ringlets and a turned-up nose. She had not long since been taken from Crofton Hall, her fashionable ladies' school at Wakefield, though it turned out to be for a purpose which no-one had imagined. Her mother had been thrown from a gig outside the kitchen window, was killed by the bursting of a blood vessel in her head, and Elizabeth settled to becoming mistress of the house, caring for her father. She was precocious and intelligent, but her only intellectual stimulus came from her circle of Yorkshire parsons and curates. She had been entranced by the idea of the new vicar even before she met Patrick Brontë. Atkinson had delivered teasing accounts of his good looks, his romantic absent-mindedness and Irish waywardness, his books of poems published, and his bravery, giving anecdotes from Patrick's Dewsbury curacy.

'The man once threw himself into the River Calder in

winter, when it was in flood, to rescue a drowning boy,' Atkinson told her.

'One Whitsuntide, when the Sunday School pupils paraded, they were held up by a party of drunks. Mr Brontë fought them in a fashion that has become a legend,' Atkinson said.

How handsome ... and forthright ... stern sometimes, humorous at others, and possessing all the manly virtues, he turned out to be.

Elizabeth Firth was fond of prattling in her diary. Her entries were short: 'I bottled some wine. Drank tea at Mr Atkinsons.' From 19 May 1815, when she recorded, 'Mr Brontë came to reside at Thornton', she more and more often wrote such things as, 'Drank tea at Mrs Brontë's', 'I called at Mr Brontë's', 'We walked with the Brontës to the top of Allerton'.

Often the whole family walked down to Kipping House; Maria leaning on her husband's arm, the children in the care of Nancy and Sarah Garrs. It was at Miss Firth's that they also enjoyed garden tea parties, Sunday midday dinners such as they could not afford at home, and cheerful Christmases.

There, Maria forgot her withdrawals from her children. There was space for her to be with them – rolling on the lawns, happy with the two-year-old Branwell climbing up her gown, Emily Jane at a year old being almost more adventurous than her elders and imitating by scrambling at her ankle; Charlotte, Elizabeth and Maria exploring the flower-beds. The children had a new mother, who laughed, with the old tendency to tease breaking through. Patrick, enraptured by this picture, would play with his son.

The Garrs sisters – little more than older children themselves – were part of this family, too. Brought up behind the shoemaker's premises in a city alley off Bradford's Westgate, for them merely to be in a garden, any garden, was paradise.

It was at Kipping House that the Brontës first heard of Haworth.

CHAPTER TWO

HAWORTH

I

'You look afraid,' Patrick remarked.

They were sitting by their fireside and there was nothing in particular to fear. Maria's life of pregnancy, commenced at a late age, had produced that look out of habit. Patrick had seen it haunting soldiers returned from the wars. He meant that her expression was keen today, as if some intuition had struck.

'My strength is breaking down. I'm always ill with something. I'm like a rusting old saucepan breaking into holes ... my life is running out through them.' Maria had been told that her fears for her health were exaggerated, but she could not lose her intuition that it was remorselessly breaking down. Through her pregnancies she, like all women, was accustomed to living in fear of death, and she could deal with that. It lasted for some months, then was over. This other terror was constant and pervasive.

'I am growing old,' she said.

'You are not old, my dear. Never, to me.'

'I am thirty-six, my love. I can no longer risk being the wife whom you need.' Her eyes brimmed. 'You are such a passionate man.'

'We must trust to God,' he said.

While God was a satisfactory prop when soothing some old lady's brow in a farmhouse, at home he was less sure. He knew he was unable to trust his animal passions to God, and they had resulted in this frightened, weakened creature who was his wife.

He went into his study. Thoughtfully, he cleaned and reloaded his flintlocks for the night's defences against robbers or post-Luddite outrage. It took him twenty minutes. By the time he had finished, set them at half-cock and taken them into the bedroom, he had decided that he must get out of Thornton.

From the first intimations in the Kipping salon that Henry Heap, the Vicar of Bradford, might advance Patrick Brontë to the 'perpetual curacy', as it was called, of St Michael's and All Angels in Haworth following the death of the Reverend James Charnock, Maria had been eager for the move. It was worth almost two hundred pounds per year and 'perpetual' meant that it was for life. Apparently it offered a larger parsonage, one not overlooked, with space around for the children to grow up in. Though it wasn't Switzerland, it should be healthier among the hills.

Firstly Patrick had to deal with the trustees of the Haworth living. In Elizabethan times they had invested thirty-six pounds in land, using the rent to pay the incumbent's stipend, and thus had acquired control. When the Vicar of Bradford wished to appoint Patrick Brontë, the trustees objected just for the sake of showing their power. Mr Heap, hoping to appease them, went over to take the service on Whit Sunday – and found the church door locked against him. The great man could only retire, spluttering.

One fine day in early summer, Patrick walked the five miles from Thornton to brave the trustees himself.

Standing in the valley, he saw the parsonage loom high up on the skyline, on a bare place to the left of St Michael's Church tower. Below it, from the backs of terraces of houses, ribbons of enclosure walls reached down to the River Worth.

Among carts and pedlars, Patrick climbed between the enclosures, where oats grew, or which held tenter frames of drying cloth. From the foot of Haworth's steep hill, he found himself shut in between dark dwellings that had hardly a gap, nor a garden. All opened onto the street. The noise and stink swamped him – drains, overused privies, manure heaps piled behind every block of houses, animal droppings, with the choking smoke of coal and peat fires blowing over it. Through doors left open to dry out damp walls and floors, and let out the fumes of woolcombers' forges, Patrick saw men sweating as they heated the iron combs for woolcombing. He glimpsed women spinning, while from upper rooms he heard looms banging and clacking. People gathered in doorways or leaned against walls to watch him. Women stood in line for water from a trickling well that smelled nearly as foul as the drains. He sensed taciturnity all about him: maybe they knew more about him than he had realized.

Before he had reached halfway up the street, he was thinking that their very natures were stubborn individuality, gruff stoicism, isolation, independence, suspicion and pride.

He discovered that most of the church trustees – the Taylors of Stanbury Manor, the Heatons of Ponden Hall, the Rushworths of Mouldgreave, the Pighills from The Brow – dwelled in what they called 'halls' and 'manor houses', some miles away; upon moorlands which beckoned him, with their light, their spaciousness, and their strong, warm brown colour, glimpsed through any 'snicket' or gap in this claustrophobic tunnel of buildings. After making enquiries at the Black Bull public house, Patrick strode on, towards the moor.

He first of all found the Heatons, who, he had been told, had lived for two hundred years in isolation at Ponden 'Hall' near Stanbury, a couple of miles beyond Haworth, with their own little factory nearby. Though not large, Ponden had gardens, orchards, farm, sheds for weaving and spinning, brewhouse and the like. He even saw a small lawn, with peacocks! It was busy with servants of house and land, and with weavers fetching warps or delivering finished cloth. Hay was being loaded into a loft above the peat store that formed the left-hand end of the building, which was dug into the bank of the hayfield. There was a yard between the track and the door, which had been left open; there was clearly no need for locks because of the prowling dogs.

'What's thy business, Mester?' a woman shouted from the door, over the barking of the dogs.

'I hope to become your new incumbent —'

'It'll be Mester Bron-*teh*, then? Thou'd best come in, sir. Come into th'ouse.'

'You'd better call in the dogs first.'

The blunt servant — she would never have sufficed at Kipping House — grabbed their collars and dragged them in. Patrick opened the yard gate and entered.

By 'th'ouse', she meant, as he knew, the main room: the habitation of master, mistress and servants, serving probably as kitchen, dining-room and leisure hall for dances and music, for all the larger moorland farms were like that.

The great fireplace had a stone mantelpiece and above were ranged guns and pistols. Suspended from the ceiling was a rack for drying oatcakes. A lad was cleaning a long-barrelled fowling piece, another was rolling about with a dog, and servants were passing to and fro. There was a large oak table down the centre of the room, and a huge oak dresser ranged with crockery. The floor was of the same stone as the yard.

Patrick had to wait to see Mr Robert Heaton. 'He's in his library!' the woman shouted, as loudly indoors as out. She spat out the words with a hint of amused contempt. The notion of a library in this out-of-the-way place amused Patrick, too. She probably meant a shelf containing a Bible, a prayer book, and an outdated novel left by a traveller.

He was offered a wooden seat in the inglenook of the fireplace, and a jug of ale, which he refused. The maidservant disappeared. After a few minutes, Mr Heaton entered and Patrick saw what he later described to Maria as 'a stocky squire of the old breed'. He wore fine woollens — because he wove them and they were his pride, Patrick supposed — but his hair was tousled, because, Patrick assumed, he did not need to comb it for fine drawing-rooms. His boots were muddy, presumably because he made no distinction between what was appropriate for field and library.

'Mester Bron-*teh*!?' Mr Heaton roared, as loudly as the servant.

'Mr Heaton!' Patrick acknowledged, in his soft, Irish voice. He stood up, smiling, and offering his hand.

'Does tha think thou's the man to follow our old Parson Grimshaw?' Again, Mr Heaton roared.

'I would try to do my duty as God directs,' Mr Brontë answered, cautiously.

'This is a difficult parish for any parson!'

'Yes.'

'Sit thee down and I'll tell thee summat abart Haworth, sithee!'

Patrick sat down again – it was as much a command as an invitation. Mr Heaton took the opposite inglenook bench and continued, in a voice still unsoftened. 'We are awkward folk for strangers to deal with, Mester Bron-*teh*, for we likes us own way! As far as we can, we do everything for usselves. We produce wool cloth from th'start to finish, clipping sheep, sorting, carding and combing, spinning and weaving, and now we're doing it in us own manufactories, sithee! It's not everywhere they do everything for theirselves, is it? We've th'same attitude t'us religion. We're homely wi' that, too. We like to mak' us *own* sense of it. Do you tak' my meaning, Mester Bron-*teh*?'

'I do, Mr Heaton, I do.' Patrick nodded, seriously.

'We're great debaters! Thou'd have to get used to that. We don't tak' owt on without thinking abart it. I dare say we're grown stubborn from having to deal wi' a difficult climate. But I'll tell thee what, sithee – I've reaped a second crop of hay this year; to look on the bright side!'

'I saw your men unloading it. It looked good hay.'

'Thou knows good hay from bad, then? Not many parsons do.'

'I am from farming stock in Ireland.'

It was a long time since Patrick had dared admit that. He surprised himself. He realized that he felt at home.

'Then thou might do well here, sithee. We're folk as appreciate a parson who can turn hay as well as he can turn the pages of a Bible.'

Patrick's next call was on Mr Stephen Taylor of the Manor House in Stanbury – a walk of a couple of miles. He found Taylor working in his hayfields with his labourers. He was standing on a hay-cart, so on this occasion was able to look down on the tall parson. It was symbolic of his position as one now able to offer Patrick Brontë a living.

'Dusta think thou's the man to follow the old parson?' Mr Taylor, too, shouted at Patrick.

Grimshaw had been dead for more than fifty years yet they were still talking about him.

'I will try to do my duty as God directs,' Patrick repeated.

'I'll tell thee summat!' Mr Taylor began, solemnly, leaning on the shaft of his hay-fork. 'In these parts folk don't like to be too dependent on outside. If thou walks through Haworth thou'll find we do everything for usselves! We've grocers and butchers, public houses and a wine merchant. We've us own clock-maker and three cabinet-makers, carters, tea merchants – surgeon – everything we need. We like to mak' us own sense of religion, too.'

'All men must make their own sense of the word of God.'

The blandness of Patrick's response, suggesting, also, modesty and humility before the great calling of ministering to Haworth, apparently scored him a success. But Mr Taylor wasn't committing himself. He evidently expected Patrick Brontë to go away, unsatisfied but subdued. The cart-horse was restless, tugging at the traces, requiring to be quietened; balancing on the shifting vehicle was tiring. Patrick was an admirer of country skills, even that of balancing on a hay-cart; but he was not to be put off. He was seeking a definite answer.

'That looks worthwhile stuff, though it's a late harvest,' Patrick commented, surveying the heap of stalks, thistles, ragwort and buttercups that passed for hay. 'Considering . . .' he added, fearful that he had been too flattering.

But he had again touched the right chord. Taylor stood erect, to his full five feet four inches. 'Eh, I'll tell thee summat! There's not a man barring mesel' can get a second crop off these hilltops in a year same as this one's bin! Heatons canna do it. It's the manurin', tha sees, and the drainage. This land's worth a pound an acre, wi' t'drainage I've laid under it, if I come to sell it ever, which I never shall—'

'I'm sure it is, Mr Taylor.'

'Have you been to th'Heatons' yet?'

'Mr Heaton came from his library to speak to me.'

'*Library!*' Mr Taylor spat. 'He's more bewks than Soft Ned. It's no wonder he canna farm.'

Mr Taylor looked Patrick straight in the eye. He spat on his palm, held it out, and said, 'I'll tell thee what, Mester Bron-*teh*! Tha seems a parson as'll know something about life hereabouts and farming. Thou go and tender thee resignation at Thornton and say nowt to nobody here . . .'

'Mr Taylor!'

'Say nowt to nobody nowhere but trust to God's providence and I'll speak on your behalf to the Heatons and such.'

The upshot of his visit was that Patrick Brontë was invited to preach a sermon in Haworth Church. But unfortunately the invitation came from the Vicar of Bradford, Mr Heap, who had anticipated the trustees. 'Nay, we'll not have that!' they declared. 'We told Mester Bron-*teh* we'd not suffer outsiders meddling wi' us religion.'

Patrick found that Mr Taylor had not the influence that he had claimed. The other trustees had organized the congregation to ruin Patrick's sermon. They climbed over the pews, laughed and whistled. They chased him down the street with catcalls. Women, filling their buckets at the wells, laughed at him.

Patrick wrote to Mr Taylor and to the Archbishop of York, saying that he was giving up his Haworth ambitions and would stay put in Thornton.

The trustees next suggested to the Vicar of Bradford that Patrick Brontë be asked to preach another sermon – this time not as the Bradford vicar's nominee but as their own, so that they could judge him again.

Patrick's reply to the trustees was equally cool:

> My conscience does not altogether approve to a circumstance of exposing myself to the temptation of preaching in order to please . . . I really am of the opinion that the best way by far is for the Trustees and some others of the people of Haworth, who are good judges of preaching, to come and hear both me and others in our own Churches at a time when we do not expect them, and then they will see us as we usually are, and such as they would find us after many years' trial.

It was as much beneath their dignity to do such a thing as it was for Patrick to make another humiliating effort at Haworth.

Poor Archbishop Harcourt of York tried to solve his problem with this disputatious parish by *ordering* Patrick Brontë to preach there. In October, therefore, he did so, once again.

There was another fiasco.

The Vicar of Bradford and the Archbishop combined their strengths – puny as they were against the determined might of a handful of Pennine clothiers – to solve the issue, and they appointed another candidate, the Reverend Samuel Redhead.

For Samuel Redhead, three weeks of the deepest humiliation in his life were about to start. The first Sunday on which he preached, the churchwardens would not allow the bells to be rung and so there was hardly anyone in the church. But they filtered in during the service, until around five hundred were present. They came in banging on the stone floor with their heavy clogs, some of them iron-tipped. Once in their pews, they were ominously quiet.

When Mr Redhead climbed to his pulpit to deliver his sermon, one of the churchwardens gave the signal, 'Out! Out!' and the congregation left with a fearful stamping. They burst into shouting at the door. Afterwards, Mr Redhead was hooted through Haworth, just as Patrick Brontë had been.

The following week, the church was crowded from the start with a mob that clambered over the pews, banged the pew doors, interrupted prayers, laughed and whistled. Again Mr Redhead was chased and insulted out of Haworth.

He now obtained an interview with Archbishop Harcourt in York. From the Archbishop's point of view, the hill people were barbarians. 'If the people of Haworth do not behave themselves, the church will be closed down and the Lord Chancellor's judgement sought in the matter!' he thundered.

Mr Redhead dared a third visit, bringing a friend.

Threats still had no effect in Haworth. This time, even on his arrival, Redhead was catcalled through the town. The same scenes as before took place in the church, so he did not even attempt to preach. He ordered the church cleared and asked the churchwardens to lock up the building, to 'await the Archbishop's pleasure'.

The churchwarden locked the door and paused with the big key in his hand, wondering if Mr Redhead would have the temerity to demand it from him. He did not do so. Instead he begged for protection on leaving the town and this he was given. Nevertheless, he and his friend left Haworth, as he described it to the Archbishop, 'Pursued once again more like wild beasts than human beings'.

There was now a further meeting between Mr Heap and the trustees. It took place in the empty parsonage. Although threatened with prosecution the trustees were still not to be cowed. Rivalries between themselves there might be; but after the passing of cock-fighting and bull-baiting, cleric-baiting was a sport that brought them together.

Mr Heap proposed the acceptance of the original nominee, Mr Brontë, who was the trustees' candidate, too – he was the most committed Evangelist, and a man who knew good hay from bad, and the price of corn. Then Mr Taylor raised a point that had not been thought of until brought up by Mrs Taylor and Mrs Beaver, after these ladies had met at Keighley market.

'I'm told that Mr Brontë has a sickly wife.'

Mr Heap groaned. He knew what Mr Taylor was getting at. Running a country living was a family matter.

Despite the big fire lit for the occasion, the long-empty parsonage was desolate and chilly, and Heap felt the damp entering his bones by the minute. He looked out of the window at the dying light and thought of the long trek on horseback back to Bradford. He wanted this business over and done with, but, predictably, Mr Taylor enlarged upon a theme that, obviously, he didn't really care twopence about.

'There's duties as can only be cared for by a minister's wife in this humble community. I'm sure thou'll understand us position, Mr Heap!'

'He has five daughters who will no doubt grow up to be an asset to Haworth,' Mr Heap responded, testily.

'We canna be sure of that,' interjected Mr Heaton, sharply. 'It's a long time off afore they'll be grown up.'

Mr Heap had come to the limits of what he could stand

from this parish. They could do without a cleric for ever, for all he cared.

'Gentlemen, once and for all tell me who you would like to appoint and you may have him!'

'We'd like Mr Bron-*teh*.'

II

Two flat carts sent over by Mr Taylor were loaded with belongings in Thornton and parishioners helped to sort out the Brontës' belongings. Many, especially the outgrown baby clothes, were given to the poor. The cats were unsentimentally tied in weighted sacks and drowned. That night the family slept at Miss Firth's on dreams of turmoiled houses, and of paws scratching in dark waters.

The tired Brontës arrived in Haworth after travelling for half a day in a gig at the head of their carts. As when they had come from Hartshead to Thornton, it was more like the moving day of a farmer than of a parson. The children held onto and fussed over the dog, except when Patrick walked alongside, and sometimes he exercised one of the elder infants.

It was a late April afternoon, showery, but of great beauty as the carts heaved up through Haworth and the sun darted out. Swathes of silver shifted down the street, and a huddle of shower-blown jackdaws gleamed. But the wet and cold made the Brontë family – all but the upright Patrick – huddle in the gig.

The arrival of a new parson was the most important event that could occur here short of a war or a coronation, and all Haworth was out, pressed against walls up the hill. It seemed to Maria that they would never make it past all those eyes – with the horses straining, pausing to add their piles to the mire, hooves struggling to grip the raised upper edges of the cobblestones. Jolted and sickly, she balanced Anne on her lap, and held a handkerchief to her nose while averting her glance from the woolcombing shops and, especially, the privies. Right at the top of the town was one that must be used mostly by the drinkers in the public houses near the church. It gave a view down the street, when the user stumbled back to his ale, or for the Brontë family, for example, to catch the back view of him as they came up. The parsonage, as Patrick had told her, was near here. It was set off a hundred yards to the left, up the gentler slope of Parsonage Lane, beyond the church and standing on the moorlands' edge. Although it was only a short distance, at least, once one climbed beyond the church, one was clear of the town. Curlews, swept off the moors by the wet breeze, came down as far as the graveyard. She heard their weird, plaintive threads of sound torn across the sky, and one of the gaunt birds dropped among the graves.

The graveyard, bare of trees, reached from the side of the parsonage garden down to the tower, and swarmed around the church. The place was smothered with dark, stone graves. They separated her new home from Haworth, making it seem that anyone came so far only in order to be buried.

Maria tightened her silk scarf around her throat.

'They're a sickly lot,' Abraham Wilkinson, keeper of the Black Bull, remarked to his wife as they stood outside with their customers, tankards and punch-glasses in their hands. As at the other five public houses, they had all been drinking for some hours. Many had come down from the hill farms for the great arrival.

'The children look as mazed as a set of strays,' said Mrs Wilkinson. 'The wife looks mard,' she added, meaning, soft; too gentle and vulnerable. 'They all look mard.'

At the Black Bull, parsons were not good news. Fifty years before, Parson Grimshaw used to come down in the middle of his service with a horsewhip to drive the customers into St Michael's to hear his sermon. According to him, a man who whistled in the street was consigned to Hell. Mrs Wilkinson could not see a lot of fun emanating from the Brontës, either.

By some standards, the parsonage was not fine, but it was almost the best house in Haworth, and certainly the finest at the upper end of town. Despite a glaze of soot from the twelve new mills in the valleys, it looked cheerful, and was of a warm, grey colour, being built of ashlar and of local millstone grit, with 'Elland flag' for the casings of door and windows, and for the front steps. Like all buildings here, it made little attempt to hide behind bushes or climbers. It was well proportioned because it had been built half a century previously. The feel of it was of a strong building that was close to the elemental, nevertheless built with craft and with an eye for elegance.

The family pulled up at the gate in the high garden wall and, while their carts went on to the back entrance, they made their way, between showers, and with what might just about be termed 'ceremony', to the front door. They mounted the house plinth, and the row of three steps. Sarah and Nancy Garrs, having arrived a day or two in advance, were waiting. They did not drop curtseys nor any other such nonsense. They stood patiently and welcomed, firstly, the dog, because it arrived first, then the children. No sort of rudeness was intended.

The interior showed the same honesty of materials as the exterior. There was stone, and ungarnished wood, with very little carving, or plaster-work. The whole ground floor, front rooms as well as rear, was stone-paved, again with 'Elland flags'. The trustees, having attended to a few structural repairs after Mr Charnock's demise, would then have left the parsonage as it was, but their wives had 'buckled to', gone over to Thornton to discuss with Mrs Brontë 'a few bits of Indian carpet' that might be ordered from Bradford, and had sent up their servants to supervise the laying of them. But they were only small pieces, and there wasn't much else in the way of decoration.

The stairs were of stone and without covering. There was wooden wainscoting. The windows were without curtains, and had wooden shutters. There wasn't any wallpaper. The walls had been stained a gentle warm grey ready for the Brontës, and one could smell the limewash: a scent at once sharp, clean and damp.

Maria, Elizabeth, Charlotte, Branwell and Emily clung to Nancy, and to Sarah who was holding Anne, while Papa and Mama advanced towards the group of men in dark suits at the far end of the passage. A moment later, the church trustees and wardens were all around the children, overbearing them like mountains, like so many black boulders. Farmers, clothiers and tradesmen of the last outpost before the long climb over into Lancashire – shouting, red-faced men – they doubtless intended to be kindly. They smelled of tobacco and dogs, had red, hairy hands the size of hams, and huge faces leering down. The children, from Maria who was six, down to Emily who was but a year and a half old, would never forget that monstrous looming.

How to distribute his family, Patrick had worked out in previous weeks, on a sheet of paper, just as he had worked out possible drainage systems for Thornton. At the front, on either side of the hall, were two square rooms, with two windows in each. Patrick took the one on the right – when looking at the house from the garden – for his study, settling his desk before the window, and looking out on his parish as he had always preferred to do. That on the left became the 'parlour dining-room'. Behind the study was the kitchen, and behind the dining-room was a store. On the upper floor there were four decent-sized rooms, plus a tiny room at the front, in the middle, over the door and passageway. For now, the parents with baby Anne slept over the dining-room, that is to the left-hand side of the house. Over Mr Brontë's study were bedded the other girls; Maria and Elizabeth in one bed, Charlotte and Emily in another. Behind this room, Patrick Branwell, aged two and a half, was given a place to himself. The two servants occupied a room behind the parents, one not connected with the house but reached by an outside stairway from the back. The tiny room, nine feet by six feet, over the stairs and between the front bedrooms, was used to hold sewing baskets and pieces of material.

With the help of Nancy and Sarah, William Brown the mason, John Brown his twelve-year-old son, and a dozen other hands – some paid and some come merely to pry – the furniture was brought in via the kitchen. Patrick heard and watched in wonderment. He himself could take care of a book but, despite his country boyhood, following his scholarly career, a hammer or a spade would have found its way to falling out of his hands.

The adults were busy for some hours. Nancy Garrs held Anne, who was breathing heavily because of the dust. She also took care of Emily. She let Branwell push her, gnaw at her, and wander some way towards the innumerable death-traps of normal domestic arrangements, the fires, the stairs, before she pulled him back. Sarah looked after Maria and also the menfolk.

The three elder children, Maria, Elizabeth, and Charlotte, ran through the rooms, poked into cupboards until they were driven off, tried to get down into the cellar but found the door locked, climbed the stairs but failed also to get under the rafters. Finally, as everyone was too busy to supervise them, they ventured into the wet garden. There was a dovecote in the kitchen yard and they looked up at the shimmering doves. There was a shed in which were kept peat, coals and wood. They found the privy, near to the rear corner of the house at the upper end of the slope. After taking a peep, they shut the door quickly on the smell. They peered into the well, which was below the graveyard wall. It was also near to the privy, and it didn't smell a great deal better. They followed the path to the front, where the scrappy lawn had a horseshoe-shaped path around it. There was a cherry tree by their father's window, and some currant and elder bushes. They went a little further, to take a look at the gravestones, then they returned.

Back in the house, Maria, behaving like an adult, took charge of Emily Jane, who kept waving at the windows, and wanted to climb onto the window-seats. At the front they looked downhill, across the churchyard and through gaps in the buildings, eastwards right down the Worth Valley to Keighley and at segments of that bright paradise, Rombald Moor and Ilkley Moor, beyond. At the rear of the house were views of uncluttered moorland.

Their home was the pivot of three segments. There was a graveyard. There was an equally crammed village for the living, falling away below. On the other side were bright, weather-wracked hills. Death, humankind and nature already enshrouded them. Their home was a plan of what would be their spiritual existences.

III

Do you think that Haworth believed its parsonage to be its most important building? The most important room, the parson's study? Or at least his kitchen where the poor might make their first call, especially on baking day? It was not. It wasn't really the church, either.

To talk about the new family and anything else that mattered, they gathered in the Old King's Arms, the White Lion, and the Black Bull; substantial public houses close to the church, the last one erected by the same builder who had put up the parsonage, and angled against the churchyard steps. These were the inns where those coming from outlying farms and halls stabled their horses and left their carts, gigs and traps for the duration of the services, afterwards taking a nip and some refreshment while the crowd dispersed, or the rain, wind or snow abated, or until someone called for them. There were many inns, because you had to drink something, and the water was mostly foul: brew beer with it, and it did not make you ill.

At the Black Bull, as elsewhere, grander folk used the front room. There was also a dark, small room at the back – the 'snug' – where the common sort of person called in for a quick one, and tended to loiter, perhaps for half a day or a day, settling onto the pine or oak benches in a smell of sour ale, wet woollens and dog. The stories from the farms were collected there, and from there the stories from Haworth spread out to the farms.

Quite unknown to the Brontë family, before they had been in Haworth for a couple of months, conversations about 'them wi' t'queer name' already hung in the air.

Patrick need not have worried as he did about the ghost of the famous Mr Grimshaw, the bewigged preacher with the plump face, the glaring eyes, the hefty shoulders – different in almost every respect from himself – who haunted his ministry. They soon decided that Patrick, with his contrasting ways, stood up to the comparison. He did not bellow and browbeat from the grand three-decker pulpit which Grimshaw had installed. He spoke without notes as confidently as Grimshaw, but softly, in the manner of his first master of storytelling: his own father, famous in County Down for recounting the myths of Cuchulain with the quiet certainty of one gossiping about intimates. Patrick sought no other way of addressing Englishmen about God. It went down well with gossipy Haworth to hear the prodigal son, or the pearls cast before swine, spoken of as if they were tales from their own farms. They called Patrick's style 'homely'.

William Brown, the mason, came into the Black Bull regularly, and so did the druggist and apothecary from across the road, Joseph Hardaker.

'Mester Bron-*teh*'s against hanging,' Brown remarked.

Brown had soon become the one who knew the Brontë family best. He lived and had his yard not many paces from the parsonage and was for ever visiting. His main work lay there, in taking commissions for tombstones.

'Against *hanging* in *Haworth*?' Hardaker laughed.

Parsons and clothiers were for ever declaring that someone or other in Haworth was ripe for hanging.

'For all crimes but murder.'

'Sedition?'

'Even that.'

'What will our lauded trustees think? That's not what they picked an Evangelical parson for. They chose him to keep us reprobates in order so we'd weave and comb more cloth for 'em.'

'He's written articles and letters to the paper about it.'

Brontë's peculiarities presented less difficulty than they would have done in most places, for Haworth folk were proud of their own eccentricities. They were used to odd parsons, too. One – William Smith – had been executed for defacing the coin of the realm, and in some quarters he was admired for it. So, though at six o'clock in the morning the new parson stood on the plinth at the front of his home and discharged pistols at the church tower, they had got used to it. They even admired him for defending his family against such as themselves. It flattered them that he could not sleep without a couple of loaded pistols by his bed. It was also satisfying to have a clear sign of where the fences were drawn up; parson on one side and themselves on the other.

The story of how Mr Brontë had been chosen for Haworth, causing articles to be written in the newspapers and placing Haworth 'almost under siege' from the Archbishop, had been polished a hundred times.

'I'm told they brought an idiot mounted on an ass into the church,' said one of the old soaks in the corner of the back room.

'How would thou know, Jack? Tha'sn't been inside a church for six months.'

'I have, tho'! I've been to chapel.'

'Which one this time?'

'The Baptists.'

Laughter again.

'They say the idiot wore six hats piled on his head and sat back to front on t'donkey as they took him round the church,' Jack continued. 'And t'next Sunday they liquored up the chimney-sweep, covered his head wi' soot, and set him on to climb the pulpit steps and kiss the parson.'

'If thou'll believe that, thou'll believe owt,' said William Brown.

'He's still very severe when it comes to God. He cut up and burned his wife's dress because it was too gaudy fr'a parson's wife,' William Brown told them a couple of weeks later.

Was the new parson's obsession with burning the tokens of wickedness right or wrong, Evangelical or just plain mean and cruel? They sucked at their pipes, they hummed and hawed.

William Brown told them: 'They say he walked to Thornton and back in his slippers. Nancy Garrs'd forgotten to clean his boots, and he'd gone without them rather than reprove her. Now that shows natural kindness.'

'He could have cleaned 'em for 'isself,' muttered Joseph Hardaker.

A titter passed around the bar.

'I don't believe it. No man'd go to Thornton in slippers. Folk'll tell you owt.'

'He's a poet. He's absent-minded.'

'He'd be visiting Miss Firth's,' commented Abraham Wilkinson.

'He's distracted because his wife is ill,' said Joseph Hardaker.

That thought turned them silent for a time. They knew what illness *was*, in Haworth.

'I can't think why he's come *here*,' Brown said.

Only Brontë's 'yonderliness' and lack of a sense of reality could explain it. The average age of death here was twenty-six.

'God bless them all, especially the little ones,' the landlord remarked.

'What are they like, the children, William?' Hardaker asked.

William Brown thought for some time. He had to be fair. He wasn't a man to shout his mouth off. He twisted his lips, sipped his ale, and twisted his mouth again, for so long that Joseph Hardaker answered for him.

'A bit odd?' he suggested.

After another pause, 'They're very odd, I'd say,' Wilkinson agreed.

'Clever, are they?'

'They're clever,' mumbled Brown, but as if cleverness was only part of the truth about them.

'They would be, being a parson's children. They haven't been dragged off the hilltops,' Wilkinson said.

William Brown, after long cogitation, delivered one, momentous word. He laid it down with the craftsman-like sureness with which he would lay a stone upon a grave.

'*Quiet.*'

They waited for more. You could hear a dog snapping at its fleas under the table.

'Quiet?' suggested Joseph Hardaker.

'You'd never know there are children in the house, they are so spiritless.'

IV

Maria had thought she was pregnant again, but after a few months it had been realized that her foetus did not move. Instead of a new limb pressing against the mother's stomach, there was a leaden lump and strange bleedings. Joseph Hardaker began grinding grains of opium in chloroform water for her.

Thomas Andrew, the new Haworth surgeon trained in Edinburgh, was called. He poked around with clumsy steel instruments, prongs and forks and what looked like lady's curling-irons, and pronounced that it was an 'evil growth'.

The nurse who was brought in hardly liked to speak about it – except, sometimes hesitatingly, sometimes throwing in the knife of a blunt word or two, to the Garrs sisters, then by whispering to the woman who came in to do some scrubbing, then to her friend at the grocer's. She muttered of a sickness that was secret, awful, specifically female, and mentionably unmentionable. Haworth had to have something to talk about.

Almost from the moment Maria arrived in Haworth she was confined to bed, where she was so restless that another bed was found for Patrick to sleep at her side.

Haworth wasn't an English Switzerland, after all, and there was little around to encourage Maria not to succumb to the pull of the tomb. Already, she had 'one foot in the grave' – as, within weeks, they were saying outside her door, and it was almost literally true. The Brontës lived in a garden of graves. If a window was open, she heard them talking about her in that very graveyard awaiting her.

The awesomeness of a person ill upstairs seeped through the house. The routines ran around it. No wonder the children were quiet. Their quietness deepened, until it seemed unusual only to strangers.

Little Maria best grasped what was happening. At seven, she was a calm, self-controlled, responsible little girl, who mostly listened, and did not argue. Days later, she gave you back what you had said, in a form you could never have put it into yourself. 'A little genius', was the opinion of her.

'Our mother is *very*, *very* ill,' she told the others.

'Will she die?' asked Elizabeth.

'Yes,' said Maria, very sensibly and adult-like.

There was no way to grow up there and not experience death powerfully; not feel it long before it was understood. The children's first playground was a graveyard. The Garrs called the children 'poor lambs', over-endearingly, and treated them as orphans already; while their mother less and less often wished to see them, for it invariably ended with her tears.

Even more than her children's affection, Maria desired their father's. Not that it was lacking. But he was preparing himself for loss. Doubtless he was diverting a flood of emotion when he loaded his pistols – gathering his excited children around – and on the following morning, at six, when the pistols had to be discharged in order to remain of use, he now went some distance off so as not to awaken his wife. Between spasms of pain, and when surfacing from strange dreams, Maria saw that her illness, a catastrophe with which he was unable to cope, made him feel guilty, angry and afraid.

She could no longer give him love, other than spiritually; and what she wanted most in the world was her husband's warm hand upon the lump – just as at one time he had liked to feel the foetuses kicking. Occasionally she asked him directly, 'Please put your hand there.' But she found it lacking in propriety to ask during the daytime, when everyone was busy, and she might have to interrupt him in his study. Also, whenever their eyes met, they showed their fear.

Were they losing their absolute trust in God? She, at any rate, was wavering.

It was easier in the dark.

Her Paisley shawl and scarf over her bed-gown, Maria generally rose in the afternoons. If it was Tuesday or Thursday, the kitchen would be warm from baking. Nancy Garrs, though only seventeen, was good at it because of Maria's training; at least she would leave the legacy of a well-run house.

Maria also came down in the afternoon because her children would be on the hills with Sarah. They were taken out on most days and Maria encouraged their rambles. More and more, she chose the lesser pain of avoiding her children. If the weather was unfit and it was put to her that she might like them brought to her, 'Perhaps they should have a lesson with their papa instead,' she would say.

The more she *wanted* to see them, the less strong she felt to bear the haunting thought that she would have to leave them. She feared their seeing her drawn features, her sweats, her quick-drawn breaths. Some mothers might have sought more, not fewer, occasions to be with their children. Maria did not have the strength, and instead she searched in her reserves of piety to be able to bear what she felt to be her cross.

One summer's day she came down, and at the bottom of the stairs turned left, as usual, towards the kitchen. As soon as she entered it she heard Patrick behind her leave his study and climb the stairs. After a moment's conversation with Nancy, she went into the passage and paused, holding the banister, listening. She heard her drawer being opened and closed upstairs. She heard the sound of metal on metal. Scissors. She climbed as fast as she could. From the door, she saw that he had laid her grey silk dress on his bed. He was cutting off the sleeves.

'*Patrick!* Patrick!'

He looked quite foolish.

'What *are* you doing, Pat?'

'Now you *cannot* wear it,' he said.

A wrenched sleeve lay half off the coverlet. She took a step or two into the room, then stopped as if the wreckage was something that frightened her.

He stabbed the air with his scissors. 'I – want – you – to – have – a – new – one!' he said; and as he had told her before several times. She had always smiled knowingly back at him. He simply didn't understand how ill she was.

She sat on her own bed, as far from the dress as possible.

'Dear Patrick, there is no point in a new dress now. It is too late.'

He had turned away from her, towards the window. When he faced her again, she saw tears.

'It isn't too late for a new dress,' he said, pathetically. A boyish smile conflicted with his tears. He had not been where she had been: for him, there was still hope.

'So now, I shall go into Keighley and fetch the dressmaker,' he said.

'*Dear* Patrick,' she repeated.

And then she heard the children entering downstairs; heard Sarah Garrs's voice, and Nancy cursing the wet dog, and Maria's, Elizabeth's, and Patrick Branwell's voices, and after a moment some burbling from Emily Jane. So she shouted them up with an eagerness that was unexpected these days; her heart beating with need for the love and support of children who were too young to give it.

Nancy Garrs stayed in the kitchen with Anne and Emily,

but Maria, Elizabeth and even Charlotte managed to rush up. Branwell, three years of age, struggled after the others. The girls' bonnets were still strung around their necks; Branwell was wearing his straw hat. They were hampered by still trying to hold one another's hands, as they were trained to do on the hills.

Reaching the bedroom, they hesitated, clearly torn between mother and father. How much of this scene would they take in? Maria wondered. Her *orphans*, as she already thought of them.

In a flash of insight she saw how odd-looking they had grown, lacking a mother's care. Maria's gown was tight because she was growing out of it. Elizabeth's was too large because it was a cast-off of Maria's that she was growing into, and so was Charlotte's, which was one grown out of by Elizabeth. Branwell's fitted him because he had no brothers either to inherit from or hand down to, and Emily's fitted reasonably well, also, for she was too much separated in years from the next elder sister to wear her old clothes immediately – they were saved up in a drawer. Otherwise, their mother saw the weirdness that Patrick never noticed. She wondered if what they would mostly remember of her would be a woman for ever giving way to irrational bouts of tears.

Maria was always being told kindly intended lies about her illness, and advised that she would 'get over it'. Elizabeth Firth turned up from Thornton and, after unnerving Maria by whispering to Patrick outside her door, came in to console her that she would 'get over' her 'malady'. William and Jane Morgan came with the same advice.

William Brown crept in to see her. His hat was in his hand as if she were already dead and he was thinking of her tombstone. His boots creaked like those of someone already polished-up for a funeral. He breathed heavily because of the dust in his lungs. He was awkward in a lady's room. He behaved as if his great, thick, stone-grey hands were an offence against her weakness. His very strength made him different. He told her, when she dragged it out of him, that they were saying in the Black Bull that Patrick had thrown the dress into the fire.

The tale was perhaps started by Nancy or Sarah – no: more likely the nurse, who was not much good, nurses never were, for what decent woman would do such work? But Maria blushed to think of reprimanding nurse or maids. What could she say? That he didn't burn it in the grate, he only cut the sleeve? The nurse would look at her with that solemn expression she could put on, and then laugh behind her back.

Maria had more important concerns. With so little time left, she asked herself many elemental questions. Does love transcend death? How? By the values it implants, which become immortal? Without her admiration for Patrick, she would be dead already; dead in life, or in her half-life. Perhaps it was that admiration, grown into love, which planted a seed in eternity.

She could still get into church on most Sundays to hear him preach. She held on to Nancy's strong arm and tried not to think, not to think, not to think, as she picked her way with the children down the slope of graves.

On days of east wind, on coming out of doors she smelled soot from the mills and houses, and the vicious tang of Haworth middens. But on days when the west wind blew she scented the moorland from behind the house. After her sickroom, she was very sensitive to outside smells. But if only there were some trees, or a few more bushes to see; something else beside those thorns and rowans, otherwise so much bareness everywhere!

After the services, she climbed back to her home, following the path curving round the lawn if it was damp weather, crossing it if it was dry. She came up to the pedimented door, the five windows above, and the heavy stone roof. She always wondered if this would be the last time that she would see it from the outside.

Her husband went into Keighley. He fetched the dress-maker. But, as she realized, it was too late. She hardly changed out of her bedwear again.

For in January, she collapsed. The latter part of winter was the worst time for everybody, when Patrick was at his busiest with funerals. From then on, she stayed entirely in her bedroom, practically existing only with the dead as they passed into the ground outside her window. They were almost the only people of Haworth who came near her, so to speak. Flashes of light, reflected from the polished tops of coffins, passed over the ceiling at which she stared for so many hours. Who are they burying now? she asked and someone told her, William Binn's fourth wife, or John Feather's son who fell in a quarry.

She hardly knew where she was. The stabs of pain banished time. The clock measured minutes and hours, but she was plunged into infinity. In that respect, pain was the same as joy. Was that strange thought a sign of her going mad with the approach of death? Pain was the same as joy in its capacity to banish time, as she had experienced happiness at Kirkstall Abbey, or at Clough House, and even at Thornton.

V

Elizabeth Branwell received a letter telling her that the six children had gone down with colds. Maria and Elizabeth had apparently caught them first by coming from the hill with wet feet at a time when everyone had been too concerned about their mother to supervise the drying of clothes. Next, one after another, they had scarlet fever.

Her brother-in-law was at the end of his tether. He should have sent for her long before!

A week later – it took her that long to make arrangements for, she imagined, two or three weeks' stay – she came up from Cornwall. A gig, hired from the Black Bull – the only providers of personal transport, she learned – met her and her trunk off the stagecoach outside the Devonshire Arms in Keighley.

It was early May and there is no worse season for being transplanted from south to north. There was still snow on the hills, and the slush of a late snow shower was thawing dirtily in Haworth, leaving soot-grimed roads. Whenever the gig crossed a passageway, or one of the dark little tunnels under the buildings, there blew a small but savage wind, with lumps of ice in it.

'That's a cold wind!' she snapped at the lad who drove the gig. The wind was like the bite of a snake.

'Sneaky,' he remarked, sourly, over his shoulder.

'Sneaky?'

'What thou might call, *treacherous*,' he explained, with what she thought of as 'a heavy phlegmatism' that she remembered from Thornton. A less appropriate manner from a member of the serving class, she couldn't imagine.

'The difference i' the weather between Keighley and here is surprising, especially at this time of year,' he said.

'The meadows have been full of flowers for a month in Penzance,' she trilled. 'The orchards are full of blossom! We had camellias in bloom in January.'

'That where thou's from, then?' He made it sound like an insult.

'Yes. I've been in a ship for three days to Liverpool – and I'm *tired*,' she said, pointedly.

'Thou mi't well be.' He sounded as though he couldn't care less.

They climbed for another hundred yards.

'I tho't thou mi't have come a long way,' he ruminated.

She guessed he was telling her to *keep* her distance that it had taken her three days to cross.

Shaken on top of the gig, she looked down into basements, their windows flush with the street drains. She wondered if the effluent trickled back in through the windows and into their beds. What would the smell of drains and middens be like in warm weather?

Level with her gaze, she looked straight into ground-floor windows or through open doors, five or so feet away, where eyes, terrifying in their calm curiosity, watched her. Several times the horse was unable to get its grip and, while it paused, she stared for several seconds into those eyes. There was nothing else to look at. Mostly they were pale and weak, damaged by spinning and weaving in a bad light, or from the glare of woolcombers' stoves. Accusing or mocking eyes, she thought, probably turned thus upon any stranger.

'Mrs Brontë's dreadful poorly,' her driver ventured.

'Yes,' she snapped. She did not intend to discuss it with members of his class.

He was silent for five minutes.

'This is t'Square,' he explained.

'Square?' She looked around for one. She would have expected a place wide enough for a market, with civic buildings, but all she saw was a crossing of alley-ways, a few tradesmen's premises, and public houses.

They turned into a narrow passageway between buildings. As she held onto her bonnet, a group of lads laughed at her – in *Parson Grimshaw*'s parish! Even in Cornwall, Elizabeth Branwell had heard of Grimshaw long before she knew the name of the brother-in-law who would take a living here. Grimshaw's deeds had been made famous through the pages of the *Methodist Magazine*. But her first impression of Haworth had not fitted her rosy picture of a Methodist's heaven. She had not expected to be *laughed* at.

Next, on her left, was the unsheltered churchyard. She thought it sacrilegious for the dead to sleep so undefended.

After a further hundred yards, with the house that the lad told her was the parsonage looming above her, the gig stopped and the youth jumped down. He helped her onto the cobbles, in what here was no longer cold rain but sleet. The elements had grown harsher every hundred yards since they had started to climb. There was no-one to meet her. He opened a gate, pointed to a wet path, and waited. He took off his cap.

'My name's Joseph, ma'am.'

She carried on waiting for a servant to appear, but the parsonage was silent as a tomb. No parish could be this primitive!

'If there's nothing else, I'll tak' your box on,' Joseph said. He waited. 'I'll be saying goodbye, then. I'd better tak' it on t' th'*back* door,' he added.

At last she fumbled in her cloak and put twopence in his hand. He thanked her, replaced his cap, and climbed into the gig.

Box, she thought. *That's what vulgar people call a coffin.*

She stepped through the garden. The flower-buds were only just bursting, in nests of snow caught on leaves of cherry tree, elder and currant bush.

We'll just have to get on with it, she said to herself.

Reaching the front door she heard Maria's scream from the bedroom above, louder even than the sigh of the weather.

The door was opened by Sarah Garrs, her face starched with alarm: but was it on Maria's behalf, or because of the visitor? Elizabeth got into the hallway and the wind slammed the door behind her. From the top of the stairs, Maria's scream subsided into moans.

'Tha mun be starved, ma'am. There's a good fire in t'parlour. And tha'll be famished. I'll bring thee in some vittals.'

Starved? Elizabeth thought 'starved' and 'famished' had the same meaning. She had no time to worry over the riddle because, immediately, there was that *dog* yapping around her heels. She'd hoped it would be dead or disposed of by now. It wanted to greet her. While Elizabeth was pulling away in distaste, her brother-in-law opened the door on her right.

'I'm sorry to meet again – like this,' she said and he smiled wanly.

He extended his big hand, but she could not reach him because of the leaping, pushing, noisy *dog*. It was amazing how pets took over houses. Sarah grasped it by the collar and dragged it off. Elizabeth at last reached her brother-in-law. Just think: for days she had been musing on the long, doleful, pitiful, begging-for-the-Lord's-mercy letter he had sent her, and had been thinking over what she would say that could measure up to it – how could *she* be expected to console a *parson*? – only to find that the first greeting had been swamped by a dog.

All was quiet now, so you could hear the moaning from upstairs.

'Her pain is terrible?' Elizabeth whispered, and touched his arm. 'Oh, Patrick, I heard her cry.'

'I have never seen such pain . . . here.' He touched his stomach. 'How was your journey?' he asked, quickly. 'May I take your cloak?'

She removed only her bonnet, keeping it in her hand because the servant had disappeared. She made gestures as if needing a fan or a smelling-salts bottle and said, 'I'm surprised we survived the Bristol Channel. I thought we'd have to abandon ship in Cardigan.'

But here she was, full of the resolutions she had formed aboard ship, to prove herself useful, to be cheering and to banish despondency.

Now she wondered if Patrick's expression suggested the saddest of sad regrets in the world, that his wife had not her own constitution.

'How are the children?' she asked.

He smiled a little, and said, 'They have recovered from the fever, thank goodness, and only have colds once again.'

'Thank goodness for that.'

Then there they were, emerging noiselessly from the room on her left – staring, huddled together, two of them snuffling with colds. Although they looked sickly, they could be worse, she thought; and it was no wonder they caught colds in this place. What a strange lot they were. They came out of the room like six moths. Already orphans. They gave one the shivers.

But Elizabeth did not know children; was offended by what she thought of as their typical effrontery, greed and selfishness. She always expected it, and felt unsure of her ground when they were *not* as she anticipated. When they were as these were. She expected treachery to follow.

'*I'm your Aunt Branwell*!' she announced, cheery and high-pitched.

In the Bristol Channel, she had thought a great deal about an epithet. She preferred it to 'Aunt Elizabeth' because it would not confuse her with her niece, Elizabeth, and it would assert the independence of her family name from the Brontës.

They responded by staring at her.

Aunt Branwell gave her nieces and nephew a quick, sharp looking-over, and decided they were much in need of her attention.

'Now tell me who is who again!' She smiled. 'I must confess, I have forgotten, you have grown so much, and it is so long since I have seen you.'

'I'm Marii. This is Lizzii. That's Tallii. That's Brannii. That's Emmii. This is Annii.' Maria pointed dramatically at each in turn. 'Annii can nearly walk properly now and Nancy Garrs says she learned to walk quicker like us all did, because of living wi' stone floors. We all wanted to get up out o' the cowld, she said.'

'*Out of the cold*,' corrected Aunt Branwell. 'Like *we* all did. *With* stone floors.'

'Yes. I think it is comical the way Annii moves from chair to chair.' Maria smiled indulgently, for all the world like a genteel adult; though she stood sloppily and spoke in an ugly, mongrel accent, part Yorkshire, part Irish.

'Well, I shall continue to call you Maria, and Elizabeth, and Charlotte, and Branwell, and Emily, and Anne. Are you all good children?'

'They are like angels, the Lord bless them!' Patrick said.

'And Maria looks like one, with her golden curls! How old are you, Maria?'

'Seven.' She pointed them all out again: 'Lizzii's six, Tallii was five in April, Brannii will be four next month, Emmii will be three in July, and Annii is one year, four months.'

'Yes, yes, yes . . .'

There were too many of them to hug them all, but 'Aunt Branwell' made a start. She got through Maria, Elizabeth, Charlotte, then she stopped at Branwell. Unlike the others who were so stiff and who moved away quickly, he clung to her dress.

'*You're* an affectionate child, aren't you!'

She found a handkerchief in the caverns of her clothing, and wiped some noses. Emily, she noticed as she wiped at her face, had such fierce little eyes.

'This is what comes of letting children run wild out of doors, I suppose. They catch colds.' She was referring to some Wordsworthian sentiments in Patrick's letter.

'Hardly running wild. They had only been for a short walk.'

'And very foolish in this climate, as you can see.'

Aunt Branwell looked around for a servant who would take the handkerchief off to the wash, but Sarah had made herself scarce, and Nancy hadn't even put in an appearance.

There was another yell from upstairs. Aunt Branwell stiffened, Patrick flinched, but the children hardly showed any expression. Their having grown used to pain, in the way children assume that anything usual in their world is normal, seemed to Aunt Branwell the saddest reflection of all.

'Well, we'd best get on with it,' she said.

'Get on with *what*, Aunt Branwell?' Charlotte asked. 'What you have just said doesn't make sense.'

'Excuse *me*!' Aunt Branwell smiled, but was confused, and affronted. 'How old did you say you are?'

'I will be five in April.' She spoke impatiently.

'Do give me your cloak,' Patrick said to Elizabeth. 'Let us go into the parlour, where there is a fire.'

There was another, even fiercer yell. Without removing her cloak, but leaving her bonnet upon the newel, Aunt Branwell bundled upstairs. She had a glimpse of Patrick, left in the hall, holding on to his two eldest daughters and seeming to be wondering if she would perform a miracle.

She burst into her sister's room – there was no doubt of where to go. The screams had turned into moans and Elizabeth saw Maria. She was white-faced, white-haired, twisting among the white sheets, alone in the big, curtained, marital bed to which her world had been reduced. Close to it was the neat, small bed where her husband slept. A nurse sat by Maria's side, apparently unconcerned, and reading a book. (Probably a *novel*, thought Elizabeth.)

She had seen feverish faces with glazed looks in the hinterland between life and death before. She had seen her father and mother die. Experience gave her the self-control to be able to kiss her sister on her clammy brow.

'I'm here, Maria. I'm here—'

But there was little point in talking. Maria was too far gone to understand. Maybe she could take in some vague impression.

Elizabeth brushed by the nurse and gave her sister a large dose of laudanum from the dark, ribbed bottle by the bedside.

As the nurse looked up to scowl at this affront, already it was clear from her face that she was going to leave.

The parsonage had been changed around even before Aunt Branwell arrived. She was accommodated in the front bed-room that had belonged to the girls, who were moved to the back room which had been Branwell's. He was given what had been the sewing-room, while Anne, at Aunt Branwell's suggestion, was moved in with her.

She dramatically altered the atmosphere of the parsonage. For a start, her silk dress was as noisy as a swarm of bees, so that one heard it, and the clogs or pattens which she took to wearing against the draughts, coming down the passageways. Doors had to be closed, windows shuttered earlier in the evening and more often, and fires had to be lit in every room, although summer was coming.

Patrick was nagged by fears of the parsonage being set ablaze by dresses brushing against the fires; his wife trapped upstairs. But they needed Aunt Branwell: once again the household was running efficiently and busily. The washing, ironing and baking were completed – *completed*, not some of it left undone – on the correct days. Her ways had to be tolerated – mostly.

Though she wanted the dog put out in the yard, she had little success with that. Everyone was against her, so she compromised by insisting it be kept in the kitchen 'until it can be got rid of altogether'. She complained of the 'impossible' servants, their disrespectfulness and of their cooking. She said this was the cause of the children picking at their food, and of Patrick's 'dyspepsia'. Her greatest grievances, as at Thornton, were associated specifically with Yorkshire – the bleak weather, the shrivelled trees, the smoky factories in 'the bottoms'.

From what she knew of Grimshaw's reputation she had expected a quelled territory, not some people behaving the worse, apparently, for his having lived. But many of them seemed either surly or to be laughing at something cruel – at a cat trapped in a well, or an unfriended person who had lost money; characteristics she found the worse for being here. Partly this was because so much else seemed exaggeratedly malevolent, the rain say, or the wind.

'Look at her feet and thou might think she's a mill-woman in her pattens. The rest of her's all silk like a countess. *"It was purchased on my behalf from Mercer's of Covent Garden!"*'

It only took a few days before they were mimicking her in the pubs. They saw something odd about all her appearances. Indoors she wore frilly white caps, having a different one for every day of the week. On Sundays, for church, her forehead spilled with artificial curls; the thrust of auburn curls managed to be aggressive and pretentious, also something to hide behind. The weakness they detected under the pretension encouraged folk to pick at her. They found fault even with her nose. 'She's got such a dainty, turned-up nose!' they remarked, sarcastically. 'A proper lady's one.' They noticed that it was the opposite of Maria's hooked nose. 'Come out of the other half of the mould,' they said. But it was combined with a firm jaw – 'Sight o' that must have put off a few suitors.'

Her complaints needled Patrick because he loved Yorkshire more and more. Its bleakness and melancholy; the tenacious endurance and, actually, the poetry of its inhabitants expressed in their humour and observant stories, and the kindness that *he* saw them showing to their neighbours. But he could not articulate these feelings clearly, even in his poems.

Especially he could not have explained them to Aunt Branwell. One glance at her made it clear that she hated the place. One sight of Patrick entering with that moody, withdrawn expression akin to the Yorkshire weather, his clothes bespattered from a long walk over the hills of which he made nothing but had evidently enjoyed, and you knew that he was akin to Haworth, and had grown to love it inescapably.

In any case, he could not have opposed Elizabeth Branwell, because the admirer of the Duke of Wellington needed her, helpless as he was in the face of his wife's sickness.

If the housewives, combers and clothiers of Haworth had looked closer at 'Miss Branwell' they would have seen that she kept a tight lid on her feelings for fear of crumpling with emotion. That trembling lip, that prickly manner, were because she was vulnerable. Most of all, she wanted to be wanted – to be of use. In the heart of a family, at least for the moment, she feared old age, she was lonely, and her thoughts sometimes drove her to keep to her room rather than let the flood through.

She stayed on far beyond three weeks. As her sister's illness worsened, she wrote letters home telling what was left of the Branwell family that she was staying. What was there to return to?

One afternoon, when there was a softness in her eye and

a tremble in her lip, Patrick drew her into his study for what she could tell would be a serious discussion. It was a good time for it because the children were out with Nancy Garrs, except for Anne, who was in the kitchen, where Sarah was smearing goose-fat on her chest for her asthma.

'I have spent my life trying to follow in the ways of God and our Saviour,' Patrick began. It was not in pride, but as one whose humility has been tormented too much. Standing in his eyes were tears, which she had never seen before. Elizabeth Branwell was not prepared for religious doubt in a parson, nor for seeing her brother-in-law as weak as a child.

'You have, Patrick. You have nothing on your conscience and I am sure you know that if you are taken tomorrow, you are prepared. But mysterious are the ways of the Lord.'

'I have climbed the ladder of improvement, as a good Christian should! I have done it for the sake of my little ones – in the interest of procreation. *So why has the Devil found his way into my wife and planted such a monstrous substitute for a child?*' He let the tears free and hid his head in his hands.

Elizabeth Branwell dared to pat his hand. The touch shook him, convulsing him like a shock from an electrical machine. He raised his helpless, begging face, and she had a glimpse of the child he must once have been. Because she herself might break down, she withdrew. In case he should respond, she buried her hand under the table, in her dress. She could not think of any text with which to console him. As usual when she could not cope, she became prickly.

'That is not the way to look at it,' she ventured.

'Then what is?'

'You surely must know best, and not I, a humble woman, but He sends all of us our crosses. It is the way in which we bear them that prepares us for eternity.' She had reached safer ground.

'This is not a *cross*. This is the Devil's infliction, Elizabeth!'

'Hush, my . . . hush.'

She almost called him 'child'.

And then, as often, their conversation was broken into by Maria's screams.

*   *   *

In the shuttered room, in the light of a candle, Patrick would press his hands together in helpless gestures that told Maria that he might not be able to cope with his fate. With bringing up a family alone.

Everyone around her was helpless. Dear Dr Andrew would sit holding her hand for long periods, as there was little else he could do. He suggested drinking brandy, or water and salt; or applying these inside her.

Patrick once started to talk of surgery, but then he began to cry.

She longed for the Lord to deliver her and thought it cruel to keep her waiting. After heavy doses of laudanum, nightmares would wake her, soaked in sweat. Twisting with agony, she had sometimes found her legs locked together.

One night – Patrick in the small bed beside her big one – '*Patrick, there is no God,*' she whispered.

He rushed to light candles and illuminate her twisted, exhausted face, put a hand to her brow and dose her with laudanum again. She just caught him saying something about 'losing' her, before she sank beneath the surface of pain.

She repeated her denial on the following afternoon. It was after he had given her a tincture of five drops of thorn-apple to quieten her 'paroxysms'. Rapidly closing and opening her eyes that, like her pores, ran with sweat, she screamed denials of any goodness existing in the world, of anything to believe in or hope for other than extinction.

Often she did not know whether it was night or day. Behind the closed shutters she might think it was the middle of the night, and then realize it must be afternoon, because she would hear – such a healthy call – 'Messis Bron-*teh*! The children'd like ta see thee, sithee! 'Ow are t' feelin' now? Messis Bron-*teh*! The children are 'ere and 'ud like ta see thee!'

Maria swam out of – out of Hell – to see Nancy Garrs's apron against the bed and the wan faces. Six of them, she remembered. There was Maria, who was growing as pious as her aunt. There was Elizabeth who shadowed Maria, and Charlotte, who was the most thoughtful and clever. Branwell was ever ready to throw a tantrum or show off, grasping the lead in their games. Emily silent. Such endless thoughts about them went round in her head, yet, because she did not wish them to see her, she peeped at them like a spy. She managed a smile as she put out her hand for the youngest, whom Nancy Garrs was holding.

'Are yee sure you're strong enough, Messis Bron-*teh*?'

'No, I'm not strong.' She fell back on the pillow. She so much wanted to hold the year-old Anne, who was crying. She cried as if her heart would break. Although, of course, she could not understand. Maria took deep breaths so as, perhaps, to recover her strength.

'Another day, mebbe,' Nancy consoled, softly.

Maria flinched. 'How's Anne's chest?' she asked. 'Her breathing . . .'

'I've rubbed 'er with the goose-fat, Messis Bron-*teh*, tho' Miss Branwell doesna like it,' Nancy whispered, confidentially. She licked at her finger several times and pointed savagely, repeatedly, at the door, as though stabbing a ghost. Her teeth were clenched. 'She doesna like nothing, that one, when it comes down to it! She's so fault-finding, Messis Bron-*teh*, sithee! She ne'er lets me and Sarah 'ave more'n 'alf a pint o' beer a day, and fetches it 'erself up from t'cellar . . .'

No doubt Nancy was glad to have something to say. There is not much you can talk about to the dying, if you cannot talk about death. Maria drifted away and clung to what she knew best and could be most sure of – her pain. That was enough for her, without domestic disputes.

Nancy saw that she wasn't listened to. 'There, come on, children,' she said, and took them away.

Maria saw that none of them looked back. They did not know her.

On going upstairs, Maria, Elizabeth and Charlotte had counted the steps aloud . . . one, two, three . . . six, seven, eight. The clock in its tall case, tall as Papa, ticked on the landing. One . . . two . . . They had fallen silent before the closed door, while Nancy half opened it and peeped round before they entered. Then she had minced forward and they had followed. In the terrible twilight there was a strange smell, sickly, musty. Stars and needles of daylight broke through the closed shutters.

Their expressions did not become elastic again until they were out of the room and the door was shut. They did not speak again until then, but once they were halfway down the stairs, they did not stop chattering, finding fault with one another – so unusual for them. Maria cautioned Branwell not to scratch the clock.

Their mother was going away, to what place they did not know, and she would not speak to them, even to say goodbye.

When they were near the foot of the stairs there came the awful cry.

'Oh, God! Where is God? There is no God!'

Papa came to his study door and looked embarrassed. 'Come in here, children,' he said, and added, 'quickly' – as if rushing them to shelter in a thunderstorm. They dashed into his study and he closed the door so that they could not hear.

He did not refer to what they had heard. He asked Emily if she'd fed the doves this morning – as she was the one who liked to totter out and offer them grain or breadcrumbs. He asked them all if they'd learned their lessons.

'To what number can you count now, Branwell?'

'What is the name of the longest river in Africa, Maria?'

They saw that Papa was frightened.

Their mother lay in an open coffin on the parlour table, among strongly scented flowers. The body had been in the parlour for seven days, for people far away had to be informed and given time to travel. There were some Cornish visitors – strange people, awkward in Haworth. There were a few well-wishers from Patrick's earlier curacies. They all stayed at the Black Bull, and came into the parsonage whispering. It was like the scratchings of mice in the attic. They moaned as they squeezed by the coffin.

'She will be with us again,' Aunt Branwell said.

'When?' Charlotte asked.

'At the Resurrection.'

There was nothing about the draped body and veiled

face that suggested their mother could not get up and do just that.

Papa and Aunt Branwell, then the children in turn, beginning with the eldest, and then the two servants, kissed Maria goodbye. William Brown closed the coffin lid.

Their mother was taken out through the front door, across the lawn, through the little gate, down the passage between graves, out of the rain and into St Michael's.

The children were haunted by the shocking coldness of their mother's cheeks. They itched in their new black clothes, black bonnets and gloves, as they followed with snivelling Aunt Branwell and damp-faced Papa; Nancy Garrs caring for Anne. Behind followed twenty others, the patrons and trustees of St Michael's. Uncle William Morgan conducted the service.

A hole called a 'vault' had been dug at the east end of the nave, on the left of the pulpit. The coffin was lowered and a great flagstone dropped on top. It was a stone like those on the kitchen, the hall and the dining-room floors; a four-inch thick stone chosen by William Brown; a stone without a fault, picked from the Penistone quarry at the back of the parsonage. Four big men, as well as William Brown, were needed to hold it.

'How is Mother to rise at the Resurrection with that on top of her?' Maria whispered to Elizabeth, when she dared speak again, as they were coming out of church. It was as if the whole of the Penistone Hill was on top of her.

Even Patrick was dazed by the mystery, about which one could preach and console, but which nevertheless remained awesome. After he returned with the others to the parsonage for an 'arvill' – the funeral meal that was traditionally a hearty affair, with roast meat, ale and wine – Dr Andrew seemed to know what was on Patrick's mind.

'Laudanum produces hallucinations,' he said. 'It is only human for great pain to cloud our souls. Surely the Lord will not hold her accountable for weakness at the end.'

'But it is part of the Lord's business to try our faith,' Patrick answered.

When every guest had gone, Patrick left Aunt Branwell with his children and shut himself in his study. He remembered the autumn woods at Kirkstall Abbey, and the first violets at Clough House, and he heard Maria saying: 'Look, Patrick, look!' He knelt on the rug before the fire and prayed.

'Lord, take my wife but forgive her who has been through too much pain! Only Thou knowest why! Lord – I ask not for understanding, only for the power of endurance and for succour. Lord—'

He remembered how none of his own family and few of his old friends had been at the funeral.

'I am a stranger in a strange land.'

After half an hour he went to find Aunt Branwell, when he heard her enter the parlour opposite. He knew that she, also, was struggling not to visualize Maria in the fiery pit. She was white-faced. Her fingers gripped the edges of the table, she walked unsteadily, and she clearly wanted to find something else to think and talk about. She had started to complain about the servants not having cleared up all the crumbs and stains, when he cut her short.

'Please do not tell anyone about your sister's denials, Elizabeth. We must leave her business with the Lord to Himself, in His bounty and wisdom.'

'What will you tell people?'

'I shall say that she had peace and joy in believing, and died, if not triumphantly, at least calmly, and with a holy yet humble confidence that Christ was her Saviour and Heaven her eternal home.'

He also had to impart to Aunt Branwell the first decision he had made about his household since she had arrived.

'I cannot sleep another night in that room!' he croaked. 'As you are staying on – *aren't you?* – we must exchange rooms. Branwell can sleep with me. Then you will have your old sewing-room back! I would like the children's cradle to go to Mrs Garrs. I have been thinking about it. I cannot bear to look at it, and Mrs Garrs is expecting her twelfth child. Will you arrange for it to be taken to Bradford?'

'I'll get Brown to help me,' she promised.

She rustled off, while he went back to his study.

Half an hour later, Brown and another man came into the house through the kitchen. Patrick heard the bumping of furniture. When he went upstairs, he found it all done. His bed lay at right angles to the wall on the left as one opened the door, and Branwell's was at right angles to the wall on his right, so that the two made an L-shaped formation; the windows were beyond the foot of Patrick's bed, and on the right of Branwell's. Aunt had moved her own belongings, together with Anne's cot, over to the other room. Henceforth, Elizabeth Branwell slept in her sister's marital bed and Patrick never again set foot in that bedroom.

Aunt Branwell's promise had been to stay 'long enough to see my sister out'. Though they had taken bets in the Black Bull that she'd only last for a week, then for a month, yet here she was, still staying on, 'For a time,' she said, 'until we are settled in mourning.'

Perversely wearing the hair-shirt of a place that irked her – she knew that might be said of her. But she loved no-one other than those children. She could not imagine abandoning them to an unbalanced upbringing, with only a widowed father.

'I am forty years of age. What else can I do?' she told herself.

'Perhaps mine is the kind of life that is spent in waiting for the undertaker,' she told herself. 'Well, we'll see.'

VI

It was Branwell who first noticed: he could not understand how Aunt Branwell managed in the privy. They already grasped so much else; Maria leading them, they followed parliamentary debates in the newspapers. But it was a mystery how Aunt Branwell managed.

Her routines were as regular as clockwork. She visited the stone shed with its two awesome pits at seven in the morning and at seven in the evening, rain or shine. The giggling youngsters heard her pattens clattering, and they would make sure to be in the yard or overlooking it. It was puzzling how she fitted inside the little shed and sat down in it and what she did with her dress and petticoats. She always slid in sideways. Invariably she came out with a look of strain.

Perhaps the strain was from the light, for she less and less often left the parsonage. As winter deepened on the heels of Maria's death in September, 'It's very icy out there,' she complained. 'At my age my bones are getting stiff, I have to be careful.' Or, 'There are strange people about in Haworth and I don't like those dark passages, what do you call them? Snickets?' Or, 'That's a "sneaky" wind, I don't think it's safe to venture out at all.'

In truth, she avoided the street because people giggled behind her back. She had to go there sometimes, to order groceries, but silences fell in shops when she entered. Her main excursion was to church with the children and servants every Sunday. It took a very fine day indeed to encourage her to tamper with the garden, and if something needed doing in the yard, washing to be hung out or water brought in, she sent one of the Garrses. On the morning that a cart came to empty the privy, she never even *looked* out of doors after seven o'clock.

Avoiding the influxes of parishioners into kitchen and parson's study, avoiding servants, children, brother-in-law, and the upsetting dog that still got free too often to greet her in the hall, she stayed a great deal in her room. If it was bright outside, she closed the shutters. She began to order her meals brought on a tray. At precise times she had pots of tea brought to her by her fire. A teapot that had found its way into the parsonage, she claimed as her own special one. It was black with gold lettering that said, 'To me to live is Christ, to die is Gain', and it had once belonged to Parson Grimshaw.

It was impossible to imagine Aunt Branwell in a privy, especially so visibly. It had been designed with two pits side by side, for the separation of master and servants, but, by lowering its height, one cubicle had been adapted for children. Therefore Aunt Branwell had to use the other one and sit upon a plank used by all adults, including the servants. It seemed the most reckless event of her day.

"The children are growing wild, and they are not yet out of mourning,' she said to Patrick when she could no longer tolerate their giggling behind her back.

'I am only too glad that they are not melancholy and brooding,' he answered amiably.

'Well, I think we need to begin their education, before they get out of hand. Something more systematic than your odd hours teaching them their ABCs and reading them stories, or letting them loose on the newspapers.'

'There I agree. Of course it is time to think about preparing them for their futures. How might we do it together? I suggest that I set aside specific hours to teach basic English, geography, history and something of the classics to the eldest, Maria and Elizabeth—'

'To the girls?'

'Why not? They all need an education, and I can't afford to send daughters to a boarding-school. Nor do I think I will find it worth sending Branwell to the grammar school. It's a long walk, especially in winter, and I can do the job of preparing him for St John's better than can the headmaster.'

'I'm sure you can best teach Branwell, but I was most concerned with my giving the girls what they need. They'll not have dowries and I doubt their turning out very good-looking, so there's little sense in bringing them up to be ladies. Beyond their ABCs, what they need is basic female instruction, I'd say.'

'I won't deny the wisdom of the ages to any of my children, Elizabeth.'

'You mean book knowledge?'

'Book knowledge, yes.'

'It'll only make them miserable if they have to marry tradesmen or farmers. I doubt it will make them happier if they marry curates or gentlemen. A woman who's read too much sets a man's teeth on edge.'

'*I won't deny them, Elizabeth.*'

They came to an arrangement. For a few hours every morning Patrick gave Maria, Elizabeth and Charlotte the basics of the learning that he himself loved – Greek and Latin; Homer and Virgil; English poetry – Shakespeare, the Border ballads, extracts of Walter Scott and Wordsworth. He read aloud to them. 'I want them to be captivated by the music, they can come to the sense later,' he said.

The geography he taught was not that of Yorkshire, but

of the heroic areas of Empire, of India and Africa. His history was not of what had created the local factories, it was ancient history, and the grandeur and glory of the French wars; Wellington, and Nelson. It was of an era that had come to an end just six years ago, with the Battle of Waterloo.

Meanwhile, Aunt Branwell, in the morning, after her penitential visit to the yard, family prayers and breakfast, taught the rudiments to Branwell, Emily and Anne. When Patrick had finished with the older girls, she gave them 'female instruction' while Patrick was busy with his pastoral duties.

She taught the correct manner of sitting in a chair, which was firmly against the back rest, hands resting in one's lap. She taught the delicate manner of blowing one's nose – which was not with a hearty trumpeting like a quarryman in a public house – and how to tuck the handkerchief away afterwards. (This skill was most important, as there was always at least one of them with a cold.) She struggled to remove their Irish-Yorkshire accents, and she taught them French, as she was quite good at it and Patrick wasn't. She gave them basic moral instruction, about which she thought Patrick was lax even in his Sunday sermons – he did not actually spell it out that they should not vex, nor argue, nor fib, nor fidget.

She told them firmly – and at least half seriously, not knowing what demons of fear she was whipping up – that such lapses might whisk one off to Hell. 'What if you should be Taken tomorrow? – What if the Lord calls you in the next minute?' she would ask when they fidgeted in the front parlour during a visit from a neighbouring parson. Sometimes she spoke with a glassy stare, and sometimes it was with a smile, teasing them. Partly.

Most important in female instruction was sewing. There was now, and there always would be, such a lot of it, and it could never be too soon to start. They were each given a workbox in which to collect pins, bobbins, buttons, reels of silk thread for embroidery, and scraps of lace that 'might come in useful'. The little magpies enjoyed scurrying about, finding bright, small things. The retrieved sewing-room was soon overflowing, while Aunt Branwell's stuffy room became like a workshop. Her black silk gown constantly needed repairs and the children's own clothes for ever required either lengthening or shortening. She taught them how to make dresses look different by turning a collar or adding a bit of lace and ribbon, or a tuck here and there. She got them into the business of trading bits of lace and ribbon with other women – women of the better sort. She had learned that a fashion was 'coming in' for relief patterns on silk, so she did embossed embroidery on her old silk dresses. She made even Emily, when she was three years of age and before she could handle a needle, sit on a stool to watch. Maria, Elizabeth and Charlotte were all old enough to lend a hand. She showed them how to make underwear, which was cut from the bolts of linen sent from Keighley; how to make shirts for father and brother; and they did rough sewing for the Haworth poor. Always, with everything, from genteel trading at the church door to sitting upright in a chair, Aunt Branwell was sensible that she was teaching them the duties of a *clergyman's* daughters.

Stitch, stitch went the prisoners.

Maria, Elizabeth and Charlotte completed samplers. 'What are samplers *for*, Aunt?' Charlotte asked.

'Stitching is for the good of one's soul,' Aunt Branwell answered.

'How does it benefit my soul, Aunt, apart from the sentiment?' Maria asked. 'And Tallii is only doing an alphabet.'

'Eight years of age is too young to be asking questions, Maria. It teaches you to be neat, and careful, and particular.'

'What has that to do with my soul?' Charlotte persisted.

'One cannot complete any task without orderliness.'

'Oh.'

'And, when one sews for others, that indeed benefits the giver most.'

Her aunt's smug answers left Charlotte, especially, unsatisfied, but she knew it was no good talking to Aunt Branwell. She had learned *that* by the age of six. Charlotte already found stupidity irksome. Wherever she came across it, in shops, in church congregations, or among her father's visitors, it set up a prickling sensation in her neck and backbone. She decided that the only spiritual benefit of sewing was to train the soul to be patient through purgatory.

Aunt Branwell demonstrated the correct manner in which to treat servants.

'It is a good idea to test honesty by leaving a penny where it might be stolen.' Aunt Branwell slipped a coin under a volume of Dr Johnson's *Lives of the English Poets* in Papa's study, and moved on in her educational tour, glacial, rustling.

'There is no such thing as a servant without a blind spot,' she announced, grandly, as if she had read it in the Bible; craning up to see cobwebs on the top of the clock on the stairs, and not minding that the Garrses overheard.

'Run your fingers over the surfaces of tables, and let them see you doing it,' she said in the parlour, and Nancy, standing by, grumbled: 'Wi' t'coal fires thou 'as, they're mucky agin in a minute and us've enough to do wi' t'slutch in t'yard and them lot traipsing it indoors all t'time. Ask Sarah what work us 'ave wi' 'em all.'

The brood behind Aunt Branwell winked at Nancy.

'Keep an account book, noting the hours they take off from duty!' Aunt instructed. 'Note down the beer they have from the cellar, and the tea they take out of the caddy. *Take care of the pence and the pounds will take care of themselves.*'

The Garrs sisters more and more seethed under Aunt Branwell's rule and would barely loosen their tongues when she was around.

Aunt Branwell pinned timetables up in her room for her own benefit, and in the kitchen for everybody else's. She indoctrinated even these crazy half-Irish children with a horror of not *wasting time.*

Only, their idea of usefully employed time was different from hers. They started to use the sewing-room for reading and writing in, and the Garrses nicknamed it their 'study'.

It was there that Maria passed on her father's lessons – the matters Patrick imparted to her but thought that the youngest would not understand.

Maria knew better.

Branwell at four and five years of age snuggled up to his eldest sister, loving her with a passion that Aunt Branwell, and maybe Papa too, if he had seen it, would have regarded as unhealthy. Together with Charlotte, Emily and even Anne, he begged to hear reports of parliamentary debates. He wanted her to read aloud Bunyan's *Pilgrim's Progress* and Milton's *Paradise Lost*, and about the exploits of the Duke of Wellington and of Lord Nelson, the Duke of Brontë, and about Byron, Shakespeare, Coleridge, Shelley and Burns: their lives, more than their works.

The Brontë children lived in literature. They lived in fantasies in which they were one creature, defensive against that other world the afflictions of which were terrifying – orphaned as they were by a death they could not understand, for which no-one really consoled them. They invented their own world in the vacuum.

Their toys were a few stray objects that found their way into the parsonage. Sarah brought them a lion of black oak that had been broken off a chair arm. 'Look what I found for yee in t'farmyard at Rush Isles. Miss Branwell sent me there wi' one of her *Methodist Magazines*, and it caught my fancy. I thought yee'd like it.'

'Can I have some red paint?' Branwell asked.

Sarah found some. He painted the lion's tongue bright red, and the broken piece of chair arm became a great inspirer of lurid tales. William Brown gave them a lead medallion, an inch and a half across, inscribed 'The William Pitt Club of Saddleworth 1818'. Papa bought them a set of alphabet blocks, two letters on each block, and on the other faces, lithographed illustrations, for example on U and V there were a Grecian urn and a viper. Sarah Garrs later gave them a small iron wheel broken off a piece of machinery in the Heatons' spinning factory at Ponden. Nancy wove for Maria a miniature basket out of rushes.

When Aunt Branwell was shut away in her room, Papa in his, and only the Garrs sisters were around to watch them, they were wild, imagining or playing out their stories.

One day, Emily went into her father's bedroom and climbed through his window, dressed as Charles II. She was already tall enough to wear one of her father's waistcoats, after a fashion. In the attic she had found a fancy plum-coloured one that he had given up wearing since his Hartshead days, and it reached to below Emily's knees. She had fastened pigeons' feathers onto an old hat she had found. By shinning down the cherry tree she enacted Charles's escape, with Branwell following. The blossoming tree was a favourite of Patrick's, and Emily struck the ground with a broken branch in her hand, Branwell tumbling after her. The servants helped rake soot from the back of the kitchen range into a tin and smother the wound on the cherry tree, then they threw the branch into the churchyard, but that was not the end of it, not by any means. Of course Patrick and Aunt Branwell detected it. It seemed the culmination of all their whisperings, secret madnesses and games – more than a body could stand.

But even Aunt Branwell had some stories for them to gobble up. Although a regular worshipper in St Michael's, she was finding her own fantasy world via the *Methodist Magazine*. She stoked her bedroom fire to furnace heat, rolled a boiled sweet in her mouth perhaps, or poured herself more tea, tugged her shawl tighter around her, sank deeper into her chair, pored over the cramped type of the tiny pamphlets with their headings in thorny, Gothic letters, and became lost to this world.

'Tell us a story, Aunt,' one of the girls might demand, while they crowded into the sewing-room, and the request would cheer Aunt Branwell no end, giving her the chance to repeat what she had read in her magazines. 'You never seem tired of stories!' she'd begin by grumbling. But she loved telling them. The children, she was finding, were warming her into life. 'Well! I have been reading about John Turton, a reprobate. Returning home late at night from playing his fiddle at a dance, he was turning matters of God and the Devil over in his mind. "Shall it be the alehouse, the fiddle and the Devil, or shall it be the chapel, Christ and Salvation?" he asked himself. He passed a fire of quickthorns in a field. Taking it for a sign, he thrust his fiddle into the flames, and he has walked with God ever since, and has become a notable preacher – watch what Anne is doing with that needle, Elizabeth!

'Yorkshire is a great place for miracles, you know. Abraham Sykes took a whole village by walking into a cottage, borrowing a washing line, standing on a chair with the rope around his neck and pretending he was going to hang himself from a hook in the beam. The housewife rushed out to call her neighbours. Thus she brought the preacher a congregation which he was able to lead to salvation. Sykes, an itinerant preacher, was by trade a cobbler, as Christ was a carpenter. Don't you think that something like that could have happened on the shore of the Lake of Galilee?'

She told them of the weaver who, on going to the alehouse half a mile away instead of to the nearby chapel, and having to walk home through the rain, caught his death of cold and was swept into Hell cursing his folly; of a woman who, after abusing the Methodists, on the next day was washing her clothes in the river when the Lord sucked her in and drowned her.

'That was in Padstow in Cornwall,' she said. 'Where your ancestors come from. There have been many miracles there, too.'

The mention of Cornwall made the poor, lonely woman dash for a lace handkerchief.

VII

'Nature is as important as books,' Patrick said, worried about the intense, indoor life of his children. 'They should be taken for a walk every fine day. Even when the weather is not over-favourable, it will do them good.'

'They'll end up with consumption,' Aunt Branwell said.

'Nonsense!' Patrick answered.

Sarah Garrs was delegated to take them, in the afternoons. They followed the track that led beyond the parsonage. Unsheltered by trees or houses and with only low field walls, it led up to the common which sloped down from Penistone Hill. It was completely open there. They could let the dog loose. They watched the clouds and shadows pass over the hills, seeing in them the animals of their picture books. They could feel the wind. They could collect feathers and pebbles, or try to pick up frail, dewed cobwebs. They came back with eggs of lapwing, partridge and quail. They once brought home a wounded blackbird which they nestled in a box until it drooped its head, closed its eyes and died, whereupon Aunt Branwell insisted on their 'throwing out the dirty creature', so they buried it in the graveyard, under a mound, with a pot of wild flowers, and a cross tied together from sticks.

Sarah eventually took them to the top of Penistone Hill. The cloud of smoke over Haworth being below them, here they could breathe, and look over the whole valley of the River Worth and the Sladen Beck. The narrow enclosures, running down the folds of the hills, lay upon the slopes like green feathers upon spread wings. They could run, or roll, or trip laughing in the grass. They found boulders and quarries where you could imagine highwaymen and Bonnie Prince Charlie hiding. Sarah was as silly as her charges.

On the top, there was a stretch of level land called Penistone Flats.

'Horse-racing used to take place here until Parson Grimshaw put a stop to it,' Sarah said.

The children imagined, not the ribaldry of the squalid poor driving mules, but a Byronic scene of Arab stallions.

'How did he do that?' Maria asked.

'He prayed for a thunderstorm. God washed out the races and they never dared hold them again.'

Sarah had errands to execute; magazines to pick up for Aunt Branwell, sermons and pamphlets to deliver, milk to collect on their way home. She was seventeen, and on their visits to the farms she was always talking about love. 'A good heart is th' best of all aids to beauty,' she said. She scrutinized her not very pretty charges, Charlotte especially. Nevertheless, she herself grabbed her chance to display a new bonnet or scarf to a lad in a farmyard.

Sarah often led them past Sowdens Farm where 'the old parson' had lived, further around Penistone Hill, and she had a love story to tell about him. She stood among cattle, pigs and poultry by the low-built farmhouse, fell into a moony trance, and sighed: 'He stayed hereabouts all his life so as to be faithful i' love. His wife died young and was buried in Luddenden six miles off, and even though he married again he still wouldna move far away.'

Taking the dog, the children started to go out by themselves. 'Make sure you stay together – hold hands all the way,'

Patrick ordered, and they became a well-known sight, the eldest leading and the youngest at the tail. They would try to get clear of Haworth quickly and unnoticed. Because the parsonage was almost out of the town, on its moorland side, they could walk directly onto open country. They almost always went westwards towards the vast stretch of Haworth Moor. On crossing the northern flank of Penistone Hill, their choices were to circle left, towards Oxenhope, or to turn right, towards Stanbury. They usually followed the more deserted walk, dipping to the Sladen Beck, and very likely crossing it at a point a long way up towards its source, possibly as far up as Top Withens. In time they went further, striking the cleft of the Ponden Clough Beck which led them down to Ponden Hall. This would be about five or six miles, and if they walked back to Haworth it would be a further two.

They would come home with their boots wet and the hems of their dresses muddy. Three times out of four they were soaked. Sometimes they got away with it and weren't scolded; Aunt would be in her room and Papa in his study. They would come in breathless, flushed, excited, perhaps screaming into the kitchen to grab some food from Nancy and Sarah and set their wet clothes before the fire. At other times, Aunt Branwell would meet them, or come in to find the kitchen full of stink and steam, and clothes ranged before the fire.

'Patrick, they'll catch their deaths!' she declared. 'It seems they've got drenched twice today. They dried themselves once while they were out, sitting in front of some weaver's fire, only to get wet through again, walking home. It's no wonder they always have colds.'

One day, Charlotte – five years of age – was brought back by a woman who lived at the bottom of the village and who had found the child standing bemused by the toll-gate.

'Pilgrim set off for the Celestial City, and I was going to Bradford,' she explained.

Patrick also took his children for walks. He showed them the structures of flowers and butterflies, and got them to watch the flights of birds. He told them the names – catechized them, almost. He bought them Bewick's *British Birds*. He wanted them to look at nature as their mother and he had done.

His children's powers of observation amazed him. They could take him out of himself with them. In the intensity of their delight, they showed the world to him more than he showed it to them. He felt he had never before seen a spider hanging in a web jewelled with raindrops until little Emily drew his attention to it.

They asked him about everything. 'Papa, which is the best wind?' Emily asked when they were on the common.

'The west wind, because it is warm, and it does not smell,' he answered.

'Why doesn't it smell?'

'Because it has not first blown over Haworth. It comes off the moors, perfumed.'

'That is a smell, too,' Charlotte interrupted, pedantically.

'I mean, it does not have an unpleasant odour, of smoke and dung.'

He took them on picnics up the Ponden Beck. In memory they seemed to have spent whole sunny afternoons, laughing, sitting by a pool and a waterfall, great flat boulders to lie upon, the heather around them.

But, sooner or later, a cloud would come over his face. Perhaps he had seen something in the features of one of them that reminded him of his wife. The mask of the father and the priest returned to replace the look of that child still within him; an inner child who could land him in foolish actions, was responsible for his selfish blind spots maybe, but who was also the preserver of his gift of wise innocence.

It was when the priest took over that he reflected that his children were a mystery – perhaps because they were almost all girls – and he wanted to know what was absorbing them when he heard them talking, laughing, and whispering behind closed doors.

One afternoon, rooting in a cupboard, he found a theatrical mask and saw how he might get to understand them. He called them into his study. He put on the mask and danced the steps of a reel, his hands above his head, while he lilted an Irish tune. When they were all laughing, he took of the mask.

'Let us play a game,' he said. 'I want each of you to wear

85

this in turn. Then I am going to ask you a question, and I want you to answer me – freely and honestly.'

The minute he said 'freely and honestly', they stiffened.

'No-one will be able to see you, and you may say anything you wish, so long as it is in truth what you think and feel. Now . . .'

He started with the youngest. The mask covered Anne's mouth and made her panic at losing her breath. Kneeling so as to be on her level, he asked, 'What do you most want in the world, Anne?'

'Age and experience,' Anne answered.

Though she was only four years of age, Aunt Branwell herself could not have given a more righteous answer. They were all so intimidated by a game which was not *their* game, that his Rousseauesque experiment in free expression had only resulted in a platitude. But Patrick was delighted with what he thought was a success.

He turned to Emily. 'Branwell is often a naughty boy,' he said. 'What should I best do with him?'

'Try him with reason,' she said. 'When he won't listen to reason, whip him.'

She had not even said *if* he won't listen to reason. She had said, *when*. One of Emily's precious possessions was a plate given to her by Aunt Branwell for her fourth birthday. It was Wedgwood, blue and white, and it depicted a little girl standing in a cart, wielding a whip. She waved it over a little boy in harness who pulled the cart. One knew it was the girl's brother because around the plate's edge was the rhyme:

> What pleasure filled my little heart
> When seated in my little cart
> To see thee act the horse's part,
> My brother.

Patrick, wondering if Branwell might have an interesting response to this cruelty shown by the fair sex, asked him, 'What is the best way of knowing the differences between the minds of men and of women?'

'By the differences between their bodies,' enigmatically,

but knowingly, answered the loner six-year-old boy who lived among females.

It was Charlotte's turn.

'What is the best book in the world?'

'The Bible.'

'And the next best?'

'The Book of Nature,' she answered, pleasing her father by remembering what he had told her once.

'What is the best mode of education for a woman, Elizabeth?'

She, also, answered as Aunt Branwell would have done: 'That which would make her rule her house well.'

Finally it was Maria's turn.

'What is the best way of spending time?'

Maria answered straight out of one of her aunt's *Methodist Magazines*. 'By laying it out in preparation for a happy eternity.'

'Can we go and play now?' Emily asked.

They scurried off to their more real inventions.

Patrick was growing more short-sighted; more afraid of dyspepsia and indigestion.

When he received the news that his mother, Eleanor, had died, only months after his wife, he seemed to be short of feeling, too, so steeled was he to deal with sorrow. He did not go to Ireland – he could not have got there until well after the funeral – and he tried to spare others by keeping the news to himself. He mentioned it briefly to Aunt Branwell, then vanished before she could lift the lid off his grief.

His children, none of whom had ever met a grandmother, he chose to tell at a time when he could be distant and calm. Consequently, the news touched them as little as if he was telling them of an incident in the Peloponnesian Wars.

But he saw in his mind the fabulous beauty of the Mourne mountains as they had spread before him in childhood. That view, blue, purple, golden, brown, was what he associated with his mother. He knew that even if he went back there, from short-sightedness he wouldn't be *able* to see the mountains as clearly as he had done in his childhood. He thought of his nine brothers and sisters, with whom he had lost contact.

He thought of how amazingly far he had climbed from the thatched cabin, stinking of roasting corn and hen-shit, at Emdale in the parish of Drumballyroney-cum-Drumgooland in County Down, to reach Cambridge and ordination as a minister. And how far God had brought him down again, taking away his wife. Perhaps for his sin of pride.

He ransacked his memory for images of his mother. He found that even then he could not evoke tears; although, he thought, it would be better for him if he could.

He studied his face in a mirror. Despite a little grey in his hair, he looked younger and more vigorous than many his age, and there was hope for him yet. While so many men fattened and developed jowls, his face was still slender.

By his bedside he removed his cravat, and his black clerical garb, undressing as far as his long flannel underwear. He laid out his gold watch, with his cocked pistol beside it. Kneeling, he prayed for his mother, and for his family.

In the following dawn, moving through the house before anyone was up to speak to him, he fired at the church tower.

VIII

While writing to thank Elizabeth Firth for her support after Maria's death, it came into Patrick's head to suggest that he pay her a visit. She had always been such a good friend, perhaps he could seek her advice and help concerning his children.

Two weeks later he walked to Thornton. It was the beginning of December and he had not seen her since Maria's funeral in September. To disguise his devastation, he bought a bottle of hair dye. This time, he made sure that Nancy Garrs polished his boots. He put on a clean cravat, and he went alone. He realized how his long stay in Haworth had been depressing him, for although the season was dank, melancholy early winter, he could not help being inspired by spring-like hope today. He descended from Thornton Heights with something of his old, light step. He entered Kipping House as he used to, through the unlocked street-door. It was as if no time at all had gone by.

Elizabeth helped him off with his overcoat. 'Goodness me, what a long cravat!' she remarked. 'Even longer than when people talked about you in Thornton.'

'My daughters have turned into skilled little seamstresses, thanks to their aunt! I asked Maria to add a little more for the winter. Now that my children are dependent on me, I have to protect myself, you know.'

'Our poetical Mr Brontë is growing eccentric!'

He laughed at himself. Yet she appeared to have spun her curls afresh for him, as if for a young man, and she wore a white bow attached to a cap that trailed a long ribbon. Her blue velvet dress, a new one he thought, carried layers of frilly epaulettes, and a lace collar of two layers. He was unprepared for his envy of her youth and for his greedy, unworthy impulse to possess it. He knew himself to be colouring. His feelings were a shock to him, there in the hallway. Unexpectedly, he felt eager to remove his elderly gentleman's cravat, and his clerical coat, into the hands of this tender young woman who so deliberately helped him herself and had dismissed a servant.

Elizabeth apologized for the 'simplicity' of the meal. There was roast pork, sprouts picked after the first frost as they should be to give them a tang, a fruit pie made of preserves lifted from the ice-pit in the garden, and cheeses. It was splendidly served. There were two formally dressed servants, standing by or shifting between sideboard and dining table. They did not dash in as the Garrs sisters did to sweep away the dirty plates. They seemed glad to serve, even if they weren't, and were not neglectful of their appearances and aggrieved, as the Garrses could be at times. Yet it was only for the two of them seated at either end of the large, elliptical mahogany table, with two candelabras, in the hour after the early December sun had set in rosy suds over the garden.

At first, Patrick had been disposed to protest about his 'plain' tastes nowadays. Since Maria's illness, food had become simply something to shovel into his mouth, while rich food affected him with much more than his previous, puritanical scruple – it actually made him nauseous. Today Patrick thought that perhaps his palate had become dulled by the Garrses' cooking and he rediscovered his appetite. There was no soot in this food. There were no burnt bits.

Here, also, there seemed no sense of secret lives – of that atmosphere which was creeping into the parsonage, with Aunt Branwell shut off, and he in his study in order to avoid talking about unhappy things, and his children secretive with their games.

Neither was Elizabeth as frivolous as she looked. Still only twenty-three years of age, she was now sole mistress since her father died, and her ability to supervise a home that was so cheerful and bountiful seemed a miracle. The kindness and the gentility of Kipping House lit up his cloud. It threw gleams of light, like reflections from Christmas baubles, through his grief.

After the servants had gone to their beds, Patrick did then take a glass of Madeira, with Wensleydale cheese. He sipped another glass of wine, and then a third. He had forgotten about his dyspepsia. With a laugh – how he surprised himself – he confided that every morning he awoke in despair and wanted to bury himself in sleep again.

'Oh, stuff and nonsense!' she said. 'You mustn't overindulge mourning. You must blow the cobwebs away!'

'I do marvel at your banishing of melancholy, Elizabeth! How you used to charm my infants! And – I confess – now my life seems worth living again!'

'I am glad I can do that for you, Mr Brontë.'

'I *must* be cheerful, for the sake of my family. Their aunt and I spend much time discussing their education. I am sure that I can best tutor Branwell for university, but I won't have the finer elements neglected for the girls, either.'

'Why not send them to Miss Mangnall's school, Crofton Hall in Wakefield, where I myself went? Miss Mangnall's own textbook shows an exemplary method for training enquiring minds. Her school is one of the finest and most progressive in the country.'

Patrick could not see how to put the important point. A 'progressive' education was fine for a lady looking forward to a marriage that would support her. How could he make it clear that, unless she who was the godmother of three of them – Elizabeth, Branwell, and Anne – came to their rescue, he had to seek an outlet suitable for girls who were plain and poor?

Patrick stayed for three days. He took walks that inspired bitter-sweet memories, he visited his old parishioners, and he talked intimately with Elizabeth.

By the time he left, he thought that God had sent him a better solution than he had at first conceived. Not thinking of himself as an 'ageing clergyman' any longer, he went home on the wings of blind happiness.

If she accepted him, would Elizabeth Firth move to Haworth? The thought brought him up short: why, no, he would leave Haworth. Her status would help him to preferment and he would apply for a better living. He could take his children to where they might not catch coughs and colds every winter.

In the heat of obsession, he wrote her a letter full of overstatement. He saved himself from a second glance at his proposal and hurried it off, via the carter who every morning took a load of wool from Haworth to Bradford, passing through Thornton.

The stupid, stupid man! How could he do such harm to their friendship!

Elizabeth Firth paced from room to room, gritting her teeth and grinding her hands as thoughts piled up, each one more resentful. She was baffled at how a clergyman who normally composed his thoughts carefully could so overstep the bounds of propriety. His letter was a garbled mixture of financial anxiety, lover's vows and sanctimonious humbug. To Elizabeth Firth at twenty-three, Patrick Brontë at forty-four seemed burned out, but she looked up to him as her second father. Didn't he realize how cruel it was to have cheated her of that? She who had lost her parents! Why didn't he think of it! He was utterly selfish. And what had he to offer *her*? The proposal was not only ridiculous. That, she could forgive. It was insulting. It was callous, and showed a terrible indifference to her dear friend, his wife.

She found herself at her kitchen door, staring through her cook so piercingly that the woman dropped a dish. At last she grew calm. She was able to sit at her escritoire for long enough to write a firm letter of rejection, and inform him that it would be her last communication ever.

It helped her composure, though it did not help her to feel kindly towards Mr Brontë, that the Reverend James Franks of Sowerby Bridge, young, unmarried and well-connected, was coming to dinner. She was very glad to see him.

Once a week, Patrick walked to Keighley.

He visited his banker, Mr Marriner and his friend, Theodore Dury, the rector. He collected the *Leeds Intelligencer*, the *Leeds Mercury*, or books from Mr Hudson, the bookseller in the High Street, or he visited the printer of the *Keighley Visitor*, Mr Robert Aked, whom Patrick was encouraging to open a circulating library – in the growing town of Keighley it was, as they said in Haworth, 'all go'.

Patrick often took Branwell with him. Not any of the girls, usually, but he believed that his son, even at five years of age, would begin to learn how the world was run from accompanying him to the places of business which he must visit.

One day, while Branwell played a lonely game of 'The Battle of Waterloo' in the shrubberies of the Rectory, Mr Dury glanced through the window and his mind strayed to thoughts of his friend's many orphaned children. 'What you need most is another wife,' he said.

'I have thought about it,' Patrick admitted, smiling, 'but wives aren't easy to . . .' He didn't like to add, 'put one's hands on.' 'To find,' he concluded.

'My sister Isabella needs a husband. I have noticed that you take pleasure in conversing with her, and not all men are of her kind.'

Patrick could not have a better solution than a link between their families. For Mr Dury's part, his sister was not very pretty, she had a mind of her own, and he feared having to keep her for the remainder of her life.

Unfortunately, Miss Dury turned out to be as prompt and peremptory as Elizabeth Firth with her reply. To her friend Miss Marriner, the daughter of Mr Brontë's banker, who might hear some gossip – or be interested in some – Miss Dury explained: 'I heard it said that my brother and I had quarrelled about poor Mr Brontë. I beg, if you ever hear such a report, that you will contradict it as I can assure you it is perfectly unfounded. I think I never should be so very silly as to have the most distant idea of marrying anybody who had not some future, and six children into the bargain – it is too ridiculous to imagine any truth in it.'

August arrived. Aunt Branwell made her own, monthly trip to Keighley. Though it was August, she was, as always, dressed in her 'coal-scuttle' bonnet, black dress, cloak and boots.

She always hired the Black Bull gig. The lad from the pub knew she expected him to be smarter than usual. No good merely removing his public-house apron, otherwise driving her down in his working clothes; and the cob had to be given a brushing, too. But then, he did not need to rehearse the latest tittle-tattle of Haworth, as he did for others who hired the gig. Miss Branwell wasn't interested in conversation. But he thought he'd give it a try.

'I brought you when you first came up here, more'n a year ago. Remember?'

'What is your name?'

'Joseph, ma'am. And I took you down town the month before last. My brother took you last month. I took you about four month sin'—'

'So you did! *I* remember!'

Joseph, insulted by her tardy memory and her indifference to Haworth matters, gave the horse a slap with his whip so that it leaped forward and nearly broke Aunt Branwell's neck.

As he expected, he was ordered to set her down in the town centre, outside the bank.

'Call for me at Miss Marriner's in exactly three hours. You are free to do as you please until then—' She suddenly remembered what happened in the month before last. 'But don't spend your time in drinking.'

'No, ma'am.'

'Nor in the public house at all.'

'No, ma'am.'

'Avoid bad company altogether. There is a new chapel for the Methodists. Chapels are not so severe as they used to be,

I believe it is quite lavish with art. It would be instructive for you to take a look at it.'

'Yes, ma'am. I'll enjoy that.'

After half an hour in the bank, seeing to the balance of her fifty pounds annuity, she sauntered through town. She liked Keighley: above a burbling river were the church, market square, shops, commercial offices and the inns, especially the Devonshire Arms, where one could obtain a superior tea. There were some factories, but never mind. It was as near as she ever came, nowadays, to the elegance of Penzance.

She could survey the fashions. Even though she was dressed in the manner of a decade before, unexpectedly she rather liked the newer clothes. The waistline was dropping. Starched petticoats were being reintroduced. Gowns were becoming fuller. She wished that she was young again.

From one shop, she ordered a consignment of china tea, and from another a bolt of linen, to be sent – 'To Haworth,' she whispered, not liking to admit to where she lived, but adding with emphasis, '*the parsonage*'.

She called at the chapel, to find out what was new from the Methodists that she could not learn in Haworth. She wondered if Joseph had reached there yet, but no, he was not around.

At last, she made it to 'Greengate', Miss Marriner's home, where she was expected for tea.

'I have news of your brother-in-law,' Miss Marriner announced, when her maid had departed after serving.

'My brother-in-law?' Elizabeth Branwell echoed with surprise, as if this was the first she had heard of even having one.

'I am told he proposed marriage to Miss Dury.'

'Told by whom?' Now, at last, the warm summer weather seemed to reach Elizabeth's cheeks.

'I am sorry to be distressing – but by Isabella herself.'

'*Isabella Dury!*'

Miss Branwell did not like Miss Dury.

'She did not accept him. She is not so foolish. Pardon my saying so, but that man – Mr Brontë – seems to be like a *horse*. I am told that he has also proposed to Miss Firth of Thornton. She is years younger than he. "No fool like an old fool," as they say. However, that is only rumour; let us hope there is no truth in it. But as to Miss Dury, as I say, I heard of the matter from herself.'

On their drive back to Haworth: 'Did you visit the new chapel?' Miss Branwell snapped at Joseph.

'Yes, ma'am, but it were shut.'

'It was wide open!'

He did not answer back. He did not need to see the huddle behind him to know how upset she was – more than she could possibly be by his not having visited a chapel, or by his having taken a little ale, after all. Because of it, he himself felt reckless and talkative, even if it had to be with Miss Branwell.

Though he tried hard, he could hardly get a word out of her. He asked her if she had liked what she had seen in Keighley and she barely answered. By the time that he handed her out at the parsonage, he felt sorry for her.

On looking over the sloven, Nancy Garrs, in her pinafore stained with stove-blacking, fruit preserve and flour, Elizabeth Branwell recalled Miss Marriner's neat maid. In disgust and despair, she went up to her room and shut the door. She threw down her bonnet. She flung off her cloak.

It was one thing for her to care for her own sister, and then the widower and his children; but to think that, had it not been for Isabella Dury having more sense than to accept, she might have had to share what had now become her home with the 'impossible' Miss Dury as its new mistress!

The fact that from time to time Patrick had thrown the glance of love at *her* made it worse. He knew well enough why she kept to her room so much; perhaps even the servants did, too! Looking at her like that – stuttering – putting out his hand – he would have proposed marriage to her, *his sister-in-law*, if it had not been totally out of the question.

Apart from anything else this fact, lodged in her consciousness like a thorn in a dog's paw, made it impossible for her to accept Elizabeth Firth, Miss Dury, or anyone else as mistress of the parsonage.

But where could she go, now? It was too late to go back to Penzance. She was trapped here for life *whatever happened*.

On top of everything else – she was starting to have bowel trouble.

She was *so* angry with Patrick. She realized that, out of being kind to him, she had become a slave of fortune. She shut herself firmly in her room.

You may think there are no degrees of firmness about a shut door. That is because you did not know Miss Branwell. She could generate an atmosphere, simply by the way she placed a used tea tray outside.

IX

There was Mary Burder left for Patrick to try.

Mary Burder, of Wethersfield in Essex, had been his landlady's niece during his first curacy. He had been aged thirty, she had been hardly more than a child, but he was handsome, and she fell in love.

Mary's guardian had sized up the position clearly enough. 'Mary,' he had said, 'if your love for your handsome Irish curate is to be consummated, he will want you to give up your faith as a Dissenter. He is of the Evangelical camp. It will be difficult enough as it is for him to make his way in the Church. It would be impossible with a Dissenting wife.'

'No! Love will overcome all obstacles!'

'Including time?'

'Uncle, what do you mean?'

'I am moving you to the farm at Great Yeldham and I forbid any meeting.'

'He will claim me from exile when I am twenty-one!' she had told her friend.

She had been eighteen. She had not seen him since. He moved from Essex to Shropshire and continued to write for a time; although he did not tell her that, wrestling with his vocation, he was by degrees turning away from her. His letters ceased when he decided that he must give her up. *For Christ's sake we are to cut off a right hand, or to pluck out a right eye*, he quoted St Paul to himself. She had been left to feel the natural anger of the jilted.

Patrick was now secure in his church. He wrote, firstly to her mother, telling her of the benefits of his Living, enquiring ingenuously after her children, asking 'whether they be married or single', and ending with the outrageous fib: 'If all be well I shall probably go into the South this summer, and may pass through your neighbourhood. I long to revisit the scene of my first ministerial labours, and to see some of my old friends.'

Elizabeth Branwell realized that Nancy had left the parsonage.

These days Nancy was often sneaking off. Elizabeth had been told that she had been caught staring at some young workmen repairing a roof. Reports had been received that she had been 'flaunting herself' – 'taking some baking from the parsonage' – to this same builders' gang where they were repairing a barn. It seemed that she had at last caught Nancy at it.

'Where has Nancy gone to, Sarah?'

'To the post office, Miss Branwell.'

'Oh.' She was a little taken aback. 'To post a letter?'

'It wouldna surprise me, Miss Branwell,' Sarah answered, sarcastically.

This could be even worse than sneaking off to a sweetheart. It was unlikely that Nancy was posting a letter of her own, as she would have to get someone to write it for her, and that would probably be known about.

The letter could be from Patrick to that fleabag, Miss Dury.

'To whom was it addressed?'

'I do not know.'

'Send Nancy to me when she comes in.'

'It were only from Mester Bron-*teh*. It'll be nowt to be concerned about.'

'I'll be the judge of that!'

'Aye, Miss Branwell.'

From her room, Elizabeth knew when Nancy had returned, because of the giggles. She overheard herself called 'a flaysome old bird'. Nancy came to the door. She found Miss Branwell bristling.

'Yes, Miss Branwell?'

'You have been to the post office?'

'Aye, Miss Branwell.'

'To post a letter?'

'Nowt else to go for.'

'To whom was it addressed?'

''Ow do I know? I canna read.'

'You did not enquire at the post office?'

''Eaven forbid, Miss Branwell, I anna nosey. It'd be none o' my business.' But Nancy was smirking.

'That'll be all, Nancy.'

Aunt Branwell truly did not know why the servants laughed behind her back. After Nancy had left, Elizabeth Branwell crumpled into tears.

When she recovered, she found Emily alone in the children's 'study'. They seemed to like the little room, making a nest in the lumber. She squeezed in, among books, newspapers, bundles of material and the part-finished sewing, and said: 'How would you feel about having a new mother? If your father . . . Papa . . . brought another one for you *to this house*?'

She could not help the slight, betraying emphasis.

'Why would he do that?'

Elizabeth smiled at her answer.

'Would you still love your Aunt Branwell?'

'My feelings for you would never be changed, Aunt, by anything that Papa did.'

Such wise words and judicious expression coming from one not yet five years of age! She hugged the child.

'You're a *good* girl, Emily.'

Patrick waited a month for a reply. Upon receiving it at last, he wrote directly to Mary Burder:

Dear Madam,

. . . I experienced a very agreeable sensation in my heart, on reflecting that you are STILL single, and am so selfish as to wish you to remain so, even if you would never allow me to see you . . . I am sure you once loved me with an unaffected innocent love, and I feel confident that after all which you have seen and heard, you cannot doubt respecting my love for you. It is now almost fifteen years since I last saw you ... I hope I may venture to say I am WISER and better ...

I have a SMALL but SWEET little family that often soothes my heart ... I want but ONE addition to my comforts, and then I think I should wish for no more on this side of eternity. I want to see a dearly beloved friend, kind as I ONCE saw her, and as MUCH disposed to promote my happiness. If I have ever given her any pain, I only wish for an opportunity to make her amends, by EVERY attention and kindness ... I cannot tell how YOU may feel on reading this, but I must say MY ancient love is rekindled, and I have a LONGING desire to see you ... And WHATEVER you resolve upon, believe me to be yours,

> MOST SINCERELY
> P. Brontë

The cheek of it – thought Mary Burder – claiming that his old love was rekindled! Out of what?

At least he admitted to his selfishness at being glad to find me single after fourteen years.

She thought of telling him in so many words that his mendacities and hypocrisy were quite phenomenal, but decided that, if she waited, an even more stinging response might spring to her mind. Her love being cauterized by those earlier years of pining, she was burning with two fires, one of anger, the other of revenge. After a couple of days during which inspired sentences lit up her life, she composed her reply:

Reverend Sir,

As you must reasonably suppose a letter from you presented to me on the 4th inst. naturally produced sensations of surprise and agitation. You have thought proper after a lapse of fifteen years and after various changes in circumstances again to address me, with what motives I cannot well define.

She paused. She gave a small, satisfied smile at the pencil drawing framed on her desk. It was of the Reverend Peter Sibree who was minister of the Dissenters' meeting-house in Wethersfield.

> From a recent perusal of many letters of yours bearing date eighteen hundred and eight, nine and ten addressed to myself and my dear departed aunt, many circumstances are brought with peculiar force afresh to my recollection. With my present feelings I cannot forbear in justice to myself making some observations which may possibly be severe, of their justice I am convinced. This review Sir excites in my bosom increased gratitude and thankfulness to that wise, that indulgent providence that withheld me from forming in very early life an indissoluble engagement with one whom I cannot think was altogether clear of duplicity. A union with you under then existing circumstances must have embittered my future days.

She paused again as another memory surfaced; that of the fears he had voiced of his advancement being hindered by her. Where had it got him? A bishopric? An Oxford fellowship? Renown as a poet? No, it was only to some bleak northern parsonage.

To rub salt into the wound, she added:

> Happily for me I have not been the ascribed cause of hindering your promotion, of preventing any brilliant alliance, nor have those great and affluent friends, that you used to write and speak of, withheld their patronage on my account, young, inexperienced, unsuspecting, and ignorant, as I then was of what I had a right to look forward to.

After a few proper consolations on Patrick's bereavement, she posted her letter.

Patrick was so shocked that it was five months before he could respond.

He did own to his weaknesses and blind spots: they lay

in the weave of his nature like slubs in woollen cloth. He realized what it must do to a woman to be left for years expecting his return, while he wrestled with his vocation. At last, swallowing his pride, he wrote back, virtually ignoring her spurning of him. His hurt, weak pleas could only make matters worse.

> I loved you, and notwithstanding your harsh and in some respects cruel treatment of me, I must confess I love you still.

She did not write to him again. She married the Reverend Sibree and produced four children, although she was thirty-five years of age when she married.

Patrick's eyesight continued to weaken. He could see as little of his surroundings as he could perceive light in his destiny. He grew reconciled to being imprisoned in a life of genteel poverty with Aunt Branwell, the pair of them on different tracks of the same treadmill.

More and more, year by year, Patrick felt the graininess of the autumns in his chest and throat. The damp did not so much rise up, or settle out of the air, as congregate – a gritty substance – in Yorkshire. Often, after he had been out on parish duties, he came home thinking he could recall exactly at what moment, in which dank Sunday School or blowy farmyard, he had felt the catch in his throat. It would stay rattling in his bronchioles and land him with another cold. He got his daughters to add yet another foot to his cravat, so that he could wind it further up his chin. Fear of an illness was the fear of a demonic ghost.

'You must wear flannel, my dears, and I, I know, for all our sakes, must guard my throat,' he solemnly advised his family.

He resolved to put aside the hope of marriage for himself, and to remember that what women saw in him was not the young man of his delusions, but the face he saw in his mirror. His children would be his security in old age. Branwell was clever enough to follow the great career that fate had denied to himself. Although the girls, with *their* looks and fortunes, had little hope of spectacular marriages, they might make satisfactory ones. If they remained spinsters, given a practical upbringing they should be able to care for him — all of them supported by a successful brother.

He would happily go to his Maker tomorrow, were it not that his life was his children's raft.

Although guilt clogged the once-pure waters of his soul in its course to his Maker, as effluent polluted the Haworth springs, what would save him, at last, would be the opinions of his children.

CHAPTER THREE

THE ELECTRIC CHILDHOOD

COWAN BRIDGE

I

Childhood was a time of happiness simply from being alive. Happy to wriggle and run and sleep without thinking of who should care for one. To rely upon someone to provide dry boots and stockings, to light the fire and put food upon the table when one came home. Happy that there was someone to run to for a hug.

Not Papa, always. Dear Papa was often weighed down and one had first to find out how he was. Hardly ever did one run to Aunt Branwell, either, but one could burrow in the lap of Nancy Garrs or of Sarah.

'I hear from Miss Marriner and others that many of the better families are employing governesses,' Elizabeth Branwell remarked to Patrick one day. 'Miss Marriner receives the news – her brother informs her. They are building mansions and filling them with art and fine things, and they require tutors and governesses. At one time, I am told, there was hardly a family within twenty miles offering that kind of employment. Now it seems that the whole district needs them. Our own girls' background suits them for such situations, provided they acquire the accomplishments.'

Aunt Branwell and he could teach them much, ranging from grammar to sewing, but for the 'accomplishments' of a governess – principally drawing, music, and French – they

103

would need to go to a school. The only alternative for a poor parson's unattractive daughters was a tumble into the chasm of domestic service.

Patrick walked thoughtfully down to Keighley, closeted himself with Mr Marriner for an hour, and returned to his study to rack himself a little longer with balancing his income and responsibilities. He decided that, at any rate for a start, he could send his two eldest, Maria and Elizabeth, to Elizabeth Firth's old school, Crofton Hall near Wakefield.

It was the first time that the family had been divided and it was like splitting a nest with a hatchet. Patrick realized it the minute he took nine-year-old Maria and eight-year-old Elizabeth, with their little trunks, out to the gig.

'They'll be back home soon,' Aunt Branwell said, as she led the remaining children indoors. She thought it best not to encourage emotional partings – children must grow up to expect them.

It was difficult for them to believe her. They felt as they had at the only other parting they had known, when their mother had died, when much the same words had been spoken, and they had turned out to be untrue.

Branwell cried. Emily said nothing – holding in what she felt, already accepting that this was the way of the world – while it dawned upon Charlotte, with a thrilling sensation, that she was now the elder sister and must be responsible.

'Let us get on with doing something,' she declared, and led the four amputated beings to retreat into their 'study'. Papa did not return from Wakefield until the following day, by which time they had woven a story about orphans.

All over the hills they were welcomed as the parson's family. They could sit at moorland firesides where primness and gentility never reached – where there was nothing else to do in bad weather or on winter evenings but tell stories. They heard such fantastic, terrible, passionate and cruel tales. If they were caught in a thunderstorm, they could sit it out and be sent home in a gig in the charge of a servant.

'Let's go to Ponden Hall,' Emily would most often beg. 'Please, Tallii – Nancy.'

'Why d'yee like it so much?' Nancy asked, once.

'It's like somewhere Sir Walter Scott would write about. The Heatons are like chieftains! Papa told me they come off the mountains long ago and settled by the stream and won miles and miles and miles of moorland.'

'*Came*,' Branwell corrected. 'How did they win them?' he asked.

'*I* don't know.'

Nancy explained. 'They married into t'farms where there was only a daughter t'inherit. Then they started making cloth. They had t'wool spun into warps at Ponden, then had weavers as far as twenty miles yonder weaving it for 'em and bringing it back for dyeing and finishing. Now they've built a spinning mill.'

It had been only recently, after the building of the mill, that they had started to term Ponden a 'hall'. That very name; the way that the Heatons owned and hunted over the moorlands; the spaciousness and appurtenances of the hall, including a library (not merely some bookcases, but a whole room filled with books); the walled orchard and garden that was a marvel to the neighbourhood, and which included a hothouse, heated with peat and coal, where the Brontë children were allowed to pick grapes; the hospitality upon which they gorged, these children who were described as 'picky' at home – the honey from the Ponden hives – the raisin brandy – the fresh-killed meat and poultry – the jellies – the greens and vegetables smelling freshly of dew and earth – Emily could have gone on endlessly listing the delights.

Ponden attracted all three Brontë children. It combined moorland wildness and an image of splendour, swashbuckling and Byronic. If they timed their rambles aright, they could drop in at mealtimes. With so many to feed at Ponden Hall already, it was always easy to fit the children around the table, while the Garrses were fed in the company of servants, tradesmen and weavers in the kitchen, where they enjoyed leftovers, or maybe thievings from the first pickings.

As they came down off the moorlands and saw the peacocks strutting, the great dogs prowling in the yard, the apples and pears golden in the orchard, and the busy court of servants, 'It's like the Ottoman's court in Constantinople,' Emily observed. She would not have been surprised if Lord

Byron, in Turkish or Albanian costume, had galloped on a white charger past the house. Tired from playing by the waterfalls, drenched perhaps, their clothes regularly torn and dirty, they would fearlessly pass the great dogs – Emily might put her arms around a mastiff's neck and kiss it – and go straight into 'the house'.

There was the huge fireplace with its stone slab, and its chimney-breast hung with old pistols and hunting guns; and with the tea caddies, painted with courting scenes, on the mantelpiece. There was the rack under the ceiling for drying oatcakes. There was the vast oak dresser reaching up to the ceiling, its racks showing pewter jugs, plates and tankards. Black, high-backed chairs stood against the walls. Although you would not say it was a comfortable room, for the floor was of stone and the ceiling was not underdrawn, it was welcoming and warm, if you had come in from a moor and didn't want to fear dirtying fine upholstery. They knew that they would be as welcome here as at home, and be greeted without fuss or pretension. To come in wet and dirty was part of the natural order of existence here, and master, mistress and servants were only concerned that the parson's children should be dry and fed before they were returned to the parsonage.

It was on a day that autumn, when Maria and Elizabeth were away at Crofton Hall, that Emily heard a haunting story at Ponden Hall.

This time, it was only Charlotte, Branwell and Emily, with the dog, who were out – Anne was at home with a bad chest, and also they were without the Garrses. They had strayed too far, were near collapsing, and were drenched from the waterfalls. The dog was bedraggled and miserable. The day was so wet that even the Ponden mastiffs would not come out of shelter, while the peacocks folded their damp displays and sheltered in the barn. But the Brontës were what few people saw: they were laughing.

Mrs Heaton rushed a man over to Haworth with a message that she was keeping the children to dry and feed them. She had their clothes put before the kitchen range and she dressed them in cast-offs and assortments. Their dog was tied to a table leg by the kitchen fire.

The long oak table in the 'house' would seat twenty people. Robert Heaton sat in a winged chair at the head, by the fire. Alice Heaton sat on his right in an upright chair that was without wings. Their year-old baby, Robert, was rocked in his cradle by a nurse, who took her food from a plate in her lap as she sat upon a stool. As usual, half a dozen stray visitors stretched down the sides of the table and around its end. There was a cousin who had walked over from Oxenhope for the shooting, there was a cloth merchant on his way from Leeds to Burnley, and there was a skilled loom-maker, whom it was politic to flatter. Among flagons of wine and jugs of beer were dishes of gamebirds and joints of meat for Robert to carve. Though the provision was lavish, nothing would be wasted, for remains would make a meal for the servants, or be turned into soups for poor weavers who came to collect their warps. The bones would be for the dogs. It was the quantities that amazed the Brontës. Meat in the parsonage was usually stewed, or handed out in small slices. A little communion wine, and some beer, was locked away in the cellar, from where Aunt Branwell, who kept the key, brought up a pint of beer each day to be shared between Nancy and Sarah, for no-one else touched it. Though fruit pies were nothing new to the children, baking having become a regular activity, what made their eyes start here were the bowls of fresh fruit, the jugs of cream, the plates of cheeses. Those who knew them only at home would have been amazed to see them laughing and giggling, amused today at being dressed like clowns in the oversized clothes pulled out of a chest; nibbling grapes, and being taught to peel an orange.

And yet to Robert and Alice Heaton they still seemed to toy with what was before them and not to join fully in the conviviality. Once Robert had seen them at a children's party held for his cousin's family in Oxenhope. They had turned up so queerly dressed, and had stood tightly together, not speaking or laughing, unfamiliar with children's games, 'hunt the thimble' etcetera. When the eldest one spoke, she had wanted to discuss a *parliamentary debate*!

Several times, Robert had watched them in his yard with the rabble of servants' children. The Brontës were more comfortable with the Ponden dogs, which terrified everyone else. In the company of other children, they stood in a huddle, stiff as spinster schoolmistresses ('already', as Robert Heaton thought, making a shrewd guess at their future careers), neither smiling nor speaking. The Ponden children were told to put it down to their being a parson's offspring, 'different because of all that God and praying', and they let them alone.

'I'll tell thee a story, sithee!' Robert Heaton bawled when they were all ready to start their meal. 'In us great great great great grandfeyther's day ...' He paused, closed his eyes and counted on his fingers, but was still not sure he'd got the number of generations correct. He looked small in his high-backed chair: very small compared with Papa, thought Emily, but he was powerful. Perhaps he shouted so much because he wasn't very big.

'Robert!' chided Alice. 'Get on wi' it! You've had too much wine already,' and she laughed.

She knew the story that was coming. It was one he'd often told, but he didn't care. If guests and hangers-on didn't want to be bored, they needn't come and gobble his food. The Brontës hadn't heard the tale. Heaton liked children, and wanted to amuse them. He opened his eyes and rocked his chair back firmly on the floor.

'We were near cheated out of Ponden. It was during the Civil War. Michael Heaton, after he had married and had two children, went off to fight and never returned. But, it seems, he hadna made a will.'

Robert Heaton laughed. He gave a crafty smile, and said, 'Now what mak' of man would go off to war and not leave a will?'

'No kind of man would,' Emily said. 'He must have made one. Someone lost it. Or burned it.'

'Aye, well,' continued Robert, a little taken aback by the child's perception of the world's mercenary ways, 'that's where Henry Casson enters the picture. He come down from Scotland, a wild, surly stranger by all accounts, driving cattle. He saw his chance wi' t'widow and stayed on employed as a keeper and bailiff. For that job it needed a stranger and a character who could face up to being unpopular, and Casson it seems was the lonely, rough kind of man for it. Eventually he married Michael Heaton's widow, Anne. I suppose she had become dependent on him to look after the estate, but he bullied her and her two children mercilessly. When they married, an inventory of the estate and goods was drawn up by her and Michael's relatives, but this, too, disappeared. It vanished just same as the will did.'

Robert Heaton carved himself a slice of apple and dunked it in his glass of wine. He brought it out on the point of his knife, making his hearers wait until he'd chewed it. Emily, Branwell and Charlotte were on the edges of their chairs.

'Casson ruled Ponden for twenty years, and had his own son by Anne. If her son by Michael Heaton, who was named Robert like me, should be so cowed as not to be able to resist, Casson's own lad, John, would inherit, wouldn't he? To make sure of it, Casson brought up his stepson to be ignorant. He couldn't even write his own name and when he had to sign a document he put a cross. He was treated like a black slave, beaten and made to shovel muck and sleep in a barn. A Caliban. He was turned into a brute so that he'd be incapable of entering polite society – a drawing-room – or a lawyer's office. Or of standing before a judge and being respected.'

Robert Heaton made his listeners wait again. A bitch whined, another snaffled bits of meat dropped under the table, and the nurse hushed the baby.

'But just afore Robert Heaton came of age, judgement was passed that the administration of the estate be granted to Michael Heaton's widow. She must have had a friend among the magistrates! A year later, Robert Heaton inherited. But he had to buy back some of his father's goods from Casson, for it's recorded he paid thirteen pounds for some of 'em. One of 'em . . .' Robert turned his chair and pointed '. . . is that great cupboard there, sithee!'

The meal was over. Alice Heaton rang a handbell. Servants cleared the remains. They didn't need to sweep the floor, for the dogs had cleaned it. The children were dressed again in their dry clothes and, in the early evening, driven home, down the Ponden carriage drive between the lime trees – the dog sitting, warm and dry, in Emily's lap – past the dark mill with barred windows, and finally back to Haworth. The September twilight seemed to deepen the savagery of the story. They carried it on, imagining Casson trying to murder little Robert Heaton. Emily thought of Casson bringing his own son, John, up to be a gentleman. 'A despicable fop' was Emily's term for him. She imagined John Casson helping with the brutalizing of William Heaton's rightful heir, and John Casson sneering at Robert Heaton for his ignorance, kicking him out to sleep above the cattle byre, laughing at him behind his back for his ignorance.

At the parsonage came the expected scolding from Aunt Branwell. Still, they didn't care. After bedtime – while Branwell slept in Papa's room and Anne was with Aunt Branwell – Charlotte and Emily, head to toe in one bed, carried on weaving one of what they called their secret 'bed plays'; one set in Ponden Hall, full of betrayals, the villainy of a 'dark stranger', a beautiful girl's love for him, and the ill treatment of a rightful heir.

II

Miss Mangnall's school at Crofton Hall was a great success for Maria and Elizabeth. They wrote excited letters home, showing off their knowledge. '*Haven't* I a pair of blue stockings!' Patrick remarked.

But he couldn't afford to keep even his eldest two there, let alone send the other three girls. He saw his children growing into savages, coming home as they had done from Ponden Hall. He conjured again with the arithmetic of providing an education, and was in despair.

'The Reverend Carus Wilson of Tunstall in Lancashire is opening a school for the daughters of poor clergymen of the Evangelical persuasion,' the Reverend Dury told him. 'It is to be called the Clergy Daughters School. The fees are only fourteen pounds per year. You would be able to afford that, Mr Brontë.'

It was crushingly put, but Patrick was used to that from fellow clergy who were wealthy.

'The scheme has attracted enlightened patrons,' Mr Dury continued.

One of them was William Wilberforce, no less. Others were Hannah More, and Mr Dury himself. There was a dozen of them, plus a patroness and sixteen vice-patronesses, made up of minor royalty, members of parliament, clergymen and Honourables.

Dury showed him an advertisement in the *Leeds Intelligencer*. It claimed, 'The great Object in View will be their intellectual and religious Improvement; and to give that plain and useful Education, which may best fit them to return with Respectability and Advantage to their own Homes, or to maintain themselves in the different Stations of Life to which Providence may call them.'

'Mr Wilson is renowned as an educationalist,' Mr Dury said.

Into Patrick's hands he put some little books entitled *The Children's Friend*. On opening their cheap yellow covers, Patrick noticed, firstly, the wood-engravings. There were crude drawings of men chained to walls, little boys in chains wringing their hands at the sight of gallows, mothers weeping over their daughters, and little girls crying by the biers of their mothers. The stories were called: *A True Account of the Punishment of Vice* and *Some Particulars of the Death Bed of a Sunday Scholar in Cornwall; Awful History of a Sudden Death*, or, simply, *Awful History*. Each could be digested in minutes, and was told in words of one syllable. One was the account of a little boy whose criminal path had begun with stealing a pin, then an apple, next a gold watch, until finally he knelt in chains before a judge who dabbed his eye with his sleeve as he sent him to the gallows.

'The Accomplishments do not seem very important to Mr Wilson,' Patrick remarked.

'Not of first importance. I don't think they will be neglected, but he has a greater aim than French and art. While Britain continues to seethe with disaffection he puts discipline, modesty, gratitude, and consciousness of sin first. He feels that the dissemination of his ideals through a corps of governesses and teachers of village schools is the best safeguard against revolution. That is why he is able to attract distinguished patronage.'

Patrick took the advertisement and a textbook home to show Aunt Branwell.

'You shouldn't be queasy,' she said. 'The morals are good ones.'

'I am led to believe that the regimen is rather strict and severe.'

'So much the better! The children have been getting more and more out of hand.'

'So long as they are strong enough for it. I am not sure that they are. Any port in a storm, I suppose. Fourteen pounds a year – seventy pounds for all of them. I don't see any other strategy for educating the girls.'

Maria and Elizabeth were chosen first. They should have been present when Cowan Bridge opened in January 1824, but all the Brontë children went down with whooping cough, then chickenpox, followed by measles. ('At least we've had no typhoid this year,' said Dr Andrew.)

Their elders studied the prospectus while they convalesced.

'The uniform is very pretty and sensible.' Aunt Branwell beamed.

The children spent their convalescence stitching their shifts, petticoats and pinafores. When both Patrick and Dr Andrew remarked that they would all recover faster in the fresh air than in Aunt Branwell's stuffy bedroom – from time to time moving from there to the cold, fireless sewing-room – Elizabeth Branwell contradicted them. 'But the children are so excited about their school, so looking forward to it!' she said, and there was no reason why they should not be. Maria and Elizabeth had enjoyed Crofton Hall.

They might next have gone at Easter, but Patrick still dithered. 'I don't think they are yet strong enough,' he told his sister-in-law.

'Why are you prevaricating?' she snapped.

'Am I?' He considered. 'I don't know. I think I must be sure that they are strong, first.'

He knew that they had to be stronger than at present even to stomach their first glimpses of Mr Wilson's booklet. Ruefully, he reflected how far Mr Wilson's ideals were from Rousseau's, put his trust in God, and one day he tested his children out with a copy of *The Children's Friend*. As he watched their eyes pass over the terrible morals, and each look at the other to see what she thought, he almost changed his mind about Cowan Bridge. Even the story of the Ark, generally shown as an image of hope – Noah, his family, and the animals saved, the dove and the rainbow above – in Carus Wilson's book was illustrated by a picture of people drowning.

Maria read aloud: 'Then the floods came, and oh! how the poor bad men did wail and howl, when they felt that they did sink in the wa-ter. They swam to the ark, and did try to get in, but they could not. The door was shut.'

Elsewhere, Elizabeth read: '. . . If the gaol does not teach him to leave his bad ways, he will be hang-ed. Did you ever see a man hang-ed? Oh! It is a sad sight! I will tell you all about it in the next tale—'

'I think that's enough for one day,' Patrick said.

Fourteen pounds a year . . . a plain and useful Education . . .

Patrick prevaricated until the summer, taking his infants on picnics, building up their strength.

One day, Aunt Branwell was waiting for them with a pair of scissors. She sat Maria, then Elizabeth, on a chair. She put a sheet around their necks.

'Why do I have to have my hair cropped?'

'A rule of the school,' she answered. 'Don't you want to be right for school?'

'But why?'

'*Because.*'

'But *why*?'

'You know what *The Children's Friend* says happens to children who ask questions! You don't want that to happen to you, do you?'

After Aunt Branwell had dressed them in the summer uniform – their buff-coloured dresses, the bits of their lopped hair sticking from under the straw bonnets that seemed to mock their prison-like haircuts – Maria and Elizabeth climbed into the gig with Papa.

The farewells to brother and sisters did not feel so terrible, second time round, and then there was the excitement of entering the Devonshire Arms where they ate muffins and drank tea. It was the grandest inn in Keighley, by the church, prominent where the straight road fell onto the town centre from Skipton, and they were taken to wait in the front room with other travellers for the Leeds–Kendal coach, which passed through Keighley and also Cowan Bridge, which was fifty miles away. They had seen the coach many times before, its passing by being one of the most exciting events in the town. Pulled by four horses, it had two massive wheels to the rear, two smaller steering wheels at the front, and was top-heavy with luggage and with travellers braving the weather for the sake of a cheaper fare.

'They are going to school,' Patrick beamed at his fellow travellers. 'At Cowan Bridge.'

'Ah! Cowan Bridge! Remote in the countryside, but the fine air will surely be good for their complexions.'

III

Charlotte's hair was hacked a month later and she, too, went to the school. Lying between the small towns of Settle and Kirkby Lonsdale, it was adapted out of a row of cottages and a small mill, by the bridge over a noisy little river: the Leck. With her Papa she was set down at dusk outside the great wall. She took in her first, overwhelming impressions, and she experienced, as after her mother's death, that fear which was as if one had swallowed a packet of Aunt Branwell's needles.

When they reached the door of the sitting-room of Miss Andrews, the supervisor: 'Papa, I don't like the smell!' Charlotte said. It was a mouldy smell, of damp walls warmed but not ventilated, and there was a stink of bad food.

It was dark before the preliminaries were over. Servants had lit candles.

'How have Maria and Elizabeth been progressing?' Papa asked.

Miss Andrews was a mean, tight, bony, dry woman, with nervous habits. 'Very well, it seems, Mr Brontë. They were not remarkable to begin with.'

'Really?' Papa looked surprised. Miss Andrews opened the admissions ledger. Having her writing in front of her seemed to calm her nerves.

'This is what was recorded when they arrived. "Maria Brontë. Reads tolerably. Writes pretty well. Ciphers a little. Works badly. Very little of geography or history. Has made some progress in reading French, but knows nothing of the language grammatically. Elizabeth Brontë. Reads little. Writes pretty well. Ciphers none. Works very badly. Knows nothing of grammar, geography, history or accomplishments."'

'May I see for myself?'

Miss Andrews handed Papa the ledger.

'Compared with some other pupils, Maria and Elizabeth seem to have received high praise,' he said, and he read aloud: ' "Reads most abominably and is perfectly ignorant of all else besides." That is for a girl of fourteen. "Reading vile." Maybe Maria and Elizabeth were overawed? They progressed well at Miss Mangnall's school in Wakefield. At home afterwards, they instructed the other little ones. Maria helped me correct the proofs of my poems when she was little more than six years of age, and in Haworth they were reckoned to be brilliant children. Perhaps you don't flatter your charges, so as to be able to encourage them with their signs of improvement later?'

Papa twinkled at Miss Andrews.

Miss Andrews looked cut to the quick. 'We do like to be able to praise them for their improvements. At any rate, our school is popular. We are expecting *many* more enrolments. You are just in time, Mr Brontë.'

Charlotte felt menaced by this lack of attainment. She had been sure that, if by no other means, her sisters and she could survive any test through their cleverness. Was what counted in Haworth not the same for the rest of the world?

Miss Andrews took back her ledger. 'Apparently they have been vaccinated for scarlet fever and whooping cough,' she commented.

Then Maria and Elizabeth were brought in. They should have been excited, as Charlotte was at meeting them. Dreadfully, they were merely polite. Charlotte could not see them quite as sharply as six weeks before – her sight was becoming yet vaguer if objects were any distance away – but she did observe that their eyes were dull and that there was no colour in their cheeks. Their complexions had not, after all, been improved by a month in the country.

Maria said: 'I hope you enjoyed an agreeable journey, Papa, Charlotte, and that you have not become too exhausted.'

She did not call her Tallii!

Papa picked them up, one at a time, raising them into the air.

'My, how you have grown!'

'I think not,' said Elizabeth. 'I think we may not have grown at all. I have had a cold.'

'I mean, you are quite like little adults! Such an improvement!'

Papa was to be accommodated in a guest bedroom. Meanwhile Maria and Elizabeth led Charlotte to the dormitory.

'Maria, what is it like here?' Charlotte asked.

Maria returned a thin smile which was more chilling than any complaint, and answered, 'I am quite sure the benefits bestowed on us so charitably will be good for us later in life.'

'I don't like Miss Andrews.'

'I'm sure she means well for all of us.'

They passed through the dining-room, which was adapted out of the central cottages. All was bare, sparse and dusty. The woodwork was painted brown or black, apart from the scrubbed tables running the length of the room. There were texts on the walls. Over the room hung the smell of rancid fat which Charlotte had noticed even in the passage by Miss Andrews's room.

'I don't like the smell here.'

'Oh, we cannot expect to dine like ladies.'

'I would love to dine like a lady.'

There was a staircase, but they did not climb it.

'The children do not normally use that staircase, which leads up to Miss Andrews's quarters, and the bedrooms for the other eight teachers and the half dozen servants,' Maria said. She had become a weird automaton, even talking about 'children' as if she was not one of them.

'Oh, Marii!' Charlotte exclaimed, and grabbed her arm. 'Marii!'

'What?' Maria leaped back. Evidently, touching did not

seem proper to her, now, and her sense of responsibility as the eldest child taught her to set an example.

In one vivid perception, Charlotte saw that the way to survive in this place was to behave as Maria and Elizabeth did, and to change as soon as possible.

'Miss Andrews does not seem a happy person,' Charlotte remarked. 'She was nervous while talking to Papa. I don't think she enjoys being a teacher here.'

'I think she does not always see eye to eye with Mr Carus Wilson, who comes down to the school once or twice a week to see how we are progressing,' Elizabeth said.

'Here is our schoolroom,' Maria announced.

They had passed through the dining-room. The schoolroom was at right angles on one end, therefore reaching down towards the river, as the cottages were parallel to the Leck. There was the dustiness of a bobbin mill, still, and the bleakness of one. As in the dining-room, there were texts on the walls, and bare wooden forms arranged this time not along the sides of tables but in groups, each around the fortress of a teacher's lectern, each of which was armed with a switch or a cane. They climbed some narrow stairs and opened a door to rows of beds, where the girls were sleeping in pairs.

'What is that noise?' Charlotte asked, and then gave her own answer. 'Some of them are crying!'

'They have not been here for long,' Maria answered – as if Elizabeth and she had been here for years.

'Did you sleep well, Charlotte?' Papa asked.

'Not too well, but I will grow used to it.' She had lain for half the night whispering to Maria with whom, fortunately, she had been allowed to share a bed. By morning she had decided to be resolute, for Papa's sake.

'You enjoyed your breakfast?'

'We had porridge.'

She avoided saying that the milk was sour and that the porridge was lumpy.

'But was it good?'

'No, Papa.'

'Well, perhaps it will get better. It hurts me to say this, but now that you are older, you must get used to some austerity, otherwise you will never be happy in your life.'

She wondered for a moment why this was not true for everyone. Some seemed to be both rich and happy.

'Miss Andrews does not seem a happy person, Papa,' Charlotte repeated. It was a last hope of being taken away.

'Perhaps she does not like the porridge, either!' he joked.

When he left, Charlotte swallowed another packet of needles. Her feeling of abandonment was worsened by seeing him shrug his shoulders.

She could not take in what she was fated to digest through a lifetime: her sure Papa, who was always to be relied on, was now leaving her, Maria, and Elizabeth, and was thinking that everything would be all right.

The school day began at six in the morning. Between seven and eight came prayers and hymns. After breakfast, always of milk and porridge, there followed lessons until noon. Between twelve and one, the girls exercised by taking a walk, or in bad weather by parading under the verandah which extended down to the river.

Dinner at one was, like all the food, worse than monotonous. The meat was often rancid. Charlotte found that there were girls – girls from southern England, who in any case did not like the north country diet of oats and milk – who chose to go without any breakfast at all for weeks, rather than eat that muck.

'The cooks despise us for our wretchedness as charity children,' Charlotte said.

Maria told her, 'You feel too deeply, and are too sensitive to what is thought of you in this life, and you imagine slights. That will not make you happy.'

But on another day, Charlotte heard kitchen hands gloating at spiders and dirt in the stew. 'Good enough for *them*,' she overheard them say. She was not imagining that.

Lessons continued until 'tea' at five. This consisted of dry bread and milk. The older girls worked on until eight, then there was more dry bread and milk before bed. Always hungry, the Brontë girls often talked of Ponden; the sides of meat, the game, the fresh vegetables, the fruit. They thought of the pies cooked by the Garrses.

Maria explained that the regime was designed to mortify the flesh and to instil endurance. Therefore discomfort was deliberate, morally enlightening, educational.

Couched in less blunt language, this was also dinned into them on Sundays, when they had to walk four miles in all weathers to Tunstall (although a church existed near Cowan Bridge) because it was where Carus Wilson preached. His preaching was as unsatisfying to the soul as the other food was to the body: it filled one up with a heavy and distasteful lump like sour-milk porridge, but gave no nourishment.

Mr Wilson stood before them in the schoolroom.

'Are you damned? Or are you of the Elect?'

They sat in little groups, Mr Wilson's visit having interrupted them as they were gathered around their teachers. After he had made his entrance, accompanied by his wife and two daughters, the pupils had turned their chairs towards the podium, the one on which the disobedient and wicked were punished.

Charlotte, Maria, Elizabeth, and the twenty other girls so far at Cowan Bridge, looked up at the Reverend Carus Wilson and saw marble; smooth, pale, and spotless. His face was carved with an unwavering glance and a slight smile, which no-one had power over.

One thing they knew, making him certainly as God-like as his appearance warranted – his side-whiskers, his firm jaw – was that he lived in a castle, in Casterton Hall, in the midst of a deer park. He also had a villa on the Lancashire coast, overlooking the sandy sweep of Morecambe Bay. Charlotte wondered how he could preach self-denial while living like that.

And how could a man who was driven through his park to preach in the church – villagers curtseying or removing headgear along his route – denounce the sin of vanity? Charlotte remembered one of his sermons: 'A little girl who had a habit of *giving way to temper*, who had *a love of dress and took a mischievous delight in idle talk*, took her *next step in evil* through *an eagerness in the pursuit of pleasure*, and by degrees ended up on the gallows.'

There he was, with his *beautiful* wife and two *beautiful* daughters who would often turn up with him – no doubt to consider how well off they themselves were – dressed in bright silks, their hair in ringlets, looking down with such hauteur upon us *charity* children with our hacked hair and our degrading uniforms!

Aunt Branwell had announced that, 'Anyone can be saved. The worst of sinners may be drowned in light, and know they have come to salvation. That is the comfort offered by Jesus Christ.' Aunt Branwell's faith was hopeful. It was cheerful, even if without humour. Wilson's faith was as black as his suits. He was a Calvinist. His belief was in the inherently damned (the 'Reprobates') or the Elect.

'Oh, how will you show that you are one of the sinless?'

He seemed to be appealing, but he was bullying. He made it seem impossible for his little girls to prove that they were without sin, and nothing that they did was ever good enough.

The sin of Mr Wilson's daughters was vanity. But Charlotte's own – she caught her breath – was envy.

Then he told them the story about a dead mother.

'Imagine two little girls who are bent over the corpse of their dead mother, laid upon a bier,' he began.

The Brontës had no difficulty in imagining it, and quite a few of the other charity girls had gone through the same experience.

'How these two poor girls cry, to see their dead mother! Imagine the scene, children. The big girl takes the sheet off the face, to have one more look. The smaller girl cries at the foot of the bed. She can't look up. They have lost their best friend. She can wash them no more; she can sew for them no more; she can talk to them, and pray for them no more. Dear children, do you yourselves have mothers? *Then thank God that He spares you*. These poor girls did not know how dear their mother was, till she was gone.'

He gazed around the room.

'They may have been bad girls! They may have made their poor mother's heart ache! And if so, they would say, "Oh!

If she would but come again, I think I'd vex her no more!"
Mind, then, dear children, that you do not vex your mother.
If God takes her from you, it may be in His wrath because of
you, yourselves.'

Maria, Elizabeth and Charlotte, harangued as if they were
criminals, could not look at one another. Of course they had
been 'bad girls' at times. Had they hastened, even brought
about, their mother's death? Was it because they were naughty
that she had wanted to see so little of them?

That night after evening prayers, Charlotte, in the dormitory, began to cry.

'Maria, do all of us here have naughty hearts?'

'Yes,' Maria answered, resignedly.

'I have been thinking of what I have done that has
been "naughty this day". I envied Mrs Wilson and her
daughters.'

'Yes, there is always something.'

'Is making up stories "naughty"? Is it "lying"?'

'Yes, perhaps it is,' Maria answered.

'Then, for what we do – you know – that way, we are
bound for Hell, and there is no way to stop it!'

IV

In late August that year, Branwell, Emily and Anne in
Haworth went down with their usual first colds before
the autumn. When they were recovering, Papa sent them
out in the charge of Sarah and Nancy, one hot, still day:
the second of September, 1824. Nancy egged them on as far
as Top Withens: a weaver's cottage four miles away, on the
moorlands towards Colne. The heather was in full bloom,
there were areas of golden dry grasses, of blood-red grasses
in the bogs, and of flowering heather, patched here and there
with specks of yellow cinquefoil. Slowly they climbed, along
the course of the Sladen Beck, until there it was, marked out
on the hillside above them by its surrounding of small, green
enclosures; a place as high up on the moorland as anyone
could live, with no track going beyond it.

To keep them going in the heat, Nancy chattered about
Top Withens. 'It was built in Queen Elizabeth's day by Jonas

Sunderland, a man in hiding. They've all been coiners, or brewing illegal whisky ever since. Or they've spent their time poring o'er t'Bible, making more nonsense than sense of it, as some do when they're too much alone. They go melancholy. They – stare.'

'Stare?' Emily asked.

'They'll stand and stare at owt, up there. You catch them at it, often. They'll sit and stare at the gatepost all day. They'll spend all morning watching the kettle. Then they'll go off and kill someone with an axe. It's the Melancholy!'

She laughed. Being from Bradford, the madness of moor-dwellers, 'mithered to death by loneliness and t'weather', struck her as amusing, and also fascinating. It was like the pleasure some took, so she was told, from visiting lunatic asylums.

'So why are we going there, Nancy?'

'There's someone I'd like to see,' she laughed.

'It's her "fancy", Patrick Wainright, who's working on t'roof,' laughed Sarah.

They reached Top Withens: a small stone shack, with walls that had the sturdiness and thickness of a fortress. It was so small that if you squeezed out of the tiny upstairs windows – a child could do it – you could leap without danger to the ground. At one end, you could almost walk out of the upstairs window onto the moor. A byre for two cows, a stable for a single horse, and a cart shed were built onto one end, a small barn and hay loft were at the other end, and between them they kept the house warm. Nearby was a spring that flooded a stone trough, a hardy ash tree, and a nest of walls enclosing small parcels of land; one growing a few vegetables, another oats, another providing grazing.

A young man was balanced on the stripped roof of the barn. He had nailed new laths across the beams. New stone tiles, drilled with holes at their upper ends, had been delivered from the quarry at Penistone, and he was hanging them on the laths. Using wooden pegs, he was working his way up from the eaves to the ridge. He waved to Nancy and she left the others. She climbed onto the field that reached nearly up to the eaves, stepped onto the roof, and joined Patrick Wainwright, setting herself down on the part of the roof he had finished, to sun herself while he continued.

The others stared into the distance. Top Withens, backed up against the moor, made one turn and look the other way. One's eye was drawn from the stones and whinberry towards the long valleys they had climbed, all awash with changing light and colour – drawn to search out the details of Haworth far below, and beyond; the tantalizing mysteries of far away. That must be what the Sunderlands did all day when they were not weaving, thought Emily.

They could hear the looms banging in the couple of bedrooms. No-one wanted to go in to disturb them in their dusty little hovel, on such a broodingly hot day, and they were at a loss what else to do.

'Let's go further up the hill,' Emily suggested.

The children, Sarah and the dog set off to climb Withens Height, which stretched upwards behind the house. Ten minutes' climb. When they reached the top, great scoops of bogland fell away on either side, so they kept to the high, dry ground, worn bare of heather or whinberry. Between the black boulders, stone was pulverized to a fine, hard sand that glittered like stars.

It was so very still – it was eerie. There seemed to be less air by the minute, presaging a storm. They noticed a faint brush of darkness over the distance in the direction of Colne. It grew larger and more ominous, like a wing approaching. The dog was frightened, whimpering, looking up at them, wanting to lick at hands and legs for comfort.

'Let's go back,' Sarah pleaded.

But she was not forceful enough and the children, fascinated by the uncanny atmosphere over the bogs, pressed on.

It was surely too early for sunset, yet as they reached some large boulders at the peak, the sky in the west turned red underneath that dusky wing.

In a few minutes, the wing of cloud, and then the red glow, swept overhead and was followed by a black band. There were distant flashes of lightning and low, rumbling thunder. There was more lightning, rapidly approaching. '*Let's go back*,' Sarah urged again, but the children were transfixed by the electric atmosphere. Anyway, it was getting too late to make an escape.

It darkened overhead now and the air stirred, for the first time that day. It turned into a powerful gust, whistling, whirling up scraps of heather, dust and grit. It grew still for another moment, then the wind returned. They found some boulders against which to huddle. It was only a moment before the storm was upon them. Large drops of rain blotched the stones. The lightning surrounded them. Thunder prowled and echoed, each clap dying in a series of ghostly roars.

A moment later, the slope of Crow Hill, below and ahead of them, erupted in explosions the like of which they had never heard of nor seen before. It threw up columns of boulders and mud from all over the bog.

As they peered through the needles of rain, a large area of the moorland came alive. It slowly turned over and moved. A bank of peat, churned up with rushes, grasses and stones, moved downhill like a massive tidal wave towards Ponden.

Branwell turned white and clung to Sarah, while she held onto four-year-old Anne, who cried at each flash of lightning, the thunder, the explosions of peat and whinberry.

'The Lord have mercy on us souls – on my mother and brothers and sisters – the Lord have mercy,' Sarah muttered. She hardly knew what thoughts to cling to, or what she was saying, she was in such mortal terror.

Then: 'Emily!' she shrieked. *'Emily!'*

The six-year-old had sprung away into the storm. Stumbling over tussocks, falling in the peat, rising and speeding on her long legs down towards the spurting stones, to the great bank of moorland a hundred yards away sliding heavily down the valley, she did not look back.

'Emily!' Sarah shouted, trying to restrain the bewildered dog who wanted to race after her. *'Emily, come back!'*

Evidently she would have carried on, without thought of danger, into the heart of the eruption. Sarah, wet, shaking, out of her mind, not able to understand what had got into the bewitched child, caught up with her as she paused at the edge of a peat gulley. She still kept her back to Sarah, and would not give her her hand. Sarah, half-demented with fear as the moorland continued to erupt, grabbed Emily under the armpits and began to drag her back uphill. The child was screaming and crying, the tears mingling with the rain on her face, and her noise competing even with the howling weather; crying, not out of fear, but out of anger and frustration at not being allowed to stay.

It was quietening down somewhat – well, it seemed to be; maybe Sarah imagined it – as she hurried her charges through the slashing rain and the wind back towards Top Withens. She was so soaked that she could feel the water trickling between her legs, as if she had dipped in a cold river. She reached the ridge, and how glad she was to see the half-finished roof below, the great stone slates shining, the tree bending and turning its leaves like silver scales in the gale! She could not stop feeling the world sliding away beneath her. Once they had dropped from the ridge, in their haste they were continually falling into peat gulleys, slipping off high tussocks of grass, and into cracks of black water; the world was still unsafe. Sarah had never imagined that the earth could shift from under her like this. She was going to be sick. She let go of the dog who fortunately, though confused, went skimming down towards the house. Yet Sarah kept tight hold of the mad Emily. She tried to keep the other children close also, and to ignore the sting of the rain, and not look behind at what terrible force or hand might be reaching for her out of the sky. The important thing was to keep hold of Emily.

Thus they slipped and slid downhill, almost as often on their backs as upright, scratching and cutting themselves on the heather and stones until they descended upon Top Withens. They reached the gate in the wall surrounding the little yard. They passed by the house window, which was shuttered to keep out the storm. The dog slipped, whining, out of the cart shed. They all poured in through the ever-unlocked door, Sarah pushing Emily in front of her.

The darkened cottage – the firelight and the rushlights flickering – with its flaggod floor, its rough, stone fireplace under the rack of drying oatcakes, was bare and severe; no rugs, but a scrubbed table, wooden chairs, crude pots and wooden spoons. The only picture on the wall was an engraving, torn from who knew what magazine, of a crucified Christ, and the only book was a Bible. Pat Wainwright and Nancy were sitting by the fire, with Tom and Mary Sunderland, and their two smaller children. At one side of the fireplace, Mrs Sunderland was praying, the huge shut Bible, with its brass clasp fastened, on her lap. She had prayed for her eldest son, the younger Tom, who was somewhere out on the moor snaring partridges, and for the Brontës and the servant. 'Pray Lord save the hay wi' no roof o'er it!' she had continued. 'Pray God stop the moor moving, dunna let it slide down o'er th'ouse! Dunna let it frighten the hens into stopping laying and the cow running dry! Lord, if we must go, give us all a safe stall in Heaven . . .'

Tom Sunderland, the father, sat on the other side of the fire, his head in his hands as he pulled at his grey locks. He was in his fifties, and the ordinary, day-by-day malevolence of the moor had defeated him through its long erosion, making him hope for nothing better than fairer weather and fatter cows in that eternity promised at chapel and at hay-barn Methodist meetings.

They all rose from their brooding lethargy to greet the drenched and dirty, exhausted party who fell through the door – Pat Wainwright slamming and barring the door behind them, the Sunderlands' children running around them like small animals.

'The Lord be blessed! Thou's restored to us!' Mary Sunderland intoned. She bent over and kissed her Bible.

'Has it quietened any outside? Is there owt left o' t'moor? Which way did it come onto thee?' Tom Sunderland poured out his questions.

'Yee must be starved!' Nancy said. She began rubbing at their chapped hands and dragging them to the fire.

As clothes were dried, what was most amazing was that not a word could be got out of Emily. The others cried, shivered, or talked hysterically. She would not answer questions. How could she explain that, after the prim sitting with a straight back in Aunt Branwell's dark room, after peering at samplers, after the gloom of death, and the partings that had seemed like death, she was freed by finding herself in all that turbulence, chaos, and violence? She simply stared – 'wild eyed' as Pat Wainwright described it later – away from the others, into the fire, as if seeing what no-one else could see, and brushing off any comfort. She would not take off her clothes. She continued to shiver, until they pulled her dress off by force and wrapped her in a blanket. Such a tall, skinny child she looked. The questions put to her died out as they began to be a little frightened, or at least in awe of her, so erect, so determined, so *stubborn*, as Sarah remarked time and again.

Tom Sunderland looked at Mary, Mary looked at Tom. How could they say it? Maybe it was something most likely to occur to lonely moor-dwellers: it began to sink in that there was something non-human about the child's detachment. The thought hung in the air that they might be witnessing the childhood of a witch.

'I fear there's a demon in her soul,' whispered Mrs Sunderland.

'Mary! Shut thee prattle, wife!'

'I'm telling thee – I've seen it afore. The Devil mi't tak' a parson's daughter sooner than another, sithee.'

Emily looked at the weaver's wife as if she thought she was a fool to believe that prayer would stop the earth moving. Evidently that was what she had been doing, because of the Bible in her lap, which she couldn't read, anyway.

'Where's our Tom getten to?' asked the father, to change the subject. 'He'll happen have found shelter somewhere. I'd better go and see if us've any roof slates left!'

He went out to comfort the horse that could still be heard kicking and whinnying beyond the wall, to inspect the hens, the drains, the fields, the spring, to peer at the bank of moor piled behind their home, and to see how much had been washed away of the long track to Haworth upon which their lives depended.

'I feel as though the earth is still moving,' Sarah said. She had said it half a dozen times already. She fled into the kitchen to be sick into a basin.

In fire, candlclight, and the continuing faint flashes of lightning, Emily remained stiff and upright, the poor grey blanket clutched around her like a dignified robe. She allowed the dog to make tentative, frightened licks at her legs. Otherwise she was alone, absorbing the lesson that it was not merely the human world that was mutable, it was the natural world also.

As Wainwright described it later: her expression was as close as a six-year-old could get to being *contemptuous*, and he claimed that he saw Emily's lips curl.

V

'It is an omen – God's warning of a judgement upon us. Something dreadful is about to come to pass,' Patrick said, after watching through the window for his children and seeing, as he described it, 'the glass tremble in the window, the heavens blacken over the moors, and, after an eerie stillness, the gale raising the dust and stubble,' and after hearing, later, of what had occurred.

The eruption left a crater eighteen feet deep and nearly three-quarters of a mile across, plus many smaller pits. Tom Sunderland the younger, who had been poaching on the lower slopes of the Ponden Valley, described 'a seven-feet-high wall of mud sliding towards me so slowly that a man had time to count his sins three times over before it arrived'. Following the course of the Ponden Beck it flooded Heatons' Mill. Fortunately the factory-children's dormitory was under the slates, so they were safe. The mud-tide destroyed three stone bridges close to Haworth and polluted the water in Leeds, thirty miles away, for a week. Poor people gathered the dead fish in sacks, and a reporter calculated that two hundred stones of fish had been suffocated by the mud.

Patrick Brontë published a letter about it in the newspaper, which brought investigators from the *Leeds Mercury*, and gentlemen of the kind who gathered in the Bradford Subscription Library, up to Haworth. Wearing tall hats that were unsuitable for the breezy hills, they climbed the moor, poked about, and wandered around. What alarmed them was not so much Patrick's announcement of the end of the world, as his describing it as an 'earthquake'. If there were earthquakes in this region, it could spell the end of the factories of the woollen industry. However, they were satisfied that the phenomenon had only been an 'eruption'.

Patrick was certain that it had been a portent. He grew angry if crossed on the subject.

His foreboding that divine justice was about to be meted out led to his conscience being troubled about all that he had done badly, or had left undone, in his forty-seven years.

He feared that he would be punished for his philandering: it had been no more than mental philandering, but that was thanks to the good sense of the ladies. In his mind, at any rate, he had betrayed his wife. He had perhaps been responsible for her death by bringing her here. These were matters he could not speak of, except to his Maker; neither could he change them. It was clear that the apocalyptic storm had come to remind him, and every sinner in Haworth, of the power of God's wrath. It was ridiculous to term it a mere 'eruption', and the first step to redemption was to accept it for what it was. Otherwise men would be repeating the mistake they had made before the Flood.

'The phenomenon in question was what justly deserves the appellation of an *earthquake*!' Patrick stormed back at the *Leeds Mercury* readers.

He also preached a sermon on a text from the 97th psalm, 'The hills melted like wax at the presence of the Lord', publishing it through the offices of T. Inkersley, of Bridge Street in Bradford.

As they were crossing to the church on Sunday, Aunt Branwell told him: 'I have been informed that Elizabeth Firth is to marry the Reverend James Franks of Sowerby Bridge.'

He looked up at the grey tower chipped with tiny gold pock-marks from his shooting at it and, once again, he felt old.

The church was crowded; the atmosphere of a revival meeting had infected the town for the past ten days. 'A reminder of the Lord's power from time to time is no bad thing,' Aunt Branwell had said. As always in Haworth, they were hushed, but not subdued, and ready to be disputatious, after the sermon if not during it. On that dark, soggy September day, the building smelled of wet kersey woollens and sodden leather jerkins. It was not at all, as Elizabeth Branwell so often reminded herself, like Mr Dury's church in Keighley, where the women and girls from the outlying places changed into light shoes in the church porch, and brought clean aprons and caps to put on, and affected to be genteel.

Aunt Branwell settled with the children and the Garrs sisters in the family pew. There came the hymns, the psalms, the prayers, then all was hushed for Mr Brontë's sermon.

Referring *en passant* to Etna and Vesuvius, he explained, mildly enough, that God sometimes created eruptions as no more than 'manifestations of his power and majesty, as for example upon giving the Commandments to Moses'.

'On the other hand,' he began, and stopped when he heard a knocking from below his pulpit.

It was a quiet knocking, but it could be heard throughout the church. Coming from the Brontë family pew, it was not something for the churchwarden, with his long staff, to deal with, in his usual manner of tapping someone on the shoulder, or tweaking a few ears. Mr Brontë saw Aunt Branwell slap Emily on the thigh, and the kicking ceased.

'The Lord sometimes brings storms as awful monitors to turn sinners from the errors of their ways!' continued Mr Brontë, a little more loudly, his temper rising.

Whether it was irritation at his daughter's misbehaviour, or was piled-up annoyance from his dispute with the newspaper, or had something to do with what Elizabeth Branwell had said to him on the way into church, for once he found himself forgetting his usual gentle story-telling manner, and he began to thunder at his congregation.

'The Lord, if he'd wanted to, might just as easily have sent the catastrophe to destroy Haworth itself!'

Knock – knock – knock went Emily, once again, so that it was heard throughout the church. Aunt Branwell slapped her again. 'Naughty child!' she was heard to say by the whole congregation. He saw Emily slip off the bench and disappear from his sight, on the floor of the pew.

*   *   *

'I have never seen such a naughty girl! She sat on the floor with her back to the pulpit and put her hands over her ears!' Aunt Branwell said.

Patrick drew twenty pounds from his bank and took Emily to join her sisters at Cowan Bridge – 'None too soon,' said her aunt.

It was also in the nick of time because the number of enrolments was increasing by leaps and bounds.

Back at Haworth, Patrick, like the remainder of his household, continued his routines. After family prayers came breakfast in the parlour. It consisted of oatmeal porridge, although Aunt Branwell might enjoy a boiled egg if their hens, that wandered around the scrap of church-owned wilderness named 'the parson's field', and roosted in the peat-store, were laying, and if the magpies had not stolen the eggs. Or they might have stewed fruit, either stirred into the porridge or eaten separately. Because Patrick had presided over the ceremony in his study, he allowed Aunt Branwell to commandeer breakfast. It was an eerily sparse ceremony with only Branwell and Anne at home.

During the mornings, Patrick set forth into his parish or gave lessons to Branwell. Aunt Branwell instructed Anne, while the Garrses did the heaviest household work and prepared dinner for two o'clock. This main meal the children most often took with the Garrses in the kitchen, while Patrick had his in his study, and Aunt Branwell was in her bedroom. This was not so much because of Patrick's withdrawal as because of Aunt Branwell's, and also because she did not like the parlour to be used in an easy-going fashion; she wanted it kept spotless in case of visiting clergy or trustees. After dinner came the children's walk on the moors, unless the weather was inclement – and what was 'inclement' Patrick and the children's aunt disagreed about, often – followed by their tea in the kitchen. The early evening hours were lonely ones for Anne and Branwell: these hours mostly spent in their 'study' were the ones when they most missed their sisters.

Lastly, after the Garrses had gone out of the house and up the stone stairs to their room at the back – part of the house and yet not part of it – Patrick climbed to his bedroom, winding up the clock on his way, loaded his pistols, removed his spectacles, placed them with pistols and watch by his bed, took a last look at his sleeping son, prayed, and got into bed.

'Ah, Sarah!' Patrick would sigh sometimes, as she removed the plate of food with which she had only half tempted him, 'An old man is always hungry, and so we are always nibbling, yet no food possesses its flavour any more. Isn't that a terrible truth, my dear?'

To Sarah Garrs, Mr Brontë at forty-seven and forty-eight seemed old indeed; and she appreciated it that he did not blame her cooking for his lack of appetite.

He seemed to ascribe everything to the will of God, and was brooding on a sense of portents – of things he had perhaps handled wrongly.

And then it happened.

Events occurred that made these dull routines seem, in retrospect, to have belonged to an age of innocence.

With the numbers of pupils at Cowan Bridge doubling over the winter from forty to eighty, there was an outbreak of 'the low fever' – typhoid – and Patrick received a message to take Maria home. He raced to the school. It was clear, even before Dr Andrew's diagnosis back in Haworth, that Maria had – worse than typhoid – consumption.

It had been summer when he had seen his daughters last. They had not been home for Christmas, 'because it was not the custom'. The new superintendent, Miss Evans, told Patrick about the epidemic. More of what had happened he learned from Maria on their way home in the stagecoach. With the rush of new pupils, the food had worsened, sanitary requirements had not been improved, and discipline had stiffened.

'On one day I had to wear a board saying I was a "slattern" because my hair was uncombed, Papa, although it was only because I felt so unwell.'

With her thin bones, her wasted and translucent flesh, Maria seemed like a tiny old woman. It was like having her mother, that other Maria, at his side again.

'Didn't you say anything to the superintendent?'

'One could not. And that is not the point, Papa!' his daughter lectured him. 'I was being slothful, too. Charlotte, you know – Charlotte especially – becomes cross when she is punished. I think that is silly. She complains that she cannot bear it, but I tell her how weak it is to complain of what fate calls upon one to bear.'

A hacking cough interrupted her speech. She occasionally brought up specks of blood. There were hectic, red patches on her cheeks.

'Miss Andrews, I thought, *was* too severe,' Maria continued. 'There was a day when I could not get out of bed. The doctor had applied a blister to my side and I was in pain, but I thought at last that I'd better try to rise. Because I was late, Miss Andrews – never mind; there is a new superintendent now, and Miss Andrews, also, surely has her place in the plan of things—'

'Do not talk so much, Maria. Let me tell you something: we have a new servant at the parsonage.'

'What has happened to Nancy and Sarah?'

'Nancy left in December to marry Patrick Wainwright. Sarah left only last week. I think she could not bear the loneliness, and Aunt Branwell's sharp tongue.' Patrick smiled. 'And she said that she missed you children. But I think that you will like Tabitha Aykroyd.'

For three months, Maria lay in the back bedroom, 'like a white statue in a church', as Anne said to Branwell.

'To step into Heaven I must be pure,' Maria said. 'I know I must, I must! If I am good, I will go to my eternal paradise.'

What else did she have to believe in? What else had been implanted in her mind?

'I am going to my Maker and that is nothing to pity me for,' she declared. 'I am *grateful*. It is only the manner of my going about which I have to be watchful.'

Maria's dignity and piety moved everyone. The only fight she put up to stay in this world was her involuntary struggle for air.

'She will have a good death,' Aunt Branwell sighed, before she burst into tears.

Aunt Branwell's overriding concern was that Maria should have 'a good death'. Maria, who had once told Papa that her ambition was 'to lay out my life in preparation for a happy eternity', was having an exemplary one.

'There is good in all the Lord's doings,' Aunt said. 'Though we may not see it at the time. That child is a great example to us. What more could be said of *any* life?'

In Maria's always-darkened room with its unforgettable, dreadful smell, and the sounds of people treading and speaking differently, and with the empty beds of Charlotte, Elizabeth and Emily, Anne witnessed the terrible moments when Maria's saintly reconciliation deserted her. She convulsed in spasms not dictated by soul nor mind, but by her body. There were times when it was apparently breaking up inside and pieces of blood came slipping out. Her face being the same white as the sheets and as her cap, only the blood on her handkerchief, or gurgling out of her mouth, was coloured. Anne imagined poppies in snow – she loved flowers, and although poppies did not grow in the Haworth peat, she had seen them in church glass, illustrating 'the Sermon on the Mount'.

There were also, and most terrifying of all to Anne, the times when Maria could not breathe. Sharp breaths followed one another as if they cut her. Then came the long gurgle like water in a blocked drain. Anne would grow tense with fear that each breath might be Maria's last.

Aunt Branwell's room, where Anne slept, was – she could never forget – also where her mother had died. In case she should lose her pressing sense of eternity, her aunt spent much of the time talking about death. Anne, in the dark – Aunt Branwell quiet at last in her bed at the other side of the room; the remains of the fire throwing patterns around walls and ceiling – remembered what she had seen of Maria's efforts to draw breath. She knew very well what it felt like. The thought came to her, quite suddenly: suppose my own breath should stop! To test it, she breathed in deeply, so that there was first a tickle, then a sharp pain in her chest. At last she let it out.

'Anne, what are you doing? You were making such a funny noise.'

'Holding my breath.'

'Why?'

'I wanted to know what it is like for Maria.'

'Goodness gracious, child, you must not do that!'

There was silence a little longer. Then that sound.

'*Anne!*'

Anne capsized her little chest. 'Yes?'

'*Stop it.*'

'Yes, Aunt.'

But she could not stop testing herself. Suppose she could not ever breathe again; for what reason was there that she should be able to? She found herself drawing breath more quickly. She was wheezing. Now, she *really* couldn't breathe.

'*Aunt – please – Aunt Branwell!*'

Aunt Branwell rushed out of bed. She lit the candle with a taper from the dying fire and bustled up to Anne's bedside.

'*I am afraid, Aunt!*'

'Do not be afraid. Say your prayers, quickly!'

'Please Lord forgive me all my naughty ways —'

'I'll get you a basin of hot water to inhale!'

Aunt Branwell went into the passage. Because there was no doorway from the house into Tabitha Aykroyd's room, she could not call the servant, so she went downstairs, raked the fire, placed a pan of water on it to boil, found a bowl and a towel.

Branwell, sleeping in Papa's room, did not have to listen to such weighty sermons about death. Neither did he look around the shadows and think: my mother died here. Maria's struggle for breath did not affect him so terribly, either.

He saw Maria as an angel, so pale, so translucent. But an angel in the house brought its own problem.

Aunt Branwell, and the lovely Tabitha Aykroyd who had come to the parsonage, although it was clear within a week that they did not agree about many things, both told Branwell and Anne: 'Heaven is within reach of us all.' The seven-year-old boy doubted it. He could not bring himself to tell anyone why. It was because one needed to be as good as Maria in order to get there. And Aunt Branwell had also, in many bedtime stories, told him about 'unworthiness'.

Since the cataclysm on the Ponden moors, Branwell had brooded on the thought that everything could be taken from him – not only his parents and sisters, but the hills, too, could

135

explode. As in the Book of the Apocalypse. His 'worthiness' for eternity was something for which he panicked, as Anne, a couple of times in recent weeks, had panicked for air in the attacks which Dr Andrew called 'asthma'.

But at last it was over. Branwell walked around the second coffin that he had seen laid out in the parlour, and was lifted up to see the waxen skin of his eleven-year-old sister looking, if possible, even fairer than it had in life, and to see the fair washed hair and the white grave-clothes. She was certainly an angel.

When the vault was opened in the church and Maria was buried, to him it was more vivid than when his mother had died, for then he had been only four years of age.

The funeral was over and guests had departed. The family and William Morgan who had buried Maria – he who had baptized her – were left in the parlour. Branwell suddenly gave a sharp, strange cry, so that the others turned, imagining someone else in the room.

He was staring towards the window, where the shutters were not yet drawn, but dusk was gathering. His lips were trembling and saliva was dripping from the corners of his mouth. He was sweating. Patrick stepped forward to catch him as he fainted, while Aunt Branwell shrieked and rushed to close the shutters.

When he came round, at first he had no recollection of anything having happened. After ten minutes he broke out of his daze and said he had seen Maria at the window, 'dressed in white . . . an angel, Papa . . . an angel, as she always was . . .'

At Cowan Bridge School, the doctor gagged on the stench from the enteritis, especially in the overcrowded dormitory and the improvised sickrooms. He did not even go near the earth closet – there was only one, for forty girls – where they were always queuing, unless they fled into the fields. He could hardly deal with it. But he tasted the food and declared: 'This porridge is not fit for pigs! None of the food is. Mr Wilson, if you are not to have epidemics of low fever, then sack the cook! Some of the children must be sent home, if they are not to die. Let the others enjoy fresh air. Take those able to travel to your villa at Silverdale, for the sea air. And – though it is not my business to advise you on spiritual matters – stop carping about death being a better place than life. For Heaven's sake.'

Even a little release from overcrowding worked wonders. The food became better. Lessons, if not sermons, were fewer. Best of all, they were encouraged to take unsupervised walks by the river, through the fields and woods. How conscious one became of the sweetness of the air!

Though Maria had gone home, Charlotte did not know of her death. Yet she was fuelled with enough anger to last her a lifetime, the many things that she could not say to Mr Wilson or to Miss Andrews hoarded away to sting any injustice or bullying in the future.

Even the fact that beauty was so abundantly *out here* – from which until recently they had been kept – made her angry. The helplessness that she observed in her teachers made her angry. Kindly Miss Evans, for instance, merely averted her eyes, and tried to ameliorate as she could, but she still had to stay and submit. She was an example of what Charlotte and Emily were supposed to grow up to be: governesses and schoolteachers not able to take decisions, not responsible, remaining all their lives like children under the bullying patriarchy of some husband, some employer, some priest.

Emily meanwhile turned in upon herself, her natural silence and mysteriousness deepening. Elizabeth seemed simply to be waiting, with a Maria-like patience.

On the same day that Charlotte and Emily were despatched to the Reverend Carus Wilson's villa, 'The Cove', at Silverdale overlooking Morecambe Bay, Patrick Brontë saw, from his study window, a gig draw up at the garden gate. Not wanting to be disturbed, he called to Tabitha.

She, with an apron around her big frame, went out to defend the parson. There was nothing diffident about Tabitha Aykroyd. She had settled 'Elizabeth Branwell's hash' during her first weeks; she had been born in Haworth and knew everything about it.

She went down to the gate and found the gig from the Devonshire Arms. There was such a sickly, miserable child in the gig. The driver told her: 'A lady I've never seen before, a Mrs Hardacre from Cowan Bridge, said I was to bring Elizabeth Brontë to the parsonage.'

'*That's* Elizabeth Brontë? That poor wee soul there?' The child could hardly stand. 'Well, thank the Lord it's a fine day.' Tabitha took the child in her arms.

'I said to Mrs Hardacre she should have come herself with the bairn, but she wouldna.' He put an envelope into Tabitha's hand, 'For Mester Bron-*teh*.'

From the window, Patrick saw the eldest of his remaining children, wrapped in a blanket, brought up the path. In a moment he was in the hallway, ready to pick her up – light as a sparrow – tears over her face – and with the same translucent, pale skin as Maria had possessed, and the same hectic blotches, and the same hacking cough, her eyes glistening with delight at being home again.

Passing Elizabeth back to Tabitha, he tore open the envelope. He found a note telling him that Charlotte and Emily were well and at Silverdale. There was also a bill. It itemized fare, guard, coachman, horse, gig, pikes and men, the fare and overnight expenses at the Devonshire Arms for Mrs Hardacre, and the cost of a couple of letters, the whole amounting to £1 15s. 10½d. Tabitha told him about Mrs Hardacre, left in Keighley because she dared not come as far as Haworth.

He simply did not have time to go to see her. After Elizabeth was settled into Maria's ex-sickroom, Patrick spent the evening making arrangements to travel to Silverdale. He envisioned the whole of his family swept away. For the first time he saw himself as some Yorkshire Oedipus or Job.

Though Patrick took the stagecoach that passed right by Cowan Bridge School, he did not stop to examine it, with now de-scaled eyes. In any case, the coach would not stop there. *There's been an epidemic*, fellow travellers murmured; evidently the whole district knew about it. They had seen the girls, robbed of all dignity – not that they'd ever had much – fleeing to hide behind bushes. Workmen would not empty the 'night soil', and the poorest of the poor had to do it. Few would go near. One saw girls being sick in the field at the back – a terrible sight.

Patrick feared that, despite Carus Wilson's assurances, he

might arrive at Silverdale too late to see his two daughters alive. That was all he thought about. It was the last day of May, yet he had no taste for the flowery countryside, nor for the view of the massive sands spread towards the sunset in the bay, nor for the artistic villa.

When he passed under the verandah of The Cove – its empty wicker chairs directed towards the sunsets over the bay – he found two much-altered children, in the charge of their tight-lipped nurse. They were frail, they were thin, as he expected; but also they were tough, they were stronger in spirit, which he had not anticipated. At the ages of nine and seven, they, too, were cauterized by the furnace of life.

'Oh, my darlings, you are well! You are survivors, eh? Is there a touch of the Iron Duke in my daughters? Why didn't you write and tell me what was happening? All that I had were reports that all was well.'

'Whatever we wrote was censored by Miss Evans,' Charlotte answered. 'There is no point in writing anything at all, if one has to tell lies.'

CHARLOTTE

I

At Cowan Bridge, Charlotte had felt the fixing upon her of a moral harness. Even at the age of eight she possessed the seeds of that view. During the early part of her time there she had often flushed with anger that she could not express. They were doing something to her mind, just as, when she was punished, they did something to her body, hurting or shaming it. In mental pain, she would turn her burning cheeks to the wall. She felt bridled, like an unhappy young horse. At times she beat the walls, the doors, or clenched her little fists around the bedposts, and she was sullen with her teachers, which did her no good.

It had been Maria who had schooled her in resignation and taught her the meaning of moral fibre. Maria was capable of saying such things as, 'To understand all is to forgive all.' It was not in the manner of Mr Wilson, pompous, insincere, and looking for excuses for his own behaviour. It was wise and consoling – at the age of eight!

Charlotte had not been able to understand her. There had been moments when she had been made angry, or baffled, and when she had been ashamed of her sister's resignation; and she had seen Emily gloat, almost, over Maria punished for coming down late. In the end, Charlotte – like Branwell, she found out later – valued Maria as a saint.

They were in the church in Tunstall one winter Sunday morning, having been marched along four miles of footpaths and slushy roads, two by two. Charlotte, with Maria, Elizabeth and Emily, had been at the front because they were among the youngest and smallest, with the tallest bringing up the rear. All were identified as orphans and beggars in their plaid capes and black stockings for the countryside to recognize them, so that Charlotte at any rate walked in undeserved shame. Every tree, farm, cottage and especially the approach to Tunstall village was imprinted on her mind because of her humiliation. She felt ashamed even under the eyes of the gypsies, the poor cottagers, and the squatters on the heaths. It was a clear day, as cold as they come, with frost in the air, the hoar of the previous night lingering in the shadows, and there was ice on stagnant pools at the edge of the river. It was a beautiful day, had they been in a condition to enjoy it.

If, when they arrived in Tunstall, they had been allowed to squat against the church wall and absorb the weak sun, they would have been all right, but nature worship was not part of their education. Hungry, cold, and with wet feet, they had to sit among what she felt were hostile and contemptuous villagers, in the freezing church, where she was angry as well as miserable. In Haworth, when they got wet feet, it was followed by a warm fire. Here, after the sermon, there was nothing to look forward to but climbing the ladder to the tiny room over the church porch where they crammed the girls in to eat the lunch they had brought with them, before an afternoon of further disgusting moralizing from the Reverend Carus Wilson. (Oh, his gloating eyes! Would she ever be able to evade them in her dreams?) Then back to school to fight for a place at the fire – or rather, to hope that some bigger girl would take pity and let her sisters and herself near it. There seemed no way out of the building. She was a partridge beating its wings in the dark box of a snare, as she had seen them do on the Ponden moors. Except that – such was her fancy – she could escape by shooting up a beam of sunlight that led from the floor to a window; a gold and rainbow-coloured, dust-grained path, dancing with thousands of dark jewels.

In the window was a serene, stately lady in blue, who was Mary the mother of Jesus. She was one who *understood all and could forgive all*, therefore she could not be touched by common human misery. Only Mary and Charlotte's elder sister Maria were above and beyond everything.

So when Charlotte made her first book, which was written for Anne after an asthma attack, back in Haworth, when Elizabeth was dead and Charlotte was now the eldest – she was the 'mother' – she wanted it to be, in a way, what Maria's words, when they had walked along the school verandah or lain in the dormitory, had been to her. She wanted it to make Anne feel better, to *be* better.

A purpose for writing had entered her heart.

The year that had passed, 1825, had been a dreadful one for the whole district. Papa and Dr Andrew, who read and swopped newspapers and *Blackwood's Magazine*, said it was because of 'industrial distress'. Firstly, Butterworths of Keighley had gone bankrupt, throwing its employees and many others out of work, then half a dozen other woollen mills had shut down.

Charlotte felt that she had learned why God had arranged the world so that the lower animals, who have to suffer so much, at least are not cursed with memory. Emily and she had reached home just in time to see Elizabeth die. There was nothing to be remembered of the year but the mourning clothes, the adults whimpering, and the moors fading from summer green, turning brown in the rain, and the water erupting from the hills in streams and waterfalls, and the daily routines, including the bitter entrances into the church where mother and two sisters lay under the nave. Visitors, coming out of duty or on business, turned up having composed what consolations they could or dared, but they had no idea of what the children's imaginations had to cope with. As they listened to Papa's sermons, they imagined the worms burrowing into mother and sisters.

Anne lay in her bed in Aunt Branwell's room, unable to breathe, emitting that terrible wheezing. It was January and from now until the spring was the most terrifying period for everybody. Even in 'normal' years, people died in numbers in January and the passing-bell rang outside the window several times every day. Was Anne's turn approaching?

The shutters were drawn. The room had a disgusting smell, brewed in stuffiness. Doctor Andrew had treated Anne with traditional remedies. The 'old wives' ones were best, he said: decoctions of the root of butterbur, the soapy scrapings of the root of black bryony which were rubbed on her chest, and asafoetida which, it was believed, also helped with the hysteria accompanying asthma attacks. Tabitha Aykroyd – whom they now all called Tabby – had Anne sitting over a bowl of steaming water, a towel over her head; which was what every cottage in Haworth did for head colds, flu, asthma and consumption.

Most of the time, Anne had Maria's resignation. Either from Maria, or from Aunt Branwell through sleeping with her, resignation had brushed off on Anne more than onto anyone else. At five years of age she talked calmly of joining Maria, Elizabeth and her mother in the earth under the great pile of stones that was the church. She seemed to accept her lonely fate of a life to be closed as soon as it started.

But when death came close in an asthma attack, and she could not breathe, she was terrified; mostly in case she should not be able to remember her prayers during that last, fatal moment that decided her eternal fate. It was fear, perhaps, that contributed to the smell in Aunt Branwell's room.

Charlotte could not talk as Maria did, could not give those dignified moral consolations, but she saw what she *could* ease her with.

She could make up a story in which Anne was the heroine.

Charlotte poked about in the kitchen. She peered around the table, her head bent, her nose inches from the surface.

'Drawer's on t'other side. I've turned t'table rarnd,' Tabby remarked, smiling.

Charlotte did not like being caught out with poor eyesight. She went to the other side of the table. 'I am looking for some paper and scissors, Tabby.'

'What does tha want 'em for? What ar't' up to, *this* time rarnd?'

'I am going to make a book.'

Tabby laughed. 'A real bewk?'

'Yes!' Charlotte snapped, embarrassed. She lifted her head at last, blushing but determined, for a large ambition burned. 'I'm making a "bewk" for Anne.'

'Bless you, I can find you paper!' Tabby rummaged on some shelves which Charlotte was too short to reach. 'I couldn't even read a bewk, let alone write one,' she remarked, wistfully.

'I'll teach you, Tabby!' Charlotte jumped up and down, clenching her fists excitedly. She was ashamed of having bristled and wanted to make amends.

'It's too late now!' Tabby was overcome, nevertheless. ''Ere's your paper. Is that enough? How big a bewk ar't' going ta make? It'll not be up to t'size of a Bible, I suppose?'

'No, it'll no' be that big,' said Charlotte – imitating the accent without thinking, as she often did with accents.

She grabbed the paper and scurried off to the sewing-room over the hallway; the 'study'. Emmii and Brannii were there, short of amusement because it was raining.

'I'm going to make a book for Anne!' Charlotte announced.

Nothing surprised them when it belonged to the realm of the imagination. If Charlotte had skipped in and said, 'We are going to Africa,' off they all would have sailed, inventing the ship, the storms at sea, the landing, and confrontations with the natives.

Tabby had given her a sheet of dirty, off-white, thickish paper which had once wrapped something from the grocer's. They all helped to rip and scissor it into four sheets, which when folded made sixteen pages. Charlotte made a cover out of a scrap of wallpaper which Emmii produced, and which she had purloined from some farmhouse on her walks because she liked the pattern of flowers. Charlotte stitched the book together, using a length of brown cotton that had been left in a needle. Aunt Branwell would have been delighted to see her sewing so willingly, then she would have criticized the clumsy stitches – two large, clumsy ones, finished with a big knot.

The stitches were all that *was* large about the book. Charlotte made it very small because it was the only way to get sufficient pages out of the sheet, and because she habitually held objects a few inches from her eyes. It was two-and-a-quarter by one-and-a-half inches. The cover was greyish white, only a shade darker than the pages, and showed one of the wallpaper's patterns – a crude, grey flower, surrounded with leaves splattered with blue spots. The fragile production would have barely filled a grown palm. It was like some delicate moth plucked from the wainscoting.

They were already used to making up stories together. Brannii's involved battles and lots of blood, Emmii's were murderous and vengeful, Anne's had saints who went to heaven, and Charlotte's invariably included the Duke of Wellington, who had become her hero. This time, Charlotte proposed a story in which Anne was central. It was decided that she must have a mother once again, and that her story must take her far from Haworth to a beautiful place.

This was as far as they got, jointly, because Papa shouted up the stairs for Brannii to come for a lesson in Latin, then Aunt Branwell wanted Emily and Charlotte to dust the parlour.

They heard Aunt's wooden shoes clattering on the floorboards. Because there wasn't space for her in the children's 'study' among the books, the sewing, the last-year's birds' nests and the newspapers, she did not enter. She called them from the door as if they were a long way away: 'Emil-*ee*! Char-*lotte*!', in a Cornish accent which they had fun in mimicking. Emily went off, but Charlotte disobeyed because she was the inventor of this story; she was in charge and had to finish it. Fortunately, Aunt Branwell was satisfied to take only Emily, and Charlotte could begin.

'There was once a litle girl and her name was Ane she was born at a little vilage named Thornton and she was a good litle girl.'

She drew a cottage. It wasn't at all like their severe-looking birthplace in Thornton, which Charlotte could not remember clearly. It wasn't like a house of the West Riding of Yorkshire at all. It was a house from a child's world.

Charlotte opened the watercolour box that she had been given on the last Christmas that she had spent at home. She coloured in a brown door in the middle of the house and windows on either side. It stood against a wooden fence, which was equally unlikely in this part of the West Riding. She scribbled in some frizzy greenery.

On other pages she did a ship with a blue sail, between brown rocks, on slate-blue water. She did a castle, a rowing-boat, and a young lady, wearing a bonnet, carrying flowers to a place under a tree. She had it in mind to draw a grave but 'No!' she said to herself – talking out loud, with her tongue between her lips.

Charlotte did show the sickroom, though. Only: it was her mother who lay in what was in reality Aunt Branwell's bed – her mother's and father's original bed – under a huge, billowing canopy. This was on the right of the picture. There were two windows, as in Anne's room, though these were not shuttered but were richly curtained. She drew a round table, on a carpeted floor.

Emerging through a door on the left was a tall, thin man, dark-faced and dressed in black. He was a sinister figure, bearing a similarity to Papa in certain moods, and also to Carus Wilson.

Charlotte continued her story: 'her father and mother was very rich Mr and Mrs Wood were there names and she was there only child but she was not too much indulged'

Without bothering to place the full stop, she paused.

It was still raining outside. The sounds which she had ignored so far, penetrated. One of them was the clanging of the passing-bell.

When she had thought a little longer, she continued.

'once little Ane and her mother went to see a fine castle near London about ten miles from it Ann was very much pleased with it. once Ane and her papa and her mama went to sea in a ship and they had very fine weather all the way but Anns mama was very sick and Ann attended her with so much care she gave her her medicine'

She thought of the sea journey because Maria – who could remember her mother whereas Charlotte and the others could hardly at all – had said that she often used to talk about her voyage from Cornwall to Liverpool and thence to Yorkshire.

It was still raining heavily, pearls of water clinging to the window. When she went out of the study, from the landing she could hear Emily singing the ballad of 'Barbara Allan' as she dusted and polished in the parlour. She had not yet learned all the words, but her singing was clear, in tune, showing a talent for music that Charlotte envied. She was wild and brave, which Charlotte also envied. It seemed in accord with her love of primitive ballads. Brannii was declining Latin verbs out loud with Papa in Papa's study. *Amo amas amat.*

From the kitchen there rose a smell of bacon stew. Whenever Charlotte came near to any meat, she remembered only the stink of rotten meat at Cowan Bridge, and she was nauseous.

Retching, Charlotte took her book into Anne. There, Aunt Branwell was sewing stupidly in the dark, sitting with her back to the closed shutters from which a few shafts of grey, soft light, like strands of silk, penetrated the chinks onto her sewing. In the firelight, her black silk dress glistened like wet streets and gravestones. There was often an unpleasant smell around Aunt in a warm room these days: like the smell of privies.

Anne was breathing dreadfully, with deep and desperate wheezes, fighting for breath, letting it out in short, feverish pants. She said it was as if spiders were escaping from her chest, wriggling up her throat, scurrying out and vanishing. She could not read the book which was put into her hands. She could only glance at it, then she dropped it onto the coverlet as another fit seized her. Aunt Branwell rose, rustled, and picked it up.

'What's this? Is it a book?' she said – being stupid once more.

She sat down again, while Charlotte bossily opened a shutter so that her Aunt could see clearly that it was a book. She also let in the sound of the bell more loudly.

Aunt Branwell held the book gingerly. Then she plunged, opening the pages brutally with her stubby fingers. She moved it back and forth, peered sideways at it and squinted. Her manner conveyed disapproval and contempt. Charlotte was afraid for her little creation, in those clumsy hands, in a bad light. She dared to open another shutter.

'Don't open too much, it lets in a draught,' Aunt Branwell said.

This annoyed Charlotte because she wanted her aunt's mind to be on the words, not on draughty windows.

'Your papa never *will* get the window-frames repaired,' Aunt Branwell continued.

She did not express one word of pleasure. Though she could hardly see them, she embarrassed Charlotte by stuttering through the first words aloud.

'"There was once a little girl and her name was Ane." Did you write this?'

She looked fiercely at Charlotte. She was not troubled by the echoes of Carus Wilson's sanctimonious tracts; it was the bad spelling she had noticed. 'Anne is spelled, A-N-N-E, Charlotte! Two ns. Spell it after me. A-N-N-E.'

'A-N-N-E,' Charlotte repeated in a voice of lead, for she was not interested in spelling. She leaned against the wall beneath the window, the rain beating above her head.

Aunt Branwell examined the binding. 'Who stitched it?' she demanded, as if a crime had been committed.

'I did, Aunt.'

'You can't do better than that? Deary me!'

'May I read it to Anne?'

That was when the bell stopped ringing. She wondered who it had been for. Was it John Fletcher, who had collapsed with palpitations after eating too much *meat* over Christmas, or was it Susan Wadsworth, who had consumption?

Charlotte took back her book and sat on the bed. Aunt smiled indulgently, having picked up her sewing once more. Meanwhile, Charlotte read her story out loud. Anne smiled at it. It seemed to calm her breathing.

Charlotte got to page two. She reached, 'her father and mother was very rich Mr and Mrs Wood were there names,' when Aunt Branwell let out a little cry, '*Oh!*'

The young authoress knew why her story had given offence, but it was too late. Although Charlotte had her back turned, she knew that her aunt had stopped moving, her sewing frozen in her hands.

Anne put out her hand to her sister, patiently, very much in the manner of wise-beyond-her-years Maria, and thanked her. Charlotte glanced over her shoulder at her aunt, who did not say anything, but who had tears on her face.

Anne had fallen asleep. Shamefaced (but why? It was only a *story*) Charlotte picked up her book and left the room; left Aunt Branwell snivelling, for there was nothing to be said to her. As Charlotte descended the stairs, Emily in the parlour was now singing 'The Meeting of the Waters'. 'There is not in the wide world a valley so sweet/As that vale in whose bosom the bright waters meet . . .' There were no other sounds from her, so she must have ceased dusting. Charlotte knew that she was in the window-seat. In the parsonage, one always knew where everyone was, and what they were doing, even without seeing or hearing them. Every little creak and tap was tell-tale when one was used to it. She could imagine Emily's very expression.

Charlotte went to show her book to Tabby. She was sitting at the kitchen table peeling apples and was about to bake a pie. The pastry was ready in a bowl. This was a crucial moment, not conducive to reading stories. Nevertheless, Charlotte said: 'I've made my book, Tabby!'

'I tho't it tewk years to write a bewk.'

Though Tabby had claimed to be unable to read, she could deal with passages of the Bible – even reading them aloud in the chapels that she attended from time to time. She had mostly learned the words by heart, but her gift for memorizing had helped her to recognize them when she saw them written down. At any rate, she could cope with the simple story.

Charlotte thrust her book under Tabby's nose. She wanted her to take hold of it but also to keep it clear of the apple peelings and flour.

Tabby pulled back from the book as if it was a fly that was pestering her. 'Nay, *I* don't have to put everything right under my nose to be able to see it,' she remarked.

This hurt Charlotte, and Tabby softened, realizing that she

had caused hurt. She put down her knife, brushed a place clear of peelings and flour, took hold of the book, put it down and peered. Charlotte stood by her side, tempted to read out the words for her, but did not do so.

The writing was too small for Tabby, also, and she made great play of squinting and of not comprehending – disappointingly, just as Aunt Branwell had done. But Charlotte had more faith in Tabby, and already had as much love for her. Though she could not clearly remember a mother, surely Tabby was like one.

After frowning and squinting, Tabby's face opened into a smile. She was blushing. 'You've written that Anne's mother's name is "Wood"!'

'Yes, Tabby.'

'Wood' had been Tabby's surname before she was married.

'Well, now! I don't know what to say. Except that I anna rich.'

With one hand she fidgeted with apple cores, and with the other hand she fiddled with the pages.

After another moment she said, 'Have you shown this to Miss Branwell?' – anxiously, yet still not able to help herself smiling with satisfaction.

'Yes, I have.'

Charlotte removed her book from the floury table that was such a threat to it. She slipped it into the pocket of the pinafore that she wore over her mourning dress. Tabby, so as not to have to talk about the book, had returned to her baking. She, like other adults, as Charlotte had noticed, hated to discuss emotional matters.

Charlotte's feelings were of pride, as well as of shame. So as not to have to admit what she had realized today about the feelings that lurked around the composition of a book, she, too, began to help with the baking.

Papa had come in from the graveyard, by the front door. He was heard stamping his boots.

'Tea! And, perhaps, some oatcakes, Tabby?' he called.

He was not appreciative of the concentration needed in order to make successful pies, Charlotte realized; he was not expected to understand, any more than Branwell was.

So that the servant would not be diverted from her baking, Charlotte placed the kettle on the fire and prepared the tea tray herself. While Tabby took it in to Papa, Charlotte amused herself by cutting out the pattern of a rose with a metal pastry cutter.

After Tabby had returned, Charlotte helped a little more. She cut another rose for the top of the pie. She watched Tabby trim the pastry from the edge of the dish and slide it into the oven, then pull back from the rush of heat from the open door, and wipe her sweaty face on her apron.

'When Mother went blind, they said it was from openin' t'door o' th' baykin' oven so many times,' Tabby said. 'She'd done it all 'er life sin' she were a girl. Dunna you fall into them ways, my lass. Find summat better for theeself. Tha mun make thyself a lady, and marry a gentleman.'

Charlotte left the kitchen, her book still in her pocket. She dared to knock on Papa's door and he called her in. He was perched in one of the upright chairs by the fireside, his tea tray on the floor. He had the expression he always wore after funerals. He gave her a warm, sad looking-over, as if he might never see her again; though she was always more glad to see that expression than his severe one, the one that had come out in her drawing. He was nibbling a dry oatcake. There was no butter, no fruit preserve nor anything like that on it. He changed his expression to a smile. 'Would you like a nibble?' he tempted her.

She shook her head. Then she remembered that, with his eyesight as poor as her own, perhaps he could not see her nod, not from across a room, so she answered: 'No thank you.' Sometimes she had thought that at a distance he could not even distinguish her from Anne; only from Emily, who though younger was so much taller.

Charlotte went forward and climbed onto his knee. She wanted to think that she was his favourite, even though she was not the prettiest.

'Goodness me, your pinafore is all floury,' he grumbled, though still smiling. She knew he was nevertheless pleased to find her domestically clad. He brushed at her front with his hand. His hand was large, freckled and sinewed, and she loved its gentle touch. It made her feel safe, and as if she had curled into a nest. Her head lay on his shoulder.

'Would you like to nibble an oatcake?' he repeated, moving his body to make her comfortable.

'No, thank you, Papa.'

'You do not like oatcakes, my dear?' he teased, affectionately.

'No, thank you, Papa, *I've told you before*,' she scolded him, solemnly. He always forgot that she didn't like oatcakes, for he was so absent-minded.

'Most people have to live on them. They have nothing else.'

She knew this perfectly well; why did Papa not understand that she did not like oatcakes because they were so dull? She liked sweetmeats. She liked what Aunt Branwell had told her were called in French bon-bons. (Or rather, she liked the idea of them. She had never tasted French bon-bons, but it was her ambition to taste them, someday.) Sometimes Papa had described the meals he had enjoyed at Cambridge, and at Miss Firth's, at a time before Charlotte could remember, and at Lascelles Hall near Huddersfield with the Reverend Atkinson, when Papa had been a curate at Hartshead. He had described what she had never seen: blancmanges and jellies arranged on damask cloths around huge displays of flowers . . .

'Papa, why does Aunt Branwell smell?'

'Charlotte! You shouldn't say such a thing. It is rude and unkind.'

So she pushed her book close to Papa's face, just as she had done with Tabby. She was about to tug at those grey locks which had started to grow around his ears now – curling over the edge of his cravat, cut into by the wires of his spectacles whenever he wore them – when he explained, mildly, with a little crinkling at the side of his mouth and eyes that she loved: 'I cannot both read your book and sit you on my knee, dear Charlotte.'

Why not? she thought. Nevertheless she left her book with him, slid down and stood a little way off, swaying in a semicircle, swinging her hands clasped in front of her pinafore because she did not know what to do with herself. She watched Papa reach out for his spectacles, which were on the table by his side, and stretch them over his nose and ears. She understood that Papa was treating her creation with great seriousness, so it behoved her to remain quiet and unnoticed.

Papa, in his turn, squinted, held the little volume at varying distances from his spectacles, pulled at the corners of his eyes, tugged at his cravat, and scratched himself. He reached into his desk drawer for his magnifying glass. Its silver mount shone as he moved it back and forth, twisted it at different angles and peered.

He came to the end of her composition. The discovery that had upset Aunt Branwell, and that had made Tabitha blush with pride, Papa simply passed over without noting its significance. He made a kindly criticism of her grammar and spellings (without expecting her to go and correct them, thank goodness) and said nothing about the drawings, but he looked pleased.

That was all the reaction Charlotte received to her first fiction.

But actually they all learned a lot about the profession of authorship.

They learned that the 'printed' word can powerfully upset people. They learned that 'disguises' can be used, not to disguise at all, but to hurt or to flatter. It was a wonderful weapon, which one could get away with using because it is 'only make-believe'.

They decided to make more books. But the incomprehension of adults convinced them that they should keep their world secret, even though it was written down.

'If we make our books really small, no-one else but us will be able to read them!' Branwell said.

This caused quite an outburst of giggling in the 'study', on yet another wet afternoon when beyond one wall Aunt Branwell was snoozing over her *Methodist Magazine*s, presumably, while Tabby was singing 'Lead Kindly Light' and banging her broom in Papa's room at the other side.

II

In the following summer Papa went to some stuffy clerical conference in Leeds. Following the clergymen's discussions of Reprobation, Election, and the Society for Providing Curates – or something like that, as he described it afterwards – he bought gifts. It was close to Branwell's birthday. Also, they were out of mourning for Maria and Elizabeth.

They were in bed when he arrived home and he tried to creep into his bedroom without waking Branwell. He put a box down and was halfway into his nightshirt, when:

'Papa!' Branwell piped up.

'Yes, Branwell, what is it?'

'What's in that box?'

'What box?'

Smiling, Papa knelt and said his prayers. Branwell could not interrupt. Papa got up. His bed creaked as he sat on the edge of it. Branwell peeped as Papa lifted his eiderdown and lay down. 'You must wait until morning,' he said.

'I won't be able to sleep.'

'It is good for you to try. You must learn patience. Have you said *your* prayers?'

'Yes, Papa.'

Before prayers and breakfast on the following morning, Branwell burst into Charlotte's and Emily's room. It was the room at the back where Maria and Elizabeth had died, and where Charlotte and Emily slept together in the one bed because it was warmer – or, as it was now summer, more affectionate. They were as intimate as two puppies in a litter and would rise sharing the same smell. Invariably they had slept upon what they called their 'bed plays', the stories they made up before they went to sleep, and because of that, perhaps, there were times in which they even shared the same dreams.

Branwell made a great noise, but Charlotte was already awake, anticipating presents from Papa's trip. Branwell would often burst in on them, saying that his feet were cold, or making some other excuse to squeeze into their tight little bed for half an hour, unknown to Aunt Branwell or Papa. Today, Charlotte leapt up as soon as she saw him, dimly, in the light from a chink in the shutters – his sloping shoulders, frail form, and a gleam of wild red hair – and with the box in his hand.

Charlotte bounced up to open the shutters. She was dazzled

153

by a brilliant June morning. But she was not too dazzled to see, when she turned round, that Branwell had opened the box and held out a set of wooden soldiers. All were carved slightly differently, and they lay side by side as if they were asleep. He was eager to show them – she realized – because his previous set of soldiers he'd had to play with by himself while Charlotte and her sisters were at Cowan Bridge, and that was nothing compared with the fun that they always had together. (For him, Anne did not count.)

By now Emily was awake, but she merely sat up, calmly. Charlotte snatched up a soldier.

'This is the Duke of Wellington!' she declared, clutching him, still with sleepy-sand in her eyes. She would have called him that even in a dream.

She threw a nervous glance at Brannii in case she had annoyed him by getting her word in first, but, thank goodness, she had not done so.

'This one is Napoleon, then!' Brannii said.

'What shall *I* have?' Emily asked, piteously.

I am sure, thought Charlotte, she is now regretting her sloth.

'*This* one is yours,' lordly Branwell told her.

'What an unhappy looking fellow you have!' Charlotte gloated.

'His name shall be "Gravey", then,' Branwell announced.

The noise aroused Anne in Aunt Branwell's room. She came in and sleepily plucked up her own soldier.

Charlotte peered at it. 'What a twisted, narrow-chested little fellow!' she remarked.

'Very like herself,' Branwell pointed out, cruelly.

'Definitely a member of the serving classes,' Charlotte said. 'He should be called "Waiting Boy". Now – what about *our* presents?'

They dressed and went downstairs. Their own gifts, they found, were laid out in the parlour, and Aunt Branwell would not allow them in until morning prayers were over, in Papa's study. They had to stand with Aunt Branwell, Tabby, and the new daily servant, Sally Mosely.

Then, minus the servants, they trooped into the parlour where Sally Mosely had lit the fire and Tabby had laid the breakfast. They saw the other presents piled on a small table, in clear view from the door. They had been placed in hope of taking their breath away, but it was an anti-climax. Charlotte went up to take a close look, but the others had eyesight good enough to apprise them from a distance. There was a toy village for Emily, a doll for Anne, and a set of black-painted ninepins for Charlotte.

As soon as breakfast was over, Brannii raced back upstairs. The girls rushed through clearing and cleaning the parlour with Tabby. They did not mind household work; they took pride in clean and polished surfaces, and it was a good time for bantering with Tabby. This time, they were impatient.

'How many soldiers are there?' Anne whispered.

'Twelve,' Charlotte whispered back and added, 'so we'll call them *The Twelve*.'

'What if Brannii won't agree?' Anne dared to suggest.

Charlotte was saved from answering because Tabby came in. She was no doubt made suspicious by their whispering and giggling.

'Such a beautiful June morning – doesn't tha wish to be out o' doors?' she teased. 'Aren't tha interested in thee own presents? Tha doesn't get that many of 'em. Or has tha some new game afoot? Is it Branwell's soldiers that have taken thee fancy? Go on, then. Off tha goes!'

Brannii had arranged them in military formation on the floor of their bedroom – paint gleaming red, blue, and creamy white; braces crossed over their shoulders; muskets and little black hats.

Their shadows fell across them – and they saw it straight away: like gods, they could move aside and let the light reach them, or not, as they willed. They towered over them with the power to make them live or die. They might change their characters, fates and names as despotically as they wished – which was as adults had always behaved towards themselves, shining upon them at one moment, disappearing for ever at the next, sending them away, bringing them back, making them stand up or lie down, killing them off.

'We'll call them The Twelve!' Charlotte announced, adding with less authority, 'Shall we, Brannii?'

He could not think of a better name, so he answered, slowly,

'Yes – and we are their *Genii*,' he added – for they had been reading *The Arabian Knights*. 'I am Chief Genii Brannii. You are Genii Emmii, Genii Tallii, and Genii Annii.'

He picked up one with a mean face and said, 'This is Alexander Sneakey.'

'This one is Monkey, then,' Emily said.

'This is Butter Crashey.'

'This is Stumps.'

Anne's eyes, normally steady with forbearance, brimmed with tears. She clutched her soldier, loving it preciously, and howled, 'I don't like "Waiting Boy" for the name of mine!'

'*I'm* going to change mine to Parry,' Emily interrupted.

Parry was an arctic explorer who was being much praised in *Blackwood's Magazine*.

'I want mine to be Ross!' Anne declared; Ross being another arctic explorer.

They were in the kitchen, six months later, on a December evening when the snow was whipped onto the windows. The kitchen, too small for the five people and two animals crowded into it, smelled of coal smoke and wet dog. Charlotte and Emily at the table had finished helping Tabby to slice carrots and onions for a stew. Anne had turned a chair around, and was kneeling on the seat, leaning over the back of it, enjoying, she said, the bright colours of the carrots.

Tabby started to cut strips off the remains of yesterday's mutton joint. Charlotte, repelled, tried to persuade her to light a second candle so that she could read. As Tabby never thought that reading mattered, she refused to do it, believing that the firelight and one candle on the table was good enough for anything that children might want to do.

In the bad light, they were at a loss. Even the dog seemed fed up with the usually entertaining children. He cast a doleful eye at them, then at the closed shutters in hope that the noise on the other side might turn into something worth barking at, and then at the cat, which was unfortunately quite content at the fireside.

Brannii was sprawled before the fire in the only armed chair, putting on the languorous air of an aristocrat. 'I don't know what to do! I'm bored!' he said.

He meant that no-one had a story to tell; for throughout the summer they had been making up stories about their soldiers, and were running out of impetus.

'Yee may go ter bed!' Tabby snapped. She took off another slice of mutton with an angry slam of the knife blade upon the chopping board.

'I'd rather do anything than that,' Brannii teased her, with a smile. He knew she didn't mean it.

'You're rather glum tonight, Tabby?' Charlotte suggested.

'An' you, miss, mi't do best be getting o'er thee fads and helping me wi' t'meat.' As she herself was busy (as usual), it irked her to have lazy children under her feet. 'You're getting as picky as thy father. Yee'll not eat this, yee'll not eat that.'

Then it came into Charlotte's head to say: 'Suppose we each had an island?'

It only needed any one of them to start a new tale, and they were off.

'I'd choose the Isle of Man,' Brannii led off.

'I'd have the Isle of Wight,' Charlotte said, quickly, before Emily got a word in.

'I'll take Arran,' said Emily, because of the Border Ballads, and Sir Walter Scott.

'I'll have Guernsey, then,' Anne said.

'The Duke of Wellington shall be the chief man on my island,' Charlotte rushed in to say before Branwell put in a claim.

'Herries shall be mine,' Branwell said.

'Walter Scott shall be mine,' said Emily.

'I shall have Bentinck,' Anne said.

Thereupon, 'The Tale of the Twelve' was converted into the epic of 'The Islanders'.

'Tabby, may we have some more coals on the fire? I'm cold,' Emily said.

'No, yee may not. It's time fer bed.'

Branwell calmly put some knobs of coal on the fire, despite Tabby's grousing.

The names of The Twelve changed many times. They flowed into one another like the shape-shifting characters in some of the old stories that Tabby told when pegging out washing, or when they were helping her clean the dishes; or like characters in the Irish tales which Papa sometimes spun – the Celtic tales of the maiden who turns into a hare to evade her pursuer, who then becomes a hunting dog, whereupon she turns herself into a salmon, therefore he turns into an otter, so she swims out to sea whereupon he turns into a fisherman.

After Charlotte's first story for Anne they repudiated any more 'Woods' in their fictions, let alone had in them Browns, Heatons and Greenwoods. There were no weavers, woolcombers, farmers, country parsons or spinsters. No-one mundane or unheroic. These were cast aside for Felix de Rothsay, Harold Fitzgeorge, Ronald Traquair and Mary Henrietta Percy. Or their characters were named after famous politicians. Lord George Bentinck, whom the seven-year-old Anne had made her 'chief man', was a Member of Parliament who supported the bill for Catholic Emancipation, while the John Charles Herries chosen by ten-year-old Branwell was secretary to the Treasury under Lord Liverpool, and president of the Board of Trade.

They knew about them because Papa and Branwell used to walk to Keighley once a week, bringing back books and newspapers, including the Tory *Leeds Intelligencer* and the daringly radical *Leeds Mercury*; while a retired clergyman, the Reverend Jonas Driver, for the sake of an excuse to go to the parsonage for a chat, passed on *Blackwood's Magazine*. From these, the children took over the famous surgeons, John Abernethy and Sir Astley Pastor Cooper, and also Henry O'Donnell.

Soon, their heroes and heroines went to live where grew palm and almond trees, where there were clear, still lakes instead of brackish moorland pools, where death was romantic and glorious, and where there were nightingales which did not sing in the Brontës' smoky homeland. For though they hid away from Haworth, they knew more than the people of the village did of the great world beyond it. They also learned about it from the illustrated 'annuals', such as *Friendship's Offering*, *The Gem*, and *The Amulet*, with engravings by John Martin, which were ordered by Aunt

Branwell, or were borrowed, being passed around 'the better houses', Oxenhope Hall, Ponden Hall and Stanbury Manor.

Issue after issue of *Blackwood's* lamented British failures to civilize Africa, and the Brontë children set out to make amends.

Branwell was reading aloud from their geography textbook: the Reverend J. Goldsmith's, *A Grammar of General Geography for the use of Schools and Young Persons with Maps and Engravings*, edition of 1823. It was much thumbed, underlined and marked; Branwell and Charlotte had scrawled drawings on the endpapers, and had inserted the names of their invented countries into the index. His voice boomed, grandly.

'"Africa is the country of monsters! Every species of noxious and predatory animal reigns undisturbed in the vast deserts, being multiplied by the sultry heat of the climate. Even man exists in a state of the lowest barbarism. Abyssinia is chiefly inhabited by degenerate Arabs and the centre, south and west, by the Negro race . . ."

'*Blackwood's*,' Branwell announced, 'suggests Fernando Po as, quote, "a site where, commanding the outlets of the Niger, Great Britain could command the trade, the improvement, and the civilization of all of North Central Africa." I propose that The Twelve set sail to occupy the Gold Coast and its neighbouring Slave Coast.'

'There is a dilemma,' said Charlotte. 'According to Goldsmith, the area is bounded in the north by "Jibbel Kumri or Mountain of the Moon", beyond which lies the River Niger and "the vast, evil Sahara Desert where live the wicked and perfidious Ashantee tribes which have recently risen against British dominion and caused a vicious war". According to Goldsmith, the Niger doesn't flow anywhere near Fernando Po. It is on the other side of the northern mountains, flowing from east to west out of Lake Chad, not north to south through the Gold Coast. Yet *Blackwood's* shows it differently. So, Brannii, which shall we choose?'

'I say we go by *Blackwood's*,' Branwell said.

'Well, I cannot think of a better place for the Duke of Wellington to restore civilization,' Charlotte said.

'And Napoleon!' said Branwell. 'For it is a little known

fact, but true, that after the Battle of Waterloo, the Duke of Wellington and Napoleon, both being heroes – and heroes understand one another – became good friends and went to rule a joint kingdom at the mouth of the Po.'

'What is it like there?' queried Anne.

'It looks like the desert,' Emily said.

'No, it doesn't,' Charlotte said. 'The colonizers have filled it with the finest buildings in the world. There are elegant ladies, and there are beautiful rivers. It is like a picture by John Martin.'

When Papa had spent £2 12s. 6d. upon an engraving of Martin's *The Fall of Babylon* it had been an event for the Brontës and for Haworth. Willie Wood, the carpenter who was Tabby's nephew, was set on to frame it, and when Charlotte had gone down the street to see how it was done she had found him gawping at it speechlessly. The picture, almost three feet long and two feet high in its frame, had been set up over the mantelpiece in Papa's study. The mass of figures writhing before the onslaught of apocalyptic fire, the fat, luscious, wailing women, the swirls of smoke around the massive towers, the fabulous, doomed city, the army advancing with bows and raised spears, and the great fireball, like a huge egg cracked by lightnings in the distance, was definitely a scene from one of their own stories.

Papa liked it, too – so did Aunt Branwell – and soon, though Papa said he could 'ill afford it', it was followed by prints of Martin's *Belshazzar's Feast*, his *Joshua Arresting the Sun*, *The Passage of the Red Sea*, and *The Deluge*, which were displayed in the parlour, in Patrick's and in Aunt Branwell's bedrooms.

Martin's landscapes and splendid cities had become those of, especially, Branwell's and Charlotte's hearts. They were as different from the low, heavy buildings and the soggy brown moors of Yorkshire as one could find. The palaces seemed made of shining air.

'They seem made of glass,' Charlotte said.

Thus they found the name of the capital of their African settlement: 'Glasstown'.

When Charlotte drew Glasstown Bay it looked like a Martin picture. Branwell brought Martin into the stories as 'Edward

De Lisle' who depicted 'The Cheif Genii in Council', of which Charlotte wrote a review. ('I before e, except after c,' said Aunt Branwell and Papa, but it never sank in.) In no time, Glasstown had a Hall of Justice and a Grand Inn. (In Haworth, Brannii was beginning to peep through the door of the Black Bull.) There was a Great Tower, similar to the ziggurat in Martin's *The Fall of Babylon*, and a 'hall of sapphire, holding a throne of gold', where genii and fairies wore 'robes of beaten gold that sparkled with diamonds'. There was a Palace of Arts and Sciences, illuminated by lamps that 'were too bright to look upon', so they decided when peering about on a dark November day, with only the promise of a candle to be lit after four o'clock.

'The city must be defended from bestial forces,' Chief Genii Brannii announced. He commandeered Charlotte's black-painted ninepins and set them out as a 'tribe of Ashantees'.

'In their uprising, they came on like a torrent . . .' Brannii roared. 'Sweeping everything aside, they burned the palm trees and laid waste to the rice fields. When they came to the walls of Glasstown, they set up a terrible yell, the meaning of which was that we should be consumed from the face of the earth and that our city should vanish away! For as it came by magic – so they declared – it should go by the same! Our answer to this insolent speech was a peal of thunder from our cannon!'

Brannii strutted and waved his arms. He stretched himself along the floor and rolled a ball towards the ninepins. '*Pquee . . . pquee . . . pqueeee!*'

All uprisings were put down bloodily, and in the end Charlotte found them tiresome. Brannii drew many pictures of them – his 'Battel Pictures'. The prancing horses and blue flags of the victors filled the top three-quarters of the paper and along the foot lay the vanquished, apparently without backbones and straight as boards. For no matter what misfortunes threatened Wellington, and Wellington's successor who was his son the Marquis of Douro (who next became the Duke of Zamorna), and Napoleon (who was replaced by Alexander Percy), their fates and the future of the arts and sciences in Glasstown were cared for by the four Genii.

Brannii invented a language for The Twelve. (Who by this time had become named 'The Young Men'.) He imitated their speech by pinching his nose and talking, sometimes like Tabby in the Yorkshire dialect, and at other times like Aunt Branwell in her Cornish one: 'Hellow! Dear! Oi tee troy bowts cawming oup tow us.' This was his phonetic rendering of, 'Hello! There! I see three boats coming up to us.' Some of it, too, was like the mummers' plays, or like the 'Pace Egg' and the 'Rushbearing' plays that were performed in the village street by rowdy drunks.

Brannii and Emmii were carried away for a whole week with inventing instruments of torture, dungeons, and a hall of judgement.

'What is it like?' asked Brannii.

Emily said: 'It has whitewashed arches, and is damp and low, creeping with spiders and green with mould. And I have the key to the door, which is at the top of the stairs.'

'Aunt Branwell keeps the key,' Charlotte interrupted, 'because you are talking about our cellar. And if you make up horrible stories I think you should ask to be forgiven when you say your prayers.'

Wickedness made Charlotte most uneasy. (Anne, apparently, even more so.) It made her want to jump out of the story before it became too dangerous, yet it also thrilled her.

Emily responded by opening her eyes wide, to be more frightening. She raised her hands in the air, stretched her fingers like claws, and, howling as they did when imitating witches, she said: 'No it isn't, it is the Hall of Judgement in Glasstown! Glasstown's enemies are tortured there! All the Cockney school of poets, Leigh Hunt, Keats and Hazlitt, because they have dared to quarrel with *Blackwood's Magazine*! A thousand children are imprisoned! The guards for thrashing them are Colonel Shaughnessy and his nephew Fogharty. And sometimes they exercise the privilege when they do not need to, for the fun of it. And Genii Brannii has a large black club with which he thumps the children unmercifully!'

'Well – the Duke of Wellington is the chief governor,' Charlotte insisted.

The stories were written down in home-stitched books

with pages sized two inches by one-and-a-half, sometimes less, each page sometimes containing as many as thirty-two lines of Charlotte's or Branwell's 'printed' writing. They were little artefacts that might break even under the pressure of breath. Hours, whole wet or snowy days, were passed in these compositions, in illustrating them, and in making the covers out of blue sugar-bags or anything else they could get hold of. The writing was too cramped and awkward for Papa to read it even with his magnifying glass.

They invented stories of incest, adultery and murder. If Aunt Branwell had read them, she would have sent for the exorcist.

It was not that there was no morality or religion in them. Figures achieved their rewards, or came to bad ends, just as they should. But, as Charlotte at any rate knew very well – and felt responsible for, because she was the eldest – their fates had not come about because they had obeyed or disobeyed precepts that would be understood by Aunt Branwell. They were the puppets of such sublime passion, or alternatively of such chthonic evil, that Aunt Branwell would have fainted to think of it, and Papa would have choked on his porridge.

They were the Brontës as they saw themselves.

III

Charlotte Brontë, wrested from home and from Glasstown, stood on the playing field at the Misses Wooler's school at Roe Head, the centre of a ring of eight girls. Miss Susan Ledgard remarked that 'Miss Brontë has a face like a lion', and it was not a compliment.

Her broad face, with its wide-set, yellow-brown eyes and its feline, crooked mouth, surrounded by her crimped, brown hair, was set upon a tiny body. If she raised her eyes, which was not often, she had the round-eyed stare of a cat at night when surprised by a light. The look was caused by her short-sightedness, but the girls had not realized that yet. Although leonine, she was not at all bold. All she managed was puzzled defiance. Hers was the look of a lioness cowed by the circus, with only a memory of not being defeated.

She had started off, not in the centre, but as one of the

circle. Apart from one or two of them who were related, the nine were all strangers to one another, because the Misses Wooler's school near Huddersfield was a new one, but they all understood this game of throwing a ball – except for Charlotte, who never even tried to catch it. Therefore they had fallen into a new sport, of setting her in the centre and throwing the ball past her, but she was supposed to stop it. 'Piggy-in-the-middle' she heard them call it. Once she had managed to catch the ball, the one who had thrown it would change places with her.

Charlotte, instead of seizing a chance for initiative and leadership, felt humiliated and at bay. Not having heard of the game before, she behaved like a fool. She could not see the ball when it was thrown: only a vague movement, which might or might not have been someone throwing. She knew for certain only when the ball was a few feet from her face, and if she had been cowardly she would have ducked. Instead, she let it pass a foot above her head, as if she hadn't noticed or as if she wasn't afraid of being hit. She was terrified.

She was next supposed to have her eye on the person who would be throwing it back from the other direction but she did not even turn round. She still kept her eyes mostly upon the ground. She wished she had a book in her hand. It was a frosty day in the second half of January and she was very cold, but she would not have minded nipped fingers if they had held a book. She wanted to think about Brannii, Emmii, Glasstown, Papa and, above all, of her beloved creation – the elder son of the Duke of Wellington: 'the Marquis of Douro'. The maddening game stole her thoughts.

The ball passed by her ear from behind, and Miss Someone-or-Other laughed. Miss Brontë raised her head for a second. The ball was thrown towards her yet again: from Miss Taylor, she just about recognized. Charlotte still did not move her arms or position. This time the throw was gentle, lower, and less dangerous. Falling upon the thick folds of her woollen skirt, the ball was lost for a second then it rolled down and settled at her feet, where she ignored it.

'*Throw it back!*' shouted an exasperated but still friendly voice a dozen yards in front of her. She thought that it came from Miss Taylor, but it could have been Miss Allison or one of the two Misses Brooke. She saw a vague, upright shape, somewhat like a huge clothes-peg but with woolly edges.

Genii Tallii bent down to the ball, then paused halfway, inspecting it as if still not sure what it was. But of course it would be silly of them to think that she could not see it from *that* distance. It was just that she was hesitating over what to do.

'*Throw it!*' another of the girls repeated. This voice was threatening and came from somewhere to the side of her. Certainly it was not Miss Taylor this time. She thought it was Miss Ledgard.

'It will not bite you, Miss Brontë!'

This was followed by a chuckle from the others. Charlotte could feel what she could not see clearly: the girls mocking her. She feared that the eight were getting to be friends by picking on her. Their homes were close together in this part of the West Riding of Yorkshire and they were mostly daughters of the new class of wealthy mill-owners for whom – as the five Misses Wooler had cleverly spotted – it was worth opening a school. Charlotte was the only pupil from far away – that is, from twenty-five miles distance – and who was a specimen of that type of freak known as a poor parson's daughter.

She felt that she could have been Zenobia, Lady Ellrington – she of her recent, first love story, *Albion and Marina: A Tale by Lord Charles Wellesley* – surrounded by the Ashantees. Where were the other genii? Where were Papa and Tabby? Where was the Marquis of Douro? She felt excruciatingly alone.

She snatched the ball, stood erect with her arm raised as if to touch the sky, and balanced the ball over her shoulder.

'Here you ore!' she shouted, straining after gaiety.

'Miss Brontë's Oirish!' mocked the extremely *nicely* spoken Miss Amelia Walker.

'We have a scullery maid who is *Oirish*,' Miss Walker added, and there was much laughter.

'"Bog-Irish", as they say. They keep their pigs in the kitchen. They keep hens in the bedroom. Don't they, Miss Bron-*teh*?'

In a temper, Charlotte hurled. She would have liked to be aiming a cannon ball at Miss Walker.

'Bravo!' sneered – Miss Haigh?

'Oh, *sod*!' exclaimed – Miss Allinson? She was another manufacturer's daughter. For Charlotte had missed everybody by yards. How could she miss everybody?! It landed among frozen grasses at the edge of the playing area and the group broke up to chase after it.

Charlotte burst into tears.

'Why are you crying?' asked the strong young voice of Miss Taylor, who had left the others and had come close by.

Charlotte was fourteen years of age. Her hair having grown again since being cropped at Cowan Bridge, it was now, like her sisters', frizzed and crimped by Aunt Branwell's curling irons.

The irons came out of the fire glowing, frightening her with a smell of burned hair about her head, and made her feel she was suffering the torments of the Inquisition. She knew her sisters felt the same as Aunt Branwell dealt with them, one by one, every Saturday evening in the kitchen; it caused the cat to flee, and Papa said – it was a kind of refrain – he feared he'd see house and daughters go up in flames. Charlotte thought she was sufficiently ignominious as it was, with her midget's stature and plain, dumpy face, so she was sure the crimping of her hair was worse for her than for naturally elegant Emily. Also, even though they were out of mourning for their sisters, all were still garbed in uniform, drab clothes. Papa disapproved of 'coquettishness' and, although Aunt Branwell could be vain, perhaps whenever Cornish memories assailed her, yet Charlotte knew – as Aunt Branwell too should have known from the 'annuals' – how ludicrous her old-fashioned taste was. But it was she who chose the girls' clothes, and they all wore the same, plain, stuff gowns, with odds and ends of lace collars and cuffs stitched on by themselves. Even in Haworth, Charlotte had known what a fright she was; if only from the looks on the faces of visitors, and from the gossip that reached from the village.

She had been sent off because her family once again hung over a precipice. Papa, strong all his life so far, had become seriously ill with congested lungs. It had continued through the summer, the autumn and the winter. He was unable to climb stairs or pulpit steps without pausing to cough and heave at his lungs. Especially at night, he tore at them to rid them of fluid, terrifying Branwell with the noise.

He had been in bed for several weeks. One day, Emily had come in — with that stare, one did not know whether of wonder or alarm, which was becoming typical of her — and said, 'I have just heard Dr Andrew say that Papa's life hangs by a thread.'

The issue of their abilities to earn their own livings had again *raised its ugly head*. They were never allowed to forget the cliff close to which walked unlovely daughters of a poor parson. It was a fall into domestic servitude at best, as ladies' maids or governesses; into early graves from poorly doctored sicknesses at worst. Charlotte, the eldest, had been sent for another attempt at training in the skills of a governess.

Mary Taylor was ten months younger than Charlotte, but ten years older in her grasp of the real world, and had enjoyed a striking upbringing. It included a sense of sisterhood with her own sex. Her father was a 'heavy-wool manufacturer' of blankets and army cloth, and a banker. Also he was a freethinker and a republican, thus scandalizing his colleagues in these Chartist days. His home, the Red House in Gomersal, was electric with intellectual dispute, and he believed that women should be brought up to think for themselves and speak their own minds. He had done a good job with Mary.

She had been protective of Miss Brontë ever since having had the advantage, with the other girls, of seeing her arrive.

That should not have been *such* a terrible ordeal. Roe Head was only just outside the boundary of Hartshead, where — Mary found out later — half the clergymen in the district were Brontë family friends. But, on this first day, Miss Brontë had not put in an appearance until late afternoon by which time the other new pupils were settled in. Mary, for example, had only come five miles; she had arrived in a smart gig that had been polished for the occasion, and was driven by a family servant. The strange little Miss Brontë on the other hand had turned up in a market cart. It seemed she had spent all day being passed from lift to lift, pre-arranged by her strategically minded father, from Haworth to Huddersfield and up the hill to Roe Head. She sat next to the driver behind the rumps of a couple of hefty cart-horses. Although the clumsy cart was covered over, a piglet could be seen poking its nose through the weave of a basket.

It had been a special misfortune for Miss Brontë that arrivals were visible at Roe Head through its three tiers of bow-windows. These were not where the front door was but on the side looking over the valley, nevertheless they offered a view of the driveway. In one bay, eight girls were assembled. They were strangers to one another, short of amusement and subjects for conversation. Miss Brontë provided both as she stepped down from the cart, stiff, cold, miserable, and huddled in her cloak after twenty-five miles of slow progress through the market towns and the mill villages. Other girls had put on some style for their appearances at a new school. Miss Brontë looked like a little old woman as she followed, not a personal servant, but the grubby, indifferent carter who carried her trunk.

'Whoever is that little fright?' Miss Haigh had giggled.

'Oh dear!' The snobbish Miss Walker rolled her eyes and waved her arms like an exasperated mama in a Rossini opera. 'That'll be Miss Brontë.'

'*Who?*'

The strange name had been enough in itself to produce a laugh. They did not know about Lord Nelson who was Duke of Brontë, any more than they knew about Glasstown – it took Mary years to find out.

'She is my aunt's godchild, though I have never set eyes on her before,' said Miss Walker. 'She lives in the mountains.'

Miss Brontë had disappeared from sight. After a quarter of an hour, she had been brought by Miss Margaret Wooler to the schoolroom door. The oak-panelled passages, the great doors, the wide staircase starting up from a spacious hall, had evidently overpowered Miss Brontë. The door swung open and she had stood there, looking down, blinking, in near-tears. Divested of cloak and bonnet, showing herself in her 'practical', old-fashioned dress, she had still looked like a little old woman to her fellows, in their pretty frocks, their lace, their bright ribbons and their neat shoes. They had interpreted her tense expression as hostility.

* * *

'I don't know how to play games!' Charlotte blubbered in response to Miss Taylor's question on the playing field, and she hid her face in a home-stitched handkerchief.

'Then don't play them!' was Miss Taylor's simple, smiling answer. She shone like a dandelion on a sunny day.

It was a revelation to learn that she didn't *have* to cultivate the affection of her peers. Charlotte smiled and tucked away her hankie. If Miss Taylor had noticed that it had been stitched at home, and had mentioned it (it turned out that Miss Taylor might well have commented; she spoke up about anything she wanted to), it would not have upset Charlotte.

They stood out in the frost, the sun shining on it. Beyond, Charlotte could hazily take in the valley of the Calder with its factory smoke thawing the frost. Whitened slopes on the far side of Huddersfield reflected a warm colour that she would have known to describe as 'chrome yellow'.

When she had been part of the game of piggy-in-the-middle she had felt trapped. Now she was aware of a spacious glow of beautiful colour.

She was no longer alone.

The other friend whom Charlotte made was Miss Nussey.

Ellen Nussey arrived at the school even later: she came after a week, but this did not disadvantage her. This was not merely because she did not have a highly-tuned imagination. (Though it was a fact that she hadn't.) It was because there was nothing in her life to cause her to feel disadvantaged. She was related to most of the oldest and best families in the district. Her home, Rydings in Birstall, only a couple of miles from Mary Taylor's home in Gomersal, stood in its own park. It possessed a rookery, and an avenue of chestnuts and limes. Her father, who like Mary Taylor's had been a cloth manufacturer and a banker, had died five years previously, leaving the family relatively straitened. It was very 'relative', and the Nusseys remained bolstered by money.

Ellen would not have known what it was to ride in a market cart. Her brother Henry had sped her over the few snowy miles down the road from Birstall in a dashing little phaeton; and the ceremonious fashion in which the elder Miss Wooler received the Nusseys might have looked like favouritism. With a woman as fair-minded as Margaret Wooler this could not have been the case, yet Ellen, on seeing the smiling, abbess-like lady – short in stature but imposing in dignity, a tight plait of hair coiled upon her head – coming right out onto the steps to meet them, had accepted it as the obeisance customarily paid to members of her family.

Despite the snow, the Misses Wooler had not relaxed their faith in the benefits of fresh air and, as on all afternoons, eight of the other nine girls were out at play when Ellen arrived. While Miss Wooler offered Mr Nussey a nip of brandy before he set off back for home, the second eldest Miss Wooler, Miss Catherine, led the new pupil to the schoolroom.

She was not intimidated by the oak panelling and the broad passageways; it was like home, and she did not notice them. Likewise, she passed a maid as if the girl did not exist. Ellen was left to browse among the volumes. The fine leather bindings and the wordy, theological titles were not what she would choose to read, yet she was impressed. She had faith in such books because of their weightiness and worthiness: they fortified what made her life comfortable and secure. She saw their school textbooks exhibited – Murray's *Grammar*, Miss Mangnall's *Questions*, Rollin's *Ancient History*, Lindley Murray's *Grammar*, and Mrs Chapone's *Letters on the Improvement of the Mind*. She found Milton and the works of Hume. She came to the conclusion that this was a very nice school.

She believed that she was alone. Not being over-endowed with curiosity, she had not even looked towards the far end of the room until she was alarmed by some sporadic flutterings, as of a trapped, tired bird. She then glanced towards the great bay-window, which was flooded with light reflected from the snow. She discerned a dumpy, ill-proportioned little figure huddled beyond the end of the table that ran the length of the road. It was weeping.

Ellen Nussey stepped towards it. She was trained to approach persons in distress, for the Nusseys were expected to walk through what *The Times* called 'the distressed districts' dispensing aid and comfort to out-of-work weavers and broken down coalminers, and just so did she approach this little creature. Yet when she reached the window it was not as when she fell upon a poor widow or an unemployed handloom-weaver. These would have solicited alms, but this creature shrank inside her grief.

'My name is Miss Nussey. What is your name?'

The little person blew into a handkerchief and snivelled through her terrible tears, 'Miss Brontë!'

'I beg your pardon?'

'Charlotte Bront-*teh*!' she said impatiently.

Ellen was too well-bred to remark upon the peculiar name. Before she could think of any more to say, the person howled out her confession, which was very precisely worded; most remarkably so:

'I have been sent here to learn to earn my living but I don't know how to play games and I am homesick!'

Ellen adopted the expression of her uncle the magistrate, when he had decided to deal sympathetically with the widow of a hanged Luddite. She answered, with a smile: 'By and by, I, too, may be in need of comfort from the same cause.'

Miss Brontë quickly tucked away her handkerchief, embarrassed – Ellen thought – because it was threadbare and, Ellen suspected from a quick impression, home-stitched. Miss Brontë blinked and pulled herself together. It was then that Ellen noticed the details that she had missed, so absorbed had she been by the aura of that extreme grief. Without any attempt to appear becoming, Miss Brontë wore a green stuff dress, patched here and there, and she could have been one of the school servants. She had an exceedingly pale face, broad in structure, but drawn, like the features of poor people after a hard winter.

'Miss Nussey, although your homesickness might be consolable, mine never can be,' she replied.

Ellen learned later that Charlotte Brontë never sought diversion from the cruelty of her awareness of herself.

'Nevertheless, perhaps we can be friends?' Ellen suggested.

'I have a friend already . . .' Charlotte began, stiffly.

'Oh.'

She spoke with such strange, simple honesty that it was shocking. Ellen lived her life on a much more normal plane of mendacity.

'Her name is Miss Taylor,' Charlotte explained. 'Perhaps,' she continued – doubtfully – 'we may all three be friends together?'

The confident Ellen took hold of Miss Brontë's hand. Without speaking, they held hands for some time, and Ellen felt the access of what she later, when she was a successful graduate of the Misses Wooler's school, described as, 'the genuine sympathy which always consoles, even though it be unexpressed'.

IV

'I, for one, have not the slightest intention of allowing my future husband to rule the roost,' Miss Walker chirped across the dormitory after candles had been blown out.

The conversation about fiancés and husbands had gone on for an hour, or it seemed to have done so to Charlotte who buried herself under the bedclothes, curled up against Miss Nussey's back.

'I do not see how it can be avoided,' responded Miss Nussey, uncertainly because she was apparently torn in her loyalties between her other schoolfriends and her bed companion.

Charlotte wished that she did not have to inflict such a conflict upon her.

Miss Ledgard said, 'If one marries sensibly for wealth and status, I, too, do not see how one can avoid giving in to one's husband – to some extent.'

'Oh, there are means available to the members of our sex,' Miss Walker added.

'Darkly spoken! Pray, what "means" are on your mind at the moment?' said Miss Haigh.

'Have you seen Miss Nussey's brother Henry?' Miss Maria Brooke attempted to change the subject. 'He really *is* dashing. *Won't* you invite us all to a party at Rydings, Miss Nussey?'

'Shut up the lot of you, you make me sick!' Mary Taylor yelled, and a pillow was thrown at her, which she returned.

Such talk regularly flew about in the darkness. It was

like the ball which others could see but Charlotte could not, in that game of 'piggy-in-the-middle'. Though cynical ambition was often the motive for marriage in Glasstown, there it was tragic, rather than mean and ignoble as it was in this down-to-earth world. Charlotte's loneliest place at Roe Head was this dormitory, despite having the warmth of Ellen's companionship as substitute for Emily's at home. If she had not found her two friends, she doubted if she could have borne it here. The only words she could bear to hear were Miss Nussey's and Miss Taylor's.

Yet Charlotte dreaded her own opinion being sought. It was all right for Miss Taylor and Miss Nussey, who seemed to be familiar with such conversations, but Charlotte had never talked of marriage in such disgustingly realistic terms.

She gave the impression that she had little to communicate on any other subject, either; not much that anyone could understand.

While the rest of the girls played games, she chose to lurk under the trees at the side of the field, short-sightedly holding a book, her face so close that it almost touched the pages. If she lifted her head, the book came up with it in a jerky movement that made the girls laugh. When they called across and asked her what she was doing, she told them of the beauty of the shadows and of the shifting patterns of light. It made them laugh.

One day she announced, dreamily: 'At Cowan Bridge, I used to stand on a stone in the middle of the stream that ran at the foot of the garden.'

'What for?' Miss Haigh asked.

'Just to stare at it.' They were still baffled so she added, 'Because it was so beautiful, and my life was not.'

'Why did you not take up fishing?' she was teased.

'I had no taste for it.'

The seriousness of her answer made them laugh further.

Her ignorance of ordinary matters was a joke. How could she possibly have *never* played 'hunt the thimble' or 'musical chairs'?

In the classroom, her showing at the preliminary tests in grammar, spelling and geography was so bad that she was mortified by being set (another rush of embarrassing tears) among younger, more backward girls at the foot of the class.

Even that wasn't evidence of the kind of simple-mindedness which they could grasp. This simpleton who was unable to spell, for example, 'peice', knew by heart long passages of Byron, and of Milton's *Paradise Lost*. While ignorant of the answers to be found in Miss Mangnall's *Historical and Miscellaneous Questions for the Use of Young People*, which her fellow pupils could deal with easily, she was a mine of answers to what left others stumped.

'Whence have we the best olives?' – when Miss Wooler briskly asked this from the section of *Questions on Common Subjects*, Miss Maria Brooke and others could tell her, almost without needing to scurry through the pages: 'From Italy, Portugal, and the southern parts of France; the oil of olives is esteemed the best and sweetest.' Ask, 'What is Fuller's earth?' and half the class of manufacturers' daughters already knew: 'An unctuous kind of marl; of great use in cleansing and preparing wool.'

On the other hand, when it came to plundering Miss Mangnall's section of *Questions Relative to the English Constitution* or her *An Abstract of the Scottish Reigns*, it was that funny little sparrow, Miss Brontë, who had learned by rote, 'Duncan, 1033. A prince of pacific temper, and great virtues; he was treacherously murdered by Macbeth.'

One day, when Shakespeare's historical plays were recommended by Miss Wooler – with reservations, and as 'a useful way of learning the succession of the English kings' – Miss Brontë took the opportunity to blurt out a summary of the whole plot of one of the 'naughty' plays, *Macbeth*. The other nine young ladies, and Miss Wooler, were breathless with shock. The Bard of Avon got short shrift from Miss Mangnall, who in her *Abstract of British Biography* chapter summarized him as 'The Poet of nature, "Fancy's Child"' and for the rest had only space to praise his editors: 'his plays have been edited by Rowe, Pope, Theobald, Sir Thomas Hamer, Doctor Warburton, Mr Capell, Mr Stevens, and Doctor Johnson, with notes.' No doubt Miss Brontë sought to impress? Doubtless she thought that what was acceptable in her barbaric parsonage would establish her among her peers at Roe Head? Out of nervousness, it seemed, Charlotte, once started, was unable to stop, and she unreeled the whole, sordid plot.

Miss Wooler pursed her lips and did not know how to stop her, either. Having herself only a hazy knowledge of a play so unsuitable for a lady's education, she was unsure at what point the impetuous pupil might crash into mention of, for instance, *women's breasts*. They were in the play somewhere.

On the second morning, Miss Brontë, her eyes red from crying herself to sleep, demonstrated her acquaintance with Sir Walter Scott's *The Bride of Lammermoor*.

Before the week was out, Miss Wooler was informed by the tell-tale Miss Walker that Miss Brontë knew the works of – Miss Walker hardly dare say it – Lord Byron. She had quoted from them in the dormitory. Her father a clergyman! Maybe one ought to write him of the dangers.

Also, there was something *morbid* about the extent of her homesickness. After lesson time, most of the girls missed family warmth and parents' love, which was why Miss Wooler commenced her 'evening perambulations', when she paced the drawing-room with the girls following her. 'Like chickens around a mother hen,' said one girl; 'like novitiates around a wise abbess,' said another, and 'like acolytes around Socrates in ancient Athens,' said a third. (Which pleased Miss Wooler, who did not possess a sense of the absurd.) Thus she encouraged a more affectionate, intimate conversation than was possible in the schoolroom. Mary Taylor talked about her cosy home in Gomersal, warm red brick in a country of cold grey stone, and about her father; his cultivated talk of travels in Italy and France, the paintings he brought home, and his salty humour concerning narrow-minded business colleagues. Miss Ledgard showed that she was not as tough as she pretended to be. Miss Walker evidently had just a little more in her head than a future of balls and romances.

Miss Brontë gave away nothing revealing about her background. Always she stared right through one, with reddened eyes about to burst. Or they were focused on the distance; presumably on that mountain parsonage from which she could not be weaned.

. . . One evening about dusk, as the Marquis of Douro was returning from a shooting excursion into the country, he heard suddenly a rustling noise in a deep ditch on the roadside. He was preparing his fowling-piece for a shot when the form of Lady Ellrington started up before him. Her head was bare, her tall person was enveloped in the tattered remnants of a dark velvet mantle. Her dishevelled hair hung in wild elf-locks over her face, neck, and shoulders, almost concealing her features, which were emaciated and pale as death. He stepped back a few paces, startled at the sudden and ghastly apparition. She threw herself on her knees before him, exclaiming in wild, maniacal accents: 'My lord, tell me truly . . .'

It wasn't merely the parsonage – it was the wicked frisson of Glasstown that Charlotte missed. She longed for its beautiful men and women, who were so different from the ugly, small person she saw in her mirror.

She would have liked to tell Ellen Nussey, Mary Taylor and the other friend whom she made, who was Mary Taylor's sister, Martha, that she was the author of several books set in Africa. She could not do it. She blushed at the thought of telling Ellen that she wrote at all, let alone what she wrote. She almost confessed to Mary, who might understand her creative writing. But she would not sympathize with it. She would never understand how one gave in to any man, even such a one as the Marquis of Douro.

For a time, Charlotte changed beds and shared with Mary. There, just as she had shared the secrets of 'bed plays' with Emily, so she discussed those of her body with Mary. Mary confessed to changes which were still a mystery to Charlotte, but which she knew would come to her – as they had already arrived for Emily, although two years younger. Horror and fear of them Mary Taylor laughed to scorn. She explained in simple words what they meant and how to deal with them, speaking plainly, as her mother had talked to her, and for good measure added more about the social burdens of being a woman.

Nonetheless, Charlotte stopped short of revelations about

Glasstown. The developments of her body were common to all females. Glasstown no-one else could understand.

Creative writing, as she already knew, was by its nature secretive – more so even than 'periods'. Writing was a way of privately admitting forbidden matters, of confessing to feelings that one was supposed not to have. It was, in essence, a sin.

While Charlotte yearned and wondered what was happening in Haworth and Glasstown, she was anxious about the responsibility that pulled her in the opposite direction. Her weakness at governess subjects, her uselessness at games or at playing the piano, made her frightened of being a failure. It weakened her like an influenza. She had to hold on to doorways before she could enter rooms. She awoke in the mornings to floods of terrible recognition. It put her off her food. Meat, especially – the other nine girls tucking into ribs of mutton – took her back to Cowan Bridge. *All* meat seemed to smell rotten. It made her nerves knot in her stomach and she felt sick.

But she needed only a week or so at the school to do as Miss Wooler advised and 'pull herself together'. She began to see the good aspects of the place. It had something of a family environment; one, like the parsonage, composed almost entirely of females, only here there were many of them, with teachers, pupils and servants.

'Roe Head is a Sapphic colony,' Mary Taylor said. 'It is a place where females are for once able to follow intellectual pursuits.'

Ellen Nussey said, 'I think that we girls can form friendships that we will find in no other spheres, by being all together here.'

Thus they offered Charlotte their different consolations – one progressive and the other snobbish.

Charlotte at last recognized that the openness and light of her surroundings – the view she saw, vaguely, which was broad and gentle, looking across lawns, rose garden, orchard, and a small park planted with trees – were physical emblems of the new swoop of her mind as it responded to the genial pedagogy of the Misses Wooler, which was all sweet reasonableness. It was as much to do with outward, visible manner as with inner substance: Miss Wooler said that the way that one walked, dressed, and behaved showed the content of one's mind.

Charlotte began to tackle governess geography and grammar with the same self-sacrificing application with which she had overcome her aversion to stitching samplers. Just as in the end she had enjoyed sewing, so she started to enjoy the systematic unravelling of French and English grammar and spelling. The other girls, who had not understood her distance from them at first, now could not understand why she worked so hard.

Because there were only ten pupils for four teachers, routines were relaxed and the girls could perform their exercises and take them to the teachers at almost any time. Tasks could be finished early so as to leave an afternoon and evening free for pleasure, but Miss Brontë would finish her set exercises and then sit by the window, studying until the light died. Even then she would try to carry on reading.

'Miss Brontë is a bat who can read in the dark,' Miss Ledgard spat, poisonously.

Under Miss Wooler's gaze, Charlotte was forced to struggle with the pianoforte. She loved music, but the piano was difficult because she could not see well; her nose almost touched the keyboard, just as when she read a book.

A sunny day arrived, when she would rather have been out in the park and orchard. Sat at the piano in the music room, every now and then she raised her head to peek at the music sheet of 'Oh dear what can the matter be?', screwing up her face and forgetting what her fingers were doing. She dared not move her hands in case she could not find the notes again. On her mind was Miss Walker's description of her. 'Have you ever seen a heron darting for a fish and lifting its head to gobble it? That's Miss Brontë playing the piano.'

'Miss Brontë, it is *either* spectacles or no music!' Miss Wooler said. 'Do you hear me?'

Charlotte's lip – as nearly always when she was spoken to contentiously, or by a stranger – was trembling. Yet she answered: 'I must do without the music then. I cannot disadvantage my appearance among the girls any further, ma'am.'

'You are exasperating! The girls do not judge you by your appearance.'

'I think that they do so, Miss Wooler.'

Miss Wooler surveyed the profile of the apparently pitiful figure whom she knew to be as strong as a rock.

'You will also have to cut your nails before you can play.'

Charlotte wriggled and did not answer.

'Or do you grow them long so as to make it impossible?'

'Perhaps I do, ma'am.'

She could not explain that she grew them as long as those of 'Lady Ellrington' or 'Mary Percy' as her secret connection with Glasstown.

It was impossible, Miss Wooler thought, to alter this stubborn person who so thoroughly contrived to have her own way.

But she made academic headway at great speed. She could mimic governess talk as well as she could that of Tabby or Papa; mimicry inspired her imagination, it made her laugh to herself.

Once a week she sent a letter home, addressed to Branwell. Miss Wooler examined the girls' letters because the composition of decorous epistles was part of their training, and she found that Charlotte's were written in such perfect Misses-Wooler English – so restrained, so emptily ornate, so different from reckless Glasstown phraseology – it was as if the language wore whalebone corsets. Thus her letters, and other accomplishments, shot her from the bottom of the junior class to the top of the senior one. At the end of the term, the brilliant Mary Taylor and she were neck-and-neck for the first prize. It was Charlotte who won the silver medal to hang around her neck.

Also her knowledge of literature from private reading came into its own when she learned to be more judicious at displaying it; though she still blushed when quoting from the classics. The girls thought that it was embarrassment at her knowledge but it was because the passionate themes – ambition, jealousy, betrayal, and unrestrained love – flung her right back into the Glasstown saga.

In some of her 'spare' time she translated Voltaire's

Henriade into English verse. One morning, day-dreaming over what she had won, what she had perhaps lost 'through the years', she scribbled on the inside of her French textbook: '*Like a vision came those sunny hours to me. Where are they now? They have long since passed into eternity.*'

V

Charlotte showed what she wanted in a man through her descriptions of the Marquis of Douro and the Duke of Wellington. The Duke was 'decisive, calm, courageous, and noble-minded'. His fictional son, 'the Marquis of Douro', was 'mild and humane but very courageous'. 'His mind is of the highest order, elegant and cultivated. His genius is lofty and soaring.'

The Marquis's appearance was 'tall and slender . . . His appearance came up to my highest notion of what a great General ought to be – the high, stern forehead, noble Roman nose, compressed disdainful lip.'

Their faults were such that, to her mind, you could call them strengths. The Duke had 'a certain expression of sarcasm about his mouth which showed he considered many of those with whom he associated much beneath him.'

While she went around Roe Head nervous as a kitten, she saw one or other of her heroes before her: a ghostly defender and friend, to terrify her enemies now that she was far from Glasstown. (Which Branwell had renamed: Verdopolis.)

> 'My lord, tell me truly, sincerely, ingenuously, where have you been? I heard that you had left Verdopolis, and I followed you on foot five hundred miles. Then my strength failed me, and I lay down in this place, as I thought, to die. But it was doomed that I should see you once more before I became an inhabitant of the grave . . .'

Her ideal man was one before whom the female person sooner or later abased herself. How could she explain that to Mary Taylor?

She never spoke of he whom she saw with her inner eye

– just as the other girls, she knew, were preoccupied with their (contemptible) images of maleness. If she came across someone who was anything like her ideal, for instance a hand-some clergyman, she stiffened and was haunted for days. She knew that the other girls were equally preoccupied because of the way they tittered and made, usually, rude comments if a male strayed into the school – the more handsome the man, the ruder the comments; though Charlotte did not do that.

One day in May Charlotte went into the orchard. It was an almost circular level of ground walled-in from the road which ran uphill to Hartshead, a couple of miles away. She let herself in through a door in the wall and paced the gravel paths.

It was a semi-forbidden place. That is to say: typical of the Misses Wooler's kindly discipline, no-one took notice of a trespass unless too many went there and did damage, in which case the punishment was slight. (Slighter than usual: for all punishments were light. A penny deducted from pocket money and given to charity. Being sent early to bed. There was nothing physical, and the most severe was the black sash which, every week, the worst behaved girl had to wear.) It was understood that girls in adolescence sometimes needed a safe place in which to walk and think alone and no-one made more use of this privilege than Charlotte.

It was shortly after her fifteenth birthday. The sunlight was filtered through pink apple blossoms, and the branches broke an enamel sky into pieces of cobalt blue. There was no wind and the sun was as warm as it must have been in that France of which she had begun to dream. The grass and the flowers breathed those odours of spring which excited every creature. A chaffinch was singing, and a migrant willow warbler. Charlotte noted these details, and the butterflies flitting, and the borders of primroses, and the perfume of the grass, because she was in love.

She did not have anyone to be in love with, but she believed she knew what the sensation was and no-one could have convinced her otherwise. She wondered about her mother when she had been in love, at Woodhouse Grove, at Kirkstall Abbey.

It helped Charlotte that she had no actual lover, for thus she did not need to be ashamed of her plain appearance; though she had done her best with it. She was wearing a new bonnet and a white muslin dress with two petticoats, that had been sent as her birthday present on the 21 April by Mrs Franks – the former Miss Firth. She felt both shy and bold, at one and the same time; and white was the colour worn by the heroine of her last Haworth story, *Albion and Marina.*

She was in a mood of pensive sadness, but it was a pleasant sensation; it gave an edge to the surrounding beauty. She sensed it as part of some eternal transcendence. She could not think of any better way of putting it.

She did not think, consciously, 'I am young', nevertheless that, also, was what she was feeling. For a time she could almost find herself beautiful, and it made her quite light-headed. Holding her skirt out, because no-one was watching, and with her long nails caught in the muslin, she walked back and forth. She feared that, if she left the warm orchard, this extraordinary sensation would vanish.

It was then that she saw him leaning against a tree. *The Marquis of Douro.*

He was far enough away for her to think, at first, that it was some effect of sunlight among the branches, or that he was a gardener standing unusually still. But no, there was no mistaking him. No lower-class gardener could look like him – tall and slender, with wavy dark locks reaching to his cheek-bones and his shoulders, and with his pallid, elongated face. He was wearing a dark blue velvet suit with tight pantaloons, a broad belt, and a jacket with puffed sleeves. His jacket and white shirt were pulled open to reveal his broad chest. No mere gardener could look so elegant, so manly.

No ordinary mortal could have had such an effect. There was a stiffening, then a weakening of her bones, so that she feared collapse. Afterwards she thought that the whole orchard had grown silent – all those tiny birds she had been listening to a moment before.

It lasted for only a second. Perhaps she blinked. She looked hard at the spot where he had been, but there was only the moss-green trunk of an apple tree. The birds had started to sing again. She was left feeling weak.

Could she ever tell anyone about it? She thought not.

Events as strange had happened in her fictions. In *Albion and Marina*, the young Marquis of Douro had fallen in love with Marina, who was the daughter of the physician to his father. The Duke had not entirely disapproved of this lowly match, but had insisted upon a period of separation to test their love, and he had moved his family from their seat at Strathfieldsaye to Verdopolis. There, the young Marquis met and fell in love with Zenobia, otherwise known as the Lady Ellrington.

On that very day, Marina came to him in a dream, begging him not to abandon her, and Douro rushed back to England. When he arrived, he found that Marina had died at the very moment in which she had appeared to him.

But that was a story.

VI

One sunny afternoon two weeks later, a servant interrupted Charlotte to take her to a visitor waiting in Miss Wooler's parlour. Charlotte expected it to be the Atkinsons' maid, whom they sometimes sent with messages, or to conduct her to their home, the Green House in Mirfield. On her last visit a tormenting 'rabble' of relatives and friends had patronized her by consoling her for the shabbiness of her 'best' frock. Something truly awful had happened next. One person, a stranger to Charlotte, had said, 'Come, child, and sit upon my knee.' Had grabbed her and pulled her onto her lap. Charlotte had been *excruciatingly* embarrassed. Was it any wonder that she ran from the room? She thought she could not be induced to visit the Atkinsons ever again. Or maybe, to look on the bright side, her visitor could be from nice Mrs Franks. Charlotte knew that Papa had once been 'sweet on her', and she had been kind to Charlotte since childhood. But it would still be a summons to a grand vicarage, full of patronizing relatives.

It turned out to be someone as welcome to her as her Marquis – though he could not be more different. It was her adored imp of a brother; he who thought himself an aristocrat, but whom she sometimes laughed at as 'Wiggins'.

He had set himself before the fireplace. 'Branwell!' she said and was stopped short by another apprehension. '*Papa . . . ?*' she began and put her hand to the little brooch that pinned her dress at the neck.

'Papa is recovering well.'

'Emily? Anne? Aunt?'

'All are well. Everyone is well. I only wanted to see you.'

Branwell's voice went strangely up and down. He twirled his spectacles in his hand. His bag was at his feet. A comb stuck out of his pocket and evidently he had just used it: he had shaped his sandy hair into a Byronic flourish, with locks over his brow and invading his cheeks. His clothes and boots were dirty. He looked tired and uncomfortable, in the room where Charlotte was now usually at ease. He tugged the cuffs of his jacket down over his wrists.

'This jacket is getting too small for me,' he said.

'I could let the hem down for you,' she offered.

For the first time in her life (she realized from the way he looked at her – and then away) he was aware of her appearance, in her white 'muslin', and with her new silhouette that seemed womanly below the waist, though it was childish above. At the parsonage, five months ago, he had treated her as he would another boy. His glances now felt slightly wicked.

'I like your new dress,' he said.

'It is from Mrs Franks. The fashion has changed and I needed something. How did you come here?'

'The summum omnium of it is . . . I walked.'

'All the way?'

'I had a lift for part of it. It was such a lovely morning that I woke up early and I was thinking of you so I left a note and set off at five o'clock. It is not so very far.'

She recognized her familiar Brannii – impetuous and romantic; thoughtless, but lovable; undisciplined, because he had never been to a school. Papa's view, that his son could best be educated by himself, was resulting in his growing up ignorant of how to behave in normal society. She wondered if anyone at home had depended upon him today. He would not have thought of it.

'I'm glad you left them a note,' she said. 'Before I came

in, I stood in the driveway and looked over the hills. Do you know that you can see to the far side of Halifax from here? If it were not for one hill in the way you would see Haworth.'

'Would you?'

It needed him to say only that for her to feel illuminated, amazed, and fascinated once again. All these months she had not heard Haworth spoken of with such meaning.

He was consoling her for the homesickness of her letters, she realized. In five months here she had half-forgotten that Brannii had once been her eyes; that he had lit up the darkness and knew her heart. All she had endeavoured to be – the Roe Head success, the young lady being prepared for her Confirmation, the future governess who would perhaps open her own school and be the security for the family – collapsed. She yearned for home, Verdopolis, and their secret, wicked life of stories.

She wondered when, or if, she would tell Brannii about seeing the Marquis.

'I don't believe you have eaten,' Charlotte said, confidently. 'I can arrange a tray of food for you.'

The bell-rope was by the fireplace, where he still stood, and she found it difficult to cross the carpet. Being deep in Verdopolis again made her giddy. She remembered how he used to creep into her's and Emily's bed. She wondered what she would do if he touched her.

But perhaps Verdopolis was over, never to be mentioned any more! It was so fragile – to be expected, she supposed, it being made of glass. And, so far, not a word had been said about it. She was hovering in a vertiginous vacuum. It was like that indeterminate moment when they were in the process of changing stories.

She brushed by him. He smelled of sweat, and of mud and dung which his boots had picked up off the road. She tugged at the bell-rope.

'Please sit down,' she said, while they waited. It was then that she could not resist touching him. She stroked the sleeve of his jacket.

He sat down and moved his bag to between his feet. Watching his awkward manner, she realized that, even if he did appear to be growing out of his clothes – and was that a slight down appearing on his upper lip? – it was she who had grown in sophistication.

She remained impatiently silent. She wanted to save the inevitable, important subject for when they would be without risk of the servant's interruption.

'Roe Head seems very comfortable,' he remarked, and then he rummaged in his bag. 'I really came to bring you a present for your birthday.'

'You walked all this way to bring me a present?'

'Yes.'

It was a block of watercolour paper and a paintbox. The box was made of pale oak. She opened it. It had compartments holding three rows of watercolour tablets, each stamped with the Prince of Wales's feathers; also a set of brushes, a lead pencil, and a pen with a steel nib. There were three china palettes, and a drawer holding two china bowls in which to mix larger quantities of washes for backgrounds. The name *G. Blackman. Superfine Colour Preparer. London.* was stamped amidst scrolls on the inside of the lid.

'Brannii! It is the most magnificent paintbox I've ever seen! Where did you get it?'

'From Bradford.'

The maid entered. Charlotte was popular with the servants, as for instance Miss Walker and Miss Ledgard were not, because she treated them as Papa insisted she treat Tabby at home, that is, as human beings. (Tabby would not have tolerated anything else. She'd die in a ditch first.) Although Misses Walker and Ledgard thought it was another of Miss Brontë's eccentricities, Charlotte was obstinate about it. So the maid smiled, as she would have smiled at hardly anyone else; the other young governesses would have regarded it as an impertinence.

'Something hot – oatcakes with honey perhaps – and tea,' Charlotte ordered, and added – because the maid was obviously wondering why they were smiling so – 'Look what I've been given for my birthday, Alice!'

When she had left, Charlotte sat on the chair nearest to her brother.

'I think that Papa has only recovered so well because he is *religious*,' Branwell said, almost disapprovingly.

'You think that is not a good thing?'

'It is a good thing, but it is not enough – for some people,' he said warily.

'Papa's strength is *unique*,' she announced, emphatically. 'His inner strength. But poor Papa does not understand the *real* world at all,' she added, patronizingly. 'He makes *dreadful* mistakes. But the strength of his religion is different. It can be quite frightening to others, for I should not think that any man was ever born with such a store of it! But I think that we should all pray to have his conviction.'

She did not confess that she had lain at night begging God for help in fulfilling her duty, and that Papa had been her model; nor that she had pleaded for forgiveness for her Verdopolitan thoughts. What would Branwell think if he knew that in her anguish she had drawn blood from her palms by tearing at them at night with her long nails? How could she confess that it had only been by crushing thoughts and feelings that she had been able to arrive at her position of calmly entertaining him in Miss Wooler's parlour, doing her duty, confident at being Roe Head's favoured one?

She had achieved her ambition, but at what cost was it to – she suddenly saw it in this way – her *real* life? Her *inner* life? How amputated, if not dead, in her role she felt; could she tell him?

Could she tell him about meeting the Marquis of Douro in the orchard?

At this moment she would risk Hell for a return to Verdopolis where everything, instead of hardly anything, was possible. She hoped that Branwell would open the subject. Possibly he had realized that Emily (she did not fear competition from Anne) was not so good at it as she herself was.

She suddenly realized: the truth was that she wanted two contradictory types of support from him. She expected him to have Papa's strength and religious integrity to save her from evil; on the other hand, she wanted him to lead her into the wicked temptations of their fantasies.

And she wanted him to carry the responsibility for it. Maybe she expected too much.

It was then that the maid returned with the tea tray piled high with buttered scones. Charlotte felt very maternal, pouring the tea.

Afterwards, they strolled on the lawn. The new spring leaves were as bright as lit candles in the wood that sank away below the edge of the field. The trees were heaving with birdsong.

When other girls walked by they addressed her as 'Miss Brontë'.

'Shame to say, Papa has been giving his support to the Reform Bill,' Branwell said.

'Poor Papa,' Charlotte answered. 'He does not understand politics.'

'But the Bill has been defeated in the House of Lords. Did you know that?'

'No.'

'Earl Grey has resigned.'

Discussing this, and other political news, their hearts seemed joined.

But the shadows of the trees were lengthening. They already darkened the drifts of bluebells below them to a sombre purple colour. Though time was running short, she still had not confided how, for the sake of her soul, she had tried to abjure Verdopolis, yet was haunted by it and wanted nothing other than to be there. She would, and she would not – 'like the cat in the adage'.

A couple of seats faced one another under a chestnut tree. She sat down and indicated that Branwell should take the second seat.

His other self was inside him somewhere, hiding; the Verdopolitan brother, with whom she could enjoy strange excitements. She must find him. The very reason she was here, squeezing herself into the mould of governess, was so that Branwell could be free to fulfil his genius. It was worth it, for her brother did have wonderful gifts; but she wanted to be assured.

She plunged, and asked him, bluntly, 'So what is happening in Verdopolis?'

She looked downwards, with an inward-seeming smile. It was one of Charlotte's two characteristic expressions. It was as if she were at that moment writing something upon her heart. It was a smile that could make one fall in love with her.

She raised her eyes, expecting to see him light up. Branwell's response was to shuffle.

'I have not decided,' he answered, irritably.

'Not decided?'

Most disappointed, she changed to her other, less attractive expression: that soft, puzzled, leonine, short-sighted stare that the girls knew so well. 'You haven't been writing?'

'Very little.'

She was bursting to tell him that she depended upon him to fulfil the ambitions that burned in her breast, but which she could not realize because she was female.

But her greater pain, at present, was – that she did not believe him. He was making an excuse. He was not *telling* her what had happened in Verdopolis because he and Emily had conspired to cut her out! She was exiled and he was lying to her, as he might to any outsider – as they all did, whenever anyone tried to penetrate their secrets.

In haste, 'Brannii!' she said. 'I was walking in the orchard and I *saw* the Marquis of Douro.'

She had confessed it without thinking. Yet once she had told him, it became the most normal thing in the world to talk about, just as always.

'Were you wearing that dress?' he responded. Then he became excited. 'Don't tell me! I know that you were. I think it was *he* who saw *you*, and that you were Marina.'

'Really?' she said.

It did not seem at all a surprising idea, but she felt that it ought to be. He was waving his arms. He kept lifting them to brush at his wild hair, which had sprung out of its Byronic grooming.

'Yes! When our so-called creations spring out of our heads, how do we know that it isn't a moment of recognition when these spirits of the real world have come forth to recognize *us*?'

Her suspicions had been unfounded – they were back in Verdopolis.

The girls already admired her artwork and she was something of a phenomenon to their art instructress, Miss Susan Wooler, who was now Mrs Carter and was the only one of the sisters to be married; she came back to give lessons during her pregnancy. She talked of 'the Renaissance'. She illustrated the proportions of the human head, using charts. She did not refer to the anatomy of the remainder of the human body, except that once or twice she remarked that 'hands are most difficult'. She set up 'still life' subjects with vases, drapes and bowls of fruit. Charlotte had to sit almost on top of them and even then she depicted them largely from invention, and from the memory of similar pictures she had copied in the past. She could do the most excellent pastiche of an engraving after Caravaggio.

In private, she used the paintbox from Branwell to enter Verdopolis through art. Her most thrilling pictures were drawn by crouching in secret corners, using a nearly dry brush, then dazzling the girls with her perfection of detail. Castles, ruined towers, waterfalls. The trouble she took – sometimes spending a month upon copying an engraving, or making a variation or an eclectic version of several of them – amazed her companions.

She drew ladies with narrow faces, with their hair in thick ringlets, with slender necks that looked so beautiful with strings of pearls around them, and with delicate sloping shoulders. Parks and country churches, sprays of honeysuckle, roses and pastoral scenes also poured out of her head. She painted yachts floating on calm, moonlit seas; alternatively she showed them tossed by storms. She made designs for lace collars and for wallpaper.

She tried not to let the other girls see the *most* thrilling of her drawings and compositions. These were the real Verdopolitan themes; subjects that swarmed unexpectedly from the back of her mind. They usually began in the form of a 'doodle' that she might make at the edge of her paper when she was undecided what subject to tackle next. It seemed then that the subject had a life of its own and *it* was indeed making use of *her*, as Branwell had suggested. Once she drew a lady, riding a dog, entering a massive, windowless obelisk. She depicted a disembodied female arm, with huge rings on every finger, each finger ending with a long red talon, such as she was allowing her own nails to become. These subjects frightened Charlotte herself; especially the ease with which she fell upon them.

Verdopolis did not only haunt her through her artwork. While she was being prepared for Confirmation in the vestry of Mirfield Church, diabolical spectres arose at the moments when they most should not do so. Among the group of girls dressed demurely in white during the Sunday afternoon class, Susan Wooler's husband, the Reverend E. N. Carter, the curate at Mirfield, would suggest that a window be opened because of Miss Brontë's hectic flush.

Every lesson she had received about damnation, from every adult she had ever known, from her father, from Aunt Branwell and even from Carus Wilson, crowded in upon her. In spiritual agony, Charlotte feared that her inability to uproot sins from her soul meant that she was beyond salvation.

She was the more afraid of these spectres because, try as she might to banish demons, she could not stop herself, through the *longueurs* of the day, from looking forward to rejoining them in her bed.

Also while she was in bed, her jealousy caused her to imagine all sorts of wicked intimacies between Branwell and Emily. She wondered if, during her absence, he had recommenced his secret old habit of creeping into Emily's solitary bed to warm his feet at night. Perhaps at this very moment they were curled up together, whispering 'bed plays' and inescapably touching – as she and Ellen Nussey did in the bed they shared in the Roe Head dormitory.

She awoke to spend her days trying *not* to think up plots involving incest, murder, and jealousy justified by its strength as a passion.

VII

'I *wish* I could for once feel like an *out and out* schoolgirl!' Charlotte said to Ellen on her last day at Roe Head. 'Let's do something naughty! Let's *run* around the fruit garden and risk a fine for trespass, Ellen!'

They had not done it. At Roe Head, Charlotte had never been *seen* to run. She had chosen the wrong person to egg her on, and she wondered afterwards if she had half-deliberately appealed to sedate Ellen, rather than to Mary or Martha Taylor, who would for certain have scampered through the orchard with her.

As it was, she realized that at Roe Head she had lost her childhood, and her last chance to express it had escaped her. With her education supposedly completed to governess standard, Charlotte went home to pass it on to Emily and Anne. At sixteen years of age, she was to be elder sister, mother, and teacher.

Aunt Branwell was proud of her. Her walk was stately, in imitation of Miss Wooler's. She had her hair tied in a bun, imitating Miss Wooler who wound her long plait upon her head. Instead of childish off-the-shoulder frocks, such as were still worn by her sisters, Charlotte had Mrs Franks's 'muslin', which shocked Haworth with the fullness of its petticoats.

And she was the superintendent of the new Sunday School that had been opened by her father, teaching and organizing other teachers.

She instructed her siblings from her own copy of the *Questions* by Miss Mangnall; a neat, leather-bound volume, it was a packed treasury of arbitrary information which, so Roe Head had taught her, constituted education.

As Miss Wooler used to walk up and down the Roe Head drawing-room, the pupils following behind as she talked, so Charlotte led hers around the dining-room table, Miss Mangnall's *Questions* in her hand.

She gave them a lesson on *Questions in Roman History*. She let them study the chapter for an hour, took the book from them, and held it as she strode round the parlour table, her nose an inch away from the text, until she flung her head back, and demanded – 'Branwell, who founded Rome?'

'Romulus, its first king,' Branwell answered, keeping pace behind her.

'Mind your dress by the fire!' Anne interrupted.

'How did the idolatry of the Romans differ from that of surrounding nations? Anne – you answer that.'

'They worshipped their gods originally, without statues, or images.'

'Correct! Emily – how were the ancient Romans trained to war?'

'On the field of Mars where they ran about.'

'That's not quite what Miss Mangnall says, Emily, but I suppose it will have to do. In fact, she points out that they ran and leaped "in ponderous armour, carried the heaviest weights, and performed all martial exercises."'

In like manner, Charlotte taught and tested them on *The English Constitution*, on *Modern Biography*, on *The French Reigns*, and on *The Most Celebrated Grecians*.

Anne was compliant. Branwell had entered an age when sometimes he would not be bossed by his sister, and he liked to show off his Latin. But Charlotte's biggest problem was Emily. She was impervious to Miss Mangnall.

'What is the use of Common Oil?' Emily just would not bother to consult the book and parrot it off.

'Name a few of the most distinguished authors since the accession of the line of Hanover.' Emily made up her own list, and it did not coincide with Miss Mangnall's, for she left out Bentley ('the critic'), Hoadley, Lardner, Warburton, Kippis ('divines'), Hawkesworth and Melmoth ('miscellaneous subjects').

'Emily, you are incorrigibly slapdash,' Charlotte told her. 'You spill blots of ink over your papers. You will not learn to spell. I've told you a dozen times, it's "kitch*en*" – not "kitch*in*". You cannot get by through stringing English grammar together in the way they speak in Haworth.'

Emily could not be argued with, nor bullied, nor shamed, nor given good examples. She treated her elder sister with a smile of superiority that was becoming characteristic. It made Charlotte squirm, for they both knew its sources.

Charlotte's womanliness was all show. Even at sixteen, nothing had *happened*, though it was only Emily, Anne, Tabby and Aunt Branwell who knew it.

Emily rubbed it in. Though two years younger, she was taller and better developed. Anyone could see that the changes had happened to her. She rubbed it in as coolly and as bluntly as Mary Taylor had, in early days at Roe Head, when she had said, 'You are rather ugly, aren't you, Miss Brontë?'

'You've not grown much, have you, Tallii?' Emily said.

Underlying all this fractiousness was a schism in the parsonage. In the aftermath of civil wars in Verdopolis, mostly conducted by Branwell, two separate states had arisen. Angria had been created out of conquered Ashantee lands east of Verdopolis for Douro, alias Zamorna, and the saga of Angria was being written by Charlotte and Branwell. Emily and Anne had then created Gondal for characters of their own. It was in the North Pacific, far from Angria, and was more like Haworth than Africa.

Meanwhile, Charlotte kept her social life up to scratch by writing letters, to Mary Taylor, and most frequently to Ellen Nussey. It was her lifeline to the intellectual world; an absorbing delight; a great discovery, only previously practised in a few, functional 'thank-you' notes and in some passionate overflowings to Branwell from Roe Head.

Her correspondence was different from, say, hotly discussing *Blackwood's Magazine* with Brannii and her sisters, which were shapeless storms of words, soon spent and forgotten except for some smarting regrets that one had not expressed oneself better. It had the deliberateness and the palpability of quiet thought. This was manna to her particular cast of mind. How beautifully writing the letter sealed her off from the expediencies of Haworth! It was both a way of relating to others, and of dwelling within her own head. She made rough drafts. She admired the form she had achieved, changing a word and refining the expression. When she sent it off, she could expect an equally deliberated response. It was almost like being published.

Charlotte's intellectual ascendancy over Ellen, in little more than a year after their first meeting when Charlotte had been a mere snivelling wretch, made her enjoy patronizing her friend. She instructed her in what she should read, and sneered condescendingly at her taste.

> I am glad you like 'Kenilworth'; it is certainly a splendid production, and in my opinion one of the most interesting works that ever emanated from the great Sir Walter's pen. I was exceedingly amused at the characteristic and naïve manner in which you expressed your detestation of Varney's character, so much so, indeed, that I could not forbear laughing aloud when I perused that part of your letter . . .

When Charlotte praised Ellen's piety, it carried intimations of her own, mysterious, guilt. It also conveyed an air of condescension. Charlotte could not help implying that Ellen's piety was due to the limitations of her imaginative life.

> . . . I could not help wishing, that my own feelings more nearly resembled yours: but unhappily all the good thoughts that enter my mind evaporate almost before I have had time to ascertain their existence, every right resolution which I form is so transient, so fragile, and so easily broken that I sometimes fear I shall never be what I ought.

Ellen never ceased to be curious about Charlotte's life in the parsonage, and about those secret, guilty matters at the back of her friend's mind. Charlotte pretended not to understand, and she claimed that her life was boring.

> 'You ask me to tell you how I have passed every day since I left school,'

she wrote, affecting an air of languorous ladyhood:

> This is soon done for an account of one day is an account of all. In the morning from nine to half past twelve, I instruct my sisters and draw, then we walk till dinner, after dinner I sew till teatime, and after tea I read, write, or do a little fancy work, or draw, as I please. Thus in one delightful, though somewhat monotonous course, my life is passed.

Nonetheless, Ellen was itching to pay a visit. Charlotte and Branwell had been to Ellen's home, at Rydings in Birstall, so they knew how *she* lived. She had to be invited to Haworth, although all at the parsonage were thrown into a tizzy at the thought of a visitor who was so grand. Nervous Aunt Branwell, although she had spent years longing for a social life with important people, made excuses to put it off.

Aunt thought it would be better to defer it until about the middle of Summer, as the winter, and even the Spring seasons are remarkably cold and bleak among our mountains.

But Charlotte at last wrote, excitedly:

Papa now desires me to present his respects to Mrs Nussey and say that he should feel greatly obliged if she would allow us the pleasure of your company for a few weeks at Haworth.

ELLEN NUSSEY

When Ellen was at last brought by her brother, Henry, to Haworth for a week, they were offered 'dinner', as it was called, although it was midday. This being a clergyman's home, there was a long prayer beforehand with them all standing for about a quarter of an hour – it felt like a full one. As Ellen stared downwards through the boredom of prayer, she noticed with sorrow and amusement that the tablecloth was darned.

The cutlery was coarse, and Mr Brontë preferred a wooden spoon. All that decorated the centre of the table was a small bowl of wild flowers; strong stems of gorse, mixed with water lilies plucked by Emily from a mill 'lodge', as Ellen found out later. Apparently, Charlotte had done her best to arrange a special spread; although, having dined at the Atkinsons, at the Frankses, at Mary Taylor's home, and at Rydings, she knew that in truth it was plain and badly cooked. She showed that she knew, by apologizing for it, too many times.

'We must eat simply because of Papa,' she explained, blushing across the table.

It was not only simple, it was dull and overdone; both the boiled pork and the vegetables. It was followed by fruit pies.

Mr Brontë did, indeed, pick at his food. 'I suffer from dyspepsia and indigestion,' he intoned lugubriously.

No wonder, thought Ellen. Yet no-one blamed the cook. Instead, they flattered their 'Tabby' as pure gold.

The ancient aunt in her black silk, who was clearly constipated — she had that overblown, anchored look — prattled on like a gourmet: 'We used to eat so very well in Penzance! My family were in the import trade, so we had plenty of luxuries. My father owned cellars on the quay for brandy and wine.' She mistily recalled the refined Cornwall of another century, but the Nusseys knew it to be as brutish, under its veneer, as the Hartshead of Brontë's day, or his Ireland. Charlotte had said that her aunt was 'a glum old bird, full of Methodist, country superstitions', but she chattered, she clinked her cutlery, and she held a napkin between thumb and forefinger to dab her lips, as daintily as if she were dining in the Pump Room at Bath.

Henry sportingly entered into their game, discoursing on the carriage and cabinet-makers, on the Palladian and Gothic styles in Yorkshire — Ellen couldn't remember it well, this men's talk, except to recall that Henry, being a student at Cambridge, turned his phrases neatly.

He turned them largely in the direction of Charlotte, to whom he had obviously taken a shine. Ellen thought he was intrigued at the challenge of taming her. Her brother was the kind of man who liked to make conquests; perhaps — oh, what a naughty thought — trying out his skills to convince himself that he had them.

Ellen was disappointed to learn that the horizons of her friend were as narrow as she had claimed. She had never quite believed, quite visualized it. The church was not a carriage journey away across a park, as at Rydings: it glowered at the windows. There was no drive and fine lawn before the house. There was a short, cobbled track between grim buildings and graves, and it led off a tomb-like village street that smelled of excrement. Parson Brontë's Sunday school for the poor was built near his parsonage, not beyond park walls where charitable institutions were placed in Birstall. The parsonage was both overheated and draughty, partly because Emily was always opening doors to let animals in and out. One's ankles would be cold and one's head would be boiling.

And how impolite were the interests of her friend's family! How socially awkward they were! The parson was inordinately fond of his study, Aunt Branwell of her bedroom, while the others spent hours in the kitchen with the servants and the animals.

Most visitors had only ever been parish ones, it seemed. Working people did not of course get beyond the kitchen or, if it was to do with the church, beyond Brontë's study. Occasionally a clergyman was entertained in the parlour, but apparently they had formed a tradition of visiting wifeless, the countryside to be traversed being so barbaric, and there never having been any wife, other than a sick one, at the parsonage to offer entertainment to a lady; Aunt Branwell, for all her quaint snobbery, did not entertain.

Ellen was used to her friend's lack of social ease. When staying at Rydings towards the end of the previous year, Charlotte had skulked in the orchard. 'She trembled on my arm as I led her into dinner,' Henry had said. But her shyness was as nothing compared with her sisters'. These could barely speak at first, and did everything to keep out of her way, while the brother, though a wild and gay enough fellow who had picked up his father's passion for guns, kept clear by, apparently, spending time on the moors with the Heatons from Ponden Hall.

Ellen had anticipated an unusual visit, but – well! To start with: there were the animals. The parsonage was a menagerie, with what appeared to be Emily's pets – cats, pigeons, the unkempt Irish terrier, 'Grasper', and a couple of geese, which were supposed to be kept in the yard but which Emily let into what the girls amusingly called the 'kitchin'. Emily stank of animals, especially when she'd been mauling the dog on a wet day, and came bedraggled into the parlour to stand in front of the fire.

Not that they were sentimental about animals. Ellen had never seen anyone as angry as Emily – the tall Irish banshee with the mad gleam in her eye, and the buck-teeth – when dog, cat or goose committed an offence.

Yet, like the other girls, she meekly and ungrudgingly performed the duties of a poor village parson's daughter. They all went through the domestic tasks which were so quaintly expected of them, although they had servants. So much sweeping, dusting, baking, carrying of water, ironing and darning of their father's and their brother's shirts went on that Ellen became afraid she'd have a sweeping brush thrust into her own hands! For such wild creatures as they were, they looked surprisingly contented with domestic skivvying.

The father, tall, gaunt, frail and white-haired, at fifty-six seemed as haggard, and nearly as blind, as Oedipus. However, no-one overshadowed him; she'd say that for him. Ellen thought of the Birstall curates as serfs of the Nusseys, whom her mother regularly called into the house to tell what to do. Brontë had the authority, the bleakness and the leanness of the Grim Reaper himself, as illustrated in one of the German engravings collected in the home of Mary Taylor.

When Ellen was awoken by his discharging pistols into the churchyard at dawn, she tried to be amused at being in a madhouse. With his poor eyesight, Brontë was the last person to be waving pistols about.

One morning, Ellen walked with Charlotte on the patch of scrappy grass, among elder bushes and dwarfed fruit bushes that they called a 'garden'. Haworth sent up its smell of middens; although, it being sunny July weather, Ellen supposed it was stronger than usual. They were discussing free will on earth versus our chances in eternity, when Charlotte stopped in her tracks. Following the direction of Charlotte's eyes, Ellen saw a row of washing hung out in the corner of the graveyard closest to the town; a narrow strip of ground hidden by the northern side of the church.

'I hope Papa doesn't spot that!' Charlotte exclaimed. 'It will put him in *such* a temper at dinner!'

Apparently he'd been feuding for thirteen years with the

Haworth women who could find nowhere more convenient to hang their washing. He had been arguing about it since he came to the living.

Perhaps – joked Ellen – his firing pistols is his way of scaring them off?

After Henry had left for home, there had come a change in Mr Brontë's and the aunt's attitudes to Ellen. She often felt that they had been talking about her. The aunt lost her ingratiating manner. She seemed to want to cause offence by taking snuff. The parson had decided to dislike her. He made her feel uncomfortable.

It seemed to Ellen that, like many selfish old people, Brontë thought that age gave him the right not to make allowances for others' feelings. His new idea of entertainment at dinner was to give an account of a parishioner who had fallen into a pigpen and, so he claimed, been eaten alive.

'A pig's teeth point backwards,' he growled through his tight mouth, over that white bandage he called a 'cravat', which almost covered his lower lip. 'Once sunk into the flesh, they cannot be withdrawn. I have it on good authority that a man, not of my congregation I'm glad to say but a Baptist, fell into a pigsty and was never seen again.'

'Papa!' Charlotte admonished, and coloured, for the umpteenth time since Ellen's arrival. 'You know that you are not bigoted! Stop pretending to be vulgar!'

'He was *devoured*,' intoned Mr Brontë, regardless, and as if from the pulpit. 'Only a few bones were left!'

Was he or wasn't he pretending, exaggerating, or inventing? Was this what, so Ellen believed, in Ireland was termed 'blarney'?

Whatever the truth, Ellen saw that he must have suffered some bitter blows to have sunk so far as to try to shock his rare visitors with coarse tales. When he stopped talking rough nonsense you could see the pain in his face, especially in the tight set of his mouth. Once Ellen had got over being shocked, she felt rather sorry for him.

His family appeared used to such tales, and Emily actually laughed; though Ellen wondered whether it was at the story or at her father's attempt to offend a visitor.

Was the parson perhaps too near-blind to realize what

effect he had? No, there was a glint behind the spectacles of the mad old Irishman.

Ellen felt she understood why Charlotte turned white at the sight or smell of meat.

It was ironic that the parson hardly touched the meat, either – as if his feelings, also, were refined.

As they reached the end of breakfast the next day, the girls were about to rise to clear the table and so forth, when Mr Brontë looked very thoughtful, very sad, and announced: 'I had my own curacy near Birstall, you know – at Hartshead.'

'I know,' said Ellen.

'Happy days!' remarked Mr Brontë.

'I'm glad to hear of it.' She feared what might be about to follow.

'But not for my parishioners! There were many troubles for them!'

'That would be at the time of machine breaking?'

'Yes. I once came on a group of men carrying a roll of carpet on their shoulders near to my church in the dead of night.' He appeared lost in the memory. 'They also had spades. It was after the raid on Rawfold's Mill. My dear wife was alive then. You know about those times, Miss Nussey?'

'Indeed I do. So what did you do, Mr Brontë?'

'I ducked behind a wall, then I followed from a distance. They went into my churchyard and unrolled the carpet. A dead man fell out. They started to dig a grave near to the tower.'

'So the authorities apprehended them?'

Mr Brontë gave her a look that would wither a stone. 'I did not inform the authorities.'

'What *did* you do? Give them your *blessing*?'

Mr Brontë shook his head. He seemed doubly old in telling this tale. The events seemed so far away. The mills were quiet, now. The culprits had been hanged or transported. So much for the fate of Combinations.

'I had a word with my sexton who, being one with them, was glad to do as I bid. He disguised the grave with sods. They were merely poor, starving people who had been punished enough already. To die in a ditch is punishment enough for any crime, don't you think? That has happened often in Ireland.'

'I think that, for some reason, your Papa has taken a dislike to me,' Ellen sighed, later.

'You must forgive him.' Charlotte's eyes misted. 'Since I went to Roe Head his health has never been good, and it can make him morose. His lungs gave way. He has crossed the Rubicon. We are all, of course, afraid of what might become of us.'

Wet days in the parsonage: those, thought Ellen, take some describing. At Rydings, people would yawn and be bored. Here they were never short of something to do.

She was amused to discover how Miss Wooler's sedate perambulations had been adapted by Charlotte. She had them all walking in pairs around the parlour table. They did their lessons that way, and they also told one another stories. Every now and then, one or other of them would *skip*. Ellen wondered what Miss Wooler would make of that.

Although they had never been to a dance in their lives, they had invented a form of Scottish 'barn dance', sometimes with music from Branwell, who had begun to practise the flute. Emily and Anne linked their arms around one another's waists, leaving Charlotte and Ellen to form the other pair. Occasionally Charlotte broke away and twirled in a pirouette. Charlotte Brontë of all people!

All of them, including the aunt in her room, left Ellen with a sense of secrets elsewhere in the house, so that she felt that she might be keeping her friend from them. Charlotte had borne an air of secrecy at Roe Head – the secrets Ellen had hoped to penetrate by coming here. Now she found that all the Brontë family were the same. They would disappear into Charlotte's and Emily's bedroom, and be heard giggling, or arguing; strange names floating through the door.

Sometimes they erupted out of the room, or their little 'study', dressed to act the stories that they had apparently been making up. They turned bed-sheets into cloaks, decorated old hats with feathers collected on walks – any old things.

Charlotte especially loved playing male parts. Forgetting her shyness, she would stiffen, swing her cloak, and roar in a deep voice. Emily, too, once painted a moustache upon her face and called herself Lord Ellrington. They made shy Anne play the female part: one Mary Percy. Branwell was someone named Alexander Percy. They tried to draw in Ellen, but, she had to confess, she was too shy.

One day, Charlotte strode into the kitchen and yelled, 'I am the Marquis' – she pronounced it *Markee*, French-style – 'I am the Marquis of Douro!' The others followed her, screaming around the chairs.

Tabby had her back to them and was bent over the fire. She turned around quickly, then raised her hands to her hair. It was Charlotte's absolute conviction that frightened Tabby. She was *not* acting. She *believed* that she was the Marquis. At any rate, it disturbed phlegmatic Tabby sufficiently to make her run out – as Mr Brontë was not at home – down Parsonage Lane and the main street to fetch her nephew, Willie Wood the carpenter, because she believed that the children had gone mad. It merely succeeded in making them burst into laughter.

They would often gravitate to the kitchen and hover around their Tabby, among the animals. It was not only dogs, cats and geese that also collected there: Emily kept a wounded lark and an injured pheasant, nestled in boxes. Through the kitchen door, left open for what they called 'folk' to come in and out, or to let free the smoke from the kitchen range, Emily's geese made their way in, out of the rain, although they were supposed to dwell in the peat-store at the end of the yard. Their snake-like necks, intertwining, hissing ferociously, would peer around the doorposts, investigating for the presence of their arch-enemy, Miss Branwell. The maid, Sally Mosely, seemed to be always mopping the floor after people, animals or birds. 'They're only talking to us!' Emily would say, and encourage the geese with pieces of bread.

They spent a whole rainy morning in the kitchen once, not at all bored, and amazingly Ellen wasn't bored either, as she would have been at home if confined in *any* room, even a drawing-room, listening to the conversation dominated by her brothers. (She had never sat with the servants: that was a novel experience in itself.) Although nothing much was done. Branwell sat in the winged chair he loved, and stretched his legs in everyone's way across the hearth. Emily was baking, rolling out her pastry with a book propped before her, behind the pastry board. She seemed almost at her happiest with Tabby.

Branwell made a remark about politics – something about the rebellion in Ireland – and it set off a discussion. Ellen couldn't follow it. They became so heated that it was difficult to make out any sense, except that they were all behind the Duke, right or wrong, and didn't like 'papists'. Charlotte most certainly didn't.

'So what is to be done?' Charlotte asked from the far side of the table, where she stood like some fantastical female member of parliament at the dispatch box, though geese tugged at her dress and her arms, like Emily's, were covered in flour.

'I don't know what we should do,' Emily said; she being the least likely to care, when it was a matter of human existence and trials, not of that strange, impenetrable world of the spirit where she mostly seemed to dwell. She shooed her geese out through the back door – more interested in talking to them, apparently, than to humans about Irish politics.

'Tha could wipe thee feet f'ra start, miss, 'stead o' trailin' muck and slutch in an' out me kitchin. And then tha could peel a pertater or summat and do summat useful. Put thy bewk down and concentrate,' Tabby suggested.

'Pill a pertater, Tabby?' Emily mocked and laughed. 'Let's all pill a pertater, everybody!'

'You, Ellen! Let's all tak' a pertater and pill it!' laughed Branwell, jumping out of his chair. The whole kitchen was laughing fit to burst, then; Sally Mosely and Tabby also, while Grasper yapped as if he was laughing too.

'Let's all pill a pertater! Let's all pill a pertater!' Emily repeated, waving her floury arms. They were helpless with laughter. Emily had to rub at her eyes which were streaming – partly because of the smoke.

'I think we've done enough that's merely useful for today, Tabby,' said Charlotte, seriously.

'The lot of you's as daft as a brush,' Tabby said. 'Why don't y'all get from under me feet and clear out o' me kitchin? Instead o' laughin' at folk at's werk to do.'

'Ellen, tha's as daft as a brush,' mocked Branwell. 'Let's all decamp and leave Tabby to her Stygian labours.'

'I'll not 'ave thee callin' *me* saucy names, my lad,' Tabby said, and they all laughed at this too, because by now they'd laugh at anything; holding their ribs, rubbing at their eyes.

'Tabby's bark's worse than her bite,' explained Charlotte. 'We're all really very fond of her.'

BRANWELL

I

Branwell watched Charlotte spend weeks copying, in pencil, the cross-hatchings of engravings, and one day she made a pronouncement that he found sad. 'Through detail, whatever one lacks in natural talent, one can make up for with industry. One may climb mountains by sheer endeavour.'

He, because he felt inspired – though without a clear objective – did not find this *courageous*. Copying, he realized, was what she did because she was short-sighted, even more so than himself. She was just as enthusiastic about art. If it were not for her being short-sighted, and for her being female, she would like to be an artist, she said.

They were all mad about art for a time, and Aunt Branwell worried about the polished surface of the parlour table. 'Aunt would worry about anything,' said Emily, patronizingly, after Aunt had left, sniffing over frustrated suspicions following one of her inspections of the girls 'busy as bees, and so quiet'. For they were a neat huddle around the table, careful with their pots of water, and there was small danger of accidents through quarrelling.

Their living so much together had produced a love of privacy, which made them careful also. Past Christmas presents had been their portable writing desks (similar sewing boxes had come with birthdays), which they usually locked, less out of distrust than to exercise privacy, and on the sloping inner lids of which they placed their drawing paper.

Also, they could hardly have caused damage because their work was on a scale not much bigger than the books they composed, and it was in the form of drawing. It was sometimes coloured in with watercolour washes, which could be a bit messy, but most often the colour was niggled in with a nearly dry brush.

They copied Martin's pictures, or birds and animals from Bewick's engravings. Branwell did some military scenes. Anne drew typical girls' subjects – flowers, and towers. Charlotte did a lady garlanded with flowers, and part of Kirkstall Abbey copied out of an 'annual'. She also continued to design lace collars and wallpapers. All the sisters depicted ladies with narrow faces, and with hair in ringlets; with slender necks and nipped-in waists. They drew ladies who were all that they themselves were not.

Charlotte evidently found some of her pictures shocking, because she tried to hide them, but they were discovered. It was never difficult to pry if one wanted to – all secrecy in the parsonage was by consent. That picture of a lady riding a dog and entering an obelisk. Why had she done it? Branwell asked. She said that she could not remember.

But even these exercises were niggling and Branwell found Charlotte's idea of art irksome. Art was grander than this.

'I've had enough of ruining my eyesight copying engravings,' he announced one day. 'Let's do some portraits of one another. Anne, will you pose for us?' – Anne being the one most likely to submit.

She was set upon a chair, her head partly draped with a shawl, one arm resting on a small table holding books. The others sat very close to her. How still she could sit! Branwell could hardly keep still for five minutes.

After they had been working for an hour in the parlour, Papa came in. He was stopped in his tracks.

'Good heavens! Aunt Branwell! Come and see!'

She was there in a minute, breathless from the kitchen. 'Has something happened? What have they spilled?! I knew it! I knew—'

'Nothing *spilled*, Elizabeth. Look at these portraits. I am amazed.'

In all three drawings, the bust was awkward and anatomically impossible; it was as unreal as the structure of the chair, off which a sitter would have slid as from a vertical wall, but it didn't matter. Charlotte had been compelled to sit so close to Anne that the perspective was lost, but this did not matter, either. Neither did her patient cross-hatching of the shawl, upon which she had spent most of the hour – her face buried in the paper, and only looking at the model from time to time – nevertheless failing to express the folds of cloth. What was important was Anne's character, grasped by all of them in their single moment of recognition. Charlotte's drawing, a side view, showed Anne's introspection, so tenderly, so poignantly, through her down-turned eyes. Branwell had caught Anne's vulnerability in a full-face view. Emily, working from the other side to Charlotte, had patiently drawn Anne as if she were an anatomical specimen, a stuffed bird out of Bewick.

Patrick and Aunt Branwell, an unsophisticated pair in visual matters, could not help being moved by any verisimilitude, as by a miracle.

Then came an incident in the Sunday school concerning Branwell; a misfortune, like any that God sends, with its positive side, thought Patrick. It decided the choice of his son's career.

All the Brontës took turns in teaching. Anne and even Emily were patient. Charlotte was thorough and could even be described as 'dedicated'. She seemed born to the role. But Branwell pulled hair or rapped his knuckles on the heads of 'numbskulls'. At last, one bold lad answered him back, 'Nay, tha'll not get away wi' that wi' me, y'Irish bastard!' and walked out.

It took courage to speak to the parson's son in that way. He must have been hard-driven. Afterwards, Branwell was excused from Sunday school duties. It was clear that he was not cut out for any profession in which he must restrain his temper.

So far, art, like music, had only been thought of as part of a general education, mainly to help the girls become governesses. Now it occurred to Papa that it might offer a future for Branwell.

'I have been facing up to the fact that my son is not cut out for an ecclesiastical career, Elizabeth. I don't think he could ever be a good pastor, it is the last vocation for the unstable. Besides, he would never flatter his way to preferment. Sooner or later he will be unable to resist telling a fool that he is one. I cannot be ashamed of such a son, can I? But there is no point in sending him to university. The artistic sphere is, I believe, more tolerant of individuality. The factory owners are spending more and more on having their portraits painted. Who knows, he might get to the Royal Academy.'

Thereupon Branwell commenced art lessons with John Bradley, a Keighley architect and a founder member of the Mechanics Institute. He was also a portrait painter, of sorts, with a studio in the upper part of his premises and in the big, high room, the north-facing half of its roof made of glass, were potted palms, easels, and a 'throne' on which a sitter could be placed among the props.

II

Branwell's arm jerked and he cut his cheek as a loud screech came from outside his door. It was Emily, who had caught him shaving for the first time in his life.

Branwell and Charlotte were being taken on an excursion to the exhibition of the Northern Society for the Encouragement of Fine Arts in Leeds. Mr Bradley had sent in works by both of them, and Charlotte's had been chosen.

After the Haworth gig, they picked up the coach at the Devonshire Arms in Keighley, taking a thirty-mile journey eastwards. Branwell, unlike his sisters, found this more exciting than the most rural part of Yorkshire, in the other direction. Frequently they sank into industrial fogs, peering through them at the fiery dramas of building sites, new mills, chimneys, bridges and scaffolding. It seemed all noise, chaos and fire, and the carriage windows were closed to keep out the sulphur and smoke. Travellers on top of the coach wore scarves around their mouths. Part-erected factory chimneys climbed into the air, and figures were clinging to many, which reached to the heights of church steeples. Papa was shocked at chimneys clustered around churches, as Charlotte was horrified at the building of mills in the grounds of fine houses. Branwell loved it all. Navvies were cutting great trenches: 'Canals,' he explained, and added, 'there are proposals for railways, too!'

'What are those?'

Charlotte had only the vaguest idea.

He could have lectured for hours. 'There's been a bill before parliament to build a public railway from Manchester to Leeds with tunnels through the Pennines . . .' Then he went off on a different tack, whispering to Charlotte. He stared at a steam boiler being hoisted off a barge, he saw the black waters of the canal reflecting the flames from a huge fire of old scaffolding and other waste timber, and he whispered: 'It is like the visions of Milton! Of Dante! Of John Martin!'

'What are you whispering about?' Papa asked. 'You are too old for that now.'

Charlotte giggled, buried her mouth in Branwell's ear and whispered back: 'Strange as the land of the Ashantees to the heroes of Verdopolis. And their faces are as black as the Ashantees'.'

They arrived in Leeds promptly at one p.m. as they knew that they would, for Papa checked the timetable with his watch. Charlotte clung to her father's arm as they promenaded by the magnificent buildings.

'London cannot be grander than this!' she said.

But here, on 'The Headrow', their own 'smart' clothes did not seem so fine.

'My pantaloons are out of fashion!' Branwell's trousers were tight, but clearly they were being worn looser. He was so alarmed, he might have been Beau Brummell.

Although Charlotte had been proud of her dress, her hair, and her shoes, now she felt like a maidservant on a day off. She was mortified by specks of soot that had blown in through the carriage window onto her dress.

They climbed a broad flight of steps. Branwell and Charlotte had never been to an art exhibition before, and when they walked in they both had the same thought: 'Verdopolis!' Branwell said, and winked.

This was their imagined Palace of Art; the high, decorated ceiling, the Corinthian columns, the polished marble floor, the buzz of ladies and gentlemen inspecting the rows of gilt-framed pictures closely packed up to the ceiling.

Branwell dashed ahead, while Patrick and Charlotte kept their distance. Branwell did not hesitate about what interested him. He passed by the duller topographical pictures – the views of local valleys with foregrounds of milkmaids and cows set against smudgy, romantic suggestions of factories. He cast a dismissive eye over portraits in stiff, outdated, eighteenth-century style. Poking his nose through the crowd, he was for all the world, Charlotte thought, like an excited spaniel rooting in a hedgerow.

'Let us go in search of *your* picture and leave your brother to his excitement,' Papa said. 'Look at him! He seems to have found his true home!'

They discovered Charlotte's picture, proudly framed by Willie Wood, hanging with other landscapes. Branwell had dashed right past it.

'I am sure it is only exhibited because it is so small, and could be slipped in,' Charlotte remarked. 'Mr Bradley said that Branwell's portrait was far too large and grand.' Gazing after her brother who was disappearing into the next room, 'I think he prefers romantic dash – never mind the subject matter,' she remarked.

'They are all unrivalled artistic productions,' Papa enthused, looking around him airily, although like both his children he was too short-sighted to take in more than an impression. 'And you must be proud to be exhibited with them. But let us move on. People will think you are vain!'

They walked on a few yards.

'Don't you think subject matter is rather more important than execution? Or do you think that the reverse is the case?' Papa asked.

'I think I admire detail the most,' Charlotte argued. 'And finish – fine glazes – rather than the daubs of chiaroscuro that attract my brother. It is a sign of his erratic nature, and of my precise one. I like to look at pictures closely.' Vanity would not allow her to admit why. 'I admire pictures, rather as I might items of fine furniture or needlework.'

Patrick gave the paintings close attention, too, peering closely for the same reason as Charlotte did. There was plenty to please him in his preference for subject matter. Incidents from the Napoleonic Wars abounded; though there were also many 'ugly' subjects for art, such as, *Navvies Building a Canal* and *A Furnace at Night*.

Strolling through the crowded gallery, he resumed his inherent sociability and peered over heads to look for acquaintances. He hoped the exhibition might be patronized by, say, his old friend Atkinson of Mirfield, or Franks of Huddersfield. Thinking of their lives, he regretted the misanthropy that had overcome him in his moorland parsonage – he had never intended it to be so.

Touched by loneliness, he suddenly took hold of Charlotte's arm. She gave a little leap of surprise, so he released it rather than tell her what had come into his mind. She relaxed, too, then, and leaned towards him, taking his arm with, perhaps, an equally excessive affection; at any rate people were looking at them.

They were smiling indulgently at the love between a father and his daughter. But he felt more than simple love. It was also possessive jealousy. Ever since watching Henry Nussey at dinner, he had grown more frightened of being left, and the crowd, that was making him regret his misanthropy, made him also afraid of the young men in it.

There were people present who never forgot the sight of them holding on to one another.

Branwell paused for a long time in front of *Napoleon's Retreat from Moscow*, before *Waterloo* and *Corunna*. There were so many battle pictures, it was as if there were a competition for them. He reached the short wall which displayed *The Battle of the Nile*, in between the corner and the opening to the next room. He pulled back out of the tightly packed group which was inspecting the six-foot canvas, in order to take in what he could of it from a distance. Then he turned his attention away, and was about to walk through the opening into the next room, when he saw it

It. He was arrested in his tracks.

Like 'Macbeth seeing the ghost of Banquo,' Charlotte

thought, even from the view she had of his back. It was the way he stiffened.

Her father was chatting, or arguing, with someone. For some time, he had been arguing his 'foolish' views on politics, as she thought of them, with various gentlemen. It was tedious. At last she was brave enough to slip her arm out of Papa's and trip towards her brother. She did not want to disturb him, yet wished to be at his side.

He took no notice of her. He was tense, and quaking a little, and maybe about to fall into a fit. When she followed the direction of his eyes, she saw such a grotesque sculpture that it made her shudder. It was a jet-black bust, more than life-size – four or five feet high. It was of a handsome young man and it managed to be both demonic and angelic. He was ruthless, with broad, shallow brow, with angry, distended nostrils, and his lips were curled in scorn. He seemed to leap forward from the plinth. The contrast between this black figure and the green fronds of a potted palm, and the white walls and columns, made it more terrifying.

Branwell walked forward in a trance, disregarding her, but she went with him, as if fastened to his arm. He stopped a few feet from the statue. Charlotte took in the encrustation of knotted veins on the mean brow of this otherwise handsome head, the demonic purposefulness in the eye, the bushy eyebrows almost meeting, and the veins collected over, rather than in, the neck. It turned out that its glossy blackness was because it was cast in iron. They peered at the inscription on a polished brass plate. It was called 'Satan', and it was by one Joseph Bentley Leyland.

'*It's Alexander Percy – it's Northangerland!*' Branwell murmured.

The very figure of his own Angrian creation.

Patrick had a difficult progress. When he found colleagues, it was not entirely delightful. He wanted to tell them about his daughter's picture, but fellow clergymen, some of whom he had not met for years, tackled him about the radical views he had expressed in letters to the *Leeds Mercury* and the *Leeds Intelligencer*. Patrick had written, not only on the abolition of the slave trade – about which few would argue – but also in favour of parliamentary reform, and he had made known his views on the mitigation of the criminal code. He had organized a petition in Haworth. The *Intelligencer*, when printing one of his letters, had felt it necessary to soothe its readers by informing them that its correspondent was 'an admired clergyman'.

He at last fell into conversation with one of the artists whose work was on show. Patrick was staring at a portrait of the Reverend John Buckworth of Dewsbury. 'Do you like it?' asked someone standing nearby. 'It's mine. William Robinson – portraitist!'

'Patrick Brontë of Haworth! Buckworth was a friend, and indeed patron, of mine, and offered me my first living at Hartshead. May I say, you execute portraits with some flair.'

Robinson's picture was as oily as spread butter, with a lot of shadowy effects in the background.

Patrick Brontë was not as impressed by Mr Robinson as a man. Although women might be unfathomable, he could size up a man. But the leprechaun was a striking limner, sure enough. Judging by Robinson's dress, he made a good living at it. He wore a tight-fitting jacket – a bit of a girl's jacket but artists were like that – of expensive cloth, and a flowing silk bow, tied underneath a winged collar.

'How did you acquire such an effective technique?' Patrick enquired, in the voice with which he might ask a fellow clergyman which college he had attended.

'I studied under Sir Thomas Lawrence,' Mr Robinson explained, smiling with satisfaction. When Mr Brontë evidently did not know who Lawrence was, 'Of the Royal Academy,' he added.

'You were at the Royal Academy?'

'I *am* an Academician,' Mr Robinson said.

Robinson seemed about to pull away from one whom he perhaps regarded as a philistine. 'My daughter has a watercolour exhibited. And I would like to introduce my son who is an artist,' Mr Brontë promptly suggested.

In the forceful way he had when he needed it, Patrick led Mr Robinson like a tethered lamb across the room.

'What other commissions have you executed?' Patrick asked.

'The Duke of Wellington, for one.'

'*The Duke?*'

'It was for the United Services Club.' Robinson spoke modestly. 'And the Princess Sophia has been among my sitters.'

Patrick gathered up his courage and asked, 'Do you take pupils?'

'I do take pupils, yes.'

'Would you consider taking my son?'

'It would depend upon how talented he is. And how enthusiastic.'

By which time they had joined Charlotte and Branwell.

Branwell continued staring at the statue, mesmerized. Charlotte confronted the man Papa had brought to them. She saw a sly little man with a weak physiognomy and romantic tufts of undisciplined hair which were not so wild as her brother's, but worn, no doubt, with the same vainglorious intention. He had a keen, if shifty glance.

'Branwell, this is Mr Robinson, a Royal Academician whose portrait of the Reverend Buckworth is exhibited!' Papa called out. Branwell turned round.

'Mr Robinson is a Royal Academician,' his father said. 'Sir, do you have a fee in mind for instructing?'

Branwell was staring at Mr Robinson with the same stupefaction with which he had looked at the sculpture; no doubt still in a daze from it.

Mr Robinson ventured to answer, ruminatively, quietly: 'Two guineas. That would be for an afternoon's session in my studio.'

Two guineas was more than Tabby was paid for a month's labour. It was a hundredth part of Patrick's stipend, therefore as much as he earned in half a week.

'We will give it some thought,' Patrick said.

'What is your opinion of the sculpture?' Mr Robinson asked Branwell.

'It is a work of sublime genius!' Branwell gushed. 'I have never imagined anything like it – well, I have imagined – I mean, I thought I would never see such a work executed, one so close to—'

Before he got lost in feelings that he could not explain, Robinson helped him out.

'It expresses the moment in Milton's *Paradise Lost* when Satan addresses the Archangel Uriel to ask him where in the universe is the paradise in which man dwells. Satan had to present himself as angelic, in order to win Uriel over to give him directions. Look at how powerfully Leyland has succeeded in expressing the paradox. In the form of a handsome and intelligent youth is the physiognomy of the dissembler, devoid of moral principle, as shown through the curling lip and distended nostrils.'

Mr Robinson waved his delicate hands.

'A figure, though damned, yet defiant – that is what I admire,' Branwell got in.

'Well, we must introduce you to the sculptor some day. He lives in Halifax.'

'*Halifax?* I never thought that genius could be so close at hand.'

'Why not? He is the son of a bookseller,' Mr Robinson purred. 'He was patronized by a local gentleman who has a collection of Greek sculptures and who sent young Leyland to London – where you yourself might well be bound. Who knows?' he suggested airily.

III

Branwell came from the exhibition aflame with art. Would he meet Mr Leyland of Halifax – would Papa find that he could afford lessons with Mr Robinson of Leeds – would Mr Robinson come to Haworth or would Branwell travel?

Portraiture still gripped him. He painted a group portrait of his sisters, on a stretched and primed canvas fetched in the gig from Keighley. He rigged up an easel out of chairs in Charlotte's and Emily's bedroom, and the project took a couple of weeks, with the breaks for housework and walks. In his mind he saw those grandiose canvases in the exhibition and did not realize how little he knew about the craft of producing them. He did not know, for instance, that periods between sittings must either not be of more than a few hours, so that the paint does not form a skin, or be much longer, for the paint to dry thoroughly. (As Branwell found out eventually: his Keighley teacher, Mr Bradley, was saving his important trade secrets to be charged up for later lessons.) A fine day came along, Branwell and his sisters went for a ramble, and on the following morning he did not understand what was happening to his fresh paint: the underpainting was not soft enough to mix with the new layer, nor was it hard enough to form an impermeable barrier, but the slightly dry surface drank up the oil, leaving the new paint looking dead.

Bradley had 'set him on' to copy his own portraits of manufacturers, or to make studies of urns and drapes, but Branwell's drawing was still poor. He knew the superficial appearance of a fashionable portrait group but had little knowledge of anatomy, or of how to analyse the structure, or of how to paint with fluency and grace. He had not even learned how to keep his colours separated, or how to mix them, so that many of them were muddied.

With unintended honesty – it came from his stiff drawing – his staring sitters looked bored and baleful. This was especially true of Charlotte, who was the one who had sat with the least expectation of a fortunate outcome. She had her 'leonine' look. All of their noses and mouths were awkwardly crooked. Branwell had portrayed the dowdiness of their hair, but unintentionally, through the muddying of his colours. In Emily he had caught an expression that seemed to say, 'Is it over, yet, Branwell? Have you done?' as she peered over Anne's shoulder. Anne was looking hopefully for escape through the window that was not included in the picture, but which had a view of the moors.

All three wore dresses of an identical style. They were their autumn ones, belted, with long sleeves and large, shapeless lace collars that flopped upon their shoulders like the petals of unwatered tulips. Aunt Branwell had chosen and had them made cheaply in Keighley. They all perforce wore 'mature' gowns now, the only differences being that while Anne's was of blue stuff, Emily's was green and Charlotte's was brown. The three girls, huddled in the picture, looked as wretched as though someone had thrown a bucket of water over them.

*   *   *

There was music, also. Branwell had lessons on the new church organ. While Emily played the parsonage's new piano, he practised the flute.

At Christmas there was a performance in Haworth Church of Handel's *Messiah*. Handel was Branwell's favourite composer and much of Yorkshire's, too – the meat of its choral societies. The conductor was Mr Greenwood, from London, who back in May had inaugurated the organ with Handel's 'And the Glory of the Lord' and 'I Know that my Redeemer Liveth'. Today, it was played by the Brontës' music teacher, Mr Abraham Sunderland, from Keighley.

The singers were powerful-chested farm-workers and quarrymen. The musicians were hard-working weavers who managed to keep their fingers delicate enough to handle a violin. They were cottagers who'd seen a grandparent's fiddle hanging on a wall since their childhood, left over from the days when a more barbaric music had been played, and now taken down for church and concert hall. The four soloists were regular singers in the choral societies. This year they included Haworth's pride, the tenor, Tom Parker, whose chest, swelling and shining in its white shirt-front, and his shoulders pulled back as if preparing to meet the foe, made the ladies gasp. There was also a marvellous, swaggering bass singer, Mr Feather from Halifax.

The players wore black coats, the women had black gowns, and the chorus was decked out in whatever it possessed, but this was mostly black, too. The weather had been bad, so there was not the full complement of performers, and Mr Greenwood had given up having tantrums over their excuses – a leaking barn roof, or a dog lost on the moors. The result was that there was a great shortage for the choir. They were also three fiddles and two basses short, but the performers they did have made up for any lack with their good spirits. Everyone agreed on that.

The men were ranked in the centre, the women flanked cither side, and the orchestra was set before them. The mouths of the chorus opened like those of eager nestlings, the fiddle bows flashed in the shadowy church, and the cellist, famed from Huddersfield to Skipton, crouched over his instrument like a lion.

The Lord shall rise upon thee, and His glory shall be seen upon thee . . .

The Heatons from Ponden, the Taylors of the manor house in Stanbury, and other local aristocracy were all in their pews, while the Brontë girls – self-conscious in their plain dresses – and their brother were in theirs. A certain amount of courting took place in the audience – eyes meeting, and nervously averted; mental notes made of whom to brush up against later, over mince pies and punch in the Sunday School. The parson's daughters were not part of that, either.

But if thoughts strayed, they soon returned. Branwell often looked up to the dark roof as if expecting to see it lifted so that God Himself might better hear this celestial music. *And lo, the angel of the Lord came upon them, and the glory of the Lord shone round about them . . .*

At the interval, Mr Feather winked at Branwell and said, 'Are you coming to the Black Bull with me, young man?'

The public house! He had never been inside one before. He had stared, fascinated, through the open door, glimpsing in its shadowy interior the shine of teeth and eyes, the gleam of woodwork and tankards. He had overheard laughter and talk of a vigour that fascinated him, until glances had been turned upon him standing at the door, and he had fled.

He had watched drunks leaving the public house, had envied and feared the place. Boys younger than he had been inside. But he was the parson's son.

Now here he was, in the dark burrow, enveloped by that odour, strong, wicked, unpleasant, yet magnetic because associated with *men*. With its fire going, the pub smelled of warm, wet wool, of old tobacco and of urine; a stench which he couldn't analyse precisely, that set him coughing and retching. But it was an initiation. 'By eck, it's t'parson's lad!' shouted hardened drinkers who had been at it since dinner time. There he was, with a tankard of strong ale in his hand. He had tasted beer before, at home, when Tabby or one of the Garrses had given him a sip of their ration. He had not liked it and could not think why it was drunk. It had been like bitter medicine. He did not like it much now, either, but he swallowed it, forcing an expression of pleasure for the sake of being with the men. Then the drink gave him pleasure. Here he was, drinking with Mr Feather!

As always in the *Messiah*, the excitement, the passion, the crescendos came in the second part. Mr Feather, who was 'nobbut a farm servant from t'tops', as the envious pointed out, sang better than he had done before. Then with what stupendous energy all rose to sing the 'Halleluyah Chorus'! All of the old, uncivilized passion of Haworth was poured into the *Messiah*.

There was a little trouble at the end of the evening when the long trills of the 'Amen', sung by so many voices, got tangled and knotted. But let that criticism pass . . .

Branwell sat through the second half filled with an unfamiliar joy, vague yet concentrated. He was light-headed with ecstasy. He sensed transcendent thoughts almost but not quite within his grasp.

And Greenwood was almost a Northangerland: tall, red-haired like Branwell, and temperamental. At the end – Branwell could hardly wait for it, to do what he had in mind to do – he rose, flushed but determined to shake the conductor's hand.

The chorus clapped and stamped its feet for the four soloists. The showy exclamation, 'Bravo!', brought from London by Mr Greenwood, was shouted – a little hesitantly, like the piping of robins in February. The soloists smilingly turned to clap for their chorus and to shake hands with the leader of the orchestra.

Branwell reached the front of the congregation and Mr Greenwood. He shook his hand with such warmth that it made the other young men in the church titter.

Finally, Papa rose to offer thanks, plus a short prayer and a blessing, not from his pulpit but from the body of his church, standing in front of the orchestra.

There was so much to talk about while walking across the dark churchyard, and in the Sunday School where mince pies, made by Emily and Tabitha, were laid out and there was a bowl of punch. The prancing and bouncing Mr Greenwood had to be compared with the more stolid and dignified conductor of last year, who had not been as good; but who was there to be found in the whole wide world of the quality of Greenwood of London? There was the fat soprano to discuss: Miss Buttershaw, the daughter of a cake-maker, who went red in the face because, poor thing, she knew that she was a joke although she could sing well. There was Miss Royd in her 'common' dress, her tinsel drapes, and her ear-rings which Miss Branwell said were made of flour paste. Mr Wilkinson, licensee of the Black Bull, said it had not been as good a concert as last year's and that he had sold less ale. And there was Tom Parker to talk about, but he, because he was a professional, saved his strength and went home.

Branwell's face was bursting with smiles and happy creases when he actually caught the *ear* of Mr Greenwood. He stared up at him with adoration.

Charlotte grew tense: Branwell's behaviour so disturbed her. She had long given up hoping that he could live up to her Marquis of Douro, but look at him! His behaviour towards Mr Greenwood was . . . she did not like to face it: 'toadying' was the epithet that came to mind as she dipped her spoon in the punch bowl and handed round the noggins, in her neat and careful fashion, meanwhile spying on her brother across the room. His manner told her that he was boasting, while Mr Greenwood listened in an aloof, politely uninterested manner, his eyes flickering around the Sunday School, looking for escape. Branwell made Charlotte feel quite sick.

As he put out his arm to touch Mr Greenwood, she had a perception which she would have given anything to banish; a stroke of disillusionment that was like a sabre cut across the cheek. She felt that its scar would last for ever.

She was ferocious with understanding. She said she had a headache, left the Sunday School early, and returned to the parsonage.

Only the pets were in the house; only Grasper came to meet her, first with a bark and then with a soft whine. She picked up the lamp left alight in the hallway and wandered about downstairs, the dog padding behind her. Her home seemed eerie, because of the thoughts on her mind. If it had not been for those, she would not have noticed it but would have been thinking of the book she was reading, or of some duty, or of something that she was going to say, or to write down.

Her shoes scuffed through sand on the floor as she went into the kitchen. While the house was empty, washing was hanging before the fire, and Charlotte's lamp cast bat-like shadows from flannel underwear and chemises. She heard the tiny wheezings of the cats, dozing in their corners. She heard coals dropping in the grate – stocks were running low and she must order a new supply.

'Good dog – stay there, Grasper!' she ordered. She went out of the kitchen and shut the door. She climbed the stairs, listening to the ticking of the clock. She did not know how she was going to face Branwell again, or ever talk about his behaviour. She hoped to be proved wrong: that he would prove not to be like that.

She went into her bedroom, unlocked her portable writing cabinet, opened her *My Angria and The Angrians*, took up 'Wiggins's' point of view, and wrote:

> Instantly I assumed that inverted position which with me is a mark of the highest astonishment, delight and admiration. In other words I clapt my pate to the ground and let my heels fly up with a spring . . . He turned round and saw me. 'What's that fellow playing his mountebank tricks here for?' . . . Before anybody could answer I was at his feet licking the dust under them and crying aloud, 'O Greenwood! the greatest, the mightiest, the most famous of men, doubtless you are ignorant of a nit the foal of a louse like me, but I have learnt to know you through the medium of your wonderful works. Suffer the basest of creatures to devote himself utterly to your service, as a shoeblack, a rosiner of fiddlesticks, a great-coat carrier – a Port-music, in short a thorough going toadie . . .'

It was not funny, really.

Why was Branwell given all the advantages in life?

Look at what had happened at the Leeds exhibition: she was the one who'd had a picture exhibited, but all the fuss had been over Branwell.

When she'd had enough of peering at her minute handwriting, Charlotte lay on her bed.

She turned the pages of half a dozen copies of the *Ladies Magazine* that had belonged to her mother, and that Charlotte kept by her. They were stained with salt water and their pages were curled and faded, for they were among the few possessions that had survived the shipwreck that had destroyed nearly everything of her mother's before she was married. They were full of old-fashioned love stories – imitations of eighteenth-century literature, *Clarissa* and *Evelina*. But they evoked a different world from the sordid one she had to put up with in Haworth – the stinking pit of it – with a brother who was a *toady*. The characters wore old-fashioned but beautiful clothes and they dwelled in fine houses with lovely gardens in the South. They were handsome and elegant, except for the villains; though she liked the villains almost as much. At least they weren't toadies. Sometimes she put villains and heroes together in a single character of her own devising, handsome but also a little wicked.

She grew tired and put the magazines aside. I wish I was not stunted and plain, with a square face and a twisted mouth. I wish I was beautiful, and beautifully dressed. Like Carus Wilson's daughters.

At last, Emily came to join her. Charlotte did not want to talk, and pretended to be asleep.

They were awakened hours later by shouting and singing. It would often happen along the path through the churchyard, where drunks went to relieve themselves, but this took place in the garden.

The noise was next in the house, accompanied by the banging of furniture. Yes, it was Branwell. He was singing one of Samuel Wesley's hymns as raucously as a tavern song.

Emily was getting up. Charlotte followed her to the stairhead. Aunt Branwell and Papa had been roused. Emily was amused by what she saw. Charlotte was shocked more than ever. In the hallway, Papa was supporting Branwell and Aunt was dabbing at the cuts that her nephew had sustained by falling about in the graveyard.

Branwell rose late the next morning and came out smirking.

He realized that his sisters had been talking about him. Papa, stern and calm, was waiting.

'Branwell, a word in my study, if you please.'

Branwell trooped in behind Papa.

His father set himself with his back to the fire, rocking on the balls of his feet, occasionally glancing at the window over Branwell's head. Papa was always more gentle than other fathers were with their sons – for instance than was the father of Branwell's friend, Michael Merrall, with whom he'd been drinking last night. Nevertheless he had an unspoken thought which Branwell could read in his eyes. It was the same thought that he read in the eyes of many older people – What sort of man are you going to become? Tabby would also sometimes look him up and down, and, when it seemed she was about to speak, say nothing. Aunt Branwell did the same. He knew that this question was hanging in the air today, perhaps not to be voiced, but certainly predicating all the other matters that would be raised.

'Now that you are sober, Branwell, can you explain yourself?'

'I was enjoying the music. I found myself led astray.' He had prepared his excuse.

'*Led* astray? As my son you are looked upon to lead others.'

Now Branwell forgot himself. 'PAPA! DON'T YOU UNDERSTAND! SOMETIMES I *HAVE* TO GET OUT OF A HOUSE FULL OF GIRLS!'

He was shaking. For the first time that he could remember, he sank into a study chair uninvited, and repeated – looking downwards towards the flames, and quietly this time – 'Sometimes I have to get away from a house full of girls.'

'Charlotte did not like your behaviour towards Mr Greenwood,' Papa said. 'She thought it improper.'

Branwell looked up, sharply. Papa did not look back at him, but shrugged his shoulders – it was almost a shudder – and tugged at his cravat, as he did when something unpleasant had to be dealt with.

'Why was it improper?' Branwell was genuinely unable to comprehend.

'She thought that the way you behaved towards him foreboded ill.'

Papa threw him a glance.

'But Papa—'

Papa looked at the window again. Branwell felt himself blushing, and looked away. Had he fawned so much upon Mr Greenwood? Yes, he had. He must not do it again.

He was desperate for art, for music, and needed to fill every minute of his life with it. He was frustrated and did not know by what – why he could not make progress – except that some infuriating mystery, some failure to understand, blocked him.

He wanted a room to paint in, instead of having to erect his easel in Charlotte's and Emily's bedroom. That created tension and he could not concentrate. He wanted a better teacher than Mr Bradley: those lessons from Mr Robinson which Papa still hedged over providing. He wanted to go to the Royal Academy in London. To Italy. He *needed* to associate with musicians, artists and poets. His only desire had been for contact with Mr Greenwood's world of music. All that he had done wrong had been to express his enthusiasm too strongly. He could not see how to say this to Papa. He did not know whether he would understand.

'Have you heard from Mr Robinson?'

'What?'

'Papa, art is my career and some day it will support all of us! All that I need is your trust, Papa! But I need the lessons!'

Spring came. Branwell spent a fine afternoon turning over engravings of London. He was so absorbed in views of the Strand, Trafalgar Square, the colonnades of Somerset House and the Royal Academy, and the shipping on the river, that if he had stepped out of the parsonage into the bustle of traffic, among those ladies and gentlemen milling around their carriages, he would not have been surprised.

When he did go out, the reality of dark and poky Haworth gave him a shock. His head, though, was boiling with possibilities there, too. By now he knew all the public houses – the 'publics' as they were called – his favourite being the largest, the nearest, and the first one he had entered: the Black Bull, where Abraham Wilkinson would chalk up his bill on the slate behind the bar until he could pay with a sub from Papa.

He was also welcome in the clubs that had mushroomed in every mill village in recent years. Should he go to the Temperance Society, or the Literary Society, or the Working Men's Tory Club (of which he was president), or the Conservative Committee (of which he was secretary), or the Boxing Club?

All the *young blades* of Haworth had grown crazy about boxing. Those who could read pored over the sporting periodical, Bell's *Life in London*, which was taken in the Black Bull. 'Put 'em up!' was a common greeting and children showed off by brawling in the street. One day, Branwell had overheard a mother, standing with folded arms over her scrapping son, shout him on with, 'If tha doesna' lick 'im, I s'll lick thee, my lad!' Branwell Brontë, alias Alexander Percy, alias the Earl of Northangerland, could go and see if any peepers had been closed, any slingers had been delivered, at the Haworth Boxing Club, which was in a dusty room above the stables in the yard of the Black Bull. He could deliver a slinger on the throat apple, lay on a black eye in great style, deliver a closer on the nose . . . No-one was looking so Branwell shadow-boxed on the cobblestones.

Or he could step into John Brown's house, which was next to the new Sunday school, halfway between the parsonage and the Black Bull, and maybe drag his friend out for a drink.

He did not want any company today. Instead, he went onto the hills. He followed his usual route down to the Sladen Beck, round to Ponden and up to Ponden Kirk. He knew every wall and farm, every crag and waterfall. It was never the same two days, not even two hours, together. The weavers' tiny fields, bright green surrounded by dark walls on the flanks of brown hillsides, seemed to him like jewels, whenever they caught the sun.

His elation at the pure air only a short distance away from Haworth lifted his spirits into – he felt – a clear perception of being at one with beauty. And one day he would be famous. He imagined visitors coming from far away because of himself. Passing by people who thought that they knew him was like being a ghost in his own body.

His sensations were mixed up with the ones of being young; of the vigour he felt unexpressed in his loins; of the desire and hope of sharing it with another, some day; of hope invested in art and music.

'Happiness,' he remembered that Papa had said to him one day, as they sat where he sat now, on a rock at Ponden Kirk, 'is impossible without courage, without integrity and a clear conscience. Remember this to your dying day, son! Happiness is within. It isn't in some place where you last found it, or in some place where you hope it will be. It is within you. It springs out of you like a fountain.

'But it is possible simply not to be brave enough to be happy. And if you ever come to be haunted by what you should never have done, you can never be happy, either.'

CHAPTER FOUR

TERRORS

EMILY

I

If the doors were open, Emily would hear Anne praying in Aunt Branwell's room. Charlotte, too, after Emily and she had giggled or scared one another with 'bed plays', closed her eyes and prayed. She lay on her back, stiff as a board, her eyes closed, and asked aloud to be forgiven.

'I don't think you've *done* anything,' Emily said, lying on her side and looking towards the window. A great, blue star was brightening in the dying orange glow of a summer evening.

'After what we've just been talking about?'

Emily laughed, and snuggled against Charlotte, who relaxed.

'You're as frightened as Anne is of being "snatched". I thought *you* were the one with the intellect!'

The doors being open because it was warm weather, Anne's prayer was wafted in, down the passageway from the front bedroom:

> 'As I lay me down to sleep
> I pray thee Lord my soul to keep.
> If I should die before I wake
> I pray thee Lord my soul to take.'

Aunt Branwell chirruped: 'That's a good girl, Anne! Now off to bed!'

It was ridiculous. Anne was fifteen. She had written some of Gondal.

'The terror of dying in my sleep after having had a sinful thought has scarred me since childhood,' Charlotte said. 'I can still hear Mr Wilson at Cowan Bridge. Can't you?'

'No.' Then: 'I don't think it matters,' Emily answered.

'For me, it is like a bullet embedded in a soldier during some old battle,' Charlotte continued. 'A bullet too deep to be removable. I'm like the old soldiers wounded at Waterloo and Badajoz we see limping around Haworth.'

'Oh, well, we must all go our own way!' said Emily, blithely. 'You had better pray again, after that outburst of scepticism.'

At his prayer meeting for family and servants in his study before breakfast, 'Thanks be to God that we are assembled this morning as on so many others in the past,' Papa intoned.

The servants, Tabby and whoever else, went into the kitchen while the Brontës crossed into the parlour; the room with the sun, if there was any. At half past seven they would be at their places.

'I'm glad we're all here again,' Aunt Branwell added her bit every morning to Papa's thanksgiving. It was as if they had been on a long journey, and it set one's teeth on edge, as the ticking of the clock could, and the sound of mastication. For a time, Branwell had shown open rebellion and scornful cynicism, but after mayhem for a week he had fallen silent. Charlotte argued. It was only Anne who never seemed to resent the daily requirement of gratitude for being alive. Emily's aloofness would often hang over the whole breakfast.

'I refuse to be grateful merely because I have not been whisked off to Hell,' she had said – but not in her aunt's hearing, for she was above crossing swords with her on the subject. The adults put her 'moods' down to adolescence; which clearly was also disturbing Branwell, but not, they foolishly thought, the other two girls overmuch.

Even Papa appeared to find Aunt Branwell's apocalyptic aubades irksome, coming after he had already given formal thanks. 'Family breakfast, and supper before retiring, are the most important ceremonies of the day. Let us make celebrations of them!' he had said, meaning: rather than making of them reminders that some of us might find ourselves in Hell, if not today, then tomorrow.

But Aunt Branwell's breakfast chair was her pulpit. She took up one side of the table, her back to the window. Facing her was Papa. On her left would be Anne and Emily, on her right Charlotte and Branwell.

'Suppose you *hadn't* survived the night?' she said. 'Suppose you'd been overcome by a sinful thought after your prayers, but just as you were falling asleep, and had been Taken, unforgiven? All because of a thought come unbidden at that unguarded moment which is Satan's hour. Emily! Are you listening to me?'

'Yes, Aunt,' Emily answered with exaggerated weariness.

'Then do not smile at me, miss!'

Aunt Branwell looked around the table. Her simple eyes were wide with horror. Her limp, plump hands on the tablecloth expressed despair.

The night before, after their bedtime prayers, Anne and Charlotte had been kept awake on sentry duty against wicked, last minute thoughts – thoughts of Gondal and Angria – until they drifted off to sleep, exhausted. Often, when they awoke, they could not remember what they had been thinking about before they had fallen asleep. It was dreadful, they agreed, if one awoke during the night and had to go through the rite of passage all over again.

'Thus you would die unredeemed by repentance. Then where would you be?' Aunt said.

'In the fiery pit,' Anne whispered back.

It seemed to Emily that Anne, even more than Charlotte, was growing into a simple Christian believer, ruled by fear, driven by a hope for eternity: an attitude that wasted *this* life.

Anne could be even more exasperating than Charlotte.

'Each morning,' Anne had told Emily, 'I feel my limbs to see if they are still there. I expect to find my soul somewhere else, so that my limbs are not part of me any more and won't do my bidding. I wake up wondering whether I am in Heaven or Hell. I am sure that one day I will find myself in a coffin, while my soul is above. One night I dreamed that my soul was with Maria's and Elizabeth's, high above the roof. As we looked down we were frantic because we could not tell you of the joy and beauty of Heaven.'

'That seems a very nice dream for you,' Emily said.

One day, Charlotte burst out, 'Aunt! I am trying to find in religion something that will offer comfort, not damn me with terrors! Surely there are some unwanted thoughts which are not so serious as to ruin one's eternity?'

The parsonage atmosphere was fraught in 1835. Charlotte was to return to Roe Head as a teacher, taking Emily as a pupil, her fees subsidized from Charlotte's pay. Branwell had written to the Royal Academy Schools in London about entrance requirements. The nest was to be broken up, as it had not been since four of them went to Cowan Bridge – an ominous precedent. Anne would be left at the parsonage without her sisters.

Charlotte's words caused Aunt Branwell to drop her boiled egg off her spoon. Her little mouth, with the whiskery hairs around it, pursed and tightened. Will Aunt Branwell dare to put into words the temptations to which our youth is vulnerable in the moments before we fall asleep? Emily wondered. You can tell by the way she is looking at our bosoms – even Anne's – what she is thinking.

'Considering the risks, Aunt Branwell is on the side of taking out insurance,' Emily said, out aloud.

When Aunt had collected her thoughts again, her description of the fires and pincers took her all the time required to recover her egg, wipe the stain off her dress, pour tea for everyone, and some minutes longer.

'Warnings of an eternal fate can be overdone, Elizabeth,' Papa chastised, mildly. 'Vivid descriptions are better left to papists and dissenters.' Instead of taking up the cudgels against Charlotte's lapse, he had put his foot in it.

'It has never been suggested to me before that there is anything akin to popery in *my* belief!' cried Aunt Branwell and burst into tears. 'I'm sorry, but I must leave the table!'

'Elizabeth! I did not mean—!'

She was standing up and quaking. 'No, Patrick! I am sorry, but it is too late. Of course you must teach your *own* children as your conscience dictates. I am alone in the world and I must make my peace with my Maker in my own way!'

She made a clumsy, rustling passage across the room and dithered before the door.

'You are *most surely* not alone, Elizabeth!'

But Papa did not rise to comfort her.

'No, Patrick! Oh, I did not think I had come to this *barren* spot to be hurt and insulted.' She went from the room. Her pattens clattered upstairs. Her door closed.

Papa contemplated Aunt Branwell's abandoned egg, her teapot and her chair, with extreme melancholy, while only the sound of Charlotte's sobbing filled the room.

'We've done it now,' Emily remarked blithely.

'We have indeed,' said Papa. 'I think one of you should go to your aunt. Anne – you, perhaps?'

Anne went to do her duty. She was near to crying, also.

After Tabby entered to clear up in the parlour, the waters closed over the disastrous breakfast and the other two girls were left, as usual, to help with the chores.

To Emily, it seemed ridiculous that the creators of Angria and Gondal should be perturbed by the snivelling of a maiden aunt. Being wise enough not to put this into so many words, she left Charlotte to the clearing up and went, sooner than usual, to the kitchen, to join Tabby at her work and to fill a pail with porridge for her dogs and cats; a smile on her face.

In church, Emily would entertain herself by watching the congregation, partly amused and in part despising them. When bored with that, she tapped her feet, *humph*ed, and itched for the time to pass. She even put her tongue out at the churchwarden with his staff. Only the parson's daughter, and one or two others, could get away with that.

She enjoyed many of the Bible stories. They were the ones of doomed people who lived lives of passion and conflict – Abraham and Isaac; Mary at the foot of the Cross; Job. Through living their fates to the full, they were raised above them – sheer passion justified them as superhuman. In these stories, Bible, Byron, Walter Scott and Shelley joined.

Otherwise, the whining, the pathetic begging that passed for prayer through three Sunday services was excruciating.

At the end she would dash for the door, grateful to be relieved of torment. For her, church was where thought and life were drowned, and on being released into the real day she felt that she had been saved once again from tumbling backwards into a hole in her head. She came out with one overriding joy: she was no longer dead. She walked into that pointed arch of light that was the porch, thinking, That's it until next Sunday! finding correspondence with her own feelings only in the wind, the light, and the crisp sense of moorland. Or, in winter, responding with excitement and gladness to the cold, rain or snow that made others hurry, grumbling, to their fires.

Until her early teens, Emily had not considered the significance of the fact that everyone did not live in a parsonage. Then her mind began to play with the differences of *her* fate. Suppose she had been born behind a weaver's loom? Suppose she had been a child of the Heaton clan? Or had been orphaned because her father had been hanged or transported, like some of the children in the Sunday school? Or had been condemned to be an 'apprentice' in a mill – one of those grubby, starved, overworked and beaten little creatures she had seen peering through the bars of the Heatons' mill at Ponden, or being marched to chapel?

Emily assumed that her life and that of her siblings would always be marked out by the rhythms of the church. Therefore she would bake for unemployed weavers, take her turn with a Sunday school class, enter cottages with gifts of baby clothes stitched in the parsonage – but she would live her real life in the interstices.

She knew without doubt what *was* her real life. As for Branwell, and for Charlotte too if she were honest (though not for Anne), it was linked to a certain wicked taste that literature and art possessed.

Emily had held racked discussions with Charlotte about it. Once, she had plucked books from their shelves, putting them down in front of her sister. She selected Byron, Shelley, Webster, Shakespeare and Walter Scott: every one of them somewhat wicked. There wasn't one that the pious of Haworth would countenance, when it came down to it.

'Remember, the *Devil* is often on the side of poetry!' she exclaimed; a mischief-making glint in her eye.

It had set Charlotte twitching, for she yearned to reconcile the passions of her Mary Henrietta Percy with Christian teaching. In her allegiance she dodged from one to the other; from the excitement of one to the righteousness – the self-righteousness, Emily called it – of the other. The result was that both tormented her. The alternatives of guilty creativity and of religion tore at Charlotte's soul. 'How can I go to lecture the Sunday school scholars straight after reading Lord Byron and writing Angria?' she asked.

Emily observed Charlotte's effort to behave with Christian resolution, watched with bafflement her struggle to suppress all else – all of that which she regarded as Charlotte's true soul – and 'Render unto Caesar that which is Caesar's' was her advice to prevent Charlotte from tearing herself apart.

Though Emily would bake for the poor and listen to sermons, she would not compromise. Seeing that the church suppressed rather than gave life and breath to the great powers that *she* felt, she solved the problem by separating her duty as a clergyman's daughter from what was more important; from that which her soul refused to allow to be polluted. That was where her real life lay.

It helped her, to take long walks.

Emily often rambled with Anne. She had been closest to her ever since Charlotte and Branwell had created Angria. The closeness had deepened as Charlotte had formed friendships at school, and Branwell had made his in the village.

The friendship grew partly because Anne and she were very different from each other. Anne was a delight for Emily to lead on a walk. As the youngest of the family, she was used to being dependent. She showed a willingness to assume that others were right, and that they could do things better than she could. This suited forceful Emily. 'You are like twins,' Ellen Nussey had observed. 'You are very different from one another, but you match.'

Now the family was to be 'scattered to the four winds', as Emily put it, Emily and Anne were sad for opposite reasons. Ironically, Anne, who was staying at home, longed to get away, but Emily, who was being sent to Roe Head, did not wish to leave even for a day. She felt pledged to the very wind in Haworth.

'I shall be losing my room!' she complained. Her room where she wrote of Gondal was the centre of her existence. 'Papa has said that Branwell can use it as his studio until he goes to the Royal Academy.'

'You will have it back when Branwell goes away.'

'It will *never* be the same again! When shall I return? Haworth will feel different. My room will not feel the same. It won't have my things in it.'

Meanwhile they climbed the Sladen Beck. At first it was between soft, green slopes; an easy walk which was to Anne's taste. Soon, it grew more difficult. Enclosure walls swept down to the stream, which threaded between rowan trees and twisted hawthorns, and fell among slippery boulders. Swampy patches had to be navigated.

Emily loved the Beck and its moods, some days falling angrily and frothing, while at other times, such as today, its pools were a warm chestnut colour, with a gleam upon the water, and a bright, happy sky dancing in its reflections. The wilder the countryside grew, the more she loved it. She longed to reach the open wilderness, the rock and heather at the head of the valley – the moorland which she had once seen erupt, defying all that humans thought that they knew and understood. To Emily that place meant beauty at every turn of her head, at every swing of her eyes, nostrils and ears.

Anne feared it. When the wind became sharper and cooler, it would mean struggle and panic for her, afraid of running out of breath. Already she was wheezing. This was irksome to Emily, as all weakness irked her. And she had to keep waiting for Anne to catch up.

Her sister reached her side and had to rest. While she was breathless and could not answer back, Emily outlined a plot for Gondal. Anne had hardly settled upon a log when Emily began.

'How do you like this for a story? Augusta Geraldine Almeida when she is a child is brought up in a palace with a companion, Angelica. Angelica falls in love with Amadeus. Augusta is jealous. She herself covets Amadeus, and because she is more beautiful and aristocratic, she steals his love away for herself. When she has secured Amadeus's love, and made it so that it is Angelica who is the jealous one, she discards him.'

'I think it's cruel.'

Was this greater cruelty the difference between their Gondal, and Charlotte's and Branwell's Angria? Anne wondered. And feared; she did not like it. Similar were the plots within plots, the plots hatching into others and losing their old selves; the passionate characters who died only to be reborn. The themes were the same ones of love, treachery, ambition, adultery and betrayal. But in Gondal, women motivated the action; that was Emily's idea of how things should be. Also the landscape of Gondal was not so exotic. It had Haworth's brown moorlands, with the heather and harebells that Emily loved. It had Yorkshire's weather – its brief summers, but much more of snow and rain; violent, drenching, and thrilling. But, most strikingly, there was this cruel streak. (And Angria was cruel enough.) People remarked on it as part of Emily's mind.

Emily laughed at her. Seeing that her sister was getting her breath back, she rose and led on, under the rowan trees.

'So Augusta now has two enemies,' Emily continued, once she saw that Anne was growing breathless again. 'These, for her own safety, she must send into exile. There Angelica and Amadeus live a life of crime, waiting for a chance to return and wreak revenge.'

The trees by the Sladen Beck thinned out until there were hardly any. There were no more enclosures either, and the moorland sides were steeper.

They reached a bridge made of flagstones upon piers. A side stream flowed in and Emily called the place, 'The Meeting of the Waters', after the Irish poem by Moore. Ahead, the main stream rose, a mile or two further on, from the spring at Top Withens. This was a spot that invited one to settle and talk – it was so sheltered, hidden, sun-warmed, and musical with the sounds of the streams.

'Meanwhile, at Regina, Augusta Geraldine Almeida takes on her second lover, the Lord Alexander of Elbe. But he dies in her arms, pining for his sunny home in the South Pacific.

Afterwards, Augusta is imprisoned in a dungeon and writes a lament for Alexander on the walls. After she comes out of prison, her next passion is for Sidonia, Lord Aspin.'

'Why is she imprisoned?' Anne interrupted.

'We must think of something.'

Neither of them could think of anything. Emily had two great, contrasting terrors: one was exile and the other was imprisonment, and her dramatic climaxes usually involved one or other of them. Exile from her inner world, she meant: Gondal, and Haworth where it grew, and imprisonment where she could not reach it.

Emily looked around at the moorlands, and suddenly said: 'What do *you* think happens when we die?'

'I am sure that we pay the penalty for our sins and, if Hell does not await us and we are redeemable, we go to Heaven.'

'I would like to return to here when I die,' Emily said. 'Here, as a spirit.'

II

Charlotte dictated what Emily needed in her trunk for life at Roe Head, and told her what to expect: she was able to impose a sense of order on her, for once.

'Emily, I *know the ropes*, as the sailors say, and you *must* listen to me.'

It was Charlotte's nature that, being small, she thrust herself forward. It was part of Emily's confidence, because of her size, not always to be overeager but to hold back and be watchful, and she let her sister have her way.

It was the end of July, and they went to Roe Head in the gig. They faced one another across their trunks. Emily wore a green stuff dress and Charlotte a blue one. They had straw bonnets, tied on with scarves.

The more Charlotte put on a schoolteacher's airs, the more it showed Emily that she herself was not the only one whose heart was not in this venture. Emily knew that her sister had admitted to Ellen Nussey that she 'earnestly envied her independence'. She meant, not Mary Taylor's brand of independence which led her to act for herself, but Ellen's 'independence' which derived from her brothers' support and allowed her to stay at home.

'Anne envies *us*,' Emily remarked, wistfully.

She was visualizing the Sladen Beck and Ponden Kirk. She had been told that there were moorlands around Roe Head, but why could they not see that it was not the same? She was thinking of her room and its view: she imagined a star-filled sky, and a wind rising. But her clothes were packed away in the chest of drawers, and – she could see it as clearly as if she were there – Branwell, with Papa helping him probably, would right now perhaps be moving their bed, Charlotte and Emily's bed, into a corner out of his way. He would be setting up his easel by her window: occupier of her place of dreams, wishes and extraordinary emotions.

The moorland balms swept over the gig, scent of gorse, sound of curlew, but they spoke only of exile. Neither Angria nor Gondal was mentioned. It was as if they were dead.

Emily's one experience of being away from home for long had been at Cowan Bridge. Going to school could only be terrifying. But she would not talk about it. Although it was the eve of her seventeenth birthday, she would not allow even that to make her feel sorry for herself. In the sunshine, she untied her scarf, removed her bonnet, shook her close-cut mop of hair that had been curled with Aunt Branwell's curling irons, and smiled.

It was on her mind to use her all-conquering, knowing smile to pull her sister back from her irritating knowingness about *everything* today, but she did not succeed. They sank out of moorland sunshine into the smoky pool of Halifax, drove through the splendours of the town centre and followed the course of the River Calder with Hartshead on the hill to the left.

Pointing to the right, 'That's Castle Hill – an ancient British fort,' Charlotte said. All the way, she had behaved like that – like the Sunday school teacher she was at heart.

They climbed left, to Roe Head. Then there took place an abrupt parting: Emily to join her fellow pupils after a brief introduction, Charlotte to her reunion with her 'wonderful' Miss Wooler.

*   *   *

As Charlotte had been a small freak among her peers, Emily was a tall one. In any case she was one of the oldest pupils. She wriggled on school benches because her long legs were uncomfortable, and in Mirfield Church because her spirit was.

'How strange is Miss Emily Jane!' remarked fellow pupils and the church congregation.

'Pinhead!'

'With a front tooth sticking out – like this!'

'Do that again, Miss Upton! You're *such* a scream!'

'Pfuff ... pfuff ... pfuff ... pfuff ... pfuff,' went Miss Upton. By retracting her chin and putting her thumb under her top front tooth, Miss Upton made a rodent-like snuffling noise that was supposed to sound like the clear-tongued Emily.

In place of Charlotte's Miss Walker and Miss Haigh, Emily now had a Miss Upton, a Miss Caris, a Miss Lister and a Miss Marriott to tease her. Because she was related to a teacher, they did not wish to like her, and she was not interested in influencing her peers. She couldn't see any need for liking, flattering, caring for, or being interested in anyone other than her family, Tabby, and characters in stories.

Charlotte had informed Emily about the dormitory conversations and they should not have been a shock. Word for word, almost, the nightly twitterings were what Charlotte had also overheard in her time as a pupil.

'I do not much mind if my husband is old, say nearly thirty, so long as he dotes upon me and lets me have my own way,' said Miss Marriott.

'Miss Marriott, you are *such* a mountebank!' screamed Miss Caris.

'Well, *I* shall not be in a hurry to throw my cap at anyone,' said Miss Lister. 'And whoever he is, I shall lead him quite a dance to get me, so as to gain control for future years.'

'I will not be satisfied with less than a thousand pounds a year. I want a London house and a private allowance for myself.'

'You will never make such a catch, Miss Upton. You are not pretty enough. What say you, Miss Bron-*teh*?'

As Emily did not reply: 'Pinhead!' whispered a distant

voice out of the dark; Emily thought it came from the bed of Miss Upton and Miss Caris.

'Miss Brontë doesn't need a husband, because she is going to be a school governess like her sister,' teased Emily's own bed companion, Miss Marriott, upon whom Emily had turned her back.

For Emily's part, it was torment to share with any of them, although she was compelled to. At night, in order to enjoy Gondal and pretend that she was back in her Haworth room, she turned her back, first on Miss Marriott, then on Miss Caris, then on Miss Lister, as each of them refused to sleep with her because she would not take part in their whispering. They decided that Emily Brontë was boring.

It was now Charlotte's turn to provoke the rows of girls with Miss Mangnall's *Questions*.

'What part of Europe was first civilized?'

'Athens; where Cecrops landed with Egyptian colonizers, and introduced order and harmony among the original inhabitants.'

'How did Theseus further promote his country's benefit?'

'He divided Athenians into three classes: nobility, trades-men and husbandmen . . .'

At long last, having Emily imprisoned behind a bench below her eye, she was able to bully her into learning the proper answer to, 'What is the use of common oil?'

'Its use in dressing wool, skins, thickening pitch, and preparing soap, is well known, and the inhabitants of the Pole find it extremely serviceable in enlightening their gloomy regions, six months in the year,' Emily answered.

You might have told that her spirit was weakening, sickening.

Excepting a method of exercising and controlling other young minds when they themselves became governesses, what had been learnt – other than arbitrary facts which were unlikely to be of use again, and if they were, were not likely to be recalled? Charlotte would catch Emily's eye mocking her for the stupidity of this exercise. Unable to laugh with her, Charlotte would blush, then become angry with one of the other girls; preferably one of those who tormented Emily. Being unjustified, Charlotte's ill temper was the greater.

Before August was out, her petulance and rages alienated Emily even though she herself had no fondness for her fellow pupils. Once, because Miss Lister could not grasp the difference between a substantive and an article, Charlotte cracked her head against the water pump. It was during the 'play hour' following the lesson; for Charlotte was still in a temper. She had meant, she claimed, merely to douse her victim, but – demonstrating the same inaccuracy that had made her conspicuous when playing ball – she caught Miss Lister's head on the iron spout.

Fortunately, Charlotte did not often show her anger so violently. As a rule she taught conscientiously. But sometimes she expressed her frustration outright to Emily.

'Fat-headed oafs!'

This was Charlotte's main subject of conversation when the sisters were able to spend time together, strolling across the fields, to or from church, or when taking a turn around the Roe Head grounds during the summer evenings.

'Dolts!' Charlotte would exclaim, slapping her tiny gloved hand on her prayer-book.

The greatest shock of all for Emily was to find that her sister was ceasing to be an intimate friend. When she talked only about the irritations of her own existence, how could Gondal and Angria be discussed?

'Miss Brontë, are you not going to eat your dinner *at all*?'

She had been picking at it for half an hour, until it had gone cold.

She had recently developed a persistent cough, and, it seemed, a mouthful of food made it instantly worse. She had behaved the same way on the previous day.

There was nothing maudlin about her resolve not to eat. There was a toughness in Emily which made her accept the inevitable. She had read of Indians and Ashantees possessed of such courage, and such philosophy, that when they knew their time had come they would silently await their ends. She had read of shamans and great kings who, in their final sicknesses, disposed of their worldly goods, then sat cross-legged upon the ground to await their fates. Such stories had meant less to Brannii, Tallii, and Annii, who had not seen how reconciliation to the inevitable was compatible with passion. Emily grasped that a calm reconciliation was the sign of having lived passionately; in fact, of having lived at all. She would rather die than mould herself to worldly circumstance and thereby be estranged from her inner world.

Delightful walks were part of the curriculum. They could go to Robin Hood's grave, not more than a mile's distance. They could stroll along the lip of the Calder Valley – marvellous views. On the far side hung meadows and copses. Most of the girls went, and Charlotte often took charge.

Emily could not be persuaded to take part. She would grimace, make an excuse, or openly refuse – she who loved walking. They came back with their mouths smeared with whinberries, with flushes on their cheeks, and their arms loaded with wild flowers. Emily remained uninterested.

Yet, as the hills daily grew a deeper purple with flowering heather, she often threw searching glances over them.

During these refusals to join in the life of Roe Head, Charlotte tried an appeal to duty, which had worked so well as a spur to herself.

'Please pull yourself together! We *have* to prepare for our work as teachers or governesses. With Brannii going to the Royal Academy, we must not be a burden on Papa.'

'Branwell hasn't gained entrance yet. He's still painting in our room.'

'But he will go.'

'He might.'

Emily was impervious to the calls of duty. Emily was stubbornly Emily.

Actually, she was thin-skinned: more than others she felt the need to defend herself.

Once it had got into Charlotte's mind to worry, she saw more to worry about. She noticed how pale she was, and her drawn face, and that she had lost weight, that she was breathless, and that her cough did not ease. The girls complained that she kept them awake at night with her coughing.

Her decline was like Maria's at Cowan Bridge.

Miss Wooler did not grasp its seriousness. Or she did not want to. How could she miss it? Charlotte thought, now that she herself had seen it.

'You must remember that you, too, pined when you first came here,' Miss Wooler said. 'Look what an excellent recovery you made. I'm sure Emily has determination and integrity, too. You can see it in her character.'

'Miss Wooler, you do not know what ails her!'

'Then what does ail her?'

Charlotte remembered Emily's glances out of the window.

'She misses her home.'

'So do all the girls! Sooner or later it is the common human lot, if we are to get on.'

'She misses it more than most do.'

'The more necessary it is for her to get over it.'

'Miss Wooler! Please! I think Emily's decline threatens to turn into a consumption if she stays away from home. I have written to Papa and he believes so, too!'

In October, the gig came to fetch Emily. It brought Anne to replace her.

When Emily dismounted in Haworth, the worse for a twenty-mile ride in an open gig, 'Oh my God, what have they done to you!' exclaimed Aunt Branwell. 'You look as though you can't stand. Where's the flesh gone from your bones? Come in, child, out of the wind. What a state to be in to face the winter . . .'

She hustled her off to her room; not Emily's room – Aunt Branwell's.

'I want my own room!' Emily cried.

'It's nowhere near warm enough whilst you are ill, child. Branwell hardly ever heats it. When you're better, we'll see.'

'I want my room!' Emily repeated as she clutched the banister, bent over, and coughed.

'Branwell needs it. It won't be for very long.'

'*I* need it.'

Branwell was nowhere to be seen – he was skulking.

'Where's Papa?'

'He's at the Sunday school in Stanbury.'

'How's Tabby?'

'Getting older. Aren't we all?'

Emily made to go to her room but her aunt, with a surge of strength that Emily did not know she possessed, pulled her away.

'Be sensible! It's chilly and dusty in there, for Branwell never lets the servants in. Your bed is made up in my room and there's a good fire ready for you. I'll bring you up some broth. Have a rest, and then we'll see.'

Emily gave in. She was weary. She was weak.

CHARLOTTE

I

Charlotte wished to be smothered in piety. Thus she would escape self-doubt.

Spiritual turbulence was part of the atmosphere these days. There were Baptists, Congregationalists and Methodists of Calvinist, Arminian, and Primitive persuasions: Moravians and Swedenborgians. At Mirfield, Charlotte saw, forming queues outside chapels and churches, the strangers come in to 'weave be steam' in the factories, their accents as strange as some of their religions. It was they who mostly provoked this air of religious unrest which Charlotte felt all about her, and of which she, in her way, was part.

Because of Papa's connection with the district, at Roe Head Charlotte was swamped with clergymen friends and advisers. Among them she was still looking for the Marquis of Douro: a man of moral stature; a last hope of someone to save her from that wicked creation who sprang into their lives on the day when Branwell, with Leyland's sculpture of Satan in his mind, transformed her earlier Douro into Zamorna and a philanderer.

If her fantasy could be good, she would be able to keep it. She could have her cake as well as eat it.

In his vicarage, she talked to the Reverend Maude, the Mirfield incumbent. She found him stretched out on a couch, nursing his spine crippled by a riding accident, and fuelling, with introspective broodings, a burning ambition to combat

Dissension. He was a good-looking man with a broad brow, strong features, and small, shrewd eyes. Charlotte especially liked his intensity. It was terrible that he was crippled.

On being shown into the book-darkened study, she found herself wringing her hands, and it struck her that she was approaching him in the spirit of a papist to her confessor.

Charlotte spoke quietly about her desire to feel her religion in her heart, and about her temptations of thought – not, thank goodness, of deed. She confessed her doubts about the power of her church to satisfy her needs. It took her ten minutes to go into the details and, afterwards, she could not remember what she had said. She was surprised at how it had burst from her.

Meanwhile he scrutinized her with his metallic eyes. No doubt, Charlotte thought, he is wondering what this small, plain, dumpy, frumpish woman is doing here. He also seemed amused – at a woman talking thus, she supposed.

'Most distressed parishioners come to see me to complain about their neighbours,' he said.

'Some of us have deeper concerns,' she answered, more sharply than she had intended.

'Your father is Evangelical?'

'As are most clergymen, I find, who care for their flocks.'

'All I meant was that he must give you a great deal to look up to. I see that you are a young lady who speaks her mind. Equally, you could be tempted into fruitless enquiries. I can tell that you are well read. Ooh! My back! Tell me what you think we should do about dissent and sectarianism.'

'Announce the truth loud and clear, I suppose, as Christ did.'

'I think that we should build a new church.'

'Mirfield Church was rebuilt only ten years ago!'

Mr Maude almost rose from his seat – leaning on the stick that he used for hobbling across the room to find a book, or to bang on the floorboards when a bell did not suffice to call his servant.

'Demolish it! Build a really fine one!' He banged his stick. 'We have the best site in town on top of this hill but it is surrounded by as many enemies as it was when it was a camp of ancient Britons! Employ the finest architect in the country! Many of our manufacturers would subscribe to a spectacle that would draw in the working population . . .'

Charlotte realized that she was wasting her time in talking to a fanatic. When his housekeeper fussed in, she was glad to leave.

She turned next to Ellen Nussey's brother, Henry, now acting as curate to the Vicar of Birstall.

When she wrote to him, she found herself in the same dilemma as with other clergymen: she could explain herself at length – at too great a length – but still not confess that the source of her anxieties was in the wickedness of her secret writings.

He paid her a visit in the teachers' sitting-room at Roe Head. Only the two of them were present.

'How very feminine and pretty it is here!' Nussey chuckled.

She realized that in the teachers' room a full-blooded man could hardly move without being in danger of breaking or upsetting something – a table with delicate legs, or that vase of wild flowers which he must guess was hers. The personality of each 'spinster' created an aura around every chair; the cushions of this one, the lace-making and bobbins of another, the stack of books by her own. The room made him feel as uncomfortable as an elephant. At least, that was what he looked like. She saw that he despised it. No doubt he thinks we all spend our time in here dreaming and gossiping of how to capture husbands, she thought.

After the maid had shown him in, Charlotte did not rise from her rocking chair; which was a child's chair, no other adult could have fitted into it. It was difficult for her to rise because, apart from the lowness of the chair, she had sewing spread across her lap. She had developed a housewifely habit of stitching whilst she conversed, and with spectacles on her nose, she was picking at the burst seams of a dress.

'I am sure this room must seem spinsterish to you,' she said, and smiled, peering over her spectacles. 'To make matters worse, you must forgive me for continuing with my tasks. Miss Wooler expects me to repair this for Miss Marriott. Please be seated, Mr Nussey.'

Despite all, Charlotte's domesticity clearly gave Nussey a

sense of well-being. When he had taken a chair (closer than she liked), she could tell of his pleasure by the way he made himself at home, stretching his leg on a footstool and letting out a deep, manly sigh; his great boots only just clear of the embroidered top of the stool. She had noticed before that men swelled with confidence when a woman was doing what she 'should' be doing; although Nussey appeared to be without need of bolstering, for he was large, tall and vigorous. She guessed that he would take his ease in any circumstances. He was made to look for a comfortable life.

But Charlotte was happy enough to have him there. She was excited by large men. They were both terrifying and comforting, to one so tiny. In their power to crush, or to shelter her, they were like God.

She had told the maid to provide spice cake and tea, and the servant came in with refreshment. The maid having left, Charlotte took further calm peeps at Mr Nussey over her sewing. She did not like the way he allowed the crumbs to collect on his whiskers. He slurped his tea. She thought it was gross.

His eyes were on her stack of books. The one on top was in French; the spine of another showed it to be the poems of Lord Byron. She knew what his thoughts would be. He would be thinking that, among such improper literature, her concern for her soul could not be as serious as all that, though she had dragged him here on a pastoral errand.

After he had swallowed two slices of cake, he brushed his fingers together, scattering crumbs on the carpet, then he referred to her letter, and advised her to put aside her doubts because, 'The good may confidently look forward to their Heavenly estate.'

She could tell that he had been talking to the Reverend Allbutt: a Calvinist, who had arrived to be Vicar of Dewsbury. Henry Nussey meant to convince her that she was one of the Elect. He did not know how often a threatening figure like that of Carus Wilson, tall, black, with the little white tie crossed at the neck, rose up in a 'daymare' to tell her otherwise.

'And some are damned whatever they do,' Charlotte whispered.

This thought touched a deep chord in her and she rocked

her chair vigorously, keeping her eyes close to her sewing, so that her spine was curved in a semi-circle, like a curled-up grub.

'Yes.'

Mr Nussey seemed insensitive to how it cut his little victim. It had perhaps not occurred to him how seriously his sister's friend could think herself damned. His smile did not fade. He looked confidently at Charlotte's bent head, not at her shaking hands.

'But how does one know who is saved and who is not?' Charlotte asked, a frown on her brow, her head still bent to hide her fear of his questioning about what *really* caused her hands to shake.

'Through inner conviction. God predestines for Heaven those of whom He has foreknowledge of their goodness. In the words of St Paul: "Those whom He predestined He also called; those whom He called He also justified; those whom He justified He also glorified." Romans, Chapter eight. One knows whether or not one is justified, because one's works are self-evidently good,' and he looked around as if for more spice cake. He really was dreadfully pompous.

'No,' Charlotte contradicted, quietly, and boldly lifted her head to look at him.

The chair he had taken had indeed been too close: from it he put out an affectionate hand, which she repulsed.

'I know that *my* works are good,' Nussey said. 'And I know that yours are, too.'

'Do you?'

'Of course they are! You teach, you look after your father and your sisters and brother. You work as a teacher so as not to be a burden. You spread only goodness all around you. Even now you are sewing and not wasting *all* your time in silly prattle with a visiting parson! You cannot imagine how often my sister talks about you; she thinks you have changed her life. You are a shining light to all, dear Charlotte. That is the test.'

'And not what is in one's heart?'

'My dear, one cannot do good in the world without a good heart to direct it. It is natural that doubts should come but, if one's works are manifestly good, be confident that it is proof that one must, *per se*, possess a good heart. That is evidence that one cannot be a reprobate.'

'Mr Nussey!' she imagined herself declaring. 'My good works cramp my soul and are leading me to a commonplace future which I cannot bear to think of. In my heart burn longings that could set fire to the world – yet they would be the expression of a wickedness that would consign me to Hell. They are not the ordinary sinful feelings of a young girl, Mr Nussey. They would make you afraid for my soul! But even if I could always suppress them – as I am doing for the present, with what difficulty a man of your temperament and limitations would never be able to understand – my fear is that, in still not being able to prevent their continuing birth in my heart, I am condemned to eternal fires. Oh, Mr Nussey! What have I, a poor, weak female, been put on this earth for, if I am only to suffer the torments of the damned for ever merely because of the way I was born?'

She forgot where she was. When she came to, she was tempted to speak her thoughts, but pulled herself together.

'If one is unsure of the heart, then set it to the wheel, Miss Brontë. Redouble the good works.'

'I try to do so, Mr Nussey.'

'But you *still* look doubtful.'

'Yes. The fiery pit is such an awful fate. For *eternity*!'

Charlotte crumpled over her sewing and wept. Henry looked uncomfortable.

'I do not think I understand you, Miss Brontë.'

'No, I don't suppose you do.'

She's already on the way to being an eccentric old spinster, if someone does not take her up and marry her, Henry Nussey thought as he left – rocking on her chair, *tee hee*ing to herself: the plain little woman.

Nonetheless, he was finding this weak little creature, who had the smallest hands and feet he had ever come across, quite attractive. Her response to his statement: 'I do not think I understand you, Miss Brontë,' continued to rankle: he had meant that he'd discovered that he'd *like* to understand her. Was she too insensitive to take a hint?

II

Charlotte and Anne returned to Haworth at Christmas. Papa and Aunt Branwell greeted them as adults, acknowledging that they had stepped into the world. Emily rushed out sure that they were as relieved to be in Haworth as she would be. Branwell was girdled in an artist's smock, his hair tousled, ready to help Tabby unload the gig. In the parsonage, a smell of oil paint was perceptible as, on certain days, the smell of baking was, or wax polish, or, in wet and gloomy periods, that of damp dog.

'We are to have our own room back over Christmas!' Emily told Charlotte. 'Branwell and Papa have moved our bed out again. Anne can sleep with Aunt.'

'I know,' Charlotte answered. 'I wrote to Papa about it and insisted.'

Branwell was still using their room, though. He had not yet gone to the Royal Academy because he had learned that, to satisfy the entrance requirements, he needed a portfolio of 'drawings from the antique' and he had not studied this with Mr Bradley, who possessed urns, drapes, and potted palms, but no plaster casts.

Charlotte had to go and inspect immediately. There were portraits of churchwardens and church trustees and their families; also 'low life' studies made up from sketches done in the pub; and friends. 'I am painting John Brown for the Masonic Lodge,' Branwell announced.

'Not posing in our room, I hope?' Charlotte said.

'There was nothing of yours here that is private.'

'*Papa!*' she appealed.

'Well, it will be different now,' Papa said – bashful, as if not sure he had done the right thing. Not knowing what further to say to his prickly daughter, he said: 'Branwell gets so absorbed, sometimes he does not come down for meals.'

'No doubt it is a great nuisance to Tabby.'

The canvases did show an increase in skill from the stiff, earlier portrait of his sisters. Charlotte knew from letters that her father, his finances relieved by her labours, had at last invested in lessons from William Robinson in Leeds and Branwell went there for a few days every week, staying over. It had worked wonders. Also, in Halifax he had met the district's most charismatic sculptor – Joseph Bentley Leyland, whose 'Satan' had almost thrown him into a fit once.

Charlotte was envious. Branwell's paints and brushes were scattered about. In the corner was a pair of plaster feet, damaged in the toes. 'Casts of Michelangelo's *David*,' he said. 'Leyland gave them to me.' On the chest of drawers which held their clothes she saw an open portfolio of engravings of London. The view across the Thames, with the ships' sails, then the boulevard filled with carriages, then the columns of Somerset House, all executed in high-toned, pale yellow tints, was as ethereal as the pictures by Joseph Martin that had inspired Glasstown when they were small children. Yet she knew that this London was a real place, two hundred miles away, which Branwell would go to but which she, she assumed, would never visit.

He had not only occupied her bedroom. He had the very male confidence to permeate the whole parsonage with a sense of his vocation. The smell of paint was everywhere. Envy crept into her, like a sense of sin; coiling through the shadows of her self like a snake.

He was writing, too. In Angria, Northangerland/Percy had committed parricide in order to inherit his father's fortune and spend it on his destructive passion, his wife, Augusta di Segovia.

'. . . thou knowest how I love thee . . . rather let me live an hour of Heaven here in the arms of one with whom I sacrifice all hope of it hereafter . . . I am Alexander Percy who thinks that years with thee are bought cheaply by Eternity.'

The passion and wickedness quite took Charlotte's breath away when Emily read it to her, in their horribly disembowelled room that night. *Why not me . . . why not me . . . why not me?*

Before the Christmas holiday was over, 'There is something I must talk about with you,' she said to Papa.

He led her into his study. He motioned her to the chair she liked best, by the fire. She loved the fatherly atmosphere of the room, the shelves of books, the smell of tobacco, and a good fire always burning.

'Papa, I would like to be an author.'

'An author?' He laughed. 'Are you not all little authors already?'

'I mean I would like to dedicate myself to it. I dread spending my life as a governess.'

'Oh.' He fell into deep thought. Lost for words, he removed his spectacles and then replaced them.

'I am finding that the light hurts my eyes these days,' he said. He seemed about to speak again, but merely sighed and fell back into his thoughts.

After a further couple of minutes, he said, 'I used to wish to be an author.'

'I know, Papa.'

His 'The Rural Minstrel' and 'Cottage Poems' were not as she envisaged her own work being. His was not dangerous. Nonetheless she grew optimistic and her expression brightened. She waited. Another minute passed. She had not taken her eyes off him.

'One is more likely to ruin one's eyes than to succeed,' he continued.

She waited for more ... for encouragement ... for the sentence beginning, 'However –' He sighed again and said, 'The imagination can be treacherous. It can seduce. It can poison the soul.'

'That is just what I am afraid of. Yet I cannot resist it!' Her tears were near the surface again.

'You must.' He tried to smile. Having been at this point himself, he must know how she felt.

'Charlotte, the raising of a church rate is opposed by the Dissenters. We now have Primitive Methodists refusing to pay. We are left with only ten pounds to keep the church in repair and pay the salaries of the clerks for the year. These parish wars are raging all over England – it is a calamitous attempt to disestablish the Anglican Church. Suppose my eyesight should weaken further? Your abilities to earn your livings are very important in these insecure times.' He smiled. 'For the time being, the future depends upon you, Charlotte. Duty is more important than passion and imagination.'

'I believe so,' she agreed, but did not mean it.

He seemed relieved that she did not show her need for

comfort; no weakness. But she kept it inside only by clawing at her palms with her nails.

'The sensual novelist is a being of depraved appetite and sick imagination,' he continued, more animatedly. 'Having learnt to torment himself, he creates an imaginary world which he cannot inhabit. He only makes the real world unbearable.'

'Branwell is given every opportunity!'

Papa smiled indulgently and said, 'Charlotte, I rely upon you to be a pillar of security, a little mother to our family.'

'I know.'

'If Branwell is not encouraged, I don't know what might happen to him, and us. I so much fear his drifting into bad company – which would be from an adventurous spirit, not any bad motive. I worry about it often. The fear of Judgement does not frighten him, it makes him worse: I think, in order to escape his fear.

'Charlotte, he has not been drinking for some time. Haven't you noticed how well-behaved he has been over Christmas? He swears never to drink again. Let us hope so, before alcohol takes a grip. Where censure fails, encouragement and sympathy might not. For Branwell to succeed in a career would be the best of all for us, would it not? There is plenty of demand hereabouts for portrait artists.'

While he was speaking, she kept thinking of how Percy/Northangerland had murdered his father.

She left the study sure that Roe Head, and then another Roe Head, was to be her fate. During the following days she took walks, alone, to think about it.

One day she came home to see burned paper in the kitchen grate. She poked at it. Her father had burned the copies of the *Ladies Magazine* that had belonged to her mother, and that had been so long by her bed.

That felt like murder, too.

'Why, Papa, *why*?'

'I did not think that they were healthy. They were full of foolish love stories.'

Before making her return to Roe Head, she wrote a poem. She confessed her blasphemy in making an idol of Douro/Zamorna, then she said goodbye in verse to her Angrian creations, one by one.

III

Charlotte was back at Roe Head. Ellen's Calvinism helped in her willed damming-up of Angria – but the dam was continually breached.

By now, Charlotte had grown patronizing towards her friend. She told Ellen what she could read in order to improve herself:

> You ask me to recommend some books for your perusal ... If you like poetry let it be first rate, Milton, Shakespeare, Thomson, Goldsmith, Pope (if you will though I don't admire him), Scott, Byron, Campbell, Wordsworth and Southey.

Then she inadvertently gave a glimpse of her sense of wickedness and shame.

> Now Ellen don't be startled at the names of Shakespeare and Byron. Both these were great men and their works are like themselves. You will know how to choose the good and avoid the evil, the finest passages are always the purest, the bad are invariably revolting, you will not wish to read them over twice.

Ellen *encouraged* Charlotte to be intellectually haughty. It happened by degrees, through hints, questions and the raising of doubts. It was clear that dependency satisfied something in Ellen's nature.

Before long, she was prodding Charlotte into criticizing her piety. The Calvinists had got all Birstall worrying about themselves, and it was ironical that Ellen should approach the anguished Charlotte Brontë for consolation.

Charlotte put her off:

> In your last you request me to tell you of your faults and to cease flattering you. Now really Ellen how can you

253

be so foolish. I won't tell you of your faults, because I
don't know them ... Oh, Ellen, how I wish my own
feelings more resembled yours!

Then Charlotte plunged into confession.

> But I am *not like you*. If you knew my thoughts; the
> dreams that absorb me; and the fiery imagination that
> at times eats me up and makes me feel Society as it is,
> wretchedly insipid, you would pity me and I dare say
> despise me. But Ellen I know the treasures of the Bible
> I love and adore them I can *see* the Well of Life in all
> its clearness and brightness; but when I stoop down to
> drink of the pure waters they fly from my lips as if I
> were Tantalus ...
>
> I keep trying to do right – but still – every instant I
> find myself going astray – I abhor myself – I despise
> myself – if the Doctrine of Calvin be true I am already
> an outcast – don't desert me – don't be horrified at
> me, you know what I am – I wish I could see you,
> my darling, I have lavished the warmest of affections
> of a very hot, tenacious heart upon you – if you grow
> cold – it's over –

Charlotte went back to beloved Haworth. It seemed an escape
from her dependency on Ellen – who believed herself to be
dependent on Charlotte.

Wasn't it all a sickness, this sisterhood in Calvin; a
poisonous plant flourishing in that shadow which was her
loneliness?

It was only an escape for a short time. The summer weeks
passed and Charlotte returned to Roe Head lacerated with
memories – less of moors and streams than of Branwell's
and Emily's enviable creative freedoms.

Emily had written Gondal poetry. It consisted largely of
descriptions of nature, and Charlotte envied the tranquillity
of her verse. Out of what did it spring?

Branwell had developed Angrian politics. There was
civil war: the monarchist Angrians had broken away from
Verdopolis, the capital. The upshot was that Douro/Zamorna

was defeated (*defeated!*), captured and exiled by Northanger-land; his son, Edward, being blinded and put to death, like King Lear's son.

'*You cannot do that, Brannii!*' Charlotte had exclaimed.

'The plot demands it,' he answered.

The only outlet left for Douro then was to break North-angerland's heart, but it was at the price of breaking his own. Douro was married to Northangerland's daughter, Mary. He divorced her, banishing her to Alnwick Castle, although he loved her. There she would die of grief. This made a great tragedy: but Douro's action was devious. It was not the manly, straightforward way in which Charlotte's hero should act.

She returned to Roe Head brokenhearted and in a state of mourning.

She sat in the bay of the Roe Head window, wearily facing half a dozen girls. She was exhausted by her futile task, by her mourning at the passing of Douro's manly spirit, and by anxiety for her own soul, still dwelling on her hero's un-Christian passions. The girls were dallying with an exercise on a point of French grammar that she had been struggling to drive home all afternoon. Sometimes their heads were not bowed to their work until she caught their eyes, whereupon they pretended to be engrossed. She knew that their exercise books, when she gathered them in, would not flatter her teaching: she had not explained well and she felt guilty.

Some months before, it would have been with visions of the Marquis that she would have consoled herself, but now her inner world was tainted. Douro was not all he should be, and anyway her phantoms were wicked.

Today, it was pious Ellen Nussey whom she saw so palpably.

ANNE

I

When Anne was living at home, before Emily returned abruptly from Roe Head, her relationship with her father had deepened. 'My dear little Anne, my baby,' he called her. They took strolls through the village and over the common; dignified walks, not wild scrambles. She would listen patiently while he chatted with parishioners. She appeared to lean on his arm, but in truth was guiding him around obstacles.

'When I look towards the light, all I see is a mist,' he said.

'We are like Lear and Cordelia,' she remarked.

He smiled down at her, forgiving her for reminding him that he was old. He was sixty. His hair was white and receding. With his height and his gaunt face, he was like a blinded hawk.

'Except that *all* my daughters are good ones.'

'Thank you, Papa.'

'But it is true! Whenever I am tempted to dwell on our losses, I remind myself of God's gift.'

They had circuited the village and had climbed back half-way up the hill. Women, gathered with buckets and washing at the well, were just out of hearing, thank goodness, when Mr Winterbotham, the Baptist minister, blocked their way. Papa was breathless from the climb; Mr Winterbotham was in possession of his wind because he was coming downhill. He was able to bawl at them, in the Haworth manner.

'By all accounts, thy son in the Black Bull has given them a fine description of London, Mr Bron-*teh*! He told them what was in every street. Described St Paul's Cathedral, and the coffee-houses where the clever folk meet. He told them that the Royal Academy didn't suit him the same as Haworth did, and the watter wasn't as sweet, either. There's nowhere like Haworth, is there, Mr Bron-*teh*!'

Anne wondered how Papa was going to get round either having to lie, or give away the fact that Branwell only knew about London from engravings. He had been no further than Mr Robinson's studio in Leeds, and next had been hanging around with the portrait painters of Bradford, in the region of Fountain Street, where forty of them had gathered in hope of picking up commissions from merchants at the Wool Exchange.

In the event, Patrick did not have to answer. He needed

to get his breath back first, and Mr Winterbotham was too set on contention to wait.

'Thou must be alarmed at the hours thy son spends in public houses!'

Mr Winterbotham was one of those who had seemed already old when young, but would still seem young when old; an unchanging look, very different from Mr Brontë's experienced-looking face. Although Winterbotham was also plebeian, unlike Patrick Brontë he had not transcended that by acquiring a conventional education, only a haphazard one, noticeable for its gaps, mistaken ideas, and the forcefulness of his prejudices. It was partly through comparing the two pastors that people remarked, 'Mr Brontë is a natural gentleman.'

Patrick always treated the Baptist condescendingly, and he was certainly not going to share his worries about his son.

'It is only his instinct for conviviality. We are all merely travellers between darkness and darkness, looking for joy on our way, Mr Winterbottom,' Mr Brontë intoned, perfect as Moses.

His calling the Baptist 'Winterbottom', in his soft, Irish way, cut Mr Winterbotham to the quick.

'Thou knows the way that William Grimshaw's son went!' Mr Winterbotham warned. He flushed, and wagged his finger as if in his pulpit. 'Thou knows what he said of himself when he inherited his father's horse? "Once it carried a saint, now it carries a devil."'

'Mr Winterbottom, you overstate your case. My son is studying for an honourable profession that has brought fame and fortune to many.'

As Anne and her father ended what should have been a delightful September walk, Anne knew that her brother's weakness dragged at Papa's days. He could no longer delight in nature because of this weight on his mind, though he would never confess it.

Anne sat with her aunt in her room, turning the cuffs of one of Papa's shirts.

Anne, who had trembled while saying her prayers because she had been thinking of Branwell's soul burning through eternity, could not help speaking of the direction in which her brother was heading.

Aunt Branwell answered, 'I am worried too, of course. But a young man has to go forth and sow his wild oats, otherwise he will never grow up.'

'And why is that not true of a girl?'

'What a silly question! Because she is a frail creature who should be looking for a husband to shelter her, one whom she will make happy in his home. She doesn't need to go into the world and take risks. She will take enough just through becoming a wife. Now thread me another white silk, and we can add a piece to Papa's cravat while we have our needles out.'

Anne bit off a two-foot length of thread, sucked the end to a point, held a needle up to the light and squinted through the eye.

'My sisters and I envy boys and men. Tallii envies them for the careers they follow. So do I. I cannot see why only men may be authors and doctors. Emily envies them for the physical things. Nobody questions it when Brannii rambles all day, do they?'

'*Anne!*'

But 'shy little Anne' could be persistent and – unlike Charlotte – stay calm.

'As for us girls being "frail" – boys do not seem to *me* to be born more able to withstand temptation, and it is cruel to think you must put their souls at greater risk. I think the dangers are as great for a boy as for a girl.'

'The things you say!'

They stitched a little longer.

'When I was coming out of church, they were talking about "Lucky Luke",' Anne said.

'What about him?'

'He lives on the moors in a shack by himself. He is dressed in rags tied about him with rope. No-one knows what he eats, but he distills his own whisky, and no-one goes near because he curses them. They say that once he used to go to chapel every day of the week, and was smartly dressed and proud. Then his wife died, his daughter was taken by cholera, his son emigrated, and he turned into a reprobate.'

'That explains it, then.'

'Papa's wife and two daughters died but he did not become a reprobate.'

'Papa is a clergyman!'

'I have heard of clergymen, too, going to the Devil. I think that something terrible can happen to anyone. Whether man or woman, clergyman or not, all can break. I do not think that men are so strong that in youth, if they live indecent lives, they should be condoned or excused. And, having said that, it also seems to me, Aunt –' Anne felt terribly brave '– that God is cruelly eager to consign us to an eternal fate merely because of the human weaknesses He has endowed us with.'

The night that Anne dreamed of Branwell with his flesh and clothes on fire in Hell, and crying for help, it sent her off on a trip to Ponden Hall.

It was a sunny autumn day and the avenue at Ponden was turning gold and orange, as were the banks of dried grasses on the moor below the belts of purple heather.

She picked her way through the farmyard and the garden where bees and red admiral butterflies danced over the Michaelmas daisies.

'Thy brother's takken his gun on ter th'tops,' she was told. 'He's gone off wi' Robert Heaton. They've heard tell of a flock of plover that's come this way.'

'It doesn't matter, I'm not looking for him,' she answered, in her soft voice.

She went into the 'house'. The indoor servants also asked if she was seeking her brother. It was assumed that she was here because she had been sent on an errand on his behalf.

'No,' she said. 'I want to speak to old Mr Heaton.'

Mr Heaton was wearing hat, gaiters, and boots, as he would do even when sitting down for a meal if there was no special company. He tilted his hat and scratched at his thin hair, a smile of curiosity on his face as if to say: *What does the parson's daughter want o' me this time? I'll bet I know.* If those were his thoughts, he was correct.

'Mr Heaton, may I sit in your library for an hour or so?'

'A dose o' this sunshine'd do thee more good, my lass, but thou can sit i' the library if thou likes.'

'Thank you, Mr Heaton.'

'I haven't none o' them fashionable novels!'

He was teasing her, and she smiled back. He led up the narrow stairs and unlocked the precious door.

'Why doesn't thy aunt set thee on to go to a ball or two? It'd do a lass more good than studying like she were a lad.'

She loved it when she could shut the door and follow her bent without check. Already breathing heavily because of the dust, she carried books to a seat by an open window. Outside a robin and a lark were singing. All the noises were lustful, occupied with immediate, practical problems. Someone was trying to reverse a horse and cart into a gateway. There came in a smell of sheep and an oily smell of wefts. Anne closed the window, the better to concentrate.

She was not drawn, as Emily was, to Mr Heaton's First Folio Shakespeare and his Jacobean dramatists, nor, as Charlotte would have been, to Chateaubriand and the classical French authors, nor as Branwell to the classical writers. She wanted an answer to the question: Was Calvin right? There was no point in seeking salvation if his behaviour was merely the symptom of his already being 'reprobated'. The books gave off a dry odour of old leather, and the dust irritated her eyes so that she rubbed at them. It prickled her nose so that she sneezed.

The sunlight inched across the window casing. As the morning went by, she breathed more slowly, heavily and noisily. She hoped that the asthma attack would hold off. What kept her going was that, as she followed clues through indexes and chapter headings, she felt a quiet, inner excitement.

She found pamphlets dealing with the Moravians, then the Universalists. *God was ultimately reconciled to all human beings, and would be reconciled even to the Devil and all the rebel angels.*

Everyone, after a purgatory, long or short, would be saved! *Hell was not eternal!* Hopelessness was transformed into hope. It turned Anne's limbs into a light and glowing fire.

But her chest had become a clogged and heavy sack. She brought the key downstairs, white-faced, strained, swallowing her breath in sharp gulps like a fish out of water.

They offered her herb teas and insisted on putting her in a gig to take her home. The driver kept looking round at her. 'Are't all right, miss?' he questioned as they trotted past the Taylors' manor house at the end of Stanbury. She had to take a painfully deep breath before she answered, none too certainly, 'Yes.'

At the same time as she was reviving in the clearer air, second thoughts were troubling her. Was she merely responding to an appeal to her desires, and not to her reason? It could be that she was merely convincing herself.

'Papa, what do you think of Universalism?'

He looked perturbed. 'What has made you interested in that? Unfortunately, Hell *does* exist. I am a tolerant man, but sectarian ideas can grow quite mad, before one realizes it. They can trickle into a family as the taint of peat or iron trickles into a well.'

'I was thinking about Branwell. I do not believe he would drink and carry on so if he did not fear himself already judged, by us and by God, and doomed in any case. Perhaps the public house seems his only rest from it.'

'The belief that all will be saved can *make* us reckless, rather than help us. It can be used by the Devil to seduce us into thinking that we may do as we wish. But you look dismayed.'

'It is all right. I am sure you are right.'

She realized that it did not occur to him that hers was more than an intellectual enquiry – that it came from her heart – that he had unwittingly cast her into Hell again.

'Emily must come home,' Papa had announced.

'She would lose so much by not finishing at Roe Head,' Anne had said, though thrilled at the prospect of her close companion returning.

'How would you like to take her place?'

'Of course I would like to, but it would not be right. You know her nature, how she pines, but she will never grow until she overcomes homesickness and learns to leave her childhood behind. Papa—'

'Anne?'

'You torture your mind with unnecessary guilt about us.'

'Do I? And how do you know that?'

He had looked surprised. But she was tired of being treated as 'the baby', supposedly lacking judgement. When she looked into a mirror, she saw a young *woman*, who might be thought pretty and intelligent, with a narrow face surrounded by a froth of brown curls, and bright eyes of a pale, violet-blue colour.

'I study your expressions. And next your mind tortures your body, and then your body in its turn tortures your mind. So you suffer from bad nerves, and that leads to dyspepsia, and I should not be surprised if the pain in your eyes is worsened by it. You become morbid and nothing that Aunt or I can say will convince you that matters are not as serious as you paint them.' She paused. 'I believe that it would be best for Emily to continue, much as she loves it here.'

When, nonetheless, Emily had come home and Anne was given her chance at Roe Head, Anne's relationship with Charlotte had been as difficult as Emily's. Charlotte, besides treating Anne as an infant, was as jealous as she was of Branwell and Emily. Anne felt it like a stone on her head. Their relationship as pupil and teacher drove a further wedge.

She lapsed into fulfilling Charlotte's expectations, becoming dependent, showing few ideas of her own.

The loneliness of not being able to share made her sickly. She developed a stammer. She still wrestled with religious fears that Charlotte did not realize she had. Anne was conscious of Charlotte's.

She had weighed up the anxieties of all in her family, and the links between them and their characters. Papa wanted assurance that there was purpose in his suffering. Aunt wanted justification for her sacrifice. Emily was unblushingly pagan. Branwell alternated between defiance and a craven fear of eternity; the latter usually when he was tipsy. Charlotte feared for her personal fate: her religion had a strong element of selfishness. Anne herself was looking to religion for guidance towards a happy, worthwhile life as an adult.

'I prefer good acts, as my passport to happiness in this world and Heaven in the next,' she declared. 'That seems closer to

God's will, which surely is to make mankind happy, rather than condemn it to waste itself by existing in fear.'

At Roe Head, the act that God was demanding of her was to pull her sister out of her fear of eternity.

'Suppose the doctrine of Calvin is *true*, Anne?' Charlotte, driven to speak at last, asked the same question that was on Anne's mind.

'I do not think so,' she answered. 'I am sure that any person can be saved, by an act of Grace.'

'But even if Calvin is not right, I do not think that *I* can be saved! For, no matter what I do, I *know* what is in my heart! ANNE – I AM DAMNED FOR EVER BECAUSE OF WHAT I CANNOT HELP!'

'There are those who tell us that God rejects *none* of His creation, therefore all are saved in the end. There is nothing, ultimately, to fear. Not according to Universalism.'

'But is it not a heresy?'

'I suppose it is.'

'Then it can't be true, can it?'

'No, I suppose not,' Anne gave in, weakly.

II

In May sunshine, from six in the morning until the afternoon, hundreds of poor people climbed past the Roe Head gate to converge on Hartshead Moor. Thousands would gather 'on the tops'. It was a holiday – Whit Tuesday – but in any case they had time to spare because the collapse of the wool markets had thrown them out of work. They were going to an 'anti-Poor Law' meeting because they were threatened with permanent incarceration in one of the new 'workhouses' – not, as previously, with a week or so of parish charity until they were employed again.

The sunshine, that made the factories and workshops seem more grimy, also lit up what the newspapers termed 'the desperation' of the poor. Yet they knew how to make a festivity of politics. There were mummers and musicians, while carts carried barrels of beer. Men ingrained with dirt, and factory women greasy with the oils of wefts and of machines, chanted verses by Shelley and sang 'Chartist hymns' – radical verses set to hymn tunes. The event was a hybrid of religious revivalist march, revolutionary army, and a fair on the move. Their banners were stretched across the road:

'No Bastilles.'

'Cursed be he that parteth man and wife.'

'England home and liberty local rights wholesum food no separation no bastilles.'

'The Poor Law is an opression it desgraces Christianity and makes humanity weep.'

At mid-morning, from nearly a mile away downhill at Colne Bridge, by the Three Nuns public house, there arose blasts on a trumpet blown by Feargus O'Connor. He was a wild, mad leader whose 'voice of brass' gave him the advantage on a moortop. The workers were stunted and pale, and Feargus strode before them six feet tall and barrel-chested: a figure out of Angria. Above his head, a banner scrawled in dripping red paint read: 'They that be slayn by the sword are better than they that be slayn with hunger.'

The Roe Head pupils and servants came out to watch. They were trapped against the wall in a suffocating smell of unwashed bodies and sweaty clothes. The young ladies had learned of the issues only from their parents and the Misses Wooler – their own families' employees would never have talked openly, as did some of these.

'When trade is good they still pay low wages so us canna save, and when unemployment comes it's th'workhouse wi' husbands set from wives, and children from their mothers. That's the worst o' it! Not bad food nor t'miserable work they set us on to. It is being separated from us loved ones! Thou cannot imagine it!'

'And we should have the vote! The creator o' wealth should have the vote!'

'That might lead to bloody revolution!' exclaimed Miss Lister.

The stifling crowd was soon too much for the young ladies. The fact of there being women among them, linking arms, laughing and singing, made it more, not less, alarming; for none of the females belonged to the 'respectable classes'. Perhaps they had been on the road since dawn and had walked a dozen or fifteen miles, dragging or carrying their children, yet their unspent force, fervent, cheerful and ungenteel, was shocking. Their stench and the hackings of the consumptives were the *real* smell and sound of revolution.

Once, following a meeting in Haworth addressed by Papa and Branwell, Branwell – who had left the Tory cause – had been burned in effigy by a Tory crowd. They had stuffed a sack with straw, stuck a turnip on top with a carrot for a nose and a red mop for his hair, put a potato in one hand and a couple of salted herrings in the other to insult his Irishness, and set the figure on a cart. No wonder the girls were terrified of real politics. They remembered why Papa always carried a gun, and recalled the talk of 'ferocious, desperate beasts'. Anne and Charlotte gagged and put handkerchiefs to their mouths. Charlotte took hold of Anne's hand and retreated.

'Goodness me, listen to this!' Charlotte announced, a week later, as she sat reading the *Leeds Mercury*. 'Have you ever heard such sanguinary language from a minister of the Gospel!'

'I don't know yet. You haven't read it to me.'

They sat by a fire in the sitting-room, where Charlotte was keeping Anne company because she had picked up a cough on that 'treacherous' spring day. Anne, huddled in a shawl, was frightened of an asthma attack.

Charlotte read aloud: '"They were not there to reason or to argue," saith the Reverend Stephens, "but were determined not to have the Bill. They will neither have the sting in its tail, nor the teeth in its jaws, but they would plunge a sword into its entrails, and dig a pit as deep as Hell, and out of the Whig filth, and rottenness, and detestable and damnable doctrines and practices, they would tumble it all into the pit." '

'No, that is not the language of the Sermon on the Mount.'

Charlotte peered over her spectacles. 'It is that of Revelations and of the Apocalypse. It is the terrifying voice of the masses!'

'What did Mr O'Connor . . . Eee-gh! eee-e-gh! ch—ck!' Anne buried her face in her shawl.

'Listen to this! "Sooner than suffer his wife or child to be torn from him, he would plunge a dagger into the heart of the man who attempted it"! I can understand Mr Stephens' passion, but . . .' Charlotte rustled the newspaper angrily. She sighed and adjusted her spectacles. 'I wonder what our radical Mary Taylor would make of it, were she here. Seven resolutions were embodied in a petition to both houses of parliament. Just look!'

'*You* have the newspaper!' Anne lifted her shining, watery eyes to the sister who never listened.

'*Poor Law!*' Charlotte exclaimed, scornfully. 'It was as much about universal suffrage! *Universal suffrage!* And about abusing their betters.'

'What did Mr O'Connor say?'

'Mr O'Connor, Mr O'Connor . . . Mr F. O'Connor . . . here we are. "Mr F. O'Connor was received with great cheering. He set out to prove that the New Poor Law Act was unconstitutional. He then proceeded to comment on the conduct of the aristocracy, who, he said, repaired to the Continent forgetting the country in which they had extracted their possessions, and afterwards returned with a piece of French cambric in one pocket, and a silver snuff box in another, and a pair of French boots on . . ." What a literary style these people have.' Charlotte pulled a face. 'All of this wretched stuff amused the crowd, apparently. "Great laughter", as the *Mercury* puts it . . .'

'Eegh . . . eegh . . . eegh . . . e.e.e.e.gh!' returned Anne.

How could Anne explain that her terror of revolution had evaporated on seeing these people with their hungry children; people with matters more pressing than the states of their souls; the passion of their lives not for fantasies, but to express their real wrongs, even though they be hanged for it?

III

It was not guilt at the wickedness of Gondal and Angria that most disturbed Anne (though there was that, too), so much as their false view of life and love. Love was not the passions of Douro, nor Angria's and Gondal's frissons of ambition and betrayal. It was what Papa had experienced: having children, educating them, and struggling with poverty. While Charlotte and Emily longed to indulge their fantasies at home, Anne wanted to express herself in the real world. She *wanted* to be a teacher, a governess.

When Anne made drawings, they were in timid, faint pencil lines. She covered them with her hand if anyone came near. They were at the foot of the verses she had composed when strolling the woodlands, and she made several during the summer holiday at Haworth, where she was both happy and unhappy, in a strange mingling. She 'doodled' again back at Roe Head.

While Charlotte portrayed handsome but androgynous heroes, or fantastically elegant ladies (sometimes with dripping talons), Anne drew cherubs. They were after Veronese and Rubens. She copied so many that she could do them without looking. Pairs floated among clouds. They gambolled among flowers. They were curly-haired and had pouting lips. She coloured them, the lips and cheeks bright red. Only some were winged.

Emily and Branwell did not seem to give a thought to Anne's scribbles, and Charlotte still took little interest in anything that Anne did. But at Roe Head, Charlotte, being a teacher, had to comment. It was very curious: though Anne sometimes openly doodled on the exercise paper that was handed in, yet when she was surprised doing it, her hand trembled.

'Anne, why do you draw babies?'

When she did not answer, Charlotte continued to stare. That cat-like stare. Anne did not feel such a need for baffled scrutiny. She felt that she understood people, whereas Charlotte, she thought, merely wished to understand them. It was those piercing looks of judgement that had begun to make Anne stammer. Being treated as a fool, made her one.

'I d—don't know.'

'Of course you know! How preposterous!'

Anne's tongue was locked in her mouth. At last she managed to say, 'They are not babies. They are ch—cherubs.'

'They look like *babies* to me.'

'They are ch—cherubs.'

'I think they are *babies*, Anne.' Charlotte almost snarled. Why was she so *discontented* with her lot? There was a smile on her lips; a knowing smile, elder-sisterly, but unpleasant enough to make Anne cry.

Charlotte's tone changed instantly, as she begged, 'Anne, Anne! Why are you crying?'

Anne crumpled. After burying her head in her lap for a few minutes she raised a tear-stained, twitching face and shouted: 'Leave me alone!' before she fled the room.

But where to? She knew that Charlotte would look for her and she did not wish to make her suffer for hurting her, but she had to hide, because she could not explain herself. She fled across the field to the wood. She hid among the bracken in a dank, brown nest, the green turning to gold fronds folding above her.

How could she express to an *elder* sister her impatience with fantasy lovers? Love was in truth a mysterious act performed with men. 'A woman's burden,' Aunt called it; it involved great pain, at best resulting in babies, but just as likely to fling one into eternity. The spirits of Anne's body, driving her into the real world of a woman, were at war with her mind that feared it.

Anne caught yet another cold in the wood. But was it not the same cold that she'd had in the spring that had come and gone all summer? There was hardly a break between them. She also had a dry hacking cough that ended in a wheeze, or a whistle.

Anne's condition brought terrible memories of Maria and Elizabeth to Charlotte.

'Dear Miss Brontë! Worrying about your sister again! She only has a cold. There is nothing unusual about it at this season,' Miss Wooler said.

After the cough had continued for a couple of weeks Miss Lister refused to share her bed. 'I cannot get a wink of sleep!' she complained.

Anne was put into a bed of her own, near the fire. Charlotte comforted her, as she had not for a long time, finding her books and papers, coaxing her into swallowing a little broth.

'Miss Wooler, Anne is *seriously* ill.'

'You worried about Emily. You behaved as if you thought she was about to die. I am sure she is perfectly all right now, is she not?'

Miss Wooler was peremptory. Did she fear that her authority was being opposed, the school being taken over? Charlotte quietened down for a time.

But, while the cold continued, Anne complained of stomach cramps, clutching the lower part of her stomach, writhing in spasms. She said she felt sick, but was not sick. It did not turn to diarrhoea or anything expected. But it continued. She could barely speak. She would not eat. The doctor visited, the Roe Head servants brewed herbal teas, but nothing did any good.

'I want to see a clergyman,' Anne whispered.

'Anne! You are not . . .'

Ludicrous as it was to think of Anne dying, yet Charlotte could not say it. *That* fear was always too close to the surface.

'Do not worry so much, Charlotte. But I would like spiritual advice.'

'Shall I ask Mr Atkinson to call?' Charlotte suggested.

'No.'

'Mr Nussey?'

'*No!*'

Charlotte went through the names of half a dozen before Anne whispered, 'The Reverend Mr La Trobe.'

'Of the *Moravian* Community?'

'Yes.'

'But why?'

'*Please.*'

Anne insisted on so little, was so little given to 'crying wolf', that when she was firm it seemed as well to let her have what she wanted.

IV

Anne had often walked by the little Moravian Community, a mile from Mirfield Church, among fields a little way above the Dusty Miller pub where the Luddites had plotted in 1811. In 1837 the pub was still noisy and riotous, even on Sundays.

Anne and Charlotte were afraid to pass by, a quarter of a century after the Luddites.

Then came the Moravians' haven of peace: among stone-walled enclosures, an island of bushes and trees holding farm, church, manse, cottages, byres and workshops. The farmhouse was low-built with a stone roof of massive tonnage, rows of tiny windows, and primitive lintels of hewn rock. Wrought-iron gates gave access to paddocks, orchard, vegetable gardens, and the graveyard.

One hundred sober, meditative people lived there. Married ones were 'brethren' and 'sisters', others were 'single brethren', 'single sisters', and there were the sweet sounding titles, 'great girls' choir', 'children's choir', 'widows' choir', and 'widowers' choir'. Titles that rang with the dignity of pioneer Christianity.

Anne preferred to go there alone, being unsure of how to explain herself to her sister. To court Dissension was alarming. Yet the Moravians drew her because they were not alarming at all. They were simple, healthy, peaceful and unafraid. She had only nodded and chatted shyly to them, while they let her wander, smiling at her, offering fruit, and their lovely spring water, sweeter than Haworth's. They did not feel the need to proselytize.

Their modest graveyard was particularly moving; Anne took great note of graveyards, having lived in the midst of one all her life. You could walk from garden and orchard straight into it. The men's graves were on one side of the path, the women's on the other, with the small, uniform stone slabs set flush with the ground. It indicated that we are all equal in the end and none is higher than another. There were no inscriptions beyond name, date and a number recorded in the Moravian register. No lugubrious fears and hopes carved in stone. No steepling piles.

She saw from this, what she sensed from their modes of living, that they were not afraid of death, just as they were not afraid of life.

So she had not spoken much with Mr James La Trobe, the pastor, until he came to see her. He was thirty-three years of age – elderly seeming to Anne; a smiling man in, at first sight, dreadful black, but softened by his smile, that of one for whom all has been resolved.

'The pain is in your stomach?'

'Below,' she answered.

'You're not . . . ?'

She blushed and turned away, angrily, so angrily. 'No, Mr La Trobe. Of course not!'

Her speech ended in a cough.

'How long have you had that cough?'

'All year.'

'You have two illnesses, but your main difficulty is spiritual. Why?'

'I am unsure of my salvation,' she whispered.

He smiled and put his hand on her brow. 'No-one need be unsure. Tell me what you know about the truth of the Bible concerning our salvation.'

'I know that it is through Jesus Christ our saviour. I also know that Calvinists say we are predestined. The Wesleyans claim that we are qualified by our works, and the Universalists tell us that all are saved, but only ultimately, after purgatory. I do not know what to think. I am worried about my sisters and my brother too and – it is all making me ill.'

It took some minutes to whisper this, with breaks in order to cough, sip her cordials and recover her breath.

'And what does your own heart tell you?'

'I do not know.'

'Then I shall tell you. It is that you are not merely so much poundage of flesh and blood. You are a unique creature, your soul winged and weightless. Nothing of the best in you can be weighed and measured. You are inspired with thoughts and feelings and intentions beyond human measurement, except in their effects. All of this is given by God. First as a loan to your earthly flesh. Later it is transformed into pure, invisible spirit. Your duty is to treasure and cultivate it. Am I not describing how you feel in your deepest self?'

Anne smiled. 'Yes, Mr La Trobe. How did you know?'

He smiled back. 'It is what we all know in our hearts. Our difficulty is to prevent its being overlaid. Listen more to your own heart, less to the laws supposedly discovered by men, and you will find the happiness of salvation.'

'You see – your sister is recovering. You had little to worry about,' Miss Wooler remarked, pleasantly.

'I had much to worry about! I still have, for my sister is *far* from recovery yet!' Charlotte snapped.

'I did not say that she had *recovered* but that she is *recovering*,' Miss Wooler said, pedantically. 'Miss Brontë, you are most unruly!'

'And you are insensitive and unreasonable, Miss Wooler! As you often are, I may say, when it comes to considering the *sensibilities* of others, rather than their mental improvement. That is one of the things it has been on my mind to tell you for a long time, and maybe this is the occasion.'

You could have heard a pin drop. You could certainly hear Miss Wooler picking at her beads. After a moment, with a grim little smile, she asked: 'What are the other matters that trouble you?'

'I think your syllabus gives too much importance to *facts*, and to *learning by rote*, and not enough to *learning by experience* and to *a wide range of reading*.'

Charlotte tapped with her finger. Finally she banged her fist on the table – a touch of her father's and her brother's temper coming out.

'Possibly it is because you think in such a way that the *discipline* of your own classes is lacking?' Miss Wooler said.

'Well! If you think so, perhaps I ought to leave the school.'

'Perhaps you should.'

Miss Wooler was the first to be in tears.

Following this – Charlotte wrote of it to Ellen Nussey as a 'little *éclaircissement*' – Miss Wooler kept to her rooms for three days. On emerging, what had always seemed to be her strong face was bloated and she was red-eyed.

Now it was Charlotte Brontë, that quivering waif of six years before, who appeared strong.

'I quite despise Miss Wooler,' she remarked stiffly to Anne.

When Papa wrote saying that he was going to bring his daughters home, it was no more than what Charlotte had decided to do in any case.

Before they left, Miss Wooler called Charlotte into her room. The headmistress was a jelly of feelings which she did not know how to express.

'I have always been so fond of you, Charlotte.'

'And I of you, Miss Wooler,' Charlotte answered, firmly.

'I do not know how matters have come to such a pass.'

'Nor do I. It would be better if you would sit calmly and speak your mind.'

She did as she was bid. 'I do not know why you have changed so much,' she said.

Charlotte had indeed changed. She had helped herself to a seat as calmly as if the room were her own.

'I have always had such a high regard for you, Charlotte.'

'And I for you. My passion got the better of me, and that is a weakness.'

'I wish you were not leaving.' Miss Wooler sighed. 'There!' she exclaimed. 'I have said it!'

She waited, like a child, to be congratulated on her confession.

Charlotte could so easily see herself as Miss Wooler in twenty years time – an unattractive old maid with quenched dreams, stranded as a governess or headmistress, rigid, and yet childish from spending all her time with children. She relented. Abandoning her stiffness, 'I will come back after the Christmas holiday, if you wish,' she said, with a slow smile.

'Dear Charlotte, please return!' And then, 'So that is settled!' Miss Wooler added, briskly, thinking that she had displayed too much emotion. 'Let us take tea together to celebrate.'

She rang for the servant and became the old Miss Wooler again, behaving as if nothing untoward had happened.

Charlotte was not the same. She was stronger.

'Let us make a pact,' Miss Wooler suggested. 'Let us agree never to speak of this unhappy matter again, but to take care to preserve our affection for one another for ever.'

'I can certainly promise to keep a place for you in my heart, but I do not know that I can promise never to speak of what matters to me. But I shall try.'

'I would have respected Miss Wooler more if she had turned me out of doors there and then, instead of snivelling for days and nights together about it,' Charlotte wrote to Ellen.

It took Anne all winter to recover; but she did not return to Roe Head, letting Charlotte go back on her own.

One clear, January morning, Anne suggested to Emily that they pile all their manuscripts in the garden and burn them. It was a day of clear frost, with a blue sky, and the bits of charred paper danced away like black butterflies.

For Emily – as Anne saw – it was the reckless fire in itself that was exciting; the gesture of setting even her own creation at naught. She joined with Anne purely because it seemed a 'dare'.

She overlooked the fact that, for the first time, Anne was taking the lead: she surely must have noticed. She did not even enquire into Anne's reasons.

TABBY

Tabby, in her sixties, was lame, having broken her leg by slipping on ice. It had appeared to be time for her to retire to the Haworth cottage where her sister lived. That was what Aunt said, but for several days the girls refused to eat until Papa and Aunt changed their minds.

Now Tabby spent much of her time in a chair before the kitchen fire, where the heat eased her leg. She smoked a clay pipe. Always she kept that eye that was at the back of her head on whatever girl was helping out. Mostly she stared into the fire. No-one troubled her about work, but in spurts she was busy night or day, determined to earn her keep. Pain and fear had aged her. 'Sometimes one catches a terrible expression,' Charlotte remarked, when she returned on holidays and saw the changes.

Patrick would often join Tabby. He ambled into the kitchen when his children (whichever ones were at home these days) were out of the house, when Elizabeth Branwell was settled upstairs, and there was something on his mind. Not matters to be resolved by reading books, but the formless, nagging worries best soothed beside Tabby's working fireplace and its cluster of pans, in the surroundings of 'her' whitewashed walls, scrubbed stone floor, scrubbed deal table, and with dog and cat, crept in for the same comfort as himself, curled together before the fire.

The proximity of 'wise old Tabby' reminded him of being in his mother's kitchen in Ireland. That memory mattered increasingly. As with all old people, his earliest memories were clearer than later ones. He could remember where his mother had kept her rolling-pin fifty years ago, when he had forgotten where he had put his spectacles that morning. 'May I?' he would ask Tabby before taking his seat. He was diffident even about moving a cat off a chair: he, the most authoritative man in Haworth. 'I thought we might smoke a pipe together,' he would suggest.

Tabby would nod, and ask if he would like the girl to make tea. Next she would rise to take down the tobacco jar (on the mantelpiece, and kept filled with supplies for both of them, on Mr Brontë's monthly account), whereupon he would insist that she stay seated; he would do it. They would pack their clay pipes, sitting on upright, spindle chairs on either side of the fire.

They had been together for twelve years. In the garden behind the wash-house was a pile of broken pipes, especially Patrick's, the long stems of which he never did learn not to hold at too great a distance from the bowl when he tapped them out on the edge of the iron grate.

It was the end of the summer. Branwell had gone to Bradford. As it was neither laundry day nor baking day, Emily was out rambling. Elizabeth, Patrick thought, was darning baby clothes which Alice Pickles, whose children had grown out of them, had left for the poor.

Patrick wandered into the kitchen. To cool and sweeten the room, the outside door was propped open, and there wafted in a moorland smell of sheep and warmed grass.

'May I?'

He moved carefully towards the chair, not sure that he would be able to see any small animal that might lie in his way. They packed their pipes. He fidgeted with a taper at the fire, lit up, and sucked for a few moments. All this time he was studied by Tabitha.

'Put on thee coat, Sarah, and tak' yon basket o' loaves to Mester Shackleton's at the foot of the hill,' Tabby ordered. After the girl had left, she said, 'Is something troubling thee, Mester Bron-*teh*?'

He smiled. 'How do *you* see my children?' he said.

Having no children of her own, Tabby had studied the Brontës with loving minuteness, but had only ever been asked advice about a cold, or a headache. She did not know how to articulate her thoughts.

'Mester Branwell – well, if I think on him, compared wi' Miss Charlotte and Miss Anne – Miss Charlotte – Mester Bron-*teh*, may I speak plainly?'

'Please, I would value it.'

'Miss Charlotte and Miss Anne worry about what mak's up a good life, but Miss Charlotte has so much anger in her, after Cowan Bridge. She wants to put th'whole world to rights. Miss Anne is more content wi' herself. But she knows what leads to ruin later, to be paid for through eternity. She often talks wi' me about what meanings we can mak' out o' t'Bible, after church when thou'rt busy, and when I come in from chapel. Mester Branwell – you don't mind me speaking this way?'

'Please go on. It is illuminating.'

'Some of Haworth is starting to talk o' the company he keeps.'

'I know, Tabby, I know.'

'But I don't know whether sermons are much use to him, for th'time being. He feels he's heard enough of them. Best leave him be.'

'I do let him be, Tabby. I fear that Judgement troubles him, nonetheless. And I try to show him sympathy, but that troubles him, too. He then drinks because he feels ashamed. Tell me what you think of Emily.'

Tabitha rubbed at her knee.

'Please try,' he encouraged. 'I promise to be patient.'

After a long pause: 'Thou should never think of sending

Emily away fr' Haworth,' Tabby said.

'It is a little too late for that,' Patrick said. 'Tabby, I am an old man, with nothing to leave my children. They must go out into the world and depend on their own talents.'

CHAPTER FIVE

LOVE

EMILY

I

Emily rambled all day mainly because, once she had climbed to a certain height, euphoria took hold of her and she could not bear to descend. Reaching the moortop she felt she had shed some form of stuffy clothing.

Her actual clothing consisted of an old cloak in winter, at other times a ragged spencer or a shawl. She wore an old pair of men's boots that she had picked up at Ponden.

She had to mix with all sorts of travellers. These days, paved causeways were being built from the hill-farms down to the mills and the wives and daughters of farmers and handloom weavers trudged along them between home and their new employment in the factories. Weavers carried warps from the clothiers' homes to their crofts. Pedlars went between hamlets on the turnpike. There were many poor and beggars.

Papa had bought her a little 'overcoat' pistol for her twentieth birthday. It was only eight inches long but percussion-fired, not an old-fashioned flintlock like his own. Hers was safe, simple, and deadly. Although neither Charlotte nor Anne had picked up their father's passion for firearms, for the past four years Emily had envied Branwell's liberty to saunter the moors with a sporting rifle, and Papa, pleased by this, had taught her to shoot at a target in the garden.

'You should not encourage her,' Aunt Branwell said. 'It would be better to teach her not to be such a fidget at home.'

Papa had smiled and answered, 'I am too fond of nature myself. I cannot bring my children up to be the same and then censure them. She always comes home pink-cheeked.'

She liked to get clear of the busy trackways and onto the moortop, among the clusters of weathered rocks; sprinklings of quartz shining like the Milky Way on the sheep-paths through the heather. As she climbed, she anticipated a sensation of beatitude. Her kin were the lark and the hawk; her lightness and loneliness linked her with their flight. She felt regal. She identified with the young Queen Victoria, ascended to the throne this year although not yet crowned and who was almost the same age as herself.

Most of all, Emily saw herself as Gondal's princess, Augusta Geraldine Almeida, for whom she had been composing poems all year. 'A.G.A.', as Emily often inscribed her poems, was tall, imperious, dark-haired, and had many lovers; while Emily herself had striking looks; tall, with an unusual combination of dark chestnut-coloured hair and cool grey-blue eyes.

She rambled in wide circles, keeping to the high contour, clear of the mills; as she had always done, but the circles were growing wider. Her routes were nearly all west or south, avoiding the factories and villages north-east towards Keighley. Twenty miles seemed nothing to her. She carried her food for the day, and her copy of Shelley, Walter Scott, Byron or some other book; and would often share her bread, or other baking, while sheltering from sun or rain or while drying her shoes and clothes in a hill farm. She wandered and circled like someone who has lost something.

Or, 'Like someone whose conscience is not clear and canna rest.' When someone hinted this to Charlotte – at the time when she was back for the summer and her sister's habits had grown a degree less orthodox – it made her angry. They had got it wrong, of course. 'The common people always do,' she averred.

The truth, as Charlotte perceived it, was that Emily had given herself to the moorlands and was able to bring less and less of herself back each time. She returned with a sense of vacancy. She became noted for her haunted look.

*　　*　　*

'Emily, what is to do?'

Aunt Branwell had come into the kitchen to find the 'hash-pan', the pan of stew, laid on the hearthstone and being licked by a cat. The fire puthered smoke and soot over pastry waiting to go into the oven. It was most unlike Emily to neglect her domestic tasks. She lifted her face from the book she was reading at the table.

'You are crying!'

Emily struggled to smile. 'It's just an old ballad that has got onto my mind.'

Her aunt rescued the pan, drove the cat out of doors, and poked the fire so that it burst into flames and would smoke less.

'Read it to me,' she demanded.

'It's called, "The Demon Lover":

> O where have you been, my dear, dear love,
> This long seven years and more?
> O I'm come to seek my former vows
> Ye granted me before.'

Emily hesitated, for her aunt, only half-listening, had been busy wiping the pie and putting it into the oven, and now she was fidgeting.

Aunt stood still and beamed.

Emily continued:

> 'O hold your tongue of your former vows,
> For they will breed sad strife;
> O hold your tongue of your former vows,
> For I am become a wife.'

After a moment, 'You should not feel things so deeply,' Aunt said. 'It can be harmful. I have known it lead to consumption.'

Her aunt left the room, her lips pursed, knowingly, warningly. Dry gulleys ran down her eroded cheeks: an old maid. Would Emily herself be such an old maid in ten, twenty years?

She returned to her book and read again, in silence, of a lady seduced from husband and babes, to sail away with her demon lover, who takes her to Hell.

But the mountains of Hell with the right lover, thought Emily, might be more exciting than the plains of Heaven.

Apart from Papa she did not *know* any actual men whom she could admire. There was Branwell, there were curates, weavers and farmers. All were inferior to the men she imagined. It was as if they were another species.

Charlotte and Anne also dreamed of men, but theirs *were* only imaginings. Emily was convinced that hers was real, although a spirit, who swept off the moorland, as the Demon Lover came off the sea. She had sensed him in the wind at the parsonage window, when the world was mysterious at dusk. He reminded her of her allegiance whenever she was unable to go out and was in danger of forgetting him, or as prayer and sleep threatened to claim her.

The west wind was her Demon Lover. He belonged to Haworth, and she would be faithful to him.

Charlotte loved to exchange tittle-tattle with Miss Wooler.

'Charlotte, you remember Mr Titus Brooke, relative of Maria Brooke whose brother married into the Halliley family of Dewsbury?'

'Of course I recall the Brookes! Maria and I shared books. We put our names in them.'

'Happy days! *Well!*' Margaret Wooler's voice fell to a whisper. '*Mr Brooke is to marry Miss Maria Patchett.* That poses a dilemma.'

'Why?' Charlotte supposed – she hoped – for some tangled love interest.

'Miss Patchett and her sister Elizabeth, who used to keep a school on top of the hill at Soyland, now have one at Law Hill near Southowram. They have a penchant for hilltops, it seems. It has forty pupils, twenty of them boarders. Maria's leaving means that there is a vacancy. There will be no problem in finding applicants. I have heard that there are twenty thousand governesses and teachers in England. But Miss Elizabeth wants someone well-recommended. It is an unusual position.'

'You are suggesting that I leave Roe Head?' Charlotte asked, startled by this apparent raising of their old quarrel.

'Certainly not! I do not know how I could manage without you. But Emily might be the right candidate. You said she is eager to try out her strengths in the world.'

'Not eager, so much as realizing the necessity of it.'

'I cannot imagine a better opportunity, nor anyone who would more appreciate Law Hill. Some might consider it an exile. Also, from what I know of Emily, Miss Patchett's – peculiarities – might suit her. I know that Emily enjoys walking. Do you think she would like to become a fine horsewoman too? It is in the prospectus.' Margaret Wooler beamed.

'We have none of us ridden but I think, yes, it would appeal to Emily.'

'Charlotte . . . I don't quite know how to put this. The habits of the Misses Patchett and their friends are rather manly and vigorous. When asked my advice about a replacement I instantly thought of Emily. As well as suiting her, the life would strengthen her constitution.'

Emily did not even need to attend for interview. Apparently Miss Wooler's recommendation was sufficient.

Her trunk was packed. Aunt Branwell bought her a fussy bonnet with bits of white lace and felt flowers stitched on it, and, with winter coming on, a new, hooded cloak. It was black, with a lining of dove-grey silk. 'Your other one smells like an old sheep,' Aunt Branwell grumbled, smiling. 'I don't know where you get to with it.'

The new cloak was voluminous. 'You know what a one you are for being out in all weathers. You'll want something to cover you up,' Aunt Branwell said. 'Besides, you need plenty of room because you are still growing.'

Aunt meant that she hoped Emily's bony form would pad out with a bit of healthy fat, but Emily was resentful. She took it that she was not being treated as a woman.

'I *am* twenty, Aunt!' were her last, rough words.

It was said as much in order to instil bravery into herself, as to reprove her aunt. As they hugged, Emily wondered why everything she said came out seemingly so contentious.

She kissed Papa gravely. She gave Anne a hug. She hugged

Tabby. Clearly, Tabby would miss her – the one of her employer's family who spent most time with her, in the kitchen. She kissed the cats and dogs. She climbed into the Black Bull gig. Before they had descended to the Haworth tollgate she had rid herself of her bonnet, crushing it under her seat.

"Ow's Branwell doing?' asked Joseph. 'We've not seen much of 'im lately.'

'He's changeable. He'll be drinking somewhere else. He spends a lot of time in Halifax with Joseph Leyland. He's been living in Bradford all summer. He has a studio there.'

'So he told us. He says he's been down London, too. He's in and out of Haworth like a dog's . . . Begging your pardon, miss. I've seen him in th'Bull only once or twice since he went to Bradford. Painting portraits there, he told us. Doing well is he?'

Emily pulled a face but Joseph, having his back to her, could not see it.

'So and so. There are too many artists, but he enjoys the ambience.'

Joseph had no idea what 'ambience' meant, and said, 'I dare say it'll pay better than writing poetry. Might go a little way towards his ale bill.' Mr Wilkinson at the Black Bull was forever grumbling about that. It was probably the reason why Branwell had deserted to a different public house.

'I doubt it.'

'If he's not to go in for the church, being a parson's son must be a bit of a problem for him. He likes to be one with the men, does Branwell. Being educated, he could have turned out a snob. He's in an awkward spot for a young man, coming from a house with so many ladies. And I've heard tell that thee young ladies are talking of opening a school in yon parsonage.'

'Thinking of it. It's Charlotte's idea. Which way are we going, Joseph?'

Emily would have known how to walk in a direct line over the hills, but the winding turnpike route was a mystery.

'Best road is to turn right by the Flappit pub, drop by the Sportsman to come out at the Ring o' Bells, then up the hill to the Queen Adelaide in Southowram. The woman at the Flappit keeps a fair ale.'

Half an hour later, 'It'll be a thirsty journey today,' he said, wistfully. He did not expect one of the Miss Brontës to suggest stopping at a public house, but one never knew.

They followed the gentle descent into Halifax.

'It's a long haul for a single horse on a warm day,' he repeated, desperately, as they clattered down towards the Ring o' Bells after their ten-mile drive. There could be seen a steep climb ahead, up Beacon Hill. As Emily could never bear ill-treatment of animals, she was happy sitting on a bench outside the 'public', drinking a small glass of ale while Joseph 'watered the horse'.

'I wonder where Charlotte, Anne and I will be in ten years time?' she day-dreamed. 'And in twenty?'

Joseph, having been in the pub and stood with his horse at the trough, harnessed it to the gig again and sat next to Emily. He spread his knees, patted his belly, and burped. He was an example of that Yorkshire coarseness which Emily hated. Yet he was happy and she, at twenty, seemed congenitally unhappy. They were a strange pair, with not a lot to say to each other.

'Is Law Hill right up there?'

'Right at t'top, behind Beacon Hill.' He told her this as if he was pleased. 'It's a strong horse as can mak' it. It's a good job thou's fond o' walking.'

Even from here, Emily could see that the situation was that of the one school in Yorkshire that might suit her. It was unique because, tucked away at eight hundred feet almost vertically above Halifax parish church, it was in the craziest of places for an 'academy' for young ladies. Only the eccentric Misses Patchett would have thought of opening one there. Before it, Beacon Hill hung with a peculiar ominousness. It was not merely that it was the site of a notorious gibbet where the corpses of criminals used, not so very long ago, to be left for the crows. It was shaped like a tombstone, and seemed as dark.

'You'd have to be fond of your own company to live up there,' Joseph remarked.

The climb was more like a cliff path than a navigable road. Emily did not need asking to walk at the side of the gig, and Joseph dismounted to lead the horse. Coal pits were driven into the hillside, and spoil-heaps were scattered about. As Emily passed by one of the 'drift' mines she saw – yes, she had to look twice, but she was sure that the creature *was* a girl. She was filthy black and about twelve years of age. She appeared at the pit mouth out of the side of the hill. She was on all fours, with a harness over her bare chest as she pulled a truck loaded with coal.

Emily gulped and was glad to pass on through the scrappy woodland that struggled on thin and poisoned soil. There followed a brief respite of light and space on the hilltop, but she felt imprisoned again as soon as she was driven through the big iron gate in the fortress walls, into the small yard between the school, which was a converted wool-warehouse, and Miss Patchett's gaunt, grey, three-storeyed home. The yard was empty because none of the girls had yet arrived back after the summer. Joseph, with the only Law Hill male, a servant, carried her trunk up the outside stone staircase to the girls' dormitory that was above the schoolroom.

In the curtained recess at the end window, given her for privacy because she was a teacher, she emptied some of her trunk. She placed shoes and boots under the bed, some dresses and her cloak on a rail, books and pistol on the windowsill. She took out her writing-desk and placed it by her bed. She left her sewing-box buried at the bottom of her trunk together with her finer dresses, careless of their becoming crumpled. She stared out of the window, which fortunately looked down the valleys. Then she went to introduce herself to Miss Patchett.

It was four o'clock in the afternoon by the time that was finished with. Joseph would be halfway home. Already she almost shed a tear when she thought of Haworth. She wondered which pubs he'd stop at. There came into her mind her lines written for Augusta Geraldine Almeida when she was in the dungeon of 'The Palace of Instruction' in Gondal, uttering laments for Fernando de Samara, who had killed himself out of unrequited love. She returned to the dormitory to pick up her copy of the poems of Shelley. She went out of the Law Hill gates and turned right.

A hundred yards away, at the junction of Law Lane, Pinnar

Lane and Howgate Hill, was an old stone signpost, two hands carved on it, indicating 'Leeds Wakefield' in one direction, and 'Halifax' the other way. She had noticed it as the tired horse passed by. Her stroll to it was of the kind she might have taken with Anne: not very far, but full of an intense, shared mood. She settled into the bank of heather at the base of the pillar – as she had always settled into such sunny nests since she had been a small child. She opened her book at 'Epipsychidion'. Or rather, the volume, dog-eared and stained by mud and the juice of moorland whinberries, opened itself.

VERSES ADDRESSED TO THE NOBLE AND
UNFORTUNATE LADY, EMILIA V—
Now imprisoned in the convent of—

Poor captive bird! who, from thy narrow cage
Pourest such music, that it might assuage
The rugged hearts of those who prisoned thee,
Were they not deaf to all sweet melody:
This song shall be thy rose . . .

    Emily,
A ship is floating in the harbour now,
A wind is hovering o'er the mountain's brow;
There is a path on the sea's azure floor,
No keel has ever ploughed that path before;
The halcyons brood around the foamless isles;
The treacherous Ocean has forsworn its wiles;
The merry mariners are bold and free:
Say, my heart's sister, wilt thou sail with me?

II

Emily was at first delighted with Law Hill. She believed she had come into her element. She thrilled to the bleakness of this high eyrie, as she had not done to the rose gardens and orchard of Roe Head. She thought that she would grow to like these girls, as she had not liked the more wilting and conventional young ladies of the Misses Wooler's school.

In her first attempts in the schoolroom, she fell over herself with eagerness.

She thought she was going to learn to ride. The yard rang as much from the clatter of horses as with that of pupils, boisterous though the latter were: they needed to be vigorous, both the boarders and those who came across the moorland. She did learn, but only barely. Riding lessons were reserved for the pupils, and riding was the subject taught by Miss Patchett herself.

She turned out to be a tartar and a 'slavedriver' – as Emily described her in a letter to Charlotte. So were her friends. There was Miss Walker of Walterclough Hall, and Miss Anne Lister of Shibden Hall. They owned textile mills and coal pits. Miss Lister claimed to be the first woman to have climbed Mont Blanc and to have descended into a coalmine (in Belgium). In the latter respect she was ignoring the women and girls who laboured in her own pits, right beneath her house and lawn, and her attitude was typical of her circle: underlings were not worth noticing, and, without a blush, she turned tenants off her farms for not voting Tory.

All the ladies were keen riders, most often found in riding habit – even in their drawing-rooms whenever Emily was sent on errands to their stony, draughty 'halls'. When Emily first walked over to Shibden Hall, at a time when Miss Lister had for a short while returned from foreign travel, Emily took her for a man – and that was from close up; not from a distance, as Emily for different reasons could be mistaken. Emily mistook Miss Anne Walker, with whom Miss Lister lived, for her fiancée. She saw them kissing. Then she realized. She was disgusted.

Other than Anne Walker, who was quite a caricature of the feminine, all of this circle of ladies tended to dress in severe, masculine black. Such items as lace bonnets, beaded reticules, fans and parasols, were anathema at Law Hill. Elizabeth Patchett, as tall as Emily, strode about her gardens, farm, yard and through the schoolroom, dressed in riding habit and often carrying a whip. Now in her forties, she was the kind of woman described as 'handsome'.

Emily was not drawn into the magic circle. Although she had her own penchant for whips and riding habits, she was revolted by these women and found herself an outsider. As bad as this, she suffered the shock of finding herself in the role of servant whenever she met them, which was generally when being sent on an errand. She, the Princess Augusta Geraldine Almeida, a *servant*! 'You are a parson's daughter?' they remarked, by way of putting her in her place.

While Miss Patchett cantered about the moors, envious Emily with her fellow teacher, Miss Hartley, found herself on duty from six o'clock in the morning until ten or eleven at night. Like every governess, she also acted as maid, running errands, mending clothes, washing the finer linen; doing everything except scrubbing and cooking, which was left to menials even lower than herself. Emily would not have minded the cleaning, but she hated sewing.

She was not good at teaching, either, for how could she have acquired the skills? She had never had any enthusiasm for Miss Mangnall, who would have made tutoring easy with her quizzes and ready-made tasks. In front of the class, Emily was awkward – not statuesque and confident, like Miss Patchett. She was not used to talking to girls of her own age other than her sisters. When, tumbling over herself on the first day, she tried to tell her pupils about Goethe, they laughed at her.

She found that the tough pupils sent to Law Hill – as much for training in horsewomanship as for anything else – if outwardly unconventional, were rigidly conformist underneath.

Unfortunately, Emily's responsibilities were not to tutor in the subjects that these young ladies found interesting, mainly horse riding and fashions. She was chiefly responsible for the 'accomplishments' of music and German. She had to give lessons in arithmetic, which she was beginning to think of as important – because Shelley, following Aristotle, took it seriously – but in which she was not well skilled. She also had to teach English grammar and spelling, at which she wasn't competent either. She had learned it by imitation from her reading, and had little understanding of its principles.

She found it hard to tell which girls were part of Miss Lister's inner circle and which were not, and she got so that she could hardly bear to speak to them.

The thought of being seduced made her cringe. When one day she caught them laughing at her projecting teeth: 'I prefer the house dog to any of you!' she yelled at her class.

At the 'back end' of the year, great sunsets blazed over the boiling and smoking manufacturing town of Halifax, below. To the east, the sun rose over curtains of more gentle hills, down the lovely Shibden Valley and beyond. Law Hill was truly a hawk's nest. Where could be more suitable for Emily's spirit?

But for most of the day she felt as much a prisoner as Shelley's Emilia or her own Augusta. The moor swept up to Law Hill School, beckoning and tempting, but she could only explore it during the daytime if she was sent on an errand, or was on one of the pretty, curriculum strolls with her pupils, which irked her. She could be alone on the hills only very early in the morning or in the late evening. It was nearly always dark before she was free.

Though tired out, nonetheless the penal indoor round made her determined to keep her vital connection with the moor. When she ought to have been recuperating for the following day's endeavour, instead she put on Mr Heaton's old boots, pulled her cloak about her, and slipped out hoping not to be noticed, nor to set horses whinnying, nor to disturb the dogs.

She scrambled upon the hills above the Shibden Valley. She got to know them when blanched and silvery, hard under foot, ice on the puddles fracturing into splinters of light under the moon, the heather stiff with rustling frost; the great moonlit banks rearing before her when she breasted a hill. It was a world of scents, too. Here wafted the smell of a flock of sheep, there of a horse left out in a frozen croft. It was magical at night. *What have I to do with Miss – and Miss – and Miss – ?* They vanished, as the frost, so real around her, would melt at sunrise.

Which was never very long after Emily, discharging her pistol a few hundred yards from the house, returned; her hacking cough rousing the dogs, firstly to bark and then to come and lick her loved hand.

She most often walked northwards, because after three

miles she reached a certain hilltop. It was as high as Law Hill. On nights when there was a full moon she could survey thirty miles square of Yorkshire from there. Westwards, across the indigo pool of Halifax, she could pick out the clump of rocks on the pass over to Lancashire fifteen miles away. To her right beyond the Shibden Valley were the hills and valleys towards Leeds. Southwards she picked out her grim prison of Law Hill. To its right spread the many folds of hill and valley towards Roe Head, where Charlotte and Anne were.

Most important of all: from this point, blocking the end of the valley further northwards, was Oxenhope Moor, and just over its crest lay Haworth. A further ten miles ahead, and she could flee the slavery of Law Hill and be home.

She came here to dream – and also to prove to herself that she could resist temptation. The shape of Oxenhope Moor, with its flat top, became imprinted on her mind as clearly as the parsonage. She stared at it to remind herself that she was strong, and that she could return to face her fate. Her dark cloak making her as invisible as a rock or a stone post, she would crouch in the frost, strong in being alone. And yet, despite all, lonely.

It was inevitable that she should come across High Sunderland Hall which lay below that same hill crest.

It was another frosty, moonlit night. She had been at Law Hill for a week and her mind, as on every day, was a tangle of resentments and 'conundrums', as Aunt Branwell called Emily's puzzling preoccupations. She could not understand her pupils' passions. She had to straighten the muddle out in the fresh air.

She reloaded her pistol. She rammed down a measure of gunpowder, followed by a ball, and set it at half-cock. She got into her boots and enveloped herself in the cloak, put the pistol into her pocket, and slipped on her gloves. She stepped into the narrow yard.

It was nearly bright as day and an iced breeze knifed her cloak. She pulled the hood up and folded it over her face, holding it to her mouth. She patted and quietened the dogs, who at first did not know her because she was covered up. By the schoolroom gable, she slipped through the big gate and fortress wall, into Law Lane.

Dark little plebeians, weavers and colliers, slipped in and out of public houses. Many were no more than children but they looked like old men. 'A boy whose backbone isn't bent by the time he's ten years of age will never make a collier,' Miss Lister said. They took little notice of Emily as she came down the road – probably not expecting surprises and delights in their lives – but some looked around afterwards, ascertaining that their vision of the rapidly walking female, glimpses of the grey silk lining of her cloak turning like water in the moonlight, was not a dream.

She walked across open moor, and through weavers' hamlets occupied by more pygmies, and past the mouths of coal pits. She sank into a valley, and climbed again. Like an apparition, the Hall was moonlit on the flank of the opposite hill.

A silky, violet sky, which the bright, high moon had robbed of stars, stood above the moor behind it. By all expectations, such a huge, grand building should not be here, in this stark setting. She saw the outline of the castellated roof and the sets of chimneys against the white moor. She saw the panes of the Elizabethan windows twinkling across its front.

'What is that?' she said, speaking out loud to herself, as she sometimes did, from being so much alone. She guessed it was almost midnight; she had been busy since six in the morning, had not eaten much, and she half thought that the mansion was an illusion caused by hunger, imagined out of her reading of Sir Walter Scott, or out of Gondal. With that thought came another one: that it was a perfect setting for a story.

She made her way towards it, following the track that led to the end gable. It turned out to be quite real, and massively so. In its buckled, grey front she distinguished, three-quarters of the way along from where she stood, a big, craggy entrance porch, and eight of the great windows. Made of small panes of leaded glass, they were at erratic angles that set up a kaleidoscopic glitter in the moonlight. Despite the grandeur, it appeared to be a working farm, with only a low wall around the neglected garden, stables and barns, and with farm carts and implements dotted about in the way typical of a farm, but not of a grand house. Battered and ill-kept, it seemed to have plenty of inhabitants. Candlelight shone behind some windows, so she did not go nearer, and did not pass under the entrance gateway, although it was open. Dogs were barking, but that did not frighten her. She kept her distance because she did not want anyone to come out and break her mood.

She was able to survey the place in peace. The gatehouse was set at right angles to the end of the building and was curiously massive; for a high wall, such as one would expect, did not continue beyond it. There was only a typical enclosure wall, three feet high, which rendered the great entrance pointless. Emily assumed that a great wall had been removed.

But it was the carvings around the gate that stirred, and amused her. There was an Elizabethan face, with straight hair – a face like Shakespeare's – blowing a horn. There were vulgar gargoyles scattered over the gatehouse at random, as if they had been brought from elsewhere, probably from some demolished part of the mansion. Above the windows were dripstones that ended in more carvings.

She drew level with the porch, which was in the same massive style as the gatehouse, with more flanking sculptures: the figures of squat, powerful males – nude, muscular wrestlers and dwarves dramatized by the moonlight. Emily had never seen a naked male before, even in engravings. She looked away from privies, and she had only seen babies, such as Brannii when he was very small. She had never known what lay beneath the fig leaves. Her education told her to be shocked. Instead, she was enthralled, forgetting time.

She longed for Him to be with her. Not a dwarf, but Fernando de Samara, Alexander Lord Elbe, Alfred Sidonia, or Julius Brenzaida; all the same man, actually, and the Gondal lover of Augusta Geraldine Almeida, alias Emily Jane Brontë. It was perfect agony to know how exciting nature would be – how much deeper – if she had a lover to touch and speak to, in the heather, on the moors at night.

Her longing was so intense that after a moment there was indeed someone present, she was sure there was, she could put out her hand and touch him; some male, hovering, whom she could not define. When she tried, he vanished.

Then he returned, beside and behind her – all around her – massive and enfolding; still but full of power; invisible but entirely real.

III

'It's a terrible night,' Miss Patchett said.

She was so tough, it would need a bad night for her to remark on it. The snow was being blasted onto walls and windows by an icy wind.

Such evenings were spent sitting around the fire telling stories. Miss Patchett would join in, stretching her booted legs before the great fire in 'the house'. Most of the candles would be blown out, leaving the firelight flickering on the faces of Miss Brontë, Miss Hartley, and the boarders. When they'd had enough of scaring one another with boggarts, 'water-wolves', spectral hounds and bogeymen, they liked to hear Miss Patchett's stories of great houses; about fortunes lost through love, revenge, greed, blasphemy and excess. Nearly always, the moral was: the danger of love.

'Tell us about High Sunderland Hall,' Emily begged.

'So that is where you have been to! Well, thereby hangs a tale. Its great days were before the Civil War, because Langdale Sunderland was one of the few Halifax gentlemen on the side of the Royalists. After the war, he was compelled to take down his wall, and he had to pay such a huge fine that he lost his inheritance. Now, it's tenanted to families of weavers and farmers who don't take a bit of care of it.'

'What sort of house would you like to live in, Miss Brontë, when you choose your husband?' she was asked. Her opinions were always entertaining.

'I would have a castle with battlements and lots of land. And I would have a handsome husband, six feet tall, with dark, curly hair and brows knit like Satan's.'

'How shocking! And where would it be situated? In Poland or Russia? In Scotland?'

'Oh, no! I only want to be in Yorkshire.'

'Have I told you about John Walsh?' Miss Patchett's voice was strong and throaty. 'He had to be buried on his own farm. Because of his blaspheming and swearing, the vicar would run away when he saw him coming, so no-one would give him a funeral service. His wife had his grave dug as far from the house as possible because she feared she'd hear him blaspheming even from six feet under the ground.'

'Tell us a story about *love* and *passion*, Miss Patchett!' demanded Sarah Oldroyd.

'Walsh's story *is* one of passion,' Emily remarked. Potentially, too, it was a story of love; or she, at least, could turn it into one.

'Let me tell you about the fall of the Walker family of Walterclough Hall,' Miss Patchett decided. 'It led to the building of Law Hill. John Walker was a wool master. He sent his eldest son to Cambridge to become a scholar and he packed his youngest son off to London to study law, where he soon died. Consumption, I expect.'

'Were they handsome boys?'

'Probably not,' said Miss Patchett. 'Oh—' She looked at Emily Brontë and, because she had been so wan, tried to cheer her by declaring: 'I think the young one was. Like Shelley, he had flowing locks and the hope of a great future.'

Everyone knew that Emily was awake half the night reading Shelley and scribbling verses, and the girls laughed.

'While they were away, that fool John Walker adopted the orphaned son of his sister – Jack Sharp. What a devil, what a cuckoo in the nest, he turned out to be! But Walker brought Sharp up to understand his wool business, in the absence of his own fop of a son who was burying himself in Cambridge libraries. Sharp first charmed, then bullied the lot of them, as he grew up. He got to know the business well, and he was a strong, wild fellow, who could more than hold his own among the weavers.'

'I think I prefer him to the real sons,' Emily said.

'He was dashing but dangerous,' breathed Miss Patchett. 'Old Mr Walker grew terrified of him. "Jack Sharp may do without me, but I cannot do without Jack Sharp," he said. Having admitted that, he was lost. One should never admit a weakness to a rascal. The upshot was that old Mr Walker felt driven out of his home. He moved to Halifax and then went even further afield, to York. He had quite forgotten the adage that "possession is three parts of the law". To hasten his own ruin, he let Sharp bully him into making over the business, and gave him the use of the Hall at a tiny rent.

'All went well enough for Jack Sharp – king of the castle – until his uncle died. Then the true son, the younger John Walker, turned up. He was as mild as his father, Sharp was pleased to observe. He had been educated to be quite out of touch with the rough ways in which affairs are conducted in these parts. He was far too gentlemanly to set about claiming his own. But then he fell in love with a lady of some mettle, Miss Elizabeth Waddington. Miss Waddington insisted on living in Walterclough Hall when they married, and Jack Sharp had to be given notice to quit. He left Walterclough with a vengeance. He took all the furniture, plate and curtains, and despoiled the remainder. He made the rightful owners wait while he had this house – Law Hill – built, which he had erected on this spot so that he could gloat over Walterclough in the valley. Imagine the bride's and bridegroom's horror when they arrived after their wedding, which was far away in Thirsk!

'Even that did not content the usurper. To wreak further revenge upon the man who had been bold enough to claim his rights, Sharp adopted a nephew of John Walker junior, Sam Stead by name, and supposedly apprenticed him to his own wool trade, just as John Walker senior had adopted and apprenticed himself. Sharp had picked on Stead because of his weak character, and he set about his moral ruin. He taught him nothing, not even to read and write, but brought him up to drink and gamble, and to be an ignorant boor, and a shame for his uncle to even think of.

'Jack Sharp himself was ruined by the revolt in the American colonies. America was the main market for his cloth, and his income dried up. When Sharp was on his way to bankruptcy, lo and behold, John Walker sold his wife's Kent estate to pay off Sharp's debts. Why he did that, is a mystery. His was too gentle and refined a nature, I suppose. Thus he himself was brought to near ruin, too.

'When Sharp finally went bankrupt, Sam Stead was taken into the Walker family at Walterclough. But he was a destroyed, ignorant character, who only taught Mr and Mrs

Walker's children to blaspheme and gamble and drink like himself.'

One day, Miss Patchett took all the girls to an exhibition of art and antiquities in Halifax, then to a concert. Emily missed it, because even over music she preferred to use her day off for another daylight look at High Sunderland Hall.

The colony of tenants paid little attention to her. Looms clattered, hens, pigs and horses were attended to, but she wandered in peace. 'Tha mun mind the dogs!' someone shouted, and that was all.

She thought of the fall of the Sunderlands, she recalled the story of Ponden Hall, and a dozen other stories of houses lost and won, and of foul inheritances. Jack Sharp, too, was on her mind. Revenge was a terribly ugly passion, she thought. But exciting, also. Supposing it had been High Sunderland Hall on which Sharp had got his 'usurping hands'?

She climbed the hill behind the Hall, to think without being disturbed. Although it was more like being drugged: a suspension of thought and will, allowing words, names, and plots to enter her mind. She knew that, if she questioned her inspiration, it would vanish; and that if words did not seem the right ones, she must be patient.

She hid in a hollow struck by the sun. Poking her arms out of her cloak, and removing her glove, she wrote in her notebook the word which had come to her as a *nom de plume* for Jack Sharp: 'Heathcliff'.

'Black hair. black browes.' (Her spelling hadn't improved greatly.) 'Six feet tall. Age 26.'

She looked down the hill, and could see Shibden Hall, sheltered in its trees, in its park at Stump Cross.

'Wuthering Heights,' she wrote: a name she had discovered by reading Sir Walter Scott. 'Thrushes Grange'. That didn't sound right, so, thinking of Stump Cross, she altered it to 'Thrush Cross Grange'.

A new story for Gondal was growing! It had found a setting; and now she hankered for it to be about love, as well as revenge. Not sordid love, but the ideal and perfect love that Shelley wrote about, and which was not usually understood by the gross world; not normal love at all.

And 'Epipsychidion' still haunted her:

> Emily,
> I love thee; though the world by no thin name
> Will hide that love, from its unvalued shame.
> Would we two had been twins of the same mother!
> Or, that the name my heart lent to another
> Could be a sister's bond for her and thee
> Blending two beams of one eternity!
> Yet were one lawful and the other true,
> These names, though dear, could paint not, as is due,
> How beyond refuge I am thine. Ah me!
> I am not thine: I am a part of *thee*.

She could see the hamlet of Catherine Slack hanging above the Shibden Valley: 'Catherine', she wrote, and after it: 'Earnshaw'.

ANNE

I

In 1842, when Joseph Leyland came to stay at the Black Bull, Anne met a strong, broad-shouldered man of stocky build, swarthy as an Italian. His large, handsome head carried a black halo of neat hair. He was flabby – from dropsy, she found – and melancholic. His eyes were brooding and watchful. Strong as an artisan, yet he was exquisitely dressed, down to a large signet ring on the little finger of his left hand. He was flamboyant, and he seemed rich, turning up in his own carriage, driven by his servant in livery. People thought him a genius because he looked and behaved like one.

Although generous towards his friends – subbing Branwell, and, she was led to believe, a circle of aspiring artists in Halifax – yet she wondered if the servant and tradesmen got paid. He was the kind of man who is generous to those close to him, and – to be kind – not only to flatterers, but to anyone for whom he felt warmth or kinship, but who is hardly aware of problems concerning the rest of the world.

Thomas Andrew, the doctor who had been the Brontës'

friend – everyone's friend – had died in the cholera epidemic that spring. Being a doctor who never took fees from the poor, he had been so much loved that his coffin had to be displayed on trestles in the street, there were so many people who wished to pay their respects. It had been Branwell's idea to commission a marble tablet from Leyland. He did not seem the best choice to carve the memorial to so modest a man, but Branwell told the committee about the sculptor's fame, and Leyland himself rammed his genius down their throats.

Though staying at the Black Bull, he made himself at home in the parsonage. He was a man to take whatever was on offer, as easily as he gave. But it was a great strain for Anne, here on a short break from her work as a governess. Branwell was no help, Tabby was lame, Charlotte and Emily happened to be far away, and, greatest anxiety of all, Aunt Branwell was very ill. Most mornings, after spending over half an hour in the privy, she was still unable to pass anything from her bowels. She came out white-faced and staggering, and once she had fainted in the yard.

'I've better things to do than argue with a small-minded committee!' Leyland moaned.

Up to a certain point, Anne could understand. He'd had Mr Heaton barking at him, and Mr Taylor from Stanbury Manor shouting, 'Haworth doesna want to waste a mint o' money, sithee!' Nonetheless, Anne was enraged at hearing him complain, while he was settled in their kitchen chair. Rage was normally a well-covered, inner state with her.

She could not help comparing him with William Weightman, her father's young curate, who was everything that Leyland was not; who was modest, concerned about everyone, and the most wonderful good fun to boot; a genius in his own way, one of exuberance and energy. He had a lightness about him, in contrast to that too solid earthiness of Leyland. Earthiness was perhaps to be expected of a sculptor, she thought, and yet, she thought again, perhaps the lack of a sense of soaring weightlessness was precisely what was lacking in his work, which remained spiritless, inert lumps of stone or iron.

'Mr Leyland, this spring has been a sad one apart from the passing of Mr Andrew,' Anne said.

'Because your sisters are at school in Brussels? Emily will be pining! I'm told she had to be rushed home from Law Hill. At death's door—'

'It has been a sad year for *the town*! Businesses have been bankrupted, the workhouses are full, and a manufacturer has committed suicide.'

Leyland waved his hand in the uncontrolled way that drinkers have, smiled at her as one who thinks himself both indulgent and wise, and said, 'You cannot take the world's troubles on your shoulders, Miss Brontë.'

She was not to be put off.

'A few years ago, Haworth held an anti-Poor Law meeting. The crowd couldn't fit in the Sunday school and we used the field we call Parson's Croft. Abraham Wildman, our Chartist, addressed it. On the table in front of him was a small piece of bread, a piece of beef two inches square, a tiny rectangle of cheese, and a potato. He held these up one by one.'

Anne picked up a potato and moved it back and forth a few inches from Leyland's hooded, brooding, drink-drowsy eyes.

'With the penknife he used for cutting his tobacco, Mr Wildman pared around the potato until it was the size for a pauper's meal. "*That,*" he told them, "is the allowance of food for a day in the workhouse."'

'Well?'

'Mr Leyland! There is a trade depression every year nowadays, and people starve in Haworth and Keighley. Some winters they die in *hundreds* of typhus and cholera. Because they are weak from hunger, they catch diseases from bad drains and polluted water. You should talk to Papa about that! He is forever fighting to move the graveyard so that it won't poison the springs. The main relief for survivors is the workhouse – other than what my father gives, or such as Dr Andrew. So you must understand why they are unmoved by your tantrums. They *worshipped* Dr Andrew.'

Before Leyland went away with his commission, the committee met in the parsonage. Anne brought their tea and cakes into the parlour and was invited to stay a little. She sat toasting bread for them at the fire, smiling to herself.

'One thing I insist on, sithee!' bawled Mr Heaton. 'We

munna pay the man in advance. From what I'm towld, he may not turn up wi' t'goods. He's let a lot o' folk down. His statues have a way of breaking at the casting foundry. He's done a *Spartacus* and an *African Blood Hound* – whatever that is – bigger'n life size. What happened to 'em? Fell off a cart! Or t'stone crumbled like mouldy flour. Th'ands and feet dropped off his *Theseus*. The bigger the statue, it seems, the more likely it is to fall.'

However, the genius delivered his marble plaque in July, after Branwell had done a lot of to-ing and fro-ing. Leyland stayed for a week, and supervised John Brown's carving of the wordy inscription, composed by Branwell. (After a crowded memorial service conducted by Papa, it was set inside St Michael's.)

While Brown chiselled his excellent Roman letters, Leyland, in the Black Bull, did not have an easy time of it. He won folk over by spending money and proving good company when in his cups. Afterwards he staggered up to the parsonage with Branwell. He threw himself around, sprawled in chairs, and smoked a meerschaum pipe. He ordered Tabby about, lame and old as she was. Being drunk, he did not know half of what he was saying.

One day, when only Anne remained in the kitchen with him – Tabby had retired, sick of him, and Branwell had gone up to his aunt – Leyland, before he fell asleep in his chair, stared crookedly at Anne and said:

'Your Branwell is a man now. Do you know that when he was a tutor in Broughton-in-Furness, the reason he left was because he fathered a child, that died?'

II

On a cold January day, Anne and Branwell sat with their trunks in the gig. They were travelling forty-five miles to Little Ouseburn; a village between Harrogate and York, where Anne was a governess – her second post.

They wore mourning for Aunt Branwell. She had died in terrible agony and indignity, with blocked bowels, the sheer pain of which stopped her heart. 'Exhaustion from constipation,' it was called on her death certificate, and

Anne had wondered if her death was not a metaphor of her blocked life.

'It's the longest trip I've ever made, in winter time any road up!' Joseph declared. 'I've bin t'*Arrergayt* afore, nivver beyond it.'

His opinion was that, instead of causing him to be frozen to death, they should have used the new railway, but Papa had thought the journey too complicated for the young couple with their luggage.

Branwell smiled sideways at his sister. She caught a certain slyness. 'Collecting together what is left of his pride.' He had failed as a portrait painter in Bradford, where he had stayed in lodgings, and he had not made it to the Royal Academy. His old teacher, William Robinson RA, had passed on, leaving his family dependent on a public subscription – one to which Branwell was too hard-up to contribute. If Robinson, who had painted the Duke of Wellington, could not make a living from art, then how could Branwell Brontë? He had despaired, dumped his easel and paints in the peat-store, and set himself to translate the Odes of Horace.

He seemed to have felt Aunt Branwell's death more than anyone else did. After his mother and two sisters, yet another female had left him. He had lost two jobs in succession. In the first he had been a tutor at Broughton-in-Furness – on the edge of 'William Wordsworth's Lakes' – and had been sacked after six months.

Because Leyland had told her about it when he was drunk, Anne did not know whether his tale of Branwell having been in love with a servant girl was true. They had all, except Emily, experienced love. Anne's had been for William Weightman, her father's curate who had died in last autumn's cholera epidemic. Charlotte had fallen for the married professor of her school in Brussels – a hopeless passion, so Anne had learned when Charlotte came home for Aunt's funeral. Nonetheless she had returned to Belgium, without Emily, and against the dictates of her own good sense, which so rarely deserted her.

How vulnerable they were all turning out to be! Although Branwell mourned so deeply, only he seemed not to suffer from love. Because of his tendency to throw a fit or go into a rage, she dared not face him with Leyland's allegation, to find out whether it was true or not that he had fathered and then deserted a bastard. Everyone hedged around tackling tricky subjects with Branwell.

His second employment had been on the Lancashire and Yorkshire Railway, becoming 'chief clerk' at Luddenden Foot. There had been absences from duty, and irregularities in the takings – due to carelessness she believed, not his thieving; nevertheless the authorities knew how often his mind had been on poetry, Greek and Latin, rather than on trains, and he had been sacked.

Branwell held forth two hands. He had that look in his eye which he had when he thought himself Northangerland. He clenched and unclenched his left hand and then his right, darting with his forefingers like Macready playing Hamlet, and announced: 'I am two men, not one. That is why I'm able to write with both hands.'

Man! thought Anne – not too unkindly, not too ungenerously, but wistfully, and returning his smile. She had known Weightman.

Anne had been a governess in Little Ouseburn, at the house known as Thorp Green, for two-and-a-half years now and had persuaded her employers, the Robinsons, to offer a tutor's position to Branwell despite his failures. He especially needed it because his aunt had left him no legacy, only fifty pounds per annum each to the girls. She had believed he should earn his own living.

But his opportunity for renewed manhood was dependent upon Anne.

Well, they had talked the theme of Branwell's weaknesses to death. Especially Charlotte. At the time when, to save the family, she might have accepted that offer of marriage from Henry Nussey in 1839, 'I *will* not marry merely for security!' she had declared. 'Ellen Nussey depends on her brothers. Mary Taylor relies on her Joe. I will not marry just because *we* cannot depend on our brother!'

'Mary Taylor treats dependency with contempt,' Anne had pointed out.

'And so do I! So I will work for ever!'

When Branwell had returned from Bradford with his tail between his legs, Charlotte had stormed at him with more sarcasms.

'I'll work as a housemaid! I *will* not be stuck between drawing-room and kitchen as a governess, not sure of my place! It is so *ignoble*! Oi surely will! Isn't that what "Oirish" girls are supposed to be when they've neither fortune nor a dependable *brother*? I won't be a cook – I hate cooking – nor a nursery maid nor a lady's maid, nor any kind of needlewoman or a taker-in of mending. Life as a plain housemaid will suit me fine! Perhaps all the talent I have is for cleaning, for making beds and sweeping hearths and dusting rooms!'

In the event, Charlotte had gone as a governess to Stonegappe, near Skipton, but soon she had been back home again. 'At least I'm saved from acting quasi-housemaid to children who have—'

Charlotte had stopped in her tracks. She had not needed to remind them, Anne especially, of what hurt the most about succouring the spoiled children of other families. Families with mothers. Families which maybe did not have their two eldest buried in the church outside the window.

After Stonegappe, Charlotte had been unable to bear yet another governess position, at Upperwood House in Rawdon near Leeds. The Whites who lived there were kind enough to Charlotte, Anne knew that. Upperwood overlooked the River Aire downstream from Woodhouse Grove, and that was why Charlotte had been even less tolerant than at Stonegappe. 'Oh, Anne! I used to take my walks where Papa and Mama went courting nearly thirty years ago and I could not bear to return and see children so happy with their *natural mother*! It was selfish of me, but I could not watch Mrs White take little Sarah or Jasper onto her knee, smothering them with love, without recalling that *we* had to make do with a dutiful aunt.'

Emily had come home pale and ill from her 'slavery' at Law Hill, hinting at sights that had shocked and repelled her. Anne had commenced her first governess post, at Blake Hall in Mirfield, and had despaired of controlling the cruel Ingham boys who did such things as taking young thrushes from their nests and torturing them.

They all wanted to stay at home, continuing their childhoods for ever: walks, domestic chores, fulfilling the duties of a parson's daughters as necessary, but escaping into the wicked frissons of Angria and Gondal. Because Tabby had retired at last to a Haworth cottage with her sister, they could legitimately spend their days on housework, or in training John Brown's eleven-year-old daughter, Martha, to do it: a well-disposed little creature in her brown pinafore, but not capable of much, yet. They refused to employ another adult because, they said, 'Tabby will surely come back.' Again – they were holding on to childhood.

'Human feelings are queer things,' Charlotte said. 'I am happier blackleading the stove, making the beds and sweeping the floors at home than I should be living like a fine lady anywhere else.'

Even Charlotte's and Emily's great adventure, of going to school in Brussels, had – paradoxically and ironically – sprung out of a desire to cement their lives in Haworth. 'Papa, couldn't we open our own school, like Miss Wooler and Miss Patchett and so many others – in the parsonage?'

Aunt Branwell had been persuaded to subsidize study in a 'school on the Continent' in order to improve their abilities with the 'accomplishments': French, German and music. It had all been inspired by Mary Taylor telling them about her visit to Brussels, and Monsieur Heger's establishment.

For herself, Anne had not been optimistic about the proposed parsonage school – *her* staying in Haworth would only result in her continuing role as 'baby'. The upshot was that only Charlotte and Emily had gone to Belgium.

When Aunt Branwell died, they had rushed home again. One term had been too much for Emily and she had nestled back into the parsonage, while Charlotte had returned to Brussels alone, baited helplessly by love.

So it was only 'baby' Anne who could have said (but she didn't say it), 'I have *chosen* to go into the world – and only I have *succeeded*.' So only she had earned the right to criticize Branwell.

His overcoat was of fancy cut, worn with a black cravat, and he rested his hands, in black gloves, upon the head of a dandy's rattan cane clasped between his knees. He had to wear spectacles all the time nowadays. They were balanced halfway down his Roman nose. To improve his five-feet-three-inches stature, he had brushed his mass of red hair into a cliff rising from his forehead. Balanced on the back of his head he wore a tall hat.

The lining of the hat had poems tucked into it; she knew this because it always held them. She also knew that his leather bag held a bottle of laudanum, and that the bag was stuffed with poems. In his trunk would be his talismanic copies of de Quincey's *The Confessions of an English Opium Eater*, the *Oresteia* of Aeschylus, the Latin version of the Odes of Horace, and his translations. They were very good. At least, Mr Hartley Coleridge thought so, Anne had been led to believe.

Their journey would take them all the hours of winter daylight, so they stopped at the inn near Bolton Abbey. It took a quarter of an hour for feeling to return to their pinched fingers and toes – a quarter of an hour of a hot fire, and, for Branwell and Joseph, a brandy punch. Anne drank tea.

'You must not expect too much of the Robinsons,' Anne advised. 'She is very worldly. The Reverend Mr Robinson pays the vicar from Green Hammerton to take his services at Little Ouseburn. He has never buried anyone nor baptized a child in his life, other than his own.

'You must not expect much of Master Edmund, either. He is not shaping up to be any kind of a scholar. His father doesn't care. It will make demands on your patience.'

Anne had said all this before, but harped on it because Branwell always expected too much.

'I assure you I will be patience itself, *quantum sufficit*.'

He believed that patience would be easy.

Their next pause was for a full meal in Harrogate. An hour was longer than they should have lingered. Over wine, ghosts were toasted: valedictions to the life that Branwell was supposedly leaving. There were anecdotes about Leyland and Branwell's friend, the railway engineer Francis Grundy; about the Bradford painters, and the members of other circles to which Branwell had belonged, ranging from a village Reading Society, to the 'boaties' on the canal. He even told stories about the Haworth freemasons. But mostly his tales concerned the group centred on Leyland's studio in Halifax. Sometimes Branwell spoke in Latin, whereupon Joseph frowned in puzzlement but also admiration, laughed like an idiot, and egged him on.

Joseph's face was red and seemed to have grown larger as the years had gone by – it was certainly fatter. His eyes seemed smaller. His face seemed to grow fatter and redder and his eyes smaller even while he was drinking.

Anne left the table and sat in the inglenook. She was thinking about the dead man whom she loved. She pulled her prayer-book from her pocket. Her fingers trembled on the pages as she heard the conversation over her shoulder.

'D'you remember t'fust time yee fell off a chair, Branwell? W'ad to carry y'ome, at finish!'

Their recycled stories were growing more fantastical. Anything seemed funny to them now, and mourning seemed forgotten, though Anne knew it was hysteria, healthy in the end, purgative. Grief did not pass. It deepened into a pool of feeling for others; wisdom – one hoped – to be drawn upon from underground.

At last they were out again, in the bright light. 'By eck, it's cowld!' Joseph declared, mounting behind the horse.

Branwell got in beside her. '*Don't worry!*' he said. 'That was my *vale vino* – my farewell to John Barleycorn. *Whoops!*'

He was in the act of giving her a slow, awkward, stagey wink when his lids closed for a few seconds, as if he had forgotten that he was winking, or was falling asleep, then he slipped sideways, and jolted awake. Fortunately, the two men were soon sobered by the cold. The horse, rested, watered and fed by the ostler, cantered out of Harrogate. They travelled through Knaresborough, across the Great North Road, and were soon approaching Thorp Green.

Anne turned over in her mind what Branwell must have meant by claiming to be two people. He did not mean that he was hopelessly divided. He meant to say that he was twice what other men were; above all, because he could choose both good and evil, so others had better beware, for his access to wickedness gave him unleashed powers. It was no doubt what he had talked about with Leyland in his 'marble works', as Leyland called his studio. If his new life should fail him, he would become as great as Northangerland by embracing folly.

Throughout her reflections, Anne remained tender towards her brother. It was costing her a reduction of ten pounds in her salary to give up one of her four charges to him, and she had done it by persuading Mr Robinson that ten-year-old Edmund was now too old for her care, and needed a classicist to prepare him for a grammar school.

The aim of her sacrifice was not merely to find Branwell employment. It was also to get him away from Haworth and the West Riding; both from its reprobate company – especially Leyland – and from the unhealthy air. From the moment she had first scented the clean air that existed away from the West Riding, she had thought it the panacea for all their problems. They would all be healthier and happier away from Haworth.

They reached the last miles of lane to Thorp Green. The frost was settling again, but the bleached fields were golden in the setting sun. The scattered farms and cottages glowed. When arriving here for the first time, she had loved the colour of the houses – the warm, pink bricks and tiles – that seemed to be blushing with pleasure. Also, she could *breathe* here. Never having been away from the factory districts, she had not known before that the air could be different in another place. She'd hardly noticed that she had been choking in Haworth, where so many were crowded together, under so much smoke. She had felt a sharp, clear thrill of hope of being well in Thorp Green. Here she might have no asthma. She could not imagine that it would not purify Branwell, too, physically and spiritually.

Moreover, every summer the Robinsons had taken her forty miles to enjoy the wonderful sea air at Scarborough.

But it had been May, not January, when she had first arrived and she had been obsessed by William Weightman. Love had grown through separation – and also, so perverse was human nature, because Weightman had been a flirt. He had sent Valentine cards to all three of them – the only ones they had ever received. All three sisters had bought perfumes from Keighley, dabbed it on and passed it off as 'nothing', and stared competitively into William Weightman's eyes. He teased them further by hinting that another woman, far away, might have his affection.

Despite his fecklessness, all other men had seemed such inferior shadows of Weightman that she had trouble with crediting any *real* existences to them; any passionate, feeling, complex, attractive existences. It was like that for her still. The only reality that other men had was as a measure of how much less they were than he – he whom Charlotte had nicknamed 'Celia Amelia', not from contempt for his virility, for that seemed superabundant, but, as Anne realized, to minimize that virility's danger.

He had been what everyone called 'a lovable man'. Anne's love for him had been the more burningly painful for knowing that her feelings were deeper and keener than were his for her; or indeed than his could be for anyone. Nonetheless she still dwelled on the dearest memories of her life; his loved face, his mannerisms, his ways of walking and talking, and his bubbling light-heartedness. Perhaps love had been the reason why even the spring flowers, strong yellows and oranges, had seemed of a particularly warm colour then.

Ever since Weightman's death, the Ouseburn countryside had been haunted by him even though he had never been here. It was because her thoughts about him here had been so intense, and it was where she had spent almost all of the time she had known him. Her deepest feelings were invested in Little Ouseburn.

They turned off to the right, between the hedges of Score Ray Lane. The sun had set and a bell was ringing in the labourers of the estate. Men and women were slipping quietly from fields and hedgerows. They were not clattering from their work in dark and dusty crowds, as they would have done in Haworth. There was no banging of metal-tipped shoes on cobblestones.

The gig entered the Thorp Green park, which had deer grazing on piles of hay put out for them under the oaks. Elm trees arched over the drive.

'Don't you love the peacefulness?' she asked Branwell.

'*Paradise!*' Branwell agreed.

They came up to the elegant, square, three-storeyed

Georgian house, with its colonnaded porch, two sets of windows on either side. They were driven up to the front door without Joseph even thinking of going to the servants' entrance. Being a friend of Abraham Wildman, the Haworth Chartist, he would not dream of turning up at the servants' entrance anywhere without protest.

'But not too peaceful, I hope. I hope there will be some company,' Branwell added, and Anne shuddered.

BRANWELL

Lamps were lit in the hallway. Branwell, second out of the gig, paused and looked into the mansion from the doorstep, while Anne, unusually for her, dashed forward. A cascade of silk dresses, yellow and white, petticoats and ribbons – Mrs Robinson's daughters of course – poured around her, crying: 'Miss Brontë! Miss Brontë!' Two servants behind his back were helping Joseph with the luggage. A man in livery addressed him: 'Mr Brontë? I'm Sewell, the steward. You're lodging with me in the Monk's House. I believe your driver's spending the night there with us, after he's fettled his horse.'

Anne glanced back. She was beaming. Thinking of the alcohol lingering on his breath, he waved her on. She vanished through a broad, mahogany door, and when the hall was empty, Sewell led Branwell in.

It was an anticlimax. Sewell led past the door – giggles and laughter on the other side of it – to another at the passage end. He found himself, hat in hand, in the kitchen: a big, echoing room, with a smell of smoke, and full of maids and pans and scrubbed tables. He was looked over and smiled at – they knew who he was. He recalled this feeling from Broughton-in-Furness: he belonged neither with them nor with their employers. He caught Sewell winking. Mr Sewell picked up a lamp and Branwell replaced his hat as he was led through the kitchen and out into a yard.

'I'm sorry to see you've suffered a bereavement,' Sewell remarked.

'My aunt, last November. And before that, I lost my close friend.'

'I'm sorry. Christ, it's a cold night. Watch out for ice.'

They trod a dark path through kitchen gardens, Branwell tapping his cane. Hard stars were netted in the trees. They passed a stable in which could be heard a violent kicking.

'Hunters,' Sewell explained. 'Six of them, fed on oats. It keeps them lively.'

They passed the coach-house – through an archway he saw a grand coach, and a small trap – the saddle rooms and the laundry, all with servants still working in them. He believed that there were ten altogether in this establishment.

'The monks from Fountains Abbey first built here,' Sewell said, walking ahead. 'It was their resting place on their way to York. One of the abbots died in the Monk's House, which was the earliest building. Their fishpond's yonder. We call it the "stew pond". Carp, some perch. Do you enjoy fishing?'

'Shooting, sir. The fishing isn't up to much in my part of the country because of poisons in the rivers from the factories.'

'I don't know how you can live with that.'

Mr Sewell led Branwell to what looked like an old farmhouse, one hundred yards away in the grounds. In the starlight, Branwell saw that it was dilapidated enough to suit his Gothic imagination. The 'Dutch' gable end was crumbling, tiles were missing, some doors were hanging from hinges, saplings had been allowed to grow at the bases of walls, and a great beech tree covered a large area of roof. A lamp had been lit in an upstairs window, presumably by whoever had already led Joseph to his room there.

'I've never seen such a place for bats and owls,' remarked Mr Sewell.

'A dangerous place for *noctambuli*, no doubt?'

'Eh?'

'For sleepwalkers.'

'That's what you call them? You *are* a gentleman, then,' Sewell commented, sourly, as he led the way up a stair that was covered with dust and chaff.

'We'd do best to divide the upper floor between us, as the ground floor's cold and damp,' he said. 'Me at this end and you at the other, we should get on well. I've lit both fires.'

Branwell saw the light down a passageway and followed Sewell towards it.

'Here's your place,' Sewell announced.

The room had been cleaned and there were curtains at the window. There was a made-up bed with a chamber-pot beneath. His trunk awaited him. An ancient wardrobe creaked when Branwell went to open it. There was a large oak table, and a small one holding a ewer and jug. There were a couple of chairs, and a mirror. All solid, oak stuff. A small faded carpet. A fire burned in the simple stone fireplace that was built in a different style in this part of the country. Odd how it varied; you could probably tell where you were by the style of fireplace.

He looked around in the pool of light, trying to penetrate the shadows.

'There isn't a shelf for books,' he complained.

'We thought you'd be working in the library. We'll find you summat, but the rats'll gnaw the bindings. They go for the glue.'

It was dusty and frugal, but Branwell liked the ghostly atmosphere. A poet's haunt.

He wondered whether Sewell took opium.

'I'll leave you the lamp while you make yourself at home,' Sewell said. 'I can find my way back in the dark. There'll be some supper in the kitchen, though I'm told you'll be dining with the children in the future.'

Cold though it was, Branwell removed his hat, gloves and overcoat before returning to the main house. He banked up the fire from the scuttle that had been filled with coals and left on the hearth. He dismembered his trunk, putting books and papers on a table, hanging up his clothes. He used the ewer to wash himself. He dissolved salt, that he had brought with him, in a tumbler of water and rinsed his mouth. Ah, that was better. He drank a glass of clean water. He combed his hair, tugged at his waistcoat, picked up his cane, gave himself a smile in the mirror, then re-crossed the still, crisp yard, past Mr Robinson's wild horses, to look for Anne, and whoever else he should meet.

He avoided the kitchen and entered through the front door – making himself at home. A lamp was lit on a table and he placed his own by it. This time he noticed the furniture. The table was gilded, French-looking. A mirror was rococo. The wall was papered, crimson and gold, embossed. The taste of the house was anything but severe. Ah! Someone, a few years ago, had made a change, and put the old, heavy Jacobean furniture in his own room and, he would bet, into the servants' attics.

How to find Anne, or Mr and Mrs Robinson? Fortunately a boy who looked ten years of age appeared – dashing in, in fact; no doubt his pupil, flying in as, Branwell imagined, his hunting-parson of a father must rush at a fence.

'And you, sir, must be Master Edmund!'

The boy stood quite still, and stared. 'My mother wants to see you in her sitting-room,' he announced. It was in that threatening tone that was familiar to Branwell from Broughton-in-Furness; the tone of a spoiled and savage little boy who had already learned – maybe from those neighbours whom Branwell had heard about, the Thompsons of Kirkby Hall – that tutors were insecure and could be quelled by pulling rank.

He found Mrs Robinson. Her hair was jet black, her skin swarthy, her eyes dark. He fancied there was Italian blood. Warm blood. Her face was more attractive than it was pretty; it was full and sensual, especially her lips. He thought of a mistress of Byron or Shelley. Anne, after describing Mrs Robinson as 'worldly', had added: 'And those with only worldly aims, pay for it with a Hell within.' That was typical of Anne, but Mrs Robinson did not look as though she suffered from a 'Hell within', or knew what one was. She looked very pleased with life and her possessions: this house, estate, family, this forest of rococo furniture. He had expected her to be wealthy in appearance, but not so fashionably attired, 'out in the country'. Ah, he remembered, York is only a few miles away. Over a green silk dress she wore a shot-silk, taffeta mantle, also green, of two layers. Her hands were decorated with rings, mostly set with emeralds.

'Mr Brontë!'

'Ma'am.'

She was so much in command that she did not feel the need to say more, but contented herself with surveying her new employee. He later thought of her as a gorgeous, resting butterfly, yet she had seemed vivacious and animated even in her stillness. It came largely from her dark and wicked eyes.

Branwell turned his attention to Mrs Robinson's hand. It was plump, manicured, as fine as porcelain, and flashed with the green, tigerish fires of her emeralds.

He raised his eyes again. Disconcerted by her level gaze, he did something rash, but typical. Blushing, he bent his head, lifted her hand and kissed it. He took even himself by surprise.

She returned him a look that was amused, curious, though still calm. His over-familiar gesture – he was still emboldened by alcohol – did not surprise or offend her. Her eyes sparkled.

Perhaps it was fate.

Anne had now only the two younger Robinson girls, Elizabeth who was sixteen, and Mary, to teach. Branwell was amazed by Anne's naturalness with them, especially when he recalled that throughout her first year she had longed to get away from her charges, who had looked down on her. Hers had been a hard-won battle, but after two and a half years, see how glad they were to be with her. She had no trouble in talking to them, and about them, as her equals. While they were present she outlined their characters as one would of children. According to her, Elizabeth was the tomboy, 'most fond of riding and spending time with the stable boys', despite which Anne thought she was the one most likely to control her passions and await the right partner; Mary was flirtatious; Lydia was headstrong, romantic and pretty and Anne feared she was going to break some hearts. 'I hope it will not be her own, nor her family's.'

Marriage was the major preoccupation of the girls and their mother. Lydia, named after her mother, and at seventeen the eldest, had been released from the schoolroom to take up post-graduate studies in the art of acquiring a husband, which meant shopping trips to York twice weekly with her mother. Branwell observed how busy and happy Anne was with the other two, in her schoolroom on the ground floor of the east wing.

It was a simply furnished room, but as Mr Robinson had also been educated in it, it had been stocked with books during Napoleonic times. Though not much added to since, yet Anne, when she was not busy teaching or sewing, seemed entertained by the volumes, many of them devotional. She could also take her meals alone in the room, or with the two girls if she wished, or with her brother. She could copy out music or write poems. She showed Branwell that she had composed many, and she confessed that she was writing a novel about governess life, based on her diary, and called 'Passages in the Life of an Individual'.

Branwell tutored the Robinson heir, Edmund, in the comfortable library, also full of old-fashioned books. But Edmund was most interested in fishing for pike. He used a long pole with live bait, a frog, perch or roach, wriggling to its death on the end of his line in the River Ouse, which was less than a mile from the house. The dreadful boy had to be kept to his Latin grammar by what little force Branwell could exert. It was a hard, wearisome task, but relief came.

'Will you come and read to me at the end of each afternoon, at about three o'clock?' Mrs Robinson requested after he had been at Thorp Green for a week. 'I like to put my feet up at that hour, and by then it is time for Edmund to take some fresh air with his father. Bring me your translations of Horace. Your sister told me about them.'

On his first visit he also brought a posy of snowdrops and celandines, plucked from where they had dared to show their early blooms at the foot of the south-facing outer wall of the garden. He had done it spontaneously, no device at all in his mind, yet his gesture pierced her armour. 'Oh, how delightful of you!' she exclaimed. He saw no vase to put them in, and as she did not suggest finding one, Branwell laid them on the edge of her table. By then she had recovered her composure.

'Sit down and read me your Horace, then. Soon I shall ring for tea.'

Thus he began to spend three afternoons each week with Mrs Robinson, when she was not in York.

The first time, when he pulled some papers from the satchel which he carried everywhere and read from the first Ode of Horace: 'As whirls the Olympic car along, And kindling wheels, and close shunned goal' – she was not impressed, and remarked that it sounded like a steam train. This led him to tell her of his work for the Yorkshire–Lancashire Railway. He described dining by torchlight with the workmen inside the Summit Tunnel before it was opened, the thousands lining the track for the first train through Sowerby Bridge, and his shaking the hand of George Stephenson when he came down on the first train, but Mrs Robinson hardly comprehended the Angrian magnificence of it all.

Then she spotted it. 'There is a drawing on your manuscript!' she exclaimed. 'Let me see it!'

He had depicted a distinguished man with curls brushed forward over his cheeks. His shoulders and the suggestion of a horse-rider's stoop were reminiscent of the Duke of Wellington. He had a marked, Roman nose, like Branwell's.

'Is it a self-portrait?' she enquired.

'It is Alexander Percy, the Earl of Northangerland.'

'*Who?*'

After this, his visits, when he talked of Northangerland, became associated with a pleasant excitement that was like the slight pricking of many warm needles.

She being so much older than himself, and of a superior station, there should not have been those sparks of sensual interest between them. Yet he felt in her a certain motherly sensuality – motherly and therefore wicked if it was carnal – which he was disposed to give in to. There seemed a promise of their exclusiveness, as if she and he were already in the net of an obsession, and after a couple of weeks he was considering the possibility of an extraordinary level of communication. It quite drowned his thoughts of Broughton-in-Furness and the dead baby. His veins were flooded with the tremendous hope of a change in his fortune. He had seen in her eyes, and had felt in her kindly teasing, the possibility of what had sustained so many poets: a patroness. It was as if she had been waiting for him to come along.

He saw less and less of Anne. She frowned on the time he spent with Mrs Robinson, and she disapproved of his

315

already shedding some of his mourning. The two of them took some meals together, generally in the company of her pretty charges; they went to church, and took a few walks. Otherwise, as she was accommodated in a bedroom near her schoolroom, they did not have to meet very often.

If only she knew, thought Northangerland.

When Mrs Robinson did not engage his attention, Branwell could discuss the classics, or go shooting, with his new acquaintance, the Robinsons' doctor, Crosby. In the evenings he wrote poems and letters in the Monk's House, or lay on his bed, perhaps lapped in opium dreams, or he went to one or other of the local public houses, sometimes with Sewell. He felt an optimism and an excitement that he had not felt in years.

Spring began to show, not yet upon the oak trees that dotted the park, but on birch, chestnut and sycamore trees, and on the banks of the River Ouse, and by the fishponds – juicy marigolds in the water, violets and primroses where it was drier – close to the church which was attended by the whole Thorp Green household. Branwell's and Anne's days had a graced quality. Outside his tutoring, much of Branwell's time continued to be filled by Mrs Robinson. When Papa paid a visit in April, he found a happy and confident son. It put him in a good mood. 'You are in a fine position to advance yourself!' he declared. 'I don't think I've ever seen you so flushed with joy and promise. I am filled with pride.'

Meanwhile, Branwell noticed that his father managed his peculiar situation, between his children's roles as servants, and his own as a man of the cloth equal to Mr Robinson, extraordinarily well. A space of time had shown Branwell how much there was to admire about his father, who could be reserved because of his integrity, yet found common ground with Mr Robinson by discussing their shared problems of church rates and dyspepsia.

Papa appreciated Mrs Robinson, too. He described her as 'charming'.

Mr Robinson would visit the library to find out how his only son was doing. He came in growling. He smelled of horses and hay, often of brandy. Though emaciated from illness, he tried to preserve the manner of the big man he had once been, still shouting and spreading himself. His first visit, in February, set the tone for the remainder.

'You must vacate that chair for me when I come in, young man,' he snapped. 'I need a comfortable chair. My years are catching up on me.'

'*Tempus fugit*, sir.'

Branwell already wondered at the miracle of such a boor capturing such a beautiful wife. He reseated himself on a hard, wooden Windsor chair, on the other side of the table at which Edmund was scowling at Caesar's *The Conquest of Gaul*. Mr Robinson sank into the great leather armchair by the fire. He almost disappeared into it. He burped.

'Dr Crosby calls dyspepsia, "The remorse of a guilty stomach",' Robinson remarked. 'Edmund, why don't you go and see that your fishing gear is in order?'

'I saw to it yesterday evening, Father.'

'Then go and see what the grooms are up to. Go on! Off you go!' When his son had left, 'I can't enjoy a damned thing any more,' he said.

'My father, also, can digest little but porridge, sir,' Branwell said sympathetically.

Mr Robinson tapped at the table and stared Branwell full in the face, inquisitorially. 'How's my son doing? Is he picking up his *amo, amas, amat*? His *amor omnia vincit*, his *dulce et decorum est, pro patria mori*?'

'Your son is making progress, sir, but it would help *him* if you would help him to see that all the world's wisdom is contained in the sayings of the Romans and the Greeks.'

Mr Robinson glared as if he hated his son's tutor. Did he – guess? But Branwell was only slightly intimidated, for the glare was what Mr Robinson turned on most people.

'That's an interesting watch that you keep playing with, in and out of your waistcoat pocket. I've not seen you with it before. Where d'yer get it?' Mr Robinson asked, and Branwell could not tell him that it was a present from his wife; just as he could not tell him about the cuff-links, the handkerchiefs, the coloured waistcoat which had offended Anne as a sign of his abandoning mourning, and the pair of boots she sent him to be fitted for on his first visit to York.

Mr Robinson came to the library approximately once a week, to glare at the tutor or throw him looks of suspicion, which meant little, Branwell soon realized. May arrived and he was still turning up for his 'confabs'. At this season, Edmund was despatched to go and rob birds' nests.

'Are you still scribbling verses?'

'I may say that I have received the praises of Coleridge and of Macaulay.'

Mr Robinson looked displeased. 'This house is pestilential with women, don't you think?' he roared.

Branwell, not wanting to pursue the implied connection between women – Mrs Robinson – and the writing of poetry, tried to turn matters by replying, 'That is not for me to say, sir.'

'They have nothing to do except look for husbands. They don't even have that once they become wives. None of them have any purpose other than to fill life with hairdressers and milliners. I've never met a woman with an intelligent occupation. Nothing in their heads. But if you don't satisfy them with frou-frou you have problems on your hands. Take my advice, young man, and don't get married.'

Mr Robinson continued his lecture for another two or three minutes, while Branwell wondered what he would make of it if he knew that his wife's head was stuffed with the voluptuous adulteries of Northangerland.

During the summer afternoons, Mrs Robinson grew intoxicated with the sins of Branwell's hero. She learned of how he had founded the Society of Atheistic Republicans, had been banished but had been ransomed by Lady Augusta Romana di Segovia who was madly in love with him; of how he had plotted his father's murder and then Lady Augusta's also, because she would not pay his fine for the deed. She was told of how, after Lady Augusta's death, he married Mary Henrietta Wharton, by whom he had three sons, whom he ordered S'Death to murder, and of how he turned to gambling and drinking after Mary Henrietta died of consumption; and of how he was executed after leading a rebellion. Born again as Alexander Augustus Percy, he abducted Lady Emily Charlesworth and was imprisoned for trying to murder her fiancé, following which he eloped with Harriet Montmorency, forsaking her for the Lady Zenobia Ellrington. And for various other mistresses, whom they discussed on gentle afternoons in Mrs Robinson's withdrawing room, or in the gardens after the weather turned warm.

It amazed Branwell that he confided what had been family secrets. But it was the inexhaustible Angria Saga, the tales of Northangerland's never-ceasing love entanglements, that was sweeping Mrs Robinson off her feet.

'My maid tells me that my husband has been holding long discussions with you in the library. What were you talking about?'

'Ladies, ma'am,' Branwell answered, thinking to tease her. 'He has a great deal of philosophy on the subject.'

'He knows nothing about us, my little Northangerland. He never comes anywhere near *me*—'

As Branwell looked at her sharply, she coloured.

'Well, now I have told you. But it is in the spiritual sense that I mean it. He never *talks* to me.' She paused, considering. 'But as for the other – you know that he is not well.'

Branwell now felt sorry for Mr Robinson, trying to throw his weight around when he could hardly stand on his feet.

She poured out the tea that had been brought five minutes before. 'Of course, you will keep this to yourself. You must not even tell your sister.'

'Of course. We do not communicate such a great deal to one another.'

'Come and sit by me.'

He sat on her *chaise-longue* and she touched his hair.

'Dear Northangerland! I am nearly old enough to be your mother, yet I love it that you come to *talk* to me – about other worlds, the worlds of your dreams. You have been in my bored life for only a few months, and, see, I am dependent on you. I want to tell you – but please don't pass this on: you may think I am well settled in this house, but no! Like you, I came from far away – Staffordshire. I was only the *second* choice as the mother of his heirs by Edmund Robinson and his family.' She appeared to wipe her eye over this. 'Their first choice was a daughter of the Thompsons of Kirkby Hall. I am sure you see how difficult that has been for me to cope with.

'You are an astounding man, do you know that? I have so longed for someone to talk to, and I have never known anyone able to talk as you do, nor able to make up such stories. Oh, promise me you will never deprive me of the sound of your voice, dear Branwell!'

'I *promise*, I promise most fervently.'

'So what story are you going to tell me today?'

'I am going to read one that my sister Emily and I are composing. In this tale, Northangerland is called "Heathcliff".'

Branwell took a bundle of papers out of his satchel.

'Emily began it when she was teaching in a school in Halifax. Then I wrote some of it. We make up the parts on moorland rambles. We walk around our dining-room table, composing. Then we write sections separately and put them together. We disagree lots of times.'

For more than half an hour – until her maid interrupted with a warning that her husband was coming – Branwell riveted Mrs Robinson with his story.

As Branwell walked back to the Monk's House, past the stable, the laundry and the saddle room, one possibility consumed him. Dyspeptic Mr Robinson, who had none of the abstemiousness of the Reverend Brontë, would not live for long. Branwell was not merely in reach of finding a patron. Perhaps the purpose of Northangerland, Zamorna and Heathcliff, was to save the Brontës' fortune through his wooing of Mrs Robinson, and for him to achieve the love of his life! That would be a turn-up for the books! Oh, that would be something!

He walked into his room singing the aria, 'See the conquering hero comes', from Handel's *Judas Maccabaeus*. Dare he? Oh, dare he? He, who had written volumes about Northangerland's consummate adulteries with the princesses who fell at his feet, could surely dare!

It was a delightful evening. Birds were singing in the orchard, while here among the simple furniture of his monk's 'cell', which he had come to love, it was comfortable, shadowy. He wrote a letter to John Brown, the mason who was the son of a mason, and his Haworth friend.

Dear Old Knave of Trumps, here I am, living in a palace where I curl my hair and scent my handkerchief like a Squire. I am the favourite of all the household, but my mistress is DAMNABLY TOO FOND OF ME! Advise me what to do! Have a word with Leyland, maybe with Grundy, who will understand.

What SHALL I DO, you old knave? For my mistress EVIDENTLY DESIRES TO GO TO EXTREMITIES!!!

She is always making me presents. Her husband is sick and emaciated. She tells me she gets absolutely nothing from him. She does not give a FARTHING for him. Dear JOHN BROWN, KNAVE OF TRUMPS – don't care one wit about your spelling but write and say what you think. Oh, it is the biggest dilemma of my life, but an EXCITING one.

He signed it, 'Jacob son of Joseph'. Brown, who had also been brought up on the Bible, would understand perfectly that Jacob in Hebrew meant 'the supplanter'.

He sealed his letter. He took half a teaspoonful of laudanum, then he lay on the bed waiting for the calm and sense of well-being to arrive. The birds ceased to sing, and he was in the soft arms of shadows. All anxiety ceased and even before he fell asleep he was lost in visions of Mrs Robinson.

They first made love by the river. In his first experience of a woman in orgasm he thought that she was throwing a fit, but when afterwards she lay still, with a degree of relaxation he had never felt in his arms before, he knew how deeply he was in love. This was not at all what he had felt with Anne Riley, the farm-labourer's daughter in Broughton-in-Furness.

On their many re-encounters, his joy in an older woman swept him off his feet. He learned new subtleties of love-making. She taught him to caress her, running his fingers from the base of her neck down her back, and along the insides of her thighs; and to rouse her with his stories.

'When you are so inexperienced, how do you manage to make up such tales?' she asked one day.

He realized that, not having any creative talent herself, she found it inconceivable that anyone should find whole worlds inside his own head. She could not grasp that one could have knowledge of what one had not personally experienced. To Branwell, this was so familiar, he had not thought of anyone else being different.

'I have a good imagination. We've never done anything else but make up stories.'

'We?'

'My sisters and I. We thought everyone was the same.'

'Get up Northangerland! We must go.'

She sat up, straightened her silks, and ruffled her curls into a resemblance of tidiness. He wondered why she had grown momentarily irritable. Was it because he had confessed that his stories were not exclusively his own?

'I love you, Lydia,' he murmured, lingeringly.

'I love you, too. Now let's be off before Edmund decides to stroll down to the river-bank with his gun.'

They walked back to the big house, where nevertheless there were no private corners for them. Even on the track through the fields they were tormented by not being able to hold hands, for some labourer was sure to see them. A shadow slipped behind bushes down the river-bank. A man who raised his hat nevertheless had the look of a blackmailer.

She was so beautiful that he found it hard to pull his eyes away. Whereas she said that she could go on listening to his voice always, so he believed that he could stare at her for ever. He was but a pair of wide-open, vulnerable eyes for her beauty to penetrate – as much now, after nearly a year, as when he had first met her.

The track ran for a hundred yards along the river-bank, where they saw a kingfisher darting. It was like a spark from a rainbow, he remarked. She told him that she believed he had the power to pull such sights out of his pocket for her – rainbows, new moons, kingfishers – for the moments were so apt when nature's most dramatic but ephemeral features appeared.

She had already told him that she believed it was he who had once set that huge, red, harvest moon to rise over the river one late afternoon; and that it was he who had once flung the full arch of a rainbow over the fields of stubble.

Calmed down at last, 'The difference between Edmund and you is that you are a poet,' she said.

'You are my muse.'

He was searching for that oneness in female company that he had known, so long ago, with his sisters. With Maria. With the mother whom he could not remember. He wanted to slake his thirst in a well of closeness. One that was deep, dark, and most dangerous.

Meanwhile, Lydia Robinson, who at the age of forty ought to have known better, was apotheosized.

But being tossed into Heaven meant she was not Lydia Robinson anymore, who had daughters, a position in the world, a substantial house, and a cuckolded husband to manage. As divine being, she came not to know *who* she was.

For the time being she was elevated by the flattery of it, that was offered so blindly.

CHARLOTTE

I

Like young doves from a dovecote, the Brontës were struck down by love – as by that hawk that had stooped, Charlotte remembered, upon one of Emily's doves one day.

Charlotte's passion was for Monsieur Heger, the peppery little director of her girls' school in Brussels: the Pensionnat Heger. An ex-lawyer, he had turned instead into a fiery advocate in the classroom. He was short in stature, dark, with dark eyes and a prominent nose. He was vain but in an attractive, manly way, and had heroic beginnings – he had fought in the Belgian War of Independence against the Dutch. He was an egoist who ruled over the *pensionnat* like a king.

It was amazing: she had gone to Brussels with the tall and reserved Douro filling her mind, and had been swallowed up by this little dictator – who happened to know the route to her heart. He was a king of the spirit. He was her intellectual hero, introducing her to French Romantic literature: to Chateaubriand, Lamartine, Michaud, and especially to

Victor Hugo, who was as shocking a taste as Byron had been at Roe Head. Charlotte could never resist a *frisson*. At any rate, not that one.

Monsieur was seven years older than she. He was the descendant of Viennese jewellers, but his father had been ruined by making an injudicious loan, hence Constantin Romain Heger's law studies had been frustrated. His first wife with their baby had died in a cholera epidemic, and he stirred Charlotte with these tragedies. He had a wonderful way with words, incisive but rich and emotional – that was the first, in fact the main, attraction.

His second wife, Claire Zoë, was a calm and practical woman who offset her husband's romantic nature, and she had brought him – Charlotte gulped at the thought – happiness, with the school, which was hers, and with their four daughters and two sons; one child born even while Charlotte sat at her master's feet. Yet, Charlotte thought, Madame Zoë did not understand her husband, she left him cold at his centre.

Charlotte clung to her passion although she knew that it could not be requited. In her fantasies, Monsieur seduced her, but in fact he had not even planted a kiss on her brow. He had shaken her hand once or twice, but it had been with gravity, in the same manner in which he had shaken Papa's hand when he had gone with Emily, Mary Taylor, Joe Taylor and herself to Brussels, (talking excitedly about visiting the field of the Battle of Waterloo). It had even been with impatience, in the schoolmasterly manner that made one think one was doing wrong.

After returning to Brussels, without Emily and against her advice, Charlotte spent a year unable to bear the sight – the *smell*, the *sounds* – of Monsieur's contentment with his wife.

She had done extraordinary things. Because Monsieur was a Catholic, in her excruciating loneliness she had gone into a 'papist' church. There she had discovered the power of plainsong to soothe demons of the spirit, transforming them into musical radiance. She had done what would have shocked Papa. She had entered a confessional box! She must have been mad. Finally she had fled Brussels.

But love did not diminish. Monsieur had taken her hand with tenderness as they parted, and she had refrained from washing it for a week. It had been as a stone remaining still warm from a hot day, long after night has fallen.

She had written about nothing but love since she had been a girl, her mind dwelling, not on the material prospects of marriage, but on what she could never think to coarsen by speaking about it, other than to her siblings: the union of souls. Now that she had sighted it, she had not expected it to leave her without peace. Never had she imagined such sharpness in loneliness as when she was able to enjoy Monsieur only in fantasy.

Back in Haworth she was hypnotized by her heart's condition, like a rabbit before a stoat, a mouse before a snake. But her love could consist only of memories – a rare evening when she had sat in the Heger sitting-room while Emily played Schubert on the piano; Monsieur lecturing on French Romantic literature – and of letters, which she composed in French.

She would begin in a way that was guarded and polite, but having spent six months bombarding Monsieur without response, she could not stop herself committing to paper what she thought was no more than a hint of the depth of her lonely affection.

In fact it was transparently reckless: '. . . for I am firmly convinced that I shall see you again some day – I know not how or when – but it must be, for I wish it so much, and then I should not wish to remain dumb before you.'

Through putting words onto paper – they were a kind of verbal mirror – she realized just how heartbroken she was.

She gulped, caught her breath, and added a postscript:

> Once more goodbye, Monsieur; it hurts to say goodbye even in a letter. Oh, it is certain that I shall see you again one day – it must be so – for as soon as I shall have earned enough money to go to Brussels I shall go there – and I shall see you again if only for a moment.

A further three months passed without word. He must think I'm a fool – I blush to think of it – I've made a fool of myself! What have I said? Has Madame read my letters – has he *talked* about me?

Nevertheless, Charlotte wrote again. Otherwise nothing happened to her, nothing could happen to her, except inside her heart and head, where love boiled.

Being fatally in love, she would never be the same person again, and the world, too, was changed, by her seeing it differently. Yorkshire and her family were transformed. She was chained to Brussels. She saw – no, she felt and she smelled the odours of the richly scented garden, the herbaceous borders, vines, jasmine, and the orchard of the Pensionnat Heger at number 32, rue d'Isabelle. She smelled the interior of her desk, into which the sensual Monsieur would blow his cigar smoke, when he left books, and an occasional enigmatic letter which she regarded as a billet-doux. In day-dreams she found herself again in the company of the foreign girls among whom she was so alone. Again, she walked out of the school, up the broad *escalier* to the magnificent rue Royale – the cavalrymen, the gorgeous ladies, the carriages – into the park by the statue of General Belliard. Again, among those fashionable people, she felt that special tang of loneliness. She looked over the tangle of roofs of the old town below. She hated Brussels all over again, and the girls, but only because of her frustrated passion; she knew that she would love it with equal fervour, instantly, were she to receive one smile from Monsieur. One moment she formed fantastic plans for going there, or to Paris, and in the next she knew that she could not go anywhere at all, there was no point to it since she could not travel with Monsieur.

When she met Mary Taylor, about to emigrate to New Zealand, Charlotte confessed. It was with a desperate hope that Mary would give her some simple advice such as she had delivered at Roe Head; something utterly obvious, that would evaporate her worries like clear, hot sun beaming upon a frost.

Mary did so. She told Charlotte that she should not stay at home, since, as she had said, she was not happy and her health was weak there.

'Think of what you'll be five years hence!' Mary cautioned. As was her way, she spoke bluntly, even callously, without meaning to; she was so impatient with anyone who was not practical. Charlotte needed such friends to balance her own, self-scrutinizing indecisiveness.

But Mary was pulled up short. '*Don't cry, Charlotte!*' she added, desperately.

The only man Charlotte could ever love was beyond reach. Her stalwart friend was sailing to the Antipodes.

She walked up and down the Haworth parlour wringing her hands.

She controlled her tears and announced, quietly, deliberately, 'But I intend to stay, Mary.'

Charlotte conceived of love as a seed in her heart, where she could either nurture it or stunt it, but still it would grow. She could not imagine doing anything other than watering it in Haworth, which was her tomb and her nunnery, while her heart was in the Pensionnat Heger.

In subsequent days she made up day-dreams in which Monsieur asked her to open a school with him in Paris; although even if he had loved her, he could not uproot because Madame owned the school and the money. (Maybe he does have feelings for me which he cannot indulge because of Madame's power?) She thought of telling him that *she* would work as a governess, a teacher, to support them both.

She imagined Madame Heger dying. Others had died around Charlotte, why should not one of them be Madame? Even then, marriage to Monsieur would carry its *frisson*, for he was a *Catholic*.

She wrote again:

> For six months I have been awaiting a letter from Monsieur – six months' waiting is very long, you know.
> I shall be satisfied with the letter however brief it be.

There was no answer to this appeal, either. She wrote yet again:

> Day and night I find neither rest nor peace. If I sleep I am disturbed by tormenting dreams in which I see you, always severe, always grave, always incensed against me.

Forgive me, then, Monsieur, if I adopt the course of writing to you again. How can I endure life if I make no effort to ease its sufferings?

All I know is that I cannot, that I will not, resign myself to lose wholly the friendship of my master. I would rather suffer the greatest physical pain than always have my heart lacerated by smarting regrets.

If my master withdraws his friendship from me entirely I shall be altogether without hope; if he gives me a little – just a little – I shall be satisfied – happy; I shall have reason for living on, for working.

Monsieur, the poor have not need of much to sustain them – they ask only for the crumbs that fall from the rich man's table. But if they are refused the crumbs they die of hunger. Nor do I, either, need much affection from those I love. I should not know what to do with a friendship entire and complete - I am not used to it. But you showed me of yore a LITTLE interest, when I was your pupil in Brussels, and I hold on to the maintainance of that LITTLE interest – I hold on to it as I would hold on to life.

I shall not re-read this letter. I send it as I have written it. Nevertheless, I have a hidden consciousness that some people, cold and common-sense, in reading it would say – 'She is talking nonsense.' I would avenge myself on such persons in no other way than by wishing them one single day of the torments which I have suffered for eight months. We should then see if they would not talk nonsense too.

Emily was sitting at the parlour table with the *Leeds Mercury* studying stocks and shares in the Lancashire and Yorkshire Railway Company. She was contemplating Aunt Branwell's investment of their legacy. Charlotte, wrapped up in her emotions, was happy to let her sister deal with it. Branwell was incapable of giving practical advice. He, too, was lost in his emotions. He was without a legacy, in any case. Papa was hardly able to read the newspaper, and Anne was still regarded as too much of a child, so the responsibility had fallen to Emily. She gave as much care to shares tables as she did to her baking or to the intricate family relationships of the Lintons and the Earnshaws in the novel she was writing. Just as she made charts of their births, marriages and deaths, just as she carefully researched the antiquated legal system that underpinned *Wuthering Heights*, so did she study the prospects of the railway companies.

'Emily, I am in love! With Monsieur Heger!' Charlotte blurted out at last. Still with no reply to her last letter, she had to speak to someone. She could not discuss it with Papa. Branwell and Anne were away. She had been considering telling Emily for a long time and now, having said it, her impulse was to rush from the room.

But her sister stabbed her with the sarcastic, crushing attitude she had developed towards Charlotte who, she said, was always lost in the sea of her feelings.

'Monsieur whom you described to me as "choleric and irritable"! "The little black ugly thing, who sometimes has the look of an insane tom-cat, sometimes of a delirious hyena". Who "but seldom assumes an air not above one hundred degrees removed from mild and gentleman-like". Do you remember saying all that to me?'

'Yes, but . . .'

'Yes, but!'

'That was my first impression.'

'What is so different about Monsieur Heger?'

'You know yourself what a fine man he is! He has passion, a fine mind and a commanding manner. In whom else does one find that combination in *real life*? And honesty! And straightforwardness! No other man is like him. No other has his integrity and his feelings.'

'Branwell, I think, is in love, too, but I do not know with whom. John Brown mutters about someone in Thorp Green, he won't say who – if he knows – but he finds it something to laugh at. And Anne still thinks about Celia Amelia—'

'Don't be angry with me! What is making you cross? Mary Taylor did not answer me like that. Please, Emily!'

How could she bear any more?

'Do you know what you are saying? What you are, in essence, proposing? What about Madame Heger and *her* happiness?'

'I would die for Monsieur,' Charlotte murmured.

'It sounds as though you would kill for him!' Emily blazed.

She folded her newspaper, got up and bustled. 'Now I must go to the kitchen!' she announced. (It struck Charlotte that she was behaving like Aunt Branwell.) 'I wish you could all be as contented as I am, but that is because I have learned to make the most of the present, and to long for the future with less fidgetiness on account of not being able to do all that I wish! I merely desire that everybody could be as comfortable as myself and as undesponding, and then I think we should all have a very tolerable time of it.'

'Emily!' Charlotte pleaded, 'You can talk that way because you have not yet felt the pain that can be inflicted by a real person. You think that my love is no more than an episode in the adventures of Douro. I can tell you, it is not!'

Poor Charlotte was about to learn, in the privacy of her comfortless soul, by the slow effort of writing herself blind, that it was not toy soldiers, tin Douros, that would make her into a great author, but her own self: the one that she was both proud of, and despised. It was by comprehending the mechanics of her own, irrational heart.

As Anne was writing a novel about being a governess, so Charlotte was composing in her head a novel about her life in Brussels. She had confronted the problem of disguise and had hit upon the notion of telling her experiences through a male character. She had not yet found out how this gender transference would work, for she was still too restless to sit composing for very long.

This summer began her temptation to flee Haworth, contradicting the instincts of a born writer to stay still, as a writer has to, scrutinizing herself instead of looking for diversion.

II

Ellen Nussey tempted Charlotte to flee. At Hathersage, in Derbyshire, Ellen was preparing the newly enlarged vicarage for her brother, Henry, who was bringing his wealthy bride to his new living. Charlotte dithered, and what finally drove her away from home was what she called 'the latest shower of curates to fall upon Haworth'. Three of them arrived in the district. She compared each in turn with her 'Dear Master', Monsieur Heger, and they were soon getting on her nerves. At last, Charlotte took the Keighley stagecoach to Leeds, made the railway journey to Sheffield, and spent three wet summer weeks at the Hathersage vicarage, next to another church dedicated to St Michael and All Angels.

Hathersage was in other ways not so different from Haworth. It was the same size, built also of millstone grit, with two factories, these ones making steel needles, and it was set in moorland. But the environs were more amiable, and less shut in. Charlotte's time there ought to prove soothing. The old vicarage was unpretentious, gentle and warm, its stone a soft, grey colour, and Charlotte thought of it as the kind of home where she herself would enjoy spending the remainder of her days, teaching in a little school, perhaps. Yet she could not imagine the pompous Henry Nussey ever fitting happily into it, despite its pretentious enlargements and 'improvements'. She wondered how he would be, lording it over weavers, spinners, and the workers in the needle factories.

She did not wish to meet Nussey and, especially, his bride, for fear she might be tempted to tell her a thing or two. She wondered if she realized that she was one of a list that had included Charlotte Brontë, a list that had been coolly written down, its candidates picked out not for passion but for useful attributes; and whether she really had, or would be able to sustain, the doll-like characteristics that Nussey had outlined to Charlotte as being required in a wife: 'character not too marked, ardent and original . . . her temper should be mild . . . her personal attractions sufficient to please your eyes'; all that Charlotte Brontë definitely was not, and all that anyone who knew the slightest thing about her could never expect her to be. His proposal of marriage had been ridiculous. She could not bear the thought of Henry Nussey, nor of his bride, she could not even bear herself, nor various provocations to mcmory, all for the same reason.

Ellen perceived Charlotte's moonstruck, apathetic behaviour, with spasms of eagerness for any diversion. The time they could talk was at night when they were curled up together in bed – it was one of the greatest delights of their meetings; 'I always look forward to our calm sleeps,' as Charlotte wrote – and there Ellen suggested: 'Charlotte – you're not in love, are you?'

She was quite put out by the asperity of Charlotte's protest.

'Ellen, I am an old maid now! I am nearly thirty, middle-aged, and too old for such nonsense!'

From her weepy exaggeration, Ellen knew that there was no truth in her evasions.

Charlotte and Ellen sat out on the lawn on one of the few dry afternoons. The maid brought out stewed pears, and Charlotte burst into tears at the mere odour of *compôte aux poires*.

Love was a hunger that pounced on the smallest morsels of memory, the more hopeless the love, the more voracious it was; and in the grounds of the Pensionnat Heger had flourished a row of pear trees, famous among gardeners throughout Belgium, which provided the girls with year-round *compôte*.

Charlotte set her basin at a distance from which she could not be affected by the redolent odour, removed her spectacles, and wiped her eyes.

'A penny for your thoughts,' Ellen said.

She was always asking that.

'I was merely thinking about Brussels. The smell of stewed pears took me back.'

Ellen stared. 'It is more than that!'

She looked very knowing. After their conversation on the previous night, it dawned on Charlotte what she might be thinking, and she coloured with embarrassment and anger. Not knowing about Monsieur, perhaps Ellen misconstrues my expression as a regret that *I* am not Henry Nussey's wife!

Tame Ellen's fascination for the half-known passions that disturbed her friend, and Charlotte's power derived from possessing a secret life, were in part what kept the friends together, yet there were times when Ellen's ignorant simplicity did cause a strain. Her absurd matchmaking between her brother Henry and Charlotte some years earlier had shown how irksome she could be. She could not be expected to understand about Monsieur, and could never be told about him.

This was especially true after the patronizing advice that she had given Ellen on the subject of love and marriage four years ago, when trying, as she sometimes did, to camouflage herself by adopting a lower level of sensibility. 'I hope you will not have the romantic folly to wait for the awakening of what the French call *une grande passion*. My good girl, *une grande passion* is *une grande folie*. I have told you so before and I tell you again – mediocrity in all things is wisdom, mediocrity in the sensations is superlative wisdom.'

After that, Charlotte knew that Ellen in return would only become sententious.

It was as cold and wet a summer as anyone remembered. Ellen tried to cheer it with such company as she could muster. The rural dean and the curate called. She dragged Charlotte off sightseeing and to visit grand houses. They had tea with Mary Eyre, a widow, at North Lees Hall, where Charlotte was consoled by the motto writ in plaster: *Vincit qui patitur* – 'He who suffers, conquers'.

Charlotte could not be saved from mooning. She regretted that she was touchy, but Ellen never quite understood how painful Charlotte's picture was of herself, especially when away from home, an insecure outsider, uprooted and planted from time to time in the bosoms of secure families whether they were friends like the Nusseys or employers. Her fate was to be a hired person, having to mind her ps and qs, to guard her temper and bridle her sensations among others' spoiled children. Her feelings when she had left home for Roe Head as a girl of fourteen had been the same as when she went to Brussels at twenty-five, for even there, despite Monsieur favouring her and offering her a post, she had felt inferior. But she was haunted by memories of her childhood when she had been an equal, happy and secure. She believed she would always be the same. That, and love, was what she would write about.

From the back of the vicarage there ran a long valley, with hedgerows, meadows and small woodlands until it was blocked by the craggy brow of Stanage. Oppressed by her secrets, by the smell of damp plaster in the vicarage, by dealing with tradesmen and hiring servants for the Nusseys, even by Ellen's company, she took walks, by herself, up the valley, which she grew to love.

She would set off along the narrow sunken lane, which was so deep that the tangled roots of beech trees hung above her head. Then she came out above open meadows, and by soakings of late summer flowers in the hedgerows. A mile up the lane it entered bare, high, unenclosed country. Looking down from there she could see the spire of the church, with the rest of Hathersage hidden in foliage. Ahead of her the first heather was in bloom, and flowering cotton grass was like drifts of snow. At the foot of the rocks of Stanage Edge she would turn left, walk another mile and descend by North Lees Hall.

The cottagers and farmers no doubt saw only a dumpy little woman in staid clothes, one belonging to a middling rank in life, her hair combed back in a severe manner. They saw a middle-aged woman without a ring – Charlotte was sure everyone noticed that, and her finger burned at its absence – walking, without any clear sense of purpose, and alone.

In fact she was with Monsieur. He was as clearly with her as, once, the Marquis of Douro had been. Everything that she looked at, if it was to have meaning and not be a mere obstacle in her way, she saw with his eyes. Her sensibility hurt her. But if she did not look out from inside his head, she felt that she was dead. The sun dashed out to light a distant field or a patch of moor; a waterfall foamed into a pool that was as golden-brown as Irish stout; and such sights became metaphors for love. She smelled the drenched countryside through her Master's nostrils. She conversed with him. She heard him speak of the flowering heather, the harebells, the moors and streams. She had asked him so many questions over two years that she felt there was hardly anything she did not know about him and, as he walked in spirit by her side, she was swamped with cares for him – how his health was, and whether he had tired himself.

She came along the lane below North Lees Hall, which she could see uphill to her right, the moors forming its background. It was a unique building in this part of the world: a thick, stone tower, consisting of three floors with a battlemented, flat roof. When visiting it earlier in the week, besides being struck by the motto, she had liked the plaster moulded ceilings, the fine Elizabethan windows, a great cupboard with a picture of an apostle on each of its twelve panels, and the spiral staircase that led onto the roof. From there one could look over the nearby rookery and across an expanse of countryside. Part of the thrill of this forbidding house, that was half castle, was the legend of the past Eyre who had confined his mad wife in the attic room. That story mingled with her dreams about Monsieur.

Her most terrible, persistent make-believe was not merely of his being free of Madame Heger (the one that had shocked Emily) for he could not be expected, even then, to find plain Charlotte Brontë attractive. Her greatest fantasy was that, being alone, he should also *need* her. As she returned to Hathersage she imagined him humbled and crippled by – Papa's greatest terror – a house fire. Blinded perhaps: then he would not be able to see how plain she was.

What mattered most in this terrible, punitive day-dream was that she should be able to 'forgive' him for spurning her, and that she should be enabled to care for him, and that it would not matter that she was plain.

Back home, she found Branwell in a dreadful state. She had not expected to have to deal with a worse than drunken brother.

'It was ten o'clock at night,' Charlotte wrote to Ellen. 'I found Branwell ill; he is so very often owing to his own fault. I was not therefore shocked at first, but when Anne informed me of the immediate cause of the present illness, I was very greatly shocked.'

'Branwell is desperately in love,' Anne explained, 'and it is disgraceful beyond what words can express. Read this.'

She showed Charlotte a letter from Mr Robinson, addressed to Branwell, which Branwell had given to Papa to save having to make a confession face to face, and about which Papa had turned to Anne. It was brief, sharp and strong. Mr Robinson dismissed Branwell for 'proceedings which are bad beyond expression' and ordered him: 'You will cease all communication for ever with all the members of my family on pain of exposure.'

'So I had to leave, too,' Anne said. 'In the last year I have witnessed behaviour so despicable as to change my whole view of human nature.'

Now Branwell – as Charlotte told Ellen – thought of 'nothing but stunning or drowning his distress of mind. No-one in the house can have rest . . . so long as he remains at home I scarce dare hope for peace. We must all, I fear, prepare for a season of distress and disquietude.'

Over the breakfast table, where Charlotte now presided, Papa spoke of love. At the moment he was hardly able to escape the theme. Branwell positively made a meal of his despair. When drunk he had threatened suicide. Even at night, he was keeping Papa awake in their bedroom with his torments at the hands of her whom Papa now called 'that vile seducer'.

'Have you heard from Monsieur and Madame Heger?' he enquired of Charlotte.

She felt herself flush. 'I'm sure that all is well there.'

Her hand trembled. She realized that Papa, who saw 'only a dim and milky cloud', had nevertheless caught sight of it.

'But you have not heard?'

'Not for some time.'

'How long now?'

'A long time.'

'I am sure you would have heard by some means if everything had not been well.'

He spoke weightily. He did not know about her love for Monsieur – at least, she did not think so – but he had suggested before that perhaps some young man in Brussels, perhaps connected with him, had stolen her heart? For she seemed so moody.

Next he referred to William Weightman. Anne still often slipped into St Michael's to sit beneath his memorial. In a deliberate manner, he remarked – apparently apropos of nothing that was part of the breakfast conversation so far – 'William Weightman was a good man! Do you remember when he bought St Valentine's Day cards for all three of you because none of you had ever received one, and went to Bradford to post them, to deceive you over who had sent them?'

They were silent for a moment, then both Anne and Charlotte started to cry.

'My children!' He looked amazed by their reaction. 'It is natural to be in love at your ages—' Papa put forth his hand and touched Anne. 'But it is damaging and foolish to be in love with the dead,' he added.

Charlotte could not stand any more of this – meddling.

'You have been talking to Mr Nicholls, Papa! I am sure he has been spying on Anne in church. He has been putting his clumsy feet into our affairs!'

ARTHUR BELL NICHOLLS

Mr Nicholls was one of that 'shower of curates' who had upset Charlotte by 'falling' on Haworth. Yet he was as tall, dark and handsome as the Marquis of Douro.

Why did these Brontë girls not respect him? he wondered. They seemed mostly to giggle and hide.

On introducing himself to Charlotte: 'You must be Mr Nicholls?' she had said. '*Bell* Nicholls,' he had answered, proudly. 'Dr Bell was my uncle, who reared me. He was headmaster of the Royal School in Banagher, one of the most famous schools in Ireland.' She had almost laughed in his face. Yet, his hair plastered down, everything trim, he knew that he looked – and sounded – the part of clergyman in a way that the incumbent of Haworth, sadly, quaintly, did not, despite his experience. Her father was unkempt – he would have seemed so to Uncle Bell. Yet Mr Brontë combined what Arthur Nicholls recognized as a native Irish manner with the quiet dignity of one who was a philosopher by nature.

The queer Brontë family would have been very surprised if they had seen Arthur this morning. After an hour in the school at Stanbury – where he taught twice weekly, and took sweets as prizes for the children as an alternative to beating the Gospel into them – he had been tickling trout in the stream above Ponden. By way of a parish visit, he had taken his catch to a moorland cottage for a widow there to cook for their lunch.

'My parish is scattered over wild country, full of dissent,' he had written home to Banagher. 'They are a wild, disputatious people, riddled with Chartism, and the incumbent is almost blind.' But he actually loved the 'primitive' people, the windswept places, and the long views down the valleys.

That morning, he had walked cheerfully back to his lodgings at John Brown's house – whistling whenever there was no-one around to hear him – had washed and put on fresh clothes, entered the church and, on seeing Anne Brontë sitting so melancholy and still beneath the plaque to the Reverend William Weightman, had changed his manner also.

He wondered himself, sometimes, why he stiffened whenever anyone who could influence his career hove into view: whether it be one of the Brontës, or another clergyman, or even one of the church trustees who, as they themselves told him in their quaint speech, were 'nobbut farmers and plain folk'.

Once, after he'd been caught 'napping', as he thought of it – playing with children, dogs and other animals, showing himself to be the country boy he was at heart – he had overheard what was said about him in Haworth. 'It's a great pity our Mr Nicholls feels he has to put on airs,' and, by way of an excuse for him, 'He's nobbut twenty-six, he'll learn!'

In the hours of deep thought assailing him in Brown's little bedroom that looked across at the church, he tried hard to work out why he switched his manner, like an automaton.

He had been taught too early to suppress the country boy in him, that was it. Though he boasted about Dr Bell, he told no-one of his life before the age of seven when his parents had died. Like Patrick Brontë, his background was a poor Irish farm. His uncle Bell had done everything to instil the necessity of hiding that fact.

He had gone on to Trinity College, Dublin, knowing Latin but having forgotten nearly all of his Gaelic, and almost weaned of an accent. He came to his first curacy at Haworth intrigued by the way Mr Brontë had resolved the difficulty of similar origins by forging a character for himself that, if eccentric, was homogenous and proud.

Arthur Nicholls could not follow that example. At any rate, not yet. He could not contemplate being a disappointment to his uncle. It was self-consciousness and dread of failure that made him pompous. But his other, childhood self kept jumping out at him.

He wanted to impress the Brontë family for another reason. The eldest daughter was inexplicably attractive. Short, dumpy, sharp with her tongue, often melancholic and withdrawn, yet there was something tantalizing beneath the surface. Apparently he was not the only person to think so. She'd had other suitors, so the brother informed him: there was one Henry Nussey, and, he was led to believe, a previous curate, perhaps two of them. She could give one a look so clear and deep that it melted the heart. He wondered if he was in love.

He had walked into an unconventional family, all round. The father had the argumentative nature of his parishioners. He got his daughters to read the newspapers to him and then dictated to them his salvos on many issues, sending off letters about the Poor Law and about capital punishment; getting heated about the local water supplies, and about apprentice-ships for poor boys. His radical activities had been reported in *The Times*. Arthur was put in mind of Milton, dictating tracts and essays to exemplarily submissive daughters. Yet these Brontës had strong characters of their own. Not only Charlotte but all the daughters, in truth, were so lit up by their imaginations that one hardly noticed their plainness.

Every one of them seemed to be in love, with a person who was not in evidence. The youngest, Anne, mooned over William Weightman. Mr Brontë confided that he believed, from her behaviour, that Emily was in love, he guessed with some young man she had met when she had been a teacher in Halifax. Charlotte, unnervingly for Arthur, was apparently infatuated with someone she had met abroad. Then there was the brother, drinking and wailing because of some unhappy love affair.

Branwell also protested about having to attend church services, and behaved badly at them — both he and his sister Emily. In any other parish, all this, from the appalling behaviour of the only son to the clergyman's eccentricities, would have seemed a very peculiar set-up indeed. Haworth took it in its stride.

'My mountain parsonage is very queer. Up in the winds at the top of the village, it is full of secrets,' he told them in Banagher.

The majority of callers came no further than the kitchen. Other visitors went to commune in Mr Brontë's study. A very few enjoyed formal tea in the 'parlour' – just as Arthur Nicholls with other local curates had done when he first arrived. (And where they had been 'baptized' with a round of insults from the eldest daughter, who had burst out with all sorts of accusations about their principles, which they had to forgive!) To enter the inner recesses was a privilege. Nicholls was forever unsure whether or not he should be where he was, and how to behave. He was divided between curiosity and a wish not to intrude, so that he trod quietly; and yet was every now and then coughing politely, or banging doors to announce his presence. If he came upon one of the girls talking to Mr Brontë, he observed a sharp change of subject matter – sharp so as to warn the blind parson.

No wonder Nicholls was uneasy and that he tried to impress them with his clerical dignity, though they laughed at him.

BRANWELL

He felt better at the first glass of whisky. His guilt dissolved. Isn't it a miracle? Ah, that's better. Isn't that much better. Another glass, and the world is beautiful – that is, the bedroom in which he lurks, in late morning, or maybe it is mid-afternoon – he does not know. The room has become bigger. It has become smaller. It holds him better. It is secure. He feels better. But, oh . . . my head . . . and that dry burning.

Papa had left – shuffling into his clothes, wearily, slowly, hesitating to speak but scrutinizing him; as Branwell knew even while he kept his eyes shut, or hid under the sheets. Just as he could hear the shuffling.

'I know you are awake! Listen to me! I will not have a repetition of your behaviour in church last Sunday. Mr Nicholls tells me you were reading a book, and winking at the wardens, or at Emily.' Branwell had been reading De Quincey's *The Confessions of an Opium Eater*.

When Papa had gone, Branwell in his nightshirt had darted out to his cache of whisky and sneaked it into the bedroom. At the third swig, or the fourth, the river was sliding by and Lydia was tying up her hair. Thank God that he did not whimper.

– He cries. He howls. He howls as if he is already throwing something against the wall. He reaches out to Lydia Robinson who is pining for him, prevented from being with him by a jealous husband.

At the sixth or the seventh swig, at any rate the one he definitely intended not to take, but which nevertheless he plunges into as if it were as harmless as spring water, he begins to spiral down, taking with him his memories of all the drinkers and the consumers of opium . . . Samuel Taylor Coleridge, Hartley Coleridge, de Quincey, Leyland . . .

He is incapable of observing himself any more. Mostly he recognizes only that it is either night or day; though making sure that he knows whether Papa is in their bedroom or not. He knows what time it is only when he counts the chimes of the clock, or he picks up on the domestic routine, or someone comes to beg him to eat – sniffing disapprovingly, of course, but generally saying nothing about the whisky-stale air, only remarking upon the hour.

His sleeps are short and frequent, the hours in bed are long as he moves from whisky bottle to laudanum jar, 'hidden' under bed or pillow, and into nightmares.

Under his mattress he keeps a kitchen knife.

He surfaces in the arms of Lydia; two drowning swimmers clutching each other as they rise out of the water. He grows aware of his sisters, Papa and Tabby whispering outside his door. He feels that he has been waking thus for a lifetime, though it has only been a few weeks since Mr Robinson's letter. He dresses and opens the door, prepared to take refuge in anger. He is often angry: it is his only defence and there have been stand-up battles with Papa, one of them after a bottle of whisky had been discovered at the back of the boot-cupboard.

'You tiptoe so as not to wake me because you think I am a nuisance!' he declares; but there is no-one around. They have vanished, or maybe they had not been there after all. He sees the passageway, the stairs, and the closed, dark doors.

(Charlotte, in her bedroom, groans and pulls a face at Emily, who continues her poem. Anne, in the parlour, trembles and hopes that Branwell will not interrupt her as she writes. Papa sighs in his study. Tabby, who has come back to the parsonage – as everyone knew she would – signals to Martha with her eyes.)

'Where is everybody!' Branwell shouts, boldly, and reaches the top of the stairs.

But one always knew what everyone was up to, as one would not have bothered to notice in a noisy household. While lying in bed, a draught might sweep the counterpane, and one knew who had opened the kitchen door – Tabby, Papa, Martha Brown, Mr Bell Nicholls, or even which parishioner. Hearing footsteps, one considered whether it was Emily's long stride, Charlotte's delicate steps, Papa's insecure ones, Anne's dainty ones, the hobbling of poor Tabby, or Martha Brown in her clogs. Nobody would be doing anything important, only going to the kitchen, the church, the Sunday school, the privy, the post office or the grocer's. But it mattered.

It was their seething thoughts, intentions, ambitions that one tried to grasp. Because of their secretiveness behind closed doors, he knew that his sisters were all writing a great deal. He longed for the days when he had been their leader, with his soldiers, while they wrote the parts he gave them in his scenarios. He longed to be marching around the dining-room table with them, discussing their work, but it was Charlotte who now led this exercise. She had engineered a *coup d'état*.

When Branwell had told Lydia about his composing a novel, he had been boasting somewhat. He had not been getting far with it. Now, in between catnaps, he had composed a list of subjects for poems. Alexander of Macedon, Oliver Cromwell, Horatio Nelson, Napoleon Bonaparte, Michelangelo and Julius Caesar.

But love's pain distracted rather than inspired him in these monumental endeavours – as it had been love's fulfilment that had distracted him from his novel, *The Thurstons of Darkwall*, at Thorp Green, and as writing ambitions in general had distracted him from painting in Bradford. He had managed a handful of couplets, such as 'A vessel lies in England's proudest port/Where venerating thousands oft resort', and that was all. The grander the ambition, the more inhibited was the execution, and all he had managed to do was to chip a few grains off a mountain of history. If that.

Love was different. About that he wrote complete sonnets, and reams of couplets. But they were a spiralling down, rather than a creative act. Where there should have been light were dark whirlpools of lines, sucking him down to wherever Lydia was.

Where was she?

When his family had packed him off to Liverpool and an excursion by ship along the North Wales coast for a few days, in the safe keeping of John Brown, Branwell had returned with a sonnet entitled 'Penmaenmawr', actually about Lydia. He had sent it to the *Halifax Guardian*, over the signature 'Northangerland', and it had been published! He wrote to Leyland that it was a secret means of reaching his lady, who would know the pen-name and pick up the hidden messages.

'She loves me to distraction. She is in a state of inconceivable agony at my loss. Her husband is cruel and unfeeling, threatening her with every deprivation of comfort for having associated with me. Please do not communicate this matter to a living soul.'

After waiting hopefully for the post (no, there was never anything from her) he would generally hurry off for more laudanum, or to the Black Bull and John Brown. There, even though he had been writing soft poetry about love for half the night, among men he expressed himself in the simple codes of sexual conquest. He had to stomach so much that in truth revolted him, in order to talk about his love at all, about his lost Lydia, and to do that had become a necessity.

It was in his letters that he was most fluent. He wrote unrestrainedly to Grundy, the railway engineer who remained a friend from his days in Sowerby Bridge, telling him, as he told Leyland, of Lydia's dreadful distress at being without him.

'Letters from her lady's maid and physician,' Branwell wrote, 'have informed me that her decay is only checked by her firm courage and resolution that whatever harm came to her, none should come to me.'

He made a drawing of her, bedraggled under her floods of tears. It was as if she had been standing out in the rain in her shift, her hair lank and undressed. 'Our Lady of Grief', he wrote on the drawing, and 'Nuestra Señora de la pena', and he sent it to Leyland as a sketch for a suggested statue.

MRS ROBINSON

When Mrs Robinson had dismissed her hairdresser, she took the parasol which her husband had bought her (though with her dark complexion she did not easily redden), left Wood's Lodgings in Scarborough, turned left along St Nicholas Terrace and paid her toll to cross the bridge over the gorge towards the spa. She could survey the whole sweep, from the castle and harbour on her left, across the bay dotted with fishing boats and sailing ships to the far, pale reach of Flamborough Head's limestone cliffs on her right. There her husband, Edmund, one of a party of gentlemen in a boat, was slaughtering the seabirds with a shotgun.

Lydia Robinson luxuriated in being 'still beautiful' – as she had overheard it put in the theatre foyer – and no-one more enjoyed being rich. After dismissing the tutor and losing, alas, a useful governess (such a to-do!) the Robinsons were taking their usual family holiday in great style. Edmund had splashed out one pound eight shillings to hire a coach to bring her four maids to Wood's Lodgings at 7a, The Cliff, and a further one pound eighteen shillings to accommodate their groom and horses. He had given her a brooch, a silk shawl, a smelling-scents bottle, a ruby pin and a diamond one. More by accident than by design, she had succeeded in making Edmund jealous and uxorious.

It had been touch and go with the tutor. It had been wonderful, too, while it lasted, and there had been times when she had been carried away. No-one else had ever called her his 'muse'. She had almost fallen for the flattery but then had steadied herself, realizing that in truth she was a middle-aged mother, with responsibilities for her daughters, and not part of that crazy epic, full of impossible and ridiculous names, created by *all* her tutor's mad family, apparently.

While realization was dawning, she had caught the servants laughing behind her back. Next they were sniggering at what they imagined was going on between mistress and tutor in church. Young Mr Brontë had frequented public houses when out of her ken. He had joined shooting parties, and taken sherry with her doctor. Heaven knew what he had said when in his cups. He had no sense of discretion.

'How is Mr Robinson's health?' he would chirpily ask his supposed muse.

'Not good,' she might answer, with something calculatedly between a smile and a serious expression on her face, to test him out, to find what he was after.

'That *is* bad news!'

'Maybe not,' she might answer, and hum a cheerful air, to lead him on. It was clear enough, she thought, what he was after.

It was when this tutor with the romantic red hair, with the captivating need and innocence, had pressed his poems upon her that she had begun to realize the deep water she had got herself into. The poems were so concrete, and they might get into anyone's hands. When, under the thin disguise of 'Northangerland', he began to send them to the *Yorkshire Gazette*, published by a York bookseller with whom the Robinsons had an account, she realized that she had to act. She had just come to terms with the fact that she had led the young tutor on in a foolish and dangerous way, and was wondering how to get out of it, when their servant Robert Pottage, who had spotted them together, blew the matter. She 'made a clean breast of it' and took advantage of Branwell's poems by showing some to Edmund.

'Oh Edmund!' she cried. 'I can see that I have done wrong, but how was I to deal with his opportuning? He would have drowned himself in the Ouse if I had not given in! Forgive me my soft heart! Please deal with it, and protect me!'

They had been going to Mr Roxby's theatre, the Theatre Royal in Thomas Street; they had seen *The Love Chase* by Sheridan Knowles, and the popular farce, *Secrets Worth Knowing*; so from Edmund's reactions, she knew that his hard skin could be punctured by her scenes. It had turned out better than she could have hoped.

She flushed a little when talking to her eldest daughter, Lydia, about it all, but Lydia herself was behaving flirtatiously with actors – especially with Mr Roxby.

'You know what men are!' Mrs Robinson laughed. 'If one learns how to, one can twist them around one's little finger.'

CHAPTER SIX

BOOKS

CHARLOTTE

It was such a fine October morning, perhaps the last of the sun before the winter. Emily had taken a walk with Keeper, the family mastiff which she had adopted. Mr Nicholls had led Papa off to see John Brown, and Branwell had not come home last night.

Charlotte, upstairs, could hear Anne coughing while she cleaned out the parlour grate, and Martha was singing as she dragged in coals. Charlotte was going through the house throwing the soiled sheets down to Tabby at the foot of the stairs. She had got as far as Emily's and Anne's room at the back of the house. She was thinking about her Brussels novel, *The Professor*, at one moment, and the next – as the mind tossed, who knew why, from the sublime to the ridiculous – she was disgusted at the dog's hairs around Emily's bed; they were over the rug where she would squat to read and write, her arm around Keeper's neck, and they were even on her counterpane, where Keeper was not supposed to go.

She saw Emily's portable writing-desk, one the same as her own, lying open next to the bed, and even that had dog hairs in it. As she pulled the sheets off, she almost knocked over the desk. It was made of rosewood, with mother-of-pearl around the lock, and a lining of purple velvet. Presumably Emily had left it unlocked because she could not be bothered to tidy up the papers and objects spilling out of it. What junk we all keep! Charlotte thought, as she bent down and delicately plucked hairs from among sealing wax, steel nibs, ink bottles, envelopes, bills for clothing and groceries. There were what looked like mathematical charts of dates and, on the same sheets, the names of the characters from the novel she was writing.

Although Charlotte knew something about what was in process of composition, having discussed it on several nights each week – she had praised Emily's descriptions of natural beauty, and had spoken of how appalled she was by the cruel passages – she had not known of the notebook which she now found, inscribed 'Gondal Poems' with lots of scratchy flourishes around it. She could not resist reading:

> He comes with western winds, with evening's
>   wandering airs,
> With that clear dusk of heaven that brings the thickest
>   stars;
> Winds take a pensive tone, and stars a tender fire,
> And visions rise and change which kill me with
>   desire –

Charlotte turned over more papers.

> Sweet Love of youth, forgive, if I forget thee,
> While the World's tide is bearing me along:
> Other desires and other hopes beset me,
> Hopes which obscure but cannot do thee wrong!
>
> No later light has lightened up my heaven,
> No second morn has ever shone for me;
> All my life's bliss from thy dear life was given,
> All my life's bliss is in the grave with thee.
>
> But, when the days of golden dreams had perished,
> And even Despair was powerless to destroy;
> Then did I learn how existence could be cherished
> Strengthened, and fed without the aid of joy.

Then did I check the tears of useless passion –
Weaned my young soul from yearning after thine;
Sternly denied its burning wish to hasten
Down to that tomb already more than mine.

And, even yet, I dare not let it languish,
Dare not indulge in memory's rapturous pain;
Once drinking deep of that divinest anguish,
How could I seek the empty world again?

Charlotte sat, not on Emily's couch – which was like that of a savage, smelling of animals – but on Anne's neat bed. She felt quite ill with excitement and envy. She knew her own verses to be stiff; like Anne, she was stuck with the forms of hymns. Emily wrote in language as sensuous as the 'Song of Solomon'. The beauty of the verses took the strength out of her legs and she collapsed before the poetry as if she had influenza.

But these days, Charlotte had only to read the word *love* and she was in tears; although in practice it would quickly prove too raw a subject for her to write about, and she would step aside from tenderness, into anger.

'*Miss Charlotte, I'm waitin' for t'sheets!*'

'Here you are, Tabby!'

She impatiently took a cloud of washing in her arms, bundled it through the door and watched it half float, half roll down the stairs. It wafted aside the cloud of dust puthering out of the parlour from the grate that Anne was cleaning. Martha Brown should do that job, Charlotte thought, as she heard Anne coughing.

'What art' up to i' theer, miss? I'm flummoxed to know.'

Tabby's shrewd, wrinkled face was staring upwards.

Without answering, Charlotte returned to pore over the notebook. She did not move for another half an hour.

By the time she descended, the wash-day kitchen looked like the beginning of a battle campaign, with the piles of separated laundry waiting for Martha to carry them to the wash-house. She was a willing and strong girl, and patient with Tabby, who was hopping about and interfering, pretending not to be lame. Anne was picking over the finer

349

linen and pillowcases on the kitchen table. Charlotte said nothing as yet about what she had found. They fell to discussing which of Papa's shirts needed darning. She said nothing about the poems even after Emily returned, though she could tell that her sister sensed something wrong.

Brontës and servants all dined together in the kitchen on wash day, being too busy for ceremony in the front parlour. Afterwards, when Papa retired to his study to bathe his eyes with alcohol, and Emily seemed about to ascend to her room, Charlotte followed to the foot of the stairs. She glanced around to make sure that Mr Nicholls, especially, was not within hearing, and admitted:

'I have been reading your poems. I wasn't prying, I was pulling dog hairs out of your desk. I found, "Sweet Love of youth . . ." and "He comes with western winds . . ." '

Emily coloured. 'You had no business in looking!' She rushed upstairs and slammed her door.

We're all growing into crotchety old maids, Charlotte thought. (Nowadays, she often thought of herself as an old maid.) She returned to the kitchen, then went out to the wash-house to help Martha carry the wet sheets to spread them on the lines in the yard. The breeze was from the right direction. It wasn't bringing the soot of Haworth to dirty the washing today. Such a sweet, blessed smell came from it, mingling with the autumn scent of moorland.

She went back into the house. Emily ceased sulking eventually and came down to help clear up after wash day. But it was some hours before she could be spoken to cordially.

When the autumn dusk was falling, and they both went out to find the washing still damp, cold, and stiffening with frost, Charlotte peeped around the edge of a sheet, smiled and said at last: 'I cannot *describe* how moved I was. Yours are not like the poems women usually write. I think the time has come! We should try to publish our verses!'

'No! They have nothing to do with anyone else!'

Charlotte could not ignore Emily's poems. They prickled in her mind. To be able to write about love like that! For complexity of feeling, one could only think of the sonnets of Shakespeare. It was as if she *had* been in love.

They were all used to imagining. Even so, was that feeling in 'Sweet Love of Youth' possible without having experienced what she herself had gone through with Monsieur? At Law Hill, had Emily . . . a great secret? Charlotte could not think of any woman who had ever written such poetry. If she had done it without experience, it was truly astounding. Compared with her poetry, Byron was flamboyant, Shelley posturing, Wordsworth was pious.

At last she spoke to Anne, who *already knew of them*!

'She writes them at night when we have been talking about Gondal in bed,' she said, simply.

'We ought to send some of our poems to a publisher!'

'Emily will never agree. If you hadn't pried, maybe she would have done.'

'But we have *always* wanted to be authors. She must be persuaded.'

'It would be a betrayal of Gondal, and that is all that matters to her.'

'Emily is twenty-seven years of age! If she is to be an author she must grow out of our games!'

'Perhaps so, but she will find it painful.'

'*No!*' Emily insisted again. They were in the parlour with the door shut tight. 'No! No! No! No! No! How can you even think of letting people know about us?'

'We could edit them so that they can't tell.'

'No! Our rhymes would be misunderstood. They would think we have been having affairs.'

'We could use pseudonyms.'

'No publisher would take our book,' Anne sighed. The light of hope lurked in her eyes nevertheless.

'Then we can publish at our own expense, using Aunt's money,' Charlotte said.

The more Emily objected, for what Charlotte thought were not overriding reasons, the more she was determined to marshall the project. Her governess skills, as well as her mothering skills, came to the fore.

Two days went by inconclusively.

'What pseudonyms would we adopt if we *did* publish?' Charlotte asked.

'I am not going to publish my rhymes, and that's that!'

'Suppose we could do it so that you could not tell they belonged to Gondal and Angria?'

Emily was silent – perhaps she was weakening.

'What about "Bell" for a pseudonym?' Charlotte suggested. 'Let's steal our curate's name!' It made Emily laugh. 'Maybe our poetry will ring like a bell. Will you agree if we use pseudonyms?'

'No.'

But she was wavering.

In the evening, the three of them were circuiting the parlour table. They had said all that they had to say about novels.

'What could we use for Christian names?' Charlotte mused.

'Nothing at all. I won't do it!' Emily was obstinate again.

'We ought to keep our own initials.'

'Stop pressing Emily!' Anne said.

'I would choose "Currer",' Charlotte announced. There had sprung into her mind a name that Branwell in his sporting rambles once spotted on the church wall at Kildwick near Keighley, which had caught his attention because it was linked with Haworth – 'Haworth Currer'. He had used it for a character in his writing: 'Haworth Currer Warner'.

'What would you call yourself if you did go along with the scheme?' Charlotte persisted.

'Ellis,' Emily said, impatiently, ferociously, treating the whole idea with contempt, saying anything that came to mind.

'Why?' Anne asked.

'No reason. I read it in the newspaper the other day. I was reading about the Ellis family of Bingley.'

'What about you, Anne?' Charlotte was triumphant. She performed a couple of dance steps further round the table.

'Acton,' Anne said.

'Why Acton?'

'It was one of the names at Thorp Green. But what about Branwell? We have not spoken to him about *his* verses.'

'If we include him, the book will never get put together at all. He will try to control it, but will show no sense. He will leave everything to go off and get drunk.'

Charlotte almost had her own way, but there were a few hitches still.

On the following day, they began to select poems and revise them – which mainly meant cutting out clues. Again they walked one behind the other around the dining-room table, reciting. Charlotte remained editor-in-chief, because Emily was still showing reluctance to participate, except by being negative, while Anne simply assumed that she would be led. Therefore Charlotte, more or less solely, decided which poems to include and the order they would be in. She decided that they would alternate their work through the volume. Each evening they discussed at least one poem by each of them.

It could turn into a stormy business. Emily might march off – now, not because of her poems being included, but because of verses that Charlotte wished to exclude, or change.

'Don't you see, you cannot publish those verses because they don't *mean* anything outside Gondal!' Charlotte remonstrated.

'Then I won't have my poems in at all!' – and off Emily went.

She was on edge, and not just during the evening editorial sessions.

Even normally, she was restless indoors – abandoning her sewing as soon as started, or going upstairs to look something up in a book. She would leave her stitching to stare through the window, for a quarter of an hour perhaps, at 'nowt', Tabby said; particularly at dusk when, as Tabby put it, 'You couldn't have seen nowt even if there'd been owt to see.'

She also went through her daily practice with her pistols in the garden – showing that same, manic intensity as Papa had at times, it dawned on Charlotte.

One day, Emily's behaviour shocked everyone. It was after Charlotte and then Tabby had been grumbling about Keeper getting onto the beds.

'If he does it again, I'll see to him myself, Tabby. I'll give him the thrashing of a lifetime,' Emily promised.

'Thou will, wilt tha? He's a big, ferocious beast for a lass to tackle. Yon Keeper's a tall order.'

They could all remember when Emily, in Parsonage Lane,

had separated a couple of ferocious dogs which a group of male bystanders would not go near. She had fetched the pepper-pot and thrown pepper into their eyes. Even so—

'I promise you, Tabby!'

Two days later, 'Keeper's on Miss Charlotte's bed,' Tabby announced. She seemed almost pleased to lay down a challenge.

Emily turned white. Her mouth set and her eyes, they believed, glowed. One read about that sort of thing. She mounted the stairs without pausing to find switch or whip. A few minutes later she was dragging the great, whining, whimpering dog by his collar down the stairs. His rear legs were locked in stubbornness, his head was pulled into his neck and after his first shock, when he was about halfway down, he began to emit frightful growls. That angered Emily even more. She dropped him at the foot of the stairs. If she should relax her hypnotic anger, take her eye off him to fetch a whip, he would spring on her, so she attacked the beast about the eyes with her fists, forgetting herself as she pummelled him, her hair dropping around her face. His eyes were bleeding before she ceased. She led the blinded, cowed, whimpering beast into the kitchen and mopped his eyes tenderly with warm water.

By writing many letters, Charlotte found Aylott and Jones of Paternoster Row, London. They would publish the poems if 'Messrs Bell' would pay the cost.

It happened at the time of the collapse of railway shares, but the more circumstances seemed to conspire with Emily's reluctance to publish, the more Charlotte was determined to reinvest some of their money in the poems project, despite the 'extravagance'.

She was very precise in her business communications. 'C. Brontë', acting as the Bells' agent, asked what the cost would be 'for an octavo volume with the same paper and type as Moxon's edition of Wordsworth'. To save Aylott and Jones from shock, she warned them that the verses were 'not the production of a clergyman nor are they exclusively of a religious character'.

She received a letter by return, addressed to 'C. Bronte Esq', informing her that the cost would be £31 10s. 0d. She sent off the manuscript of the poems of Currer, Ellis and Acton Bell, and then, not so much waited on, as prodded her publishers over the next couple of months.

All that winter, while they waited for fame, anxieties crept about the house like the invisible draughts. Charlotte's life again hung on waiting for the post; it used to be in hope of hearing from Monsieur Heger, now her life's blood was her correspondence with Aylott and Jones. The responsibility of being the eldest in the family scared her, sometimes.

Their anxieties blew up into disputes. While Emily blithely wanted to continue risking their legacy in railway shares, Charlotte enquired of Miss Wooler about investing in life insurance policies. Emily's interest in shares, as they were all beginning to see, was in the mathematics, not really in profiting from it; she had that peculiar character of seeming practical and calculating, and then doing nothing, being as resigned to fate as Spinoza. But none of them wanted to quarrel with her whose temper was like her father's, and Charlotte dropped her insurance plan – she said, because she had found out that the 'terms for female lives are very low'. So, after more poring over the newspapers, the legacy stayed where Aunt Branwell had put it, in the York and Midland Railway Company and in the Reeth Consolidated Mining Company.

They had Papa's blindness to worry about. Charlotte would sit for hours, talking and reading to him. He suffered from not being able to ramble about the hamlets and farms, and hated to be dependent upon Mr Nicholls who (very patiently, Charlotte had to admit) helped him up the pulpit steps, and so forth, and took upon himself many burdens which were not usual for a curate, to make it possible for Papa to keep his living. She was overwhelmed by waves of love for him in his pathetic vulnerability, wanting her to read 'Ecclesiastes' or the 'Book of Job' while she, candidly, would have preferred the 'Song of Solomon'.

Her own poor eyesight enabled her to read or stitch only in daylight. After four o'clock in the afternoon they could only talk, unless Emily played the piano. The hours dragged. Charlotte felt the terror of darkness closing in on them all.

'Papa, don't you think I should talk to an oculist about an operation?'

In his blank, grey eyes, with the film over them, the firelight picked out a frightened expression. Then they calmed and Papa recovered his usual bravery. His big, if not practical hands, the inheritance of generations of labourers, again gripped the chair without a tremor.

'—Merely to ask whether an operation would be successful?' she continued, softly.

She went to Mr Carr in Leeds – a surgeon who was a relative by marriage of Ellen Nussey – and stayed with her friend, sharing Ellen's problems as a break from her own. As Ellen had one brother who was mad and another who was alcoholic, they had much to share. They discussed growing into 'old maids' and contemplated the examples of spinsters who had, nevertheless, led good and satisfactory lives. Miss Wooler, for one.

But Charlotte could not calm her inner fear. It was all right for Ellen Nussey: despite two of her brothers going to the bad, she still had a secure elder brother to take care of the family.

Charlotte again feared their being thrown out of the parsonage. This year, Papa had been unable to lead the Sunday school 'scholars' and teachers around the village on their anniversary, managing only to deliver their sermon. He had not been able to take part fully in the installation of a new set of church bells – having missed out on the evening dinner in the Black Bull. He had missed laying a foundation stone for Oxenhope's new National School. Every Sunday his congregation saw how feeble their parson was when he had to be led through his church and up his pulpit steps.

It irked Charlotte that, because Emily was so fatalistic, the responsibility to act fell upon herself.

She also grew bitter at seeing Emily, for reasons she did not understand, sympathizing with their depraved brother.

When Charlotte came home from her bittersweet visit to the Nusseys with the good news that eye operations 'were often successful', she found Branwell in bed, drunk, after he had touched Papa for a guinea.

'He told me he had pressing debts,' Papa explained, wearily, weakly.

'He hasn't discharged them! He's spent your money in the public house. You should have known what would happen, Papa!'

'I suppose I did. But he gets into a fury if crossed. The night he asked me for money, I cannot tell you how often I was woken up. He has such dreams, Charlotte. When he wakes me, for a moment I don't know who or what is in the room — some beast. It is awful. The noise he makes. The things he says. Even though I did not believe he would pay his debts, I thought it best to give in to him.'

'And so the liar is victorious!'

'It seems so.'

'Not for the first time, either! Do you remember his pretending it wasn't he who had hidden a bottle of that disgusting whisky in a boot in the cupboard?'

'Calm yourself! Though he who tells an untruth thinks he has got away with it, he pays the price of being distrusted. We must pray that it does not become tragic for Branwell. He can neither be faced, nor abandoned, in the condition he is in, and I cannot turn him out of my room, for anything might happen to him in the night. I hope he will reach the bottom of his folly and begin to grow wise. Then we will all be able to forgive, and love him gladly. He will be the better for his experience and we too will all be the richer for it.'

Papa fumbled in his suit. 'A handkerchief, my dear, my eyes are sore.'

Papa might be excused, but Emily ought to have prevented this from happening. Charlotte turned her fury upon her sister.

She did not know whether to scream, cry, or shout. 'I have been in to see Branwell. He is stupefied, lying on his bed, incapable of answering! Papa thinks he will grow wise through growing foolish. I cannot talk to Papa about it, he is too weak, but why oh why did you let him get money as soon as my back was turned?'

'Yes, he is a hopeless being,' Emily said, quietly, and almost blithe in her acceptance. 'It is no use any of us trying to prevent what he does.'

BRANWELL

Tabby had to confront the gossip, about Branwell, about the letters for the parsonage, whenever she hobbled down Parsonage Lane.

She did not, any more, go further than West, the grocer's, and Holmes, the butcher's, but the twittering awaited her as soon as she turned the corner by the church.

It was John Greenwood, the bookseller, who had set it off. By trade a woolcomber grown too ill to support his family, he had a stationer's shop which supplied the parsonage. He talked about the quantity of paper and exercise books that were bought by Miss Charlotte. Then there were these letters and parcels up from London.

The more it became the opinion that three eccentric old maids lived up at th'parsonage, the more defensive Tabby grew. 'Folk should mind their own business,' she told them, huffily, and she described the Brontës as the most ordinary people; baking, washing, cooking, and reading their prayer-books.

Nonetheless, she worried. There had been four of these letters and parcels that she herself knew of. Folk gave even her, Tabitha Aykroyd, such looks.

She spoke to the parson.

'I don't know what's wi'em now,' she said.

'Why, Tabby?'

'The letters that come for "C. Brontë Esquire".'

Patrick laughed. 'They'll have another school scheme in mind. They'll tell us about it when they're ready.'

Neither could Branwell miss the change in his sisters. Behind the parlour door, shouts of anger or fun would burst out. He heard their footsteps patrolling around the parlour table.

Branwell, although shuffling, unwashed, hardly caring that he did not know night from day, still possessed that occasional, uncanny self-possession, with flashes of intuition, characteristic of the mad and doomed before they plunge back again under the waters.

He would appear at doorways to make pronouncements apropos of nothing of concern to anyone else at that moment.

One day, when the girls were dusting and polishing, Branwell lurched to the door in a cloud of the illegally distilled whisky that he drank, and other foul odours that, Charlotte said later, 'You could set fire to'.

'If you must try to publish poetry, I cannot stop you with my good advice!' he said.

He stumbled, straightened himself against the other side of the doorway, and continued, 'The days of Byron and Walter Scott are over. Frances Leyland told me that Moxon didn't want to publish even Wordsworth, because the market has so declined. Not Elizabeth Barrett Browning . . . not anyone. You're wasting your time! The novel's the only writing that'll pay these days. *I'm writing a novel.*' He stumbled off, laughing to himself.

How had he guessed . . . what had he seen . . . what had he been told in the Black Bull? He knew that was what they'd be thinking. He stumbled towards the kitchen, then out to the privy.

The truth was that for him the parsonage was not a place of creativity. It was one of frustration and loneliness. Sometimes it was the theatre of his most stupid anger against it, simply because it was not the public house.

The 'public' was warm, it was kind. It seemed that only in a drinking den was he sane and free. He walked right past the church where it had once been his delight to play the organ. He might call at John Brown's, but he did not want to bump into Mr Nicholls, and was ashamed before Brown's wife and teenage children – one of whom, Martha, might tell tales at the parsonage – so he was most likely to go straight to the Black Bull.

There Brown was still likely to be his most patient listener: the big man, fatherly by nature, who would put his arm around him and present a positive, humorous view of things.

These days, Branwell had graduated to the circle in the back room, among those old men who, when young, had watched the Brontës arrive and had seen them grow up.

His hands had begun to shake on the glass. His memory was blurred. His complexion was like mouldy flour. They had watched all that happen, and yet he held his own among them. His sisters might despise him, but he understood the common man as they did not.

'Folk are talking about your ladies up at the parsonage!' Greenwood remarked. It was largely to get Branwell off the subject of the rich and beautiful lady who was pining for him, about whom they had once been all agog but in whom they were now ceasing to believe. 'It's no-one else's business, but folk mak' it so – the way folk do. They talk about the parcels that arrive and the letters from London addressed to C. Brontë *Esquire*.'

'It's a mistake,' he told them – ashamed to think that he himself could not get a book published.

However, the dreadful morning in May arrived when Charlotte put into his hands a slim, green, printed volume, cloth-bound, with a design on the cover like an Elizabethan rose-garden. In its centre was the gold tooled lettering:

POEMS
BY
CURRER, ELLIS,
AND ACTON
BELL
4/-

'You have done this without me!'

'It would seem so, Branwell.'

She looked – how would one describe her expression?

'Don't look so – maddeningly superior! You have left me out because I am the only one without a legacy and cannot pay!'

'I cannot tell you how much I despise that remark, Branwell. You – a *man*! I do not feel "superior". I feel sad. I was thinking of the old days when . . . oh, never mind.'

He had mistaken her look. What had been on her mind had been a yearning for the days of fantasy. He saw it now.

She wished he *had* been part of the book. He had brought her back to earth with a jolt.

She went out of the room and left the book behind, but it would not open for him. The green covers, lifted half an inch, fell back into place as if made of lead.

'Even though in the public house they laugh with you, and admire your turns of phrase, behind your back they all *pity* you!' spat the triumphant authoress, with anything but pity in her eyes. She was tigerish with hate, and with lust for revenge. Having constant toothache, she was never in a good mood this summer.

'How do *you* know that?' he blustered. 'You who go nowhere, so that everyone thinks of you as a cranky old spinster!'

'Because that is how they talk about you when you are not there, you fool! That is what Martha Brown hears when she goes home! That is what Tabby hears *ad nauseam* at the grocer's and at the butcher's!'

It was true. Often, what drove him to the point of keeling over was that expression on his friends' faces which showed that they had moved from amusement to pity, and that they despised him for not being able to hold his drink. It made him worse. When he came to, on the following day, perhaps after being sick in the graveyard or even in a corner of the kitchen, though he had forgotten almost everything else, even how he had got home, yet he remembered those expressions vividly.

'You did not write to me like that from Brussels,' he remarked, wistfully anchoring himself in the last affectionate words from her that he could remember.

'And you did not answer me!' she spat.

He remembered how pathetic, how sad her appeals had been. 'Be sure to write to me soon, and beg Anne to inclose a small *billet* ... it will be a real charity to me. Tell me everything you can think of ... In the evenings when I am in the great dormitory alone, having no other company than a number of beds with white curtains, I always recur as fanatically as ever to the old ideas, the old faces, and the scenes in the world below.'

Now she knew that he had not responded because of his infatuation with Mrs Robinson, and hadn't had time for her.

'You have no pride!' she hissed.

He put his head in his hands. 'Tragedy engulfs us.'

'And what are *you* going to do about it? Why don't you get some work? Haven't you realized the state that Papa is in?'

He usually tried to slip home quietly, taking advantage of Papa's being able to see so little. If he came in without too much shouting, Papa might not lecture him.

He crept upstairs and into the bedroom with his shoes in his hand. Through a drunken blur, his mind jumping with memories of the night's fun, he took in the pathos of it: a candle was left alight for him, not by his own bed where he might knock it over, but safely by Papa's.

He had dropped his trousers and was pulling off his shirt.

'Branwell?' Papa whispered. His voice was dry, crow-like, old. He put out his hand, but Branwell did not take it. He rarely could, or would.

'Papa?'

Every advice and warning had long since been delivered. He did not want any more. He sat on his bed, which was at right angles to his father's, and pulled on his nightshirt. Candlelight and the dying fire enabled him to make out window shutters on his right, the table holding the ewer beyond the end of his bed, the chest of drawers on the left-hand side of the fireplace, and Papa propped up, pale-faced and sharp featured. He was like some night-hawk, with scrappy, white hair like a crest of feathers. Papa blew out the candle and said: 'Try to pray, for once.'

The request was met with a cheerless silence. Then with the rustling of Branwell getting under the quilt.

'Branwell, I do not *blame* you. You must understand that. I have been foolish, too. I once cut up a dress of your mother's. It upset her dreadfully. I wanted to force her to wear a new one, to make her happy. She knew it was too late. I only succeeded in reminding her of it. Branwell!'

'Yes?'

'I too have been foolish in love.'

Patrick told his son about Mary Burder. He confessed about Elizabeth Firth and Miss Dury.

'I was desperate . . . I do understand how you feel. I still do not forget your mother. I can't go into our room – Charlotte's room – even now. It's no good hoping to forget love. One does not do so. It is not merely a matter of enduring it, either. I know how painful it is at the moment. But your attitude towards all others whom you come to love will be richer for your past experience. Mark my words, son. When this purgatory is over you will think of it as a gift from God, for you to pass on for the benefit of others.'

'How do I start to recover?'

'Gather up your pride, firstly. For that, you must face up to yourself. Are you listening?'

'Yes, Papa. I could do *so much* if I had a legacy like my sisters—'

'Branwell! You are at a crossroads and may go one way or another. Either downhill, thinking that no good can come of your life because of the harm that has been done to *you*, or you can think of what you are doing to hurt those who truly love you – whether the sacrifice you expect from *them* is worth *their* while. Then you might list what good you might do in the world, with all your advantages. That will work miracles . . .'

Branwell had fallen asleep.

For part of the day he pecked away at his novel, *The Weary Are at Rest*. In it, Northangerland seduced Maria Thurston: the wife, longing for love, of a dissolute husband.

He acquired a little other work for himself. Leyland was farming out more of the tedious parts of his commissions – the lettering, the construction of mounts and bases – to John Brown, and Branwell busied himself as a go-between, which gave him an excuse to write letters to the sculptor. He badgered his old acquaintance, Grundy, the engineer, with laments and requests for help in finding a position on the railway again. His remaining pride was the perverse one of keeping these endeavours secret.

When he felt himself to be recovering, an unexpected

caller turned up and felled him. Enoch Thomas, who now kept the Black Bull, sent up a message that 'Mr Allison from Thorp Green' was at the pub asking for Mr Branwell Brontë. Branwell had no doubt that he was being brought the news he had been awaiting: his loved one was ready.

Mrs Thomas and her customers fell silent as Branwell walked in. She motioned him to a private room. There Branwell saw that Mrs Robinson's coachman was wearing mourning, and panic struck: she had died of love!

However, Allison put him at ease.

'Your late master has passed away,' Allison announced and waited to see how the news was being taken. He studied the excitement and hope on Branwell's face, then added, 'It was dyspepsia and phthisis, according to Dr Crosby.'

Branwell sat down overcome with delight.

'I have a message from the mistress. If I were you, I'd take a glass of brandy.'

'I've brought no funds, I left in such a hurry—'

Allison rang the bell with a gesture more of contempt than sympathy, ordered brandy, and awaited its arrival before he spoke again. He studied Branwell in the calculating manner of one surveying an unlikely contestant who was about to enter a boxing booth.

'It concerns Mr Robinson's will.'

'I am not interested in her inheritance!' Branwell protested.

Allison had the mildly bullying manner of a lawyer, or some other official who is compelled to take command of grief.

'The point of what it is my painful duty to communicate is, Mr Robinson has put his affairs in the hands of trustees to ensure that his instructions are carried out. He has left his elder daughter, Lydia, out of his will, on account of her absconding with Mr Roxby, the Scarborough actor, and has divided everything between his son, his two other daughters and his widow. However, every penny of it goes instead to the trustees if she, Mrs Robinson, communicates or has anything at all to do with you, sir. If I may speak man to man: you will understand her distress. I have heard of her thinking of entering a nunnery.'

Branwell had begun to emit frightening noises from his

throat. Little clicking noises, like a nervous tic on his tonsils. His trembling hand reached to pour another brandy. Allison did it for him, and continued.

'This move controls the mistress's future and that of her daughters. Mr Robinson has chosen trustees who do not hold you in any great favour. You might think them the villains in the piece, so to speak. It is not for me to say. But for the lady's sake, sir, I'm sure you do not need me to tell you – you being the man you are – what you have to do.' Mr Allison stood up, evidently anxious not to be delayed by the inevitable scene. 'She sent you this,' he said, looking away, and handing Branwell an envelope.

He tore it open and found no letter – evidently Mrs Robinson was being cautious – but five pounds.

Allison apparently knew the contents, and had been commissioned to communicate what Mrs Robinson had the discretion not to put on paper, for he said, 'She expects you not to go talking about her all over the place.' He winked. 'If you keep quiet, there might be more of the same coming your way. And she wants no more poems in the newspapers! Get my meaning?'

Allison left. Branwell twitched more violently, then he collapsed. From the bar, before they rushed in, they heard a sound which Enoch Thomas described as being 'like that of a bleating calf'.

Later, only the mad old Angrian ideal came to the support of Branwell's wrecked pride: it is better to be wicked than to be pitied. And *anything* that sprang from the Infernal World would, he had no doubt, draw his sisters' sympathy again.

The five pounds was spent in a month. He went to Halifax and treated Leyland, for a change. Then he turned to opium, either smoking it or taking it dissolved in alcohol as laudanum, which was cheaper than other drink, also he could get it on Papa's medicine account without having to wheedle for a sub on pretence of having pressing debts. In any case, a bottle of it was kept in the kitchen and Charlotte was regularly soaking a cotton pad with it to place on her aching teeth.

After taking opium, passages from Angrian chronicles which he had composed ten years before rose up with dreadful realism. One night, collapsing after a last glimpse of his father's head sagged in heavy slumber, the sight entered his nightmare mixed with the blinding of Zamorna.

> Ernest, aye, his son, his oldest son, holding him in his arms, just as if he were going to baptize him; the priest, one Quamina, at hand, and right red iron in his paws; whereon, we stand, and here we go, have at it: then in goes the iron, first into one eye and then into the other hissing and searing to the brain . . .

One early evening, Anne smelled smoke and on entering Papa's bedroom saw Branwell's coverlet on fire. Returned from drinking all afternoon, he was asleep on top. He had moved the candlestick to his own bedside. It now lay on the floor. Evidently he had swung his arm to extinguish it, had knocked it over without realizing, and had fallen asleep again. Anne took in the sight of his wide-open mouth, his sprawled arms and legs, the flames licking up to consume the bed, and fled for help.

Emily was already brought to the door by the smell of smoke. Instead of wringing her hands she grabbed his arm, dragged him off the bed and pushed him, stumbling and bewildered, to abandon him in a heap in the corner by the door. She poured the contents of the ewer over the bed, pulled off the sheets, tried but failed to stamp out all the flames, rushed downstairs for a bucket of water from the kitchen, and returned to douse first the bed again and then her brother – with relish, it has to be said.

Charlotte appeared. 'Thank God that Papa was not in bed!'

The fire extinguished, they ignored the shivering, half-conscious wreck of their brother struggling to come to terms with another blow to his pride, and tried to clean up the room and change the bedding before Papa knew about it.

Alas, Papa had been alarmed, too. He stumbled upstairs, bruising himself, praying loudly for everyone. All that he had most feared had come to pass! It was several minutes before he could take in Charlotte's assurances that all was well, it was a minor matter – for he could hear Branwell screaming and carrying on, and Anne in tears.

CHARLOTTE

The Manchester Royal Infirmary looked like a manufactory, with a clock set above four rows of barred windows, but it had neat formal gardens. Inside was a smell of gas from the new form of lighting. Down the whitewashed corridor, they passed a woman in a bloodied apron carrying a bucket that held scraps of human limbs.

Unlike Emily, Charlotte tried not to look around. But even she could not keep from glancing at the line of poor people in the dispensary, and into a dormitory where she saw two women in a bed, one without an arm and the other declining, she thought, from a consumption. In the waiting-room, people were white with fear, and crying. Though Papa would not see this before his operation, he would hear, and he would smell the odour of butchery and vomit.

Following the suggestion from Dr Carr, Charlotte and Emily were hunting down an eye surgeon. They had heard of the eminent William James Wilson. Apprenticed in Lancaster to Mr Braithwaite (a Quaker, and the inventor of a celebrated opium mixture known as 'Black Drop'), Mr Wilson had eventually studied at St Bartholomew's Hospital. He was at present staff surgeon at the Infirmary. He was also a gynaecologist, as well as being founder of the Manchester Institute for Curing Diseases of the Eye, a couple of miles away, where they had already searched.

Mr Wilson was not at the Infirmary either, which was as much a relief as a disappointment. Charlotte and Emily at length tracked him down to his rooms in Mosley Street.

Theirs had been quite an exploration. Charlotte was determined not to leave the strange, overpowering, commercial city before completing her errand. Emily hummed cheerfully as she went along, (nothing of the 'Sister of Mercy' about her!) driven, it seemed, more by curiosity than by mission, and easily outpacing Charlotte on stairs and streets. But by now, because it was a hot day, they took a cab, even though Mosley Street was only a short distance away from the Infirmary in Piccadilly.

Mr Wilson's waiting and consulting rooms, fortunately, were not an abattoir. There was a scholarly atmosphere designed to create confidence; only here, instead of the theological works that the young ladies were used to, were medical tomes, and charts of eyes and other organs. There were eyes in jars, pickled in formaldehyde.

They met a man who was not prepossessing in appearance, being a little paunchy from lack of exercise, but warmth, generosity and understanding lit up his features. What remained of his fair hair was brushed over his bald crown, and forwards towards his cheeks, romantically. He was charming, smiling, and witty. Charlotte, susceptible to such men, liked and trusted him at once. She knew that Papa would trust him too.

She removed the piece of camphor which she was sucking in order to ease the pain in her back teeth. She did not intend to leave the discussion to Emily. When she had explained about Papa's age, circumstances, status and condition, 'I have been told by Dr Carr of Gomersal that an operation called "couching" might bring relief,' she said.

'I don't believe in couching,' Mr Wilson answered. 'In couching, the clouded lens is merely pushed out of the line of vision. It is the simpler operation, but it is rarely permanent. When his age makes it too late for any operation, your father's blindness might return. The only effective way is to remove the lens.'

'I do not want him to suffer—' Charlotte started to say.

'Then that is the operation we must have!' Emily interrupted. 'When should we bring him?'

'I cannot operate on a cataract until it has hardened, so you must bring your father for me to inspect it. If it is firm, I can remove the lens – only from one eye, for fear of infection rendering him totally blind. Should that happen, he would still have one eye left. To minimize infection, and for other reasons, your father would need to stay motionless for at least four days with his eyes bandaged, and a further four weeks mostly bandaged, with little movement. Someone, preferably a loved one, must stay with him. I could find you lodgings for that and for the performance of the operation, if you wish me to.'

Charlotte was glad to hear that it would not be carried out in the Infirmary. Throughout the interview, she stared at the surgeon's hands, watching for a tremble. They were firm, and after a few moments she judged them to be sensitive. She felt that she had not had dealings with such men since Monsieur. She sighed for the lack of them. She would like to write about such men. She lifted her eyes.

'What would it cost?'

'My fee would be thirty pounds. If you took up my suggestion of rooms, which belong to my retired servant, Mrs Ball in Boundary Street, she would charge perhaps one pound per week for your month's stay. Then you would need a daily nurse, for perhaps fifteen shillings per week.'

Charlotte added it up to a quarter of Papa's annual stipend. It was worth it. She arranged to bring him.

'What are you thinking?' Emily asked as they sat in Victoria Railway Station.

'I was thinking that right now Monsieur and Madame Heger will be taking their vacation,' Charlotte answered, dreamily.

Three weeks later, Charlotte took Papa to the barber's. She had his hair and bushy eyebrows trimmed. That evening, she cut his toenails and fingernails. At the thought of restoring his eyesight, she was in Heaven. 'Old and infirm people have few sources of happiness, fewer almost than the comparatively young and healthy can conceive; to deprive them of one of these is cruel,' she had recently written to Ellen.

Late August grew even hotter, yet on the following morning Papa insisted on wearing a suit of black wool and on being muffled in his cravat. Nowadays he was able to take so little exercise that he did not feel the heat as others did. After helping him into his coat, Charlotte stood on the second step of the stair to brush his shoulders. He turned round, smiling, for her to do his front. She led him out to the gig.

From Keighley they were now able to travel on the railway. 'I *wish* you could see the beautiful station they have built!' she said. A railway servant took their bags and she led Papa through the ticket office. When going to Manchester with her sister they had economized by travelling second class, but this time she booked them into one of the upholstered first-class compartments.

'The train, Papa!' The monster with the long black boiler and the tall smokestack, hauling a set of blue coaches, came hissing, panting and squealing up to the platform.

As they rattled through the scenes of Branwell's disgrace in the Calder Valley, trickles of sweat ran down Papa's balding temples: mostly, she thought, from fear. One could not tell easily, not being able to see his expression behind dark spectacles. The old man, nearly seventy, sat upright and firm. His mouth was set. His hands were steady upon his knees. Would one guess that he was a clergyman? Perhaps. Or – from the white, ragged hair, the scraps of white side-whiskers, the unpretentious dress – one might think of him as a scholarly gentleman, neglectful of himself but with, she hoped it would be thought, a loving daughter.

'I trust our home will be safe,' he remarked.

'Branwell won't set fire to it again. Emily will see to it.'

Travelling round a curve, the train swayed and shook. Papa tensed.

'At what speed are we travelling, Charlotte?'

'Fifteen miles per hour?'

He was thoughtful for a few minutes. He seemed to be staring at the valley. He shifted and swayed with the peculiarly regular rhythm of a train – not at all like the jolting of the Haworth gig – then he said: 'We are lucky to have a curate as competent as Mr Nicholls.'

'Yes, Papa.'

'He is industrious. Yet he seems not to be popular.'

'That is because he gives himself airs, and lacks a sense of humour.'

He ruminated for a further quarter of a mile, and said: 'In our parish, with so many Dissenters, a Puseyite curate may not be such a wise choice. His not attending the concert in memory of Thomas Parker because our great singer was a Baptist did not endear him to many.'

'Hush, Papa! Do not worry about Haworth now!'

There was another pause.

'I wish I could study this miracle of the railway,' he said. 'Such a boon – animals need no longer be mistreated!'

'That is what Anne says.'

'Improvements' had always thrilled him, but all he could appreciate of this one was the rocking, the sense of speed, and the gusts of smoke pouring in, forcing the passengers to close the windows although it was a hot day.

At last she helped him descend into the hubbub of Victoria Station. Thankfully, she found a porter to care for their trunk and force a way through the ugly crowd: two coach lengths away she could see the third-class passengers, rude and boisterous, disembarking from their open carts, their faces 'black as Ashantees' from the smoke and sparks. Though guiding Papa yet the little woman in her pale yellow 'summer muslin', who hardly reached above his elbow, appeared to be leaning on his arm, as always when they went out together. She found a cab to take them to Mr Wilson's.

The specialist seated Papa in an upright chair and removed the dark spectacles. He lifted the magnifying glass which was on a cord around his own neck and examined the old man's eyes, meanwhile chatting about Haworth. Apparently Papa's eye was excellent for an operation. Mr Wilson suggested one in a few days' time.

It was news which they welcomed and also dreaded; though knowing of the possibility, and having brought sufficient clothing and money for a stay, Charlotte had half expected to be returning to the parsonage for a while.

'How on earth will Emily and Anne manage with Branwell?' was the first thought in Charlotte's mind.

After a night in a hotel, by the weekend they were installed in Mrs Ball's lodgings in Boundary Street, where fast-growing Manchester thinned into the countryside.

Having to wait a few days, Papa and Charlotte kept an isolated vigil, for it happened that Mrs Ball and her husband were absent in the country. There was no-one else in the small lodging house, but Charlotte was too much in a panic to notice that Papa and she were lonely. She had to organize the housekeeping, and ordering provisions and cooking had always been Emily's responsibility.

She did not care what she herself would eat: pain leapt

through her gums as soon as her teeth touched anything. Papa would only require beef or mutton, and bread and butter washed down with tea. But a nurse had been commissioned and Charlotte was worried about satisfying *her* tastes, which she was sure would be fussy ones. She was sure that the nurse would invent a hundred ways of hinting that Miss Brontë was strange, using this to bully her; and that she would complain, wanting different food from what was given her. Or she would justify all the tittle-tattle about nurses: 'an unreliable, underpaid class, dragged in off the streets' and 'drunken thieves, likely to ill-treat patients'. It was Charlotte's disposition to fear the worst of the lower orders and she had been terrified of meeting this ghoul of her imagination who haunted operating rooms.

Charlotte had fastened back the windows in hope of catching a breath of air. Through the hot, still streets on the following Tuesday morning, Mr Wilson's carriage could be heard from far off as it turned from Oxford Road into Boundary Street. She could not have explained why she knew it was Mr Wilson, but she was not surprised when he pulled up at the door. She peered down from the upstairs room and watched him descend through a rabble of children. One of his assistants carried his surgical bag. His other apprentice bore a larger bag holding she did not know what. The nurse, whom she had not yet met, came last, carrying the gentlemen's cloaks and hats.

The front door was open and they entered without knocking, as medical gentlemen do. Charlotte waited at the top of the stairs. They were solemn except for Mr Wilson. He was incongruously flippant, she supposed in an attempt to put everyone at their ease.

As the three gathered around Papa, arranging their paraphernalia, the nurse introduced herself and handed Charlotte a package. Emily had posted it on from Haworth: it was the manuscript of her novel about Brussels, *The Professor*, returned from yet another publisher.

Their poems, although receiving a generous review or two, had sold only two copies. *Wuthering Heights* and Anne's *Agnes Grey* were still going out to publishers, but they had been to so many, Charlotte had little hope left. Chances of financial salvation through literature being dashed, she tried not to think about the operation's vital importance for other reasons besides Papa's health and happiness.

'Stay with me, Charlotte,' Papa pleaded. 'Where are you?'

'Of course, Papa. Here I am.'

They were going to slice off the lens of his eye with a scalpel. From fear of making some movement, even a sneeze, which might disturb the surgeons' concentration, she would have chosen to flee the room. Instead she went to assure her father with the touch of her hand. With her other hand she stroked his brow.

Meanwhile, Mr Wilson was putting on a filthy old coat caked with blood, and an assistant was arranging scalpels on the table. One had a small, heart-shaped blade. Another was an ornate little scimitar. There was a cranked spatula, and one was shaped like a fish knife, with a blunt end. The other assistant was taking dark glass bottles out of his bag.

'Would you like laudanum?' Mr Wilson said.

Papa refused.

'Alcohol?'

'Maybe a little brandy.'

Charlotte liked to see the relationship that had developed between Mr Wilson and her father. It expressed her notion of how men should be with one another – firm, kind, equal, humorous and bold. When they were like that, or seemed to be so – maybe she had illusions – she felt happy to be a woman.

While Patrick swallowed a glass of brandy and was laid flat, Charlotte took up her position, far enough off not to interfere, close enough to rush forward if he were in agony. Upon seeing the surgeon's arrival she had already closed the windows, but she still remained afraid of street noises. Suppose there should be pandemonium from a runaway horse, a street accident, or even, in this hot weather, a thunderstorm, causing the surgeon's hand to jolt?

Her own hands were trembling, like Papa's. She could see all that was being done. While an assistant used tweezers to hold the eyelids apart, Mr Wilson applied belladonna to the pupil of the left eye. Papa clenched his fist.

For some minutes, Mr Wilson worked with his scalpels. He made an incision with the heart-shaped knife, enlarged it with the midget fish knife, then raised the lens with the spatula. He virtually squeezed the lens from the iris, wiping it off the blade, into the dish.

Papa's eyes were bandaged and he was laid back on his bed.

There had been no mess and Charlotte wondered why the surgeon had worn the dirty old coat. He being quite a dandy, she supposed it had been from custom, or affectation. She supposed that surgeons had to put on sanguine airs, which they might not feel, in order to be able to perform their dreadful duties. She had been told of student doctors being sick, or having to rush from the theatres with their hands over their ears to cut out the screams.

The two assistants seemed relieved and pleased.

'I have never known anyone show such fortitude as your Papa,' Mr Wilson said. 'Now he must lie under the bandages, and move or speak as little as possible for four days to allow the incision to heal. It will try his patience, but it is important. The greatest danger is of the cuts reopening and of a haemorrhage.'

'My father has great spiritual strength,' Charlotte announced proudly.

'I think so. If there is any great pain, or signs of blood from the eye, send for me immediately.'

During the following days, the nurse proved to be clean and orderly, but as critical and suspicious as Charlotte had anticipated, and an obsequious snob. Charlotte, fortified by her prejudices, neither liked nor trusted her. The nurse applied the leeches required – eight to Papa's temples one day, six on another – otherwise Charlotte employed her as a maidservant and, since she did not wish to go out herself, sent her to do the shopping.

Charlotte did as much of the actual nursing as she could. She shaved Papa, washed his face, and inspected the edges of his bandage for signs of bleeding. She spooned soups into his mouth. She believed it would be less humiliating for him if it was she who aided his bodily functions, and safer should he slip, so she helped him from his bed, the blindfold still over his eyes. His hands shook when she helped him – they shook more than they had when Mr Wilson had carved the lens from his eye. Papa was having it branded into his soul that old age and sickness are obscenely without dignity, and help is not possible. To what extent was it *fear* that made one praise God for his 'mercy'? Charlotte wondered.

Her toothache kept her awake through the hot nights. She tried tincture of myrrh. She used a piece of cotton soaked in Friar's Balsam. When Mr Wilson visited, he gave her a small piece of zinc, recommending her to place it on one side of the tooth, with a piece of silver, a small coin for instance, on the other, explaining that the metals in conjunction produce sufficient electricity to numb the pain. Awkward as it was, it seemed to work for a short time.

But when she moved close to Papa's face, as she had to several times a day, she saw, mixed with his gratitude, his automatic revulsion from the smell of her diseased mouth.

She barely left the hot, airless house. She felt tethered to it, to him, to her duty. If she thought he was asleep, she crept around the room.

'Is that you, Charlotte? What time is it?'

'Five a.m., Papa.'

'I knew it was dawn for I heard a bird singing.'

'Are you comfortable?'

'Yes, but it is strange to hear the birds and to remain in darkness.'

'Hush, Papa, you should not talk.'

He picked up every sound, for instance that of a quill upon paper, and made meaning out of every silence, such as the one telling him that Charlotte had not moved for an hour.

'Are you writing, Charlotte?'

'Yes, Papa.'

'I thought so. Not a letter, surely? You haven't moved for an hour.'

'It is a miracle what you can do without your eyes! I am sure that, if you say so, it has been precisely an hour. Do you know that the way you preached for exactly your usual half-hour, without being able to consult your watch, is the talk of Haworth?'

* * *

Time, even the distinction between day and night, was almost banished. The shutters being always closed, and Papa needing her in the night as much as in the day, and with her toothache, she, like Papa, had taken to catnapping every few hours.

She might have grown irritable. Why, despite her creeping about their lodgings, did he seem to know more about what she was doing than if he'd had his eyesight?

What sustained her was that she had a book in her mind. On the day following the operation, in the first one of a package of small, square exercise books which the nurse had been sent to purchase, she began *Jane Eyre*. The rejected *The Professor* spurred her to it.

Because of her short-sightedness, she held the paper a few inches from her face. She wrote sometimes in the neighbouring room for the sake of the better light there, and sometimes in the room with Papa, by what little light crept in between the shutters, or by a candle, which was kept far away from him. The experience she was going through was having the effect of focusing her past life. Everything – the loss of her mother and her sisters Maria and Elizabeth, Cowan Bridge, and Monsieur Heger – came under her lens, sharpened, not diminished, by tiredness, silence, anxiety and the pain of toothache.

She picked over her feelings as she had once done in the confessional in Brussels; although her own soul gave back answers richer than mere advice to change her faith. She discerned that her life had been a tussle between the drive of passion and the pull of duty. Through writing, she also realized the extent of her anger. Her life should not be without outlet because she was plain, dumpy, and a woman! She should not be dependent upon men, when they could turn out to be such contemptible articles as Branwell or Henry Nussey!

Anger made these days and nights bearable. The moment she stopped writing, she fell into a paler, a more anxious world. There the anger was still present but it was shapeless, not formed in fiction, and poisonous.

On lifting her eyes from the page, her toothache seemed to return. So did her longing to be home; and her knowledge that home was not a place of rest. Branwell's state still had to be faced, and her fear for Papa and the future.

When she broke off to send a letter to Ellen, she wrote, 'I long to get home, though unhappily home is not now a place of complete rest – it is sad to think how it is disquieted by a constant phantom, or rather two – Sin and Suffering – they seem to obscure the cheerfulness of day and to disturb the comfort of evening.'

She told Ellen nothing about her novel. But, realizing what a paradise the act of writing it was, she fled back to it, with cramped fingers.

When she looked across at Papa, it occurred to her that it was a sort of blindness that had condemned her sisters and herself to Cowan Bridge.

Perhaps, also, from the constant dimness of these rooms, twilight and blindness were infecting *Jane Eyre*. Even daylight scenes were turning out seeming to be twilit, and often wintry.

Four days went by and she hardly stopped writing, day and night. Papa lay with as much silence and patience as he could muster; it was considerable. There was no sign of blood leaking from his bandages and he did not complain of pain. All the signs were good.

She wondered what he was thinking.

On the fifth day, Mr Wilson came to remove the bandages. The two assistants, the nurse and Charlotte, waited for Papa to tell them whether or not he possessed his sight.

'I see a faint light. Yes, shadows.'

Charlotte's heart sank, thinking the operation was a failure.

'That is all right,' Mr Wilson said. 'There is no sign of infection, nor anything clouding the eye, and there has been no haemorrhage.'

The eyes that had been tantalized with a little light were put under bandages again.

'He should still be kept in near darkness, without movement, but in a few weeks' time a little light might be introduced. His sight will strengthen steadily, do not worry. Congratulations, Mr Brontë!'

After two weeks, the bandages were removed permanently. Papa said he could distinguish the outlines of objects, and movements around the room.

As the nights felt chilly, with both of them being so still, a small fire was permitted at last, from the glow of which he had to be screened. He was allowed to talk a little more. He was now able to observe as well as hear the scratching of her pen.

'You never stop writing,' he said.

'I, too, need to occupy my mind.'

She expressed herself lightly, but the thought of Papa's shock if he should read *Jane Eyre* made her go hot. Contrasting the courage and honesty of a child with the cruelty and hypocrisy of an Evangelical clergyman was as iconoclastic as – what she would move onto next – showing what a woman really felt and fantasized about, compared with the angel she was supposed to be.

She never ceased to feel the pangs of an old maid's fate. She recalled that, at the *pensionnat*, one of the teachers had been a spinster, ten years older than Charlotte, who used her brothers to take messages to unmarried men in hope of saving herself, as she put it, from 'losing all natural feeling as a Sister of Charity' – which was the only alternative to marriage that she could see for herself when her work as a schoolteacher was no longer wanted. Charlotte had told Mary Taylor about these frantic notes, and found herself declaring, vehemently, 'I hope I shall be put in my grave as soon as I am dead!' Today, she saw that the parsonage might become her nunnery, and that it might be Papa who would wall her in, to die before she was dead.

Passion could be stronger than righteousness, and didn't she know it. Papa, and all her friends – Ellen Nussey probably, Mary Taylor certainly – would believe that in *Jane Eyre*'s love scenes she was indulging something unhealthy. Haworth would think she had composed what it was presumptuous for a woman to write. That would be easy for them to say. She knew that she was plumbing, not a cesspit of indulgence, but memories that were her well of creativity.

Three weeks of writing passed, and anger gave way to sensuousness. Douro and Monsieur Heger had come into the story, transformed into Mr Rochester. When she described a garden at dusk, and the scent of a smoking cigar, it was,

without her realizing it, as sensual as the love-making that
was not within her experience.

> Sweet-briar and southernwood, jasmine, pink, and
> rose have long been yielding their evening sacrifice
> of incense: this new scent is neither shrub nor flower;
> it is – I know it well – it is Mr Rochester's cigar.

'I think I caught your expression then!' Papa said. 'You
were smiling!'

'Yes, Papa. It is because you are improving day by day.'

'Instead of caring for an old man, you should be leading
the life proper to a young woman. Above all, I want you to
be *happy*.'

' "He who suffers, conquers." That was the motto writ in
North Lees Hall at Hathersage. I have never been able to see
anything when I have been happy. Don't you think that, by
being unhappy, one understands what one cannot see when
one is cheerful? Amelia Walker at Roe Head was always
laughing her silly head off but she never saw anything. It
is in the bright light of happiness that one is blind, Papa.
I have come to see everything when looking into my own
mind because I could see no light anywhere else.'

'How wise you are! But this is all such a sacrifice
for you.'

'I have learned the difference between the law of passion
and the law of duty. Do you remember that I came to you
ten years ago to tell you that I wished to become an author?
Then, I wept at your answer. "Duty is more important than
passion," you told me.'

'But maybe duty is a passion, too.'

PATRICK

As Patrick lay with bandages over his eyes he realized that,
except for his family, the dead were more real to him than
the living. Charlotte told him she was amazed he could lie
for weeks without occupation, but he had already entertained

himself for a whole year by summoning ghosts. He pictured his old friends, the Reverend John Buckworth of Dewsbury, Heap of Bradford who had offered him the Thornton living – clergymen also afflicted with blindness – Dury of Keighley, and Hammond Roberson who had defied the Luddites. How fresh and hopeful the world had seemed when all whom he had known had been energetic! Ghostly, deceased clergymen moved about the air in Boundary Street like so many bats with smiling faces.

With his inner eye he saw women whom he had loved. Elizabeth Firth, who had passed away, played again with his small children on the lawn of Kipping House. He thought of Mary Burder, and wondered whether she was alive or dead. His dear Maria was summoned, sun-dappled in a grey silk dress as they picnicked on cheesecake and claret among flowering heather at Kirkstall Abbey. The same grey dress . . . no, better not pursue that memory.

Charlotte would lift her eyes from those exercise books she was filling, and ask what he was thinking.

'I was thinking how marvellous it is that you have patience to sit with your old father, and never complain.'

'I have something to occupy me, don't worry.'

Or he answered, 'I was wondering how Emily and Anne and Branwell are faring. I wonder how Branwell is.'

Anything but share the womb of bright memories where he really lived, and from which her youth made her remote.

On a sweet September day, he returned to Haworth with open eyes. Still vague though everything was – and spots danced before his healing eye, which Mr Wilson said did not matter – it was a delight to see the colours of the compartment, and Charlotte's crimson dress.

The train plunged through the Summit tunnel into the Calder Valley. He saw that the plain of Lancashire, with its monotonous rows of redbrick buildings – mean, to his way of thinking – had changed to Yorkshire's stone, out of which could be carved columns, pediments, and sculptures. He had never before delighted in the sheer warm flush of brick, and then in the blackberry-coloured indigos of sooty stone. Even from behind dark spectacles, he was able to enjoy the purple dash of heather in bloom, misty swathes of it winging over the hills as the train sped by. In past years, though it had been clearer, it had never been as vivid. He wanted to convey from the pulpit his delight in sight.

Coming up through Haworth, he knew his parishioners, but not so many as in the earliest years. It was mostly the older inhabitants whom he recognized. He was still dwelling on memories. It was evening, and he saw a light in the window of an end gable. To him it did not belong to the new inhabitant. It would always be Dr Andrew's light no matter how many years had passed since he had died.

Patrick had no wish to retreat from his parishioners, but it was happening inevitably, and he wondered if they would understand.

Anne and Emily, greeting him from the gig, did not consist, any more, merely of the feel of arms around him, and of helping hands. He could see their expressions: Anne's pale face and Emily's flushed cheeks; both, he feared, unhealthy symptoms. There was Mr Nicholls, standing in the lane. Tabby was at the door. Branwell? Oh, surely not retired to bed so early? What? He had been there most of the day?

Emily helped him upstairs. Her silence was fateful, he knew. They entered the bedroom and the stale smell hit him.

Patrick held out his hand. His son had climbed out of bed only upon hearing them on the landing. Had he been too far gone to remember that his father was coming home?

Patrick could hardly bear to look at his son, revealed to him at long last. His once handsome red hair had receded, revealing what seemed huge, gaunt temples. His lips were shaking, his eyes were damp. His face showed all the signs of weakness which had been masked by the vitality of youth the last time Patrick had been able to see him clearly. His manner was both unsure, and cocksure.

It was the revelation of the inner Branwell that was most shocking. His guilt was not merely at being caught in bed. It was guilt at the price he was exacting from his family, and the impossibility of justifying it, that showed in the face which God had given Patrick the light to see again.

What would it take, how long would it be, O Lord, before his son realized that to be useful and independent on earth was more worthwhile than whatever he thought he achieved through his half-baked posturing, which tore himself and others to shreds? The frightened boy was rigidly defending himself against the truth – which he could not be told.

Patrick ruffled his son's now lifeless hair, smiled and put his arm around his shoulder.

BRANWELL

They got through Christmas without pandemonium. 'Out of funds, Branwell?' Charlotte suggested, scornfully. It was true that he had no money, but since Papa had returned home and seen him – this had been the nadir of his shame – he had also been trying to turn over a new leaf. Why would only Papa and Anne give him credit for it?

They passed the anniversary of Maria's birthday in January with no more than the usual stresses of memory. Once they had got through Elizabeth's birthday on 8 February, they could hope to have survived once again. Winter, as not just those in the parsonage knew, was a season for self-defence, for pulling up the drawbridge, shutting out the draughts, avoiding contagion and cold, wet feet. By conserving oneself – with the brief flare of Christmas for relief – one survived.

Then Branwell changed and put a strain on everyone. Bottles were again discovered in strange places. Gin was found by Martha Brown in the iron pot for boiling washing in the wash-house. Charlotte came across whisky in the flour bin.

It was the end of January. Outside the window were icicles and frosted trees. At mid-morning, as soon as Branwell came downstairs, having missed breakfast, and shortly after Martha Brown had disturbed him when doing her rounds to relight the fires, Papa called him into his study. Branwell was about to shut the door behind him for what he knew would be another humiliating interview, but Charlotte was following, and behind her Emily and Anne trooped in, ominously, to join the tribunal.

A whisky bottle stood on Papa's desk and Branwell's eyes

became fixed upon it. Papa touched the bottle and announced: 'Tabby found that in the oven.'

'What? How – !?'

'The baking oven. Suppose it had exploded?'

He then spoke of the gin in the wash-pot, and the whisky in the flour bin, illegally distilled whisky that would probably poison him. These were subjects not brought up before for fear of putting Branwell in a rage.

'How did they get there?' Branwell asked.

'You tell us.'

'I've no idea!'

'*Liar*,' irresistibly sprang from Charlotte's lips. Branwell saw denunciation lurking in Papa's quivering features, too.

Branwell was not lying – not exactly. He had been, in a sense, hiding the bottles from himself, as much as from them. Not wanting to be tempted by the sight, yet he had placed them in reserve, in case of need in the middle of the night or in the morning before they were stirring at the Black Bull. He had never confessed that there were times when, if drink was not available, he had been tempted to break into a house or into Mr Thomas's wine store. Hiding drink was better than the alternatives of creeping around Haworth, a thief, or trying to justify his openly keeping a reserve of alcohol at home. He hid them in ridiculous places because he was always half-seas-over when he did it. He'd have to be, because he brought the bottles home from the public. Who else but a drunken idiot would put a whisky bottle in an oven? And then forget to retrieve it? But how could he explain all that to them?

'I am not lying! I had forgotten them! I suppose I must have put them there – but I don't remember – well, I think I do now – as a matter of fact: would I have left them to be found on wash day if I'd remembered they were in the pot?'

His excuses were met with silence.

Sensing hope of victory in their bemusement, he said: 'Anyway, what *is* this? An inquisition? Do I have to be spied on in my own home? Is that what you've all come down to?'

'Branwell!' Papa began. 'In early December, we had to deal with the visit by a sheriff's officer from York with a writ for payment of debts to the landlord of a public house. We paid up, but we did hope that the threat of the debtor's prison hanging over you for a week might frighten you into fresh ways. It seemed to. "I promise I will change! Look, I have not touched a drop for three weeks," you told us. It surprised us all by lasting even longer than that. We were so hopeful. So what happened?'

'Your boastful promises were as unpretty a sight as your abject squirming is now,' Charlotte added, crushingly.

For a time he had been as high as a kite on sobriety, he remembered. He had been as high as he had ever been when drunk. Now he was back drinking heavily and – as Charlotte was eager to tell him – they had known it would happen.

'Where did the money come from?' asked Papa.

Branwell began to twitch.

'You had better sit down and tell us,' Papa added.

Branwell collapsed like a sack of potatoes. His fingers fluttered on the chair arms, itching to put themselves around an invisible glass. He realized what he was doing, bit his fingers, buried them between his knees, and said, 'I received my payment from Leyland for helping him deal with John Brown.'

'He could not have given you much,' said Charlotte.

'I had more on account.'

'Humbug!' Charlotte interrupted. 'You told us a few days ago that you had not been to Halifax since well before Christmas, and that you had stopped keeping bad company. We assumed that meant Leyland. Leyland has not been in Haworth, that I am aware of. You had a visitor from Thorp Green, though, last week. Dr Crosby, wasn't it? Had that something to do with your funds?'

'It had nothing to do with it.'

'That was when you started to backslide,' Papa remarked.

'*Did Dr Crosby bring you money from Mrs Robinson?*' Charlotte insisted.

'*No!*'

'Swear to it!'

'We must believe you, if you say so. There is no need to swear,' Papa said, calmly.

'Even if Dr Crosby had brought me money, would it be

unfair to receive some compensation from her who has done me such wrong?' Branwell gestured wildly. Quite out of control.

Dumbfounded, they stared at him.

'But it is not entirely her fault. It is fate, too,' he added. 'I, at least, forgive her.' He put his head in his hands.

Papa said, 'It is charitable of you to think so kindly of —' He paused. '*That vile seducer!*' He mopped at his eye. 'What is so dreadful, is to see you wasting your youth. You are at the prime of life, and the snake in the Garden, so to speak, is that you do not realize it. You do not realize it. That is tragic.

'Now let us say a prayer, and remember the Day of Judgement.'

When it was over, all Branwell could think about was a drink to calm his nerves. Whenever they put the fear of God in him, it drove him to drink. Each fresh lapse became another item on his moral bill to be paid on Judgement Day. The growing size of his account, too, drove him to drink. Seeing that the fear of Judgement had achieved little, they next shamed him with their sympathy and pity: that, too, drove him to drink. Then they went back to the Last Trumpet. Terror drove him back to the Black Bull, or to Leyland's studio. To disguise the fact that he had been drinking, he was complicating his life, going here, going there, on 'errands', on escapades which he put in the light of artistic endeavours – simply because he dared not go home in the state he was in. Once he had begun to lie about his drinking, it became easy to lie about everything.

Tabby had described it as 'a descent into a cellar'. He realized that alcohol and laudanum had taken over his nature. They dictated that he should lie and steal to feed the habit. They teased him by permitting him to make promises and then defeating them, thus weakening him further, morally, and gaining a greater grip. Even as, high and excited by sobriety, he had continued to make promises, he had begun to hide further bottles around the house. 'The demon drink', Papa called it, and never had he spoken a truer word.

Branwell fought the call of the Black Bull for most of the day. The girls scattered to their housework or whatever, and Papa left with Mr Nicholls. At one point Branwell went into the kitchen to tease and gossip with Tabby, for old times' sake, but he was a twitching jelly in the chair.

He returned to his bedroom. He took the carving knife from under his mattress, felt the edge of the blade that, for years, he had watched Tabby sharpen on the kitchen step, and the fact that he felt so calm about killing himself, and that no-one had yet discovered the knife, it would be there waiting for him, gave him the courage to carry on with life; in so far as lying on his bed and taking laudanum – in search of a relief that was cheap and would not impart the smell of alcohol to his breath – could be called 'life'.

In the early evening, he at last went to the Black Bull, for one glass only, but he knew that the first glass was like putting a noose around his neck and stepping off a ladder. If he could not resist the first, how could he fight off the second, and then the third? As John Brown often said: 'First the man takes the drink, then the drink takes a drink, then the drink takes the man.'

He sat alone at a table and had already drunk a quantity of brandy before Brown came in. He was now master of the Freemasons' lodge which Branwell had deserted. Like his father, he carried himself with the majesty of a workman who knows his job. He *built* his life, solidly. He was a good person to confess to, and Branwell began to hold forth about Mrs Robinson. He talked as if it were the continuation of a conversation that had been briefly interrupted; one of as absorbing interest to Brown as it was to himself. As Mrs Thomas had said, 'When Branwell's in his cups, he'll talk to the dog about Mrs Robinson, if no-one else will listen.'

'John, sit down, sir! Doleful news! I have tried to communicate with her again but those surrounding her, who hate me like hell, sent Dr Crosby to return my letter unopened. He told me to resign myself to never seeing her more, though once I could not imagine such a thing! She, too, is weighed down by sorrow, but resigned to her doom. She is an angel, who can do no wrong. But she is confined and pining. Apparently, when Crosby mentioned my name, she fainted. Yet I may not see her even one more time to console her, less she lose all, all! I once had reason to think that I would become her husband! That hope is *gone*. She talked of entering a nunnery. I cannot imagine what it will cost to tear the memories from my heart. They rush in like memories of sunlight to a man who has lost his sight.'

'Cheer up, old son. Where there's life there's hope.'

Branwell continued to confess. 'I make promises and I break them. I mean to give up drink, but I can't. All day I think of that glass of –' He waved his hand. 'Whatever. The very sight of an empty glass on a shelf provokes me!' He was thoughtful for a moment. 'At home, they call her "the vile seducer".'

'That's a very sensible attitude to drink,' Brown laughed.

'No – *Lydia*! My *Lyd-i-a*!' Branwell howled her name like a dog. 'My family regards me as their *caput mortuum*,' he moaned.

'Eh?'

'That is what Emily calls me. *Caput mortuum* – the thick matter which remains after distillation.'

'Thou old sinner!' John Brown laughed. Perhaps he would have slapped Branwell on the back, had his chest not grown so sunken, his whole form frailer and thinner of late.

Branwell raised his eyes and gave utterance to his greatest loss of all. His voice was like an echo in a cavern. 'John, I have lost my sense of beauty in the world. I look upon it with the eyes of a dead codfish.'

'It could be worse.' John Brown sniffed and suggested, 'Thou should leave home for a while. Get away from them spinsters. Condemnation and guilt – it's no good, sithee!'

'John Brown, sir, you dear friend! You dear friend!'

Branwell recalled John Brown leaving the Black Bull – his decisive back going through the door, 'to a home that did not make his life a misery by condemning him', as Branwell put it to himself. He remembered nothing else until after his own departure, when he was brought to by the icy air.

He grew conscious of the millions of stars. Of the murderous slipperiness of the road. Did he recall putting his arms around the trunk of a tree, talking to it because he thought it was Lydia?

His last clear thought was that he would be quite without hope – without means – when Papa died. Mrs Robinson's erratic funding would not last for ever. If only Aunt Branwell were alive, she would understand his financial predicament, now!

The following morning, he was sick in his bed. It was after the others had risen. There was so much coughing in the house nowadays – they all had colds or bronchitis – that no-one took notice of his retching. He slept again in his vomit, and it took him by surprise when he awoke.

He used the chamber-pot – which Martha had not emptied after Papa – then he bundled up the sheets and piled them by the door. This wasn't a simple operation. He had to concentrate on every step.

It was bitterly cold, yet for some reason Martha had not been in to light the bedroom fire – but then, he knew the reason. Hesitating to wash himself, fearing he would not be able to handle the heavy jug of water and the ewer, he first rubbed at the frosted window, almost falling through the pane before he steadied himself. It was all gold outside, the sunlight on an ethereal wonder of melting frost. He thought he remembered a black bundle that had been someone – a fellow drunk or a tramp – sleeping out in the graveyard last night.

He turned back to ewer and jug. There was thin ice on the water. He plucked it out and did not know where to put it. He dropped it onto the floor. His nightcap fell off his head into the bowl as he was washing. Floundering after his nightcap, he trod with bare feet on the piece of ice, jumped from the cold, slipped, and banged his knee against the stand.

His whole life seemed a tragedy. Again he felt like killing himself. He almost cried, as he fished out his nightcap with fingers that could hardly hold it.

There was no doubt that he should get away. Not even Tabby had patience with him any more, and he dreaded what she would say about the state of the sheets.

He realized that Brown had it in mind that he should obtain another tutor's position, one where they did not know him and so would not envelope him in an atmosphere of accusation that was like sleeping in his own vomit.

Instead, he left home to find company in Halifax. What he had told neither his family nor John Brown was that Dr Crosby had softened his fateful news with twenty pounds as the reward for keeping quiet. Enough to maintain him for some months. He strode with gritted teeth, his bag over his shoulder, on a chilly, ten-mile walk towards sweet depravity. He was as determined on this as was Pilgrim when setting off for the Celestial City.

Leyland's 'marble works' was in the centre of town, close against the Piece Hall where wool merchants sold their cloth. Branwell loved this great noisy shed, smoky with dust, the light filtering through a glass roof. Two assistants were going through a limestone block with a two-handled saw. Among other blocks of stone and bins of clay, there, emerging eerily out of white marble, was a life-size, reclining, dead body, its arms crossed: the figure of an archbishop which Leyland was executing for York Minster. On the walls were ghoulish drawings of it – drooping hands, drooping legs. They already looked like ancient parchments because of the thick dust that collected within a week. On a platform was a life-size 'Hercules' modelled in clay, the muscles bouncing off the flesh, where it was not covered by damp rags.

Leyland might tamely advertise himself in the *Halifax Guardian* as maker of 'monuments, busts, tombs, tablets, chiffonier slabs, and marble chimney-pieces', but even these turned out looking demonic. Also in course of execution were the capitals of two stone gateposts. On three-foot square blocks, serpents writhed around the beaming faces of sun-gods. At the expense of much expert chipping at the blocks, which had originally been a foot longer on either side, the serpents' heads, with eyes and jaws more like those of savage dogs, wove terrifyingly through the air.

Most of these sculptures had hardly advanced since Branwell had last been here a couple of months before. His friend was running out of impetus. He was slumped in a chair, dressed in his smock and biting on his meerschaum pipe, blowing the aroma of shag through the dry air. His eyelids sagged from dropsy. It all added to his air of melancholia.

Branwell realized that his friend was amazed to find him still alive. He then remembered the storm of self-obsessed letters he had sent from Haworth through this winter. They were maudlin letters, decorated with drawings of tombstones and gallows, and with Leylandesque pictures of himself as a martyr bound to the stake among flames, or in chains heaving himself out of the earth – a Prometheus who was thick-necked, barrel-chested, and muscle-bound, only recognizable as Branwell Brontë by his features. Or he depicted himself and cronies falling backwards off chairs, breaking tables, scattering glasses; humorous balloons of speech bursting out of their mouths. These were the only drawings he'd done in years and his ability, like Leyland's, had fallen off. They had shown a mind near the end of its tether, one full of anxious volition that petered out. Branwell knew it.

The sculptor became animated. He put down his pipe and lumbered to his feet. 'You're as thin as a rake, my friend,' he said. 'Christmas hasn't fattened you at all. What's this coat?' He tugged at it. 'It fits you no better than a cast-off, man. You'd better have some soup. I've not much else.'

As a matter of fact, Branwell was thinking of getting *him* out for a drink – and of paying. It was hard to talk in the studio with the workmen present.

'Let me take you out. Shall it be the Talbot or the Old Cock?'

'Not today.'

Half an hour later, after the soup which they took with the workmen, they set off for both public houses. Because of his swollen legs, Leyland found it difficult even to stand. But the Talbot was just a few yards from the studio, and from there they had to climb only a few more steep yards to the Old Cock.

Before the afternoon and evening were over, they had picked up the landscape painter and keeper of a beer house, Wilson Anderson; the gilder, Joe Drake; the conductor of the Halifax Choral Society, Dan Sugden; and William Dearden, 'the Bard of Caldene'.

They anticipated their gloriously foul and spendthrift ends, ill health and the reprobate's Hell, and complained about the world in glorious style. Branwell poured out his heart about Mrs Robinson and said that her grief would be an excellent subject for a sculpture, all of which he had said before, in letters. Leyland sighed about his commissions, which were mostly for dull and petty 'tradesman's art': memorials and gateposts. They took their time paying even for that, and never stopped complaining. The statue for York Minster was costing him a fortune in outlay. He was running into debt, had dispensed with his carriage and groom, and regretted that he had not set himself up in London.

They went back to the studio. The assistants had left. They revived the stove, found battered chairs and dusty couches, and smoked opium. Leyland forgot his debts. Even while sprawled among his great works, he forgot the cost of executing them, the marble, the casting, the wages of assistants and the expense of carting statuary about the country, while clients kept him waiting for payment. Money started to fall from his pocket: half a sovereign which Drake needed to buy gold leaf, and the train fare for Anderson to go to a Leeds exhibition.

At last, Leyland began to sob.

When the others had sifted off into the night, Branwell bedded himself down behind the sculptures and slept, through nightmares, until he awoke among them also – emerging from stone, draped in damp rags – in the studio.

He was awakened by the arrival of the assistants, in a bad mood because they had not been paid. He felt they'd make sure Leyland's sculptures fell to bits, out of spite. They'd square up faulty blocks of stone, so as to have something to laugh about in the pub. Leyland, faced with their grumbling, fidgeted with the ring on his little finger.

Meanwhile Branwell went out to the privy, came back, sipped some dirty coffee, and, coughing from the dust, ventured into the street.

His night in the studio had been so potent that the town, seen from the step of the barn-like door, suggested Hell. Perhaps Leyland had sited his studio in the Square for this view. Down the slope, he saw the sooty tower of the parish church, pinnacles at its corners, and it looked like a black, black-eared, devil-animal, with its two belfry windows for eyes as it poked up out of the tangle of wool merchants' premises, craftsmen's cottages and Elizabethan houses of the old town. Furnaces glared, and there was a great clattering from under some tall chimneys. On the far side of the church, beyond the river and the railway, the soot rose up Beacon Hill to a line like a dirty tidemark round a trough; a line upon which coal pits opened, and from which coal carts trickled down the hill.

The winter had followed a trade slump, the slump had led to strikes because the price of potatoes and bread had risen and wages had not, but strikes helped the manufacturers – they had nothing to employ workers for, so it was a saving to them. The power-loom workers had held out for three months, then returned for the same wages, or for even less than they had been paid before. The lives of the really poor – poorer even than those on starvation wages – had become Hell. Branwell and his friends had spent the previous day talking about art as if they were on Parnassus: but look at this.

He saw the unemployed every day during the following weeks of his drink-blurred, opium-blurred stagger around Halifax. He saw the poor react to despair with abandoned joy, reckless violence, bizarre humour, a drily expressed pride in endurance, but mostly, just like himself, in a spirit of self-destruction. They lay in heaps suffering opium nightmares – just as he did, and for the same reason: laudanum was cheaper even than ale. They would eat anything. They begged shamelessly, and yet blazed with aggression. One of them looked for someone to punch, and another for someone to complain to or accuse. In the streets he went native in a world which gentlemen rarely looked at. He half-realized what a privilege this was, but if he pulled himself together to write at all – which he did, sometimes – his mind was on Lydia Robinson.

It was for the same reason, almost, that his sisters did not give written expression to what they, equally, could see when they stepped out of doors in Haworth during that terrible winter. It was, largely, because they were all in love – maybe with ghosts, spirits, memories, the dead; maybe even with themselves; but in love.

Branwell's sympathies were with the gentlemen who lived on the hills. As the poor grew poorer, the rich were more ostentatious than ever. Their mansions were becoming grander, while the racked poor – except for the radicals – *took pride* in the ostentations of the rich.

It was as if they needed them to give hope to their own lives. *Everyone* was proud that not only mills and mansions but even the memorials in the graveyards were growing more massive and ornate by the year.

Leyland and his friends fell into the maelstrom of excess as if they would die tomorrow. They got around a bowl of punch before the great Elizabethan fireplace in the panelled upper room of the Old Cock. They talked endlessly, wittily, although they had forgotten most of it by the next day. But after a week or two, as Branwell's money ran out, it dawned on him how little he had to offer the company of artists and of gentlemen relaxing from their businesses. He realized that his story, of a parson's son who had been curiously employed as a railway clerk and who had enjoyed many other adventures, including his tales of 'going to London', had become tiresome. They laughed at him more than with him.

Neither did these drinking excursions alleviate his jealousy as Leyland's hanger-on. Except that Leyland had this great studio, and had the sense to pursue a straight line of action – sticking to sculpture, not dodging between one art and another as he himself had done – they did not seem to be any different from each other. They were both plunging into alcohol, rushing out for that first fatal drink. No different from each other – except that Branwell had been unlucky.

He could be high for hours, then he collapsed. Remorse, sickness, and, above all else, absence of hope, would hit him when he awoke, some time between the middle and the end of the morning. Then it was as difficult to get out of that dusty bed behind the statuary as if he had been bolted to it.

He had used Lydia's money to try to make himself happy by destroying himself: this reflection hit him one day, when sunlight brought a touch of spring to the hills above Halifax, and stabbed him with the memory of another need. Even in the smoky town, a bird leaving a roof – that whirring, and the light shuttled in feathers – reminded him of partridges and plovers on the hills above Ponden.

To clear his head in the mornings he sometimes climbed up past the coal pits to Law Hill. The light would strike a far hill in a particular way, lighting up a bright green enclosure high among the brown, and the sight would reach his heart. A resolution to give up drinking and dissolute living struck again. Perhaps he would keep to it, this time. He would try.

After having been absent for a month, one early spring day Branwell had to go home.

ANNE

Anne and her sisters thought that they knew curates. They came and went through Haworth and Keighley, useful and jolly sometimes, often hard-working and reliable, like Mr Nicholls. Mostly, during their years between student freedom and pastoral duties, they were in a state of spiritual adolescence. They were callow youths of the spirit. When being entertained, they jumped about like fleas. They lived in lodgings found for them with easily put-upon people, and they pestered their landladies by visiting one another, expecting to dine on lavish meals. Over port, they began by arguing about differences of doctrine and, as they drank more wine, sank to complaining about the toughness of the beef and the overboiling of the potatoes, before descending to making fun of one another's origins, or their sentimental affairs, and to imitating one another's accents, particularly if they were Scottish or Irish. They would create such uproar that you would expect it to end with duelling pistols, but you could count on their being the heartiest of friends by the next morning. They had only been practising their oratory, as young swallows do their wings.

When Haworth grumbled that Mr Nicholls was slow to move on to his own living, perhaps out of a romantic attachment to the elder Miss Brontë, Charlotte claimed that she had no time for curates and that was that. 'The lady doth protest too much', or words to that effect, many thought.

Although the Brontë daughters looked down on 'the species', secretly they always hoped for worldly – not spiritual, never spiritual – salvation from them. Marriage – to be blunt. While curates never arrived without seeming to preen themselves at the thought of three virgins in the parsonage.

When Mr Collins had arrived to be Mr Busfeild's curate in Keighley he already possessed an Irish swagger and had a firm, soft voice that affected the ladies. Though he was married, that had not put any off fawning on him; his wife was a shadowy person, easily overlooked. At the parsonage, it had been Charlotte who had most praised him at the time. She had pointed out that he 'was one of the most stentorian voices to speak against the Dissenters'.

In November, a stricken Mrs Collins had come to Haworth parsonage.

Although she had from the beginning appeared a hurt and hunted creature, this had largely been put down to the fact that some are so, by nature. But after she had climbed the muddy routes from Keighley with her child – Tabby said that 'the poor woman slunk in like a beggar, ashamed to look even me in the face' – she spent an hour with Papa and, it appeared, gave him a different version of Mr Collins. Papa had paid for the gig to take her back to Keighley, and then had told Charlotte what he had heard; Charlotte being the only one of them at home in that autumn of 1840, seven years before.

Mr Collins had turned out not to be any kind of man at all. He had become a reprobate – drunken, extravagant and profligate – beating his child for irritating him, beating his wife when he could not get hold of her savings and, when he could not face the outrage of Keighley and of his rector, disappearing to Manchester or Leeds for days. He even deserted for a trip back to Ireland, leaving a trail of carnage there, too. Mrs Collins had looked as though she had been in a mill accident.

Charlotte asked Papa what advice he had given her.

'I told her to leave him for ever and go home, if she had a home to go to.'

It was one of those stunning advices that Papa sometimes delivered. Telling a woman – her husband's property – to desert him and steal away with his heir! It certainly amazed his daughter.

'With his child!?'

'For the *sake* of their child. It was not easy to say.'

'I wonder that she could ever have married a man towards

whom her feelings must always have been much as they are now,' Charlotte remarked.

'Many of us were taken in by Mr Collins.'

'But she must have known him better than we did.' Charlotte claimed that she had always had reservations about him, despite his bold manner in the pulpit. 'It is often such diabolical creatures as Collins who prey on susceptible women. I wonder why it is that we like them?'

'And vice versa,' Papa remarked.

In the event, the advice had proved even harder for Mrs Collins to take than it had been for Papa to give. She did not leave her husband. But neither did she break. She became a marvel of suffering and martyrdom in Keighley, until Mr Collins was dismissed by Mr Busfeild and the family left the district.

Mrs Collins had disappeared for nearly seven years and had been forgotten. She turned up on another April evening, after Branwell had returned from his exploits in Halifax. Martha came in to announce that 'a reyther lady-like woman wi' a child wished to speak in the kitchen'.

Mrs Collins was strained and thin, but calm, which she had never been in Keighley. The clothes of her little girl and herself were modest, but decent. She said she had stayed in the kitchen because she was shy of meeting Mr Brontë, from wishing she had taken his advice in the first place, and from having fallen so far beneath his station that she would find it difficult to converse with him. Nevertheless she was persuaded to stay for tea.

The tea things having been cleared away, Tabby nursed the little girl in the kitchen to keep her from hearing the details of her mother's story. It took her a couple of hours to tell, sat in front of the parlour fire, among a great deal of coughing, for all at the parsonage had colds. Papa had bronchitis and Branwell, thin as a rake, yellow-skinned and mad-eyed, was coughing also. Anne thought that their visitor would think that they, too, had survived the winter only by the skins of their teeth.

The Collinses had moved to a lodging house in Manchester where Mr Collins never stopped bewailing his ill fortune. She had been afraid of his coming home at nights, if he *did* come home. When three days had passed and he had not returned, she realized that her daughter and she were abandoned, without money. They survived only through the kindness of the lodging-house keeper.

'There is many a Christian hypocrite who would have turned me out of doors, as I know to my cost by now, and my husband had no care or thought of whether that was to be my fate,' Mrs Collins declared. 'I have no idea where on earth he is. Perhaps he is in Ireland, though I hardly think so, for he has disgraced himself in his homeland, too.'

'If I were you, I would not try to find out where he is, and I would keep my whereabouts secret,' counselled Papa.

'I do not intend to let him know! I could not endure ever to see him again,' Mrs Collins declared.

Apparently, with the help of her landlady she had managed to 'pull herself up by her bootstraps', and was now keeping her own boarding-house in that very district of South Manchester where Charlotte had stayed with Papa. In penury, she had passed through the fire of learning who her friends were, and had emerged, not broken, but dignified. Although thinner, she was – as Anne put it – distilled.

At half past eight Papa sent Martha for the gig, and Mrs Collins and her daughter returned through the dark to the house in Keighley where she was visiting with friends.

Papa went to bed at nine, as usual. The others continued to sit around the ashes in the parlour grate. They waited until they heard Papa wind the clock on the landing, and shout down, as always, 'Don't stay up too late, children!' and close his door. Then they heaped more coals on the fire, blew with the bellows, and fell to discussing Mr Collins and his kind.

For he was not the only curate to have disappeared. There had been James Smith, who had been Papa's curate once and Mr Busfeild's later. Reprobates seemed to come with the drinking water in Keighley.

'Do you remember our handsome Mr Smith?' Charlotte said. 'The stories of ditches and gates he had leaped on horseback after hounds?' The previous spring, being ill from the district's regular miasmas – enteritis, cholera, vomiting, coughing: the usual spring plagues – he had decided that he must leave or die. He had absconded with the charity funds and returned to Kells in Ireland. There famine had struck, once again. His next plan was to set sail for Canada, there to be a lumberjack, or travel further west after gold.

It was remarkable that while three frail girls could survive here, a strong man could not. Why was it men and not women who so often broke – vanished – *went off the rails*, as the new expression had it, Anne wanted to know? She reminded them about Lucky Luke, the once upright Methodist who had turned into a moorland recluse, whisky-sodden, dressed in rags and cursing his Maker. She recalled others whom they knew, or knew of, who simply, one day, broke. It had often been the most upright men, too. It was as if the firmness of their outer natures disguised their inner frailty.

It was not that women's lives were less hard than men's, for wives of child-bearing age stared at death every year. They lived as dangerously as soldiers, as could be seen in any graveyard through the lists of some men's two, three, maybe four wives killed in childbirth. Neither was it that women were stronger, Anne believed.

Perhaps women endured through being permitted to express their feelings more readily? They did not have to fortify themselves, in silence, for the trials of business – but for natural crises, to which, perhaps, God was more sympathetic and helpful. And they had more of a shared community of help, advice and talk. At any rate she heard the 'old wives' gossiping, and saw them popping into one another's houses with salves. They were not competing, not crowing if a 'competitor' came to a bad end; and were not despised for weeping.

Through the discussion, Branwell continued to be restless. He had been so all evening, getting up and leaving the room, biting his fingers, crossing his legs one way and then the other. He burst out at last. 'You are turning into nothing but old maids, complaining about being old maids, and proving it by twittering about old maid subjects most of the time! You start on about who has married or should marry whom, and whether your bits of lace might get crushed in the post or be stolen at the post office where you think they open your letters. You worry about how to get your copies of *The Sunday Scholar's Christian Year*, and take the huff because some old maid has something better to do than trail to Haworth. And you have no knowledge of the world at all! That is the only reason why you are so shocked.'

'It's true that I have no knowledge of the world,' Charlotte admitted. For Branwell's outburst was mostly directed against herself; it was she who had plagued them with worries over the lace she had posted to Ellen Nussey, and who had 'taken the huff' because Ellen had made excuses not to visit. 'But Collins's behaviour has been disgraceful. No-one should put up with that.'

She was hinting at Branwell's carryings-on. Judging by his exaggerated manner, he knew it.

'The saddest thing would be if Mr Collins never comes to see the error of his ways,' Anne said. 'He deserves our compassion for that.'

Touching Branwell's conscience apparently made him smart more than insulting him would, for he left the room in a great storm.

Now they could turn to talking about books.

When Anne tried to use the careers of Mr Collins and of their own brother as examples of why one should not expose the doings of such a monster as Heathcliff without censuring him in the novel, without pointing out the moral, Emily laughed in her face. 'People are what they are, and there's no help for it. As you have said yourself, "truth carries its own instruction",' she said.

But 'truth carried instruction' through the way it was interpreted and Anne could sense Emily's admiration for her monster.

Anne was growing ever more impatient with all her three siblings' praises of wickedness and passion, and with their beliefs in fantasy figures. Heathcliff and Mr Rochester were youthful dreams, innocuous then, but poisonous when taken seriously beyond childhood. It was what had led to the unimaginable: her brother committing adultery with his employer. He was ruining his life by seeing himself as Northangerland, the spiritual cousin of Heathcliff and Rochester, and by being in love with a fantasy: just as Mrs Collins's misguided love had proved almost fatal to her.

For Branwell's 'Mrs Robinson' *was* a fantasy. Anne, being in correspondence with her daughters, knew truths that Branwell could not be faced with. Unable to manage the estate, which had been dealt with by her husband, she had sacked her servants, sold Thorp Green, and now she was flapping around the north Midlands – her original homeland, in the local papers of which she had been astute enough to announce her husband's death – looking for husbands for her daughters and for herself. Anne's former pupils described in detail the marriage market in which Branwell's 'pining Lydia' was such an assiduous trader. They were upset at being 'treated as prize cattle', preened and combed for display at dinners and balls. Elizabeth complained of their mother's extravagance; the visits to London or Buxton for gowns, and the expenses, ranging from carriages to hairdressers, which depleted their dowries. She had taken Anne's advice to refuse one wealthy suitor – who had cost the expenses of a London 'season' to hook – because she did not love him, and at this moment she was being made to feel ungrateful, selfish, wilful, and a burden. She described it as a wearing away of her spirit that was like the drip drip of water which would wear away a stone.

On the day following Mrs Collins's visit, Anne settled to writing a new novel, in which neither women nor men would be Byronic figures, larger than life. It was based on Mrs Collins, her survival, morally and physically, and the saving of her child by what most would consider the depraved as well as the illegal act of taking him away from his father.

Anne had lain awake half the night plotting it. She gave her heroine, Helen Graham, a son rather than a daughter, thereby being able to deal with another of her preoccupations: the care with which boys should be brought up; at least as much care as girls, if they are to turn out well. Helen would marry her husband although knowing his weaknesses, and against her better judgement, but driven by the passion of love; consequently she would consider it no less than her moral duty to return when he was ill and needed her.

It was as she herself had pined for William Weightman despite knowing his fecklessness and fickleness. If they had married and he had turned out to be like Mr Collins, she believed she might have left him in order to save herself, and certainly for the sake of a child, but she would never have deserted him in spirit. For her love could not have ceased, so she would have kept what watch she could from a distance, and returned if he needed her. Like Mrs Collins's actions, it would be misunderstood by most people. Consequently she would make Helen Graham a strange figure to her new neighbours, as no doubt Mrs Collins was in Manchester with her child.

She called her story, *The Tenant of Wildfell Hall*.

When she told Charlotte about it, her sister said, 'I wonder if Branwell would feel flattered if he knew that we are all writing novels about unredeemed men, and putting him under the microscope for the details?'

CHARLOTTE

I

Wuthering Heights and *Agnes Grey* had seemed unpublishable, but when news arrived that Newby had agreed to issue them upon payment of £50 deposit for each, Charlotte's first thought was one of outrage at such a disadvantageous arrangement. She was also stung that her *The Professor* was still circulating without success – separately from her sisters' novels, ever since she had received it back in Manchester during the previous August.

Then she wondered what Branwell would make of the published *Wuthering Heights*, when he stumbled across a copy, at some time when he was sufficiently *compos mentis* to settle to reading for more than half an hour, and recognized something of himself in Heathcliff's self-destructiveness.

'Well, what if?' Emily asked. 'He won't dare tell anyone who the authors are. He'll be too ashamed.'

'He will when he's drunk.'

'No-one is going to believe that we have written novels. Even when he's sober they wouldn't believe him, let alone in his drunken ravings.'

Then came Charlotte's deliverance.

She sent off *The Professor* to Smith, Elder & Co. of London.

She found their address on an old copy of Aunt Branwell's beloved 'annual', *Friendship's Offering*. It seemed that they published novels as well as moral and scientific works.

Charlotte was hopeful and yet hopeless. In the manner of the hopeless, she did what she could to make sure that she would fail. She sent the manuscript from Keighley railway station without changing the wrapping paper in which it had been returned from four other publishing houses. She merely altered the address, thereby showing that others had not been interested in it. Her inner voice whispered that she would thereby gain the victory of proving herself right about her own hopelessness.

However, before a month was out, she received a two-page letter from Smith, Elder. Although not offering to publish *The Professor*, they rejected it in the most considerate fashion and informed her that they would look kindly upon any other product of her pen, particularly a novel in three volumes. Having almost finished one by then, Charlotte soon walked to Keighley with the manuscript of *Jane Eyre*.

It was August and the warm weather made her feel optimistic. Humankind was cheerful in the fields and on doorsteps. Windows were open in the clattering lofts of weavers. It was different on the edge of Keighley, now much altered: childhood's metropolis had bloated to twice its size. She had to walk between great mills, and through a settlement of the Irish driven from Ireland by successive potato famines, and through districts of prostitutes and beggars; places she could smell better than she could see them. But the heart of Keighley was richer than ever, and other changes were for the better. The splendid new church in the 'Perpendicular' style was half completed, and she could admire the elegant though still unglazed windows.

She went to the railway station. She loved going there. It was like a villa in the Dutch/Tudor manner, with Dutch gables, and barley-sugar chimneys for the waiting-rooms, and the loveliest of porticos. It had the warmest associations – less of her own few journeys than of meeting Ellen Nussey, and from there going for tea at the Devonshire Arms before they made their way to Haworth. Perhaps in the future she would look upon it happily for another reason. She was far more hopeful than when she had come here with *The Professor*. She felt most important when she handed in the parcel; though worried because the station was too small a depot to be able to deal with the bureaucracy of a prepayment. 'Wait a moment,' she said. 'Can you let me have pen and paper?' She enclosed a letter:

> If, when you acknowledge the receipt of the MSS., you would have the goodness to mention the amount charged on delivery, I will immediately transmit it in postage-stamps. It is better in future to address Mr Currer Bell, under cover to Miss Brontë, Haworth, Bradford, Yorkshire, as there is a risk of letters otherwise directed not reaching me at present.

She made her way back half a mile to the Devonshire Arms, holding a handkerchief to her mouth for her toothache. People whom she knew wished her a good afternoon. 'Glad to see you in town, Miss Brontë.' There were also well-wishers whom she was less pleased to meet, such as Mrs Sykes the haberdasher from whom she bought the child-sized underwear which she was obliged to wear: it was demeaning to meet Mrs Sykes today. She could not make these people out until she was almost on top of them. Then she put on as blithe a manner as she could, with her gums raging, and wondered what they would think if they knew what she had handed over at the railway. It made her quite light-headed.

She lost her courage for a moment upon spying Mr Busfeild, and dodged around the other side of the market. Even Ellen Nussey, let alone the polite society of Keighley, would believe she had written something wicked. That was what they would think even if it had been composed by a man. It was most presumptuous from a woman.

Her mind was alive with the more dangerous passages of *Jane Eyre*:

> Do you think, because I am poor, obscure, plain, and little, I am soulless and heartless? You think wrong! – I have as much soul as you, – and full as much heart! And if God had gifted me with some beauty, and much

wealth, I should have made it as hard for you to leave me, as it is now for me to leave you. I am not talking to you now through the medium of custom, conventionalities, or even of mortal flesh: – it is my spirit that addresses your spirit; just as if both had passed through the grave, and we stood at God's feet, equal, – as we are!

'Good afternoon, Miss Brontë. A *lovely* afternoon. Perfectly *lovely*.'

Mr Barwick, the hairdresser who also taught music, beamed from his doorstep, no doubt wondering about her flush and attributing it to the walk he would guess that she had taken through the fields; for everyone knew that the Brontës, from the father down to the youngest, were always walking. It was believed that they were too poor to afford a gig very often. Charlotte paused and chatted, for all the world as if she had not just posted off *Jane Eyre*.

She reached the Devonshire Arms, at the corner of Church Street, with its memories. Memories were so much on her mind because everything might change, soon. Her relationship with everyone would alter if *Jane Eyre* was published and it came out who had written it. She had her secret identity to hide behind, yet the risk was – spicy. That was the word for it; and she savoured again the delight of writing as a form of secretiveness.

She asked for tea, celebrating with a treat that cost three shillings – which was half of a woman's weekly wage for seventy-six hours of labour in a factory. When it was served, on a silver plate, she asked for a little laudanum and soaked a corner of her handkerchief to put it on her aching tooth. Was it laudanum, or hope, that went to her head?

II

Mr William Smith Williams, reader to the publishing house of Smith, Elder and Co., came into their office in Cornhill, late, tousled, but excited. 'I had a sleepless night finishing *The Autobiography of Jane Eyre*,' he explained.

George Smith, junior, laughed at him. It was more with delight than with worldly cynicism. They were both new to publishing: George Smith because, at twenty-three, he had just entered his father's firm, and Williams because his adventurous and energetic young employer had recently scouted him out of the drudgery of clerking for a firm of lithographers, in his spare time from which he wrote drama reviews.

'If you think I'm a fool, I would like *you* to read it!' Williams demanded. He called for strong black coffee, and felt at his unshaven chin.

Mr Smith took the manuscript home, intending to get up early on the following morning, Sunday, and give himself a taster before setting off for the jaunt he had planned with friends into the country. Work and ambition came first. He was transforming the worthy family firm, which had mostly been kept afloat by the tedious 'annual', *Friendship's Offering*, and had started to publish scientific works, Charles Darwin's *Zoology of the Voyage of the Beagle* and *The Collected Works of Sir Humphrey Davy*, while John Ruskin had joined the publishing house with *Modern Painters*. What young Mr Smith wanted most, though, was novels, of the kind that one couldn't put down.

He was a bachelor, living with a doting mother, sisters and brothers, and after breakfast it was easy for him to slip away into his study without, as he put it, 'a wife and children to pull faces if I do not give them enough attention'.

Fortunately, Mr Bell's handwriting was, although not 'copperplate', very legible. The spelling, punctuation and grammar were bad, but Smith was soon so delighted that he was already making his editor's marks on the manuscript. Being free to spend his day alone if he wished to, he found himself cancelling his engagements one after the other; first his excursion and then his lunch, satisfying himself with a sandwich and a glass of wine in his room.

He was absorbed by the story's energy, its iconoclasm, the author's involvement with his characters, and by his insights into women's feelings. What sort of man is this? he wondered. He is either a genius or a hermaphrodite. He excused the fact that the author did not have much perception of how men felt; or at least, not as he himself felt. It did not seem to matter when set against the range of the book, from realism about an abominable school, to the 'Gothic' strangeness of a lover's voice heard from miles away across the moors at night.

He finished the novel after dinner. Following a long day spent with the work of an author on whom he had never set eyes, he was so caught up with this unusual 'man's' imagination as to see his familiar surroundings through the author's eyes.

The thought crossed his mind that it was by a woman, and he smiled. Maybe he was suffering from exhaustion, or from those two or three glasses of wine.

After being so long immured with such a sensual, enveloping description of love, he was glad that he slept undisturbed.

In the following week, after a little reflection on business matters, he sent off a letter offering Mr C. Bell c/o Miss Brontë a sober deal: one hundred pounds for the copyright.

Jane Eyre was published in October. It caused such a fuss that the scurrilous publishing firm of T. C. Newby, into whose hands Emily and Anne had fallen, ceased dragging its feet over bringing out *Wuthering Heights* and *Agnes Grey*.

'They won't be popular works, and we already have the Bells' money,' Mr Newby had said. He now changed it to, 'The name of Bell is on everyone's lips and anything with that name attached to it will cause a stir. If we confuse matters sufficiently, the public might even mix up Ellis and Acton with Currer Bell and think they have new works by the author of *Jane Eyre*.'

Mr Williams started to send packages of newspaper cuttings to Haworth.

> *Jane Eyre* is a remarkable novel . . . in all respects very far indeed above the average of those which the literary journalist is doomed every season to peruse. It is a story of surpassing interest, rivetting the attention from the very first chapter . . . This is not merely a work of great promise, it is one of absolute performance . . . It is one of the most powerful domestic romances which has been published for many years.

Wuthering Heights didn't do badly, either, as they found when Newby sent similar packages.

> It is not every day that so good a novel makes its appearance . . . it is impossible to begin and not finish it; and quite as impossible to lay it aside afterwards and say nothing about it . . . We strongly recommend all our readers who love novelty to get this story, for we can promise them that they never have read anything like it before.

'Emily, what *have* we done?' Charlotte bit her lip, trying to restrain her pride but failing.

'Oh, dear,' responded Anne, but with a smile.

Emily, rolling pastry, doubled up, giggling.

Charlotte coloured while bundling up the washing. Nowadays, when asked a question, she was often speechless – her mind was so far away.

And no-one, in London or Haworth, knew who they were! The famous author Thackeray, for instance, wrote to Mr Williams, who posted on the letter:

> I wish you had not sent me *Jane Eyre*. It interested me so much that I have lost (or won if you like) a whole day in reading it at the busiest period . . . Some of the love passages made me cry, to the astonishment of John, who came in with the coals . . . Who the author can be I can't guess . . . if a woman she knows her language better than most ladies do.

Finally, he decided: 'It is a woman's writing, but whose?'

The Brontë spinsters looked at their neighbours and thought: *They do not know*. They imagined being read by the Nusseys, by Miss Wooler, and by the Yorkshire clergy. They visualized people unknown to them, in drawing-rooms, or whiling away long journeys, reading their novels. There was the sense of a great world opening up before them.

It was not the same for Anne. *Agnes Grey* was ignored or despised – rather as Anne had been for much of her life, it dawned on Charlotte. The best that was said of it was, 'It is a simple tale of a governess's experience and trials of love, borne with that meekness and met by that fortitude that ensures a final triumph,' and: 'It leaves no painful impression on the mind – some may think it leaves no impression at all.'

How strange that the tide of encouragement should turn. It was impossible to say what caused it. However, Charlotte began to think that the verdict on Anne, of 'leaving no impression', was an enviable one, as further reviews harped upon the 'painful impressions' made by *Jane Eyre* and *Wuthering Heights*.

It began in November when a cutting about *Jane Eyre* arrived from the *Spectator*:

> There is a low tone of behaviour (rather than of morality) in the book; and, what is worse than all, neither the heroine nor the hero attract sympathy . . . The plot is most extravagantly improbable, verging all along upon the supernatural, and at last running fairly into it.

She also had to face the pain of the cutting phrase.

> It is 'high life below stairs' with a vengeance, the fashionable world seen through the area railings, and drawn with the black end of the kitchen poker . . . The language she puts into the mouth of Blanche Ingram would disgrace a kitchen maid.

Reviewers looking for something fresh to say? Charlotte knew how easy it was to write in that waspish, negative fashion, because she had done it herself. It was childish and belonged to her own childhood, when they were composing their own '*Blackwood's Magazine*'. This did not prevent the review, and others like it, from hurting. She was angry for a moment, while in the next she claimed, 'It does not matter, I am above that sort of thing!'

This was to Emily, who was indeed above it, in a sense. That is, although she was just as hurt as anyone would be, yet it was how she expected the world to treat revelations of her secret life.

Then Charlotte collapsed into depression. She found that

she could not write anything all day. She started some sewing, but everything was going wrong; she pricked her finger, and the winter light died too soon so that she could not even see. She could not *think*, other than about the cruel phrases from the newspapers, and of how to answer them. The world was robbed of beauty, and she was listless.

She lit the lamps and tried to console herself by thumbing through her book, hoping to find what was good about it. She tried to catch herself by surprise, and to read her over-familiar words as if she had not seen them before. She often did this when revising, trying to judge them as if someone else had written them.

'I looked, and had an acute pleasure in looking, – a precious, yet poignant pleasure; pure gold, with a steely point of agony: a pleasure like what the thirst-perishing man might feel who knows the well to which he has crept is poisoned yet stoops and drinks divine draughts nevertheless.'

The reviewer who was able himself to describe the act of looking into a pair of eyes might have the right to castigate her for writing 'with the black end of a kitchen poker'! It was so unfair!

She was almost angry with *herself*, as the world turned grey, and time seemed endless, and all effort seemed worthless – because of a *book review*! Whereas she *knew* that she should feel gratitude for inspiration which was beyond that 'reviewer' . . . that . . .

She turned again to Emily for comfort, but Emily was being mauled, also.

> We know nothing in the whole range of our fictitious literature which presents such shocking pictures of the worst forms of humanity . . . It casts a gloom over the mind not easily to be dispelled.'

> The author of *Wuthering Heights* has evidently eaten toasted cheese.

> How a human being could have attempted such a book as the present without committing suicide before he had finished a dozen chapters, is a mystery.

While lurking in the provinces, instinct told them what was happening. As they were the talk of London, or at least 'Currer Bell' was, they were being punished for shunning society. Only they were not yet old enough to stay above it. They walked with a new thrill, sharper than any foreshadowed by their childhood thrills: that of notoriety. Emmii, Tallii and Annii were being described *in the newspapers* as being beyond the bounds of society and religion! Intelligent men were writing that authors of such works must surely want to cut their own throats!

There was increased speculation as to whether the 'Bells' really were male. Ladies wrote that such coarseness and brutality could not have sprung from the female soul, or, if the authors were female, they were outcasts from their own sex. The *Mirror* complained that 'Religion is stabbed in the dark'. Lady Eastlake wrote that *Jane Eyre* was:

> pre-eminently an anti-Christian composition. There is throughout it a murmuring against the comforts of the rich and against the privations of the poor, which, as far as each individual is concerned, is a murmuring against God's appointment.

After fulminating against its 'ungodly discontent', she continued,

> We do not hesitate to say that the tone of mind and thought which has overthrown authority and violated every code human and divine abroad, and fostered Chartism and rebellion at home, is the same which has written *Jane Eyre*.

Charlotte a Chartist!

Meanwhile, *Jane Eyre* was still selling, and she realized that secret notoriety would overhang her and her family for the remainder of their days.

She was in the parlour, seeking distraction through her new novel, *Shirley*. Anxiety exhausted her. She spent as much time sinking onto the couch, wiping her brow like, she imagined, one of those feeble lady reviewers who criticized her.

She overheard Papa saying to the postman in the hallway: 'I tell you, there is no such person as "Currer Bell" in the parish. The only one of that name is my curate, Mr Arthur Bell Nicholls. Perhaps you should take it to him at Mr Brown's house.'

'I have left letters here for Mr Bell before,' the postman insisted.

Charlotte rushed out. 'Please leave it here. I know who Mr Bell is.'

'You do?'

She laughed, as they often did at Papa's many puzzlements. 'Wait a moment,' she said and rushed upstairs. She gathered some reviews from her writing cabinet. She had to think quickly about choosing them: there were flattering ones, as well as bad ones, which it was not wise for Papa to see. The one that described *Jane Eyre* as 'not merely a work of great promise, it is one of absolute performance' could not be shown because of the sentence following which called it 'one of the most powerful domestic romances which has been published for many years'; its reference to 'romances' might send Evangelical Papa through the roof – or so she feared in her keyed-up state, recalling the day when he had burned the love stories that had belonged to her mother. They had all been worrying for ages about whether or not to tell Papa, before the Bells were unmasked and news of it got to Haworth; and about how to tell him.

She found him in his study. He blinked at her. Having closed the door, she stood by it, ready to run out if she should burst into tears. She clutched the bits of cut paper.

'Papa, I have been writing a book.'

He had returned to his reading, passing his magnifying glass over *Graham's Domestic Medicine*, and as she waited for his response she wondered if he was thinking of Branwell and reading about delirium tremens.

Without lifting his eyes, he answered, 'Have you, my dear?'

'I would like you to read it.'

'I can't read manuscripts. My eyes . . .'

'But it is printed!'

He looked up at her and said, 'I hope you have not been involving yourself in any silly expense.'

'I think I shall gain money by it. Only I want to keep it secret. The author, you see, is supposedly one "Currer Bell", which is my pseudonym.'

He was amused. 'Do the others know?'

'Emily has published too. As "Ellis Bell". And Anne, as "Acton Bell".'

'Goodness me! What does Branwell call himself?'

'Branwell hasn't published anything.'

He looked unhappy, so she said quickly, 'May I read you some reviews?'

'Please do.'

She quoted to him for five minutes. 'My word,' and 'Goodness me,' he interjected from time to time.

'So will you read the book, Papa?'

'You might leave it, and I will see if my eyes will take it.'

The day wore on. She noticed that he did not leave his study, and she hoped that he was as absorbed as she had been told Mr Smith had been.

At tea, he seemed to intend not even to raise the subject. It was a calm meal, Branwell was not at home to create a rumpus, and they could have talked. She assumed that he did not like it. Or maybe he was too annoyed because Branwell had not published anything. He had not even commented on that. It meant that his disappointment was very deep.

As they were about to leave, he gave his verdict:

'Children, Charlotte has been writing a book, and it is a better one than I expected. A little naughty, but in fact really very, very good.'

III

Ellen Nussey in a letter hinted that Charlotte was the author of *Jane Eyre* and Charlotte wrote back in a fury.

> If any Birstallian or Gomersallian should presume to bore you on the subject, – to ask what 'novel' Miss

Brontë has been 'publishing' – you can just say, that you are authorized by Miss Brontë to say, that she repels and disowns every accusation of the kind. You may add, if you please, that if any one has her confidence, you believe you have, and she has made no drivelling confessions to you on the subject.

Yet Ellen could not help noticing that she did not actually deny that she was Currer Bell. She only refused to acknowledge it. Therefore curiosity was roused further. They were all gossiping a great deal about 'Currer Bell' in Gomersal and Birstall – in the drawing-rooms, on the church steps – and it was hard to leave the matter alone.

'I found such extraordinarily familiar things,' Ellen said when they met. She wore her timid, tempting smile; an old maid's trap, seeming so harmless that it drew one's confidence. 'I had a strange sense of what I can only call, as the French say, *déjà vu*.'

'Such as?'

'The school is so like your descriptions of Cowan Bridge.'

'Perhaps Mr Bell was foolish enough to send a daughter there.'

'The Eyre family was in Hathersage. I remember you were struck by the name.'

'Now you are being fanciful!'

'Much of what Jane says is so like the way *you* talk. Once it got onto my mind, paragraph after paragraph was like the things you say.'

'Now you are being *completely* fanciful! It is not like me at all.'

'Then you have read it?'

'Papa has a copy.'

'What did you think?'

'I thought that far too much fuss is being made of it.'

'Mary Taylor wrote to me from New Zealand about it.'

Charlotte had posted a copy off in January, many months ago, consumed by excitement and not thinking of Mary's communicating with anyone else, but trusting, it appeared, too much in her discretion.

'How is Mary?'

'She is changing from her timber business to buying and selling cattle. Isn't it amazing that she should receive such a book out there? She did not say who had sent it.'

'It could have been anyone. It probably drifted in as a stray in her import agency. Did she tell you what she thought?'

'You know Mary! For her it was not outrageous *enough*. Nowhere near outspoken enough about the condition of women. She said it was all romance and she couldn't understand what the fuss was about.'

'I quite agree.'

'Whoever "Currer Bell" is, I'm sure he knows Cowan Bridge,' said the Reverend Thomas Crowther of Cragg Vale, who had also sent his daughters to the school. 'He has got that devil of a place to a tee.'

'I should not be surprised at that,' answered Patrick.

After Crowther had left the parsonage: 'You quite take *me* by surprise, Papa,' Charlotte said.

'Why, Charlotte?'

'Because of your audacity in lending Mr Crowther *Jane Eyre* and then asking for his opinion – while I was present! Suppose he had found out who I am? You realize that I am notorious?'

He chuckled. Then – 'It really does upset you, doesn't it?'

'Papa, none of us realized how unusual our upbringing has been, until I was publicly blamed for being "unladylike" and "unChristian". I feared *Jane Eyre* might be shocking, but not as much as the newspapers say. On the other hand, I did not expect that you would be so amused. And proud of me. I was delighted at your enthusiasm for entering a conspiracy with me. It is strange and wonderful to walk invisible and learn what people really think. But now you are tempting providence.'

'I hope I've brought you up not to take too much notice of the world. You have told the truth. You should be proud.'

'Thank you, Papa.'

She left it at that, but remained prickly. To say it 'upset' her had been an understatement. Charlotte could think of little else but her notoriety. It was only through absorption in yet more writing that she was able to escape it.

Only when she was writing well did she feel well – even though it was work that she supposed would make her yet more notorious. Charlotte wrote – as she had written *Jane Eyre* in Manchester – as the only way to shut out what was painful in her life, from toothaches, to the spectacle of Branwell drifting from bad to worse.

But worrying did neither him nor herself any good, and as an author she had become self-disciplined enough not even to notice whether he was in the house or not. She appeared impervious to his complaints of nightmares, of being ill and lovesick.

But whenever she reached the end of a stretch of writing, the thoughts that she had been ignoring overwhelmed her and she felt as exhausted as if she had been digging coal. She might lie on her bed, but more terrors preyed on her there, so most often she turned to domestic tasks. She became Miss Elder Sister, Miss Practical Housekeeper, and went out to help Tabby and Martha. She went into Haworth to help with parish duties. She valued the routines that had always been part of her life. That was Aunt Branwell's legacy.

Whether outside or at home, the question she asked herself about everyone she met was: *Does he know?* or *Has she read it?*

Tabby and she might be, say, cleaning the parlour, when it would dawn on Charlotte that for several hours, on and off, all that she had thought of was, Has Mr Greenwood guessed?

She lived with her unsolved dilemma as if it was the shadow of yet another sick brother. To her, now somewhat lessened, obsession with Monsieur Heger, she must add the fresh domination of something she would have never imagined: the lie she was living. Henceforth she and her sisters would live under the cloud of being notorious, though secret, authors.

CHAPTER SEVEN

REQUIEM

BRANWELL

I

'Every step that I should take to make things better, John, instead I go the opposite way. It seems that I *try* to make things worse. I get up in the morning—'

'When wert thou last up i' th'mornin'?'

'All right, in the afternoon. Have another drink, on me this time! When I wake up, I feel that I'm dying, and vow I'll never drink again, but instead of eating good bread and drinking water to clean my system, as I intended, I bloat my stomach with mutton stew and make for the alehouse. I set out for the moors but instead I dive downhill to Halifax. Always downhill! It is like taking that first drink. Even before I've finished it, I know I'll not resist the second. I've already given in to my fate.'

Branwell waved his glass, and put it down after spilling some of his beer. The hand he held it in was shaking. He hid the other trembling hand beneath the table. He returned his attention to Brown as if he had just discovered him in the room. He seemed startled, then fixed him with a glaring eye and announced, so that half the Black Bull heard him: 'This is the Devil claiming me, John! He grabs my arm at every good intention! Draws me to him! I cannot help myself!'

'Cheer up, old lad. Things are bound to mend.'

But Branwell was not to be thwarted of his tragic role.

'I've been happy for months on end, then *always* I destroyed it! Some of my happiest times were spent walking with Dearden and Grundy. It was Paradise. What happened? Because of my love of beauty and art I neglected my work and, behind my back, my assistant cheated the railway company.' He grabbed John's arm, desperate not to lose his sympathy. 'I'm not a thief! Someone else stole, John, it wasn't me!'

'Oh, my friend, I know it weren't thee. It were bad luck.'

'I see a beautiful girl and am tempted to court her. For a few days I forget what I perfectly well know. When I believe I'm in love again, I learn the truth: that in the state I'm in, I'm a joke to her.'

'It canna be that bad,' John Brown said, but without conviction.

'It's what happened at the Ovenden Cross!'

'Nay!'

'Yes! Listen to me, John! I thought I'd charmed the girl, you know!' Branwell's eyes glistened. Clutching at straws, he wanted, if not some girl, then a man, his friend, to assure him that he could indeed still woo the female sex, as at Broughton and Thorp Green. 'But she was only fooling with me.'

'*Nay!*'

'In the presence of beauty, I have the strangest sensation – *I do not feel it!* For that, you need to be in love. Then you are part of life, not shrivelled up inside yourself.'

He looked at his friend crookedly and said: 'You're not *glad* to see the parson's son going to the dogs, are you?'

For once, John was embarrassed. Almost nothing disturbed his calm, but this did. 'Why should I be glad?'

'Some are, in Haworth!' Branwell's hands shook more violently. He banged the table, tears came, and he added, 'Not you, no, sorry. But it makes some feel better to see those above them brought down low!'

There was a huge silence. It lasted only seconds, but seemed longer, and to quench the room.

'Oh, gi' o'er thy fancy talk! Stop feeling sorry for theesen. Look at Nathan Hartley yonder. He's happy because he'll have a chance to drop in at a few alehouses when he takes a load from Bridge Mills to Halifax tomorrow morning. I'll tell thee what'll do thee good. I'd say I'm lucky wi' my battles wi' John Barleycorn because I always have work to do in the morning, and it gets the ale out of my system. Come and work wi' me for a while.'

Branwell met this with an unbelieving stare.

'I know thou can't do much, but thou can fetch and carry and talk to people on the job. It'll stop thee fretting. It's fine, frosty weather we're having. Just to stand about in the fresh air in my yard'll be good for thee. Even that might put some flesh on thee and help thy suit to fit thee. Thou's a bag o' bones, man. Wi' thy hands shaking like that, we'll keep thee away from hammers and chisels for a time, but thou'll soon improve.'

Branwell promised to join Brown on the following day.

On getting out of bed the next morning, his resolve brought a spring to his step and he could not imagine why he had ever been irresolute.

A little inner voice tripped him up. While rooting through a drawer, and halfway to choosing his trousers, he stubbed his toe and the voice reminded him that he was a failure, while his sisters were successful.

When he tried to close the drawer it jammed part way and he had not the strength to deal with it. He broke into a sweat, of the kind that often woke him in the night. His eyes prickled with tears. The voice told him that, in his wretched state of health, his ambition to be a working man was absurd. Sometimes he could hardly pull on his shoes.

Instead of clothes suitable for Brown's workshop, he put on his best. He muffled himself up in topcoat, scarf and hat, sneaked across the graveyard to come out at the rear of the Black Bull so as not to have to walk past Brown's house, descended the hill to the yard of Bridge Mill and hitched a lift on Hartley's cart-load of wool to Halifax. It was all as simple as the Devil could make it. The Devil had placed the carter in the public bar last night, and thus had arranged the transport.

The Devil decided to tease him. On seeing him white-faced and sunken-cheeked, and on hearing his cough as he waited in the frosty yard while the horses were fettled, Nathan was inspired to declare that he would not take him.

'Thou'd do better seeing Dr Wheelhouse,' he told him.

It made Branwell more determined not to be thwarted. 'I'm going to Halifax to *see* a doctor, a specialist, don't you understand, sir?'

'Then why didn't thou say so in the first place? Thou'd better wrap th'orses' blanket round thee shoulders, and let's hope it doesn't cloud over and snow.'

Branwell knew this was a reckless journey. While travelling over the frost-bound hills, he let out small dry coughs, which hurt his ribs. He feared that Leyland would not be overjoyed to see him. He had little money left. He was fearfully unsure of how he was going to return home. In 'the old days' he would have walked, but he knew he'd never be able to step out that distance any more. But nothing could stop him when the Devil was inside him.

On reaching Leyland's 'marble works', he was so relieved by the sculptor's welcome that he forgot his direful reflections.

He could not later recall much of this stay in Halifax. He upset a table in the Talbot, breaking the landlady's punch-bowl. No-one seemed to mind at the time. For some reason, the pub was still happy to extend credit – the antics of the artists brought in the high-spending merchants from the Piece Hall.

All his friends were prepared to let the world go hang, and Leyland was in despair. The Dean and Chapter of York Minster had at last advanced fifty pounds towards his statue provided he would guarantee to deliver the work in four months' time, but this seemed unlikely. Not much more had emerged from the stone since Branwell was last in Halifax. Was there a big toe, and the beak of a nose, defined?

Anyway, the money was already spent, partly in paying off debts. Suppliers and clients were dunning him. Without paying his bill, he could obtain no more marble on credit. A gentleman was pestering him to send 'a cart and a man' to take away the chimney-piece 'which is now an eyesore in my drawing-room', for the marble had crumbled and cupids had tumbled onto the carpet.

Leyland made fun of his stack of letters, filed on an iron spike and growing dusty, but he was only trying to be gamey. Only in the mornings, when Branwell woke up on the studio couch, did he convey the truth. He was too weak, his ankles were swollen, and he could no longer stand for hours nor sustain the hard work demanded – for *his* sculpture in particular. 'Do you know how much marble has to be chiselled away to leave standing a proud nose like the archbishop's? Do you know how much is wasted to carve that projecting toe in its death throes? And are the philistines prepared to pay for this waste?'

In the sober light of mid-afternoon, Branwell watched Leyland going to the public house – his walk now an even more exaggerated roll, because of the swelling in his legs – and he wondered what on earth would become of the great sculptor. But in consequence, he found himself in the unusual role of comforter. It did him good. He thought that, when it came to it, his ambitions were as great, and he as wordsmith could match Leyland the craftsman.

Happy and glorious in his talk, he forgot that he was ill and neglected. He felt, briefly, that joy which had been his until leaving Thorp Green. To restore even a moment of it made life worth living. If they should all die tomorrow, what did it matter?

'Bravo, Branwell! This is better than being swamped with petticoats in Haworth, eh?'

'I'll tell you what! My sisters are setting out to be something in the way of authors, too. Tell no-one of this, mind. You know that there's a novel called *Wuthering Heights* causing a stir? By "Ellis Bell". Ellis Bell is my sister, Emily. She sent it to the publishers. But I wrote it.'

His companions froze like the sculptures around the studio, staring at him, waiting for more, and he felt his own face freeze, too.

Then they clearly decided he was talking drunken nonsense, and changed the subject.

After a couple of weeks, Branwell coughed his way home, hitching lifts on other wool-carts. His wallet was empty. He did not remember having run up debts, but his bills pursued him through the spring.

For long enough, it hardly mattered. His main literary form these days being the slippery begging letter, he exercised the art on public house landlords, and he also asked

Leyland to placate or put them off 'until I am next in Halifax'.

More pressing was the Pennine winter, typically persisting with 'sneaky' winds and rain through February and March, so that everyone in the parsonage caught flu. All were in bed, in turns, in pairs, in trios. For one terrible week all five of them were ill. Each time Branwell posted a letter to Leyland, he wondered whether in truth he would ever be in Halifax again.

II

No more sharing of the joys of translating Greek: Patrick's conversations with his son had dwindled to discussing emergencies and crises. In their room each night they had swum through the warm pool of shared experiences, and now they were on the rocks. Patrick had given up expecting his son to say his prayers before he slept. He had found it best not to remind him of them. On other nights, though, Branwell was fervent in his pleas to God. They were the nights when he was hallucinating, when he saw rats scurrying across the floor and goblins sitting on top of the chest of drawers, and there was nothing Patrick could say or do. He would listen, and hope that his son would sleep soon, and achieve a blessed peace. His main help was negative. He kept the candle by his own bedside and in other ways took care that his son did not set the house on fire. He tried not to distress his daughters by letting them see the extent of their brother's collapse. He did not speak of his disappointment. He bore his cross alone – he who had counselled so many to share their burdens. He talked to Branwell only about what they could not avoid discussing.

Their conversations usually took place with Patrick sitting up in bed, just able to make out the form of his son, who generally did not look towards him but was humped under his quilt and facing the other way, towards the window. This was left unshuttered these days, because Branwell was afraid of the dark, and because he often had to stumble around the room during the night.

'Thomas Charnock, the son of my predecessor the Reverend Charnock, has hanged himself. He was found in his dressing-room,' Patrick announced one night. Better than letting Branwell find out about it in the public house was to seize a moment when he was relatively sober.

'No-one knows why he did it. No woman seems to have been involved. "Melancholia", it is assumed. It takes many on the hills in winter. A dreaded mystery. If only he had shared it with his father!'

He waited in hope of his son's saying that he would never end his life in that way. In the past, Branwell had threatened to cut his throat, to slash his wrists, to stab his heart, 'where *she* lies buried', so that the family had discussed hiding the kitchen knives.

'It is the worst fate to overcome a father,' Patrick said. 'Especially a clergyman, who has to face the fact that he has not managed to pass his faith on even to his own son. Brannii – if you ever despair, please turn to me. Promise.'

'I have often turned to you! I have had debts, but when I asked you—'

'And they have been paid, over and over again. But—'

'But! I do not want to talk any more. I want to sleep.'

Summer arrived, still cold, still wet. On one of its endless, twilit afternoons, when Tabby was in the village, Emily despite her lingering cough was getting soaked by walking Keeper through a drizzle, Martha Brown was at her father's, and Charlotte and Anne were catching up with Sunday school business neglected because they had been busy with literary affairs, Patrick caught his son in the kitchen and saw his chance to get something unpleasant off his chest.

Only a member of the family would have thought this an opportunity to discuss anything. Branwell was shivering, yet sweat poured from his forehead and his face was red. He had a cough – as they all had. Anyone else would say he should be in bed, but no-one knew better than Patrick that Branwell was even more tormented there. One would be advised to call the doctor, but Dr Wheelhouse had grown impatient. There *wasn't* any hope of finding Branwell sober: only perhaps less inebriated than usual. He was peeling an apple, and Patrick's attention became fixed on his shaking hands holding the knife.

'Stop staring at me!' He dropped the knife, scrambled after it, and cursed.

'Let me help you,' Patrick said, quietly, still hoping not to rouse his son, but it did not work.

'I can peel an apple!'

Patrick held back. When at last the apple was gouged and peeled – wastefully, as he observed, and the peel dropped onto Tabby's scrubbed floor – he felt he dare hand out his bad news. Thus, strategically, they had to deal with Branwell. It was no use raging at him any more.

'I have had a letter from Mr Nicolson of the Old Cock Inn in Halifax. Apparently he has asked you several times to settle your account from last January. He says that if it is not paid he will issue a court summons.'

'I don't understand!'

'Don't you?'

'I have paid him already. It must be a mistake!'

'How have you paid him?'

'Through Leyland.'

'There is no need to fear a court, then. Or perhaps Mr Leyland has neglected to pass the money on? I believe he is careless in financial matters. Sit down, Branwell, please. It will be much better. Do not upset yourself further – please. There is no problem without an answer. Have you put him in charge of *all* that you owe?'

'Most of it. Some of it.'

Branwell sat with his head in his hands. His twitching hands made unexpected darts up his cheeks. They were like devils running.

He took away one hand and fumbled for a piece of apple. He managed to hold it, but could not find his mouth and gave up the effort, collapsing on the table. He was turning red again, and shivering. He was going to have another fit of delirium tremens and Patrick had to get him to bed. He held his son under the shoulders, surprised at how easy he was to lift. It was like lifting a bird off a nest. Under the loose clothes, he was all bones, and easy even for an old man to get upstairs. It was as if he flew, or blew.

It was harder to stop him talking: an endless logorrhoea mixing Latin, Greek and English, only half intelligible, cursing his fate, expressing terror of God and of dying. He jumped at a sound from the kitchen. 'What is that?' As if he thought the Devil had come for him.

'Martha returning, I expect.'

At the head of the stairs, Branwell claimed that black rats were running across the floor.

'Try not to talk so! Rest yourself. Be calm.'

Almost carrying the frail thirty-year-old, Patrick was taken back to Branwell's childhood. He got him onto his bed, where he would still not stop talking, especially about the rats. He said they were among the shadows in the corner of the ceiling.

'How much do you owe Mr Nicolson?'

'Ten shillings will keep him quiet.'

'We will find it tomorrow, Brannii.'

Patrick could not think of any more to say. He feared that his son might be worse than he had realized.

Crossing the hallway, Patrick met Emily, who had a hacking cough and flushed cheeks. Her clothes and hair were bedraggled. Following came Anne, crouched over her own aching chest. She was nagging Emily to change her dress. His frail daughters were arguing in such an overwrought way. Adding his mite of persuasion to get Emily to change her clothes, Patrick followed them into the parlour where papers and writing cabinets were strewn over the table as if it were an office. A fire burned, but it was low. He pulled the bell-cord to summon Martha to bring more coals. When Martha had done so, Emily was prepared at least to dry herself before the fire, even if it was no use trying to get her to change her dress when she did not wish to. As her clothes steamed around her, she leaned on the mantelpiece and coughed into her fist, frighteningly – it was so dry, from so deep in her chest – but he dared say nothing about it. She had such a temper, and giving vent to it weakened her further.

Charlotte rambled in, wanting to know what the family was up to; squinting and peering in the dim light that had hindered her reading, writing and sewing all day, and which was why she had gone out to the Sunday school.

'I am terribly afraid that Branwell might be developing a

consumption,' Patrick announced, now that they were all together.

He sent Martha to fetch Dr Wheelhouse, who took his time in coming. He was not pleased.

'I fear that my son has a consumption,' Patrick told him.

Impatiently, Dr Wheelhouse clumped up the stairs. For a minute, he examined Branwell from the doorway. Patrick was right behind him.

Wheelhouse approached the bed. 'He's in a drunken stupor! His very skin exudes alcohol. Mr Brontë, I have twenty cases of consumption in Haworth – all worsened by this wet summer – but your son has nothing more than flu, aggravated by his dissolute habits.'

Ten shillings was only a fraction of what was needed for Branwell's debts. Once out of bed, he got as far as Brown's. Ever since he had not turned up for his day's 'work', he had avoided seeing him. A month had gone by. It was not necessary for him to be shifty. John laughed – he had always liked Branwell for being mercurial – and picked him up as he had when they had been little more than boys, pretending to wrestle.

He put him down instantly, with a look on his face as if he had seen a ghost.

'What is it, John?'

'Friend, thou never weighed much in thy prime, probably only about nine stone. Now I'll wager thou's no more than six, or six and a half.' He spoke deliberately, with one eye closed; the manner of an expert at calculating weight and mass. 'Thou's shivering like a newborn pup, man. Like a chicken that's lost its feathers.'

'When are you going to Halifax again, John?'

'Wednesday next.'

'Will you give this envelope to Mr Nicolson? As you see, I cannot get there myself. He will probably tell you it is not enough for what I owe, but *please* assure him . . . *please* . . . this is most important . . . *that the rest is to follow for certain!*'

'All right, don't upset thyself so.'

'You don't understand!'

'Yes, I do.'

When Branwell was halfway back to the parsonage, he turned to find Brown staring after him.

He wrote to Leyland.

> My Dear Sir, – Mr Nicolson has sent to my Father a demand for the settlement of my bill owed to him, immediately, under penalty of a court summons. I have written to inform him that I shall soon be able to pay him the balance in full – for that I will write to Dr Crosby and request an advance through his hands which I am sure to obtain, when I will remit my amount owed, at once, to the Old Cock. I have also given John Brown this morning Ten shillings which John will certainly place in Mr N.'s hands on Wednesday next.
>
> If he refuses my offer and presses me with law, I am RUINED. I have had five months of such utter sleeplessness, violent cough and frightful agony of mind that jail would destroy me for ever.
>
> I earnestly beg you to see Nicolson and tell him that my receipt of money on asking, through Dr Crosby, is morally certain. If you conveniently can, see Mrs Sugden of the Talbot and tell her that on receipt of the money I expect so shortly I will transmit her the whole or part of the account I owe her.

He then wrote to Lydia, 'via Dr Crosby'. The undying love that he swore above his signature 'Northangerland' made him feel better while he wrote, but worse after he had finished – the difference was so great between the dash and glory of Northangerland and the frightened, ill and lonely Branwell who was not as certain of Mrs Robinson's continuing generosity as he had pretended.

He went out to post his letters, and to call at the druggist's. In the post office, they were talking about the recent revolution in France. Woolcombers, weavers and housewives cared about King Louis Philippe's flight to England, but Branwell took no interest. It was a steamy day after weeks of rain and that mattered more to a man with an ailing chest. The manure heaps were stinking. There was even an odour rising from the trough at the spring, which had flies skimming over it. In his own mouth there was phlegm. He imagined some damp, cruel prison waiting for him. He could hardly climb the gentle slope by the church wall. He blamed the weather. He made it to his room, closed the shutters and removed his spectacles. Yet again, he spat blood into the chamber-pot. He put on his nightshirt and collapsed back into bed. His skin seemed to be creeping over his bones. He was both sweating and shivering.

His life's dilemma presented itself with appalling clarity. With his lack of vocation for following his father's path into the church, nothing of what he had loved and learned, the classics, art, literature, suited him for the world in which he might have earned his living. He should have studied mathematics and engineering, then he could have succeeded on the railway, or he could have worked in the mills. His passionate nature – his innocent nature because he had been brought up unusually, among girls, and without ever going to school – had led him astray when he had been a tutor, so his career was blocked in that direction. What could he do? There was no way out.

He took laudanum and saw several visions. One was of Success, who appeared as a dark female. Ah, he understood . . . she was the Muse and he only had to write down what she dictated! He would be inspired, as Handel was when composing the *Messiah* during a few weeks, as Goethe had been when writing *Faust*!

He fumbled at his bedside for pencil and paper . . . they were usually there . . . but there was nothing.

His Muse turned into a dark spider scurrying across the wall by his bed, then over the ceiling. It was the size of a crab. He bundled himself under the covers, strangling his twitches, muffling his screams.

'I'm afraid the old man and I have had a bad night of it together,' Branwell said – boasted – when he reached the kitchen at the end of the following morning.

Charlotte's mouth drew tight. She turned from him to continue putting wrapping paper on the fire.

'What has the postman brought?'

His sister's manner was so hostile, these simple words were like thistles in his throat.

'A parcel.'

'No letter?'

'Not for you. Were you expecting one?'

'Yes . . . no. Was it interesting?'

'Only some books.'

Only some books. At one time, that would have been the most exciting, shared event on earth.

'It is no use expecting your Mrs Robinson to write to you,' Charlotte snapped. 'Do you know what she is doing now? No, you have no idea. Anne knows, because she has letters from her daughters, but she doesn't dare tell you. Your Lydia has been having an affair with Sir Edward Scott, an old man only waiting for his wife to die – which she has now done, making way no doubt for the second Lady Scott. I am sorry that it sets you snivelling, but you have to get over these things, as I have had to do.'

She left him to it, stunned under her blow.

When he thought no-one was stirring in the hallway and up the stairs, he made his way back to bed. At the foot of the stairs, Emily appeared from the parlour – from where he could hear Anne crying.

Emily, despite her cough and livid complexion, smiled at him. 'You should not have left your bed,' she said.

She took him firmly by the arm. As she bent over him with sisterly warmth, he was aware of the yellow cinquefoil flower pinned between her breasts. Waves lapped over him from the shores of Gondal.

'We *are* a feeble lot!' she laughed.

'Why is Anne crying?'

'She has the reviews of *The Tenant of Wildfell Hall*. "There seems in the writer a morbid love for the coarse, not to say brutal," one said. "The work seems convincing proof that there is nothing kindly or genial in the author's powerful mind," said another. But you must stay in your bed until your flu is better. I'll bring you up some soup.'

He looked at her with a dog's gratitude. 'Thank you, Emily.'

Gratitude was so untypical that she was taken by surprise. 'Why? I have done nothing.'

'Emily!' Charlotte shouted from behind the half-closed parlour door. 'Books, Emily! Books!'

III

Charlotte sat at the head of the breakfast table, her head full of metropolitan matters. Her mail included letters from William Thackeray, George Henry Lewes, and the authoress Julia Kavanagh. Branwell might think himself a proper little Northangerland when throwing his weight around in Halifax, but that summer Anne and she had been where he had never managed to get to – and where Charlotte herself had been more than once, on her way to Brussels – *London*.

They had set off to clear up a confusion created by Anne's and Emily's publisher, Newby, who, through claiming that Currer, Ellis and Acton Bell were all one person, hoped to tack his publications, especially the latest one, *The Tenant of Wildfell Hall*, onto that comet, the mysterious author of *Jane Eyre*. To destroy the scoundrel they had begun their impetuous trip by marching into Smith, Elder's office and announcing themselves as women; two plain, dull women in comically provincial dress at that. 'Currer and Acton Bell' had then been round to shock Newby.

In their few days they had been taken by the handsome George Smith to see *The Barber of Seville* at Covent Garden. They had been to the Royal Academy and to the National Gallery. They had brought presents home for Emily, Tabby and Martha, but Charlotte had refused to look for something for Branwell, and, as Anne had thought that 'too cruel', they had softened the insult by not bringing anything home for Papa, either.

It was irksome, this morning, to have to think about a malingering brother. Charlotte complained about the empty place, family prayers missed, a spoiled meal, and added, bitterly: 'Branwell gets out of his bed easily enough for the poet. He leaves the house without trouble when he thinks we aren't watching. Though he was too "ill" to come to church, he nipped out to an assignation with John Brown. I caught sight

429

of them as I was coming out of church and I asked Martha if she knew what they were doing. Martha gave this to me.'

Charlotte then read aloud Branwell's note, which he had told Martha to take to her father.

'Sunday. Noon. Dear John, I shall feel very much obliged to you if you can contrive to get me Five pence worth of Gin in a proper measure. Punctually at Half-past Nine in the morning you will be paid the 5d out of a shilling given me then. Yours, P.B.B.'

'Where was the shilling to come from?' she added.

'From me, of course,' Papa told her. 'I had promised him. It was better than finding it taken from my bedside drawer – as happened a week ago. Yes, I know it is shocking, but you must not, you *must* not, say anything to him about it, for shame will make him worse. He steals to feed his habit – the greedy demon inside him. It is not immorality. He is upright in other matters. This is a sickness, requiring a gentle inoculation of the disease's constituents. He told me that he wanted to go to Mr Greenwood's for writing-paper and, like you, I thought that in this fine September weather it would be good for him to take a stroll.'

'There is neither reason nor sense to be had from him any more!'

'We are all without sense or reason at times.'

Francis Grundy responded to Branwell's letters by turning up at the Black Bull and arranging for a meal for the pair of them. The new landlord, John Sugden, was itching with curiosity when the railway engineer asked him to send a message up to the parsonage.

In a cheerful private room, with crimson curtains drawn against a melancholy September night, the fire sparkling upon cut-glass, silver, and china upon a white damask cloth, Grundy waited.

Branwell, a mass of dank red hair surrounding a yellow face that was dry and shrivelled, eventually peered round the door, as if fearing an enemy. His eyes, normally small and unimpressive, were enlarged, swelling behind his spectacles and staring intently, madly. His forehead bulged from his receding hairline. Although his clothes were washed and ironed by his sisters and Tabby, he was unshaven and had dressed haphazardly. His hair was uncut and uncombed. His lips were not so much trembling, as shaking. So were his hands.

Grundy rose and did not so much shake Branwell's hand, as gently feel those bones that were as frail as a bird's. Branwell's sharp coughs obviously hurt his chest. He cut off Grundy's excuses: too busy at work to answer your letters – thought I'd give you a surprise, and revive the spirit of the old days—

'The old days have left me in a sorry state,' he quavered.

Grundy led the shivering wreck to the fire, which he poked into a blaze. He relieved Branwell of his loose black overcoat that made him look even more like an angel of death. Leaving him standing over the fire, he went to hang the coat next to his own behind the door; which he closed, noticing that the Sugdens, the maid, and other customers were prying. He had then to lead Branwell from the fire to the table. Otherwise, it seemed, he would simply have gone on staring into the flames. Grundy suggested, first, a glass of punch, then said he had ordered game soup followed by a side of beef with vegetables. Branwell had trouble in getting the glass to his mouth. It chattered against his teeth.

He smiled at last. Smile! It was a cheerless mockery of transient joys.

'I haven't eaten anything but broth for a long time,' he said.

Grundy pulled the cord to summon the maid, and wondered how he would get through the evening. But Branwell turned more cheerful by the glass and the mouthful. His hands grew steadier. They worked through the soup, the meat, the vegetables.

'Perhaps I could still obtain work on the railway?' Branwell suggested, wistfully. When Grundy did not reply, he added, 'Maybe it's but a foolish dream.'

Another pause, and he said, 'Whenever death comes, I am ready, Francis! It is solely due to you-know-who.'

They finished their meal. They took more punch. The

maid, whose curiosity was not being satisfied, was growing less courteous.

They sat for more than an hour. They talked of old friends. In an erratic switch, Branwell was turning every memory into fun. Grundy encouraged it.

But Branwell's attention wandered. It was often impossible to understand what he was talking about.

Grundy rang for the bill. The hour or so that had dragged now seemed to have sped by. Branwell's manner changed back to what it had been when he had arrived. He had evidently enjoyed a brief respite from Hell.

He got up and strode over to his coat. Out of the pocket, he drew something wrapped in a towel. He placed it on the table. He unrolled it and there was Tabby's knife. He sat down again, put his hands across the table and held Grundy's hands.

'When your message came, I thought it was Satan sending for me, from the Black Bull where he has waited for me so many times! I thought you were the Devil! I meant to stab you, until I heard your voice!'

Grundy put on his overcoat. His own hands were shaking now. He helped Branwell into his coat. It appeared he was going to leave the knife and towel behind. Grundy made a bundle of them, and pushed it into Branwell's pocket. They went into the Square.

'Haven't you a hat?' Grundy asked.

'No, I have – lost it.' The words sounded like an echo from down a well.

Grundy led his friend by the arm up Parsonage Lane. A candle was burning in the central upstairs window of the parsonage.

'Emily lights it for me,' Branwell explained. 'When we were children, we used to call that room our "study". We made our books in there.'

Grundy stopped outside the yard gate. He knew he would never see Branwell again.

'Won't you come in?' Branwell begged.

'I'd better not. I have hired the gig to take me to Keighley. It would keep them up too late at the Black Bull.'

He had to turn away quickly from Branwell's bowed head, and tears. He could not look back as he returned to the Black

Bull. The Sugdens were waiting for explanations. He could not avoid giving some, as they were providing his transport to Keighley late at night.

Grundy told them: 'All through the evening, I sensed that he was frightened – not of me nor of anything that might come into the room, nor even of death, but of *himself*. Of the eternity to which his own self had destined him.'

Branwell managed an expedition into Haworth on the following day. It was one of those warm September days with gentle veils of mist and a moist scent of peat coming off the moorland, and birds singing in the garden. He was tempted out by a false promise of spring. He reached the Black Bull corner. Then he had to be helped home by whoever was nearby, which happened to be John Brown's brother, William. He could not mount the doorstep unaided. Emily and Papa got him upstairs, while Dr Wheelhouse was sent for.

'Thank you, Emily – Papa – I do not deserve it,' Branwell said.

To hear him expressing humble thanks was extraordinary. It was eerie.

Wheelhouse examined the shivering, yellow sack of bones, touched him here and there, listened, and knew it was what he had seen in dozens of Haworth cottages.

He went with Mr Brontë into his study and pronounced Branwell near to his end. He was embarrassed at his previous wrong diagnosis, and wanted to hurry away from the steady gaze of Patrick's contempt.

Papa went upstairs to his son. The white face was tiny, the skin shrunk to the skull, and the skull in its nest of red hair was filled with big eyes lifeless like rain pools. How small he seemed, he who in his rages had seemed large. Already the bed seemed only half occupied, for there was such a small hump under the sheets. Only the sheets held his son down from immediately floating off to – where? There was no hope expressed in the face; only the resignation that had crept over Branwell during the last few days.

'My son, our last hours are with us,' Patrick said. He hardly needed to give Dr Wheelhouse's verdict.

'I know where I am bound.'

'No, my son. No. No. No! There is forgiveness even in the last hour.'

It was through sheer effort of will throughout most of the night that Patrick Brontë led his son towards confession. His was the effort of a man belonging to that breed whose wills were as strong as any on earth: those clerics of England who modelled themselves on the Duke of Wellington and Lord Nelson. The story of Branwell's life was unwound, so much of it unknown to his father. 'At that hour which we all must reach and yet which we so rarely conceive,' – as Patrick expressed it later – he did not try to persuade his son to save his strength, but to talk. Of the illegitimate child in Broughton-in-Furness, of the adultery in Thorp Green, and of warnings he had shunned.

Patrick spent most of the night kneeling by the bed, other than when he had to move – for a glass of water, the chamber-pot, or to put coals on the fire. Otherwise, between each confession he prayed for perhaps five minutes. 'There *is* no hope for me,' Branwell said, more than once. He spoke with utter simplicity and Patrick had to guard himself from the useless regret that they had not talked thus ten, five, three years ago.

At some moments they simply shared the sight of the stars. In the dawn over Rombalds Moor, there was – of all stars – Venus. The universe seems to have a way of creating symbols at moments of crisis, thought Patrick.

By that time Branwell, though racked, appeared to have a sense of beatitude and Patrick, too, felt changed.

Charlotte found herself pacing the house alone. She went in to see Emily and Anne – Emily was asleep and Anne was praying – and in to Papa and Branwell. There she immediately felt she ought not to intrude. She went down the stairs, where the clock whirred and ticked, and into the kitchen where cats stared in alarm, Keeper let out a growl of surprise, and cinders dropped with what seemed a doomful clatter in the grate. Finally she entered the parlour – the study that had excluded Branwell. She walked around and around the table.

She was still up at six o'clock, when she went down to Brown's house to inform them of her brother's last hours and to ask Mr Nicholls to take Papa's service: for it was Sunday morning. They did not need to be told. John had heard rumours in the Black Bull and elsewhere, and they had seen lamps moving in the cracks of the shutters in the parsonage all night. Mr Nicholls put on his topcoat and returned home with her.

'You should be wearing more than a shawl, Miss Brontë.'

That was all that was said – whispered – by either of them. But she was surprised at how comforted she was to have him sharing, she knew, some of her thoughts; at any rate, the pity for Branwell. She realized that she could not think of any other man – any other person – she would rather have as comforter. She was glad that he would be there, for Papa's sake, and she could not think what accumulation of impressions she must have absorbed, unrealized, for her to form thoughts so contrary to what she had said of him. As she let him go in alone to see Papa, she flashed him a smile. She saw that he was grateful, and she could not think why on earth such a handsome man should be fond of her.

John Brown came shortly after. He stayed for an hour, and left the bedroom expressing surprise at Branwell's peacefulness.

'He didna once mention Mrs Robinson. He carried all the blame himself,' it was reported that he had remarked to his wife.

There was no church for them this morning. The family crammed itself into the bedroom at nine o'clock. They witnessed the extraordinary sight of Branwell praying and whispering 'amen' to the prayers of his father.

His death throes lasted for nearly half an hour. Then he leapt up – almost out of the bed – so that they all jumped back. It seemed he was leaping for the sky through the window. Papa being closest, Branwell grasped him around the neck, and both fell back onto the bed. The fingers slipped from Patrick's neck.

Charlotte got up to close the shutters. She saw folk on their way to church, and she wondered what sermon Mr Nicholls would preach. She had the unexpected confidence that he would not let her down.

She ushered Papa into his study. 'I do not believe that any of us will ever sleep again,' he said. She closed the shutters there, too, and left Tabitha to sit with him.

Martha was sent to fetch one of the Haworth widows who washed corpses; there were several such widows, though some of them only gave their services during epidemics. Martha helped by bringing the hot water, and dashing off to Mr Lambert's for unguents. In haste, before rigor mortis set in, the body was washed, and dressed in Branwell's best nightshift which Anne had taken from the bottom drawer of the chest in the corner. His jaw was tied up with a scarf. Emily snipped off locks of hair to be kept in envelopes and lockets. They each wondered why they were dry-eyed.

Moving woodenly, Charlotte was the only one to almost collapse. It was the knife that she found under Branwell's mattress.

She did not tell her sisters about it, and perhaps she never would. Then she broke down, and had to make for her bed.

John Brown tolled the passing-bell. He did wonder if he had been as kind as he might have been to his friend. All by himself in St Michael's tower, it came back to him what Branwell had said once when they were both drunk. 'You're not *glad* to see the parson's son going to the dogs, are you?' It was one of those unguardedly true things that drunks and fools (sometimes the dying, too) could come out with. First of all it had offended and shocked him – made him want to protest – then his conscience had told him, as it did now, that he had indeed glorified in his strength, and the family sprung from his loins, in comparison with the son of the most important man in the village, with all his advantages.

But, by eck, he'd been good for a laugh many a time in the—

Tabitha Aykroyd closed the remaining shutters in the parsonage.

'I've been doing this night and morn for twenty-four years,

sithee,' she whispered to Martha, who fastened the latches because Tabby was too crippled to straighten up. 'I did it th'first time four years before thou were born, and I never thought I'd be wearing mourning and closing the shutters for the house's children.' She said the same to her brother William Wood, the joiner, when he came to measure the body.

By candlelight in the darkened house, the women – themselves frail, except for young Martha – unpacked mourning dresses, funeral gloves, veils and bonnets from where they had lain for six years in drawers following Aunt Branwell's passing. Charlotte was still in bed, but in the kitchen the clothes were spruced and ironed by Tabby and Martha, Emily and Anne. Lace collars, cuffs and hem guards were repaired. The fine black wool from Keighley was lovely to touch and to fold, and like silk.

They all still wondered where their tears were.

Wood stayed up all night to make the coffin and on the following day John and William Brown helped to manoeuvre it through the house. Finally they laid it in the parlour among strong-scented flowers, such as were available; chrysanthemums and late-flowering roses.

How dreamlike was this day, and the next. Perhaps this numbing was God's consolation. Behind the shutters, they moved so quietly, shadowy in black, with so little to say. A pale face sometimes loomed in candlelight or firelight. The parsonage was a grotto to the dead and dying, haunted by priestesses.

Charlotte, still in her bed days later, started to weep at last and she stifled her tears in her pillow.

Anne came into the room. Charlotte looked at her and burst into full flow. Anne caught it from her, brought it downstairs, and passed it on to Tabby, Martha and Papa like an infection. It seemed that only Emily was immune.

After the long day and night of straining his will on behalf of his son's soul, and after lying sleepless in the bedroom with the corpse until Wood had made the coffin, Patrick ghosted the house, calling like a lost bird, 'My son, my son!'

Mr Nicholls picked up all of Patrick's duties and spent

much time with him. Patrick was unsure whether or not to try to let loose his own emotions, blow a hole in the wall of the dam, and he could see that his curate was unsure, also. It was very strange: that sense of silent appeal hanging between them in Patrick's study.

At last, 'He was such a gifted boy,' Arthur Nicholls said.

'Such a waste.' Patrick could hardly speak at all.

'His poems. His classical studies. I know that his translations were much admired. He had such a love of life.'

'Such a waste.'

'But you are fortunate in your wonderful daughters.'

'Such a waste. Such a waste . . .'

Dr Wheelhouse visited Charlotte. 'It is bilious fever,' he told Patrick, who could hardly take it in. 'In fevers, the mind as well as the body should be kept easy. Everything that disturbs the imagination, furthers the disease. It is most important with any fever to give the mind solace.'

The parishioners came to peer into the open coffin, at the body lying among preservatives and sickly scented flowers. There were men from the pubs looking shifty with their hats in their hands. There were church trustees, in dignified sorrow. How few women came – thought Patrick – for a young man so fond of them, and undone by a woman.

With Mr Nicholls's help again, Emily and Anne coped with the arrangements for the funeral: the tea and the invitations. A white, embossed card was printed. It showed a Roman tomb, draped, and a rose-bush whose petals and leaves seemed to be weeping – so automatic was the practised art of memorial artists – but it gave Branwell's age wrongly.

Patrick managed to write to William Morgan, Branwell's godfather, to ask him to conduct the burial service, relying upon him for warmth as well as solemnity. It is often the most jolly of men who are most able to rise to solemn events.

Branwell was carried across the garden and let down into the family vault. Morgan spoke of Branwell's noble appearance in death, and of a life frustrated of its promise. He talked of his old friendship with Patrick and with Branwell's mother.

Those mourners who were family, associates and friends

paired off again for their procession back to the parsonage. Patrick and Morgan were at the head, Anne and Emily came behind. Tabby and Martha, John Brown and his wife, the Heatons, the Taylors, and the families of other church trustees wound across the graveyard, through the wet grass, on a damp and changeable, 'sneaky' day.

'I *wish* they had got his age right on the card!' Emily hissed to Anne.

'Hush, Emily –' Anne touched her sleeve.

'Thirty instead of thirty-one! Why couldn't Charlotte have looked after *something*, instead of leaving it all to us and taking to her bed?'

'It was Mr Nicholls who kindly arranged for the printing, and he could not be expected to know exactly.'

'Charlotte or her Mr Nicholls, it's the same thing!'

Emily's impulse was to stride ahead, but she realized in the nick of time that she should not do so at a funeral. Instead, the trivial incident of the card broke the dam of her tears. For the first time she released what others had given way to days before.

Along the narrow way between the graves, they were approaching the gap in the wall that led into the garden. After just one quick stride, she had to wait and lean on Anne's shoulder, but only lightly and for a second, and then she clutched the wall.

A knot of mourners formed to support her. After a moment she controlled herself sufficiently to be able to move again. The gush of tears, brief but powerful, had left her clutching a pain in her side.

The procession had broken up. Most followed the dry path that curved around the lawn, meeting the ends of the path that ran across the front of the house, while others, including Emily, and also Anne – not because she thought it wise but in order to stay with Emily – walked in a straight line to the front door, across the wet lawn.

Upon reaching the hallway, Anne went straight up to see Charlotte, who was still in her bed.

Emily refused to go. With the other guests, she went instead into the parlour, though she loathed the smell of the ham and other cooked meats, and she anticipated the conversation which would start piously and drift towards coarseness. Funeral teas were all like that, even in a parson's family.

She ought to have changed her shoes. She merely leaned on the mantelpiece, her damp dress steaming before the fire. Tired out – it hit her now how tired she was – she crouched down, in a cloud of steam from wet wool. Her legs were cold in wet stockings. Her feet were very cold.

IV

I have been in bed long enough! Charlotte thought. Me, taking to my bed! Oh, no!

Two days after the funeral, she asked Martha to get out her mourning dress and help her put it on. She had chosen the day that the shutters were opened: it was as near to being a cheerful moment as could be expected. She groped her way down the stairs. Papa and Anne were pleased to see her, Tabby was, Martha was, and she expected a welcome from Emily – who had barely been up to see her all week.

She tried to put Emily's behaviour down to overtiredness, grief, and the cough and the cold she had caught at the funeral. But Anne, too, was ill with a severe cough, and so was Papa, who was seventy-one. These two had been up to sit with her.

They were doing the ironing in the kitchen. When Emily's baleful resentment – there was no other way to think of it, and it was partly what had kept Charlotte in bed – drove her away, she went to sit by the parlour fire. Huddled in a shawl, she shivered and sweated. Her stomach still trembled from all her heaving, and her bowels were exhausted.

Martha brought her writing cabinet and she wrote to her new correspondent in the bright world of literature, Mr Smith Williams.

> We have buried our dead out of sight ... It is not permitted us to grieve for him who is gone as others grieve for those they lose. The removal of our only brother must necessarily be regarded by us rather in

440

the light of a mercy than a chastisement. Branwell was his Father's and his Sisters' pride and hope in boyhood, but since Manhood, it has been otherwise . . . I do not weep from a sense of bereavement – there is no prop withdrawn, no consolation torn away, no dear companion lost – but for the wreck of a talent, the ruin of a promise, the untimely drear extinction of what might have been a burning and a shining light . . . There is such a bitterness of pity for his life and death – such a yearning for the emptiness of his whole existence as I cannot describe.

Articulation so fine and graceful not only *expressed* feelings, it also smothered them. The finer the net of articulation, the less were certain other reflections able to filter through.

She felt Emily's resentment so cruelly because – she knew without its having been talked about – what caused it was her own harshness towards her brother.

Death had at a stroke transformed Charlotte's regard for Branwell. Her contempt had evaporated in the instant that life had fled, when he had seemed made of wax; a queer ghost of himself. She was back with the residue of the admired boy.

'All his errors – to speak plainly – all his vices seemed nothing to me in that moment, every wrong he had done, every pain he had caused, vanished,' she wrote.

The memories of her unkindnesses had descended, squawking like a demonic flock of starlings, at that moment when she had turned the mattress and seen Tabby's old carving knife. There had been no escape by taking to her bed, hiding the knife under clothes in a drawer.

Also: worse than Emily's balefulness and disapproval, worse than guilt – exaggerating that guilt – was what Charlotte had glimpsed in the kitchen. Emily walked differently, hunched over and slow, with one hand hovering under her ribs, until she winced, catching her breath, afraid to let it out; next clutching her ribs tightly, and white with pain.

EMILY

I

Emily would not talk about it.

'Emily, you look hot!' Charlotte suggested, and her anxiety made her so forceful that it sounded like a complaint.

'Are you feeling cold all of a sudden?' she questioned on another occasion. 'Why are you holding your side?'

'Stop spying on me!'

Speaking caused her to catch her breath.

'Your cough and cold have not improved in a month. We must fetch Dr Wheelhouse.'

'I'll have none of your poisoning doctors!' Emily tried to shout. It ended in a whisper: 'Look what happened to Branwell.'

Tabby said, 'I still think a bowl o' steaming water's the best thing for lungs. But if thou'll do nowt for theeself, there's no good in other folks bothering.'

That amused Emily enough for her to try the remedy they had known since childhood. For a time, Anne and she regularly sat side by side at the kitchen table, towels over their heads, breathing in the steam.

'I've sent Martha out for some fennel root,' Tabby said another day. 'I'll mak' thee an infusion in warm water.'

'Tastes like poison,' Emily said, still laughing.

'Anne's supped hers well enough. Add a drop o' milk if thou's too fancy for't, miss.'

Tabby had seen 'galloping consumption' before – the perspiration on the brow, the skin hanging yellow on a starved body. Mary Feather had died of it when she was sixteen and, even an hour before she passed away, she did not admit to having anything worse than a 'chill'.

Emily had her own way of ending such interviews: she crouched down and talked to majestic Keeper, or to tiny, silly Flossy – Anne's spaniel whom Emily had appropriated. When she communicated with her animals, you knew there was no way to get another word out of her.

Charlotte consulted Dr Wheelhouse secretly.

'She has a dry cough – feels hot and then cold – a tightness in her chest. Her palms are clammy and hot.'

'Any blood in the spittle?'

'I don't think so.'

'If she will rest herself —'

'She *will* not rest. No-one can persuade her to.'

'Well, try not to excite her passions. A consumption—'

'*Consumption?*'

'A consumption is often aggravated by violent passion, or by exertions of the mind, or by grief and brooding. Do all that you can to avoid arguments and to make her cheerful.'

Cheerful!

'I cannot help feeling much depressed sometimes,' Charlotte wrote to Ellen:

> I try to leave all in God's hands . . . but faith and resignation are difficult to practice under such circumstances. The weather has been most unfavourable for invalids of late; sudden changes of temperature, and cold penetrating winds have been frequent here . . . I could not, and would not, leave home on any account.
>
> These things make one *feel* as well as *know* that this world is not our abiding-place. We should not knit human ties too close, or clasp human affections too fondly. They must leave us, or we must leave them, one day.

Patrick had watched his son 'cry wolf' so often that he had not believed death was coming. He now saw Anne ill, and never complaining – but at any rate she took advice. Emily, also, was outwardly calm as if death were not on its way, and it apparently deceived others, though not himself.

'Emily is the dearest thing, the nearest to my heart in the world,' Charlotte said. 'I cannot bear to think —'

'Others in our family have been afflicted similarly,' Papa interrupted. 'With them I persisted in hoping against hope, though they are now where hope and fear fluctuate no more.'

'Emily, you are the dearest thing on earth to my own heart!' Charlotte repeated, this time with the anger of frustration, during one of their strained conversations in the parlour. 'But all you offer is your basilisk smile. You must realize you are hurting us. You are treating us with the contempt that Heathcliff threw upon those who loved *him*.'

Remonstration got her nowhere. She went back to her sewing, to the newspaper, or to a book, sent perhaps by Mr Williams. They had difficulty in talking about anything these days.

Mary Robinson, now married, paid a visit with her sister. They came in a carriage, wearing bright dresses, and they chattered and clung to Anne as if they were still children. Charlotte supposed the fuss was to drown their associations with Branwell's downfall, but it could not cheer Anne who remained as solemn and wretched as Cassandra, preoccupied with hiding what was prophesied by the pain in her chest.

Charlotte doggedly continued with *Shirley*. 'I wrote *Jane Eyre* to keep my mind busy during Papa's operation, and I could not put the book down. Now I write *Shirley* so as not to think of other matters, but it is like lifting stones. Yet it does its work. Once I get started, it absorbs me, but after an hour or two, if I pause I collapse altogether,' she told Anne.

Anne was writing poems. Emily was tinkering with her old Gondal stories and hesitating over a fresh novel. For them to be writing together by the parlour fire at least made it seem that they were restoring the happy days, but there was little heart in it; the greatest benefit was that it saved them from talking. Like sheep tracks in a fog, conversations got lost in that cloud of disagreements better not explored at the moment. Day after day, the three women in black sat in the parlour and picked at their writing boxes, at their sewing, and at each other.

One dark afternoon, Anne said wistfully, 'If only we could go to Scarborough, we would all be better, I am sure.'

'Risky at this time of year,' Charlotte answered.

Anne, who seemed as ill as Emily, put down her mending and cuff-turning with an exasperation worthy of Charlotte, and continued with quiet emphasis, 'The air is so clean in Scarborough.'

'Papa is too old to travel and he cannot be left. He needs us to care for him, poor, frail trio though we are.'

Anne turned to Emily. 'Though it's the wrong season for

bathing we could go to the spa, and the castle, and the rotunda. The light is beautiful on the sea! We can afford it.'

'I am not leaving Haworth! Perhaps the wind will change and it will be good—'

On the settee she clutched her ribs, arched her humped back and craned her neck, 'Like a dying swan,' Anne thought.

'It is all so quiet!' Charlotte remarked, once again. 'The house seems empty without Brannii making his noise. He has left a great hole and we are all tiptoeing round it.'

Patrick began to avoid the parlour dining-room. It was as he had shunned the bedroom since Maria had died there twenty-seven years before. The parlour was even more potent. Opening the door one evening, he saw his three daughters, in the candlelight and the firelight, turn towards him their waxy faces that wore the masks of the Fates and he felt a trespasser.

'I had a strange sensation that I have not felt since I was a boy, when three women would gather around a body at a wake,' Patrick confided to Mr Nicholls as they sat on either side of the fire in the study. 'You must have seen that, Arthur. They were so quiet and still, in a place where I have so often found them busy and chattering. I felt I was intruding in a place which my daughters were making sacred.'

Such thoughts affected him at dinner or breakfast. He looked at their attempts at cheerfulness – one day it was a few sprigs of autumn heather that Charlotte had found in flower, Heaven knew where – but he could not get out of his mind his image of a sacred cave to the dead, the three young women in black keeping watch around the fire.

A day later, when they all happened to be in the kitchen, he said, 'I think we should take our breakfast and other meals in here. Tabby has so much to do. Haven't you, Tabby?'

'It's none so easy for me to keep up appearances any more.'

'And we don't eat much. We all seem to prefer soups, and liquids.'

'No!' Charlotte protested – but did not know how to continue.

The change was not a revolution, except in the admitting of it. They had been drifting into this arrangement ever since troubles had beset them. For weeks they had eaten as mice do, creeping here and there, nibbling or sipping as their feeble appetites allowed them. Only at morning and evening prayers were they for certain together – a twice daily affirmation before God that they were still alive – but at meals, if one or other was absent, or if food was left, no-one questioned it. But the formal abandoning of the parlour was a step towards retreating from the social life which, ironically, was at long last within their grasp. Their place of creativity was being given up to grief and mourning.

'Perhaps we may entertain in the spring,' Papa consoled Charlotte.

It was in that patronizing manner he had shown since they were children, and she knew, as she had when she was a child, that nothing would come of it.

II

Emily knew what would cure her. After Branwell's funeral an east wind persisted and she needed the one from the west, warm, sweet and herbal off the moorland, to carry away the miasma of the Haworth middens. The way she spoke and wrote of it, she was awaiting the coming of a Messiah.

Though she slept little because of coughing and sweating, she continued to rise at seven, soon after Martha had cleaned out the grate and lit the fire. She opened her own window shutters, usually before dawn. As she approached the window, she was listening. In her rear room, facing the moorlands and the south-west, she would hear the wind arrive. Morning after morning, it prowled from around the corner and through the bushes, coming from the front of the building and the town. A month passed. Still no breath on her shutters – not unless, on more violent mornings, it rose in an eddy from the yard.

The west wind became a test of her fate. If it came, she would live. It would fill her lungs. It would fill her imagination. It *was* her imagination. She felt that she could not write until it inspired her, literally inspired her, and became the breath in her body.

She had been trapped by life's supposed values. She was

expected to find a husband among farmers and curates. Just look at the Heatons, the Pighills, the Taylors, Mr Nicholls and the other curates who had been and gone, all either loud-mouthed or tight-lipped! It made her flesh creep to think of such lords and masters! It was cynical of Him to give her and her sisters imaginations and then expect them to submit to that!

The one way to defy it, and all the contradictory vicissitudes of a God-given destiny, to exercise free will, was to choose one's moment of dying.

There were known to be people who had taken to their beds, sometimes for years, holding on to their resolve to die after some heartbreak or failure. You could go into cottages and find them, lying among rags or quilts, waiting to die of their broken hearts.

Emily saw herself doing the same, except for one thing: the possibility of a drift into an inept bedridden state in which there was no choice but to suffer. She determined to be decisive.

In December she gave up waiting for a blessing from the wind. One relatively mild afternoon she decided on a last act of defiance against the weakness in her body, by taking a deliberate farewell of the moorlands.

Normally, Mr Nicholls called to exercise Keeper. This afternoon, 'I'll take him on the common,' she said, 'I want to sit in the sun for half an hour. I'm feeling better and it will do me good.'

Holding Keeper's lead, she let him pull her along, instead of almost outpacing him as she used to. From the back of the parsonage she followed the track along the flank of Penistone Hill; she could not climb to the top of it. Because the easterly wind was light, she soon outwalked the smells of the town. The winter sun was sinking ahead of her. She breathed in deeply, until the sharp pain returned. Walking for a hundred yards at a stretch before resting, seeking out hill flanks that caught the sun, she reached the Sladen Beck.

The day was calm enough for her to be able to hear the streams and the melodies of waterfalls far off. The low sun threw up banks of shadows against golden cliffs of grass. There were warm-brown, distant hills. She sat by the Sladen

Bridge and said goodbye to it all. She committed to her soul the details of this last day – 'Yearning for it through the walls of an aching heart; but really with it, and in it,' as she had expressed it through the mouth of Catherine Earnshaw. When she had done, she turned her back and, without looking over her shoulder, struggled home.

She closed the door and found food and water for Keeper. Too tired to climb the stairs, she went to lie on the sofa in the parlour. Charlotte and Anne were pleased because they believed she had been taking Dr Wheelhouse's advice of 'fresh air and moderate exercise'. She did not tell them that she would not leave the parsonage again.

Having negotiated a pact with sickness, Emily adjusted to the changes in her habits, appetites and feelings. Breathlessness on encountering a draught from an opened door. Palms sweating while she tried to do the ironing or to play the piano.

She haunted that place where she had been as happy as on the moorland: the kitchen, with Tabby. Of the sisters, she had been the one most contented there. What joy she felt from watching the fire, from the sight and sweet smell of a scrubbed stone floor, from ranks of cleaned and polished utensils, from the chatter and company of servants and casual visitors, and from animals!

She had a craving for the acid taste of citrus fruits; a craving as unreasonable as that of a pregnant woman. 'Oh, Mr Nicholls, if you could bring me some oranges, I would be so grateful.' She had a childish faith in Locock's Cough Wafers. They eased the soreness and the ulcers in her throat which had recently developed. If she asked for something, they had the satisfaction of doing their duty and then they left her alone. She hid what she could – her greenish-white phlegm, which tasted of salt and was flecked with blood; the frequency and paleness of her urine; her diarrhoea that started in the beginning of December. Branwell had complained of such symptoms of consumption, but in the tumult of his ravings no-one had taken notice. She remained adamant about refusing 'poisoning doctors'. When Mr Smith Williams sent a parcel of books, among them a work on homoeopathy, she read it as if it were a matter of mere curiosity to her. 'It's only another form of quackery,' she pronounced lightly.

She coped with the tension between her sisters and herself by mostly refusing to admit that she was ill at all. Whenever the air crackled with mutual frustration, Emily climbed to her room. She paused more and more frequently each day. Sometimes she reached the top on all fours, after resting several times, pausing on the top stair to inspect her swelling feet and ankles protruding from the hem of her black dress.

Sitting by her window, choosing most often her favourite hour when dusk gathered on the slope of Penistone Hill, over Stanbury Moor and Oakworth Moor, Shelley's 'Ode to the West Wind' rang in her mind.

> If I were a dead leaf thou mightest bear;
> If I were a swift cloud to fly with thee;
> A wave to pant beneath thy power, and share

> The impulse of thy strength, only less free
> Than thou, O, uncontrollable! . . .

She had not the energy to continue her new novel. She let it lie, a bundle hidden in a clothes drawer. What new literary work she did was mostly tidying up. She sifted through her poems, tinkered at revisions, and burned many in the grate on evening after evening. So much of what she had written was about yearnings for lost love, although she had known no-one beyond her family and Tabby. It was her inner man whom she had lost.

She made a start at fresh poems, but burned many of those too, and did not finish anything. She examined her old drawings. She noticed how many blasted pine trees and ruined towers were among them.

No west wind came to rescue her.

Maybe the truth was that she could not write without Brannii? Even though his companionship, as both audience and conspirator, had been missing for many years, there had always been his token presence.

Anne wore a small, rectangular silver locket, with a tiny

glass window in it, for the plaited strands of Branwell's hair: the locket bounced and gleamed on her dress when she coughed. Emily, apart from the mourning dress which they all wore, showed no memorial of him. Instead she had this hole in her heart – the lost promise of childhood – which swallowed the poems and novels she might have written. It swallowed her inspiration, as a cave might swallow the wind.

Wry towards Tabby, impatient with Charlotte, practical towards Anne – to whom she gave the care in her sickness that she should have exercised on herself – yet Emily had little to say.

Anne had deserted their Gondal epic which had contained the whole world. She now shared a bedroom – nay, a bed – with Charlotte, and there was no way to communicate with her any more.

Charlotte, also, would never understand *Wuthering Heights*. Her sisters were too conscious of the cruelties, especially the accumulation of incidental cruelties. Emily's novel had people hurting themselves and each other, then falling in love because hurting and being hurt was a thrilling bond and a passion. That was what Anne pointed out. She did not see that it was through the energy of the cruel, the implacable and the remorseless that Emily's intuition of what 'lay beyond' could be expressed. It was only possible through a character who her sisters and the reviewers told her should not be allowed to exist. But they were the very feelings that had disturbed Emily all her life. Heathcliff – as she had admitted so many times – *was herself*. Under the flail of Christian teaching, she had found that the exciting drive to be cruel made life vital.

One could also, if one read carefully, see her own struggle to separate herself from such self-love. That was expressed in Cathy's efforts to love Edgar. Emily could show that in novels, but how on earth could she talk about it?

That was why she had always had very little to say. She had been dumb at Mrs Collins's visit. She had appeared dumb when any serious subject – politics or religion – was being considered. Sometimes her consciousness of having nothing acceptable to say had embarrassed her, making her awkward – like an adolescent whose provoking body outstrips her mind.

By now, she could control herself. She disciplined her spirit behind an enigmatic smile. Let them worry about *that*: better than their being horrified at what she might say.

She was half in, half out of this world, people had said. 'It allus looked as though t'other world was waiting to claim her back,' they said of her. She had hated to hear it, apart from at some weaker moments when it had flattered her vanity, and she had enjoyed being special. Now, light-headed and near death, she wondered if maybe it was true. Such people, though rare, were not unknown. They generally died young, much younger than she was. If she was one of them, she should be quite proud to have reached the age of thirty. Her sort were physically weak but mentally and spiritually brilliant from birth. She knew her worth, was proud but not vain.

'I feel so much better today!' Emily declared one afternoon. 'I feel I could take a walk.'

She did reach the garden. A little restored energy was so exciting! When she returned, she slept well.

In the morning, though, she went to the window and still saw no evidence of the west wind. Only a few dry leaves scattering across the yard from the east.

She moved to the fire to comb her hair. Pulling strands from the comb, she let both hair and comb slip. A draught sucked the hair like smoke into the chimney and the comb dropped onto the hearth. As she was about to pick it up, she fell, but managed to clutch the mantelpiece and call out.

Martha came first. She smelled the burned tortoiseshell, and saw Emily who had reached the edge of the bed.

'The comb, Martha . . . !'

Martha rescued the charred comb.

'Thank you, Martha. I'll be all right now.'

'Nay, miss. You've gone white!'

Charlotte had arrived. 'Emily, oh my dear Emily – oh—'

'It's all right, Tallii – I'll dress myself.'

'You must stay in bed – you should see yourself—'

'I don't want to see myself!' She was pulling at her clothes.

'Let me help you dress, then.'

'No!' She shrugged Charlotte off. When she gave in, Emily smiled, not a warm and outward smile, but an inward one – her 'basilisk smile'.

Memories of trying to interfere when Emily was determined on something, as for instance when she had thrashed the dog, made Charlotte hold back. She hazarded a joke: 'I expect you'd be wanting to feed the dogs again, if you could.'

On the previous evening, Emily as usual had gone to feed Keeper and Flossy with a mixture of meat scraps and bread in her apron, but at the touch of cold air in the kitchen passageway she had all but collapsed against the wall. Even then, Charlotte and Anne, rushing to help her, had been brushed aside.

'Yes, I would like to feed Keeper again.'

They watched, boiling with emotion, as Emily pulled on her clothes. They went downstairs with her, hardly daring to touch her. Martha went ahead in case Emily should fall. Charlotte descended at her side, ready to hold her. Papa, Anne and Tabby were waiting in the hall. Some field of inhibition kept all five at a distance as Emily edged, leaning against the wall, into the parlour.

She lay on the sofa. Cushions were brought. She could not eat anything. She took liquids – weak tea, the juice of an orange, fennel root, and finally barley water, sipping these throughout the morning while sisters and father sat with her. She hardly had strength to be impatient, but such as she had, she expressed as irritation at her own feebleness. She coughed. Coughed. Coughed. Tearing at her lungs. She tried to sew. The sewing dropped from her hands. At last she agreed that they might bring Dr Wheelhouse. They got her upstairs – Martha, mostly, carrying her. In her room, although it was a winter's afternoon – 19 December – the sun was shining.

As Dr Wheelhouse arrived, she began her convulsions.

Charlotte and Anne arranged for the preparation of their sister's body. They snipped her hair to be put into lockets, into envelopes buried in drawers, and given to those few who had been given the opportunity to love her.

They organized a modest funeral. Obituaries, funeral cards,

gloves and a simple tea. She would have wanted as little church pomp as possible. It was Nicholls who arranged for William Wood to measure Emily for her coffin. It was only sixteen inches wide, she had become so wasted.

Arthur Nicholls led what was left of the Brontës out of the parsonage. Patrick, and Emily's mastiff, Keeper, walked at the head, behind the coffin. Then followed Charlotte and Anne. Then Tabby and Martha.

The bitter wind, that made it dangerous to linger, rattled on the panes as the congregation, huddled in a bond of recognizing how cruel the east wind was in Haworth, gathered around the hole below the pulpit, reopened by John Brown.

Nicholls thought of how deeply he was caught up in this family, and this town. It was becoming like home. He would never have expected it. Before the stern old man who was his clerical superior, and the dumpy little woman whom he was daring to admit to himself that he loved, and the other frail little Brontë, he declared:

'There is a purpose in all things, in all our sayings and doings! We, who remain, must look upon the death of Emily Jane Brontë as our faith counsels us to look upon all affliction. As we learn from the lessons of Abraham and Isaac, and of Job – the purpose in her, and in our, suffering is to fortify us who remain, and to strengthen our wills –' He looked directly into the eyes of those novelists and poets, and continued: '– to bear witness to our afflictions, that others might benefit from our wisdom'.

ANNE

It was 5 January, seventeen days after Emily's funeral, and almost Anne's twenty-ninth birthday. Charlotte had called in Mr Teale, the Leeds specialist in consumption, to examine her with his stethoscope as she lay on the parlour sofa, a large fire burning in the grate. Charlotte looked brittle – a bag of nerves – going to pieces with despair. Then she went off with Mr Teale for a conference with Papa in his study.

Ellen Nussey had come to bring comfort and she waited

for the verdict with Anne, who, unable to sit still, walked around the room on her arm, flushing each time she reached the fire. Ellen tried to cheer her by saying she looked 'flushed with good spirits'. But the sharp pain in her side returned when she came to the door and its draught. What an innocent-sounding name for the vile wind that had once blown weakened Emily right over, in the passageway when Tabby opened the front door.

'If we could go to Scarborough, I am sure we would *all* get better,' Anne said. (Why would Charlotte not agree? Is it because it is *my* idea, not hers?) 'I love Scarborough! I have been so happy there.'

Anne heard Papa's door open, and two men's deep voices saying their farewells; Charlotte's voice, and that of Tabby summoned from the kitchen to fetch Mr Teale's coat; and the brush of the front door opening.

Charlotte and Papa came in. Anne felt cold shivers when she looked at Papa. His dark glasses prevented one seeing into his eyes. His mouth was turned down. How grey, old and worn he looked, aged by a decade since the autumn, and by another ten years since this morning. The old can lose their strength in minutes. He sat on the sofa, his clothes merging into the black. He was stiff and upright as if on a dangerously fast phaeton. He beckoned her. His head was close to her bosom. He reached out with both hands and buried his face in her sleeve.

'My *dear* little Anne—'

She was already in the later stages of consumption.

Her deepest fear was not of death nor of pain. It was of committing the sins that she had seen tempt others near their ends: those of denying God's existence, or of suspecting that He was a perpetrator of cruelties.

Papa, after Charlotte and Ellen had slipped away, prayed with her. Then he told her: 'Your mother found her affliction so cruel that she denied the existence of God. It is a memory I have never been able to face.'

'I know I am young, but I *cannot* doubt that all mankind will be redeemed. You must not be anxious about Mama's salvation! She was driven by too much pain. But I know I shall not deny God.'

She did not know it. Two days later she wrote a poem:

> A dreadful darkness closes in
> On my bewildered mind;
> O let me suffer and not sin,
> Be tortured yet resigned.
>
> Through all this world of blinding mist
> Still let me look to Thee,
> And give me courage to resist
> The Tempter, till he flee . . .

It was through fear of committing the sin of pride that Anne followed the remedies proposed. Emily, refusing all 'poisoning doctors', had chosen to die – out of pride. Anne had seen the suffering it caused others. So she allowed them to apply 'blisters' to her side: hot poultices that were supposed to draw the illness to the surface and sweat it away. She swallowed carbonate of iron, and cod-liver oil which she told them tasted like 'train oil' and which made her feel sick. She wore the cork-soled sandals that Ellen Nussey sent as a protection against the cold floors, and she struggled with the 'respirator' also sent. She went through the unpleasantnesses calmly, until it was clear that in fact they were weakening her.

Her patience masked inner panic.

She generally felt better in the mornings, worse in the afternoons, worst at night. Changes in the weather had more than ever before become the subject of scrutiny since Emily's decline: a spell of sunshine, an early spring, might bring Anne life, while rain, cold, or a sharp frost could mean an early death. She opened doors and approached corners with trepidation, afraid of some fatal blow from the other side.

They dithered endlessly over granting her what she really wanted. Papa actually admitted, 'Mr Teale told me that a change of scene is useful in the earlier stages and he even suggested Scarborough.' Then he added, 'But – my dear Anne it is in the *early stages*. I fear – I fear – you know, the strains of travel, the strange beds, the strange place. They could be too much.'

Yes, if only they had let her go earlier! Now, they could not understand one another. For their sakes she could not admit that hope of cure was not any longer foremost in her mind. What she wanted was Scarborough to be her last experience on earth. So she continued with the charade of considering the potentialities for a *cure* there, hoping to wear them down.

She engaged in battles over the practicalities. Who could go with her – as it would mean leaving Papa alone if Charlotte went? As consumption could take a bad turn, for example from a change in the weather, what if the worst happened away from home? Charlotte continued asking such questions, clearly in anguish, for some months – just as she had dithered when Ellen had tried to get her to go to Hathersage years before.

Ellen was brought into the fray, via letters. It was suggested she might act the host to Anne in Birstall, since she so much wanted a holiday from Haworth; or be her companion to a watering place – perhaps even Scarborough. Anne realized that she had turned the tide. They were now discussing, not whether, but when.

Her suggestion of May was rebuffed.

'The weather is generally inclement then. It would be better in June and better still in July.'

She sensed what was going on. Ellen wrote to her thus because Charlotte was manipulating matters behind her back. Why was her sister so opposed to Scarborough but not to some other place? It could only be because it was not her own idea. But Anne remained firm, in her gentle way. Even the handwriting of her reply remained positive.

> The earliest part is often cold enough, I acknowledge, but, according to my experience, we are almost certain of some fine, warm days in the latter half when the laburnums and lilacs are in bloom, whereas June is often cold and July generally wet.

Then two hundred pounds unexpectedly fell into Anne's lap from the death of her godmother, Fanny Outhwaite. It was decisive. Charlotte, Ellen and Anne could purchase maximum comfort, travel first-class rail, and book lodgings in the grand place where the Robinsons had always stayed, at Mrs Wood's, 2, The Cliff.

They could not make the journey without delaying for a day because of a confusion that seemed ominous. Ellen had gone to Leeds to meet them but they had not set off because Anne was unwell, the excitement being too much for her, Charlotte had decided. There was no way to get a message to Ellen, who sat for some hours watching the trains arrive. That was when she was confronted by omens. She came to Haworth on the following morning in a fluster and Anne overheard her tell Charlotte, 'I watched two trains arrive. Out of both they unloaded coffins, and put them on hearses.'

At last, they caught the train. They stayed over at York. Trees and bushes laden with flowers bent over the walls of the archbishop's garden. The golden front of the cathedral was sunlit. They went inside, where it was as cold as winter; coloured light dancing over floors and pillars. Anne stared upwards. 'If finite power can do this, what is the . . .' and to say any more was too much for her.

She revived out on the precinct, restored in her determination to make the prelude to her death as happy a memory as possible. She was over-eager for them to enjoy this city, which she knew well but they had not visited before, and she used the remainder of the afternoon to buy them presents, although she had to be wheeled around in a Bath chair hired from the hotel. What a joke: she was like some old dowager at a spa, a blanket wrapped around her shoulders; coughing and dribbling, with her chin stooped into her chest. From time to time, Ellen or Charlotte wiped her mouth with a handkerchief. She had another blanket around her legs. Only her shoes, hands and face peeped out.

Charlotte and Ellen chattered, hysterically full of the holiday spirit, seemingly taking their lead from her. She was glad it was so, but she did find their talking about her from behind the Bath chair unnerving. She herself could say little, for it put her out of breath.

But what lugubrious crows they would look in gay Scarborough if they did not lighten their mourning dress! Anne was determined they should have what was required for a season at a resort. From Thorp Green, she knew what these were. She dictated to Charlotte a list of what she would purchase for them all: bonnets, gloves, ribbons, combs, stockings of black silk, and corsets. She had in mind a stage of semi-mourning – purple in place of black – for shawls and ribbons for Charlotte and herself, and some decorated straw bonnets, hopeful of sunny weather. More summery clothes altogether for Ellen. 'No, I owe you a *treat*, Ellen – you have been so kind to me.'

Anne collapsed in the draper's. Her head drooped, hopelessly.

Charlotte was looking keenly at her. Ah, the novelist's scrutinizing eye, noticing her sagged cheeks, no doubt, and how thin her wrists and hands were!

'Take me back to the hotel,' Anne said. 'I am so tired.'

At Scarborough they had a sitting-room and, above it, a double bedroom, on the top of St Nicholas Cliff looking towards the east. The fine, tall house was in the centre of the bay. When they arrived, Anne, leaving her companions fussing behind her, went through to the sitting-room window and stared at the great calm sea below, between the horns of the castle on its promontory to her left, and the white arm of the cliffs of Flamborough Head to her right. A rim of sand curved below, with only a few bathing machines on it at this time of the year. Beneath the castle was a shipbuilding yard and a harbour, mostly crowded with fishing boats, but there was a great schooner in the bay, a few sails unfurled for its drift in on such a calm evening. Another schooner was tied up in the outer harbour.

Although the other two were busy unpacking, she begged Ellen to come and open the window. It was so instantly thrilling – that window with sky and sea spread in it – after the climb up from the dark street-side of the house. They stood behind her, worrying about the damp evening air, while she was entranced by the blast of seaside hubbub. Odd how it could be harsh and yet calming – the sharp cries of the gulls, a dog yapping at the sea, and the lapping of the tide. And the access of sea-scent and light, merging into a single element of salt and brilliance! In that moment she felt that she would live for ever.

The next minute she gave way, was beaded with sweat, shivering and hot, and felt a pain that would not let her breathe.

They closed the window, helped her to climb further up the stairs, put her to bed and drew the curtains. Charlotte and Ellen were to share the double bed while Anne had her cot. Mr Teale had ordered her to sleep apart from Charlotte because of the contagion. It had rendered her comfortless.

In the morning, there was the dawn over the sea! When Charlotte drew the curtains, Anne saw a brighter light on her ceiling than ever was in Haworth. Her energies revived and she put down to tiredness her slight irritability of the previous day, when they had seemed rather *too* enthusiastic about dress purchases and the delights of Scarborough that she herself had suggested.

She still wanted, so much, to show them the town. It was the only recompense she could make to them for their doleful duties. She had noticed that Scarborough was burgeoning with enterprises that had not been here when she had come with the Robinsons; an expansion, she supposed, because of the railway. 'Let us go to the museum!', 'The church!' 'The castle!' 'The gardens!' 'The harbour!' 'The beach!' 'The spa!'

'Oh, but it is all far too much for you,' responded Ellen.

Did Anne imagine a slight complaining tone?

'No, not at all, it is good for me.' Anne paused, as she did after every few words, to draw breath. 'They revive so many happy memories – of when I did not realize I was happy. Because of my difficulties. Because of Branwell's carryings-on – but I was.'

It was hard to say more. Charlotte comforted her.

At last they settled on going to Harland's Baths: that would do her most good and be least likely to tire her, being only a quarter of a mile away.

From the door of the lodgings, which faced away from the sea, they entered an elegant square, where carriages passed around an oval garden. They turned left, through a deep shadow cast by the morning sun. Once beyond it, as they burst into the light by the bridge, there was a spectacular view over a ravine. On the right was the gorge with the botanical gardens, the rhododendrons in bloom, and on their left that view into sea and rising sun. They crawled along so slowly that even elegant strollers outpaced them, but no-one could have been more excited. And it was as warm as summer. Anne felt the gloom scoured away by the salt air and by the spectacle of water and light. She felt that her fatal sickness was something she had dreamed.

She pointed down into the gardens. 'I do not think there were so many rhododendrons in flower even when I came with the Robinsons, although then it was midsummer.'

'All especially for you,' said Ellen.

Beyond the bridge, along the cliffs, birds were singing. All over the land it was as if many springs of song were rising. It was a very Heaven. She would be well!

They descended the steep slope into the gorge.

Ellen's patronizing comment – 'All especially for you' – was upsetting her. It was extremely trivial and she should not let it trouble her. It was not good for her recovery, and indeed it was simply because of her sickness that she felt so vulnerable to their moods and to the nuances of what they said.

They hovered at the entrance to the baths.

'Why don't you leave me with the attendant and explore the town without my hampering you? I would love to show it to you but I don't think I can.'

'No, Anne. We are not leaving you!'

'The very idea,' said Ellen.

'I know you are shocked, but I promise, I would not suggest it' – She paused to collect her breath – 'were I not certain that I am well enough. I feel so well. Please, Charlotte! You know, I am sure it will be good for me to be responsible for myself.'

She did not add: 'For a change.'

Charlotte hesitated, looking at Ellen.

'Go on, Charlotte. You are such a ditherer! You might think of me as the baby—' Anne began.

'Nonsense—'

'But at least I know my own mind!' Anne laughed, but it hurt. She made a gesture, almost as if she felt strong enough to give her sister a push.

The tears glistening on Charlotte's eyes then were, she thought, ones of huge hope for her restored strength.

'Go on, Charlotte. I shall be quite well.'

'We will come for you in an hour,' Charlotte said.

'I do not know how long I would like to stay. I'll make my own way back. *Don't worry!* I feel so well. Or someone will help. Go on, Charlotte. Ellen – take my sister away, will you. I'll be back at Mrs Wood's for dinner.'

They were persuaded to leave her. She soaked herself for an hour, with the attendant's assistance. She dressed and began her return.

Looking at the ascent, her courage failed. The mood of the day was different now. The birds had quietened, the light was grey and soft. Where had Charlotte and Ellen got to? She made her way by holding on to railings, creeping a few feet, and resting. She collapsed at the gate of Mrs Wood's and a maid came to help her in. As the girl helped her upstairs, 'Don't tell my companions that I fell, please!' she begged. 'Nor the other servants, in case it gets back to them. Promise me!'

When she burst upon Charlotte and Ellen there was the faintest whiff of a sense that she was disturbing a conversation, although they made a great fuss of her.

Charlotte said, 'We went as far as the harbour, then had a look at what was on at the theatre, then —'

'I'm very tired. I must rest before dinner. I've been foolish. But it was such a beautiful day.'

She rested for an hour until dinner. In the afternoon they went onto the sands. Only a couple of hardy gentlemen were bathing; no lady was risking the chill. The donkey carts were out, though, to race people along the beach. Anne took a ride and the lad in charge received a shock, no doubt, when she insisted on holding the reins herself, 'so that he will not be driven too hard'.

Sunday. They simply would not let her go to church after the exhausting adventures of the previous day. Neither would they go by themselves, although there was a church, Christ Church, next door.

In the morning, Charlotte wrote a letter to Mr Smith Williams. Anne had seen her write several already. So far as she knew, Charlotte had written only once to Papa.

Ellen Nussey read Mrs Gaskell's *Mary Barton*. Charlotte had been sent it by Mr Williams and it had upset her because it anticipated her own *Shirley*; the labour that was still occupying her, with diminished concentration. She was at the stage of transcribing a fair copy. Anne had read both *Shirley* and *Mary Barton*, which was also about workers' unrest in northern England, but written from a point of view that Charlotte did not share: that of understanding for the factory workers and the poor. Anne could never forget how Charlotte had claimed that the social concerns of *The Tenant of Wildfell Hall* were an unsuitable subject for Anne, dealing with matters about which she was supposed to know little.

Feeling tensions whirling in the air, Anne escaped to the window, staring at the sea and hoping to benefit from the breeze. They were blessed by the weather. The sea was still calm. Minute by minute its tints were changing, from those of a peacock's feathers to those of a silver, fluttering bird, as the sun climbed higher. When it was overhead, and the ship that had been on the horizon had reached the harbour and docked, and the sailors were rolling barrels off its deck, the ladies were called to dinner.

Afterwards they descended to the promenade, but soon Anne had to sit on a bench. She begged Charlotte and Ellen to go on without her and visit 'the Gothic Saloon' a little way off: the building holding the spa spring, at the foot of the cliffs, and which they had been talking about. It looked like a child's model of a medieval fort, with battlements, and towers at its corners, and one taller, more slender tower carrying a Union Jack.

'Are you sure you will be happy with only your thoughts for company?' Ellen asked.

'Oh, yes, I don't need anything more.'

For the better part of an hour, Anne stared at the sea. At children with a nursemaid. She patted a dog.

Imagine not seeing the sky, not hearing the cry of the sea, even in memory. One cannot imagine it. Eternity – one cannot conceive of that, either. I know it exists, but I cannot actually imagine time that does not have a beginning or an end. I don't think I can truly imagine a number much larger than a hundred – maybe not even that. Neither can I see the world as existing without me. Eternity, even a number bigger than a hundred – or my non-existence – it is vanity to believe that I can grasp them. Because man conceives and does so much, he believes he understands much more. The truth is that, rather than being within reach of God's spirit, he is closer to the animals, who have no sense of dying, of numbers, of eternity. Man has just enough understanding to fear.

She felt unbearably lonely and unhappy. Then they came back for her. It was a terrible labour to climb back up the steps.

That evening they would not leave her to go to church, either. She felt hurt that they could leave her at the baths and, with even less pressing, while they followed up their interest in the saloon, but would not go to the church that was only next door. Did they feel they had enough gloom and piety from being with her? Was she doing just what she had not wanted to do: spoiling a holiday for them?

Turning her back, saddened to feel thus when she would have to leave them soon anyway, she sat at the window yet again. The sunset, which was behind her, inland behind the cliffs and the hills, must have been of great brilliance for it cast a luminosity to the eastern horizon, and threw the colours of a pearly shell over the calm sea. She stared for an hour. All at once she knew that she would probably never see another evening.

She did not miss Haworth. She reflected that, if she had not been such a weak character, she might have come to live here, or in another place like it, long ago, and thus have saved her life or at least have lived longer. Others left bleak northern houses for brighter lives elsewhere. Charlotte would have done so, merely if her foreign professor had whistled.

The light had died. Sea and sky were like charcoal. There was only the gleam of lamps on fishing boats and of the first stars, some of them splintering in reflections on the sea.

'Help me to the fire,' Anne said.

They dragged her, chair and all.

'Could we take a train home in the morning?' she asked. If only they had appreciated the *quiet* delight that she might have taken in being here – so long as they had sustained her.

'I don't *want* to leave Scarborough,' she said, though it was half a lie. 'But if I die here it will be difficult for you so far from home.'

'Let us talk about that in the morning.'

Her night was calmer than she had expected. At any rate, she was able to muffle a great deal, and she slept.

She had dressed herself by seven o'clock. That is, she had dragged off her nightgown and pulled on a shift and combed her hair. She had to rest every minute – everything seemed so heavy – but it seemed an improvement. She needed hardly any help. She remembered how well Emily had been shortly before she died, when she had taken a walk in the garden, surprising herself and everyone. Anne opened the door, stood on the landing and looked down the perilous flight.

'I'm afraid to go down.'

'I will carry you,' Ellen said.

'No!' said Charlotte.

'Why not?' Anne laughed – laughed! 'I don't *weigh* anything, and Ellen is stronger than you. Why don't you go back in, so that you don't have to watch?'

Anne had an authority as never before. At any rate, Charlotte obeyed.

Ellen descended a couple of steps. 'Put your arms around my neck. I'll carry you.'

'What if I *am* too heavy?'

'You won't be.'

Anne collapsed upon Ellen's shoulders. They lumbered down the stairs.

At the bottom, Anne's head dropped like a stone upon the top of Ellen's head. Her eyes closed and she was still.

When she came round, she found herself in the big armchair that she had made her own. Ellen was on her knees before her, looking terrified.

'I thought it was over! You suddenly became heavier!'

Anne put her hand out. 'It could not be helped. You did your best.'

They held a subdued breakfast, Anne as usual sipping a glass of boiled milk, though she was without the strength to come to the table. She was grateful for every breath. You could hear every one. She was conscious of each: of how long it lasted, the pain that came with it.

Through the rest of the morning, they read and talked quietly in the room.

Anne felt that they were all waiting for her to—

Awful as it was, it was too strong a feeling to be ignored. It was extraordinary that she felt calm. Only: she knew that if she moved at all, the little flutterings of breath would turn to knife stabs and finish her. Clearly they all realized that death was in the air. Anne saw that it was she who must give voice to it.

'Do you think we might still take a train and return home in time?' she asked again.

It was so impossible, so desperate, that Charlotte realized the inevitable had to be faced. She went out to have a doctor summoned.

When he came, Anne asked him bluntly, 'Tell me how long I have! The truth, please. I am not afraid.'

He looked into her eyes. He asked her questions. He examined her with a stethoscope. He said, quietly, 'You have little left of a lung. I fear the angel of death is with us.'

You could hear laughter, loud talk, and the clinking of plates from beyond the door.

'Thank you for being honest.'

'I'll return in an hour,' he said.

She had seen, with Branwell especially, how little pride was left during the approach of death. But she had not forgotten her resolve to keep her dignity and not fall into sin.

She felt that she was nothing – a mere scrap of thistledown that could blow away into the sea if the window were open. How could she then expect to feel anything? The worst she suffered was an uncomfortable restlessness in all of her body. *Lie and wait for death to come*, she told herself. Her breathing would simply stop.

William Weightman – Papa – Haworth – seemed to belong to another life that she had lived, once. Especially strange was that she could not grasp the thought of Papa.

'I shall be joining Emily and Branwell before you,' she said.

She swam out of her thoughts to see Ellen and Charlotte

looking at her intently. Perhaps they had been doing so for some time.

Was she now about to blow away, out of the window, over the sea? Indeed, she was rising – they were lifting her – and she was sinking again, onto the sofa.

'Is that better?'

'Yes. But ease . . . will be . . . my Redeemer.'

The doctor had arrived again. He did not examine her with his stethoscope this time. He was like a clergyman, merely giving comfort.

'She is so tranquil,' Anne heard him say.

Had she already died, thus to overhear herself being talked about? Was this the ante-room of purgatory or paradise? Everywhere was calm enough. There were sounds from far off, which she remembered from a distant past – lodging-house sounds, pans being clattered and maids laughing. But there was Charlotte, crying at the doctor's words.

'Take courage,' Anne said. She tried to smile and wondered if she succeeded.

She did not make a further sound.

Charlotte leaned over and closed her eyes. A maid appeared at the half-open door.

'Dinner's served!' she announced.

CHAPTER EIGHT

CATHARSIS

CHARLOTTE

I

Charlotte's absences from Haworth created guilt about Papa. The habit of staying away had begun over a year ago in Scarborough, after Anne died. Having arranged for the gravestone on the cliff in the grounds of St Mary's Abbey, she had stayed on for a week with Ellen, astonishing herself with her inability to return and give support at home. It had been more diverting to observe Ellen, pitiful in her waiting for a husband to come along, and declaring her maidenhood by wearing girlish dresses. The spectacle of her hoping for some eligible gentleman to present himself – in the saloon, on the bridge where she paid her toll in order to promenade, or at the rotunda museum – yet petulant because the season was not starting, took Charlotte's mind off her sorrow and guilt. Observation was what a novelist *did*, she reflected, and it was one of her faults that she did not do enough of it, looking mostly inwards.

After Scarborough, because its pleasure-loving atmosphere was getting on her nerves, she had got Ellen to compromise by leaving for the quieter resort of Filey, a few miles south. When they grew irritable with one another even there, Ellen had agreed to move on to Easton Farm, Bridlington, with the Hudsons, who were Nussey family friends. In all, immediately following Anne's death, Charlotte had stayed away for nearly a month.

Her lengthy absences, then and since, merely worsened the atmosphere she had anticipated waiting for her back home – the silent parlour, the faint disapproval emanating from Papa and, a little more strongly, from Mr Nicholls. So, even when back in Haworth, she had communicated mostly with Ellen: the one whom Anne had asked to 'be a sister to Charlotte in my place', or so Ellen had declared. Sharing a bed had been a great comfort and she had missed it nightly since. She would flee to the Nusseys' just for that. As she wrote to her:

> Sometimes when I wake in the morning – and I know that Solitude, Remembrance and Longing are to be almost my sole companions all day through – that at night I shall go to bed with them, that they will long keep me sleepless – that next morning I shall wake to them again – Sometimes – Nell – I have a heavy heart of it . . .

Since Anne's death, she had not caught up with knowing who the new Charlotte Brontë was, and her travels were in search of her. How could she stay with Papa who only wanted the old Charlotte, his 'Tallii'?

Papa's worrying in itself drove her away. 'Do not fail me, Charlotte!' – his pathetic words when Anne had been ill rang in her ears, strengthening her at times when she was already strong – and weakening her, if she was already weak. Her nerves became wound up. She found herself holding her sneezes in check for fear he would ask her if she had a cold. 'It's like living under a sword suspended by a horsehair!' she had exclaimed.

Now she was returning from the second trip she had made to London. It was July 1850, and after the anniversary of Anne's death. Now out of mourning, she had hired a Keighley dressmaker to fit her out completely, from underwear to cloak. She had also decided to dress her hair in tight bandeaux. Instead of her previous curls there were two flat partings, one on either side of her face, in order to narrow the forbidding breadth of her brow. Nevertheless she was not impressive. Her tiny size was a joke. She had been led to believe that

Harriet Martineau, the famous feminist, had described her as 'the smallest person I have ever seen outside of a fair'. Some months before the earlier trip to London, most of Charlotte's teeth had been removed by Mr Atkinson, the Leeds dentist, and she still did not have much confidence to open her mouth when in society.

Charlotte could chill a room with her depression and anxiety. The Smiths had arranged several dinner parties in her honour, and at the earlier ones, on her first London trip, she had been unable to eat anything all day beforehand, her throat tight with nerves.

At one early dinner, major literary critics from the *Athenaeum*, the *Spectator*, the *Atlas*, the *Examiner* and *The Times* had been assembled. They were not all generous-minded. A few days earlier, *The Times* critic had written off the recently published *Shirley* as 'commonplace and puerile ... at once the most high flown and the stalest of fictions'. The newspaper had disappeared from the Smiths' morning-room that day, but she had begged to see it. George's mother had given it to her, and seen her weep. So at the dinner she had said little until, after a long silence followed by whispering around the table, she had been driven to shock them. At the time, Macready's performances in *Macbeth* and *Othello* were the talk of London. She had been to see them and, goaded for her opinion, she declared, hotly, 'Anything more false I could scarcely have imagined!' She went on, in gummy fashion, to instruct her distinguished new acquaintances that in London they knew nothing about tragedy or Shakespeare, although they could deal with farce well enough.

William Makepeace Thackeray had been present; a large, happy man, with a twinkle behind his spectacles. He looked around with a confident stare. He had met her before, and had taken her under his wing. Now he tried to tease her out of her embarrassment. The grim ceremony of dinner being over, the gentlemen were beginning to light up as the ladies retired. Mr Thackeray sniffed the air, twinkled at her and remarked, 'I suppose you have perceived the secret of our cigars!' It was a reference to the potent scent of Mr Rochester's cigar in *Jane Eyre*. This delicate way of saying that the gentlemen were all wooing her was meant to flatter and amuse, but in fact it had stung her with its levity.

Now he himself had recently given a dinner for her at his home in Young Street, Kensington. Various literati had been assembled: Mrs Crowe, Mrs Proctor, Miss Adelaide Proctor, Mrs Elliot, Mrs Brookfield and Miss Perry. She had seen them watching her from the window as she descended from the carriage on the arm of George Smith. She remembered the way she had been gazed at as she had arrived at Roe Head nearly twenty years before.

After a fuss in the entrance hall, she had been led in between the towering figures of Thackeray and Smith. There, too, the silence created by her entrance had crushed her. They had been amused. For some reason they had stared at the top of her head, as if implying that she was missing another foot of stature. Or was it what she wore on her hair?

Mr Thackeray introduced her as 'Currer Bell' and, out of nervousness again, she had turned on him. At that moment the name had not suited her mood.

'I believe there *are* books being published by a person named "Currer Bell", but the person here is Miss Brontë and I see no connection between the two!' she snapped.

That had done it. Despite the candlelight, the warm fires, the silver and the gorgeous dishes, the occasion had turned arctic. The more they waited for her to say something shocking or brilliant, the deeper she froze. They had continued to stare at the top of her head, while she remained hypnotized by the tablecloth. Eventually they had withdrawn to Thackeray's study where Charlotte had thrown herself onto the sofa and managed some sincere conversation with the children's governess, which no-one could overhear. Mrs Brookfield at last moved into battle.

'Do you like London, Miss Brontë?'

The room had fallen silent, all of them assuming that she must speak at last. They waited a moment while the tension knitted Charlotte's brow and her lip trembled.

'Yes,' she answered in a quiet voice.

In the great silence following: 'And no,' she added.

Soon afterwards, Thackeray was seen in the hall with his hat on. He left the ladies to it and went to his club.

Some days later she had her portrait painted by George Richmond. She went to the first sitting in terror, dressed as she had thought best: a simple dress with a small lace collar, a ribbon round her neck and tied in a slack bow, her hair pulled to the back of her head in bandeaux, and wearing the same hairpiece that she had worn at Mr Thackeray's dinner. The minute she had taken off her bonnet, Mr Richmond had said, bluntly: 'What on earth is that pad of wool on top of your head?'

'My hairpiece, Mr Richmond. I thought it flattering.'

'Is that what made them laugh at you at Thackeray's? Please take it off, Miss Brontë.'

She trembled. Then she burst into tears – again.

After he had apologized and comforted her, 'Miss Brontë,' he had said, smiling, 'I am used to nervous sitters, and there is one thing I must insist on before we begin. You mustn't look at the portrait before I have finished.'

She had not found the posing difficult. She simply drifted into her comfortable dreamy state. She kept her lips together to hide her lack of teeth, and her head slightly tilted as Mr Richmond had instructed. When the portrait was ready, she saw that although he had flattered her greatly, giving her a slender neck and a more narrow face, yet he had still conveyed her look of constant anxiety.

But what made her burst into tears once more was that its expression of comprehending wistfulness made her so like *Anne*.

Or so she thought – Anne, or one of the others, being constantly on her mind – and being so short-sighted, too, she was constantly seeing one or other of them in someone else's features.

Now, returning from London, she had to accustom herself again to the great, grey casks of the mills along the railway, more of them being built every year; the tall chimneys raining soot. It being fine midsummer weather made it worse: here, she entered a smoky cloud. Trees were eaten away while in full loaf.

From the station, prying Keighley had to be passed through. She was sure that at the post office they opened the letters of their notorious authoress. She walked to the Devonshire Arms, took tea and hired a cab. It was what she regularly did. Her cover, 'Currer Bell', having been blown since Anne had died, she could no longer walk up the main street of Haworth in peace. It was different from their adolescent discomfort when going past the wild-looking woolcombers, sweating and ruddied by their stoves, and past the weavers and the spinners, which had been like walking by the pens of strange animals. Now the problem was not that Charlotte's life was private: it was that it was public.

There had been a meeting at the Haworth Mechanics Institute about her books. As half of Haworth had rushed to the Keighley Mechanics Institute for *Jane Eyre* and *Shirley*, they had decided to cast lots for who should borrow them, allowing two days for each person and imposing a fine of one shilling 'per diem' for keeping them any longer. Chartism might have had no success in parliament, but it had taught Haworth to organize a queue before the trough of learning.

Busybodies had started to appear 'in our wild hills', seeking her sources of inspiration and pestering the blind, geriatric parson. Charlotte hoped that they would soon stop coming. Those connoisseurs of authors, Sir James and Lady Kay Shuttleworth, had been astounded to learn of a famous writer ten miles away from their residence, Gawthorpe Hall. They had been to the parsonage, expressed shock at her gloomy situation with a misanthropic old father – 'Miss Brontë, how can you bear to be buried away? Because of *him*, you say?' – and offered to whisk her off for display at the London season. (At that time, even the idea of it had scared her to death.) Clergymen had called to complain that they believed themselves the originals of some of her notorious characters; also to leave with Papa sly invitations to bring his daughter to dinner, although they were total strangers. The curates she *had* satirized in *Shirley* soothed themselves by crowing over their colleagues' portraits – thus showing themselves to be very much as she had described them – while Mr Nicholls had been reported as 'rolling on the floor with delight' in Brown's house over the depiction of himself as 'Mr Macarthey'.

To cap it all, an ageing spinster, not *au fait* with literary gossip, but supposing 'Currer Bell' to be a gentleman like Mr Rochester, had written Charlotte a love-letter.

How well she could see herself as that spinster; for only literature had saved herself. As Mary Taylor had written: 'Look out then for success in writing. You ought to care as much for that as you do for going to Heaven.' It was out of respect for that salvation, and for other reasons too, that she liked adopting her authorial *alter ego*, even outside her books. She still signed letters in his name to her publisher and others, and sometimes spoke as 'Currer Bell' when she was in London, and elsewhere, if it suited her to.

Now Haworth had to be faced, its smoke, its stink, and the clatter of its stony ways.

As her cab drove past Bridge Mill at the bottom of the hill she saw John Greenwood, his staff in his hand and, judging by his determined walk, setting off for a long journey. He stared at her as if he had seen a ghost. Then he signalled frantically for her to stop. She halted the cab, although not worried about his fluster, because it was his way to be over-serious about parsonage affairs. Greenwood felt that he was an intimate, who owed them a debt of gratitude. The woolcomber who had set up a stationer's shop was one of the bookish artisans of Haworth, 'with a mind too keen for his frame', as Charlotte put it, and she had made use of her connections to help him open a bookshop too, starting with Smith, Elder's books. It was he who had suggested the fine for holding on to her novels. He would do anything for one of the Brontë family.

She learned from him that Papa had worked himself up into a state during her absence – the last days of which she had spent with Ellen Nussey – and he was sending Greenwood to walk the ten miles to Birstall to find out how she was and what she was doing.

'It's said that after thou'd been to London thou'd gone on t'Edinburgh wi' a young man!' John Greenwood let out in his panic.

It was Martha's gossip, probably, or maybe Tabby was becoming less scrupulous with secrets now that she was old.

By the time Charlotte arrived at the parsonage she was annoyed with Ellen. It was, of course, she who had sown this unnecessary commotion, by writing to Papa. As Charlotte had feared, the servants were caught up in it. Tabby was very cool. While Martha went off to deal with the luggage, she remarked: 'We hear thou's been up t'Edinburgh as well as down to London, miss.'

Charlotte had gone away because advantage was being taken of the good summer to replace the roof and she wanted to escape the dust, noise and confusion: that was all. It was none of Tabby's business.

'I am more concerned about how you have all fared through the re-roofing, Tabby.'

'They made a lot o' slutch and din wi' it but we had to put up wi' what come. Th'Mester's been all right. Me and Martha've made do.'

'Is it watertight now?'

'It didna come through on me and Martha when it rained. I were tired o' putting us buckets under t'drips.'

Charlotte, being too short-sighted to see how the roof had looked when she came up Parsonage Lane, and in any case not having the skills for inspecting a stone roof, had not been able to judge for herself.

While she disrobed and sniffed the air for damp and dust, Tabby was following her into the parlour, feeling the textures of the fine clothes passed to her: a silk shawl, and an expensive bonnet with a whole meadow of felt flowers around the brim. She still seemed disapproving. Charlotte ran her hand over furniture, and over the stair newel post. She even stooped to the dining-room floorboards to inspect for dust.

'If thou thinks it's mucky, thou should a seen it when us had us roof off,' Tabby grumbled. 'Bits o' lathes everywhere, stones dropping through, nowt covering the roof half the time though they put canvases on at neet, and all t'shouting and banging from dawn to dusk. I'd swear they made such a to-do so as notice'd be taken that they were no' laiking. Th'Mester's been coughing. That'll not surprise thee, will it, miss?'

'Yes, it does surprise me. I thought I had left him in good hands and in good health.'

'He were. He wouldn't still be after all th'carrying on, though, would he?! It's th'Mester should a been sent away fra holiday, not —'

'Tabby!'

'Aye, miss, it's none o' my business.'

Then her father came in.

'Papa!'

'Charlotte! My dear! Oh, my dear! Oh, my dear! I thought I heard you. Did you have an exciting time? We were so alarmed. Ellen wrote that you were not well.'

He spoke so formally; was so much the provincial clergyman. It struck her after London's snappy conversation. There, a new style was in vogue. It relied on hyperbole, concision and absurdity, and the circle she had joined were leaders of it. Nothing could be more removed from the Yorkshire and the Irish forms of eloquence.

Papa had made his appearance so quietly behind her. A tall, dark, thin shadow. How quietly the old drifted. She was aware above all else that the parlour was dark, and that her father was half blind and stooping. He held her and she stood on her toes, lifted her face, and kissed the cheek that he bent down to her. But she could not prevent her terror of the parsonage descending, in a deluge of realization, drowning her memory of London, Edinburgh and George Smith.

'I'll mak' thee both some tea, sir,' Tabby said, coldly.

'Yes, please, and some cake, Tabby.'

'I only had a cold, Papa. What about your chest? Tabby said you, too, were starting with a cold.'

'It will be all right when fires have dried out the new plaster. Who was this young man who whisked you off?'

'It was *very* wrong of Ellen to alarm you, Papa! Don't be afraid, I have no suitors! Mr Smith is eight years younger than I. He is only my publisher who had to make a business trip. A handsome young man has more dashing prospects than to tie himself down to a provincial old maid with no beauty or elegance.'

'I would not describe you as short of elegance. Nor of beauty. Look at you! As well as I can see, you look sparkling and fashionable. I would fall for you were I a young man. You remind me of your mother. Well, you are back. You are back.'

He sank into a chair by the fire and poked the coals in the homely manner of some old farmer or squire making a visitor welcome with a blaze on a summer's day, though with no pretension at all.

'How is the new roof? I can still smell damp, and dust in the air.' She smiled. 'I suppose I'll have a month of turning out drawers. Dust will have got into everywhere.'

'Brown tells me that the roof looks as straight as a billiard table now! He made sure they did not re-hang any raggy slates. A good man. They brought a great many new slates from the quarry, and there is no more damp by my bedroom chimney. One of the workmen was a Catholic. I told him to persist in his belief and all would be right in the end. We seemed to get on well with the workmen.'

Tabby came in with a tray of tea, scones and cake. She was biting her lip. When she had left, 'Tell me how you found London and Edinburgh,' Papa said.

Charlotte had written that she had been to the opera, and to an exhibition at the Royal Academy, where she had admired Landseer's depiction of Wellington at Waterloo, and also Martin's canvas of the 'Last Man', 'the red sun fading out of the sky, and the foreground made up of bones and skulls'. Yet again, she had been regressing to Angria and childhood, she reflected: to the Tallii whom he knew. But she was guiltily aware that she had not written to him as fully as to Ellen. It had been a dutiful letter and she had been unsure of what to tell him. At last she had hit upon the theme of her visit to the zoological gardens. Then she had described animals, birds and snakes, until she had filled a judicious number of pages.

Her problem then had been what it was now: she avoided the subject of her literary life because her notoriety would grieve him. This had grown tenfold after it had been revealed that 'Currer Bell' was a woman. There had been much guessing beforehand; a game that had at first delighted her. Because of the way Grace Poole in *Jane Eyre* stitched on curtain rings, 'The author is either a woman or an upholsterer,' Harriet Martineau had apparently said. Then it had turned into anything but a game. The reviews of *Jane Eyre* had grown truly poisonous – the ones written by women. The *Quarterly Review*'s Elizabeth Rigby had written that the author 'must have forfeited the society of her own sex'. When

Charlotte was so foolish as to dedicate a second edition of *Jane Eyre* to Thackeray, she had not known that Thackeray's wife had been mad, like Rochester's wife. The gossip then was that 'Currer Bell' had been a governess in the Thackeray family. Charlotte could not tell Papa that, when she went into the society, she walked into the burrows of vipers.

The worst of it was that she had no-one to share it with – no Emmii, no Annii. How could she tell Papa what she really felt in dazzling company?

She now gave an edited version, while he ate his cake and drank his tea, in that bird-like way of old people.

'I met Mr Thackeray.'

'How did you like him?'

'I'd say he is a distinguished and formidable gentleman, but not handsome. Indeed quite ugly.' He did not look at all like the Marquis of Douro, nor even like Mr Nicholls.

She seemed to think a little longer; although she had rehearsed what she would say on the train. 'A most kindly genius – but too satirical. He does not have the right sense of his high calling. He treats it in the style of a mere workman. I had to quarrel with him over his faults.'

'Tell me about Mr Smith!'

'He is a young man with a cool head for business. He has less understanding of the heart. He teases the ladies, but as I am old enough to be his mother, I may tell him so.'

She had in mind another incident that had hurt her at Thackeray's dinner party. George Smith had been flirting with Miss Proctor. On the way back to Gloucester Terrace she had said to him, pointedly and also, she feared, in a hurt voice, 'She would make you a very nice wife.' 'Whom do you mean?' '*You know whom I mean.*'

'You – old enough to be his *mother*?' Papa queried.

'Well – I'm old, anyway. He took me to the ladies' gallery in the House of Parliament,' she added.

As they had not been allowed to sit together, and as he had feared that she would be bored in this male preserve, he had arranged that she should flash him a look when she wished to leave. He had come to take her away sooner than she had expected, explaining, 'There were so many eyes, and I could not keep staring at the ladies! I was sure you would have had enough of our speeches by now.' He knew nothing about the fiery politics of Angria, and the parsonage disputes.

'I was not at all bored. I think it was some other eyes that were signalling to you!' she had teased him. He'd been flirting again, and, although she was 'old enough to be his mother', she was jealous.

Before her father asked her about that visit, 'You are not smoking your pipe today,' she remarked.

'I have given it up for the time being. It affects my chest.'

She looked at him slyly, smiled, and told him, quietly: 'I met the Duke of Wellington.'

'You met the Duke!' Papa was alert again.

'Through Mr Smith. He took me to the Chapel Royal one Sunday, as I was sure to catch him there. Afterwards Mr Smith took me on a walk on which I was bound to meet the Duke on his way back to Apsley House. I passed him twice.'

'Did you speak?'

'No, there was no chance for that.'

'Well, well, well. What did you think of him?'

'He was a grand old man. He was all that he should be. Mr Smith promised he would send his portrait. He also commissioned my portrait from George Richmond. An RA. A most eminent portraitist.'

'Bless my word! Tell me about it.'

'It was very tiring. Millais wished me to sit, also, but I could not face it.'

'And Edinburgh? How was that?'

She became fully animated at last. 'We saw Arthur's Seat and the monument to Scott and his home at Abbotsford and his restored abbey at Melrose . . . I was as happy as I have ever been in my life.'

She had said it before she realized what it implied. As she continued to blather on to cover up her mistake, she felt her face grow hot. Yet she blundered into more revelations.

'Mr Smith hired a driver who knew every nook and corner and was better read in the Waverley novels than I am. London is a great, rumbling, rambling, heavy epic. Edinburgh is a lyric – clear and vital as a flash of lightning.'

Papa looked at her keenly. 'I believe that Miss Nussey

dissuaded you from taking an even longer trip with Mr Smith to Loch Lomond and the Highlands?'

She was blushing. 'Miss Nussey can be a silly old spinster at times! But, yes, she did point out rather forcefully what people might say. Although Mr Smith was only being kind to his author.'

II

Autumn came with its inescapable melancholy – it did not need the anniversaries of those deaths. In parlour, kitchen or bedroom, among objects that had been familiar to her all her life but which now had the light of strangeness cast on them from her moods and from the quiet of the house, Charlotte would sometimes stand, a frozen pillar, not knowing which way to turn, lost in arctic wasteland.

She would have given the remainder of her life to be with Emily and Anne again for a day. Authorship was pointless without them, and she wrote little. Reflections strayed into her mind, threads drifting on a breeze, and she thought that she could apply them in a novel. There were times when she felt that her pain was precious and to be recorded; moments when a sensation was articulated, thrusting into the light like a spring crocus bursting from under frozen earth ... something to apply in the account of another life, set somewhere else ... but she could not be much more creative than that. She had sketched three chapters about a chillingly named 'Lucy Snowe', whom she could not decide whether to call 'Frost'. Lucy was an orphaned waif in the house of her godmother, Mrs Bretton, who was a portrait of George Smith's mother. Then Charlotte had dried up.

She now refused to go far from Haworth, as a penalty for managing to do no more than tinker with a novel. 'I ought to be put in prison and kept on bread and water in solitary confinement till I had written a book,' she wrote to George Smith.

It was ironical that never had there been so many strangers, affable and beaming, hunting her out in her fastness and breaking into her concentration. They invariably assumed that, having been given a glimpse into a soul made public in books, they had a personal relationship. There she would be, perhaps returning from her Sunday school, crossing the churchyard on one of her perambulations and talking to Emily, relying upon nobody's overhearing; the thought of life's brevity hurting her, like a nail in her shoe. In the next moment she was looking anxiously towards home because she had spotted some stranger, in the garden, or in the lane near the gate. She knew what they wanted and what they were thinking. Could that middle-aged little figure be Charlotte Brontë?

Sometimes it pleased her to tease by walking past with a knowing smile, then going into the parsonage to wait until they knocked. Or she would find them already inside being bossed about by Tabby, her janitor, who was getting used to pretentious folk, become supplicants for once in their lives. Or they would be sitting with Papa. He had taken up his pipe again and would sit smoking by his study fire, his spittoon in the grate.

Proud of his daughter, he tried to be courteous to strangers, but sometimes he could not keep it up. If he realized that they were not interested in him, the twinkle died and a bitterness showed. His visitors were made to feel awkward. Like his daughter, he liked to tease. He would ask their opinions on every subject under the sun, ranging from the provision of curates to the provision of drains. If he did not like them at all, he sat them alone in the parlour with the newspaper to wait for half an hour.

'I fear they write me up in their memoirs as a fierce old eccentric and misanthrope,' he told Charlotte with a smile.

Once, there came the Reverend Andrew Cassels of Batley. 'He looks no more a vicar than I do,' Martha said. His clothes reeked of his bad habits – smoke and alcohol – and he tried to drag Charlotte and her father off to the Black Bull. How could she explain to such a man *what it was like* in the parsonage? Before the two clergymen started to quarrel, which might become the talk of Haworth – Papa was growing increasingly irascible these days – she drew Cassels off into the parlour. There he winked and leered, and indulged in the vulgar conversation he thought he could get away with, with the author of *Jane Eyre*.

In contrast there came John Stores Smith, an aspiring young author from Halifax. A couple of his friends had attended Haworth Church to stare at her; Smith's own line, however, was more respectful and sensitive than many. He did not hold forth as if he were Rochester and she Jane Eyre. He genuinely admired her creativity and so she entertained him well, giving him dinner in the dining-room parlour. A quite amazing welcome from her.

She realized then that she had not eaten a meal in company, other than Tabby's, for nearly a week. Nowadays Papa had his brought into his study on a tray, while she took hers alone in this parlour, or joined Tabby and Martha.

She chatted with her visitor for a couple of hours. He brought her up to date about Halifax, for although she knew about London, and about the doings of the titled and the famous, most of her native province beyond Keighley had become a mystery to her. They were soon enjoying a homely giggle about some of those whom Branwell had known. Ah, it was good to be in comical Yorkshire, after all! She felt herself grow hysterical. But, as usually happened, the gloomy note fell. She asked about Leyland.

'Didn't you see the obituaries? He died in a debtor's gaol.'

'Thus are the mighty fallen,' Charlotte commented, without pity.

She sent Smith off with the advice not to try to seek his literary fame in London. 'As for most of those who call themselves literary men, avoid them as a moral pestilence,' she told him.

After he had left, she realized what this new Charlotte Brontë was whom she had been seeking. Angria had died, and within the space of a year she had grown into a stately and cynical old maid, aged thirty-four.

Nonetheless she received proposals of marriage. Not from Mr Nicholls, who was rather maddening – a man as big as he was, looking at her so sheepishly and, to mix her metaphor, with such bovine stares. Nor from the source from which she had hoped for salvation from loneliness and the burning memory of Monsieur Heger: from George Smith – ridiculous as it seemed, and about which she herself had set the gossip in motion.

One of her offers was from an employee of the publishing house: the chief clerk, James Taylor, who had wooed her with regular parcels of books. Papa took a liking to him when, before leaving the country to represent Smith, Elder in Bombay, Taylor came up to Haworth to propose. He first approached Papa.

'I do not think it would be a happy move to go out to India, Charlotte,' Papa mused afterwards. He had probably hardly slept all night from trying to imagine her in Bombay.

'But I believe Mr Taylor could be returning in five years' time. A temporary separation is a good test of an engagement. I have been thinking. If you were to marry, I would be happy to move into lodgings, so that I could be cared for and not be a burden.'

In five years, she would also be too old to bear children. An engagement now, for consummation then, would take away the danger of her dying in childbirth. Was that what was in Papa's mind?

Anyway, such a solution wasn't even to be contemplated, so far as she was concerned.

'I cannot abide Mr Taylor!' Fiery anger lit her famously soft eyes, and she admitted, 'He looks like Branwell!'

Once again she had blurted out her true thoughts before realizing it. Taylor was red-haired and small. That was why Papa liked him – and why she did not. He had literary connections nearly as strong as George Smith's, and that was enticing – when thought about from a distance. Close at hand, she despised him. 'Were I to marry him – my heart would bleed – in pain and humiliation,' she wrote to Ellen.

Also: a young poet, Mr Sydney Dobell, who had praised the Brontës' novels in a review, wrote to present himself as Charlotte's soulmate, and to invite her to Gloucestershire.

Ellen commented, enviously, 'For a woman who constantly complains of her ugliness and loneliness, you have had a great many seeking your hand. Five, that I know of. My brother Henry. That curate – Bryce. Everyone says that Mr Nicholls is a follower. Mr Taylor. Mr Smith.'

'You talk a great deal of nonsense, Ellen, and Mr Smith is certainly not a follower. He is the kind of man who would not be a "follower" of anybody. He is his own man. A leader.'

'Oh, I see!'

'Although he has suggested that I take a trip with him up the Rhine.'

'Charlotte! That is tantamount to a proposal!'

'Nonsense, he was merely being kind.'

'What was your answer?'

'That it is out of the question. All London would gabble like a flock of geese.'

In part, she boasted to make Ellen jealous. That was something else she had not been able to resist since her girlhood. The other reason was that, still, she was seeking consolation in fantasy.

The depression was palpable. It was choking. After injections of sociability, she fell into its clutches. It was waiting for her as soon as she was alone. Her inability to work fed it. Everything that happened to her fed it. Proposals of marriage that she had to reject only made her more lonely. It seemed a trap. Whatever her struggles, it tightened its jaws.

As she could make no progress with her book, she responded to her publishers' suggestion of bringing out a new edition of her sisters' novels. They would arrange the business matters with Newby, if she would edit the works. She agreed that *Wuthering Heights* and *Agnes Grey* should appear, in a single volume, but *The Tenant of Wildfell Hall* 'hardly appears to me desirable to preserve' she wrote, waspishly. 'The choice of subject in that work is a mistake: it was too little consonant with the character, tastes, and idea of the gentle, retiring, inexperienced writer.'

She had already altered their poems, substituting her own words, and removing some of the sting and pain from the last poem that Anne wrote by replacing a whole verse with one of her own. Revising *Wuthering Heights* and writing a preface, she found herself possessing Emily and Anne again, as she had when she had been their older sister. Now, she mothered their work.

One September day she went into the garden with a

manuscript bundle. It was a dry day with no wind, ideal for a bonfire. She burned letters and poems. Having suppressed *The Tenant of Wildfell Hall*, she now burned Emily's unfinished second novel which had been left among clothes in her drawer. She stood among flames and charred paper by the graveyard wall, and she thought how typical of them all had been their ways of dying – Branwell protesting and creating turmoil, Emily simply deciding to do it and making herself responsible for it, Anne hoping to disturb no-one but passing away in a lodging-house where she was not even noticed. How typical would be her own death, also, she was sure: however it was to come about, she had firstly taken charge of the family's reputation.

Only when she went indoors did she think, *Oh God forgive me!* She collapsed into 'a depression of spirits well-nigh intolerable – for one or two nights I scarcely knew how to get on till morning – and when morning came I was still haunted with a sense of sickening distress.'

She escaped again, invited to the Lake District to stay on the shore of Lake Windermere where the Kay Shuttleworths had rented a house. There she met Mrs Gaskell whose *Mary Barton* had forestalled her own *Shirley*. Nevertheless she felt no rivalry, only rapport and, incredibly, very quickly, little shyness. Mrs Gaskell was rich, happily married, had children, was beautiful and full of poise – everything that Charlotte was not – yet Charlotte was at ease with her.

'Papa and I dine alone, sit alone,' she told Mrs Gaskell, too soon for it not to be a shockingly intimate revelation. Only a very lonely person would give so much away, so soon. It was especially shocking to Mrs Gaskell with her rich family life.

'I know that my death will be an early and a lonely one,' she also confessed to her, on the lawn by the landing-stage one day. 'I have no relatives left to nurse me, and Papa cannot bear a sickroom.'

It added to the assessment which Mrs Gaskell had already formed. With her extraordinarily cramped look, with her tiny, tight shoes, her tight little gloves, and with her habit of lurking in corners of the great drawing-room rather than entering into conversations, Charlotte was that type of retiring

Sunday school teacher in whom seethe all kinds of perverse, romantic passions. Only, in Charlotte Brontë's case, she being a genius, this was taken to extremes.

One day, when Charlotte was about to enter the drawing-room, she overheard Lady Janet Kay Shuttleworth remark to Mrs Gaskell: 'Nowhere could be worse for her than being stuck in that gloomy parsonage with that mad old father – such a monster – in that village of little grey houses where nothing will grow, right up that terrible hillside.'

'Tell me more!' said Mrs Gaskell.

'He bored me to death about water supplies and *drains*. Blames the whole sickness of the town on it. All sorts of things are said about his peculiar ways and his fierce temper. The nurse who tended his wife when she was dying told me he smashed the furniture and cut up his wife's—'

Charlotte interrupted and confronted the look of pity in their eyes.

In fact they knew nothing about her. She had led them to believe that she had had no childhood. Because she could not tell them about Gondal and Angria, they could not know how marvellous it had been. She realized what she had been doing in talking to Mrs Gaskell: she had been recreating her life in order to make it a model for the fiction which she was, stumblingly, conceiving about herself as Lucy Snowe or Frost. She had remade herself and her life, so that she could study them. Now she was not sure how to get out of it.

How could she tell them that Papa was actually quite amiable, that he had been a wonderful father for them, and that the parsonage was not really bleak? Mrs Gaskell might understand how novelists recreate themselves, as props for their characters, but Lady Kay Shuttleworth, with her already fixed antipathy to Papa, never would.

'Charlotte, my dear, we were discussing what to do for your depression,' Lady Kay Shuttleworth announced.

'We did not mean to insult or offend you,' said Mrs Gaskell.

'A revelation cannot be hidden again! That is what is always so terrible. You must live with it. It is not like a dog's bone that can be buried.'

'You *must* get away,' advised Mrs Gaskell.

'I do get away. I am here.'

'I mean, more permanently. The world is yours for the choosing, now that you are famous. Immuring yourself in a life of self-denial for the sake of your father is not healthy. Physically. You are so frail and dainty and sensitive. We fear you could fall victim to a consumption. And emotionally it will narrow you as an author,' said Lady Janet.

'My spirits are in Haworth,' Charlotte answered.

She had that dreamy look which she had possessed when she had said more or less the same thing to Mary Taylor, on the eve of her friend's leaving for New Zealand. Mary Taylor, from what she had written since, had realized how powerful the gravitational pull was; disapprove of it though she might. Mrs Gaskell and Lady Janet seemed to think it only a mood of the moment; part of her temporary mourning which, she being Charlotte Brontë, would *have* to be extreme. She had spoken too simply, quietly, almost off-handedly, for them to grasp the importance of what she said. In fact, she had come out with one of those statements the truth of which sticks like a burr once it is in the open.

An hour later, all were involved in another round of the socializing foisted upon them by Sir James, who was forever lecturing on how to enjoy oneself, on which were the finest views of the lakes. No matter what anyone else wanted, there had to be a trip huddled on the lake in the rain with an inspector of schools, or an expedition through storms and mists, around hairpin bends over precipices. He fancied himself a perfect friend for one who was grieving; but he was exhausting. Wearing himself out with his high-pitched nerves, he had suffered nervous illness, and he wore others out, too.

Jollity was no help to her. She could pull herself together as much as she liked, doll herself up for visiting London or elsewhere, but fate stalked her still. Nothing that happened outside her mind mattered to her. The only place for her to look was within.

III

Because of her ever worsening eyesight, Charlotte could not read or write after dusk, when neither fire nor lamplight was bright enough. More and more, she sat alone in the 'dining-room parlour', knitting perhaps – socks and mittens for Papa, for Tabby, for the poor – because that was mechanical, and she did not need to look at it, and it occupied her shaking hands, which she thought looked more and more shrivelled, like birds' claws. If Mr Thackeray and the Duchess of Westminster could see me now! She could sit for an hour at a time. She fell into a trough where she was mesmerized.

When restless, or when a spasm of resentment against her fate took hold of her, she got up and walked around the table two or three times, slow and soft-footed, fearing that any noise might drive away the beloved ghosts.

Whenever she could not sleep at night, she came downstairs, stirred the parlour fire and again walked around the table. She was the keeper, the gaoler, of her own past. She counted the turns she made. She talked softly to Emily and Anne.

She composed her novel in her head in the evenings. She slept upon scenes and characters so that she lived and became them in her sleep. She wrote in the mornings. *Villette* was a novel more like a dream, its coincidences dreamlike, improbable. Among its surrogate lives – 'Paulina' based on Mrs Gaskell's chattering daughter, Julia, 'Paul Emanuel' representing M. Heger, 'Dr John Graham' for George Smith, 'Mrs Bretton' for Mrs Smith – Charlotte was a poor spinster looking for love, spinning a tale of how her own life had worked, or could work, out.

She had had the parlour redecorated while away on her last visit to London, had it hung with curtains, but the flowered wallpaper, the deep crimson fabric instead of bare wooden shutters, did not succeed in lightening the atmosphere. She put the blame for her discontent upon the Keighley manufacturer who had failed to dye the fabric properly. The fact was that the minute she raised her eyes from the paper it was as if she awoke and fell into another life. Emily was half-sitting, half-reclining, on the black sofa against the wall opposite the window. Her sister rose, went to the window and stared at the chimney-pots on the other side of the graveyard, at the Black Bull and John Brown's house, examining by the smoke which way the wind was blowing. 'It will soon change,' Charlotte told her. Anne was—

No, it was all horribly untrue. Charlotte had no child such as Paulina/Julia to help her relive and pass on her childhood with Emmii, Brannii, Annii. She would never have her own son or daughter. Almost her only friends were old maids like herself who either imagined love or despaired of it: Ellen Nussey, Mary Taylor, Miss Wooler.

The winter of 1851 to 1852 was vile, when she began seriously to work on *Villette*. Such howling, savage bites of cold and wind pierced the windows, and left crusts of ice on chamber-pots, that it seemed a monster was curled around the parsonage, trying to crush it, or to insert claws and teeth. For weeks, snow plastered itself on walls and window-sills, giving only tiny glimpses of graveyard and village with no-one out there. Rags were stuffed under doors and around windows but still the candle flames flickered in the draughts. Dressed in overmantles, the two remaining Brontës haunted the house, which stank of candle grease and confined animals.

Then Keeper, Emily's dog, died. Very nearly on the anniversary of her death, the beast, which had been sickly ever since, suffered a restless night and was dead the next morning. Thereupon Flossy, Anne's spaniel, wandered about looking for a lost companion – like every other creature of the parsonage.

Charlotte became ill. Out walking one day in a chill wind, a pain struck her in the side. It stayed with her and grew severe enough, together with other symptoms, of fever and a burning chest, for her to call a doctor.

This time it was Dr Ruddock. He diagnosed a liver complaint but Papa and Charlotte, remembering the medical horrors of the past, thought they knew better. They believed it was Charlotte's turn for consumption. The doctor prescribed mercury pills, but they made her worse. Yet more of her teeth became loose, her gums were painful, her tongue swelled, and her mouth filled with phlegm. She scoured Papa's *Domestic Medicine* and on realizing that she was also suffering from mercury poisoning she refused any more pills. Emily had been quite right in dismissing 'poisoning doctors'.

The weather of Charlotte's inner world was appalling, also. While Papa fumbled along icy roads to sit for hours by deathbeds, she remembered, with a sickening thud of guilt, her complaint to Mrs Gaskell that he 'cannot bear a sickroom'.

She wrote in fits and starts. Through the winter, she took her forsaken heroine Lucy Snowe to 'Villette', alias Brussels, to become a schoolteacher in a *pensionnat*. As Charlotte's feelings about Brussels again rose to the surface, she had to revise and revise, finding that each revision intensified the novel, spiralling down into the heart of the emotion.

Writing about that city, she was caught on the tines of love on the one hand, vengeance or satire on the other. Her fictional school was on 'rue Fossette', the *little ditch*, in 'Villette', the *little town*, in the country of 'Labassecour', the *poultry yard*. The school was a place of secretiveness where the proprietor, Mme Beck, spied, made a wax impression of the key to Lucy Snowe's writing cabinet while she slept, kept the door hinges oiled so that she could creep about undetected, and did not permit others to carry candles around in the dark.

Once Charlotte had let out the poison of her hatred of 'Mme Beck', or rather, Mme Heger − purely because she was her Dear Master's wife − could she then turn to the purer and more creative springs of love?

There arose another dilemma. Having brought into her novel the two men of her life, represented as M. Paul Emanuel and Dr John Graham Bretton, she had to resolve her love for them, and the problem was that it was so recognizably close to life.

How was her publisher going to take being a character in the very novel he was to edit and publish, his relationship to his authoress examined, its outcome prophesied?

In the summer before the autumn in which she began to write *Villette*, Charlotte had spent a month in London and there had occurred a decisive event at the theatre. George Smith had taken her to see the French actress, Rachel − who was supposed to be shocking, as *Jane Eyre* was. Charlotte had seen her twice. In the second performance, especially, as Camilla in Corneille's *Horace*, she had seen Rachel seem to 'tear apart the earth and let out glimpses of Hell'. She grappled as if with a tiger, and it had been one of the most powerful experiences of Charlotte's life. But George was unmoved. He made a strange comment. He separated the woman, Rachel, from the artist, saying that he admired the first and not the second. At that moment Charlotte saw only too clearly that he made the same separation in her own case. Only, in her case, he admired the artist – but not the woman. In the theatre foyer she had searched his face with the blank stare, neither laughing nor crying, of one who has longed for love and has realized that it does not exist. But who still holds on to a thread of hope.

She now wanted to go nowhere else with him; any joy in that was dependent upon her innocent assumption that her love was returned.

He had tried to behave as if he had not noticed any change. But she was sure he was aware of it, because of a brusqueness in his manner, mixed with a judicious kindness. She rejected his pity; just as she could not bear his brusqueness following the joy of intimacy. There was a dull cloud over the remainder of her London visit and she soon left, first for Manchester, where she stayed with Mrs Gaskell at Plymouth Grove, and then home.

It was clear from the beginning that, no matter how much she wished it, Lucy Snowe could not marry Dr John. She feared the admission of it, the committing of it to paper that George Smith would read.

In the spring, on the anniversary of Anne's death, she went, alone, to Filey where she had stayed with Ellen after Anne had died. Was this indulgence in past pain a good thing? She turned this over in her mind, on the train, in her long walks on the beach, or standing on the cliffs, and on trips to Anne's grave.

Running away from her novel was making her worse. She felt ill just from that. I can always go straight home, she told herself. Yet she stayed for a month, although, it being early in the season, the place was half deserted, and it happened to be very cold.

But one exceptional day when it chanced to be sunny she hired a bathing machine and took a dip for the first time in her life. Shuddering, she bent her knees so that her voluminous bathing-dress floated about her in great white petals. She bent her head low enough to look along the surface of the water towards Flamborough Head. She listened to the symphony of waves. She saw rainbows caught in the spray. She smelled the salt tang. She found herself smiling. She was thrilled by a sensuality she had not felt in a long time – maybe never before.

What is my old maid's body for? Is it really too late?

For a moment – with the little waves lapping her breasts – she thought of Mr Nicholls; his long slow stares, and his stammeringly expressed kindnesses. It was not the first time that she had thought about him.

She stood up: she was too cold. In her clinging shift she retreated into the bathing machine that smelled of damp wood and salt. My real sensuousness, she thought, is that of suffering. It always has been. She realized that she had indeed done the right thing in coming here, to be lonely, and discover that truth about herself.

She had also followed the right instinct for her novel. When she returned to Haworth, she worked with new energy at *Villette*. She had already plumbed depths of pain in volume one – which she had completed a few months before – and which had ended with her description of turning, in despair, to a Catholic confessional.

She saw her pain as like a fruit, rich, ripe, tasty. As like a body she made love to – as she imagined love. She even mirrored its sensuality in the imagery of a continental garden in summer; the garden of the *pensionnat*, at twilight, scented and mysterious, with love-letters thrown down from a casement.

Summer came and she stumbled into more difficulties. She began to write again in August, and had finished the book in a surge by October.

She wrote of swallowing tears as if they had been wine. When she described Dr John taking Lucy to a concert, jealousy was the thrill.

Describing him glancing at a 'Juno' in the audience,

'cold, rounded, blonde, and beauteous, as the white column, capitalled with gilding, which rose at her side,' she remembered the chill that had run through her when George Smith had been flirting at Thackeray's house. It had been as if she had suddenly died; had fallen out of life.

She also imagined perfect happiness.

> Some real lives do – for some certain days or years – actually anticipate the happiness of Heaven; and, I believe, if such perfect happiness is once felt by good people (to the wicked it never comes) its sweet effect is never wholly lost. Whatever trials follow, whatever pains of sickness or shades of death, the glory precedent still shines through, cheering the keen anguish, and tinging the deep cloud.

Although truth would not allow it to be Lucy Snowe's happiness: not with either of the men she loved.

It became Dr John's happiness with Paulina.

Meanwhile, as she was writing, Mr Nicholls was doing something very queer, very queer indeed. He passed by the parlour window with a strange, twitching motion, not looking where he was going, but squinting in at the parlour window, grimacing out of embarrassment. A man of his bulk, which made him so fine a sight in the pulpit, looked especially awkward doing this. He had no sooner passed out of sight than he came back again, squinting over his other shoulder this time, winking and leering, his walk made awkward because he seemed not to know whether to linger or to hasten. Ten minutes later he was back again, presumably having been lurking in the graveyard.

She put down her pen and went to the front door, not knowing whether to be amused or annoyed. She stood on the front step, looking at him fidgeting. He was arrested ten feet away from her, his mouth open as if an egg might pop out.

'I did not wish to disturb you,' he explained.

Surely the man could not be in love?

She smiled. 'I *am* busy,' she answered.

He smiled back awkwardly, and said, 'Mr Brontë hopes for a happy ending!'

'You have been talking about me to Papa?' she said, brusquely.

Judging by his pained expression, she might have stabbed him.

'Only about your novel. A happy ending would cheer him up.'

She shut the door on the importunate curate, more hastily than she would have done had he not looked such a lovesick clown, and returned to her work, most upset. To discuss her novel *was* to discuss her, for her book was her life!

Because Papa's eye had become dreadfully inflamed and he had grown almost blind once again, she had been reading *Villette* to him and when he had begged, 'Please give Lucy Snowe a happy outcome!' she had replied, 'It is not what I have in mind for her, it would not be in accordance with truth.' But now she relented. A little. For the sake of Papa, aged seventy-five and with only herself in the world, she conceived an ambiguous ending. This was so as not to sacrifice, for those able to see it, the essential truth: that there could be no reliable happiness in life for Lucy Snowe. Paul Emanuel was at sea in a cataclysmic storm. Lucy Snowe was waiting for him on shore. The readers could decide the outcome for themselves.

IV

Could I create a happy ending? Charlotte wondered, as with Tabby and Martha she went demurely into church on Whitsuntide morning in 1853.

The reviews of *Villette* were on her mind. Miss Martineau's had been deeply wounding, summarizing the novel as 'intolerably painful . . . the author has no right to make readers so miserable'. The famous feminist had also castigated her for suggesting that females view the world with only one interest, that of love. Charlotte had been compelled to give up her budding friendship with Miss Martineau.

Thackeray had been personally insulting, so Charlotte had been led to believe. 'It amuses me to read the author's naïve confession of being in love with two men at the same time, and her readiness to fall in love at any time. The poor little woman of genius! ... a noble heart longing to mate itself and designed to wither away into old maidenhood with no chance to fulfil the burning desire.'

That might be the end of her friendship with Thackeray, too. George Smith, in his unconscionably light-hearted manner, had left her dangling with his opinion. Doesn't he understand how I feel? I want to know if he thinks Dr John *should* have married Lucy Snowe!

Everything seemed to change after finishing a novel. They marked out phases of life. After years of immersion in *Villette*, the river of life had moved on, and she stepped out of her book a different person; one made to some extent by the work that she had completed, which had been begun in order to settle certain questions. The same kinds of changes in her had happened after *Jane Eyre*.

Charlotte's gloved hands, projecting from her dark cloak, clutched her prayer-book to stop their trembling. Her head was ducked under the peak of her bonnet. Coming into church out of a sunny day and blinded by the dark, soon she made them all out, by squinting at them through the corners of her eyes. Good morning, Mr Lambert. Mrs Lambert. Good morning, Mr Sugden. Mr Brown. Mr and Mrs Greenwood. Mr Heaton.

The minds of the congregation were less on God than they should be, she was sure. This was not only because many had read *Villette*, in the way simple people read novels – as autobiographies, if they seemed close enough to fit. It was also because Haworth had been gossiping about Mr Nicholls's behaviour since before Christmas. He had made a spectacle of himself after she had rejected him. One reason she had gone to London for a month had been to avoid the rumpus.

In between Tabby and Martha, Charlotte walked to the pew below the pulpit, by the family vault. The organ was playing. She put her prayer-book on the bench and, like her companions, knelt in silent prayer, her eyes buried in her gloves.

She sat back and removed her gloves, prepared for the two-hour-long communion service. She stared towards the pulpit, away from the eyes that watched her; if they were not watching Mr Nicholls, about to officiate for his last time ever. He began to chant. He was in control of himself, thank goodness, and the service for morning prayer had begun.

Mr Nicholls had been one of the few who would sit with Papa – who had grown so blind and inward-looking that he had not a great deal to communicate.

One night last December, after sitting as usual for a couple of hours, Mr Nicholls had come out of the study at nine o'clock, supposedly to make his way home to John Brown's house, but instead had tapped lightly on the parlour door. At that late hour, Charlotte knew what it would be about.

He came in shaking and pale. He could hardly get his words out. He had anything but a hopeful expression as he looked down on her in her child's rocking-chair, in dim candlelight, by the fire; the knitting dropped from her hands. He was so intense and mad, his face and eyes catching fire in the candlelight, he had looked as though he would stab her rather than, at long last, ask her to marry him. As he explained that he had suffered for months and had to know her answer and settle the matter, he had talked like a character in a novelette. He had not wished to disturb the writing of her book, he explained. 'Do not answer me right away unless you wish to! But I crave leave for some hope, no matter how long it takes you to decide!' He clearly did not know whether to sit, or kneel, or remain standing. He stayed on his feet.

'Have you spoken to Papa?'

She did not look up. He was so very towering, it would hurt her neck.

'I did not dare before asking you.'

'I will give you my answer tomorrow.'

She rose and took his arm, although she hardly came higher than his elbow, and helped him out. She led him to the front door and closed it behind him – not able to bear to watch him go, reeling and sobbing, towards the gate.

She went in to speak to Papa. He was sitting calmly by the fire, smoking. His room was twilit. He, also, did not need a light. Two near blind, vulnerable people.

'Mr Nicholls has asked me to marry him. I told him he would get his answer tomorrow.'

She expected Papa to oppose such a marriage but she had

not anticipated his wrath. Dropping his clay pipe into the fireplace, where it smashed, he stumbled to his feet and turned, hovering above her, tall, gaunt and fierce, with feathery wisps of hair. Here was another great, tall creature lowering down upon her with ferocious passion! Even before she had indicated what her answer might be, Papa was put into a rage she had never seen in him before; although she had heard, from 'Uncle Morgan' and others, of the tempers of his youth. The veins in his temples stood out. His face reddened and she feared a recurrence of the apoplexy that had troubled him in the summer.

He claimed that Nicholls was a bounder and a rake for going behind his back; that his was the behaviour of an unprincipled army officer, not of a curate; that the match would degrade her on the brink of a great career; that Nicholls had neither money nor prospects nor even honour.

Anything but express the thought that really brought him agony. That was too much to come out with.

He spluttered and coughed. He heaved into the spittoon – his aim was certain, although he could hardly see it.

'I shall answer Mr Nicholls in the negative tomorrow,' she said, to quieten him and get him to bed.

On the morrow, she went down to Brown's house and gave her refusal. Mr Nicholls stiffened in the face of her rejection: as, no doubt, he thought he should.

Yet the memory of his stormy behaviour, corrected by such manly fortitude, was almost causing her to change her mind. She was now attracted to, and certainly full of curiosity about, this evidence of both passion and dignity in a man whom she had thought of as nothing more than a bland and reliable curate.

Being rooted in such equivocal thoughts, her refusal somehow suggested to him that he had reason to hope. That was what Charlotte learned he had told Mrs Brown – who was sentimental.

'Well!' Charlotte said, 'I thought I was merely being kind and trying not to provoke a scene.'

She kept to her rejection. Yet, through her friendliness whenever she could not avoid meeting Mr Nicholls, she also showed that she might be open to second thoughts. As she was almost the only person who *was* warm towards him, it was bound to feed the fire.

Virtually all of Haworth took the side of their well-tried, helpless, blind old parson. Where more than half the wives died in childbirth, they did not need it spelling out to them what ultimate tragedy it was reasonable for Mester Bron-*teh* to fear. After his loss of wife and five children, the thought of his last surviving daughter, such a frail little thing, marrying that great big man was awesome. Awesome. Without Martha Brown telling what she overheard at her place of work, they knew what the conversations would be between parson and curate.

John Brown, in the Black Bull and elsewhere, said of his lodger, 'If I had a gun I would shoot the man!'

'Hush, John!' Mrs Brown answered when he declared such feelings at home. 'Doesn't tha think it's terrible for Mr Nicholls, too, to love a woman he'd be likely to kill?'

Martha was in tears from thinking of Mr Nicholls's dilemma.

Charlotte kept this Angrian script alive by putting it about that, for her part, she 'thought that he was more sinned against than sinning'. To anyone who would listen, she praised his qualities, for example the strength and reliability that would make him a good husband for *someone* who would appreciate them.

Of course, it got back to him. Baited thus with hope, he upset Mrs Brown because he would not eat. He avoided the church and his parishioners as much as he could. They avoided him, too. There was such a hangdog melancholy about him that no-one wished to speak to him. A great, brooding, Celtic figure. 'You felt he might chase you with an axe,' they said in the pub. He was once found sobbing at the parsonage gatepost.

Tabby quarrelled with Martha, saying that she was disgusted at his collapse, 'such a big, strong man, and a clergyman to boot'.

Papa would not speak to him at all. The only comical element in it all was to see those two avoiding one another, by going round opposite sides of the church; to see Mr Nicholls hovering at corners if he spied Mr Brontë.

Mr Brontë said that he wished he would take up another situation, as he could never trust him any more. 'And I wish that every woman may avoid him for ever, unless she is determined on her own misery!' he burst out to Mr Heaton.

Nicholls then made arrangements to go to the Australian colonies as a missionary for the Society for the Propagation of the Gospel; they were practical at least to the extent of his writing to the six referees he needed. But even in that he grew irresolute. Torn between what he should do and what he desired, 'he behaves as if he is burning in his soul', it was remarked. This seemingly rock-like and determined man, shaken to his foundations by that little woman, asked to remain in Haworth after all. He asked for the rescinding of his resignation from the curacy, but Patrick would agree to this only on condition of a promise not to 'approach' Charlotte; one that Nicholls could not possibly make. Finally, he cancelled his application to go as a missionary. Instead, he was now to take up an offer of a curacy at Kirk Smeaton near Pontefract.

They had sung the psalm, 'Jubilate Deo', and had moved through the Creed of Saint Athanasius and the remainder of the Whitsuntide morning service, followed by the Litany. 'Good Lord, deliver us,' and 'We beseech thee to hear us, good Lord,' Charlotte had repeated, a dozen and more times. The congregation was like a murmuring flock of birds.

Nearly an hour had gone by. As well as staring at the windows in a blank dream of hope, her eyes sometimes catching what she tried to avoid – that spot where her mother, three sisters and brother lay – Charlotte also could not avoid watching Mr Nicholls to some extent, and even catching his eye. Papa would not come to the service, but unfortunately she had to be present, for someone from the Brontë family had to be here on Whit Sunday. She feared Mr Nicholls would break, he was so brittle.

Those who had not registered for communion left the building. Mr Nicholls was hovering before the table spread with a white linen cloth for the wine and the bread. He, too, must be especially weighted with the thought of communion as a ceremony of reconciliation for 'those betwixt whom malice and hatred reign', and she felt uncomfortable at imagining their thoughts held in common. It was too intimate.

He began the Lord's Prayer, and he still seemed firm. It was when he came to, 'Almighty God, unto whom all hearts are open, all desires known, and from whom no secrets are hid', that he first notably faltered. He stumbled on through the ten commandments. Then he became weak, white and nearly voiceless.

Soon, he would be due to press the bread and wine to her lips.

A churchwarden whispered to him: something that could not be overheard, but it looked stern, and Mr Nicholls made a great effort. Women by her side along the communion rail were sobbing quietly. If anyone had sympathy with Mr Nicholls in his passion's dilemma, it was the women. It was a most terrible scene, and Charlotte began to sob also. Never before had she met a man capable of the passion that resided in her own heart! She would never have suspected it.

She had written to Ellen that, in refusing Mr Nicholls, she had not been able to decide whether she was 'losing the purest gem', or whether she was 'escaping the yoke of a morose temper'. She decided at last that he was the former. With this thought in her mind, she looked up at him while he, with superhuman effort, put the bread to her lips. Bread turned into flesh, wine turned into blood.

He will be back, she thought. My husband.

But she did not know if this was a feeling to be relied upon as a support in life, or a literary one, the voice of her books.

ARTHUR BELL NICHOLLS

I knew I had one strength: I had promised that, if she forsook her freedom for my sake, I would take care of her Papa. I was the agent of providence, as she saw.

Winning her over was a long drawn-out battle, made the more difficult because she used her father's wrath as an excuse for dithering. In truth she was unwilling to lose her total dedication to authorship, but what is that compared with its accompanying fate of withering away, an old maid like some of her friends – like Miss Nussey? Together with the news of George Smith's marriage, my promise about her Papa sealed the matter. It was not easy to make. Among all the other abuse hurled against me, apparently he had thundered that he would never, never have another man in the parsonage.

My wife-to-be had a cold at the wedding. It was held at eight o'clock in the morning, on the 29 June 1854, a quiet, dull Thursday. Only the night before, Patrick, who at long last seemed to have grown reconciled, had apparently declared that he would not come to it. There was hardly anyone else present, either. A boy was sent to the top of the hill to watch out for the arrival of the vicar of Hebden Bridge, who was to officiate, for my own landlord in Oxenhope, and myself. The lad was then to run for the parish clerk. I caught the old fellow lacing his boots up in the lane.

After the women had raked through the prayer book to find out what to do about Patrick Brontë's obstinate refusal to give away his daughter, the office was performed by one

500

of the only two guests whom Charlotte had invited: Miss Wooler. The other guest was her bridesmaid, that perpetual bridesmaid, Miss Nussey. Tabby and Martha Brown were there, of course, and Martha had taken it upon herself to raid the town for flowers. There was a great deal of snivelling over the wedding breakfast, from colds, and from emotion. Charlotte had dressed prettily, in white muslin traced with green, and a white bonnet with more greenery, so that people said that the little creature looked like a snowdrop. But you'd think the whole affair was another funeral.

It was our honeymoon that made the difference to us. You'd be amazed at the effect actual passion had on her. As soon as we were married it became, 'Arthur thinks this . . .' and 'Arthur says that . . .'; 'Arthur is ready for us to take a walk . . .' and 'Arthur has come in, I must end my letter now.' People smiled at first, then found it irritating. I encouraged it. You will understand why I wanted to be sure of her; and our honeymoon, via North Wales to Ireland, was, I unblushingly confess, designed to acquaint her with her lord and master's background, which she hardly knew. She visited my college, and all my haunts. My home in Banagher made her eyes pop, I can tell you. It was the kind of house she had normally entered as a governess. She met my relatives, and the servants who had attended me since childhood. She had not, after all, stepped down in the world. (We did not explore her own antecedents in Ireland.)

Along with her publisher, George Smith, whom she had told that she wanted no more to do with after he married, she appeared to abandon . . . abort . . . her writing, and set it at nought. Before my return to Haworth to pursue my courtship of her, which was not many months after my leaving, she had worked on The Story of Willie Ellen. It was a tale with a disembodied spirit, a spirit of place, among its characters. It also had a housekeeper modelled, like Nelly Dean of Wuthering Heights and other genial servants in their books, on Tabby. It had a dispossessed child, his loss of fortune and ill-treatment reminiscent of the histories of Ponden Hall and Law Hill. It was as cruel a story as you could imagine, with dreadful descriptions of floggings – you can see why I needed to watch over my wife.

(Except for Anne, they were all of them as cruel as they were tender, in their minds.) Nevertheless, Willie Ellen *was so much like something by Emily that I wondered if it was in fact hers; her worked-up manuscript. Charlotte also began a novel entitled* Emma. *She managed about twenty pages of it; it lost its energy when Smith married. The central character is a school pupil, spoiled under the assumption that her father is wealthy. When it turns out that he is an imposter, she is seen as a different person, although, unless you define people by what they have, she is not in truth any different to what she was. What she is, is a sleepwalker, able to reveal herself only in fits and madness.*

Mr Thackeray and others have found this story promising. The odd thing is that it is the same abused child, Willie Ellen, who when grown up appears as mentor and guardian of the misunderstood girl in Emma. *Whether* Willie Ellen *was originated by Emily or not – they spent their lifetimes passing stories back and forth to one another, in any case – with hindsight it seems that both tales were part of a grand design which my wife was too weak or too diverted, or maybe too sensible – too determined not to make herself unhappy by dwelling on misery at her writing-desk – to finish. She once impulsively read the manuscript of* Emma *to me, her eyes shining, and I was pained to see them cloud over when I commented that I thought it was backward-looking, being another novel set in a school. Then: 'What is the matter?' I asked, in surprise. 'I was thinking how much I miss talking to Emmii and Brannii and Annii,' she replied. She substituted the happiness of being a curate's wife, which was hardly different from being a parson's daughter, only there was more of it.*

There were times when, looking at her across the table, at Sunday school teachers' teas, or when we visited the Devonshire Arms, I saw that she was restless. I mean, her spirit was restless. She had habits that showed it. She would pull at her fingers. As she realized, this drew attention to their small size. Her smallness and constraint were features that she was always exaggerating – tight shoes and gloves, neat collars – as if to say, 'So you think I'm small and tight-laced? Think it, then! The loss is yours!' I believed that she was missing in me those undisciplined feelings I had once shown, those 'Angrian' emotions as I learned they were, when I had clutched her gatepost, weeping; when I had all but collapsed in church. I supposed she thought – or desperately hoped – or convinced herself – that these would make me a partner to her writing. I sympathized with it, without quite understanding, but authorship made her life, and therefore my life, dreadfully public – her presentation of it. Well, I ask you, doesn't a man have a God-given right to possess his wife? Isn't that what holy matrimony is for?

I learned much about my wife, by the way, from her letters to that Miss Nussey. Naturally, if I could not put a stop to them, I had at least to insist on seeing and censoring them, and, for what it was worth, making Miss Nussey promise to destroy what she received. Otherwise, I told Miss Nussey firmly, my wife would definitely not be allowed to write to her any more. Letters are dangerous hostages to fortune. I grew embarrassed by my own letters, in which I had wooed Charlotte when I was in Pontefract, but it was easy for me to destroy those, when Charlotte became mine. I think I won the battle over her letters to Miss Nussey also. I think the element of foolish confession dried up.

'My life is so different now. For the first time I have stopped waiting for letters every day,' she said to me once.

One day she went out carrying a tin box. It was under her cloak, but I had caught sight of her slipping it under the folds, though I said nothing. I saw her go along West Lane, onto the moors. 'Where have you been?' I asked, awaiting her at the door on her return, well over an hour later. Although it was a sunny winter's day, her feet were wet from trailing through the grass, and her cloak was insufficient to protect her in December. It was a dangerous time – there was much sickness in Haworth. She was shivering. This time, she showed a trace of irritation, although I always enquired into what she had been doing, where she had been, or where she was going. 'It was such a pleasant day that I walked along the Sladen Beck.' I took her cloak from her; for Tabby, who would have fussed, had then become seriously ill with diarrhoea, like many others. My wife had returned without the tin box, but I didn't mention it. I happen to know what was in it. I had *made it my business to know. Letters, from Emily and Anne and Branwell, perhaps even a few from M. Heger, who I know remained her true love. (A spouse sees that kind of thing: he gave her words, whilst I merely made her happy.) She had buried them somewhere along the Sladen Beck. She had buried her romantic past, where Emily before her had buried her spirit.*

It was after this that my wife became seriously ill, with 'morning sickness' but also with the same symptoms that killed Tabby at the age of eighty-four in the following February, a month in advance of herself. I wonder if my wife caught the illness from her?

Though vomiting and weakening over a period, death took her by surprise. Once, overhearing us pray for her in her delirium, she whispered: 'Oh, I am not going to die, am I? He will not separate us, we have been so happy.'

But He did. She was a few months pregnant, and He did.

After Patrick Brontë's death, four hundred and eighty-five lots went under the hammer at the parsonage. Patrick's replacement, the Reverend Wade, a Brontë hater – and perhaps chosen in preference to Nicholls for that – was in haste to be rid of it all, and of Nicholls too; to smother the Brontës' remains with a new church, its main pillar over their tomb.

Without pretensions, Arthur Nicholls left by the back way. The gig, holding Nicholls, Patrick's dog Plato, and a brass-bound trunk, descended Parsonage Lane. Watched by the families of Brown and the other tradesmen near the church, it turned downhill through the gauntlet of parishioners who had sent him off with a gold watch and with their ambiguous thanks. Many claimed that Brontë fame would not serve God's purpose in Haworth. Nicholls's face remained impassive, square, strong and rock-like, circled by dark, neat hair and a thick, curly beard. At Keighley, he took a train for Liverpool, boarded ship to Dublin, and went seventy miles west, home to Banagher. He made the return to Ireland that Patrick had never made.

Nicholls had experienced enough of 'livings'. He became a farmer. He *seemed* to *live*. But no-one was sure of it, for he had taken with him several of Charlotte Brontë's dresses, manuscripts and drawings, a wallet holding the little books from childhood, and the last living creature from the parsonage, Plato. What did he want these for, other than to dwell upon the past?

Martha Brown came to serve him. Even after Nicholls had married again (his cousin) he talked mostly to Martha. She now waited on an old man with a shock of white hair who went through the cattle markets of Banagher exuding a ferocious air of self-containment. He dwelled on memories that he did not talk about, except to Martha.

At the end, he talked about the future – the eternal one. The clergyman who had renounced holy orders upon leaving Haworth would drink whisky, whisky and stout, or whisky and stout and tea, alternately from a row of mugs and glasses ranged before him in the Irish fashion, and would mutter, softly, 'I wonder how it will be?' He wondered if death would be a release and if he would be with her again in the spirit. Charlotte and her sisters, especially Emily, had seemed to believe that love was not of this world, but was a visitor, a spirit coming here to be embodied. Love was a migrant, often to be mauled, mangled, and soon buried – as they had seen it happen, in the bitter lives of the farms, in the clothiers' old halls, and through the mendacities of some men who had wooed them.

Nicholls believed in an afterlife for love – it must be so, after the intensity of the brief experience that Charlotte and he had shared. His love had been a fever developing for lack of cure. It had become the more heated when he had learned how capable of love she was. To the end, he could not forget, firstly, her love for George Smith, and secondly for her little Belgian professor, both of whom were apparently so much cleverer than himself, more vital and imaginative. Above all, Monsieur Heger had been *unobtainable*, because he already possessed a family: a life of which Charlotte, like her own mother, had been thwarted. (Charlotte died at the same age as her mother. Wasn't that odd?) When Nicholls and she had begun to launch the small ark of their marriage upon the tide of Patrick Brontë's fury, she had started to love her husband. That was when it became intense. Their experience had been the flame of the world. Love wasn't anything you could touch, except either to burn yourself at it, or to extinguish it; which was what they all wrote about, those – girls. But Arthur Nicholls waited impatiently for the joy of being in that flame again, in Eternity.

In the fifty years that followed Charlotte's death, Arthur Nicholls never talked much to his new wife about how he felt. Yet she understood. He died in 1906 and, to the shock of a miry little Irish town, before she buried him she laid his coffin in the dining-room under the portrait of Charlotte Brontë that had been executed so flatteringly by George Richmond in 1850. Through the three days of an Irish wake he awaited his soul's journey beneath a portrait of the woman who might have borne the only child he'd ever have. The only Brontë child at all.

H.G.: THE HISTORY OF MR WELLS
Michael Foot

'A WONDERFULLY RICH, INFORMATIVE,
ENTERTAINING AND CHALLENGING JUSTIFICATION
OF THE MAN. THIS DELIGHTFUL BOOK SHOULD BRING
A NEW GENERATION OF READERS TO THE
ENJOYMENT OF WELLS' UNDOUBTED GENIUS'
Allan Massie, *Daily Telegraph*

H.G. Wells was one of the intellectual giants of his time.
Famous on both sides of the Atlantic for his best-selling
books and prolific journalistic output, he played a leading
role in the important controversies of his turbulent age.

As a personal friend of Wells in his youth, and strongly
influenced by him in his own political beliefs, Michael Foot
is uniquely placed to bring new life to one of this century's
most colourful and controversial heroes. From the fight for
women's rights to arguments about democracy and
communism to a liberation from Victorian values of sexual
morality, Wells was never far from the burning issue of the
day. He lived through both World Wars and the Russian
Revolution and his work reflects the great changes that the
world was undergoing, creating such popular classics as
The Time Machine, The War of the Worlds and *The
Invisible Man.*

'ILLUMINATED BY GENUINE PASSION AND
UNDERSTANDING'
Peter Ackroyd, *The Times*

'GENEROUS, ERUDITE AND PERCEPTIVE'
Roy Hattersley, *Mail on Sunday*

0 552 99530 4

BLACK SWAN

DINA'S BOOK
Herbjørg Wassmo

'THE GREATNESS OF THIS BOOK IS ITS GUT-
WRENCHING PORTRAIT OF A WOMAN FOREVER IN
THE GRIP OF HER PAST'
Los Angeles Times

Set in Norway in the mid-nineteenth century – a land of short, blazing, idyllic summers and dark, frost-rimmed winters, of mountains, bear-hunts, and hazardous sea voyages – *Dina's Book* centres around a beautiful, eccentric and unpredictable woman who bewitches everyone she meets.

At the age of five Dina unwittingly causes her mother's death. Blamed by her father and banished to a farm, she grows up untamed and untaught. Her guilt becomes her obsession: her unforgiving mother haunts her every day.

When she finally returns home she is like a wolf cub, tamed only by her tutor, Lorch, who is able to reach her through music. Married off at sixteen to a wealthy fifty-year-old landowner, Jacob, she becomes sexually obsessive and wild. Jacob dies under odd circumstances and Dina becomes mute. When finally she emerges from her trauma, she runs his estate with an iron hand. But still Dina wrestles with her two unappeased ghosts: Jacob and her mother. Until one day a mysterious stranger, the Russian wanderer, Leo, enters her life and changes it forever . . .

'A MASTERPIECE THAT LIGHTS UP THE SKY LIKE A
MEGASTAR'
Verdens Gang, Norway

'AN EXPLOSION OF A BOOK – A UNIQUE TALENT AND
A WONDERFUL EVOCATIVE POWER'
Politken, Denmark

'A NOVEL THAT WILL STAY WITH YOU FOREVER'
Kristianstads-bladet, Sweden

0 552 99673 4

BLACK SWAN

KNOWLEDGE OF ANGELS
Jill Paton Walsh

SHORTLISTED FOR THE BOOKER PRIZE 1994

'AN IRRESISTIBLE BLEND OF INTELLECT AND PASSION
. . . NOVELS OF IDEAS COME NO BETTER THAN THIS
SENSUAL EXAMPLE'
Mail on Sunday

It is, perhaps, the fifteenth century and the ordered
tranquillity of a Mediterranean island is about to be
shattered by the appearance of two outsiders: one, a
castaway, plucked from the sea by fishermen, whose beliefs
represent a challenge to the established order; the other, a
child abandoned by her mother and suckled by wolves, who
knows nothing of the precarious relationship between
church and state but whose innocence will become the
subject of a dangerous experiment.

But the arrival of the Inquisition on the island creates a
darker, more threatening force which will transform what
has been a philosophical game of chess into a matter of life
and death . . .

'A COMPELLING MEDIAEVAL FABLE, WRITTEN FROM
THE HEART AND MELDED TO A DRIVING NARRATIVE
WHICH NEVER ONCE LOSES ITS TREMENDOUS PACE'
Guardian

'A BEAUTIFUL, UNSETTLING MORAL FICTION ABOUT
VIRTUE AND INTOLERANCE'
Observer

'A RICHLY DETAILED AND FINELY IMAGINED
FICTIONAL NARRATIVE'
Sunday Telegraph

0 552 99636 X

BLACK SWAN

THE INFLUENCING ENGINE
Richard Hayden

The engine is running. I can sense it. A charge in the air. A smell like iron, like a storm approaching. The dust swirls in spiral patterns on the floor. The engine is running.

The year is 1812, and in the wake of the French Revolution, London is possessed by political ferment. Into this melting pot steps an innocent, John Bellingham, who believes that he has been wronged by the government of the day. Imprisoned in Russia for five years, and faced with financial ruin and a collapsing marriage, he embarks upon a journey into the world of the dispossessed, seeking the reparation that is his right.

But there are many pitfalls for the unwary traveller in this unfamiliar landscape, not least those agents provocateurs who seek to harness the unwitting to their own political ends. As Bellingham struggles to maintain his dignity, sanity and his marriage, he is lured into the ragbag cabal of revolutionaries, lunatics and loners who believe they possess the ultimate political weapon . . . *the influencing engine.* Having lost control of his life once already, he is quickly in danger of doing so a second time . . .

The Influencing Engine takes the reader on a dark journey into the murky chambers of the nineteenth-century political underworld and uncovers a spider's web of intrigue and deception, from which no-one is likely to escape unscathed.

'A THOUGHTFUL AND PROVOCATIVE NOVEL'
Daily Telegraph

0 552 99677 7

BLACK SWAN

SWEET THAMES
Matthew Kneale

'RAW IN CONTENT, ELEGANT IN TREATMENT . . .
RICHLY ENJOYABLE'
David Hughes, *Mail on Sunday*

It is 1849. A major cholera epidemic threatens London.
Working unsupported by employer or public authority,
Joshua Jeavons, engineer, is completing his great drain plan
for the capital. When the deaths begin, he works even more
furiously, driven by a bold vision – a London freed of
rotting sewers, cleansed and reborn, and he, Joshua Jeavons,
hailed as the discoverer of the source of the killer disease.

Then his beautiful young wife Isobella, a paragon of female
virtue, suddenly disappears and Jeavons must turn his
attention to new and even more perplexing questions. Why
her coldness? Why her absolute refusal of his attentions
since the first night of their marriage? Could certain
unthinkable accusations, made anonymously against
Isobella in a series of letters, actually be true?

Jeavons' search for the answers to the mysteries that
surround him leads to the shores of the Thames where only
sewer-scavengers thrive; to glittering Haymarket cafés where
high-class prostitutes ply their trade; and finally to the
dangerous heart of London's slums. What he finds there,
amid poverty, disease and death, will shatter his ideals and
strike at the core of everything he has ever held dear.

'EXCELLENT . . . THE GRADUAL UNFOLDING OF THE
PLOT IS SUPERBLY DONE'
Mark Illis, *Spectator*

0 552 99542 8

BLACK SWAN

A SELECTED LIST OF FINE WRITING
AVAILABLE FROM BLACK SWAN

99588 6	THE HOUSE OF THE SPIRITS	Isabel Allende	£6.99
99618 1	BEHIND THE SCENES AT THE MUSEUM	Kate Atkinson	£6.99
99632 7	NATALYA, GOD'S MESSENGER	Magda Bogin	£5.99
99572 X	STRANGE ANGELS	Andy Bull	£5.99
99531 2	AFTER THE HOLE	Guy Burt	£5.99
99628 9	THE KNIGHT OF THE FLAMING HEART	Michael Carson	£6.99
99686 8	BEACH MUSIC	Pat Conroy	£7.99
99587 8	LIKE WATER FOR CHOCOLATE	Laura Esquivel	£6.99
99482 0	MILLENNIUM	Felipe Fernández-Armesto	£14.99
99530 4	H.G.: THE HISTORY OF MR WELLS	Michael Foot	£7.99
99479 0	PERFUME FROM PROVENCE	Lady Fortescue	£6.99
99589 4	RIVER OF HIDDEN DREAMS	Connie May Fowler	£5.99
99599 1	SEPARATION	Dan Franck	£5.99
99616 5	SIMPLE PRAYERS	Michael Golding	£5.99
99677 7	THE INFLUENCING ENGINE	Richard Hayden	£6.99
99605 X	A SON OF THE CIRCUS	John Irving	£7.99
99567 3	SAILOR SONG	Ken Kesey	£6.99
99637 8	MISS McKIRDY'S DAUGHTERS WILL NOW DANCE THE HIGHLAND FLING	Barbara Kinghorn	£6.99
99542 8	SWEET THAMES	Matthew Kneale	£6.99
99660 2	STEPS	Jerzy Kosinski	£5.99
99569 X	MAYBE THE MOON	Armistead Maupin	£5.99
99577 0	THE CONFESSIONS OF AUBREY BEARDSLEY	Donald S. Olson	£7.99
99536 3	IN THE PLACE OF FALLEN LEAVES	Tim Pears	£5.99
99636 X	KNOWLEDGE OF ANGELS	Jill Paton Walsh	£5.99
99673 4	DINA'S BOOK	Herbjørg Wassmo	£6.99
99591 6	A MISLAID MAGIC	Joyce Windsor	£4.99